CHARLIE BROWN

AND FRIENDS

Other *Peanuts* Kids' Collections

Snoopy: Cowabunga!

Charlie Brown: Pow!

Woodstock: Master of Disguise

Snoopy: Contact!

Snoopy: Party Animal

Charlie Brown: Here We Go Again

Snoopy to the Rescue

Snoopy: What's Wrong with Dog Lips?

I'm Not Your Sweet Babboo!

Snoopy: Boogie Down!

Lucy: Speak Out!

Charlie Brown: All Tied Up

Snoopy: First Beagle in Space

CHARLIE BROWN

AND FRIENDS

A PEANUTS™ Collection

CHARLES M. SCHULZ

Andrews McMeel
PUBLISHING®

Peanuts is distributed internationally by Andrews McMeel Syndication.

Andrews McMeel Publishing
a division of Andrews McMeel Universal
1130 Walnut Street, Kansas City, Missouri 64106

www.andrewsmcmeel.com

www.peanuts.com

22 23 24 25 26 SDB 15 14 13 12

ISBN: 978-1-4494-4970-4

Library of Congress Control Number: 2013942906

Made by:
King Yip (Dongguan) Printing & Packaging Factory Ltd.
Address and location of manufacturer:
Daning Administrative District, Humen Town
Dongguan Guangdong, China 523930
12th Printing—3/14/22

ATTENTION: SCHOOLS AND BUSINESSES

Andrews McMeel books are available at quantity discounts with bulk purchase for educational, business, or sales promotional use. For information, please e-mail the Andrews McMeel Publishing Special Sales Department: specialsales@amuniversal.com.

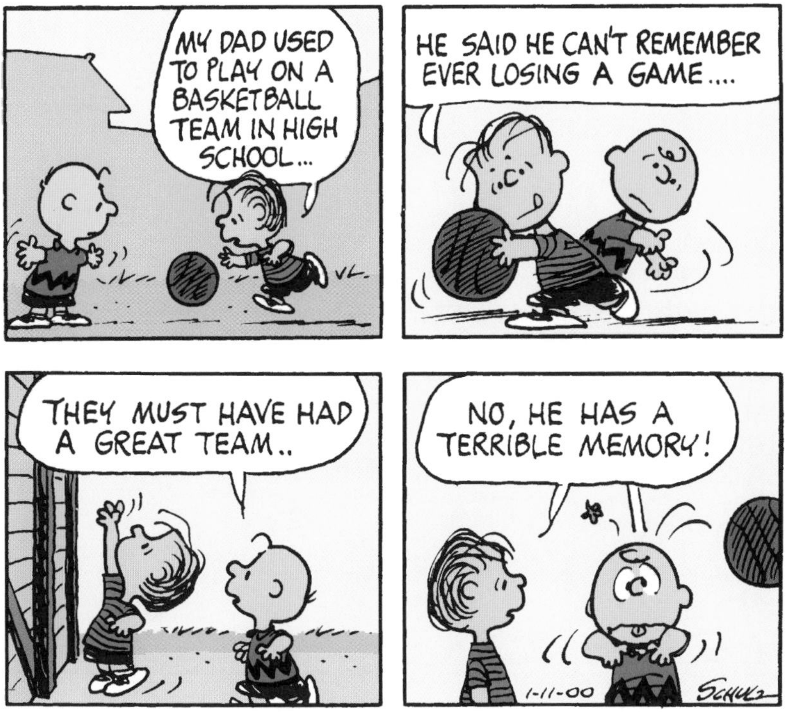
MY DAD USED TO PLAY ON A BASKETBALL TEAM IN HIGH SCHOOL...
HE SAID HE CAN'T REMEMBER EVER LOSING A GAME....
THEY MUST HAVE HAD A GREAT TEAM..
NO, HE HAS A TERRIBLE MEMORY!
1-11-00
SCHULZ

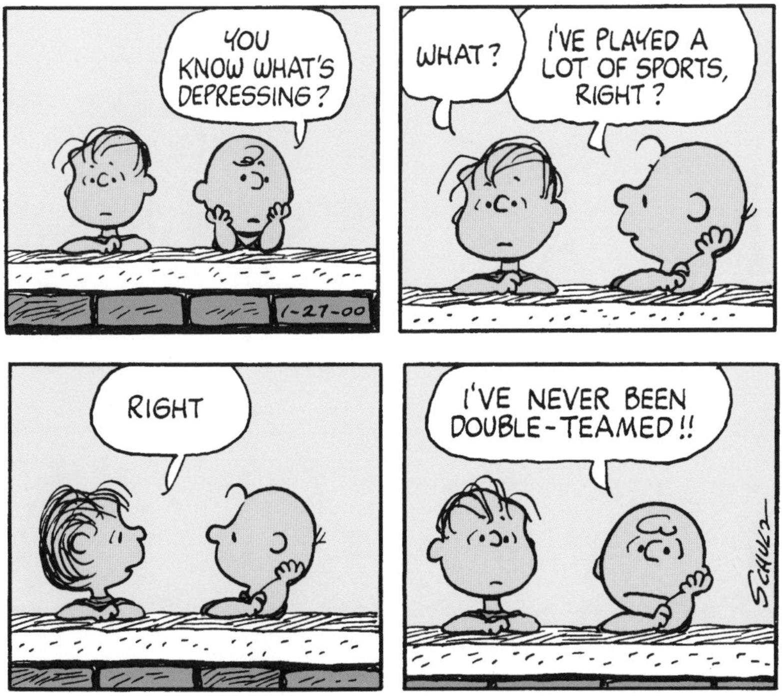
YOU KNOW WHAT'S DEPRESSING?
1-27-00
WHAT?
I'VE PLAYED A LOT OF SPORTS, RIGHT?
RIGHT
I'VE NEVER BEEN DOUBLE-TEAMED!!
SCHULZ

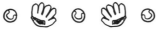

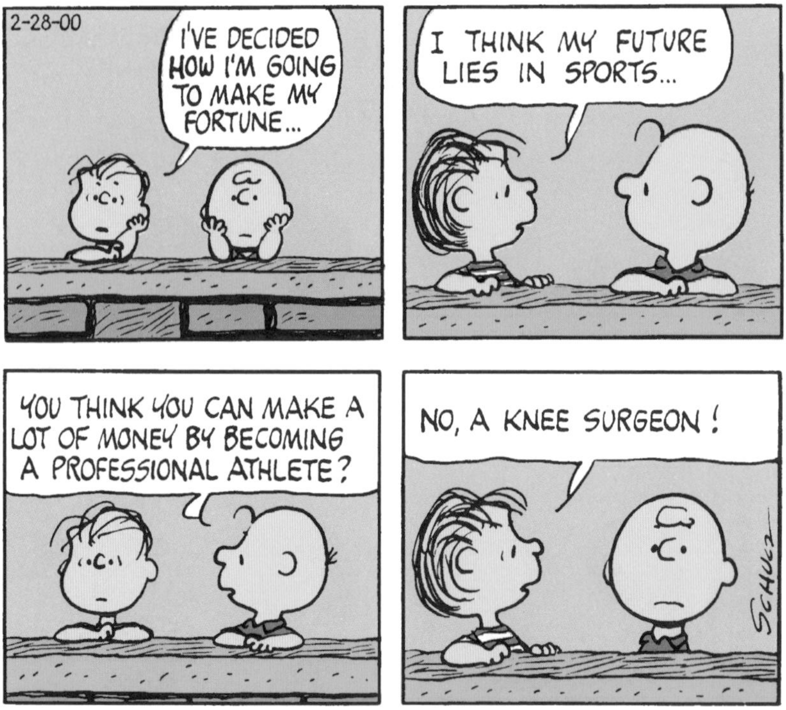
2-28-00
I'VE DECIDED HOW I'M GOING TO MAKE MY FORTUNE...
I THINK MY FUTURE LIES IN SPORTS...
YOU THINK YOU CAN MAKE A LOT OF MONEY BY BECOMING A PROFESSIONAL ATHLETE?
NO, A KNEE SURGEON!
SCHULZ

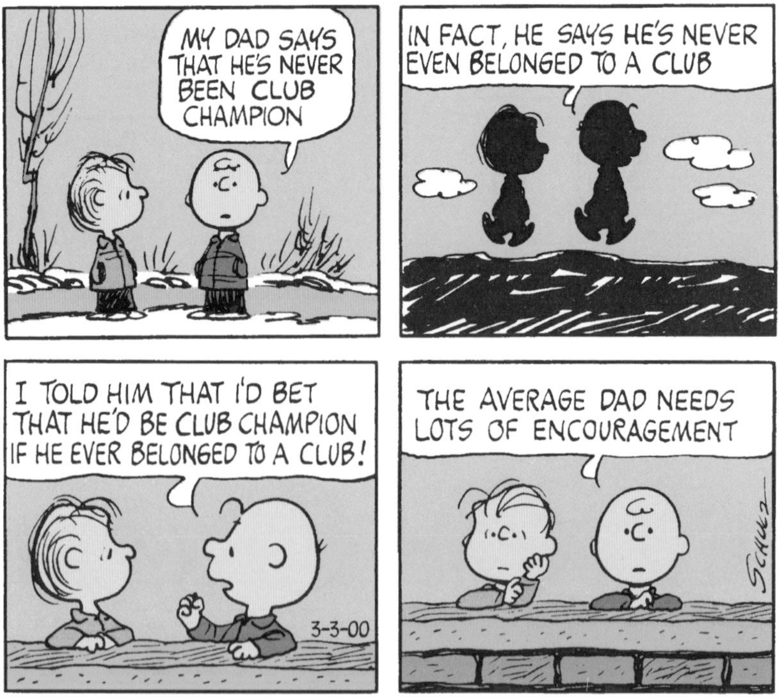
MY DAD SAYS THAT HE'S NEVER BEEN CLUB CHAMPION
IN FACT, HE SAYS HE'S NEVER EVEN BELONGED TO A CLUB
I TOLD HIM THAT I'D BET THAT HE'D BE CLUB CHAMPION IF HE EVER BELONGED TO A CLUB!
3-3-00
THE AVERAGE DAD NEEDS LOTS OF ENCOURAGEMENT
SCHULZ

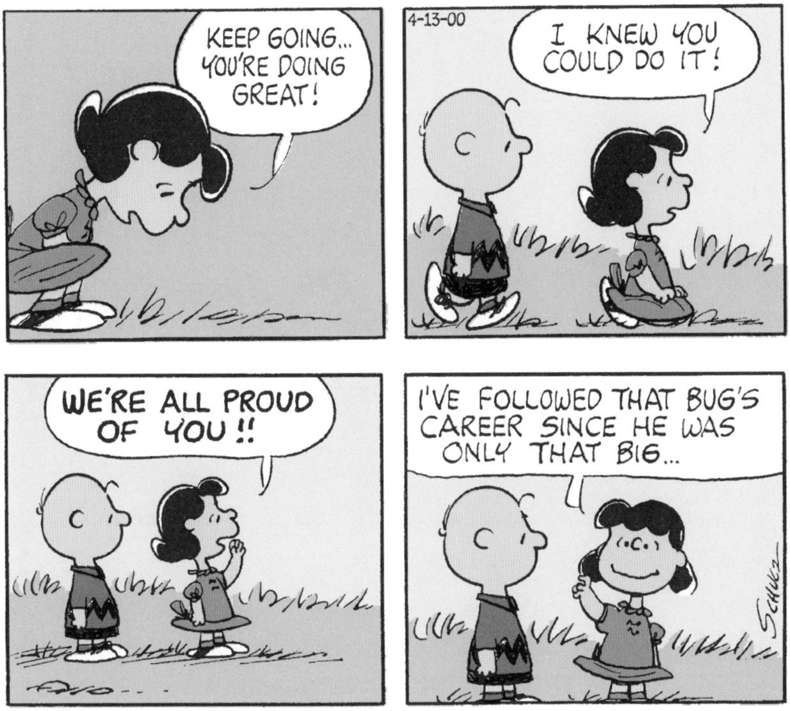
KEEP GOING... YOU'RE DOING GREAT!
4-13-00
I KNEW YOU COULD DO IT!
WE'RE ALL PROUD OF YOU!!
I'VE FOLLOWED THAT BUG'S CAREER SINCE HE WAS ONLY THAT BIG...
SCHULZ

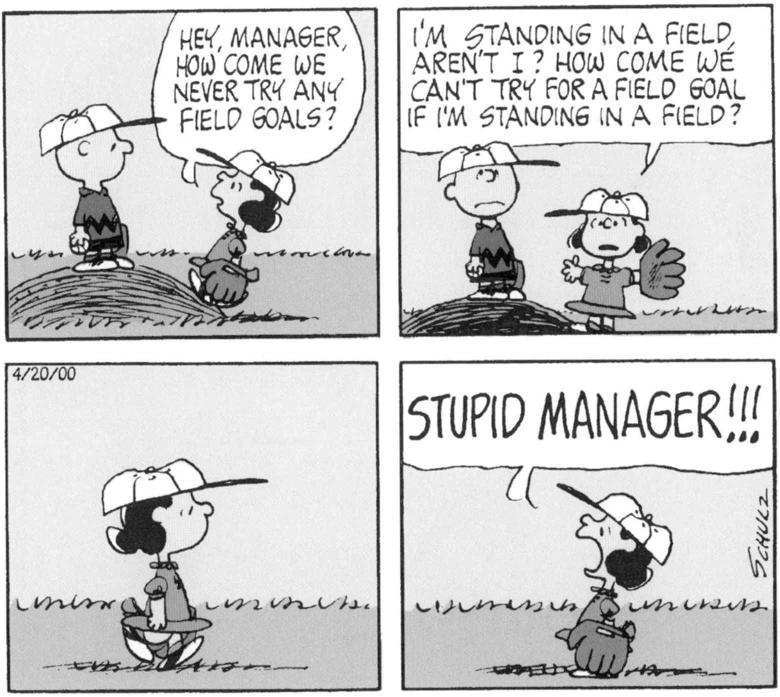
HEY, MANAGER, HOW COME WE NEVER TRY ANY FIELD GOALS?
I'M STANDING IN A FIELD, AREN'T I? HOW COME WE CAN'T TRY FOR A FIELD GOAL IF I'M STANDING IN A FIELD?
4/20/00
STUPID MANAGER!!!
SCHULZ

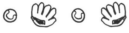

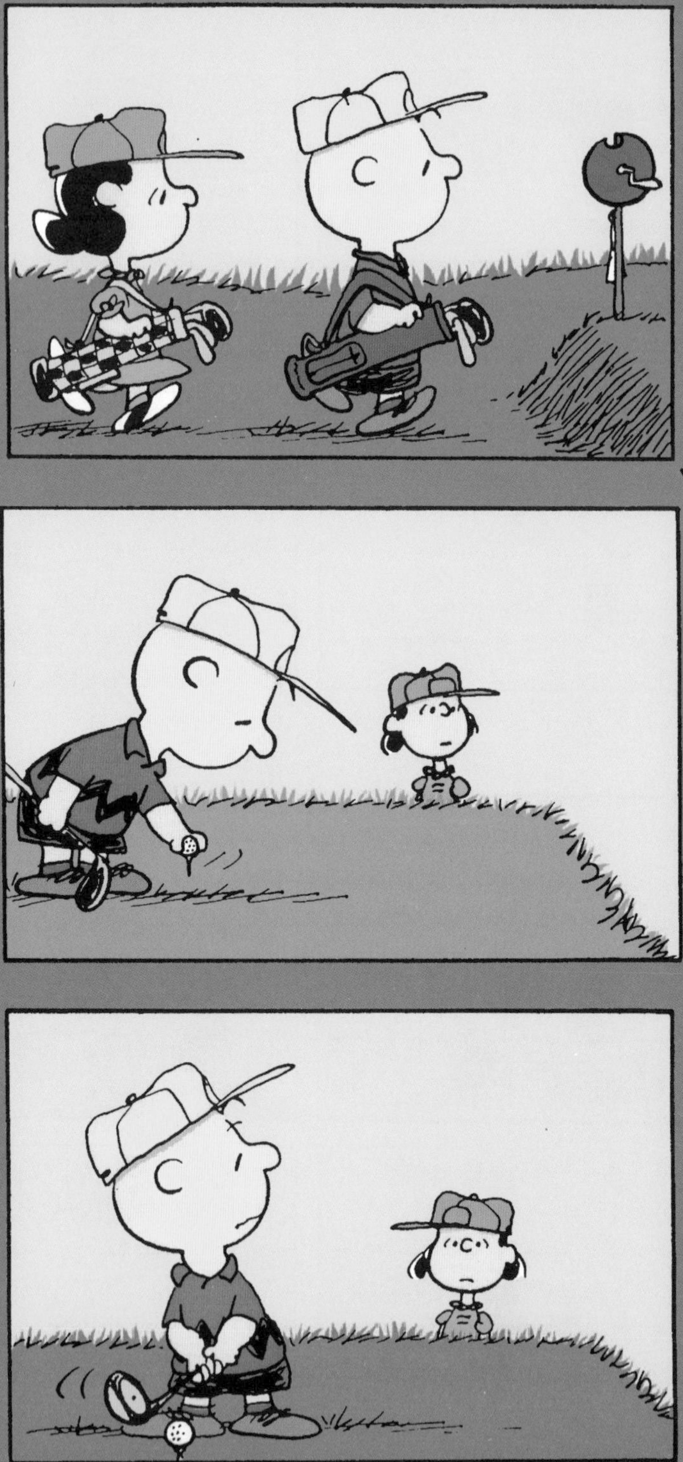

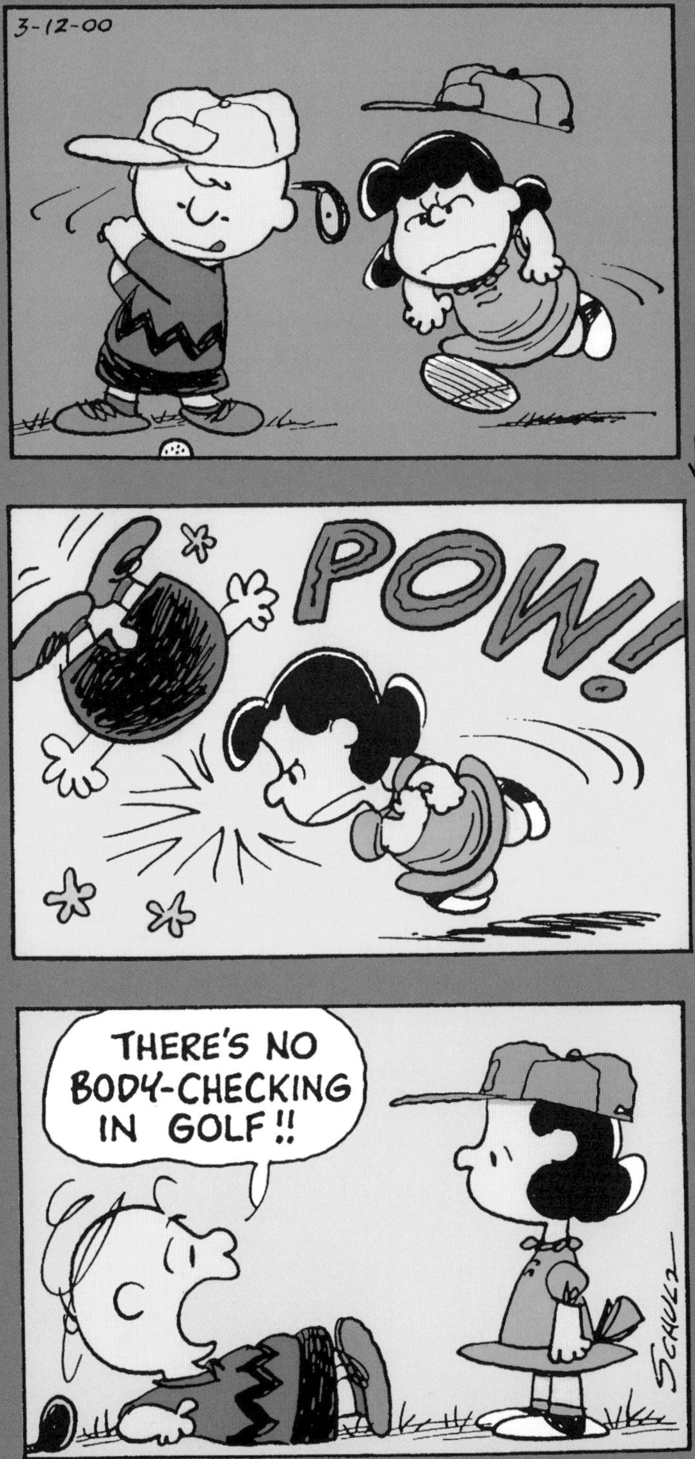
3-12-00
POW!
THERE'S NO BODY-CHECKING IN GOLF!!
SCHULZ

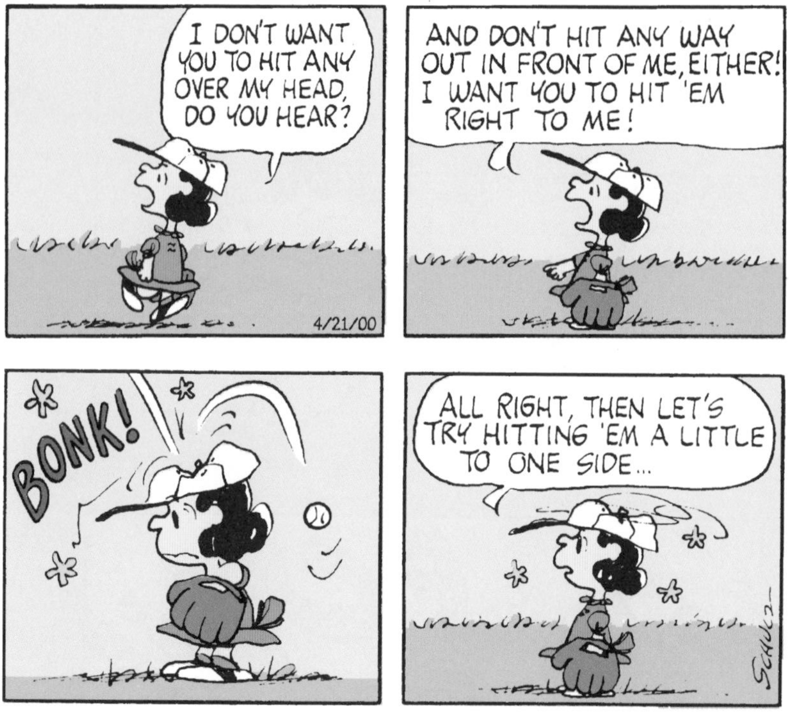
I DON'T WANT YOU TO HIT ANY OVER MY HEAD, DO YOU HEAR?
4/21/00
AND DON'T HIT ANY WAY OUT IN FRONT OF ME, EITHER! I WANT YOU TO HIT 'EM RIGHT TO ME!
BONK!
ALL RIGHT, THEN LET'S TRY HITTING 'EM A LITTLE TO ONE SIDE...
SCHULZ

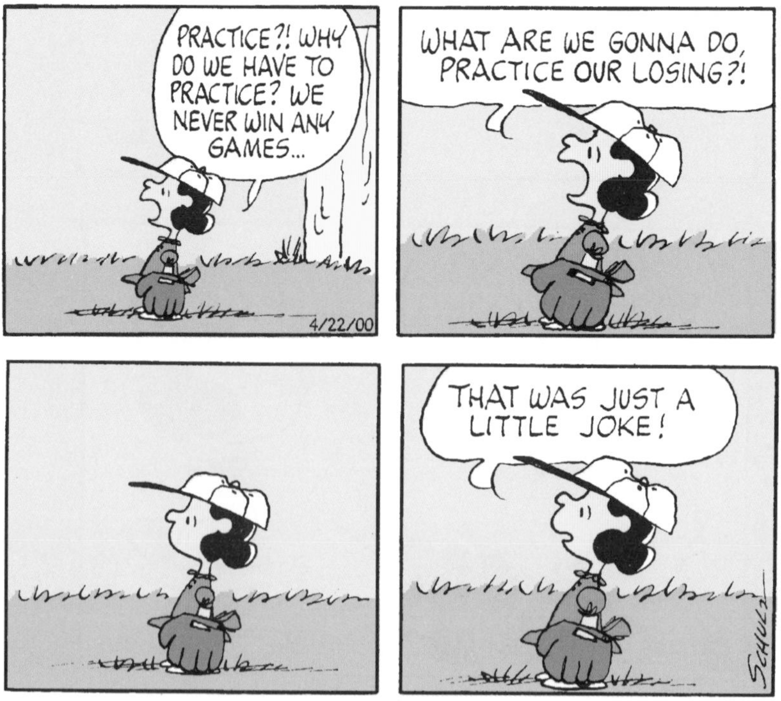
PRACTICE?! WHY DO WE HAVE TO PRACTICE? WE NEVER WIN ANY GAMES...
4/22/00
WHAT ARE WE GONNA DO, PRACTICE OUR LOSING?!
THAT WAS JUST A LITTLE JOKE!
SCHULZ

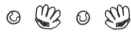

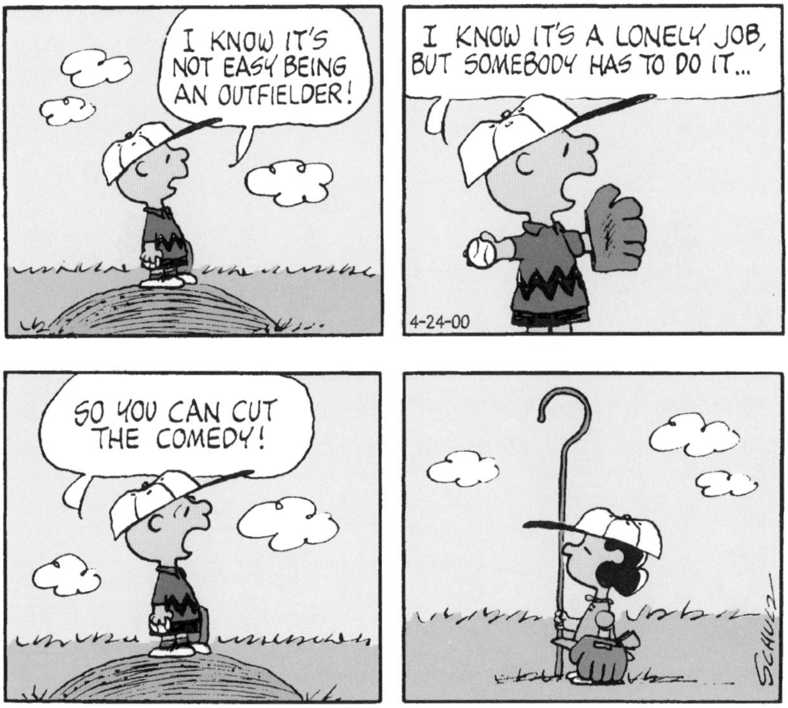
I KNOW IT'S NOT EASY BEING AN OUTFIELDER!
I KNOW IT'S A LONELY JOB, BUT SOMEBODY HAS TO DO IT...
4-24-00
SO YOU CAN CUT THE COMEDY!
SCHULZ

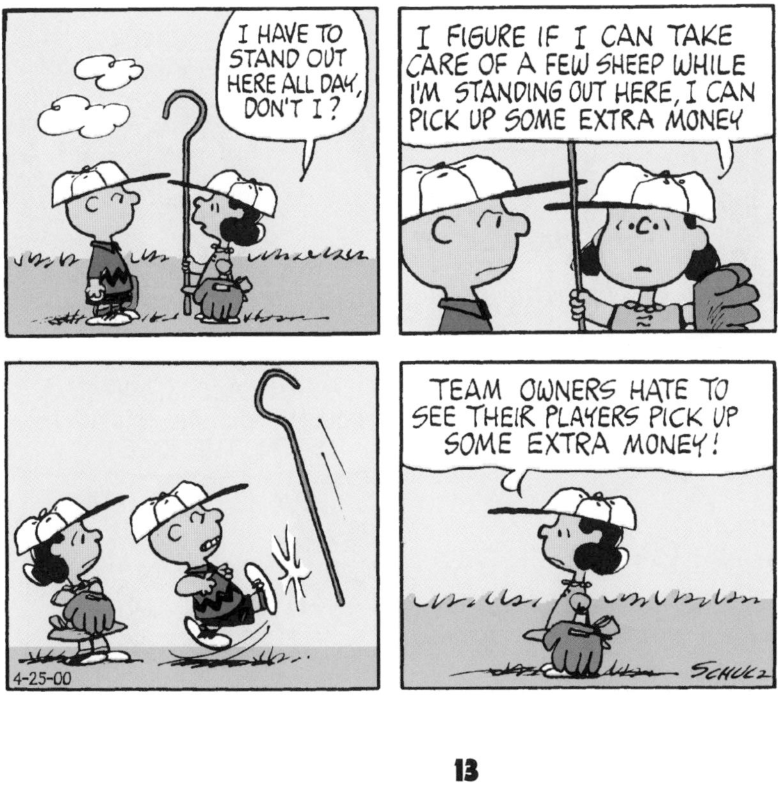
I HAVE TO STAND OUT HERE ALL DAY, DON'T I?
I FIGURE IF I CAN TAKE CARE OF A FEW SHEEP WHILE I'M STANDING OUT HERE, I CAN PICK UP SOME EXTRA MONEY
4-25-00
TEAM OWNERS HATE TO SEE THEIR PLAYERS PICK UP SOME EXTRA MONEY!
SCHULZ

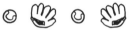

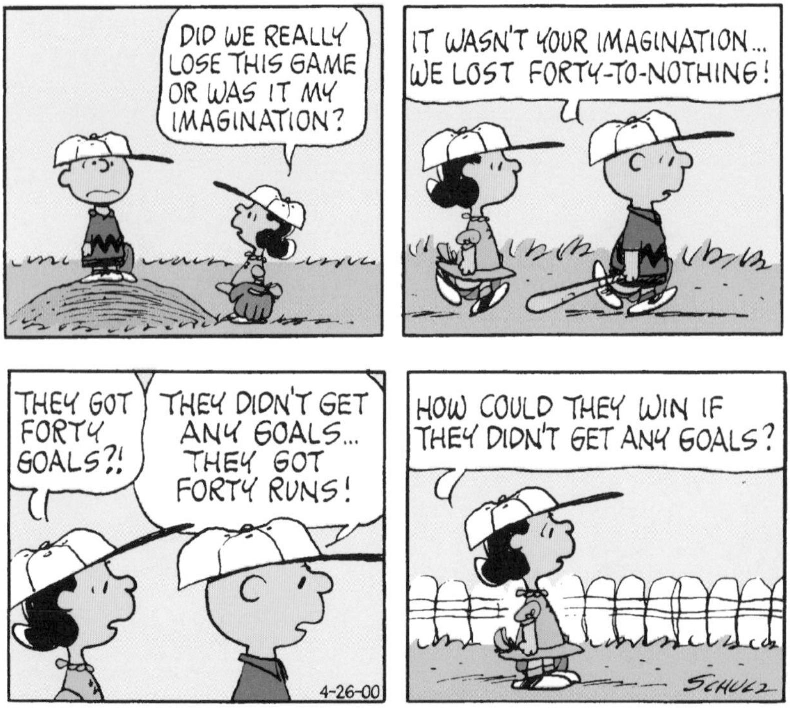
DID WE REALLY LOSE THIS GAME OR WAS IT MY IMAGINATION?
IT WASN'T YOUR IMAGINATION... WE LOST FORTY-TO-NOTHING!
THEY GOT FORTY GOALS?!
THEY DIDN'T GET ANY GOALS... THEY GOT FORTY RUNS!
4-26-00
HOW COULD THEY WIN IF THEY DIDN'T GET ANY GOALS?
SCHULZ

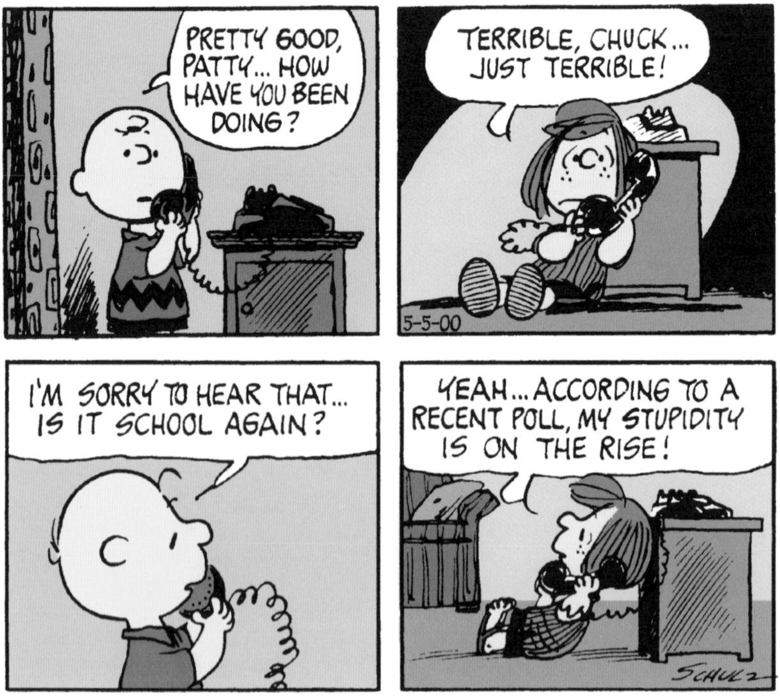
PRETTY GOOD, PATTY... HOW HAVE YOU BEEN DOING?
TERRIBLE, CHUCK... JUST TERRIBLE!
5-5-00
I'M SORRY TO HEAR THAT... IS IT SCHOOL AGAIN?
YEAH... ACCORDING TO A RECENT POLL, MY STUPIDITY IS ON THE RISE!
SCHULZ

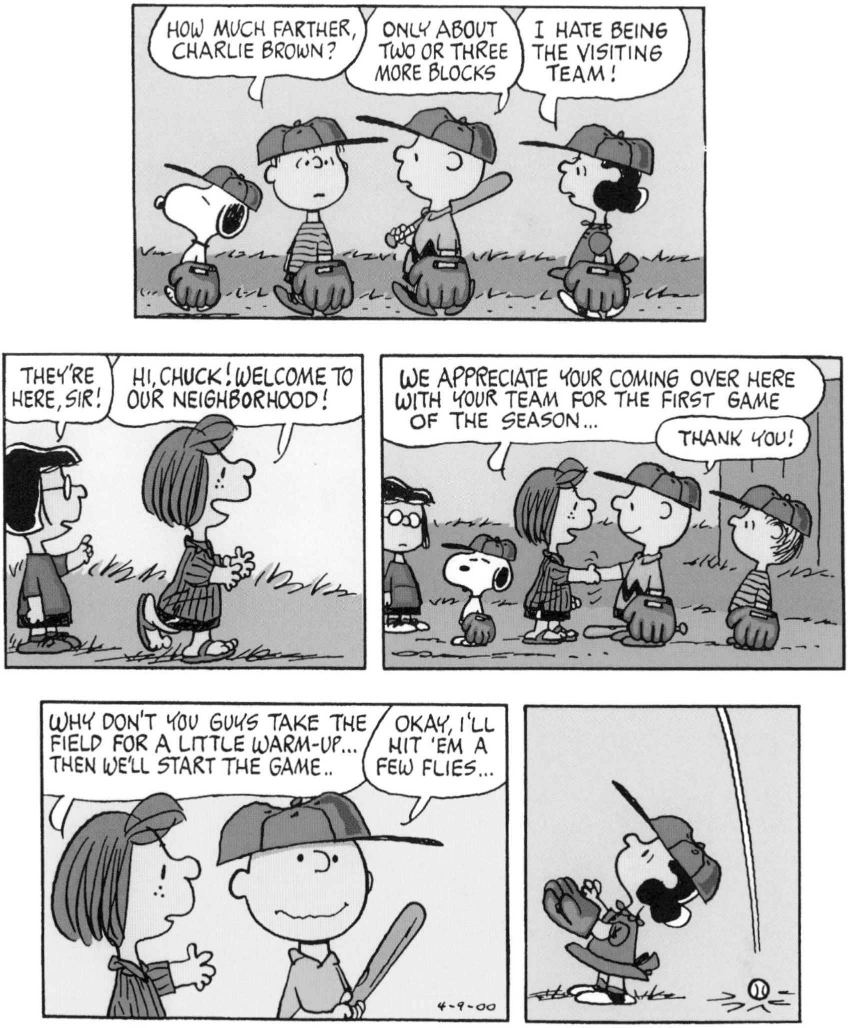
HOW MUCH FARTHER, CHARLIE BROWN?
ONLY ABOUT TWO OR THREE MORE BLOCKS
I HATE BEING THE VISITING TEAM!
THEY'RE HERE, SIR!
HI, CHUCK! WELCOME TO OUR NEIGHBORHOOD!
WE APPRECIATE YOUR COMING OVER HERE WITH YOUR TEAM FOR THE FIRST GAME OF THE SEASON...
THANK YOU!
WHY DON'T YOU GUYS TAKE THE FIELD FOR A LITTLE WARM-UP... THEN WE'LL START THE GAME..
OKAY, I'LL HIT 'EM A FEW FLIES...
4-9-00

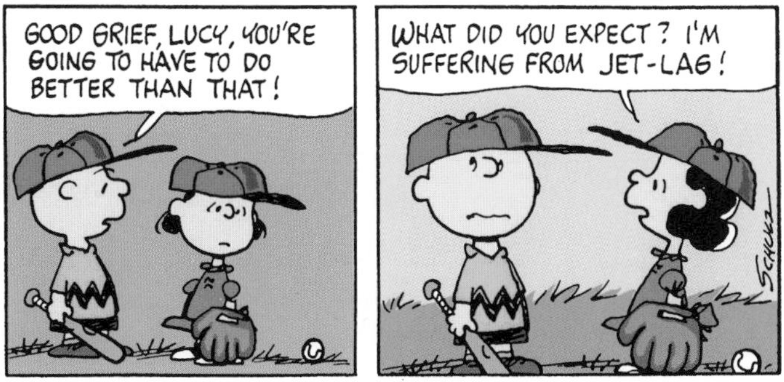
GOOD GRIEF, LUCY, YOU'RE GOING TO HAVE TO DO BETTER THAN THAT!
WHAT DID YOU EXPECT? I'M SUFFERING FROM JET-LAG!
SCHULZ

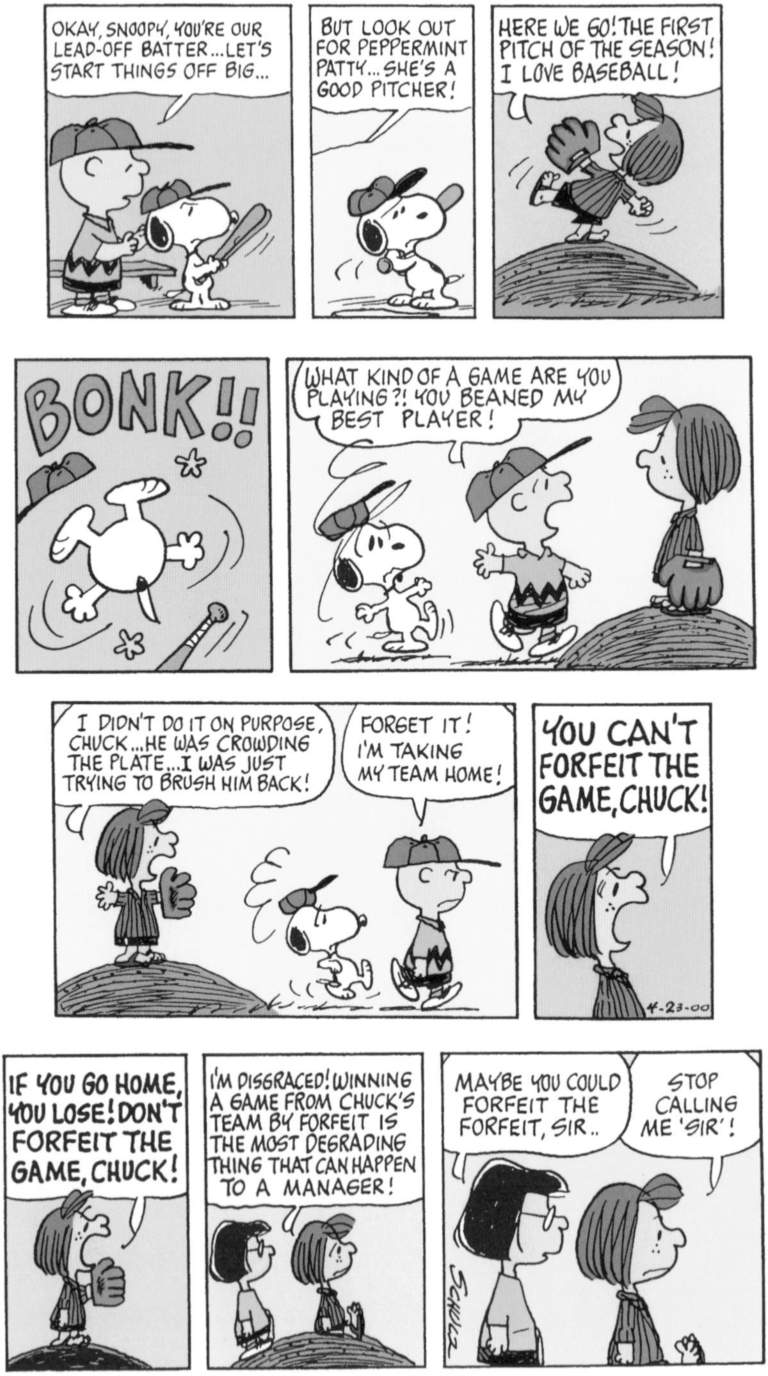
OKAY, SNOOPY, YOU'RE OUR LEAD-OFF BATTER...LET'S START THINGS OFF BIG...
BUT LOOK OUT FOR PEPPERMINT PATTY... SHE'S A GOOD PITCHER!
HERE WE GO! THE FIRST PITCH OF THE SEASON! I LOVE BASEBALL!
BONK!!
WHAT KIND OF A GAME ARE YOU PLAYING?! YOU BEANED MY BEST PLAYER!
I DIDN'T DO IT ON PURPOSE, CHUCK...HE WAS CROWDING THE PLATE...I WAS JUST TRYING TO BRUSH HIM BACK!
FORGET IT! I'M TAKING MY TEAM HOME!
YOU CAN'T FORFEIT THE GAME, CHUCK!
4-23-00
IF YOU GO HOME, YOU LOSE! DON'T FORFEIT THE GAME, CHUCK!
I'M DISGRACED! WINNING A GAME FROM CHUCK'S TEAM BY FORFEIT IS THE MOST DEGRADING THING THAT CAN HAPPEN TO A MANAGER!
MAYBE YOU COULD FORFEIT THE FORFEIT, SIR..
STOP CALLING ME 'SIR'!
SCHULZ

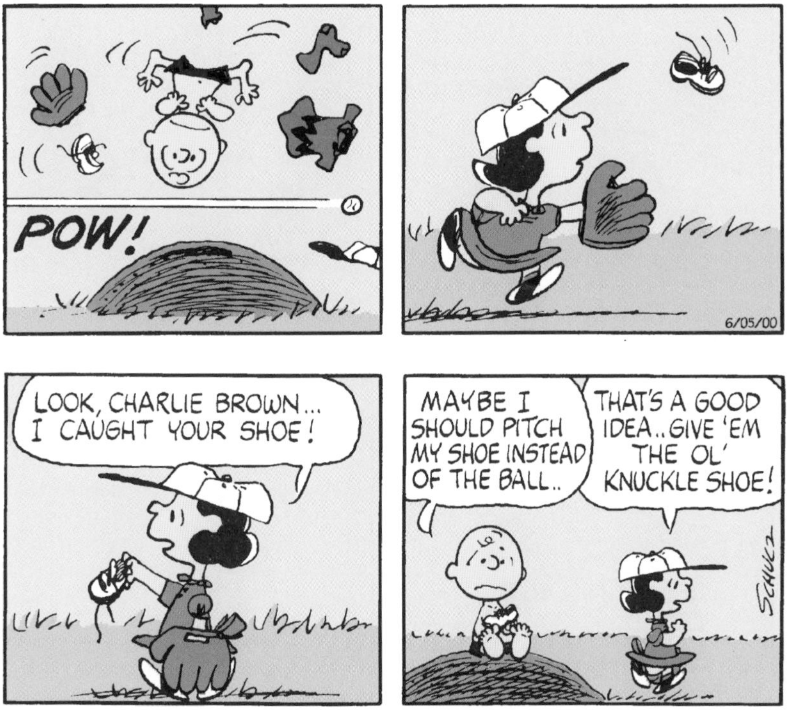
POW!
6/05/00
LOOK, CHARLIE BROWN... I CAUGHT YOUR SHOE!
MAYBE I SHOULD PITCH MY SHOE INSTEAD OF THE BALL..
THAT'S A GOOD IDEA..GIVE 'EM THE OL' KNUCKLE SHOE!
SCHULZ

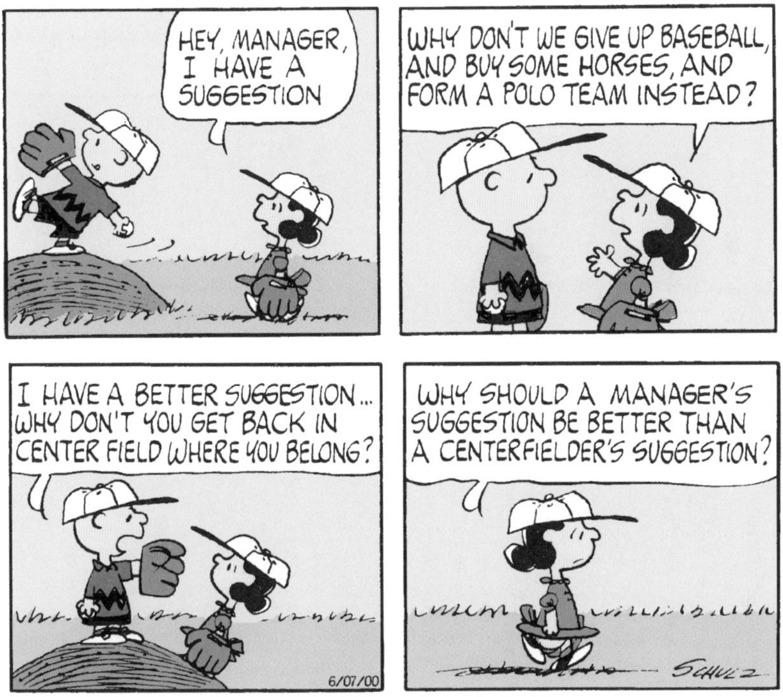
HEY, MANAGER, I HAVE A SUGGESTION
WHY DON'T WE GIVE UP BASEBALL, AND BUY SOME HORSES, AND FORM A POLO TEAM INSTEAD?
I HAVE A BETTER SUGGESTION... WHY DON'T YOU GET BACK IN CENTER FIELD WHERE YOU BELONG?
6/07/00
WHY SHOULD A MANAGER'S SUGGESTION BE BETTER THAN A CENTERFIELDER'S SUGGESTION?
SCHULZ

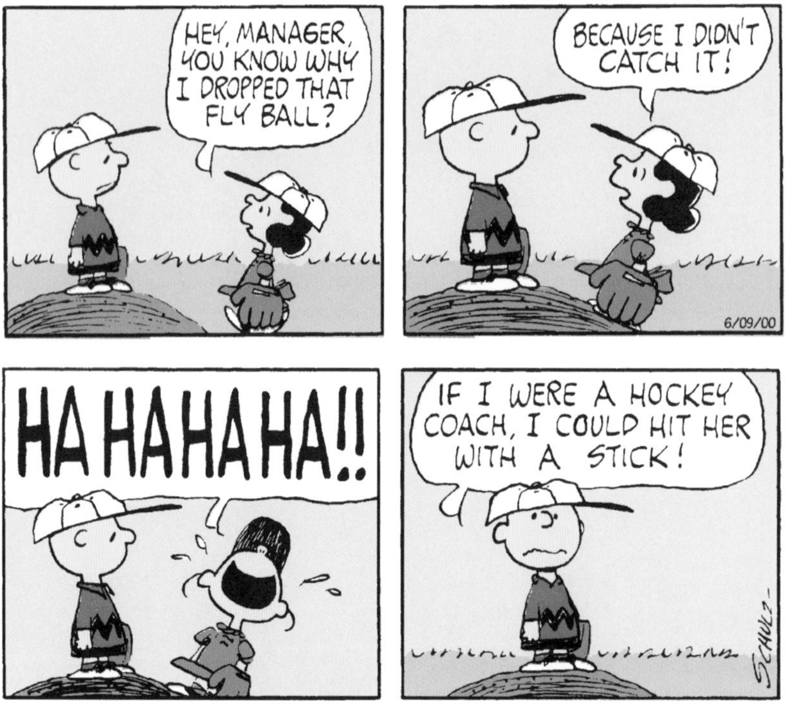
HEY, MANAGER, YOU KNOW WHY I DROPPED THAT FLY BALL?
BECAUSE I DIDN'T CATCH IT!
6/09/00
HA HAHAHA!!
IF I WERE A HOCKEY COACH, I COULD HIT HER WITH A STICK!
SCHULZ

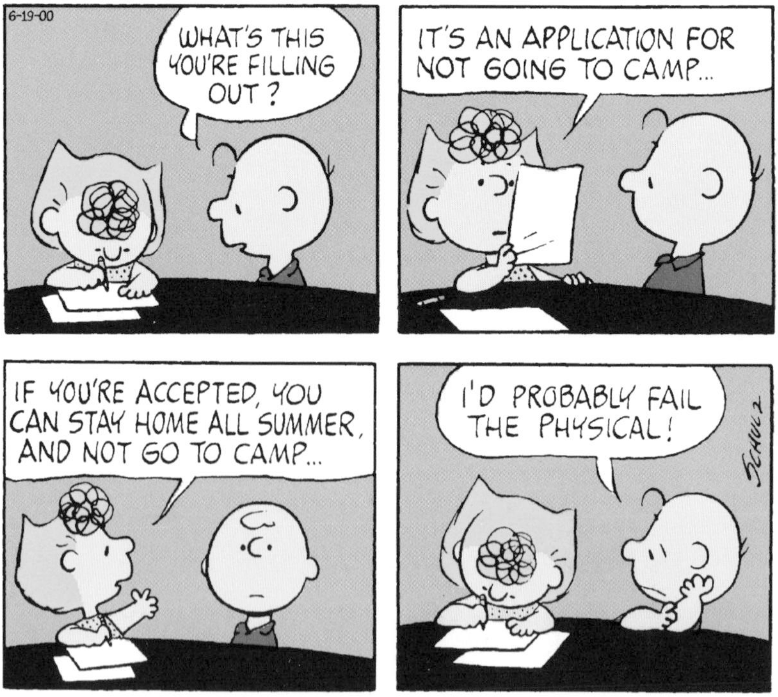
6-19-00
WHAT'S THIS YOU'RE FILLING OUT?
IT'S AN APPLICATION FOR NOT GOING TO CAMP...
IF YOU'RE ACCEPTED, YOU CAN STAY HOME ALL SUMMER, AND NOT GO TO CAMP...
I'D PROBABLY FAIL THE PHYSICAL!
SCHULZ

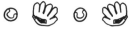

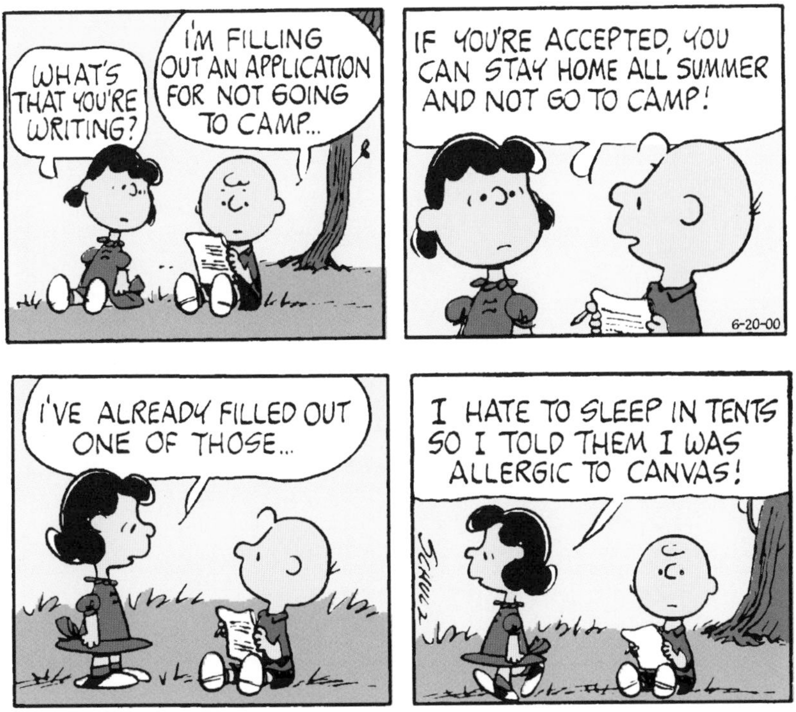
WHAT'S THAT YOU'RE WRITING?
I'M FILLING OUT AN APPLICATION FOR NOT GOING TO CAMP...
IF YOU'RE ACCEPTED, YOU CAN STAY HOME ALL SUMMER AND NOT GO TO CAMP!
6-20-00
I'VE ALREADY FILLED OUT ONE OF THOSE...
I HATE TO SLEEP IN TENTS SO I TOLD THEM I WAS ALLERGIC TO CANVAS!

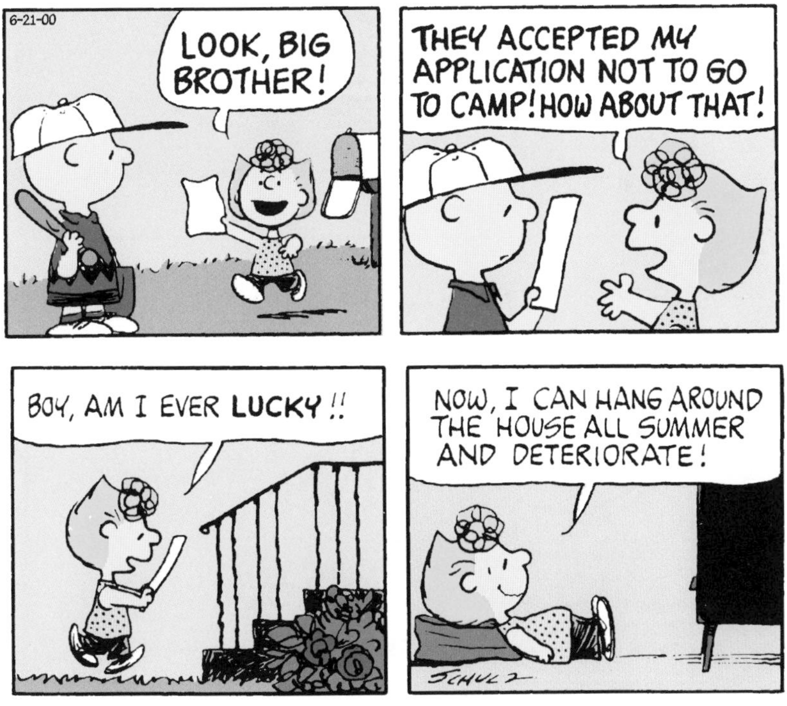
6-21-00
LOOK, BIG BROTHER!
THEY ACCEPTED MY APPLICATION NOT TO GO TO CAMP! HOW ABOUT THAT!
BOY, AM I EVER **LUCKY**!!
NOW, I CAN HANG AROUND THE HOUSE ALL SUMMER AND DETERIORATE!

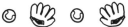

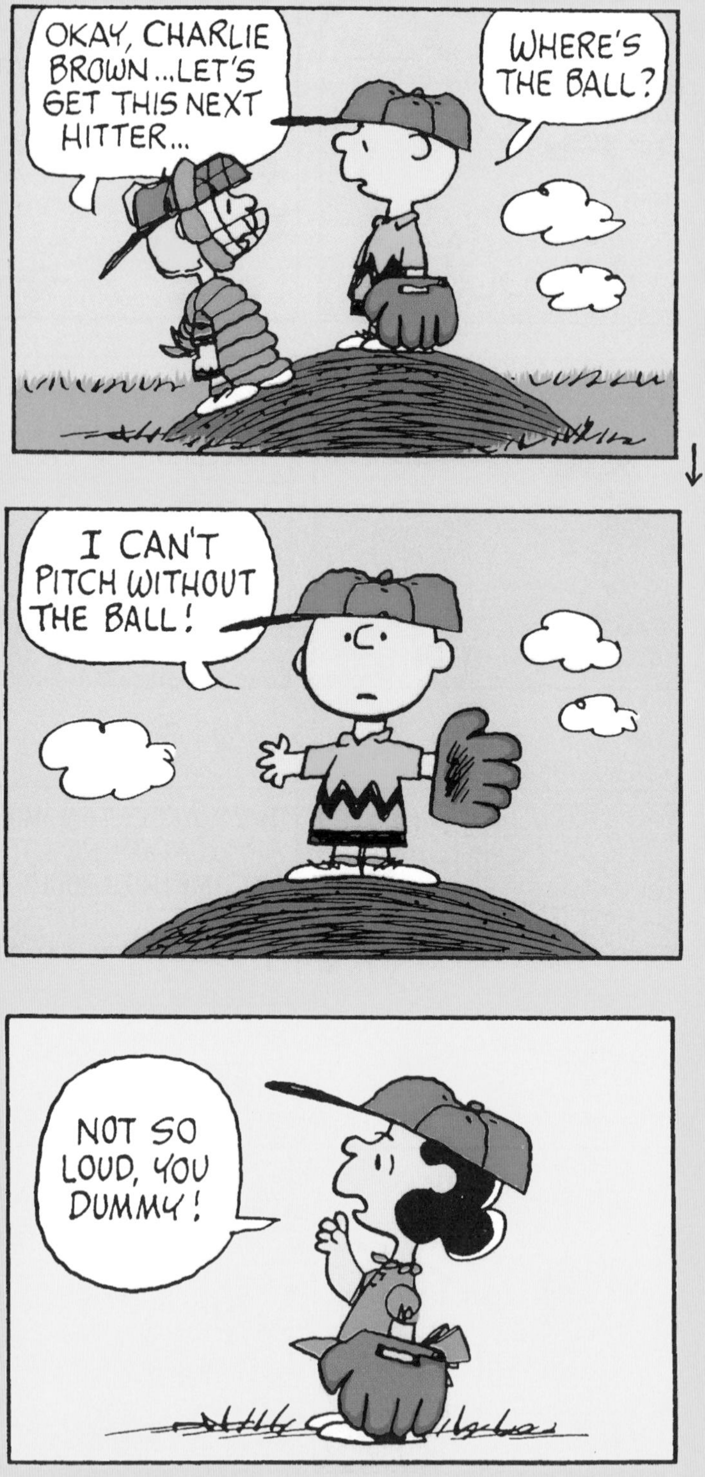
OKAY, CHARLIE BROWN...LET'S GET THIS NEXT HITTER...
WHERE'S THE BALL?
I CAN'T PITCH WITHOUT THE BALL!
NOT SO LOUD, YOU DUMMY!

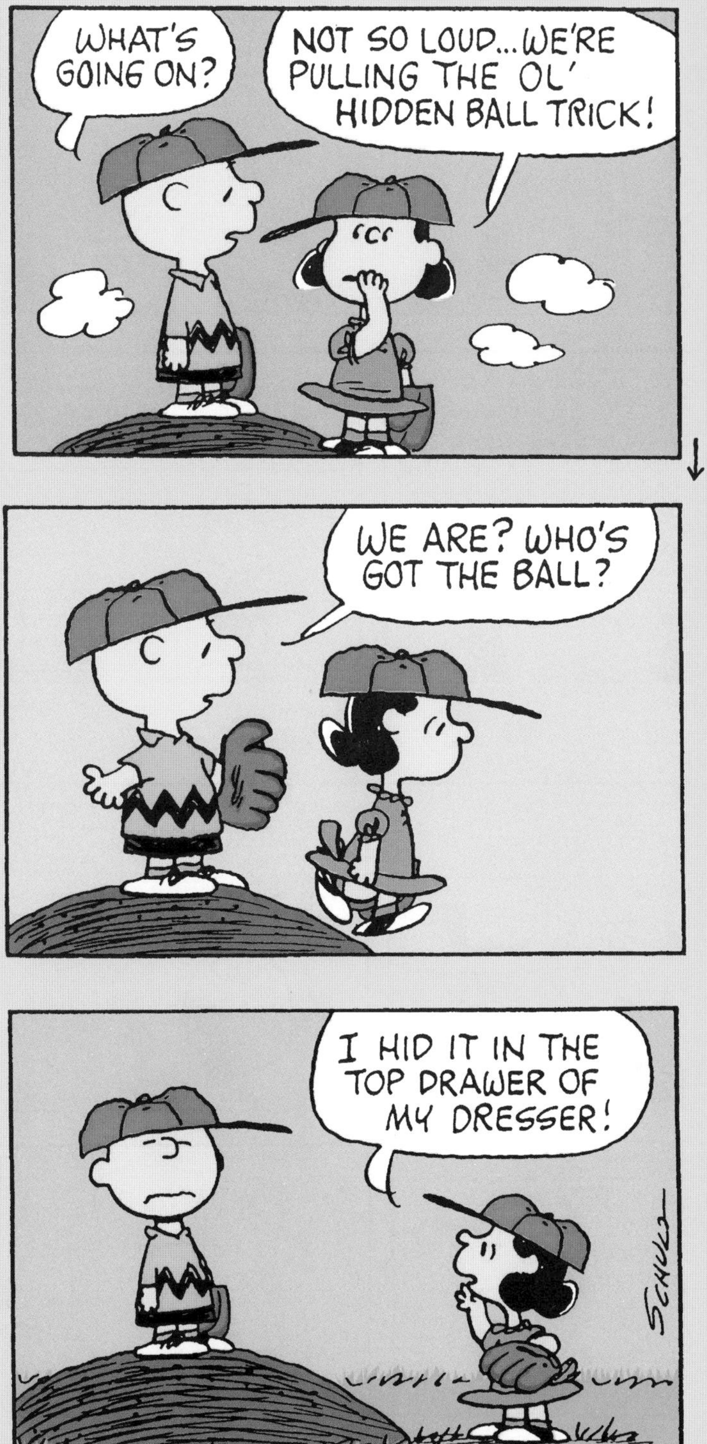
WHAT'S GOING ON?
NOT SO LOUD...WE'RE PULLING THE OL' HIDDEN BALL TRICK!
WE ARE? WHO'S GOT THE BALL?
I HID IT IN THE TOP DRAWER OF MY DRESSER!
SCHULZ

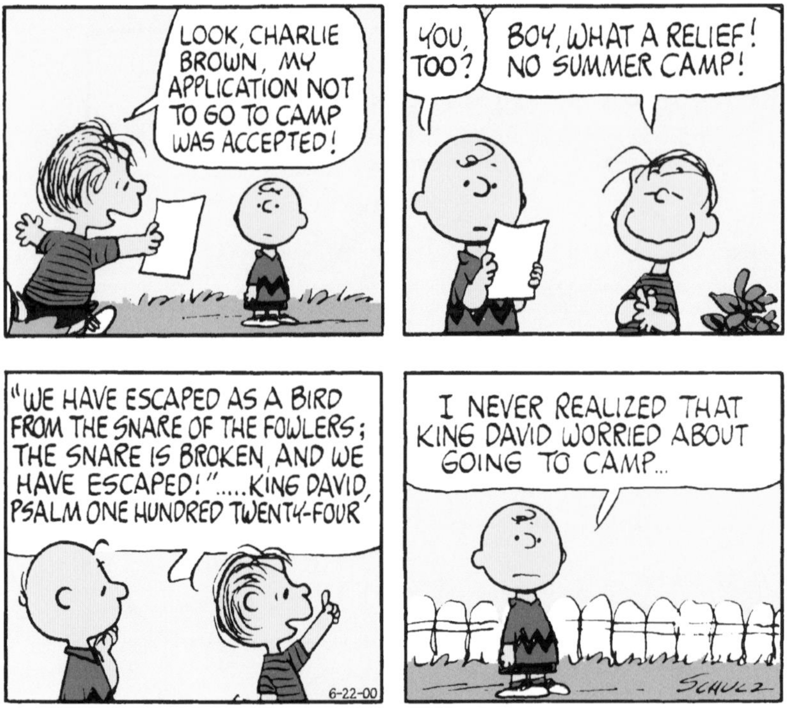
LOOK, CHARLIE BROWN, MY APPLICATION NOT TO GO TO CAMP WAS ACCEPTED!
YOU, TOO?
BOY, WHAT A RELIEF! NO SUMMER CAMP!
"WE HAVE ESCAPED AS A BIRD FROM THE SNARE OF THE FOWLERS; THE SNARE IS BROKEN, AND WE HAVE ESCAPED!".....KING DAVID, PSALM ONE HUNDRED TWENTY-FOUR
6-22-00
I NEVER REALIZED THAT KING DAVID WORRIED ABOUT GOING TO CAMP...
SCHULZ

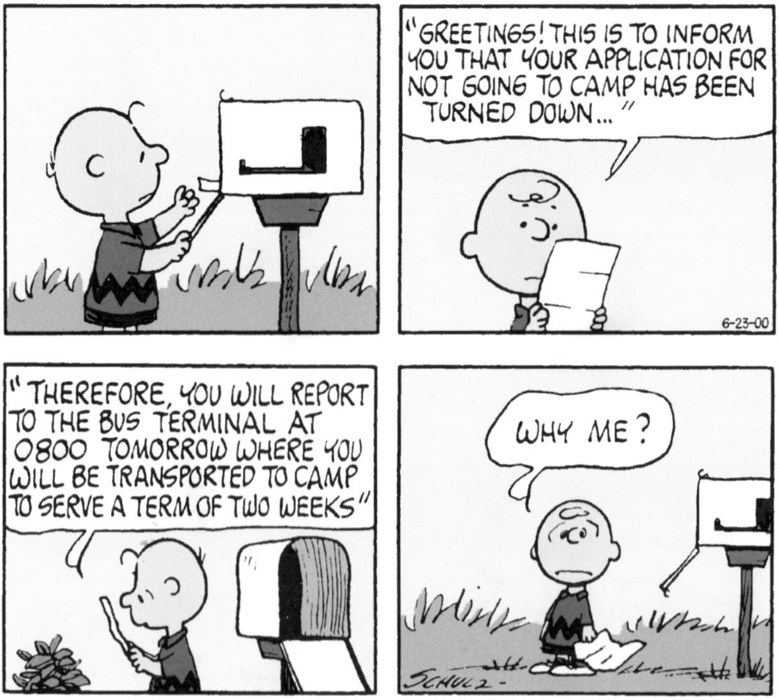
"GREETINGS! THIS IS TO INFORM YOU THAT YOUR APPLICATION FOR NOT GOING TO CAMP HAS BEEN TURNED DOWN..."
6-23-00
"THEREFORE, YOU WILL REPORT TO THE BUS TERMINAL AT 0800 TOMORROW WHERE YOU WILL BE TRANSPORTED TO CAMP TO SERVE A TERM OF TWO WEEKS"
WHY ME?
SCHULZ

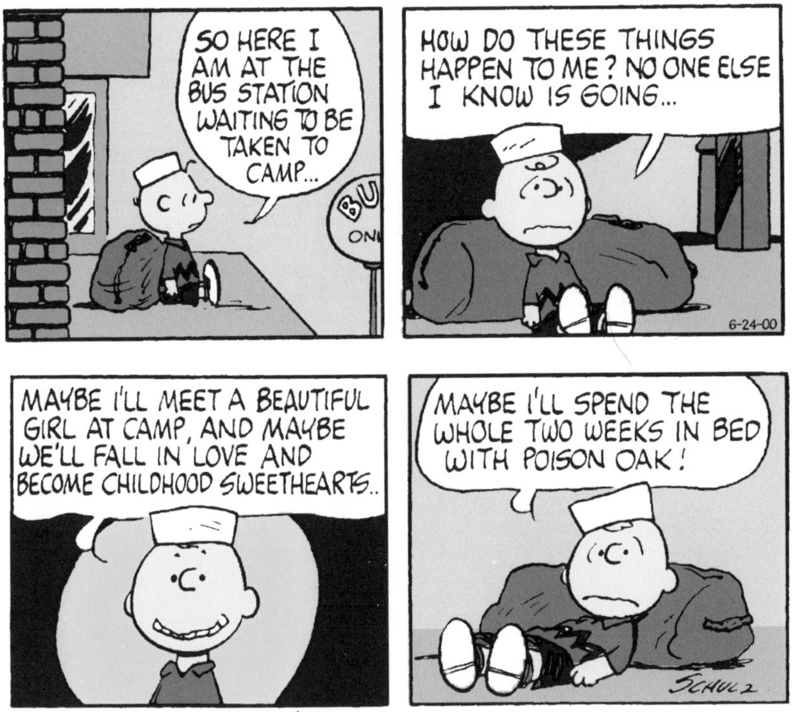
SO HERE I AM AT THE BUS STATION WAITING TO BE TAKEN TO CAMP...
HOW DO THESE THINGS HAPPEN TO ME? NO ONE ELSE I KNOW IS GOING...
6-24-00
MAYBE I'LL MEET A BEAUTIFUL GIRL AT CAMP, AND MAYBE WE'LL FALL IN LOVE AND BECOME CHILDHOOD SWEETHEARTS..
MAYBE I'LL SPEND THE WHOLE TWO WEEKS IN BED WITH POISON OAK!
SCHULZ

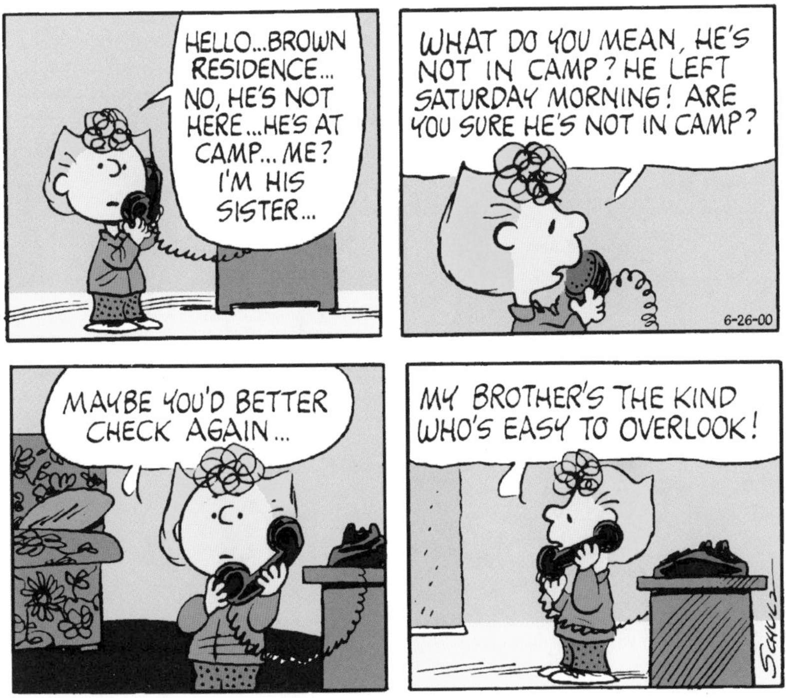
HELLO...BROWN RESIDENCE... NO, HE'S NOT HERE...HE'S AT CAMP... ME? I'M HIS SISTER...
WHAT DO YOU MEAN, HE'S NOT IN CAMP? HE LEFT SATURDAY MORNING! ARE YOU SURE HE'S NOT IN CAMP?
6-26-00
MAYBE YOU'D BETTER CHECK AGAIN...
MY BROTHER'S THE KIND WHO'S EASY TO OVERLOOK!
SCHULZ

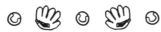

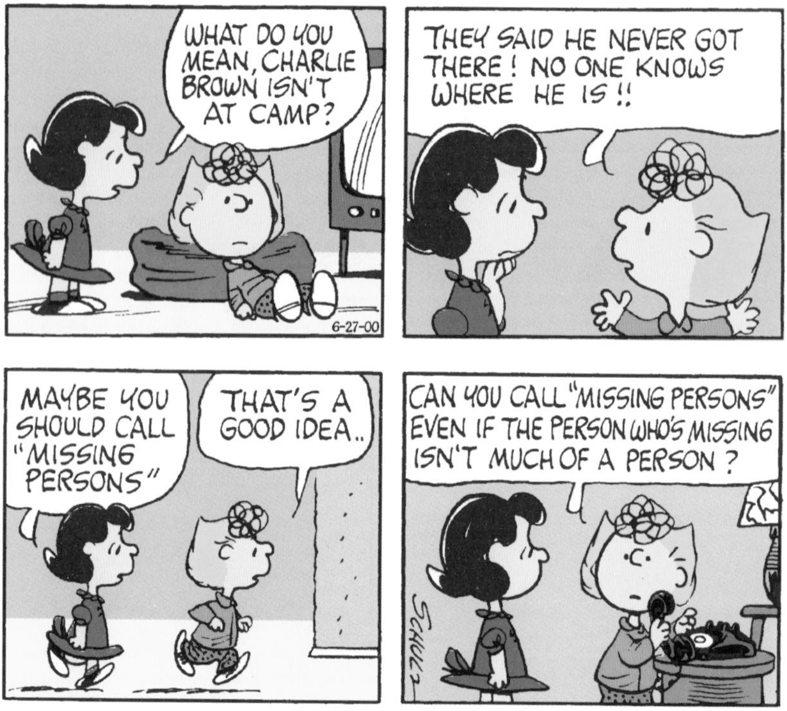
WHAT DO YOU MEAN, CHARLIE BROWN ISN'T AT CAMP?
6-27-00
THEY SAID HE NEVER GOT THERE! NO ONE KNOWS WHERE HE IS!!
MAYBE YOU SHOULD CALL "MISSING PERSONS"
THAT'S A GOOD IDEA..
CAN YOU CALL "MISSING PERSONS" EVEN IF THE PERSON WHO'S MISSING ISN'T MUCH OF A PERSON?

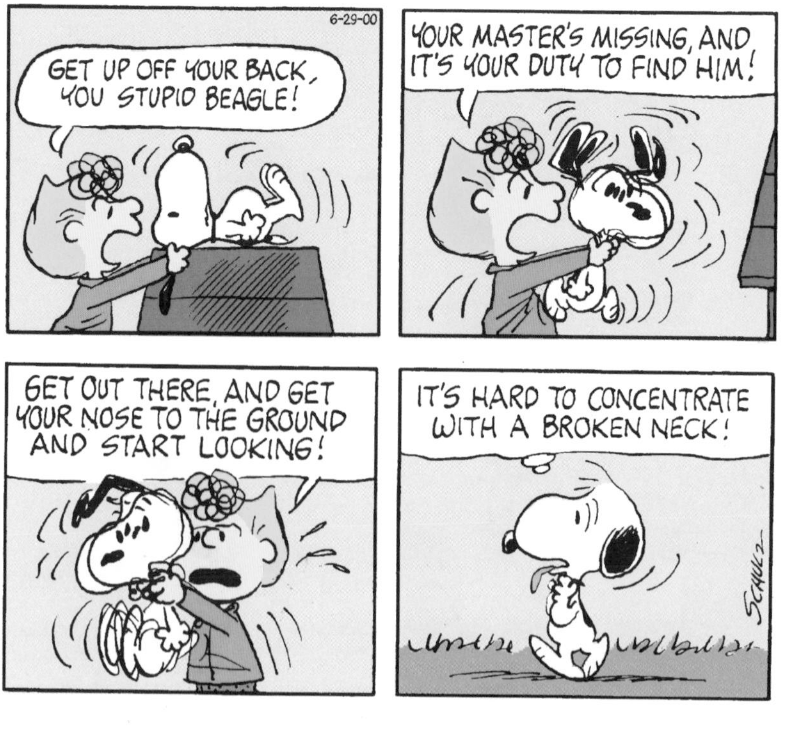
6-29-00
GET UP OFF YOUR BACK, YOU STUPID BEAGLE!
YOUR MASTER'S MISSING, AND IT'S YOUR DUTY TO FIND HIM!
GET OUT THERE, AND GET YOUR NOSE TO THE GROUND AND START LOOKING!
IT'S HARD TO CONCENTRATE WITH A BROKEN NECK!

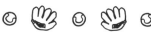

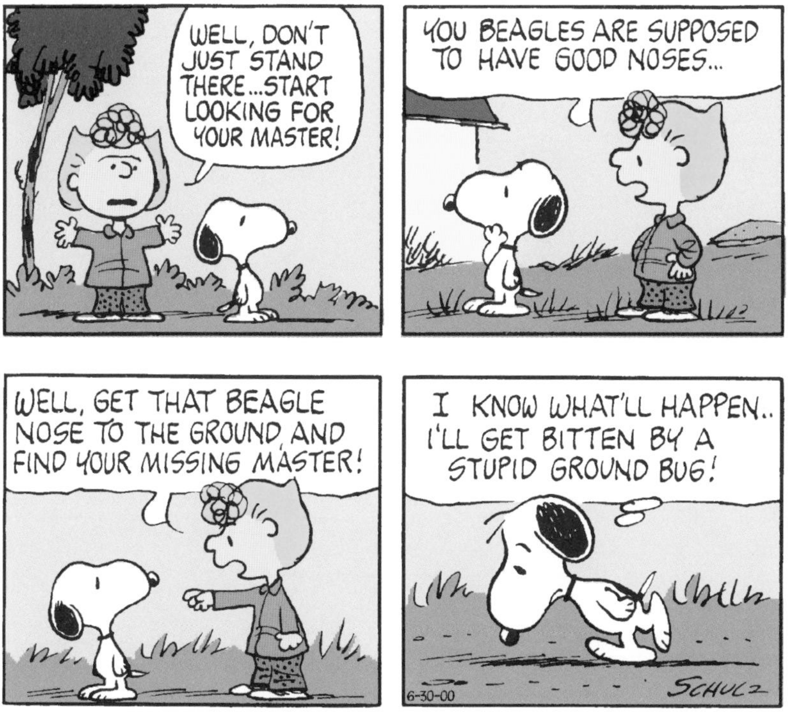
WELL, DON'T JUST STAND THERE...START LOOKING FOR YOUR MASTER!
YOU BEAGLES ARE SUPPOSED TO HAVE GOOD NOSES...
WELL, GET THAT BEAGLE NOSE TO THE GROUND AND FIND YOUR MISSING MASTER!
I KNOW WHAT'LL HAPPEN.. I'LL GET BITTEN BY A STUPID GROUND BUG!
6-30-00
SCHULZ

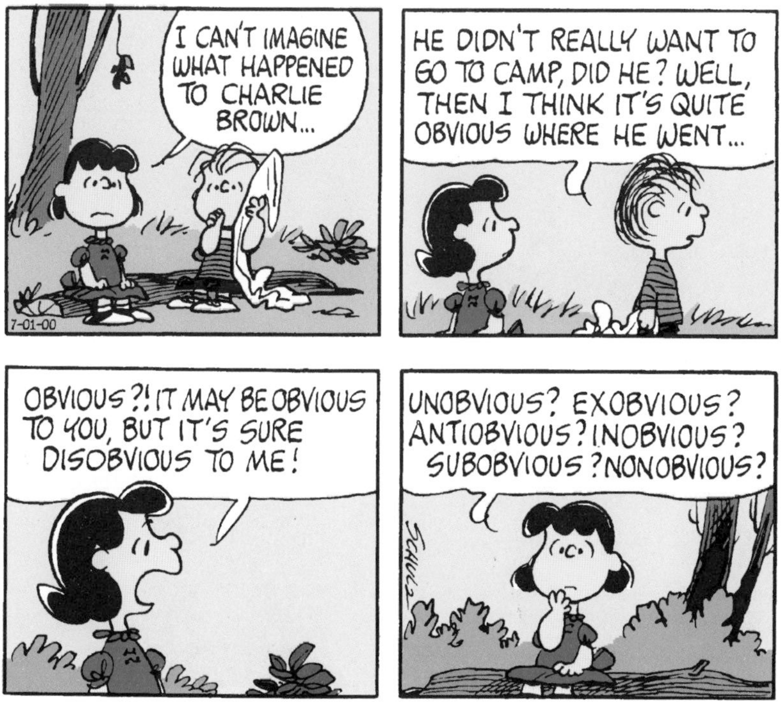
I CAN'T IMAGINE WHAT HAPPENED TO CHARLIE BROWN...
7-01-00
HE DIDN'T REALLY WANT TO GO TO CAMP, DID HE? WELL, THEN I THINK IT'S QUITE OBVIOUS WHERE HE WENT...
OBVIOUS?! IT MAY BE OBVIOUS TO YOU, BUT IT'S SURE DISOBVIOUS TO ME!
UNOBVIOUS? EXOBVIOUS? ANTIOBVIOUS? INOBVIOUS? SUBOBVIOUS? NONOBVIOUS?
SCHULZ

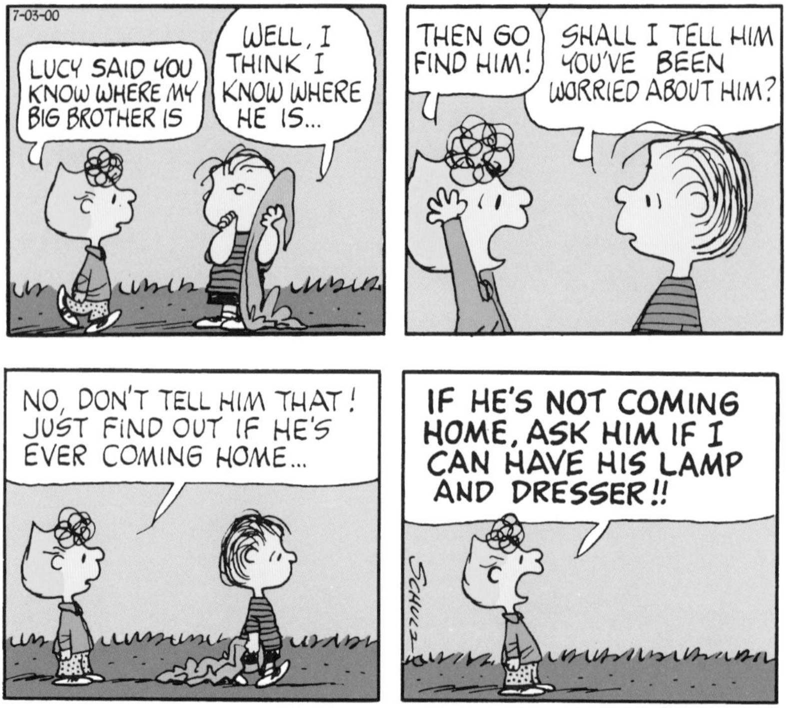
7-03-00
LUCY SAID YOU KNOW WHERE MY BIG BROTHER IS
WELL, I THINK I KNOW WHERE HE IS...
THEN GO FIND HIM!
SHALL I TELL HIM YOU'VE BEEN WORRIED ABOUT HIM?
NO, DON'T TELL HIM THAT! JUST FIND OUT IF HE'S EVER COMING HOME...
IF HE'S NOT COMING HOME, ASK HIM IF I CAN HAVE HIS LAMP AND DRESSER!!
SCHULZ

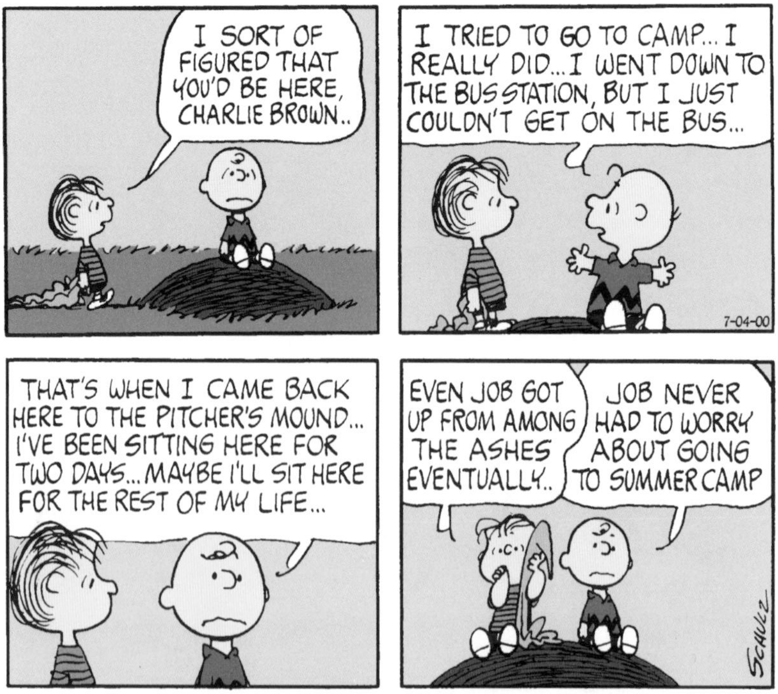
I SORT OF FIGURED THAT YOU'D BE HERE, CHARLIE BROWN..
I TRIED TO GO TO CAMP... I REALLY DID... I WENT DOWN TO THE BUS STATION, BUT I JUST COULDN'T GET ON THE BUS...
7-04-00
THAT'S WHEN I CAME BACK HERE TO THE PITCHER'S MOUND... I'VE BEEN SITTING HERE FOR TWO DAYS... MAYBE I'LL SIT HERE FOR THE REST OF MY LIFE...
EVEN JOB GOT UP FROM AMONG THE ASHES EVENTUALLY..
JOB NEVER HAD TO WORRY ABOUT GOING TO SUMMER CAMP
SCHULZ

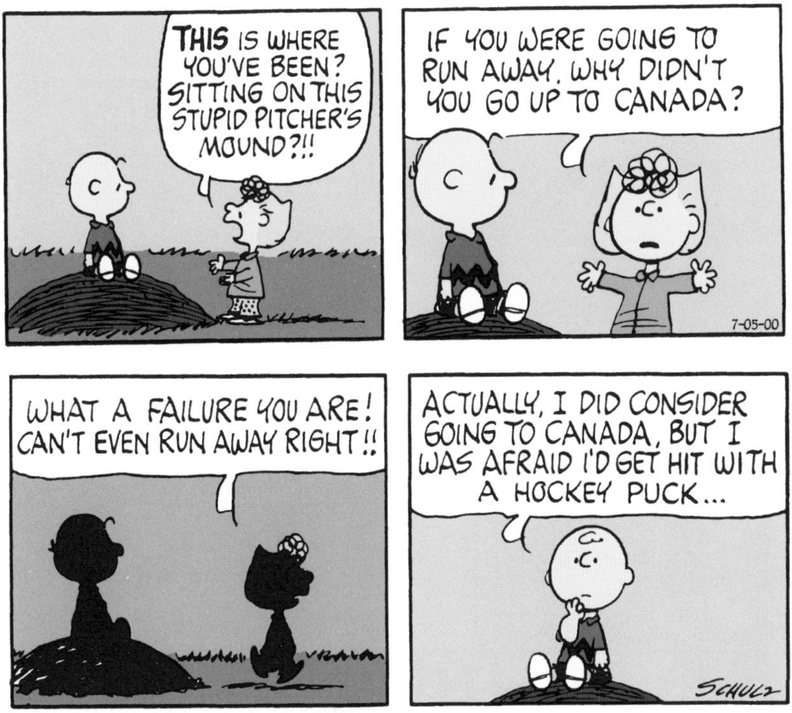
THIS IS WHERE YOU'VE BEEN? SITTING ON THIS STUPID PITCHER'S MOUND?!!
IF YOU WERE GOING TO RUN AWAY, WHY DIDN'T YOU GO UP TO CANADA?
7-05-00
WHAT A FAILURE YOU ARE! CAN'T EVEN RUN AWAY RIGHT!!
ACTUALLY, I DID CONSIDER GOING TO CANADA, BUT I WAS AFRAID I'D GET HIT WITH A HOCKEY PUCK...
SCHULZ

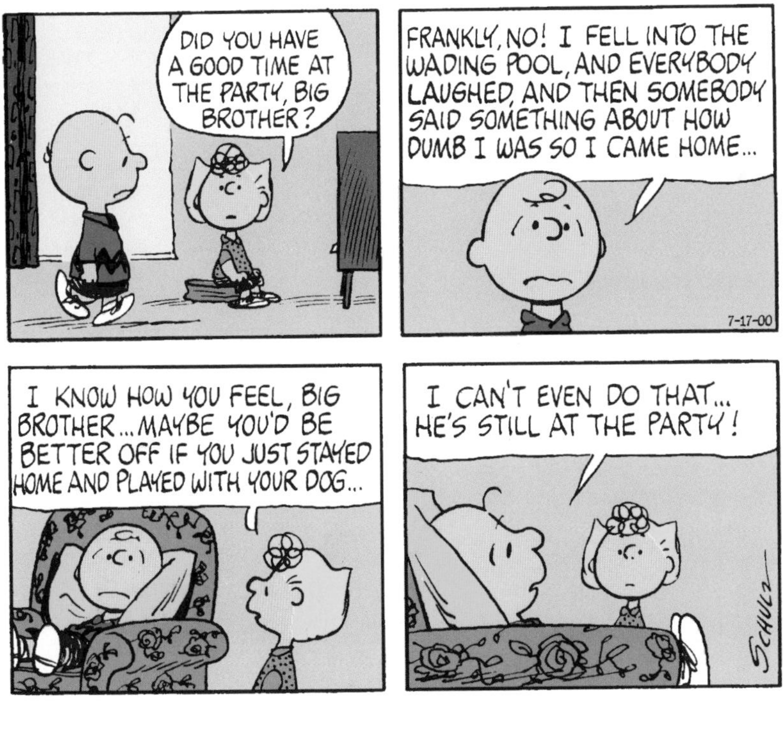
DID YOU HAVE A GOOD TIME AT THE PARTY, BIG BROTHER?
FRANKLY, NO! I FELL INTO THE WADING POOL, AND EVERYBODY LAUGHED, AND THEN SOMEBODY SAID SOMETHING ABOUT HOW DUMB I WAS SO I CAME HOME...
7-17-00
I KNOW HOW YOU FEEL, BIG BROTHER...MAYBE YOU'D BE BETTER OFF IF YOU JUST STAYED HOME AND PLAYED WITH YOUR DOG...
I CAN'T EVEN DO THAT... HE'S STILL AT THE PARTY!
SCHULZ

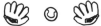

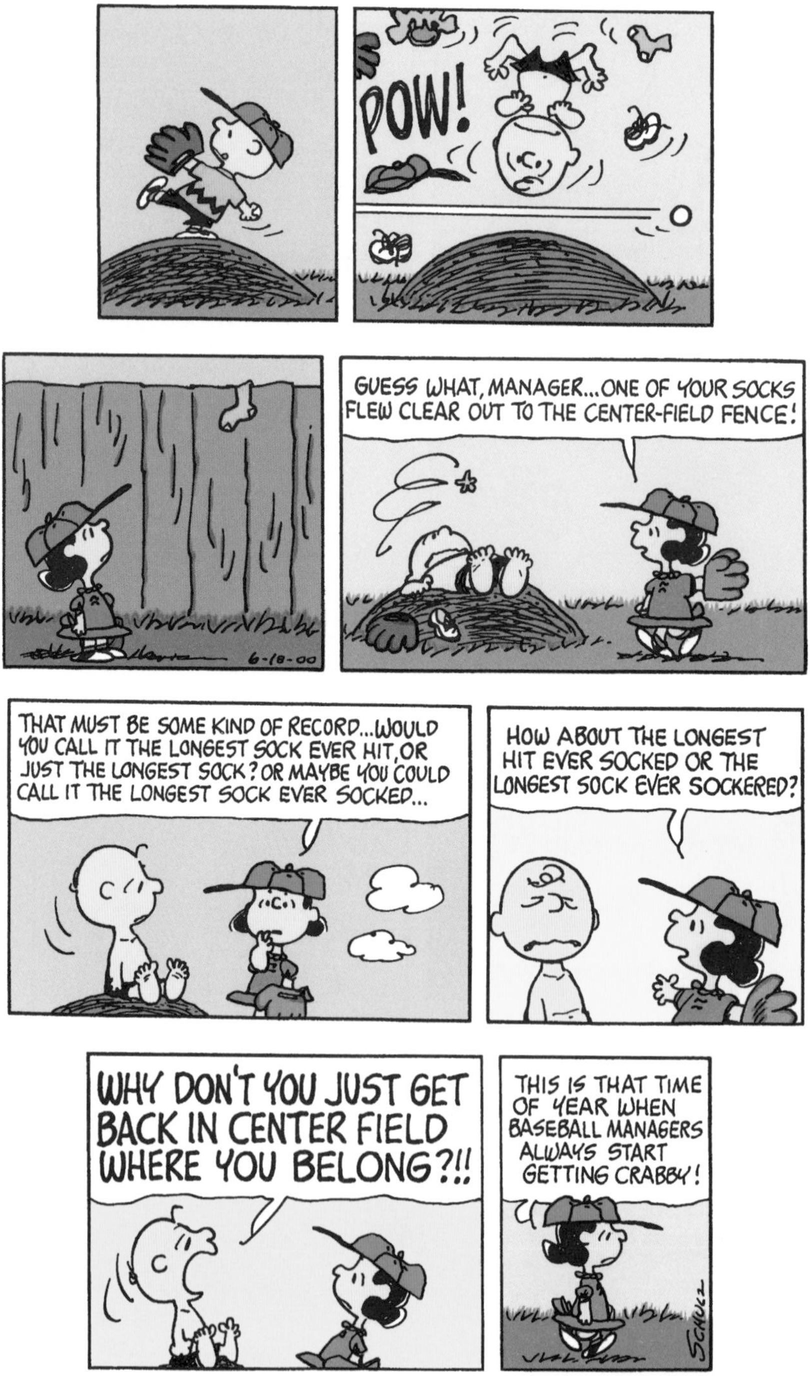
POW!
GUESS WHAT, MANAGER...ONE OF YOUR SOCKS FLEW CLEAR OUT TO THE CENTER-FIELD FENCE!
THAT MUST BE SOME KIND OF RECORD...WOULD YOU CALL IT THE LONGEST SOCK EVER HIT, OR JUST THE LONGEST SOCK? OR MAYBE YOU COULD CALL IT THE LONGEST SOCK EVER SOCKED...
HOW ABOUT THE LONGEST HIT EVER SOCKED OR THE LONGEST SOCK EVER SOCKERED?
WHY DON'T YOU JUST GET BACK IN CENTER FIELD WHERE YOU BELONG?!!
THIS IS THAT TIME OF YEAR WHEN BASEBALL MANAGERS ALWAYS START GETTING CRABBY!
6-18-00
SCHULZ

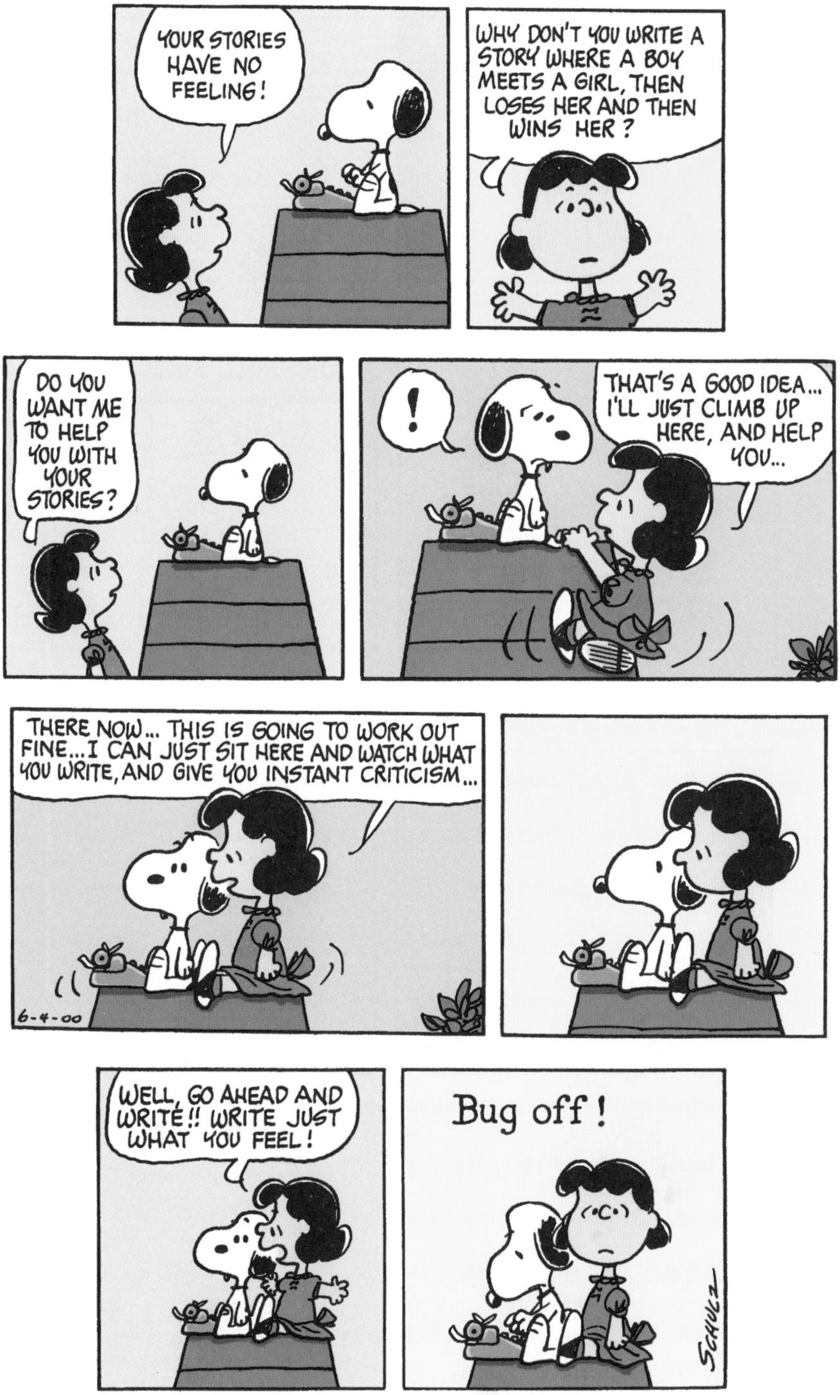
YOUR STORIES HAVE NO FEELING!
WHY DON'T YOU WRITE A STORY WHERE A BOY MEETS A GIRL, THEN LOSES HER AND THEN WINS HER?
DO YOU WANT ME TO HELP YOU WITH YOUR STORIES?
!
THAT'S A GOOD IDEA... I'LL JUST CLIMB UP HERE, AND HELP YOU...
THERE NOW... THIS IS GOING TO WORK OUT FINE...I CAN JUST SIT HERE AND WATCH WHAT YOU WRITE, AND GIVE YOU INSTANT CRITICISM...
6-4-00
WELL, GO AHEAD AND WRITE!! WRITE JUST WHAT YOU FEEL!
Bug off!
SCHULZ

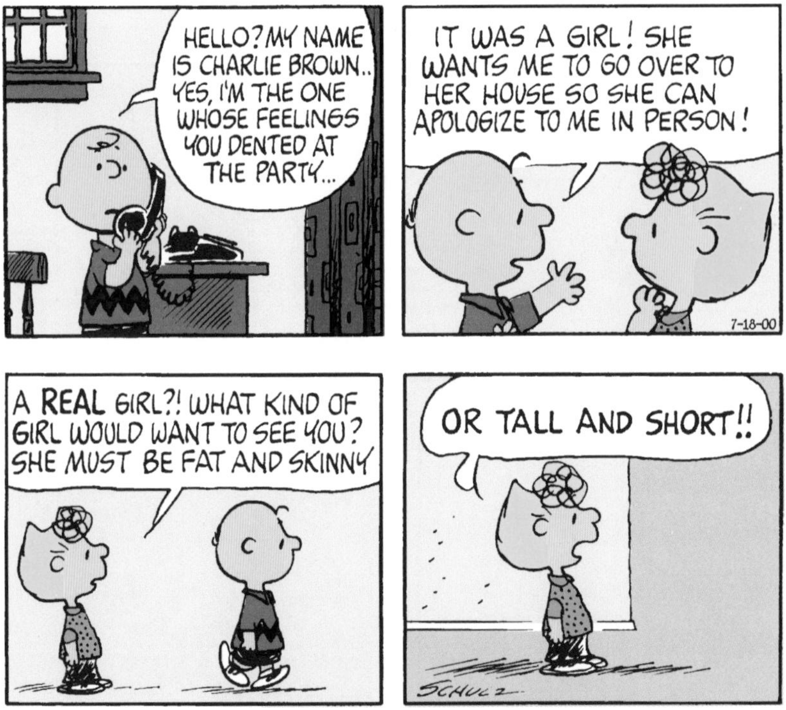
HELLO? MY NAME IS CHARLIE BROWN.. YES, I'M THE ONE WHOSE FEELINGS YOU DENTED AT THE PARTY...
IT WAS A GIRL! SHE WANTS ME TO GO OVER TO HER HOUSE SO SHE CAN APOLOGIZE TO ME IN PERSON!
7-18-00
A REAL GIRL?! WHAT KIND OF GIRL WOULD WANT TO SEE YOU? SHE MUST BE FAT AND SKINNY
OR TALL AND SHORT!!
SCHULZ

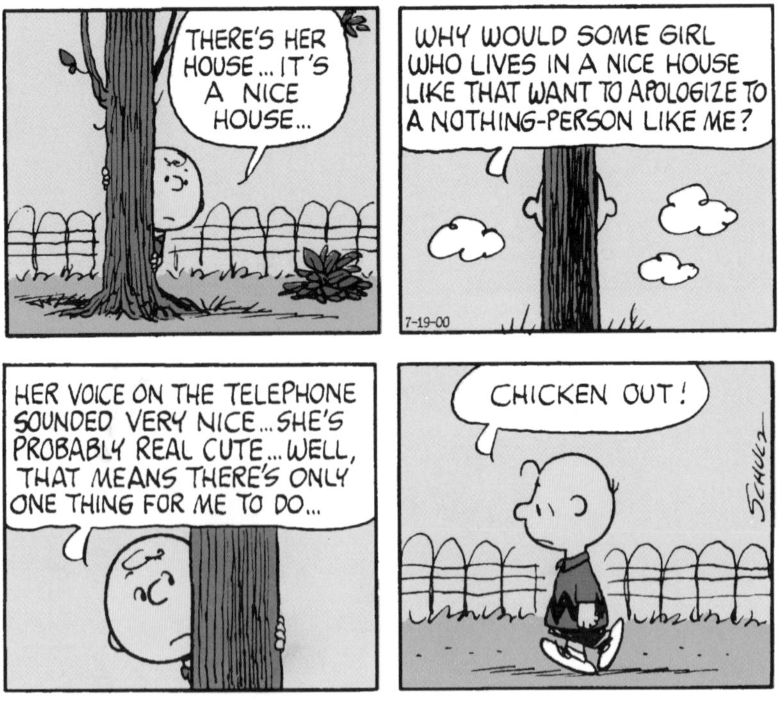
THERE'S HER HOUSE... IT'S A NICE HOUSE...
WHY WOULD SOME GIRL WHO LIVES IN A NICE HOUSE LIKE THAT WANT TO APOLOGIZE TO A NOTHING-PERSON LIKE ME?
7-19-00
HER VOICE ON THE TELEPHONE SOUNDED VERY NICE... SHE'S PROBABLY REAL CUTE... WELL, THAT MEANS THERE'S ONLY ONE THING FOR ME TO DO...
CHICKEN OUT!
SCHULZ

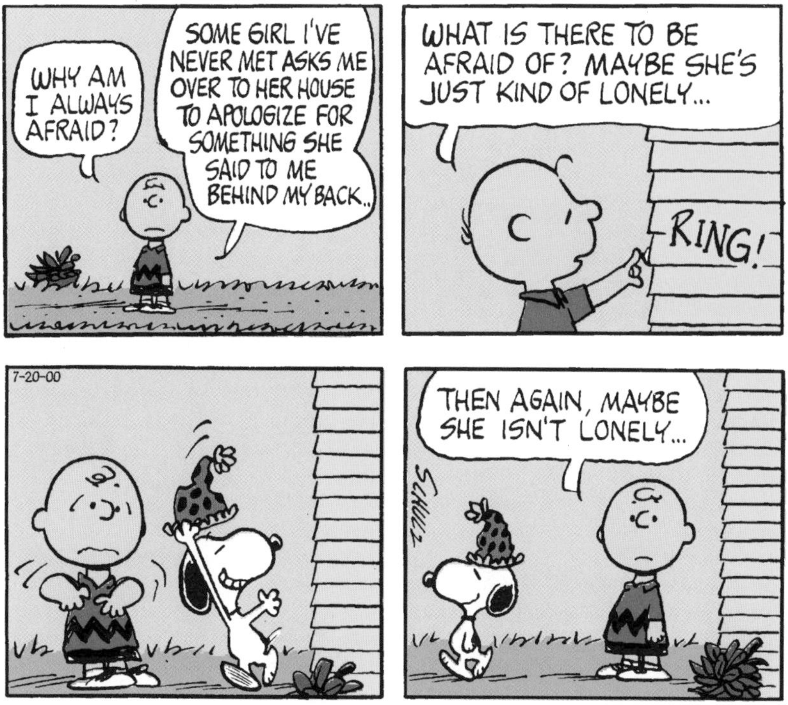
WHY AM I ALWAYS AFRAID?
SOME GIRL I'VE NEVER MET ASKS ME OVER TO HER HOUSE TO APOLOGIZE FOR SOMETHING SHE SAID TO ME BEHIND MY BACK..
WHAT IS THERE TO BE AFRAID OF? MAYBE SHE'S JUST KIND OF LONELY...
RING!
7-20-00
THEN AGAIN, MAYBE SHE ISN'T LONELY...
SCHULZ

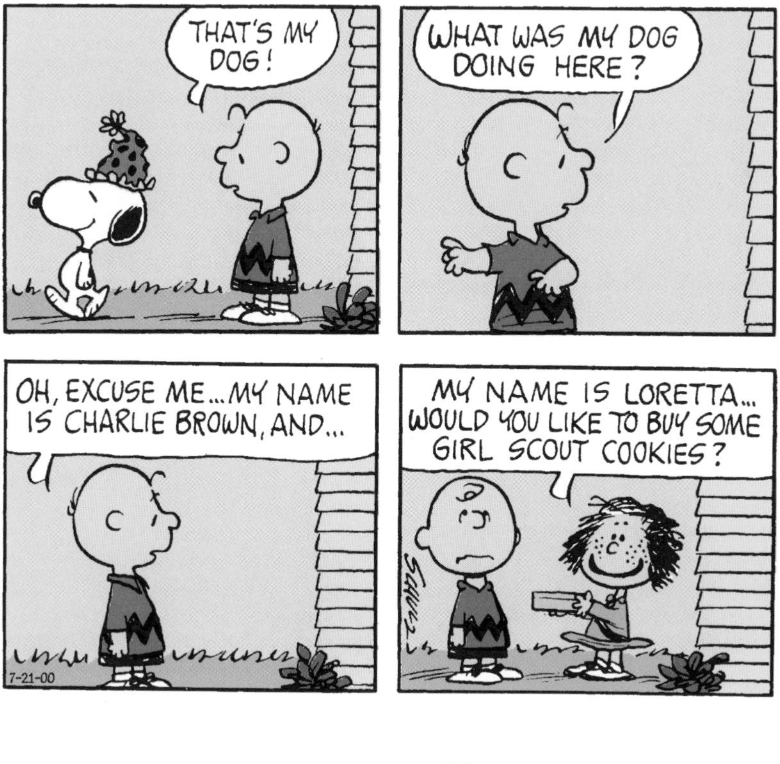
THAT'S MY DOG!
WHAT WAS MY DOG DOING HERE?
OH, EXCUSE ME...MY NAME IS CHARLIE BROWN, AND...
7-21-00
MY NAME IS LORETTA... WOULD YOU LIKE TO BUY SOME GIRL SCOUT COOKIES?
SCHULZ

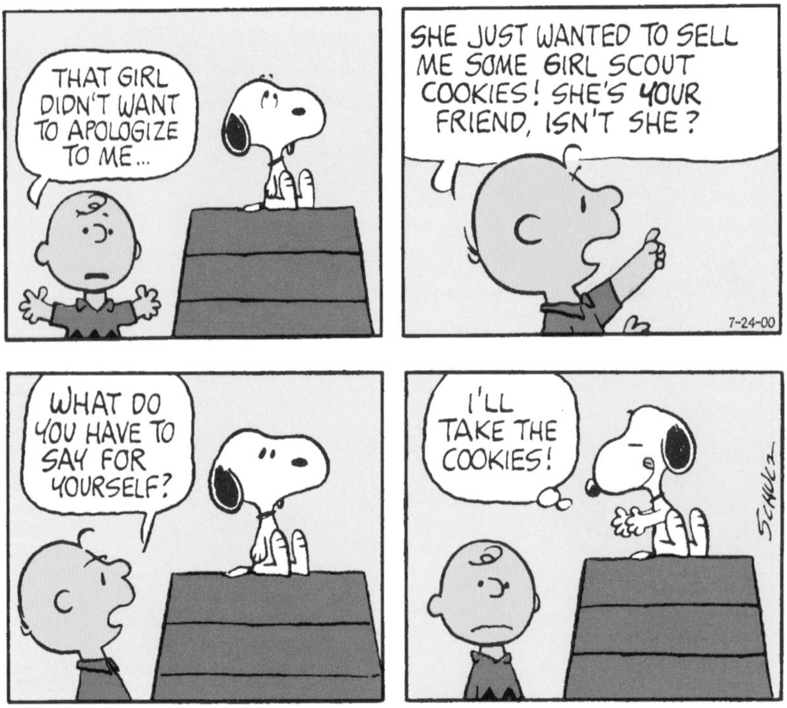
THAT GIRL DIDN'T WANT TO APOLOGIZE TO ME...
SHE JUST WANTED TO SELL ME SOME GIRL SCOUT COOKIES! SHE'S YOUR FRIEND, ISN'T SHE?
7-24-00
WHAT DO YOU HAVE TO SAY FOR YOURSELF?
I'LL TAKE THE COOKIES!
SCHULZ

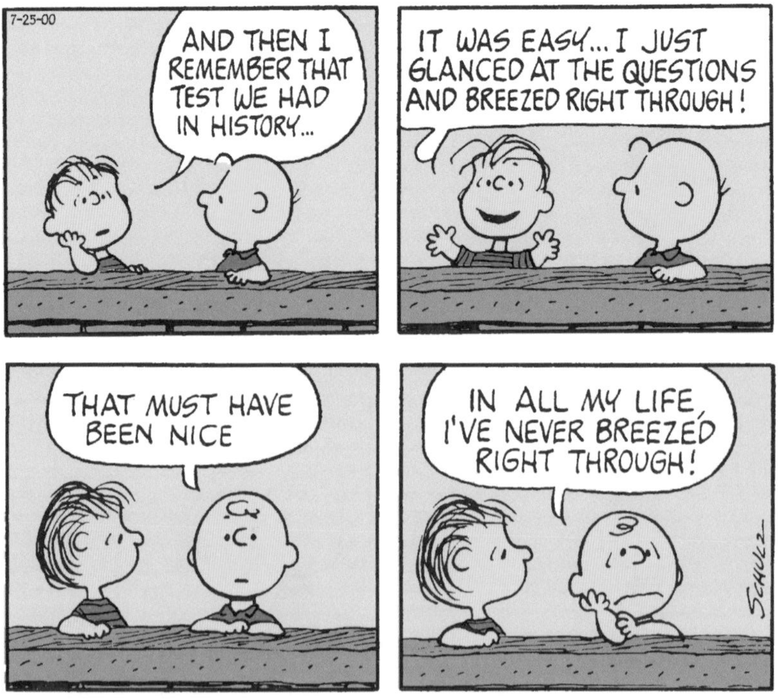
7-25-00
AND THEN I REMEMBER THAT TEST WE HAD IN HISTORY...
IT WAS EASY... I JUST GLANCED AT THE QUESTIONS AND BREEZED RIGHT THROUGH!
THAT MUST HAVE BEEN NICE
IN ALL MY LIFE, I'VE NEVER BREEZED RIGHT THROUGH!
SCHULZ

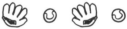

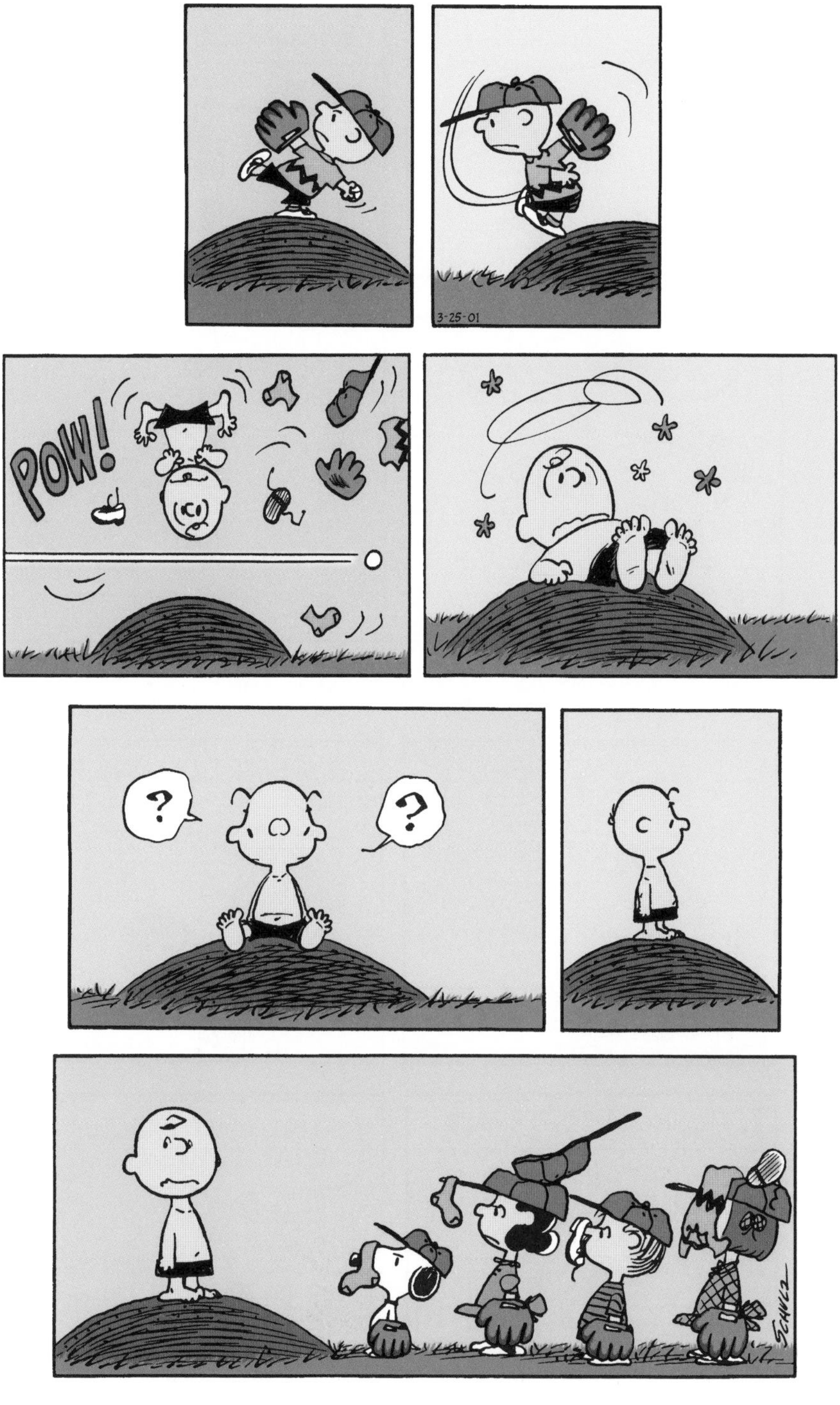
3-25-01
POW!
?
?
SCHULZ

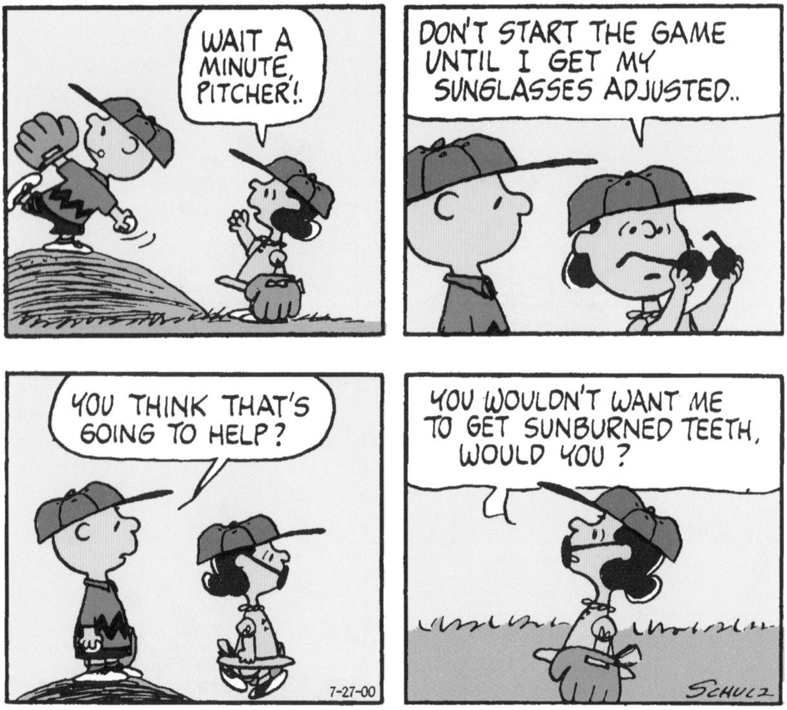
WAIT A MINUTE, PITCHER!.
DON'T START THE GAME UNTIL I GET MY SUNGLASSES ADJUSTED..
YOU THINK THAT'S GOING TO HELP?
YOU WOULDN'T WANT ME TO GET SUNBURNED TEETH, WOULD YOU?
7-27-00
SCHULZ

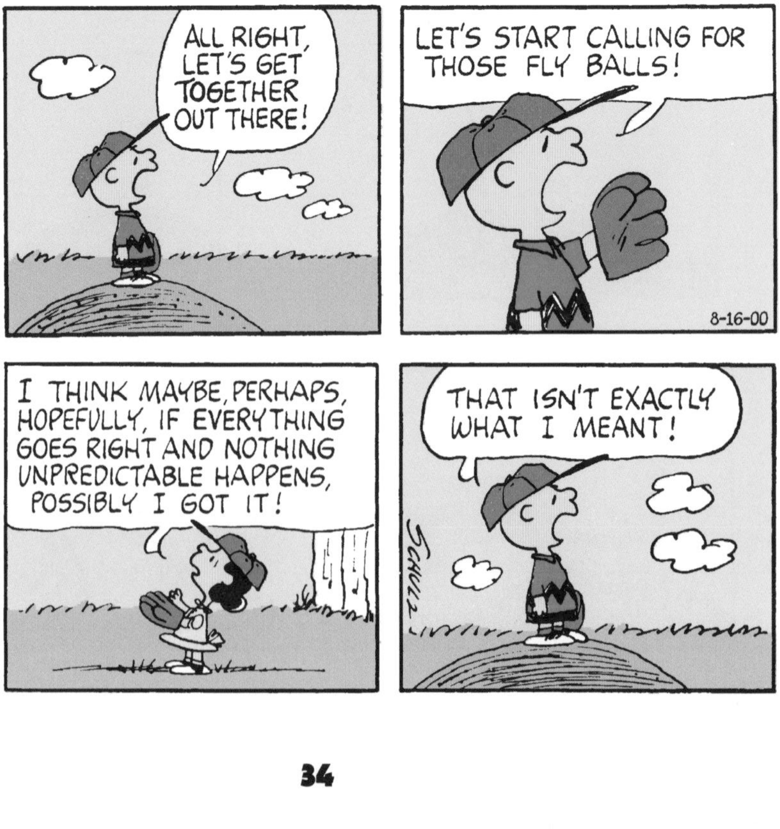
ALL RIGHT, LET'S GET TOGETHER OUT THERE!
LET'S START CALLING FOR THOSE FLY BALLS!
8-16-00
I THINK MAYBE, PERHAPS, HOPEFULLY, IF EVERYTHING GOES RIGHT AND NOTHING UNPREDICTABLE HAPPENS, POSSIBLY I GOT IT!
THAT ISN'T EXACTLY WHAT I MEANT!
SCHULZ

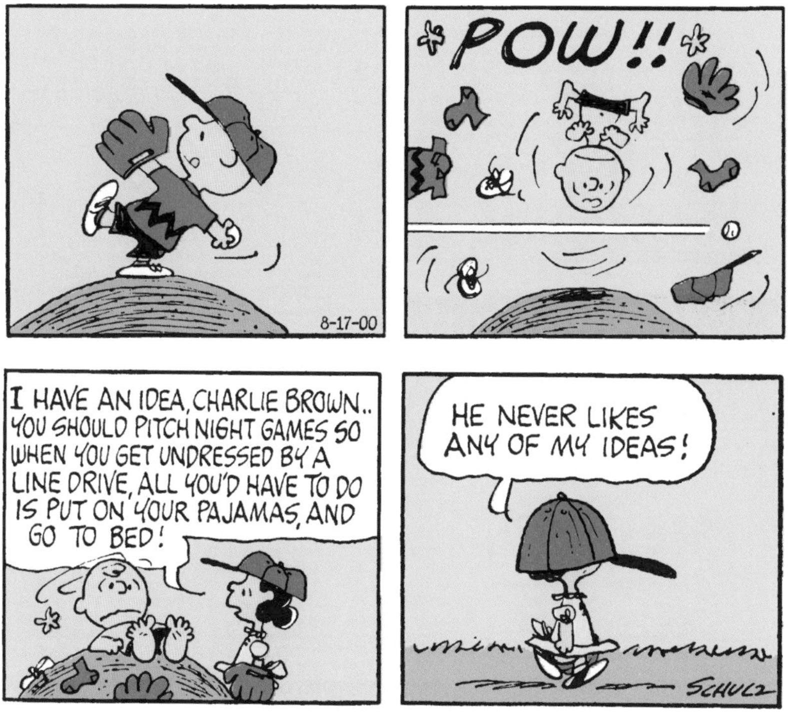
8-17-00
POW!!
I HAVE AN IDEA, CHARLIE BROWN.. YOU SHOULD PITCH NIGHT GAMES SO WHEN YOU GET UNDRESSED BY A LINE DRIVE, ALL YOU'D HAVE TO DO IS PUT ON YOUR PAJAMAS, AND GO TO BED!
HE NEVER LIKES ANY OF MY IDEAS!
SCHULZ

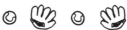

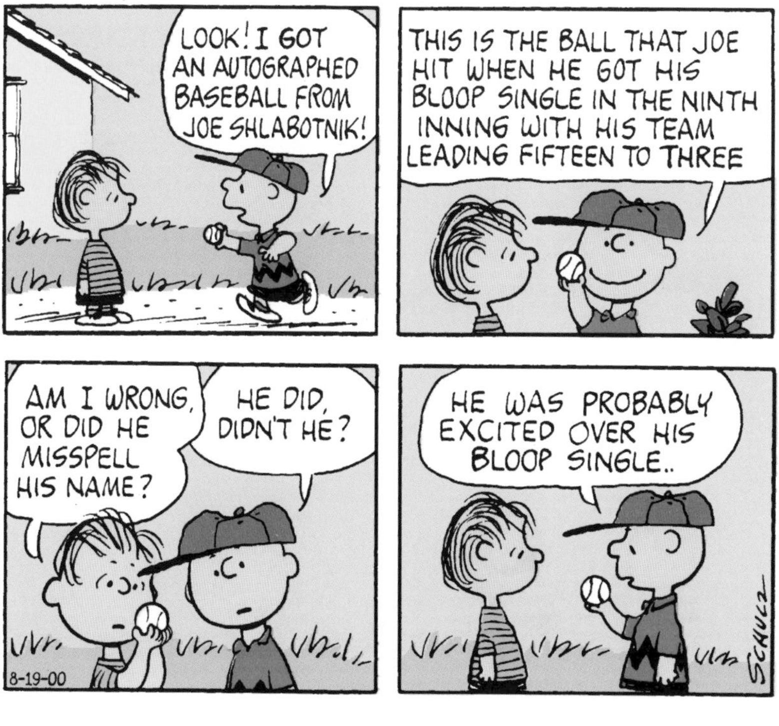
LOOK! I GOT AN AUTOGRAPHED BASEBALL FROM JOE SHLABOTNIK!
THIS IS THE BALL THAT JOE HIT WHEN HE GOT HIS BLOOP SINGLE IN THE NINTH INNING WITH HIS TEAM LEADING FIFTEEN TO THREE
AM I WRONG, OR DID HE MISSPELL HIS NAME?
HE DID, DIDN'T HE?
8-19-00
HE WAS PROBABLY EXCITED OVER HIS BLOOP SINGLE..
SCHULZ

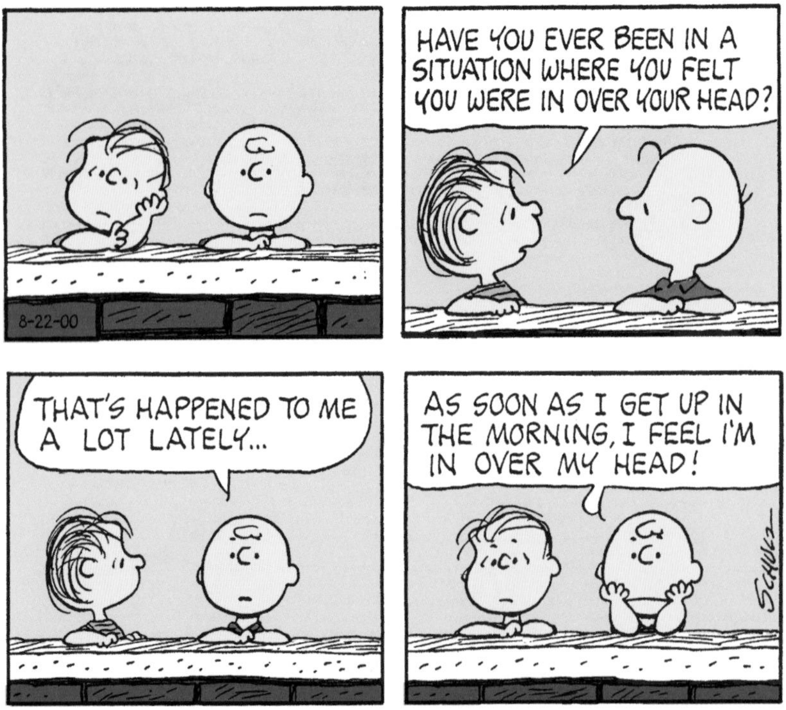
8-22-00
HAVE YOU EVER BEEN IN A SITUATION WHERE YOU FELT YOU WERE IN OVER YOUR HEAD?
THAT'S HAPPENED TO ME A LOT LATELY...
AS SOON AS I GET UP IN THE MORNING, I FEEL I'M IN OVER MY HEAD!
SCHULZ

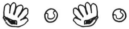

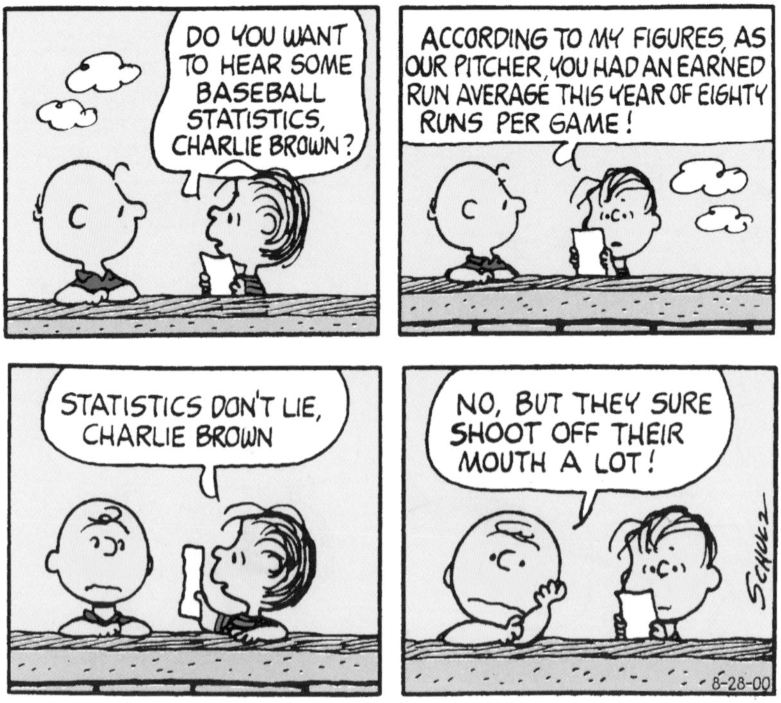
DO YOU WANT TO HEAR SOME BASEBALL STATISTICS, CHARLIE BROWN?
ACCORDING TO MY FIGURES, AS OUR PITCHER, YOU HAD AN EARNED RUN AVERAGE THIS YEAR OF EIGHTY RUNS PER GAME!
STATISTICS DON'T LIE, CHARLIE BROWN
NO, BUT THEY SURE SHOOT OFF THEIR MOUTH A LOT!
SCHULZ
8-28-00

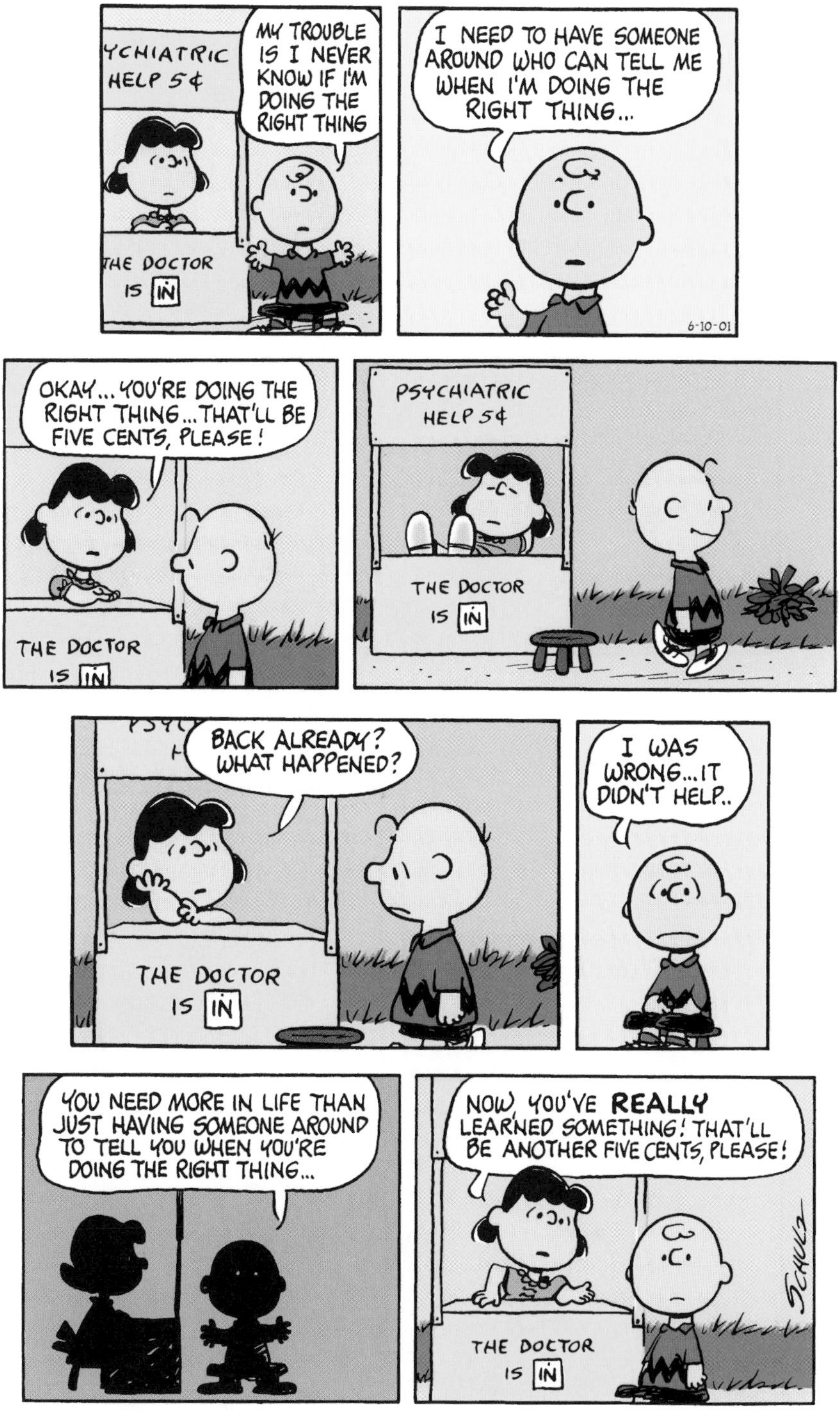
YCHIATRIC
HELP 5¢
HE DOCTOR
IS IN
MY TROUBLE IS I NEVER KNOW IF I'M DOING THE RIGHT THING
I NEED TO HAVE SOMEONE AROUND WHO CAN TELL ME WHEN I'M DOING THE RIGHT THING...
6-10-01
OKAY... YOU'RE DOING THE RIGHT THING...THAT'LL BE FIVE CENTS, PLEASE!
THE DOCTOR
IS IN
PSYCHIATRIC
HELP 5¢
THE DOCTOR
IS IN
BACK ALREADY? WHAT HAPPENED?
THE DOCTOR
IS IN
I WAS WRONG...IT DIDN'T HELP..
YOU NEED MORE IN LIFE THAN JUST HAVING SOMEONE AROUND TO TELL YOU WHEN YOU'RE DOING THE RIGHT THING...
NOW, YOU'VE **REALLY** LEARNED SOMETHING! THAT'LL BE ANOTHER FIVE CENTS, PLEASE!
THE DOCTOR
IS IN
SCHULZ

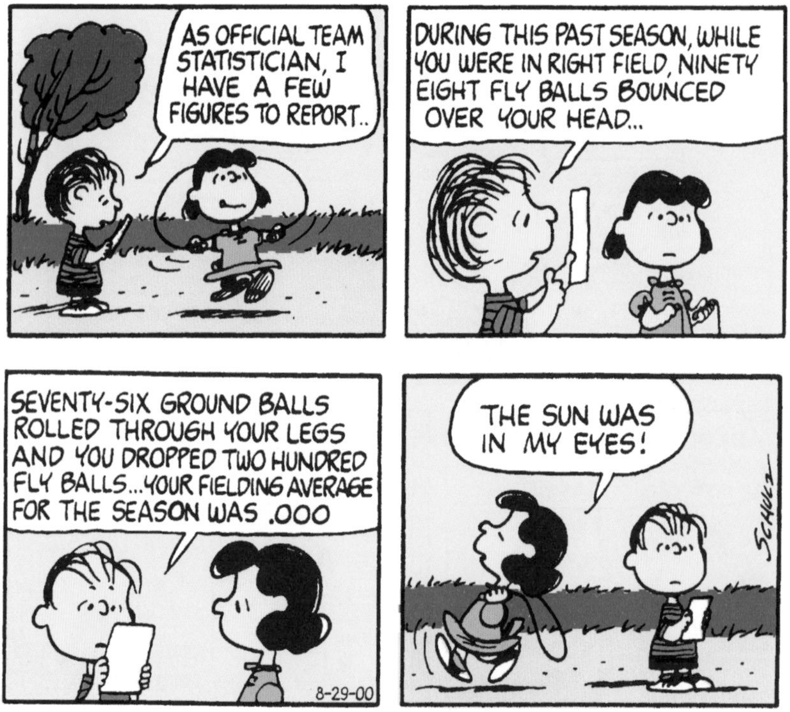
AS OFFICIAL TEAM STATISTICIAN, I HAVE A FEW FIGURES TO REPORT..
DURING THIS PAST SEASON, WHILE YOU WERE IN RIGHT FIELD, NINETY EIGHT FLY BALLS BOUNCED OVER YOUR HEAD...
SEVENTY-SIX GROUND BALLS ROLLED THROUGH YOUR LEGS AND YOU DROPPED TWO HUNDRED FLY BALLS...YOUR FIELDING AVERAGE FOR THE SEASON WAS .000
8-29-00
THE SUN WAS IN MY EYES!
SCHULZ

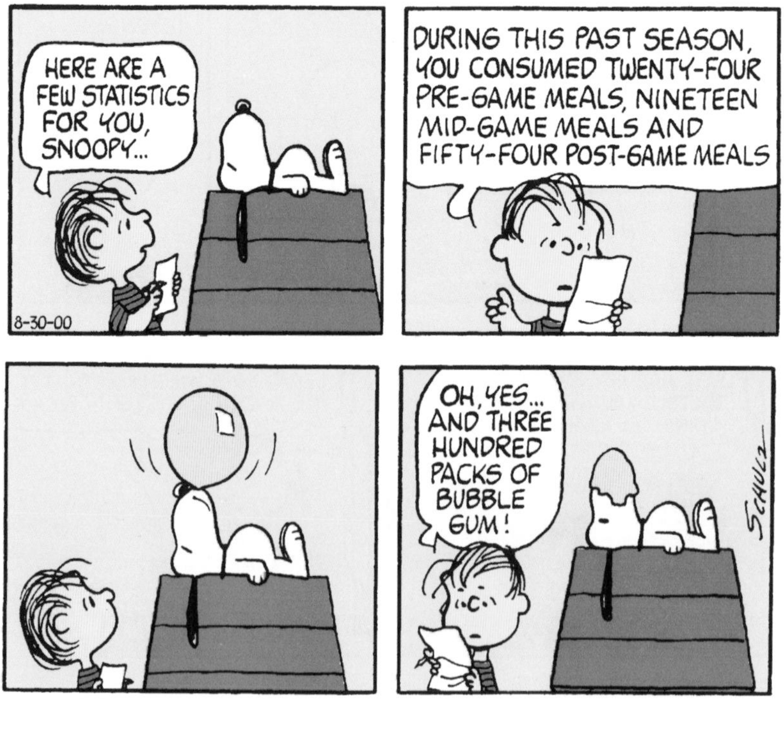
HERE ARE A FEW STATISTICS FOR YOU, SNOOPY...
8-30-00
DURING THIS PAST SEASON, YOU CONSUMED TWENTY-FOUR PRE-GAME MEALS, NINETEEN MID-GAME MEALS AND FIFTY-FOUR POST-GAME MEALS
OH, YES... AND THREE HUNDRED PACKS OF BUBBLE GUM!
SCHULZ

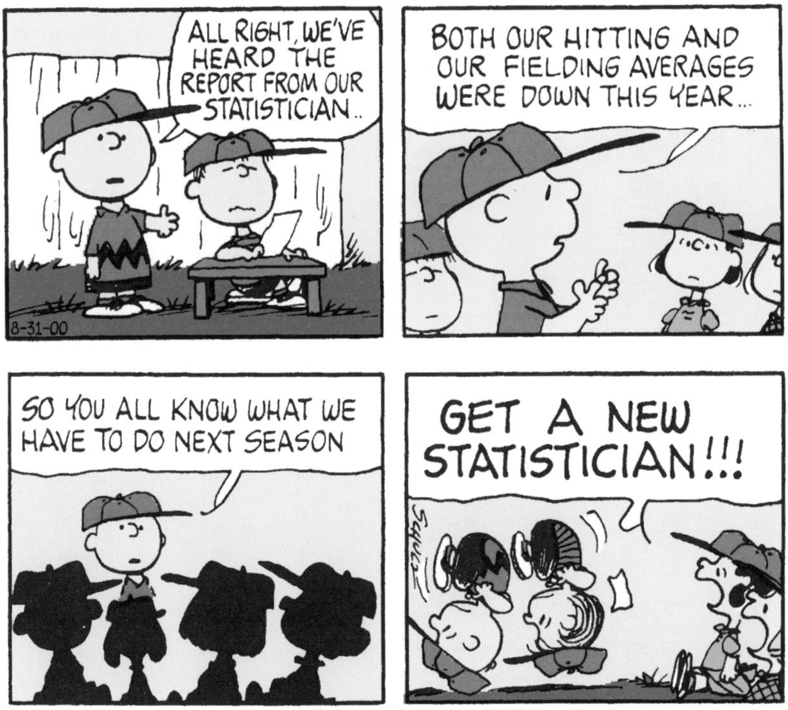
ALL RIGHT, WE'VE HEARD THE REPORT FROM OUR STATISTICIAN..
8-31-00
BOTH OUR HITTING AND OUR FIELDING AVERAGES WERE DOWN THIS YEAR...
SO YOU ALL KNOW WHAT WE HAVE TO DO NEXT SEASON
GET A NEW STATISTICIAN!!!
SCHULZ

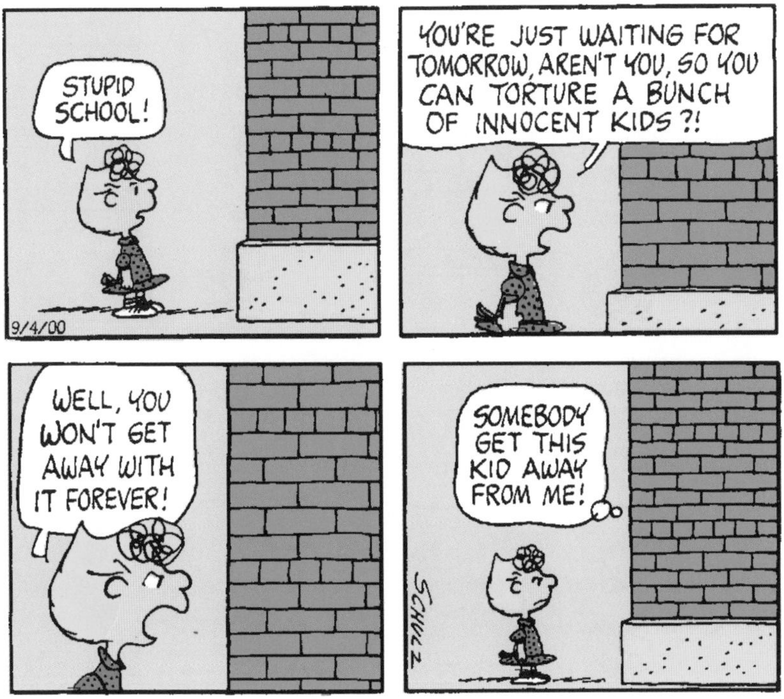
STUPID SCHOOL!
9/4/00
YOU'RE JUST WAITING FOR TOMORROW, AREN'T YOU, SO YOU CAN TORTURE A BUNCH OF INNOCENT KIDS ?!
WELL, YOU WON'T GET AWAY WITH IT FOREVER!
SOMEBODY GET THIS KID AWAY FROM ME!
SCHULZ

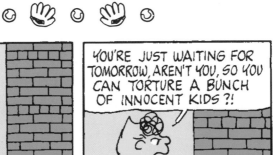

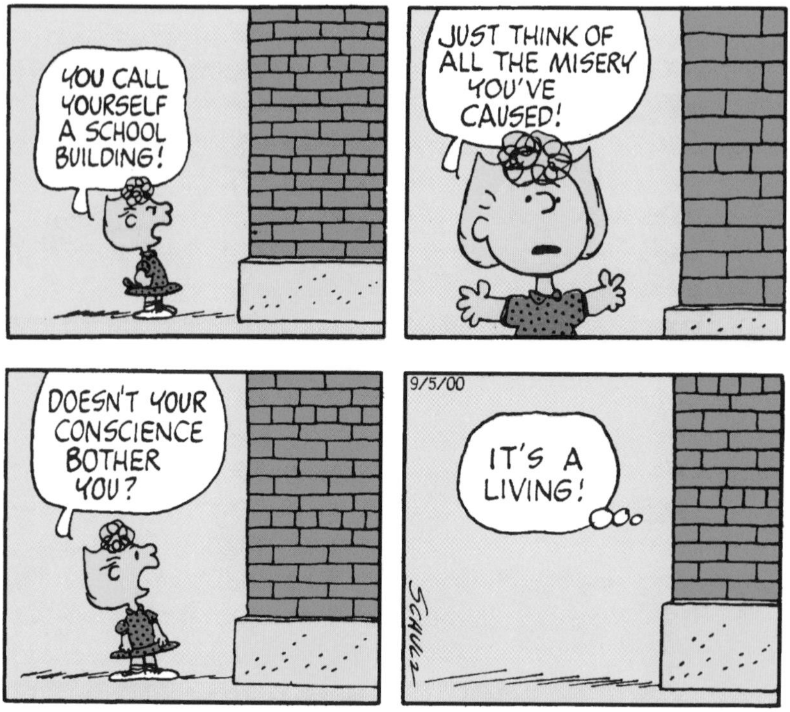
YOU CALL YOURSELF A SCHOOL BUILDING!
JUST THINK OF ALL THE MISERY YOU'VE CAUSED!
DOESN'T YOUR CONSCIENCE BOTHER YOU?
9/5/00
IT'S A LIVING!
SCHULZ

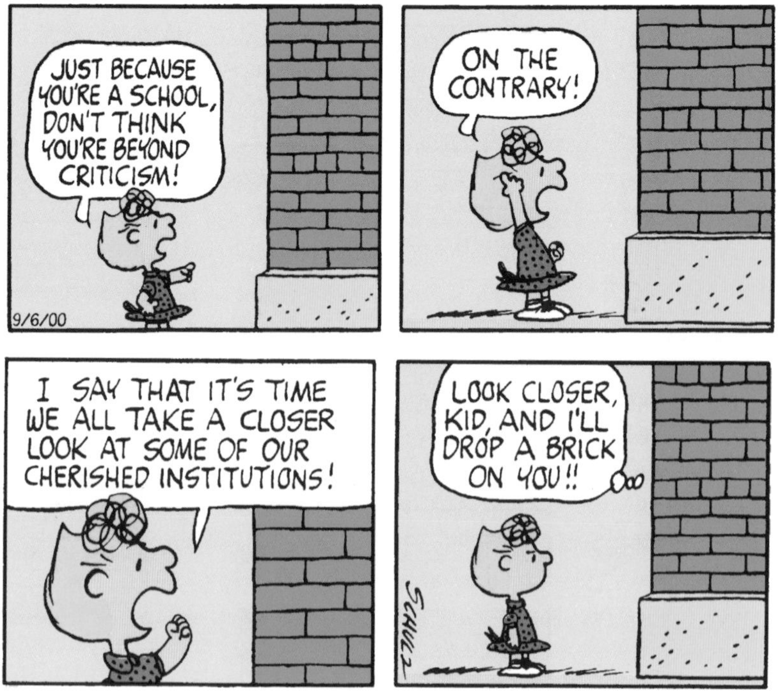
JUST BECAUSE YOU'RE A SCHOOL, DON'T THINK YOU'RE BEYOND CRITICISM!
9/6/00
ON THE CONTRARY!
I SAY THAT IT'S TIME WE ALL TAKE A CLOSER LOOK AT SOME OF OUR CHERISHED INSTITUTIONS!
LOOK CLOSER, KID, AND I'LL DROP A BRICK ON YOU!!
SCHULZ

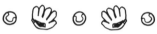

I'LL HOLD THE BALL, CHARLIE BROWN, AND YOU COME RUNNING UP AND KICK IT..

NOPE, I REFUSE! YOU'LL PULL THE BALL AWAY, AND I'LL COME CRASHING DOWN AND KILL MYSELF!

BUT YOU CAN'T BACK OUT NOW... THE PROGRAMS HAVE ALREADY BEEN PRINTED...

PROGRAMS?

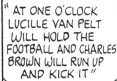

"AT ONE O'CLOCK LUCILLE VAN PELT WILL HOLD THE FOOTBALL AND CHARLES BROWN WILL RUN UP AND KICK IT"

SHE'S RIGHT..IF THE PROGRAMS HAVE ALREADY BEEN PRINTED, IT'S TOO LATE TO BACK OUT...

THIS YEAR I'M GONNA KICK THAT BALL CLEAR OUT OF THE UNIVERSE!

10-15-00

AAUGH!

IN EVERY PROGRAM, CHARLIE BROWN, THERE ARE ALWAYS A FEW LAST MINUTE CHANGES!

41

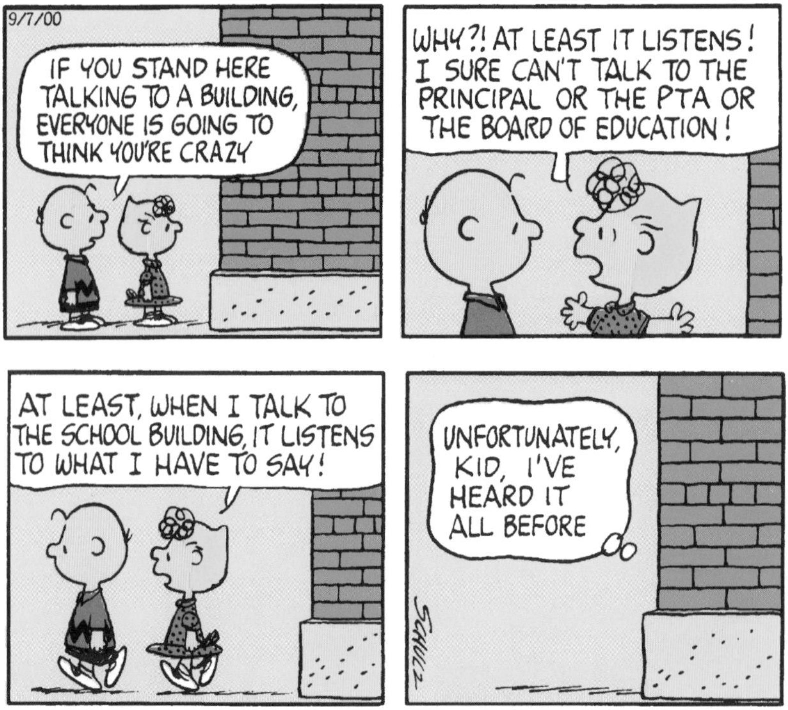
9/7/00
IF YOU STAND HERE TALKING TO A BUILDING, EVERYONE IS GOING TO THINK YOU'RE CRAZY
WHY?! AT LEAST IT LISTENS! I SURE CAN'T TALK TO THE PRINCIPAL OR THE PTA OR THE BOARD OF EDUCATION!
AT LEAST, WHEN I TALK TO THE SCHOOL BUILDING, IT LISTENS TO WHAT I HAVE TO SAY!
UNFORTUNATELY, KID, I'VE HEARD IT ALL BEFORE
SCHULZ

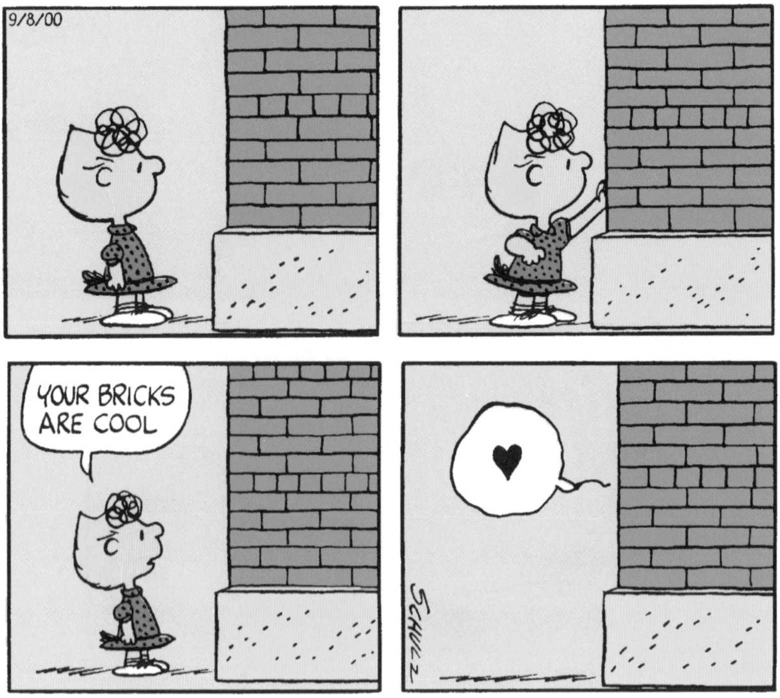
9/8/00
YOUR BRICKS ARE COOL
SCHULZ

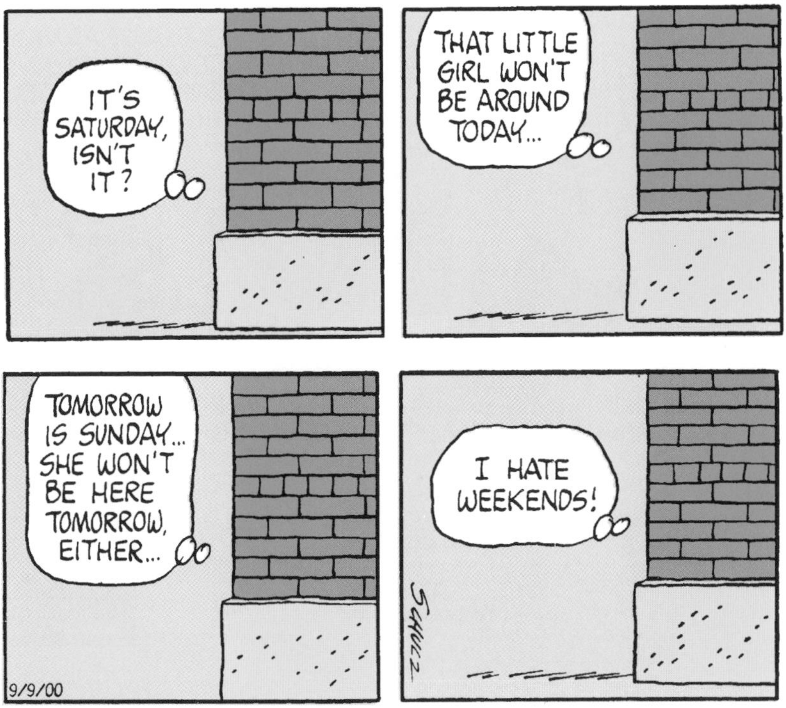
IT'S SATURDAY, ISN'T IT?
THAT LITTLE GIRL WON'T BE AROUND TODAY...
TOMORROW IS SUNDAY... SHE WON'T BE HERE TOMORROW, EITHER...
I HATE WEEKENDS!
SCHULZ
9/9/00

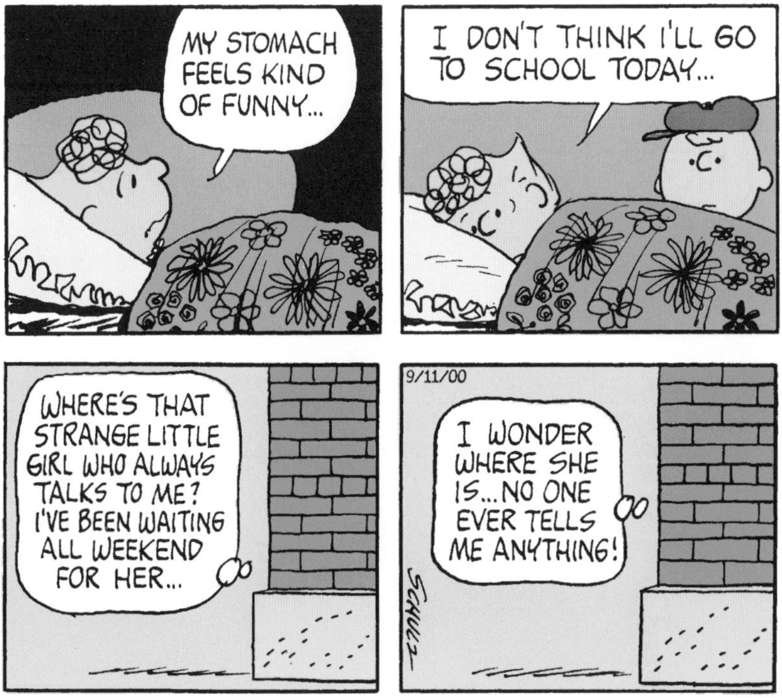
MY STOMACH FEELS KIND OF FUNNY...
I DON'T THINK I'LL GO TO SCHOOL TODAY...
WHERE'S THAT STRANGE LITTLE GIRL WHO ALWAYS TALKS TO ME? I'VE BEEN WAITING ALL WEEKEND FOR HER...
9/11/00
I WONDER WHERE SHE IS...NO ONE EVER TELLS ME ANYTHING!
SCHULZ

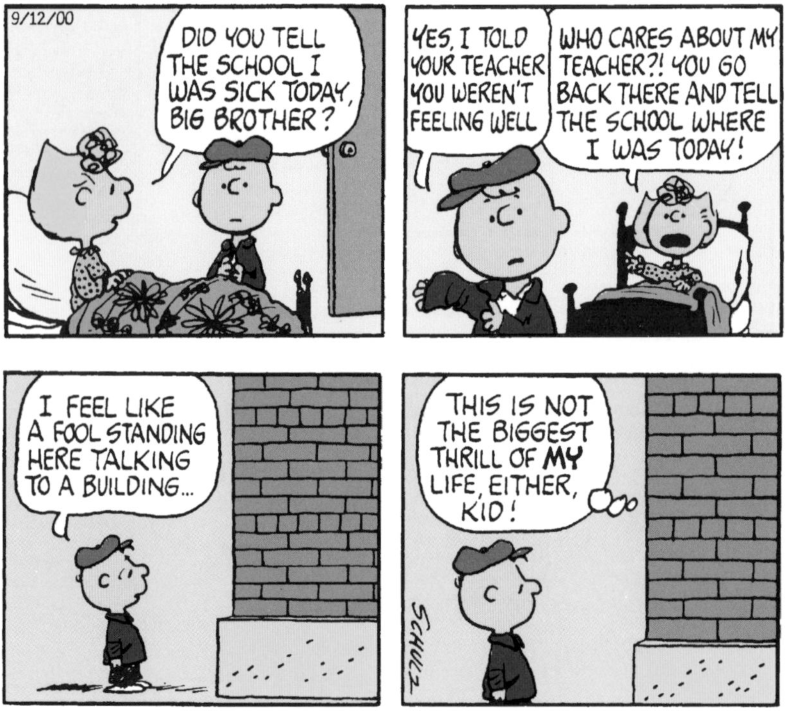
9/12/00
DID YOU TELL THE SCHOOL I WAS SICK TODAY, BIG BROTHER?
YES, I TOLD YOUR TEACHER YOU WEREN'T FEELING WELL
WHO CARES ABOUT MY TEACHER?! YOU GO BACK THERE AND TELL THE SCHOOL WHERE I WAS TODAY!
I FEEL LIKE A FOOL STANDING HERE TALKING TO A BUILDING...
THIS IS NOT THE BIGGEST THRILL OF **MY** LIFE, EITHER, KID!
SCHULZ

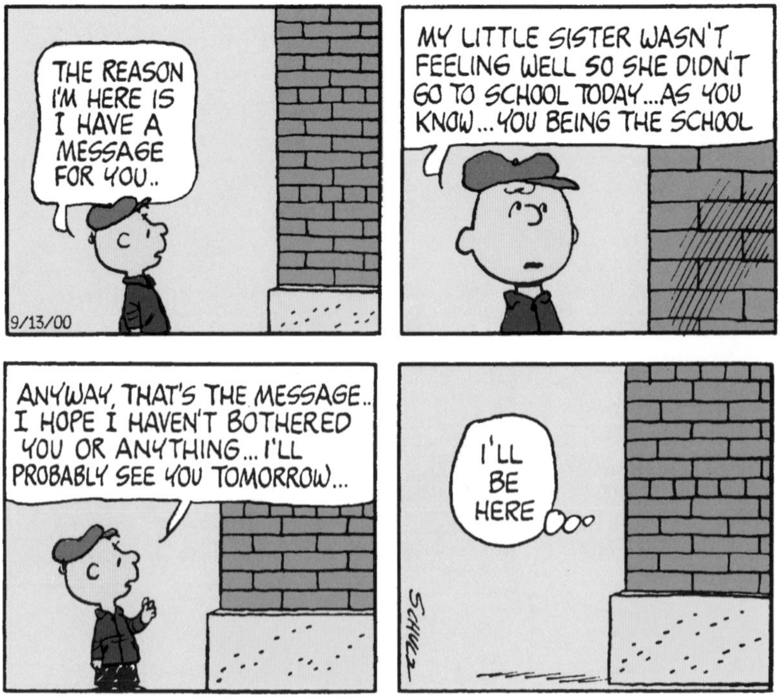
THE REASON I'M HERE IS I HAVE A MESSAGE FOR YOU..
9/13/00
MY LITTLE SISTER WASN'T FEELING WELL SO SHE DIDN'T GO TO SCHOOL TODAY...AS YOU KNOW...YOU BEING THE SCHOOL
ANYWAY, THAT'S THE MESSAGE.. I HOPE I HAVEN'T BOTHERED YOU OR ANYTHING... I'LL PROBABLY SEE YOU TOMORROW...
I'LL BE HERE
SCHULZ

9/14/00

DID I JUST SEE YOU TALKING TO THAT SCHOOL BUILDING?

I DID, DIDN'T I? YOU'VE FINALLY CRACKED UP, HAVEN'T YOU, CHARLIE BROWN?

YOU HAVE TO BE CRAZY, YOU KNOW, TO STAND AND TALK TO A STUPID BRICK BUILDING!

BONK!!

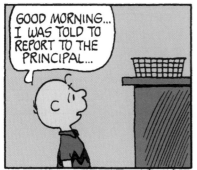

9/15/00

THE PRINCIPAL'S OFFICE? ME?! YES, MA'AM..

I HATE GOING TO THE PRINCIPAL'S OFFICE! I ALWAYS HAVE THE FEELING THAT I'LL NEVER COME BACK, OR THAT NO ONE WILL EVER SEE ME AGAIN...

GOOD MORNING... I WAS TOLD TO REPORT TO THE PRINCIPAL...

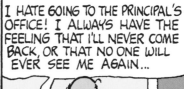

AM I ALLOWED ONE PHONE CALL?

45

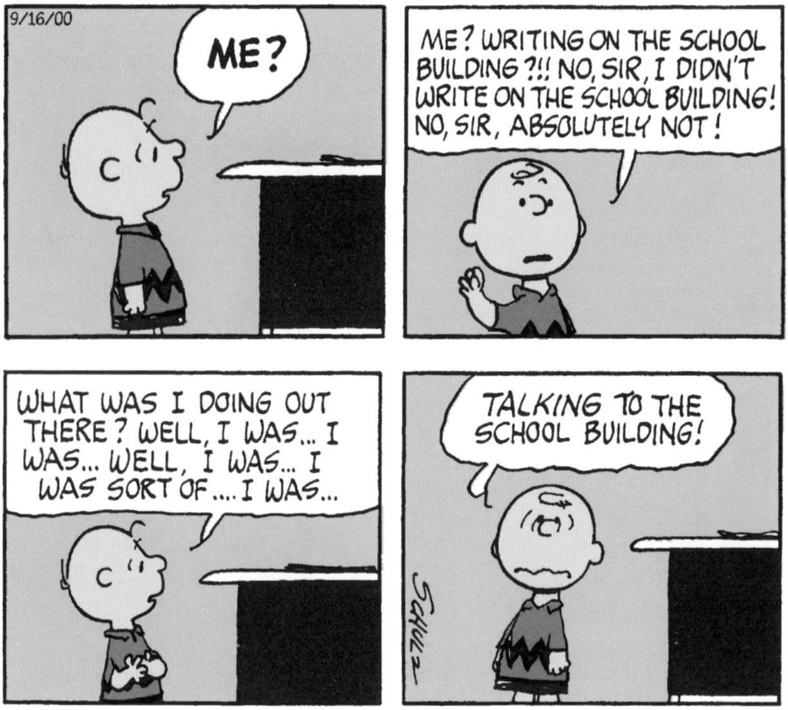
9/16/00
ME?
ME? WRITING ON THE SCHOOL BUILDING ?!! NO, SIR, I DIDN'T WRITE ON THE SCHOOL BUILDING! NO, SIR, ABSOLUTELY NOT!
WHAT WAS I DOING OUT THERE? WELL, I WAS... I WAS... WELL, I WAS... I WAS SORT OF.... I WAS...
TALKING TO THE SCHOOL BUILDING!
SCHULZ

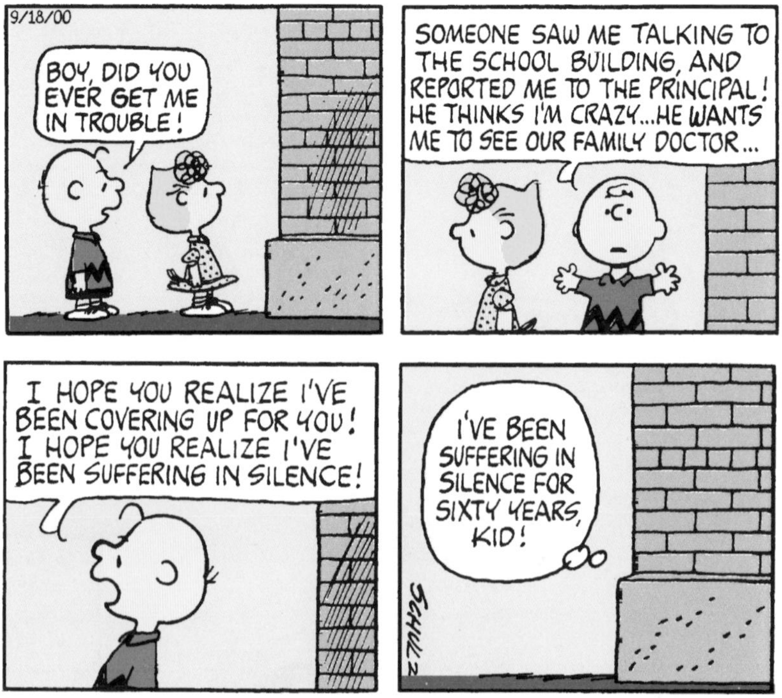
9/18/00
BOY, DID YOU EVER GET ME IN TROUBLE!
SOMEONE SAW ME TALKING TO THE SCHOOL BUILDING, AND REPORTED ME TO THE PRINCIPAL! HE THINKS I'M CRAZY...HE WANTS ME TO SEE OUR FAMILY DOCTOR...
I HOPE YOU REALIZE I'VE BEEN COVERING UP FOR YOU! I HOPE YOU REALIZE I'VE BEEN SUFFERING IN SILENCE!
I'VE BEEN SUFFERING IN SILENCE FOR SIXTY YEARS, KID!
SCHULZ

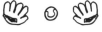

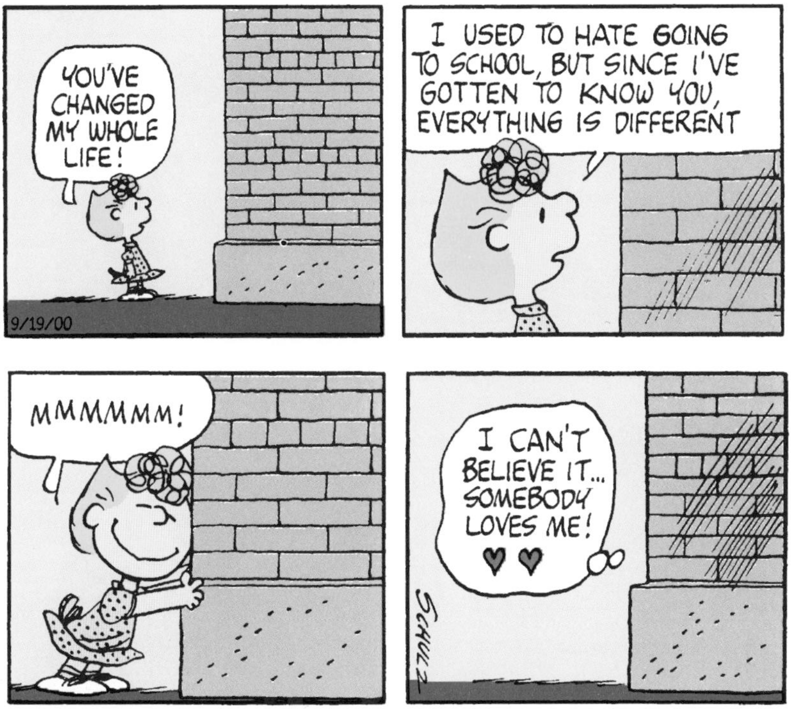
9/19/00
YOU'VE CHANGED MY WHOLE LIFE!
I USED TO HATE GOING TO SCHOOL, BUT SINCE I'VE GOTTEN TO KNOW YOU, EVERYTHING IS DIFFERENT
MMMMMM!
I CAN'T BELIEVE IT... SOMEBODY LOVES ME!
SCHULZ

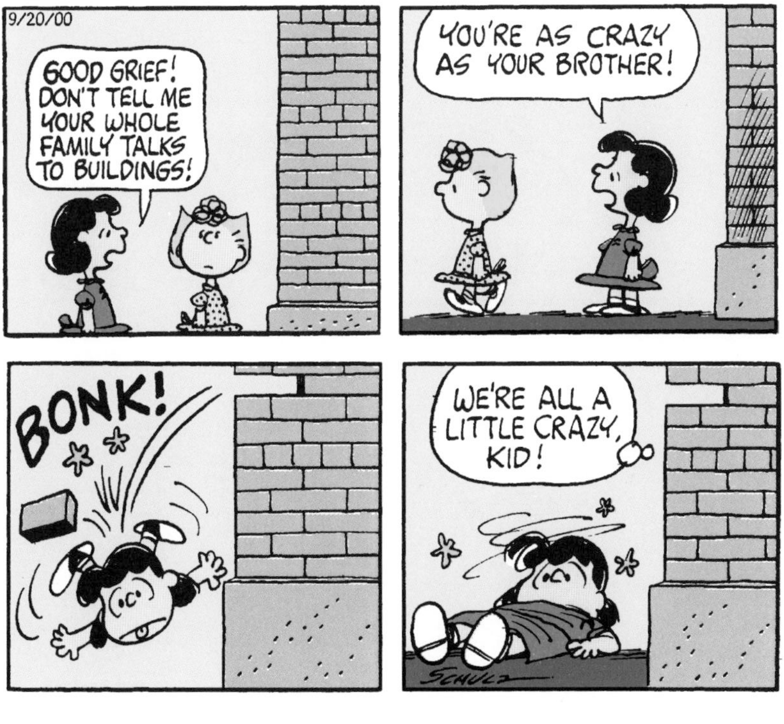
9/20/00
GOOD GRIEF! DON'T TELL ME YOUR WHOLE FAMILY TALKS TO BUILDINGS!
YOU'RE AS CRAZY AS YOUR BROTHER!
BONK!
WE'RE ALL A LITTLE CRAZY, KID!
SCHULZ

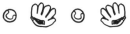

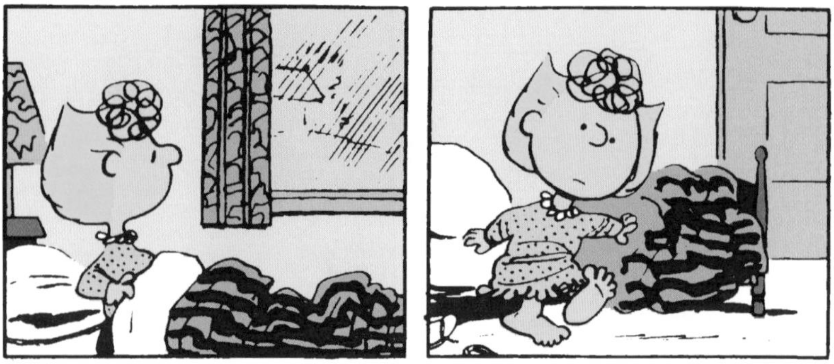

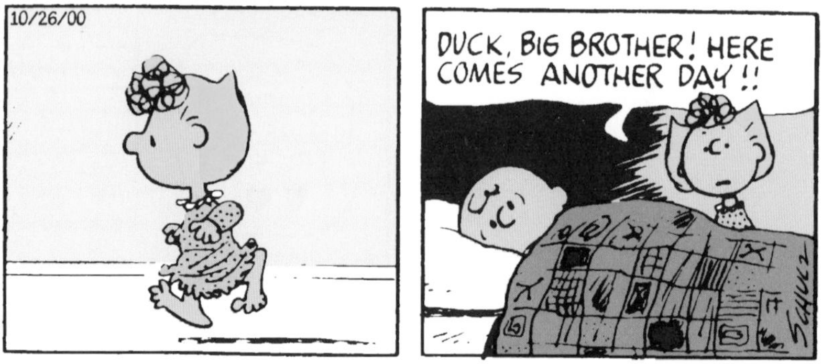
10/26/00
DUCK, BIG BROTHER! HERE COMES ANOTHER DAY!!
SCHULZ

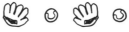

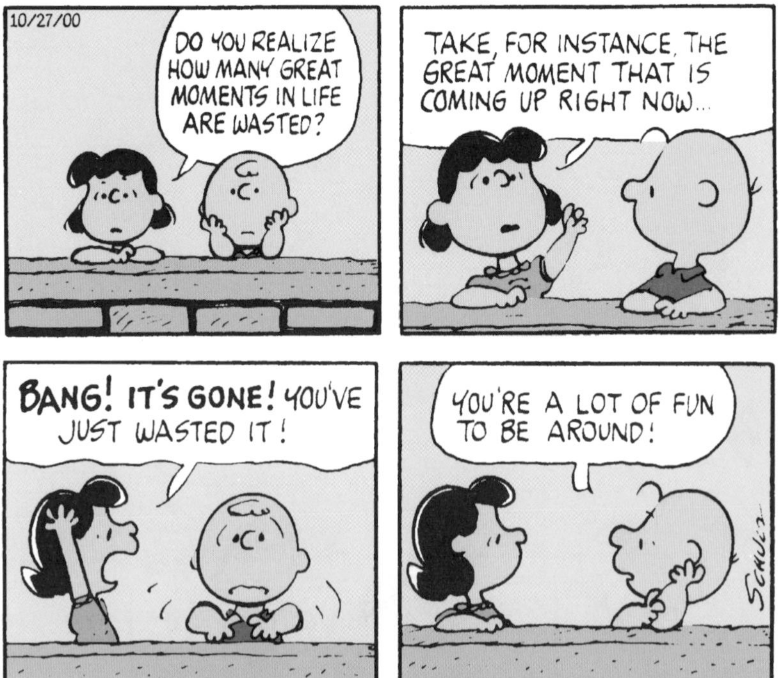
10/27/00
DO YOU REALIZE HOW MANY GREAT MOMENTS IN LIFE ARE WASTED?
TAKE, FOR INSTANCE, THE GREAT MOMENT THAT IS COMING UP RIGHT NOW...
BANG! IT'S GONE! YOU'VE JUST WASTED IT!
YOU'RE A LOT OF FUN TO BE AROUND!
SCHULZ

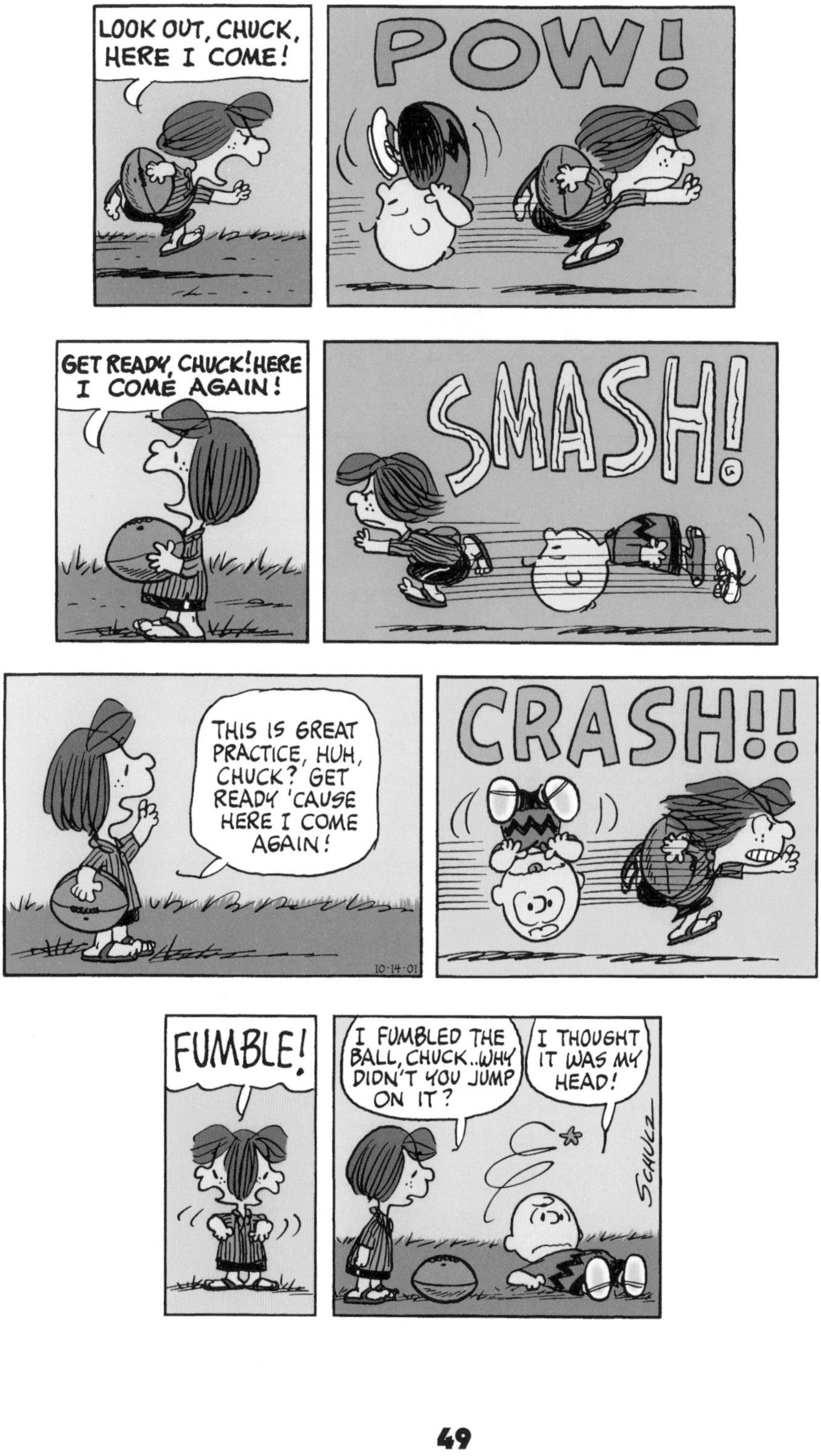
LOOK OUT, CHUCK, HERE I COME!
POW!
GET READY, CHUCK! HERE I COME AGAIN!
SMASH!
THIS IS GREAT PRACTICE, HUH, CHUCK? GET READY 'CAUSE HERE I COME AGAIN!
10-14-01
CRASH!!
FUMBLE!
I FUMBLED THE BALL, CHUCK..WHY DIDN'T YOU JUMP ON IT?
I THOUGHT IT WAS MY HEAD!
SCHULZ

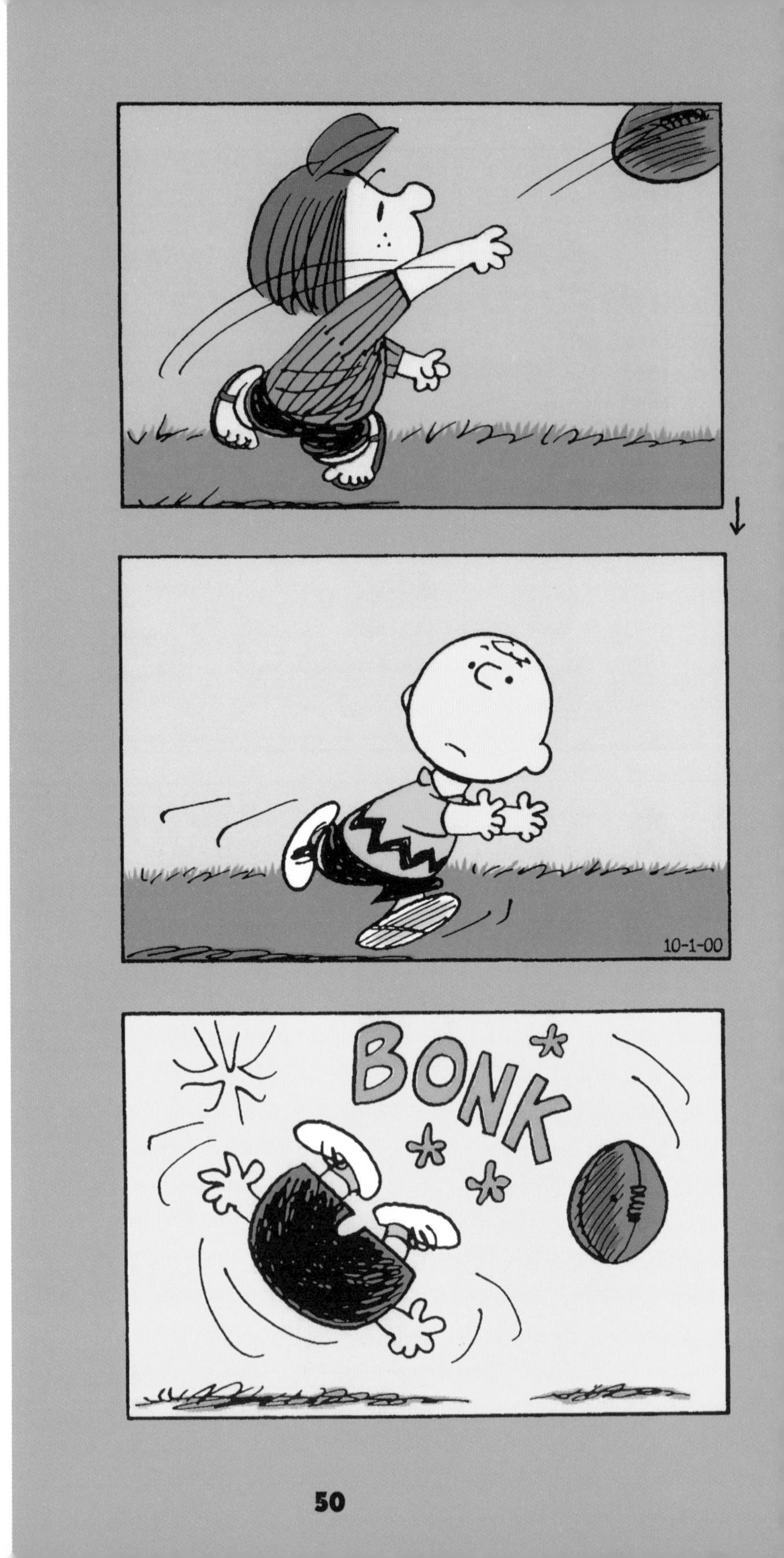
10-1-00
BONK

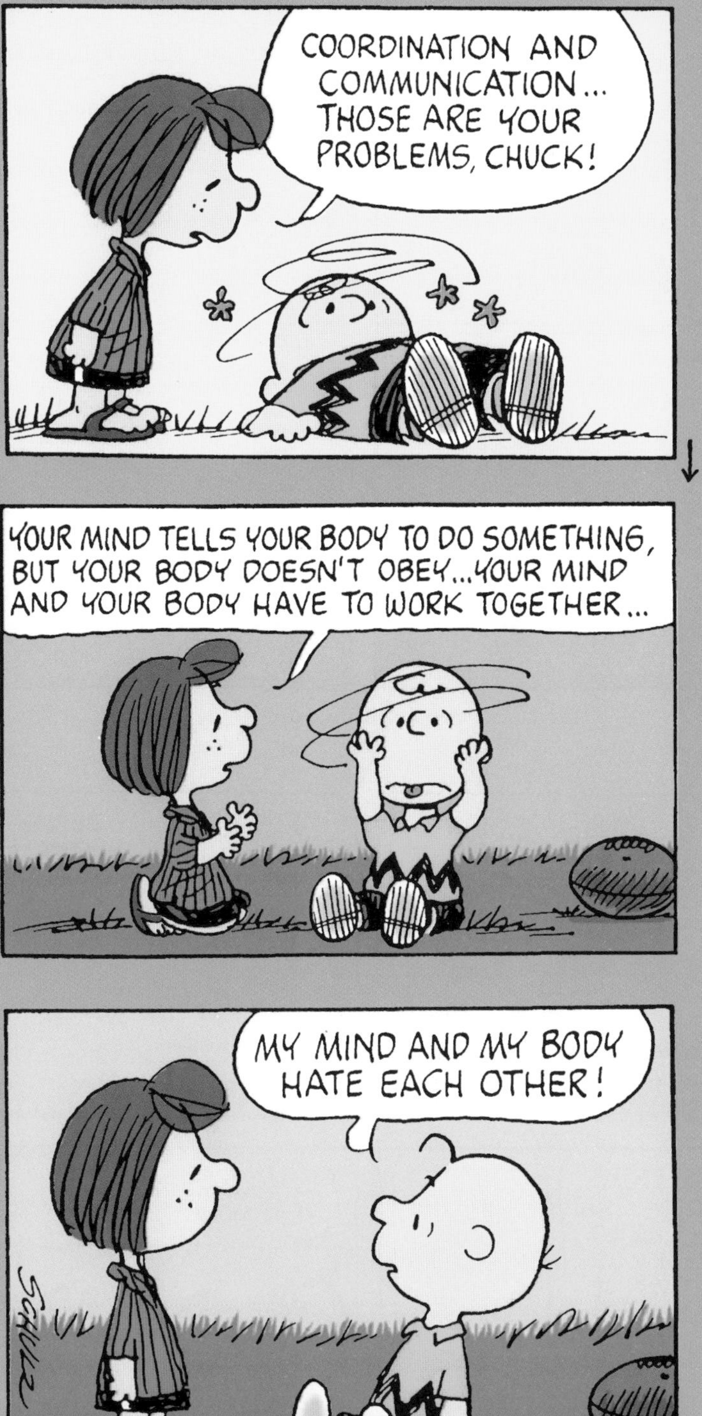
COORDINATION AND COMMUNICATION... THOSE ARE YOUR PROBLEMS, CHUCK!
YOUR MIND TELLS YOUR BODY TO DO SOMETHING, BUT YOUR BODY DOESN'T OBEY...YOUR MIND AND YOUR BODY HAVE TO WORK TOGETHER...
MY MIND AND MY BODY HATE EACH OTHER!
SCHULZ

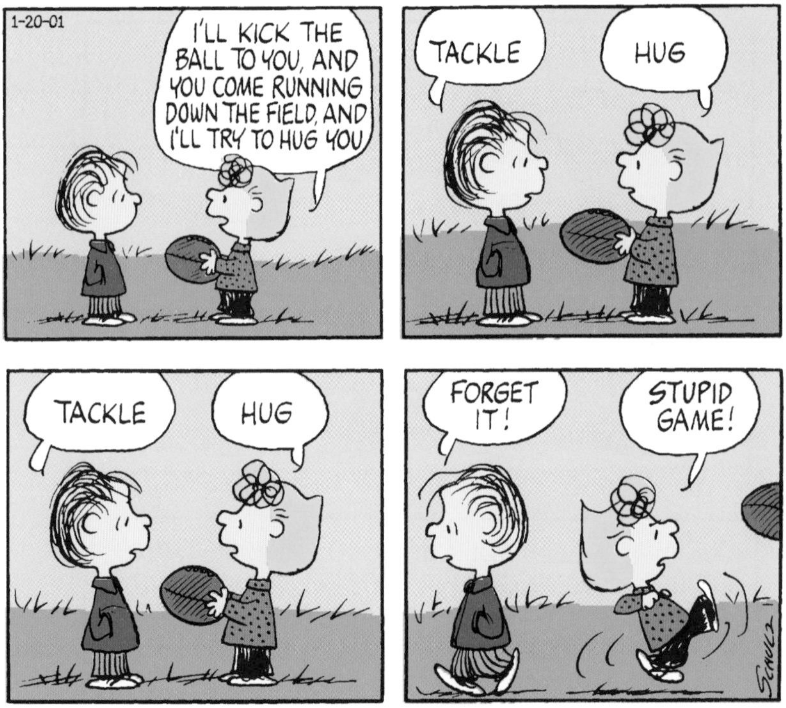
1-20-01
I'LL KICK THE BALL TO YOU, AND YOU COME RUNNING DOWN THE FIELD, AND I'LL TRY TO HUG YOU
TACKLE
HUG
TACKLE
HUG
FORGET IT!
STUPID GAME!

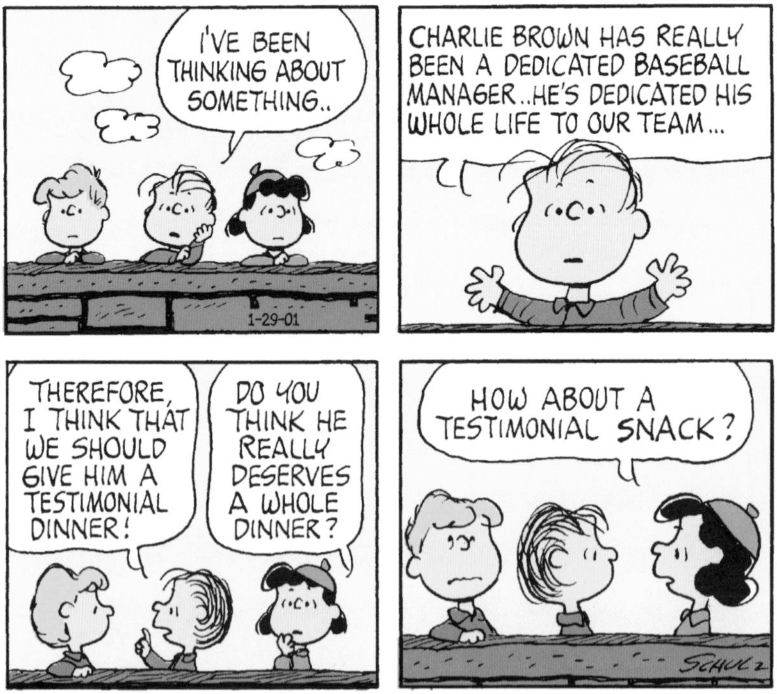
I'VE BEEN THINKING ABOUT SOMETHING..
1-29-01
CHARLIE BROWN HAS REALLY BEEN A DEDICATED BASEBALL MANAGER..HE'S DEDICATED HIS WHOLE LIFE TO OUR TEAM...
THEREFORE, I THINK THAT WE SHOULD GIVE HIM A TESTIMONIAL DINNER!
DO YOU THINK HE REALLY DESERVES A WHOLE DINNER?
HOW ABOUT A TESTIMONIAL SNACK?

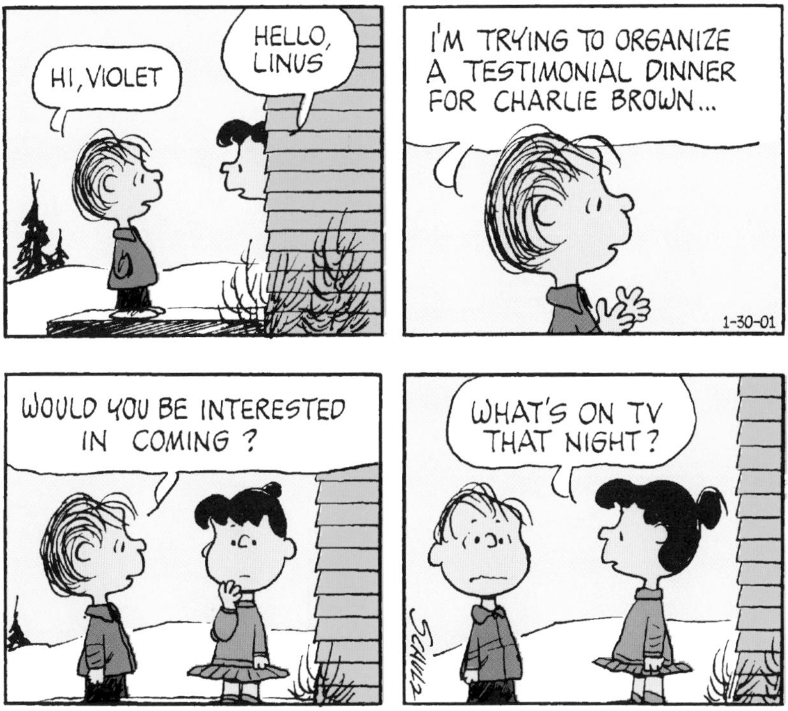
HI, VIOLET
HELLO, LINUS
I'M TRYING TO ORGANIZE A TESTIMONIAL DINNER FOR CHARLIE BROWN...
1-30-01
WOULD YOU BE INTERESTED IN COMING ?
WHAT'S ON TV THAT NIGHT ?
SCHULZ

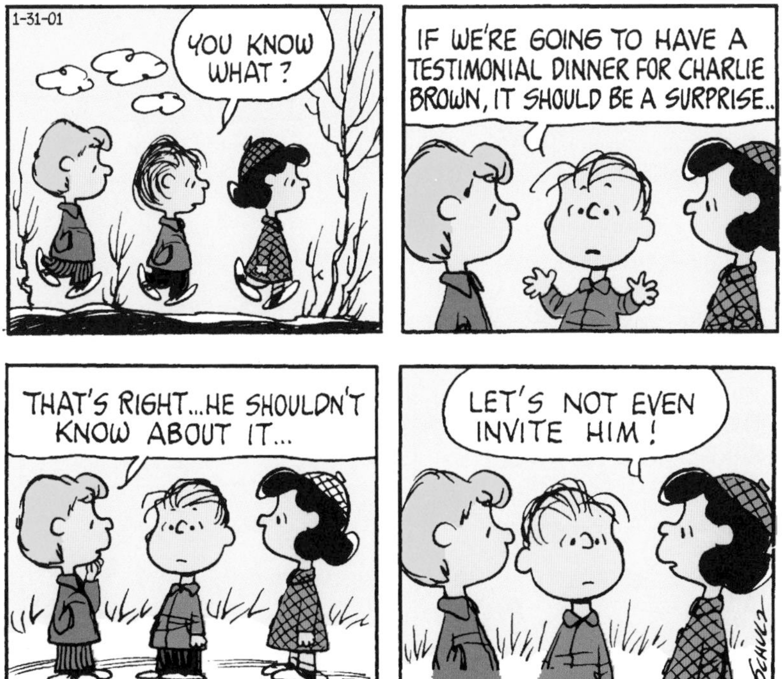
1-31-01
YOU KNOW WHAT ?
IF WE'RE GOING TO HAVE A TESTIMONIAL DINNER FOR CHARLIE BROWN, IT SHOULD BE A SURPRISE..
THAT'S RIGHT...HE SHOULDN'T KNOW ABOUT IT...
LET'S NOT EVEN INVITE HIM !
SCHULZ

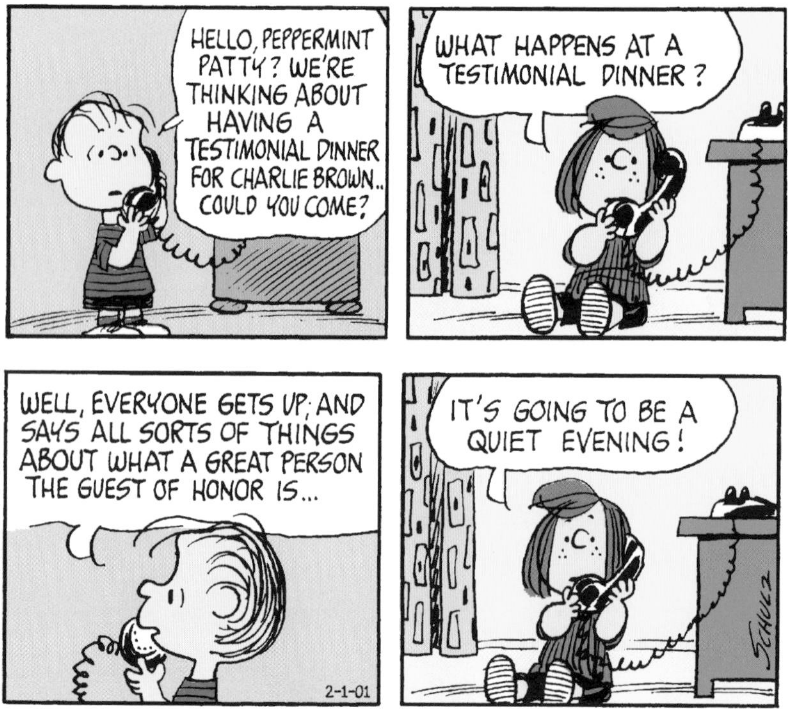
HELLO, PEPPERMINT PATTY? WE'RE THINKING ABOUT HAVING A TESTIMONIAL DINNER FOR CHARLIE BROWN.. COULD YOU COME?
WHAT HAPPENS AT A TESTIMONIAL DINNER?
WELL, EVERYONE GETS UP, AND SAYS ALL SORTS OF THINGS ABOUT WHAT A GREAT PERSON THE GUEST OF HONOR IS...
2-1-01
IT'S GOING TO BE A QUIET EVENING!
SCHULZ

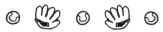

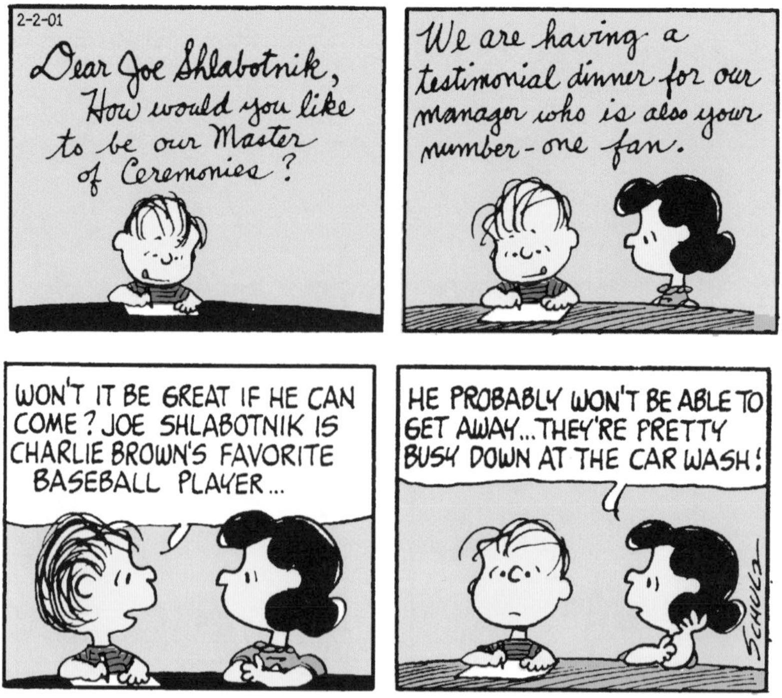
2-2-01
Dear Joe Shlabotnik, How would you like to be our Master of Ceremonies?
We are having a testimonial dinner for our manager who is also your number-one fan.
WON'T IT BE GREAT IF HE CAN COME? JOE SHLABOTNIK IS CHARLIE BROWN'S FAVORITE BASEBALL PLAYER...
HE PROBABLY WON'T BE ABLE TO GET AWAY...THEY'RE PRETTY BUSY DOWN AT THE CAR WASH!
SCHULZ

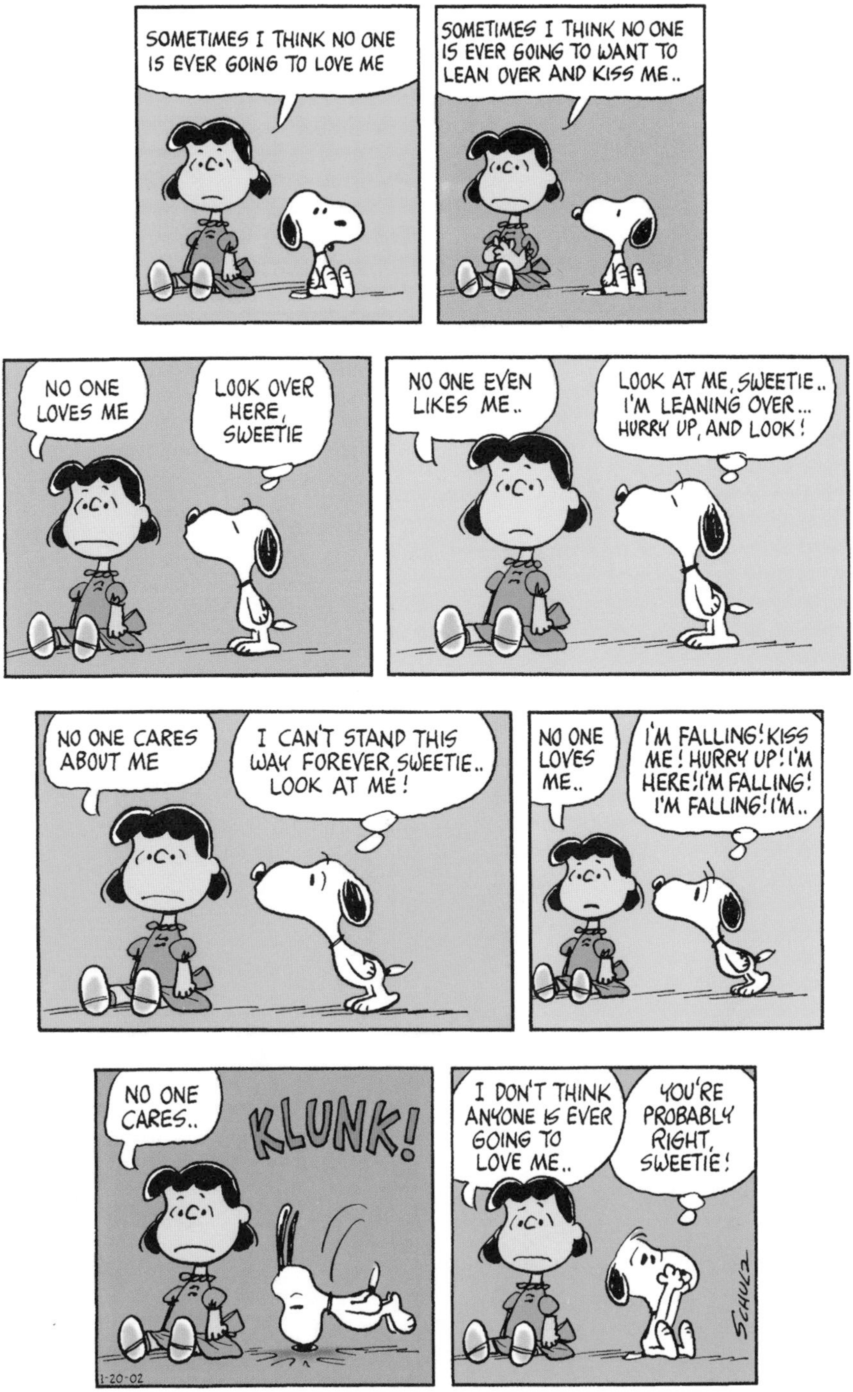
SOMETIMES I THINK NO ONE IS EVER GOING TO LOVE ME
SOMETIMES I THINK NO ONE IS EVER GOING TO WANT TO LEAN OVER AND KISS ME..
NO ONE LOVES ME
LOOK OVER HERE, SWEETIE
NO ONE EVEN LIKES ME..
LOOK AT ME, SWEETIE.. I'M LEANING OVER... HURRY UP, AND LOOK!
NO ONE CARES ABOUT ME
I CAN'T STAND THIS WAY FOREVER, SWEETIE.. LOOK AT ME!
NO ONE LOVES ME..
I'M FALLING! KISS ME! HURRY UP! I'M HERE! I'M FALLING! I'M FALLING! I'M..
NO ONE CARES..
KLUNK!
1-20-02
I DON'T THINK ANYONE IS EVER GOING TO LOVE ME..
YOU'RE PROBABLY RIGHT, SWEETIE!
SCHULZ

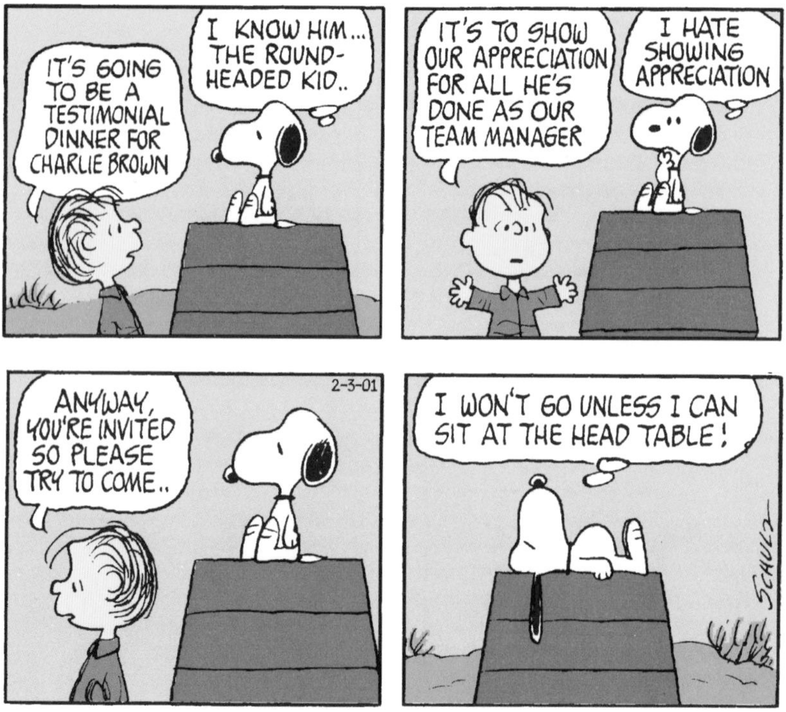
IT'S GOING TO BE A TESTIMONIAL DINNER FOR CHARLIE BROWN
I KNOW HIM... THE ROUND-HEADED KID..
IT'S TO SHOW OUR APPRECIATION FOR ALL HE'S DONE AS OUR TEAM MANAGER
I HATE SHOWING APPRECIATION
2-3-01
ANYWAY, YOU'RE INVITED SO PLEASE TRY TO COME..
I WON'T GO UNLESS I CAN SIT AT THE HEAD TABLE!
SCHULZ

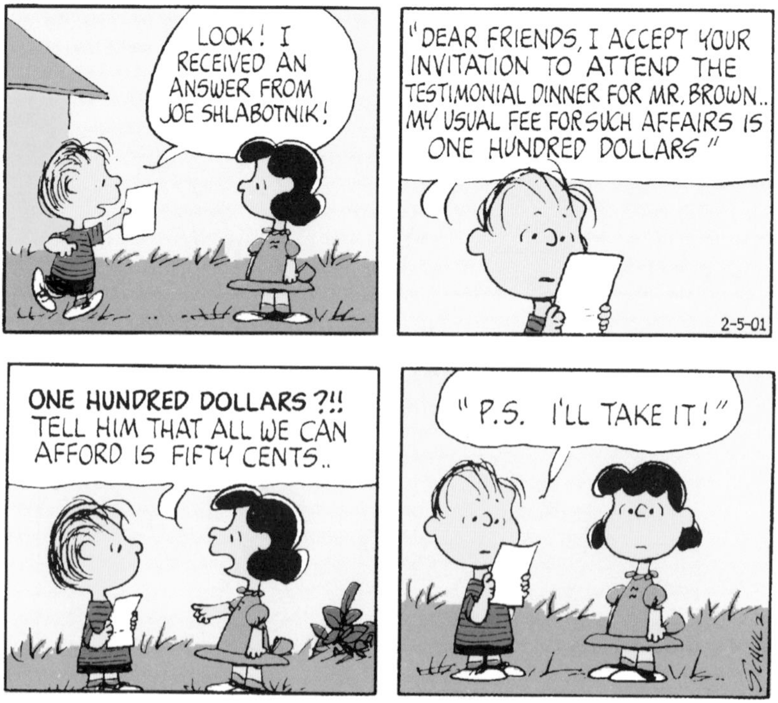
LOOK! I RECEIVED AN ANSWER FROM JOE SHLABOTNIK!
"DEAR FRIENDS, I ACCEPT YOUR INVITATION TO ATTEND THE TESTIMONIAL DINNER FOR MR. BROWN.. MY USUAL FEE FOR SUCH AFFAIRS IS ONE HUNDRED DOLLARS"
2-5-01
ONE HUNDRED DOLLARS?!! TELL HIM THAT ALL WE CAN AFFORD IS FIFTY CENTS..
"P.S. I'LL TAKE IT!"
SCHULZ

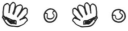

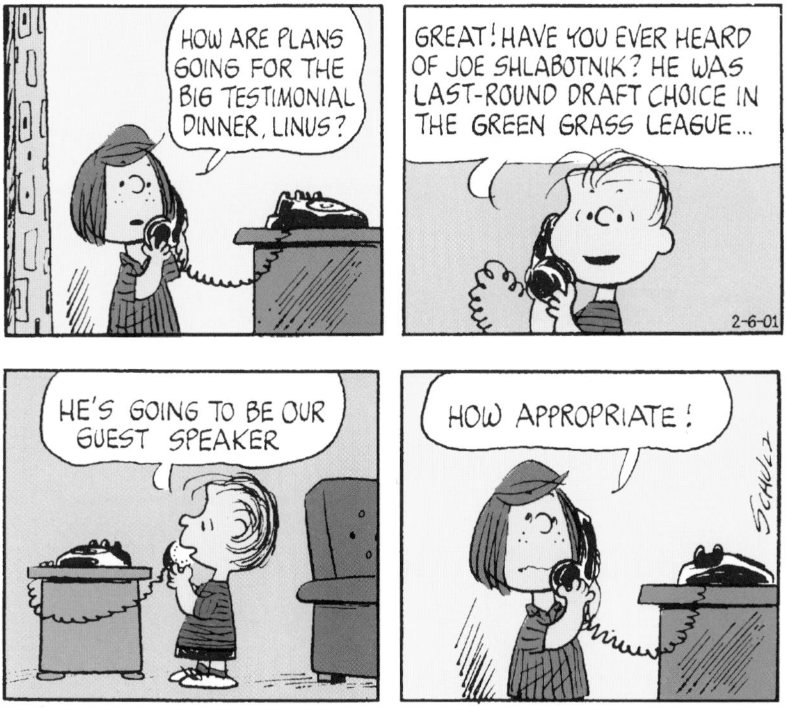
HOW ARE PLANS GOING FOR THE BIG TESTIMONIAL DINNER, LINUS?
GREAT! HAVE YOU EVER HEARD OF JOE SHLABOTNIK? HE WAS LAST-ROUND DRAFT CHOICE IN THE GREEN GRASS LEAGUE...
2-6-01
HE'S GOING TO BE OUR GUEST SPEAKER
HOW APPROPRIATE!

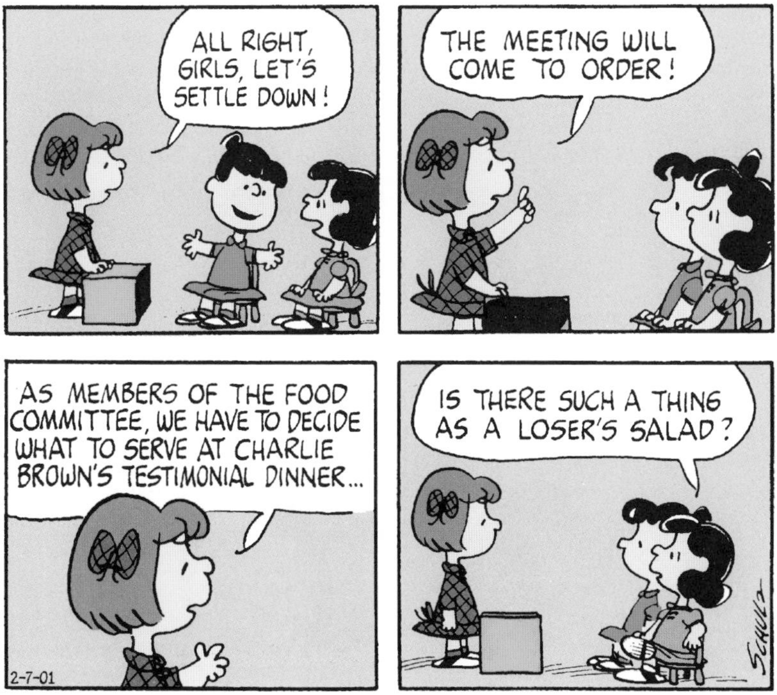
ALL RIGHT, GIRLS, LET'S SETTLE DOWN!
THE MEETING WILL COME TO ORDER!
AS MEMBERS OF THE FOOD COMMITTEE, WE HAVE TO DECIDE WHAT TO SERVE AT CHARLIE BROWN'S TESTIMONIAL DINNER...
2-7-01
IS THERE SUCH A THING AS A LOSER'S SALAD?

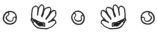

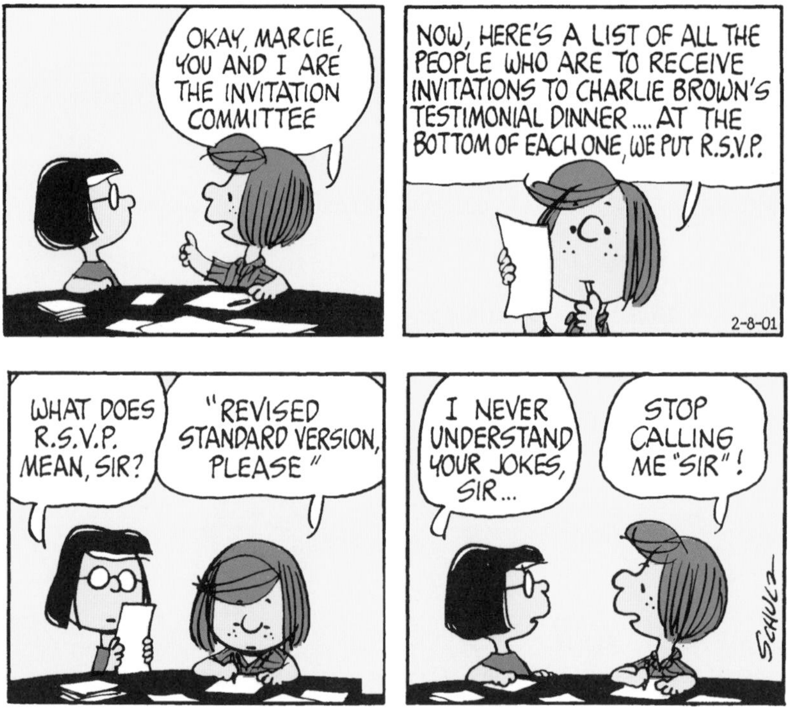
OKAY, MARCIE, YOU AND I ARE THE INVITATION COMMITTEE
NOW, HERE'S A LIST OF ALL THE PEOPLE WHO ARE TO RECEIVE INVITATIONS TO CHARLIE BROWN'S TESTIMONIAL DINNER.... AT THE BOTTOM OF EACH ONE, WE PUT R.S.V.P.
2-8-01
WHAT DOES R.S.V.P. MEAN, SIR?
"REVISED STANDARD VERSION, PLEASE"
I NEVER UNDERSTAND YOUR JOKES, SIR...
STOP CALLING ME "SIR"!
SCHULZ

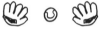

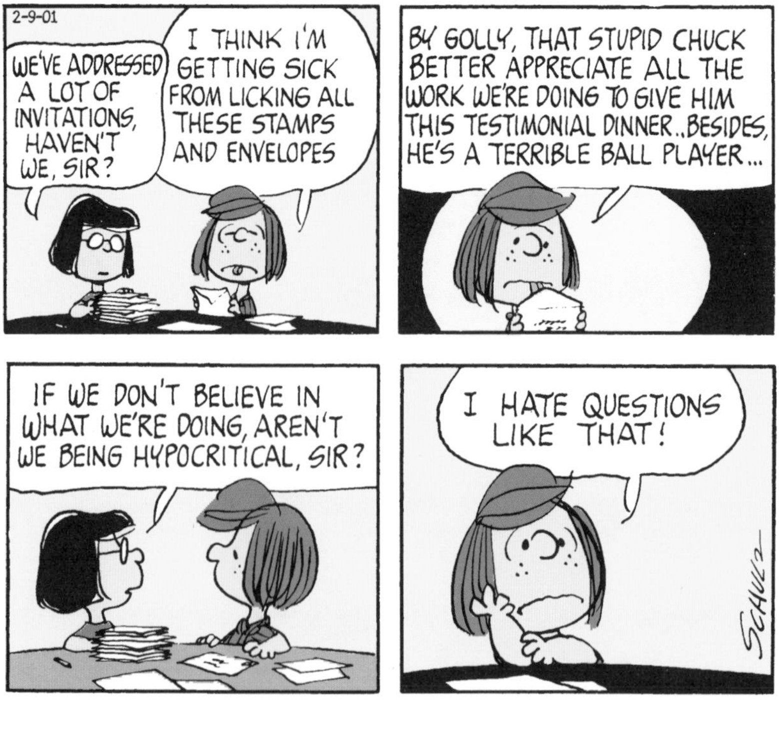
2-9-01
WE'VE ADDRESSED A LOT OF INVITATIONS, HAVEN'T WE, SIR?
I THINK I'M GETTING SICK FROM LICKING ALL THESE STAMPS AND ENVELOPES
BY GOLLY, THAT STUPID CHUCK BETTER APPRECIATE ALL THE WORK WE'RE DOING TO GIVE HIM THIS TESTIMONIAL DINNER..BESIDES, HE'S A TERRIBLE BALL PLAYER...
IF WE DON'T BELIEVE IN WHAT WE'RE DOING, AREN'T WE BEING HYPOCRITICAL, SIR?
I HATE QUESTIONS LIKE THAT!
SCHULZ

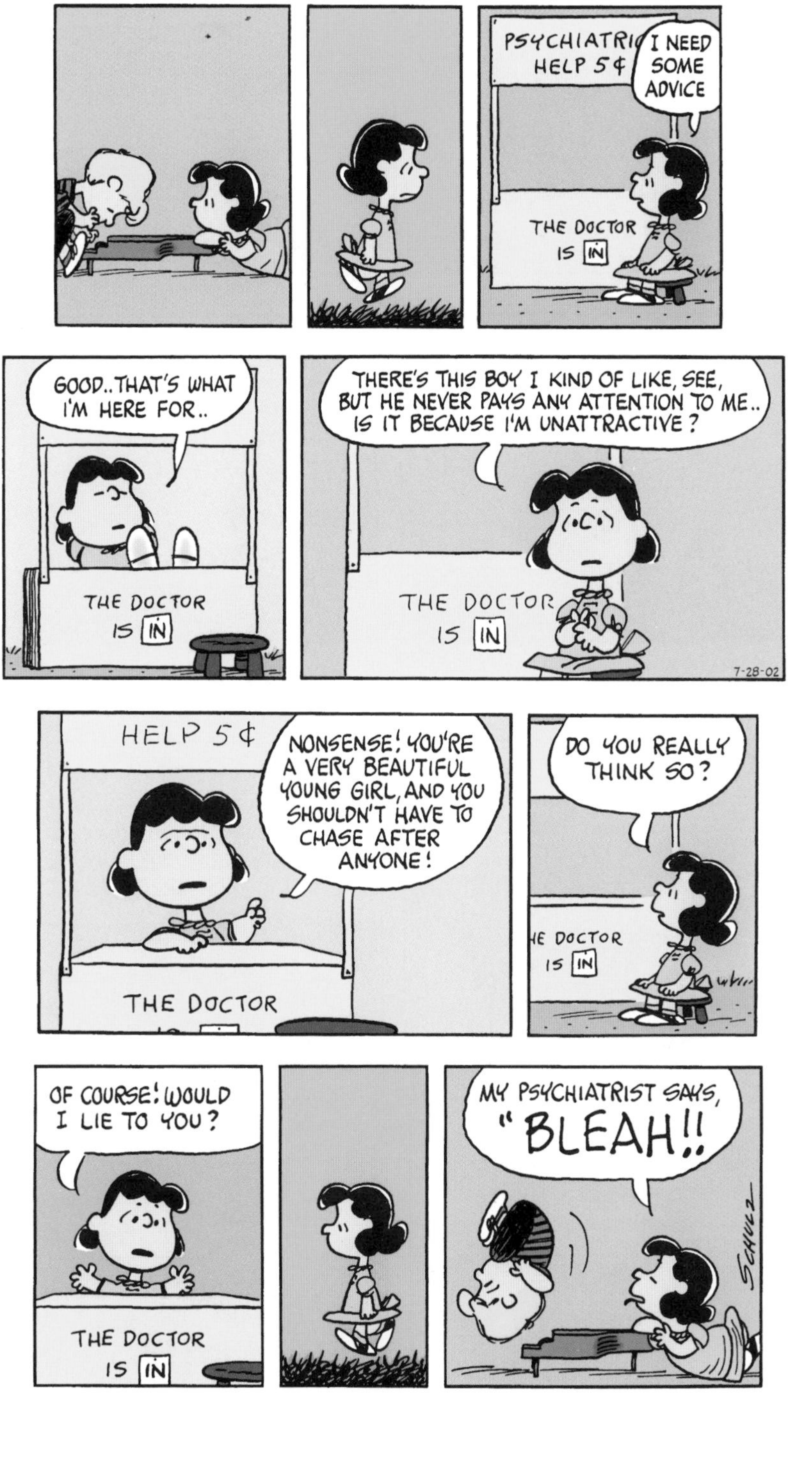
PSYCHIATRIC HELP 5¢
I NEED SOME ADVICE
THE DOCTOR IS IN
GOOD..THAT'S WHAT I'M HERE FOR..
THE DOCTOR IS IN
THERE'S THIS BOY I KIND OF LIKE, SEE, BUT HE NEVER PAYS ANY ATTENTION TO ME.. IS IT BECAUSE I'M UNATTRACTIVE?
THE DOCTOR IS IN
7-28-02
HELP 5¢
NONSENSE! YOU'RE A VERY BEAUTIFUL YOUNG GIRL, AND YOU SHOULDN'T HAVE TO CHASE AFTER ANYONE!
THE DOCTOR
DO YOU REALLY THINK SO?
HE DOCTOR IS IN
OF COURSE! WOULD I LIE TO YOU?
THE DOCTOR IS IN
MY PSYCHIATRIST SAYS, "BLEAH!!"
SCHULZ

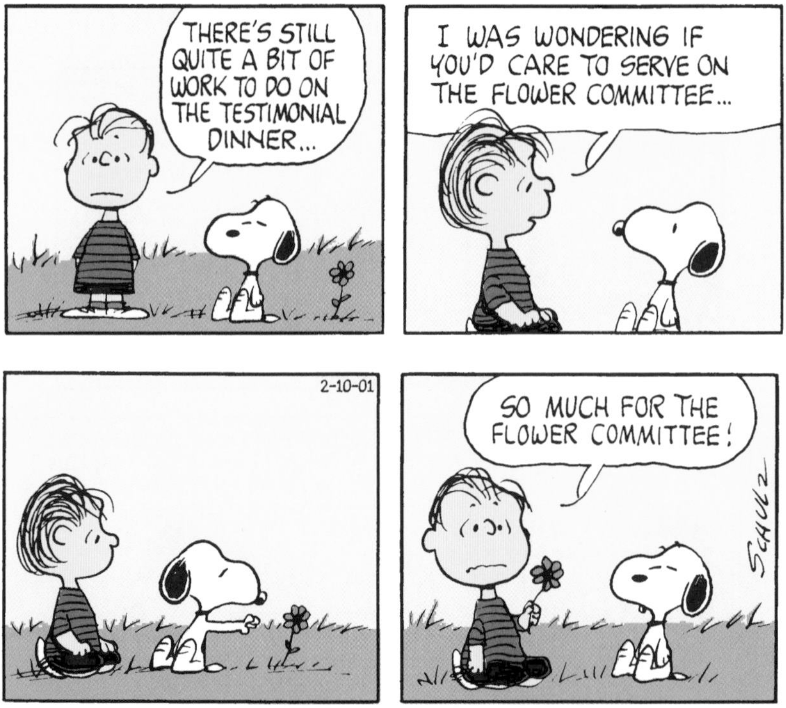
THERE'S STILL QUITE A BIT OF WORK TO DO ON THE TESTIMONIAL DINNER...
I WAS WONDERING IF YOU'D CARE TO SERVE ON THE FLOWER COMMITTEE...
2-10-01
SO MUCH FOR THE FLOWER COMMITTEE!
SCHULZ

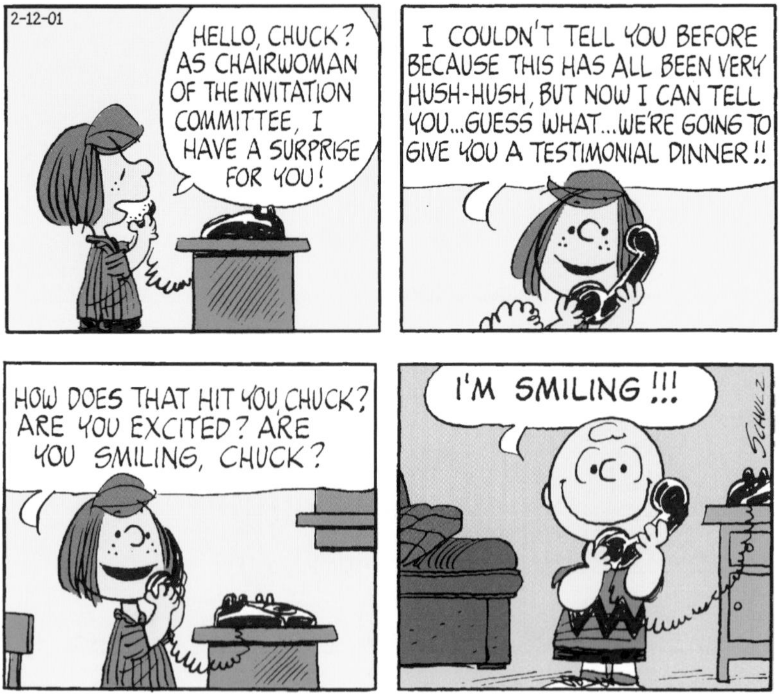
2-12-01
HELLO, CHUCK? AS CHAIRWOMAN OF THE INVITATION COMMITTEE, I HAVE A SURPRISE FOR YOU!
I COULDN'T TELL YOU BEFORE BECAUSE THIS HAS ALL BEEN VERY HUSH-HUSH, BUT NOW I CAN TELL YOU...GUESS WHAT...WE'RE GOING TO GIVE YOU A TESTIMONIAL DINNER!!
HOW DOES THAT HIT YOU, CHUCK? ARE YOU EXCITED? ARE YOU SMILING, CHUCK?
I'M SMILING!!!
SCHULZ

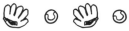

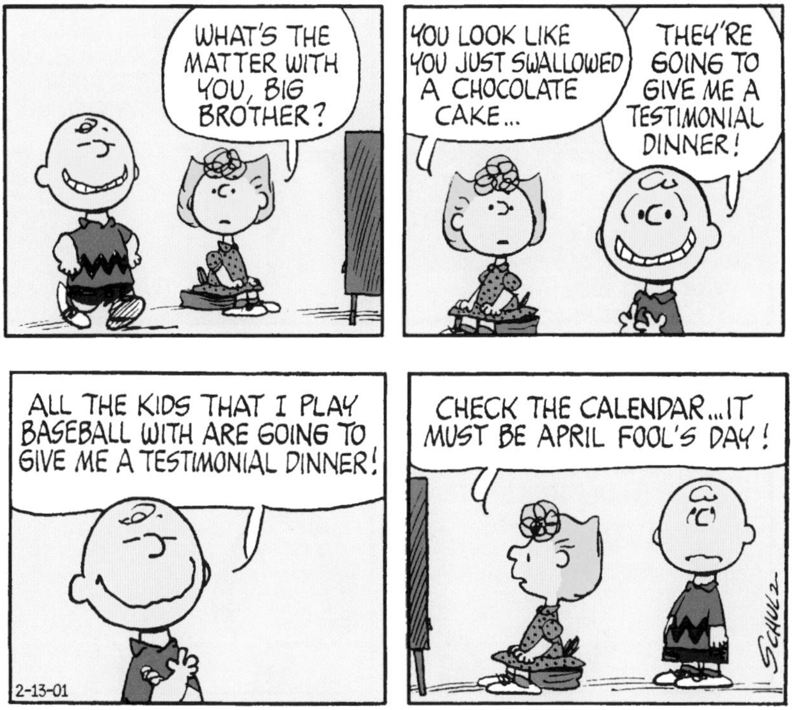
WHAT'S THE MATTER WITH YOU, BIG BROTHER?
YOU LOOK LIKE YOU JUST SWALLOWED A CHOCOLATE CAKE...
THEY'RE GOING TO GIVE ME A TESTIMONIAL DINNER!
ALL THE KIDS THAT I PLAY BASEBALL WITH ARE GOING TO GIVE ME A TESTIMONIAL DINNER!
2-13-01
CHECK THE CALENDAR...IT MUST BE APRIL FOOL'S DAY!
SCHULZ

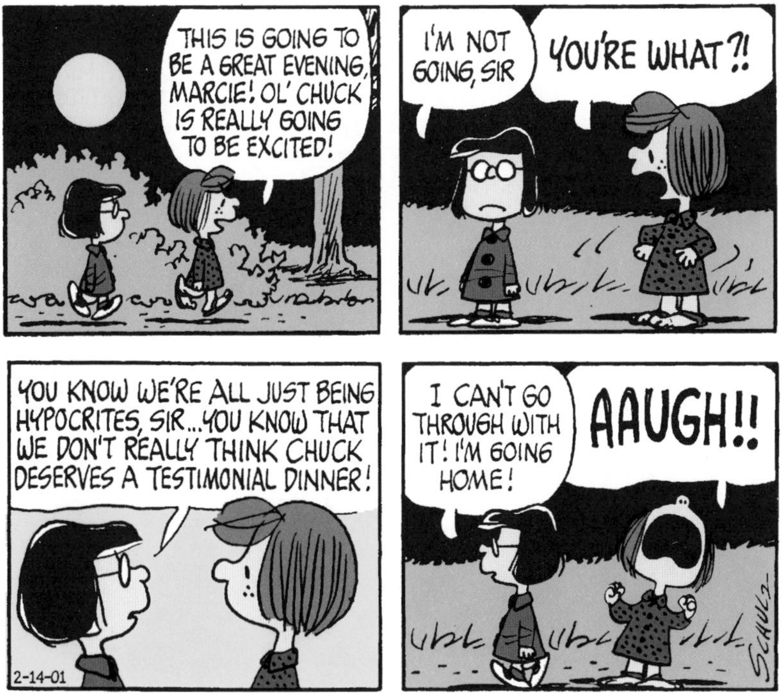
THIS IS GOING TO BE A GREAT EVENING, MARCIE! OL' CHUCK IS REALLY GOING TO BE EXCITED!
I'M NOT GOING, SIR
YOU'RE WHAT?!
YOU KNOW WE'RE ALL JUST BEING HYPOCRITES, SIR...YOU KNOW THAT WE DON'T REALLY THINK CHUCK DESERVES A TESTIMONIAL DINNER!
2-14-01
I CAN'T GO THROUGH WITH IT! I'M GOING HOME!
AAUGH!!
SCHULZ

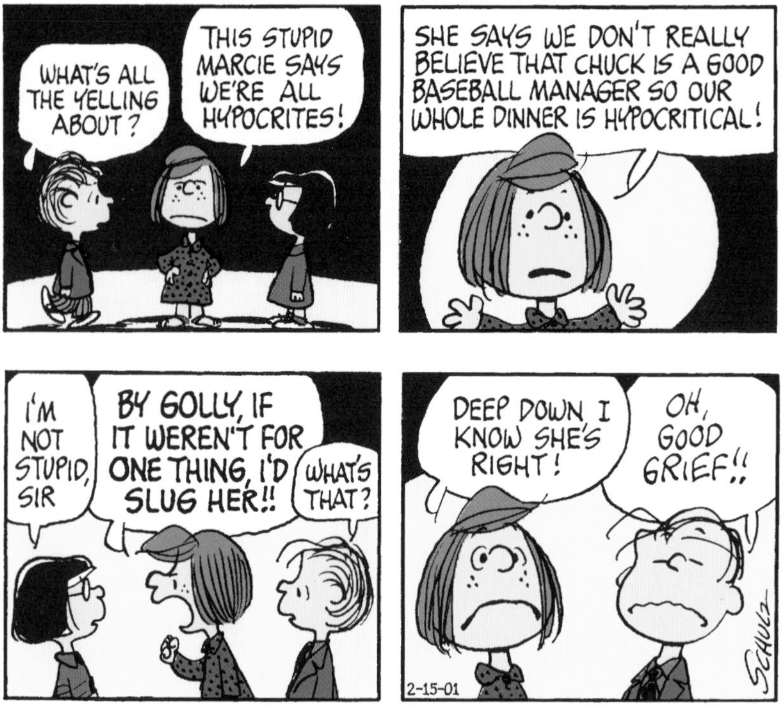
WHAT'S ALL THE YELLING ABOUT?
THIS STUPID MARCIE SAYS WE'RE ALL HYPOCRITES!
SHE SAYS WE DON'T REALLY BELIEVE THAT CHUCK IS A GOOD BASEBALL MANAGER SO OUR WHOLE DINNER IS HYPOCRITICAL!
I'M NOT STUPID, SIR
BY GOLLY, IF IT WEREN'T FOR ONE THING, I'D SLUG HER!!
WHAT'S THAT?
DEEP DOWN I KNOW SHE'S RIGHT!
OH, GOOD GRIEF!!
2-15-01
SCHULZ

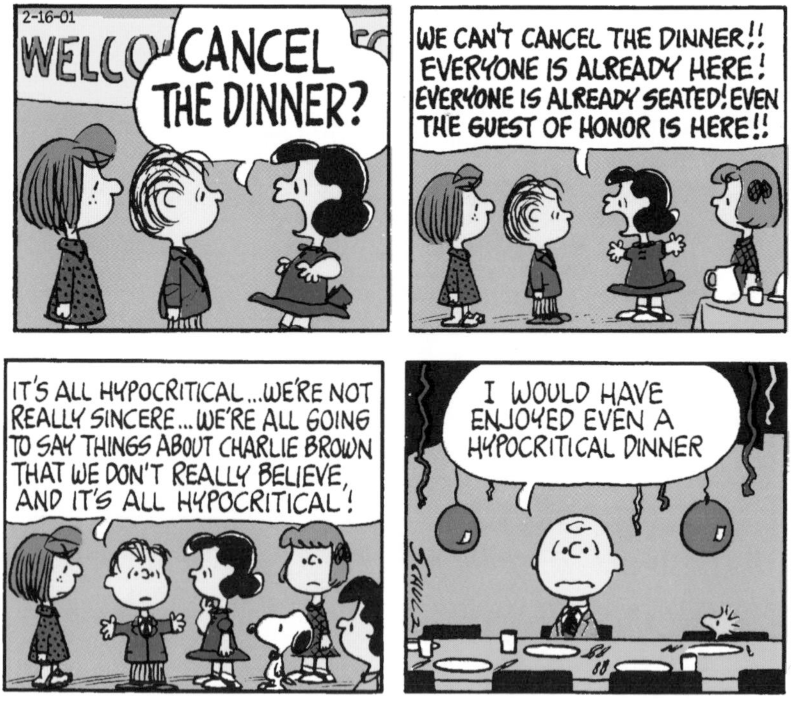
2-16-01
WELCO
CANCEL THE DINNER?
WE CAN'T CANCEL THE DINNER!! EVERYONE IS ALREADY HERE! EVERYONE IS ALREADY SEATED! EVEN THE GUEST OF HONOR IS HERE!!
IT'S ALL HYPOCRITICAL...WE'RE NOT REALLY SINCERE...WE'RE ALL GOING TO SAY THINGS ABOUT CHARLIE BROWN THAT WE DON'T REALLY BELIEVE, AND IT'S ALL HYPOCRITICAL!
I WOULD HAVE ENJOYED EVEN A HYPOCRITICAL DINNER
SCHULZ

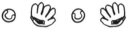

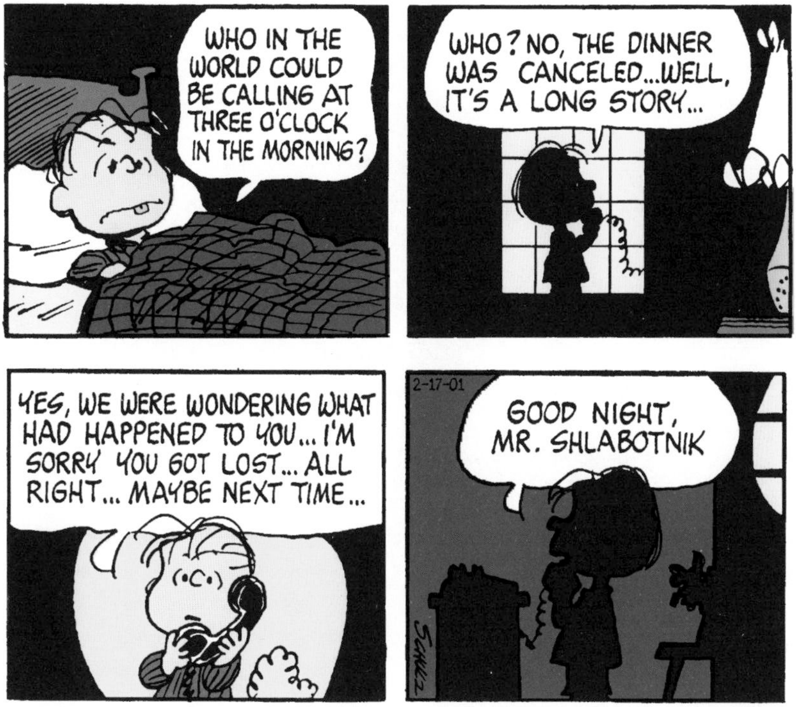
WHO IN THE WORLD COULD BE CALLING AT THREE O'CLOCK IN THE MORNING?
WHO? NO, THE DINNER WAS CANCELED...WELL, IT'S A LONG STORY...
YES, WE WERE WONDERING WHAT HAD HAPPENED TO YOU... I'M SORRY YOU GOT LOST... ALL RIGHT... MAYBE NEXT TIME...
2-17-01
GOOD NIGHT, MR. SHLABOTNIK
SCHULZ

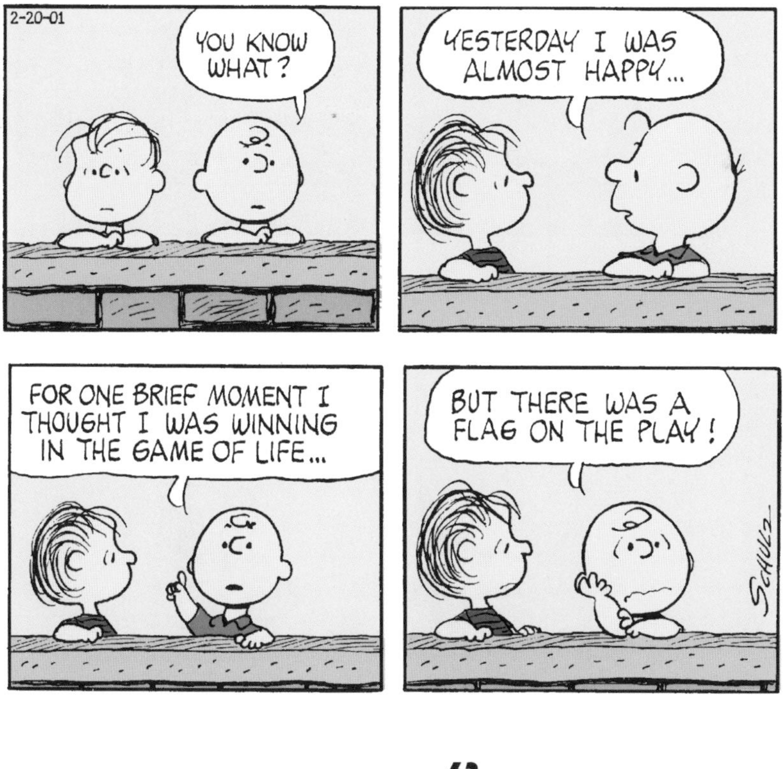
2-20-01
YOU KNOW WHAT?
YESTERDAY I WAS ALMOST HAPPY...
FOR ONE BRIEF MOMENT I THOUGHT I WAS WINNING IN THE GAME OF LIFE...
BUT THERE WAS A FLAG ON THE PLAY!
SCHULZ

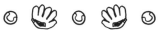

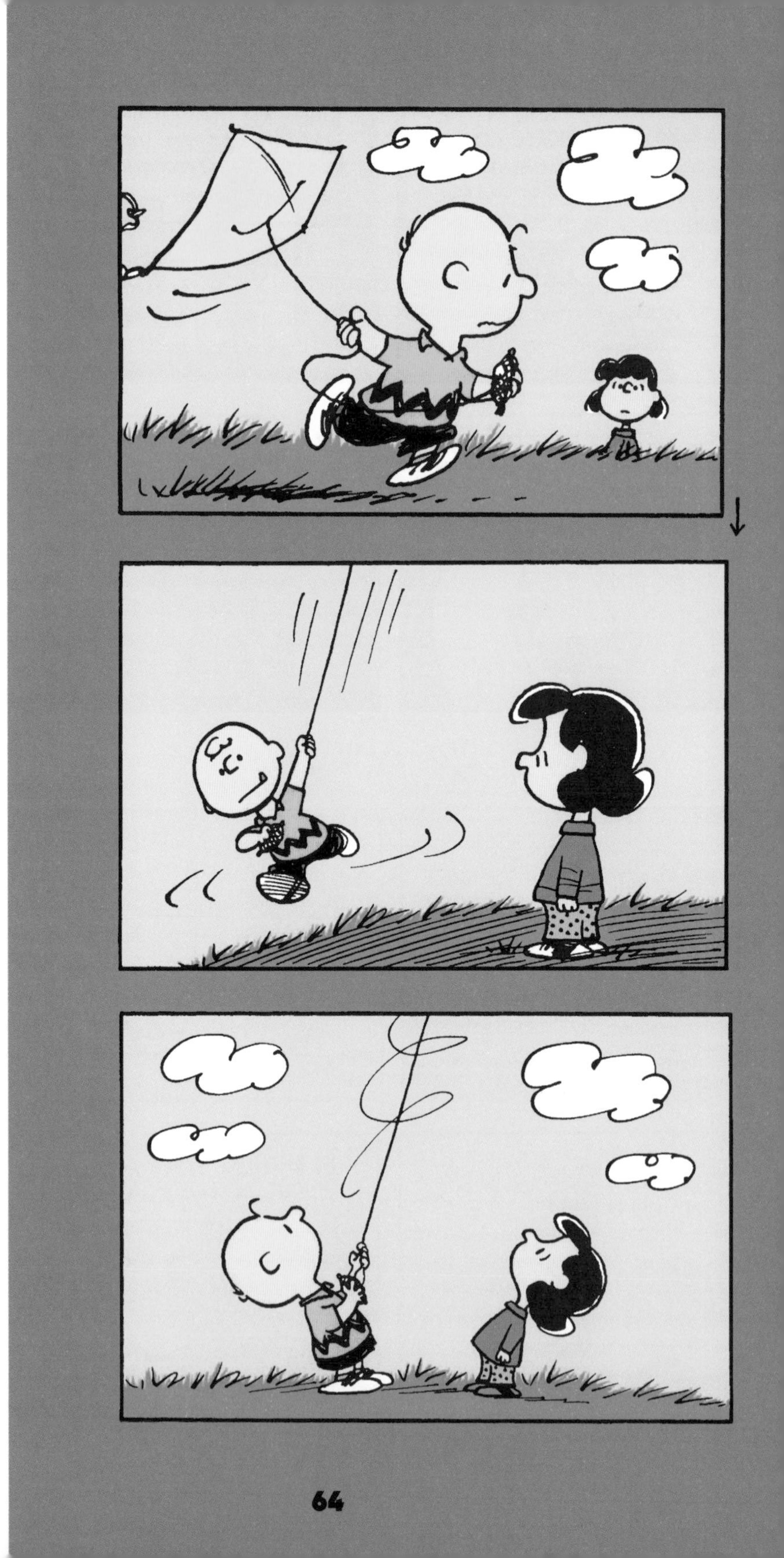

YOU KNOW WHAT MAKES KIND OF A GOOD HOBBY? SAVING STRING!

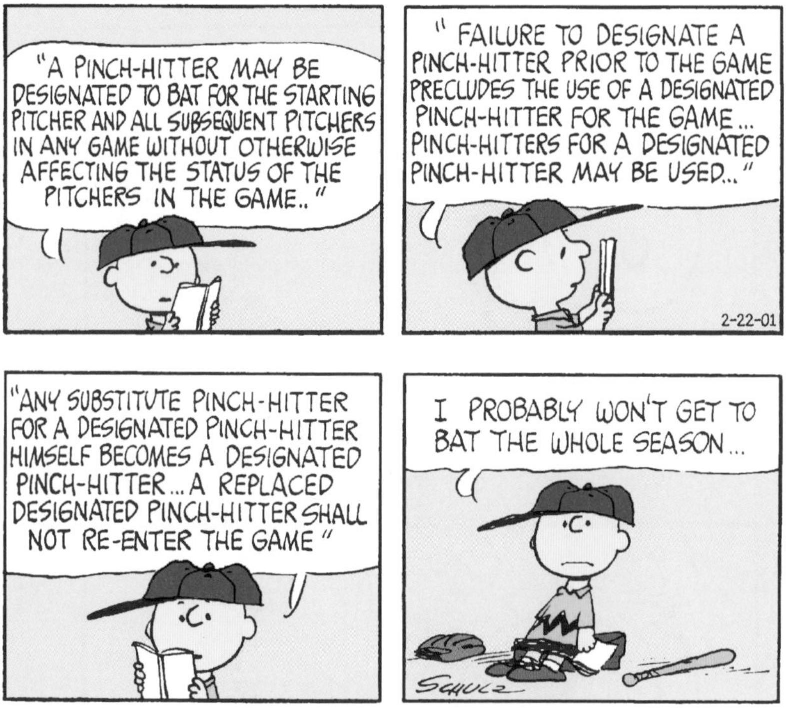
"A PINCH-HITTER MAY BE DESIGNATED TO BAT FOR THE STARTING PITCHER AND ALL SUBSEQUENT PITCHERS IN ANY GAME WITHOUT OTHERWISE AFFECTING THE STATUS OF THE PITCHERS IN THE GAME.."
" FAILURE TO DESIGNATE A PINCH-HITTER PRIOR TO THE GAME PRECLUDES THE USE OF A DESIGNATED PINCH-HITTER FOR THE GAME... PINCH-HITTERS FOR A DESIGNATED PINCH-HITTER MAY BE USED.."
2-22-01
"ANY SUBSTITUTE PINCH-HITTER FOR A DESIGNATED PINCH-HITTER HIMSELF BECOMES A DESIGNATED PINCH-HITTER... A REPLACED DESIGNATED PINCH-HITTER SHALL NOT RE-ENTER THE GAME"
I PROBABLY WON'T GET TO BAT THE WHOLE SEASON...

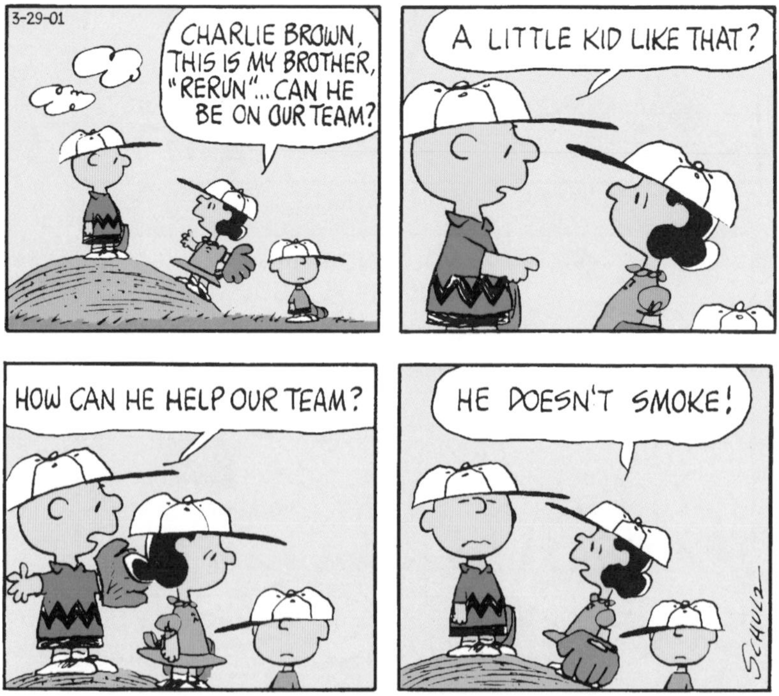
3-29-01
CHARLIE BROWN, THIS IS MY BROTHER, "RERUN"... CAN HE BE ON OUR TEAM?
A LITTLE KID LIKE THAT?
HOW CAN HE HELP OUR TEAM?
HE DOESN'T SMOKE!

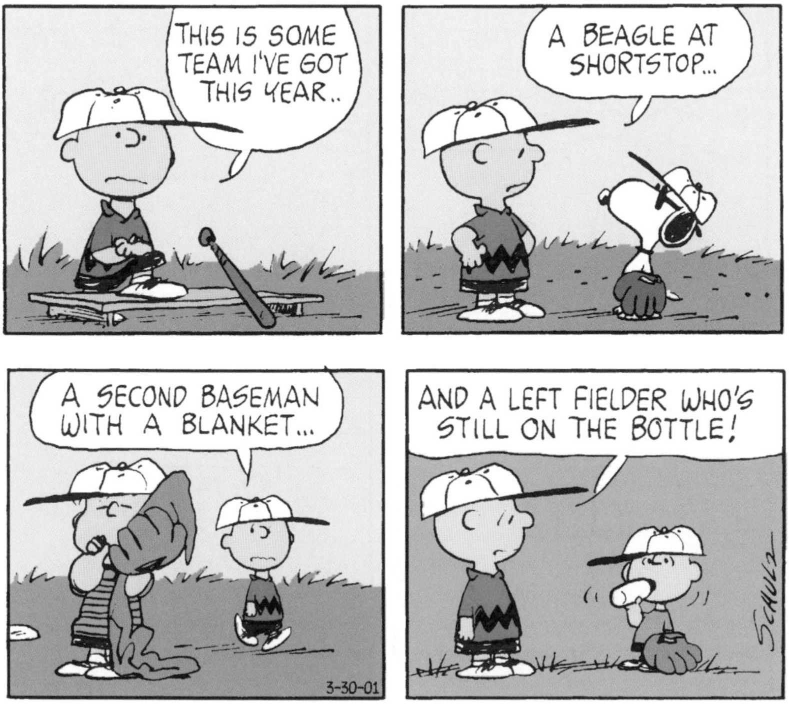
THIS IS SOME TEAM I'VE GOT THIS YEAR..
A BEAGLE AT SHORTSTOP...
A SECOND BASEMAN WITH A BLANKET...
AND A LEFT FIELDER WHO'S STILL ON THE BOTTLE!
3-30-01
SCHULZ

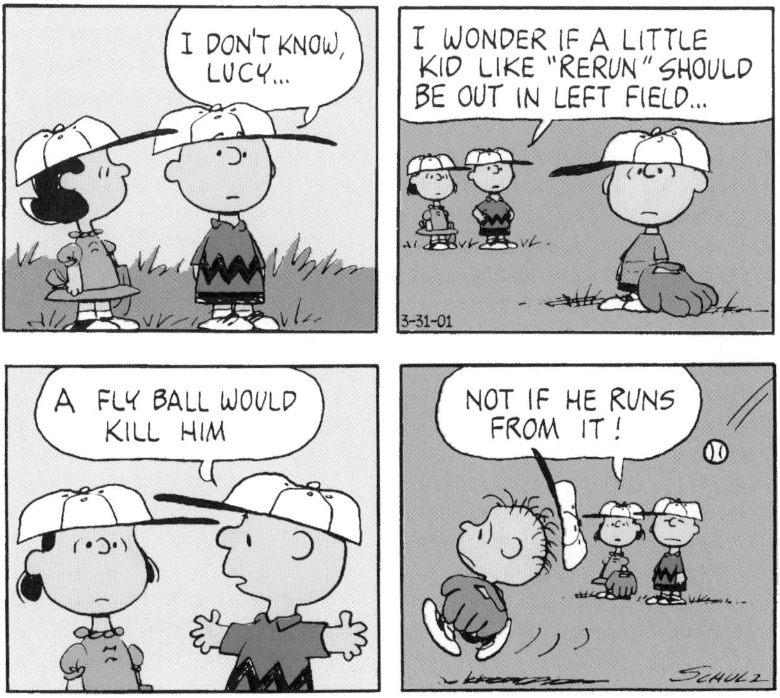
I DON'T KNOW, LUCY...
I WONDER IF A LITTLE KID LIKE "RERUN" SHOULD BE OUT IN LEFT FIELD...
3-31-01
A FLY BALL WOULD KILL HIM
NOT IF HE RUNS FROM IT!
SCHULZ

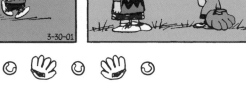

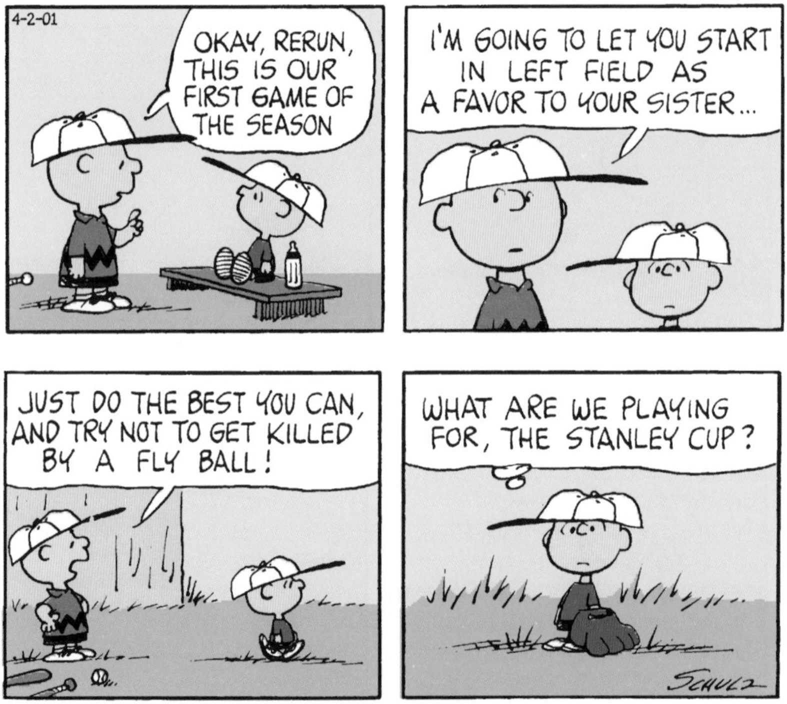
4-2-01
OKAY, RERUN, THIS IS OUR FIRST GAME OF THE SEASON
I'M GOING TO LET YOU START IN LEFT FIELD AS A FAVOR TO YOUR SISTER...
JUST DO THE BEST YOU CAN, AND TRY NOT TO GET KILLED BY A FLY BALL!
WHAT ARE WE PLAYING FOR, THE STANLEY CUP?
SCHULZ

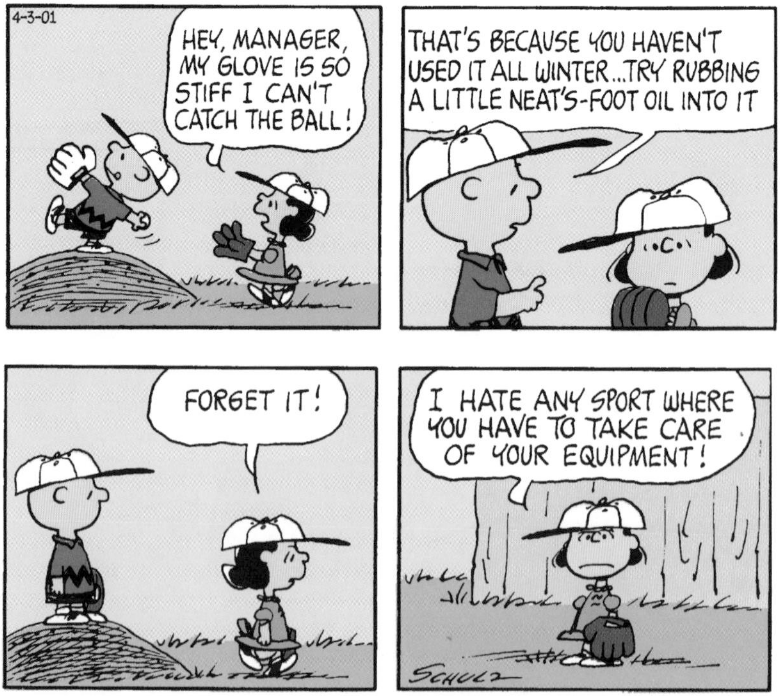
4-3-01
HEY, MANAGER, MY GLOVE IS SO STIFF I CAN'T CATCH THE BALL!
THAT'S BECAUSE YOU HAVEN'T USED IT ALL WINTER...TRY RUBBING A LITTLE NEAT'S-FOOT OIL INTO IT
FORGET IT!
I HATE ANY SPORT WHERE YOU HAVE TO TAKE CARE OF YOUR EQUIPMENT!
SCHULZ

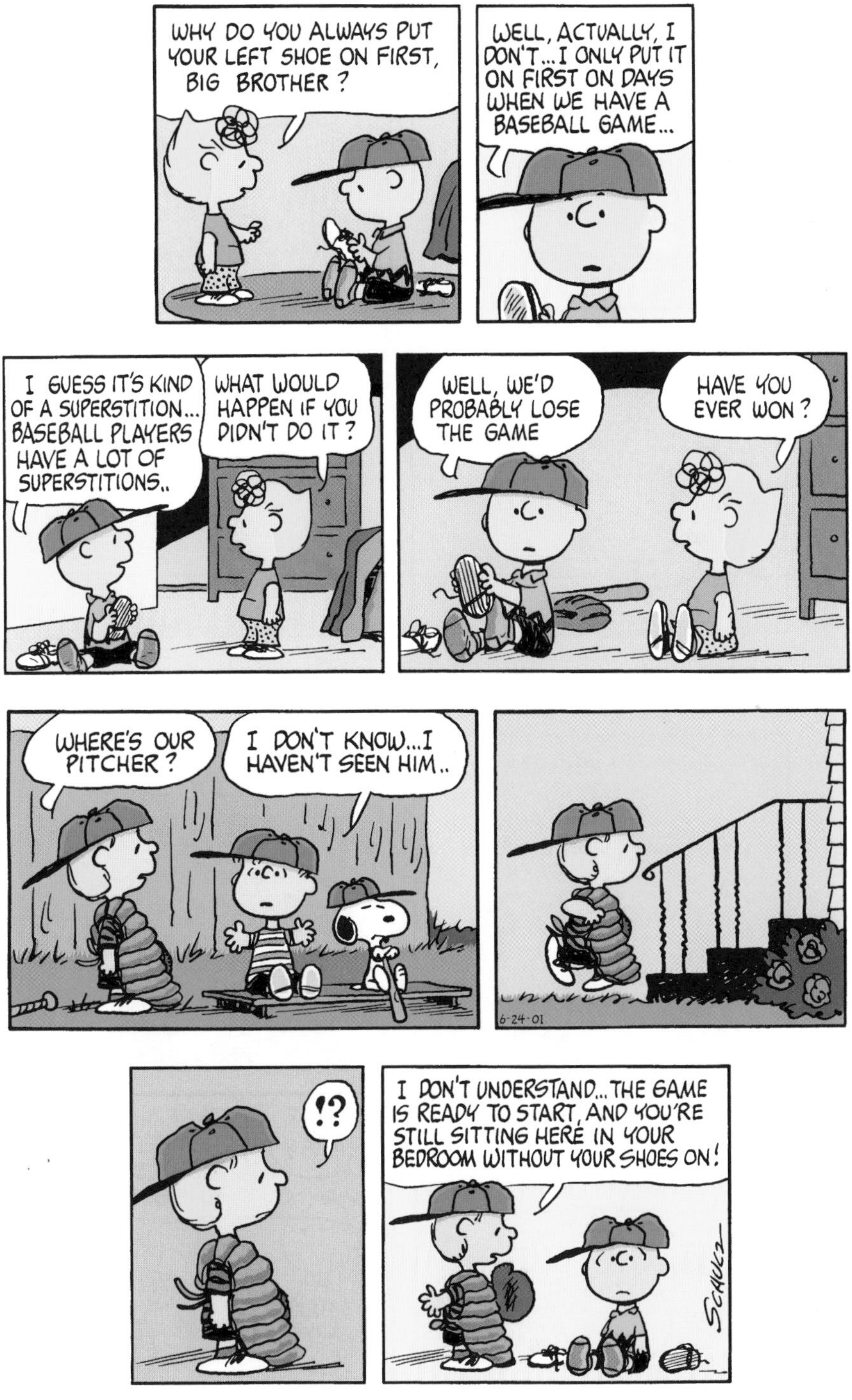

WHY DO YOU ALWAYS PUT YOUR LEFT SHOE ON FIRST, BIG BROTHER?
WELL, ACTUALLY, I DON'T... I ONLY PUT IT ON FIRST ON DAYS WHEN WE HAVE A BASEBALL GAME...
I GUESS IT'S KIND OF A SUPERSTITION... BASEBALL PLAYERS HAVE A LOT OF SUPERSTITIONS..
WHAT WOULD HAPPEN IF YOU DIDN'T DO IT?
WELL, WE'D PROBABLY LOSE THE GAME
HAVE YOU EVER WON?
WHERE'S OUR PITCHER?
I DON'T KNOW... I HAVEN'T SEEN HIM..
6-24-01
!?
I DON'T UNDERSTAND... THE GAME IS READY TO START, AND YOU'RE STILL SITTING HERE IN YOUR BEDROOM WITHOUT YOUR SHOES ON!
SCHULZ

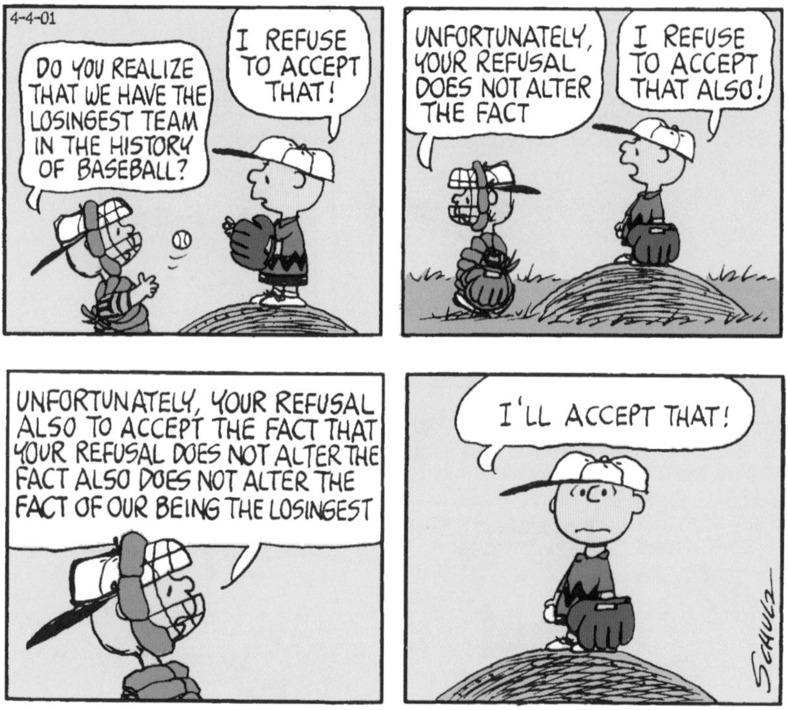
4-4-01
DO YOU REALIZE THAT WE HAVE THE LOSINGEST TEAM IN THE HISTORY OF BASEBALL?
I REFUSE TO ACCEPT THAT!
UNFORTUNATELY, YOUR REFUSAL DOES NOT ALTER THE FACT
I REFUSE TO ACCEPT THAT ALSO!
UNFORTUNATELY, YOUR REFUSAL ALSO TO ACCEPT THE FACT THAT YOUR REFUSAL DOES NOT ALTER THE FACT ALSO DOES NOT ALTER THE FACT OF OUR BEING THE LOSINGEST
I'LL ACCEPT THAT!
SCHULZ

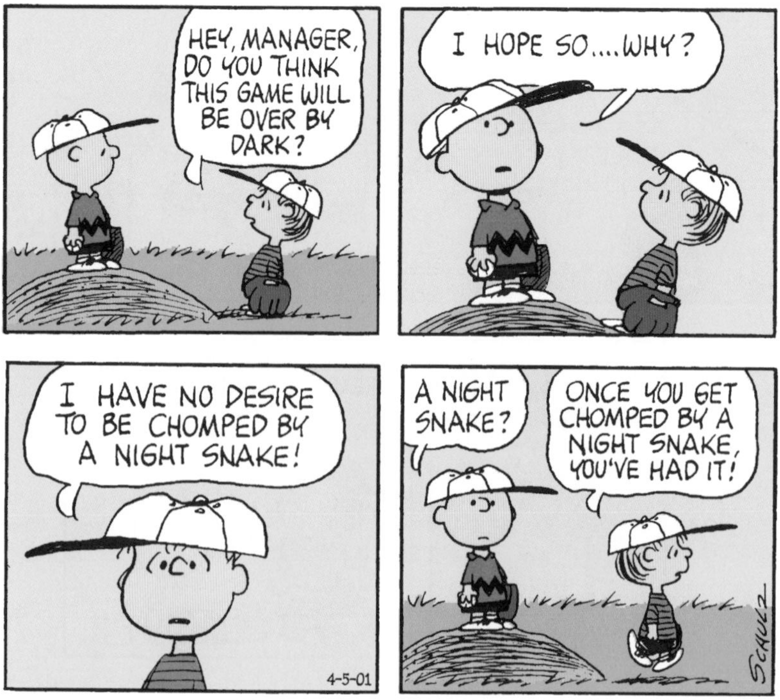
HEY, MANAGER, DO YOU THINK THIS GAME WILL BE OVER BY DARK?
I HOPE SO....WHY?
I HAVE NO DESIRE TO BE CHOMPED BY A NIGHT SNAKE!
4-5-01
A NIGHT SNAKE?
ONCE YOU GET CHOMPED BY A NIGHT SNAKE, YOU'VE HAD IT!
SCHULZ

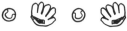

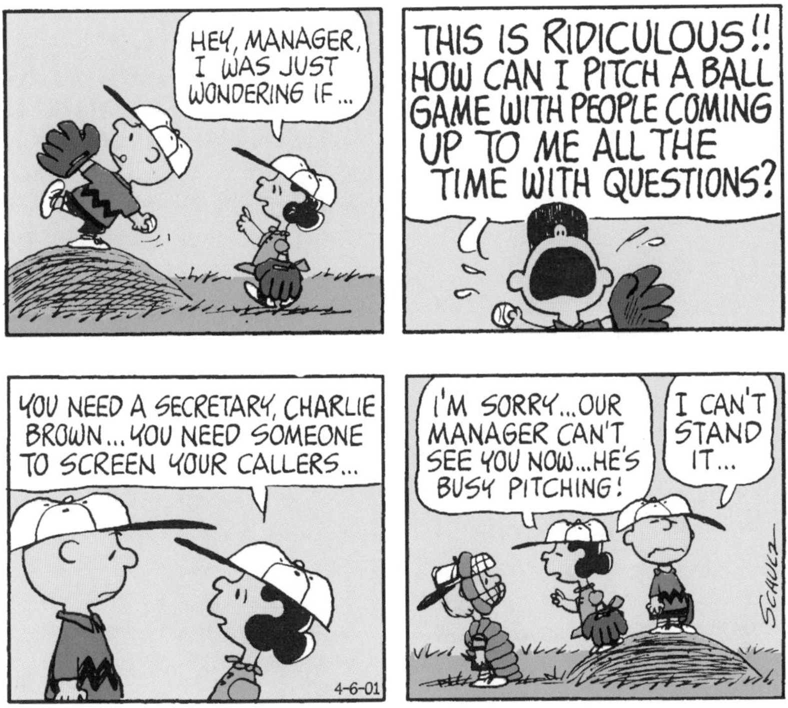
HEY, MANAGER, I WAS JUST WONDERING IF...
THIS IS RIDICULOUS!! HOW CAN I PITCH A BALL GAME WITH PEOPLE COMING UP TO ME ALL THE TIME WITH QUESTIONS?
YOU NEED A SECRETARY, CHARLIE BROWN... YOU NEED SOMEONE TO SCREEN YOUR CALLERS...
I'M SORRY...OUR MANAGER CAN'T SEE YOU NOW...HE'S BUSY PITCHING!
I CAN'T STAND IT...
SCHULZ
4-6-01

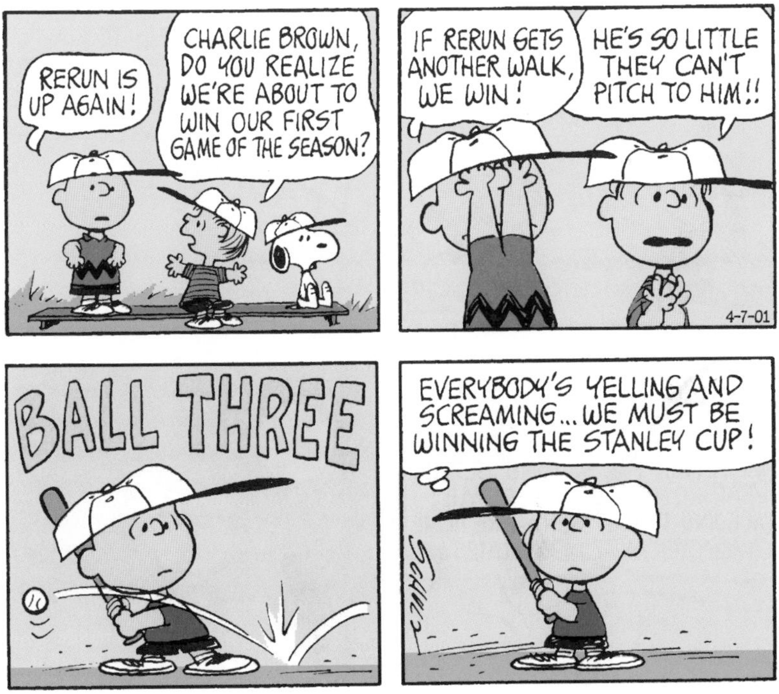
RERUN IS UP AGAIN!
CHARLIE BROWN, DO YOU REALIZE WE'RE ABOUT TO WIN OUR FIRST GAME OF THE SEASON?
IF RERUN GETS ANOTHER WALK, WE WIN!
HE'S SO LITTLE THEY CAN'T PITCH TO HIM!!
4-7-01
BALL THREE
EVERYBODY'S YELLING AND SCREAMING... WE MUST BE WINNING THE STANLEY CUP!
SCHULZ

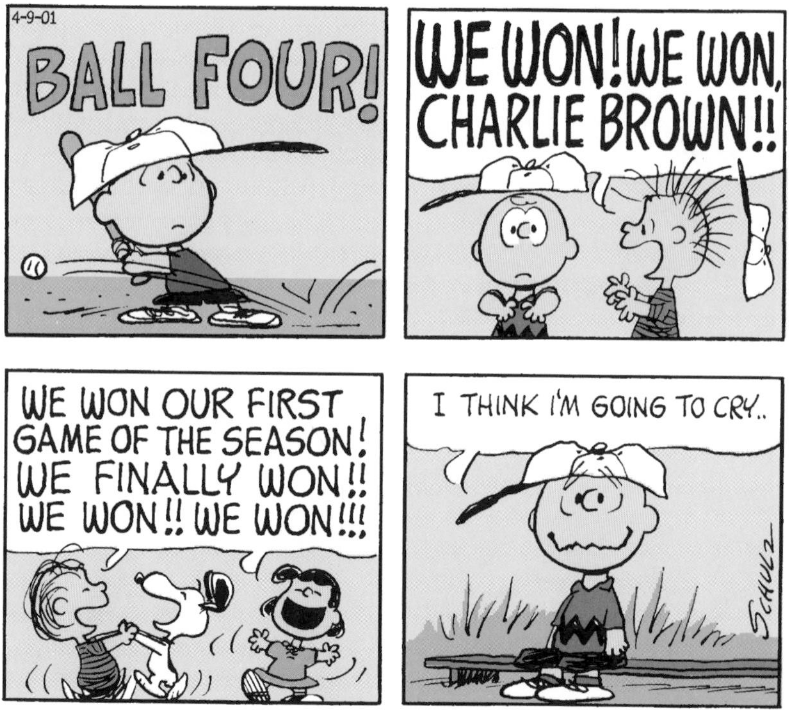
4-9-01
BALL FOUR!
WE WON! WE WON, CHARLIE BROWN!!
WE WON OUR FIRST GAME OF THE SEASON! WE FINALLY WON!! WE WON!! WE WON!!!
I THINK I'M GOING TO CRY..
SCHULZ

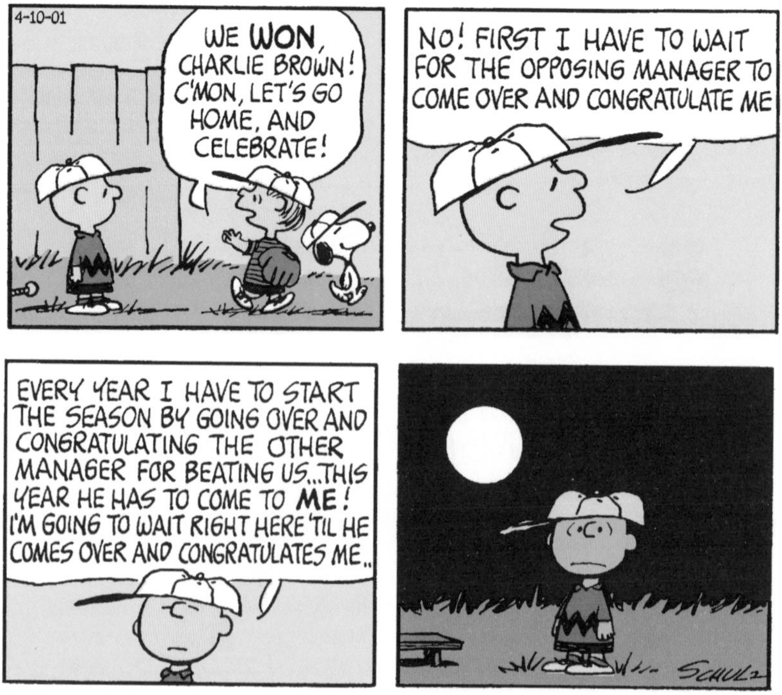
4-10-01
WE WON, CHARLIE BROWN! C'MON, LET'S GO HOME, AND CELEBRATE!
NO! FIRST I HAVE TO WAIT FOR THE OPPOSING MANAGER TO COME OVER AND CONGRATULATE ME
EVERY YEAR I HAVE TO START THE SEASON BY GOING OVER AND CONGRATULATING THE OTHER MANAGER FOR BEATING US...THIS YEAR HE HAS TO COME TO ME! I'M GOING TO WAIT RIGHT HERE 'TIL HE COMES OVER AND CONGRATULATES ME..
SCHULZ

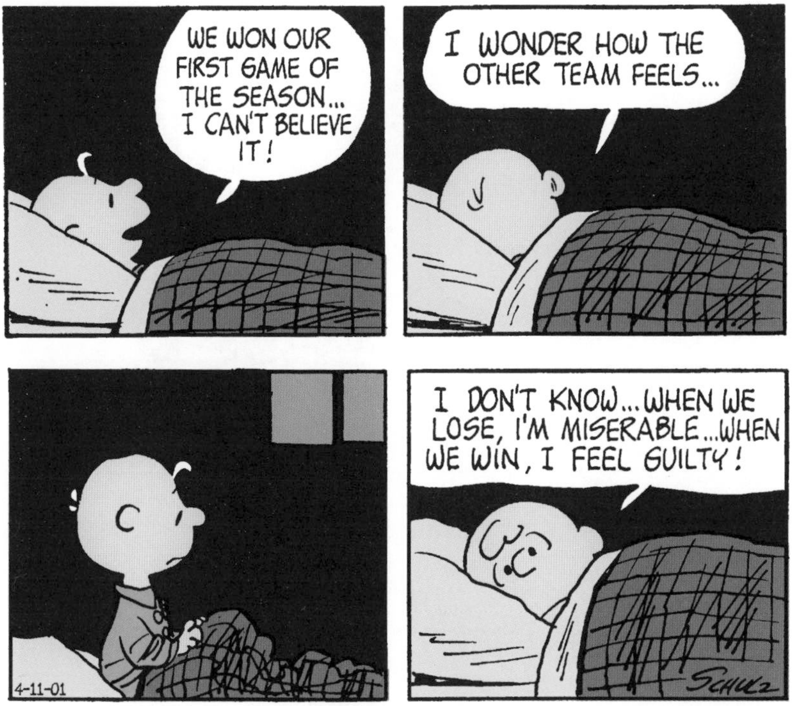
WE WON OUR FIRST GAME OF THE SEASON... I CAN'T BELIEVE IT!
I WONDER HOW THE OTHER TEAM FEELS...
I DON'T KNOW... WHEN WE LOSE, I'M MISERABLE... WHEN WE WIN, I FEEL GUILTY!
4-11-01
SCHULZ

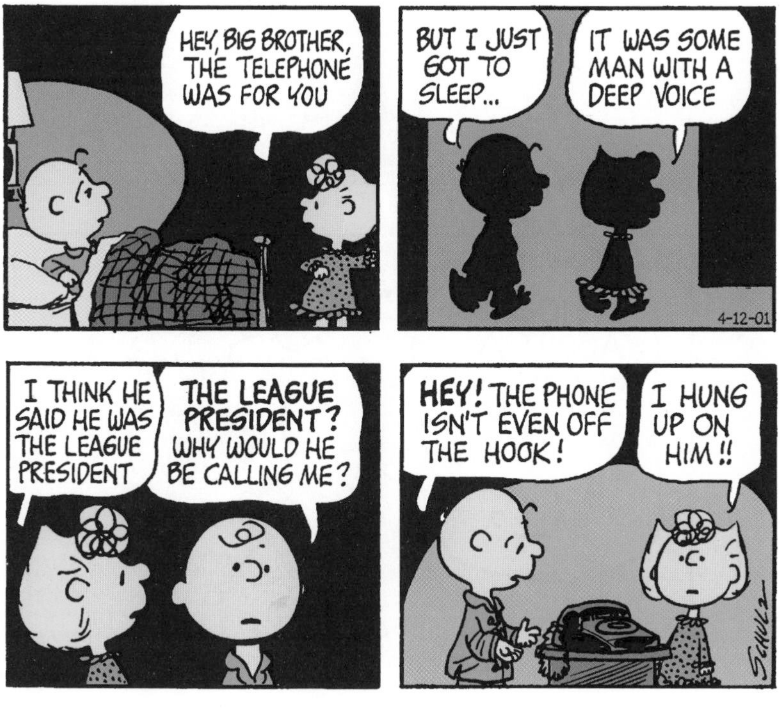
HEY, BIG BROTHER, THE TELEPHONE WAS FOR YOU
BUT I JUST GOT TO SLEEP...
IT WAS SOME MAN WITH A DEEP VOICE
4-12-01
I THINK HE SAID HE WAS THE LEAGUE PRESIDENT
THE LEAGUE PRESIDENT? WHY WOULD HE BE CALLING ME?
HEY! THE PHONE ISN'T EVEN OFF THE HOOK!
I HUNG UP ON HIM!!
SCHULZ

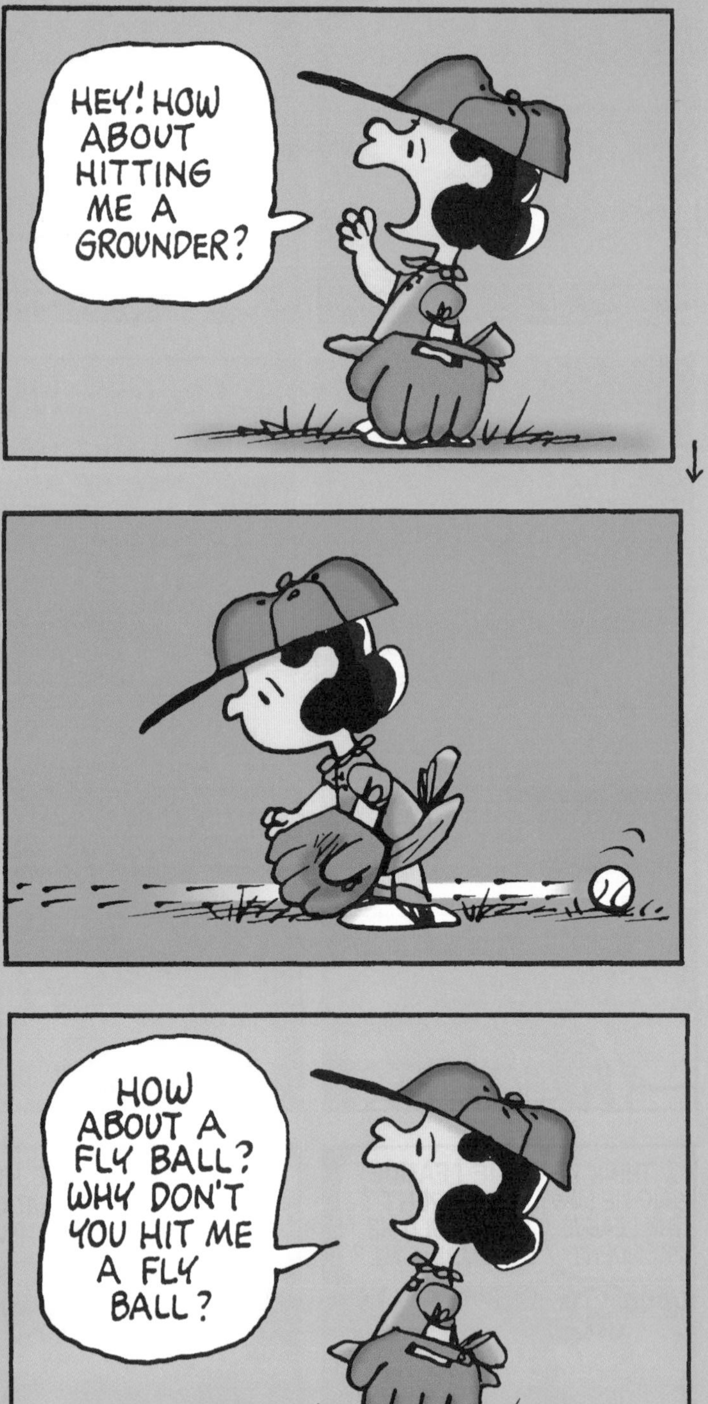
HEY! HOW ABOUT HITTING ME A GROUNDER?
HOW ABOUT A FLY BALL? WHY DON'T YOU HIT ME A FLY BALL?

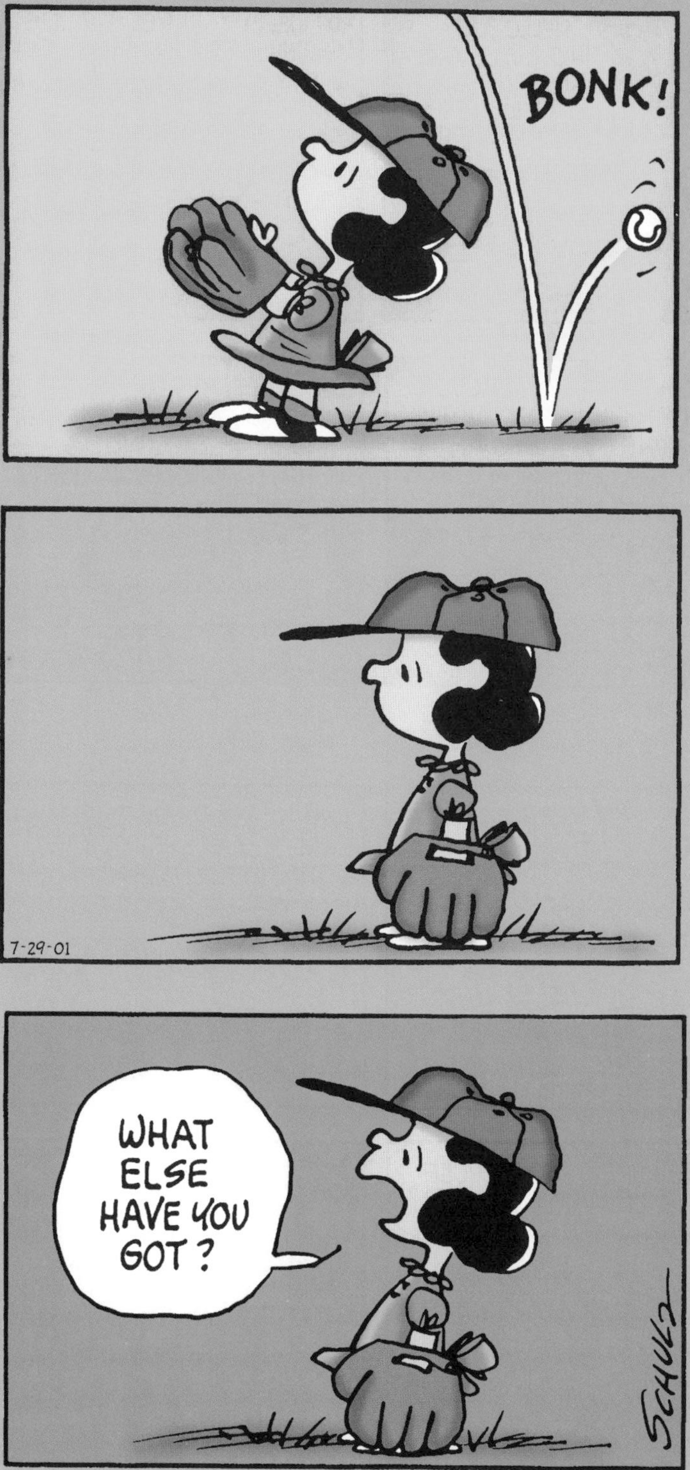
BONK!
7-29-01
WHAT ELSE HAVE YOU GOT?
SCHULZ

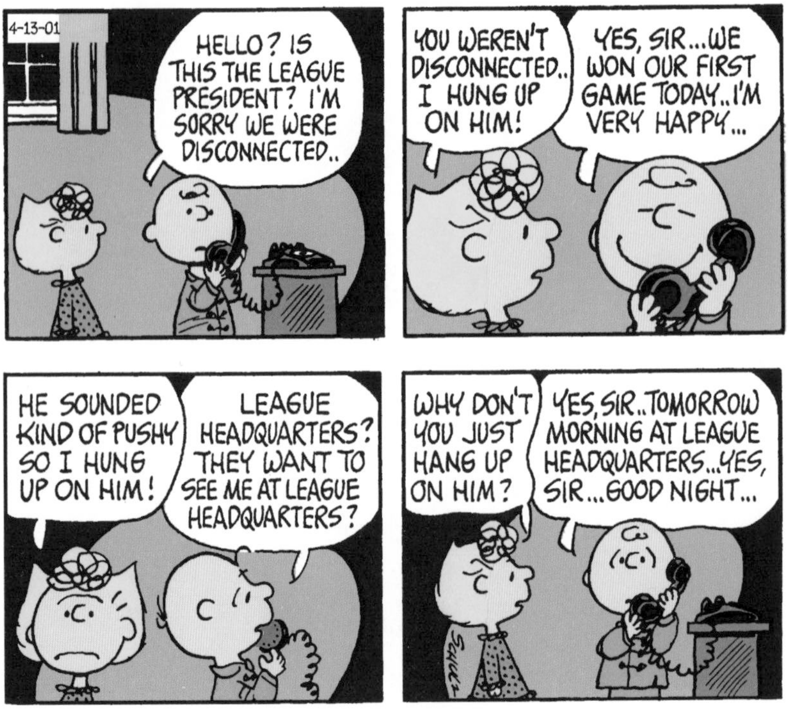
4-13-01
HELLO? IS THIS THE LEAGUE PRESIDENT? I'M SORRY WE WERE DISCONNECTED..
YOU WEREN'T DISCONNECTED.. I HUNG UP ON HIM!
YES, SIR...WE WON OUR FIRST GAME TODAY..I'M VERY HAPPY...
HE SOUNDED KIND OF PUSHY SO I HUNG UP ON HIM!
LEAGUE HEADQUARTERS? THEY WANT TO SEE ME AT LEAGUE HEADQUARTERS?
WHY DON'T YOU JUST HANG UP ON HIM?
YES, SIR..TOMORROW MORNING AT LEAGUE HEADQUARTERS...YES, SIR...GOOD NIGHT...

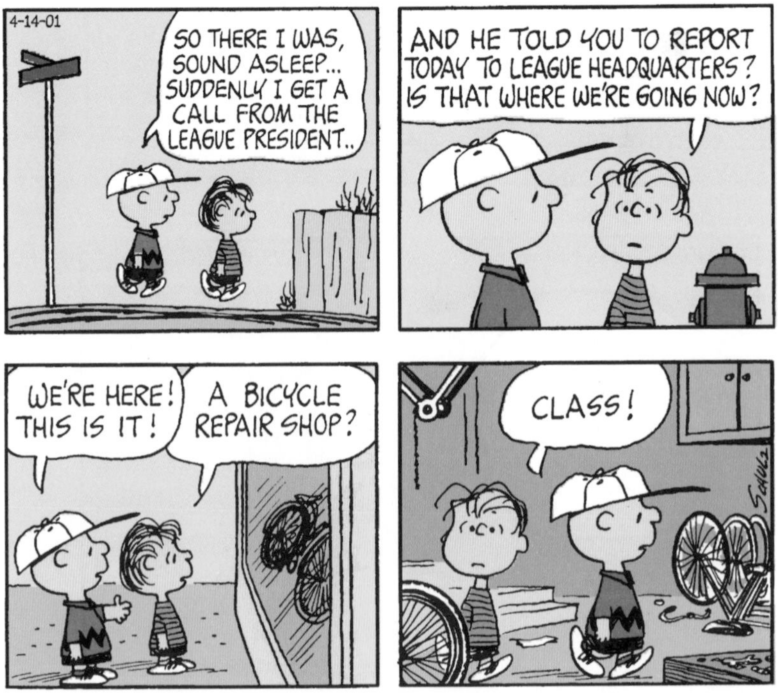
4-14-01
SO THERE I WAS, SOUND ASLEEP... SUDDENLY I GET A CALL FROM THE LEAGUE PRESIDENT..
AND HE TOLD YOU TO REPORT TODAY TO LEAGUE HEADQUARTERS? IS THAT WHERE WE'RE GOING NOW?
WE'RE HERE! THIS IS IT!
A BICYCLE REPAIR SHOP?
CLASS!

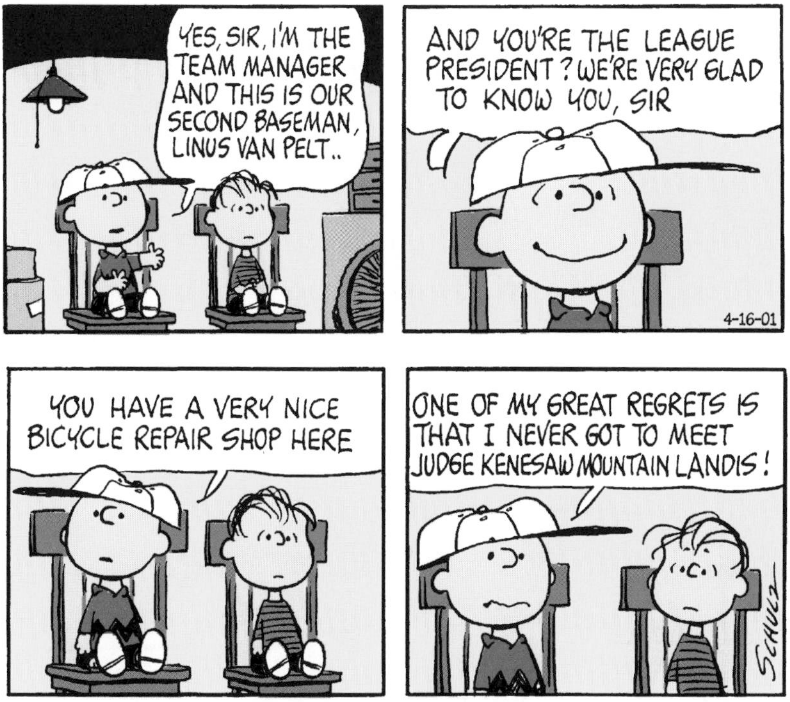
YES, SIR, I'M THE TEAM MANAGER AND THIS IS OUR SECOND BASEMAN, LINUS VAN PELT..
AND YOU'RE THE LEAGUE PRESIDENT? WE'RE VERY GLAD TO KNOW YOU, SIR
4-16-01
YOU HAVE A VERY NICE BICYCLE REPAIR SHOP HERE
ONE OF MY GREAT REGRETS IS THAT I NEVER GOT TO MEET JUDGE KENESAW MOUNTAIN LANDIS!
SCHULZ

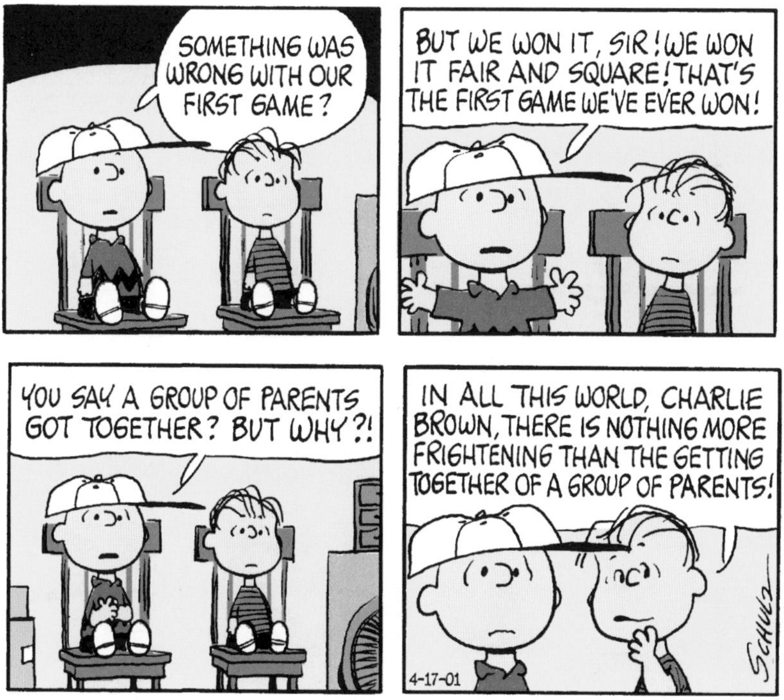
SOMETHING WAS WRONG WITH OUR FIRST GAME?
BUT WE WON IT, SIR! WE WON IT FAIR AND SQUARE! THAT'S THE FIRST GAME WE'VE EVER WON!
YOU SAY A GROUP OF PARENTS GOT TOGETHER? BUT WHY?!
IN ALL THIS WORLD, CHARLIE BROWN, THERE IS NOTHING MORE FRIGHTENING THAN THE GETTING TOGETHER OF A GROUP OF PARENTS!
4-17-01
SCHULZ

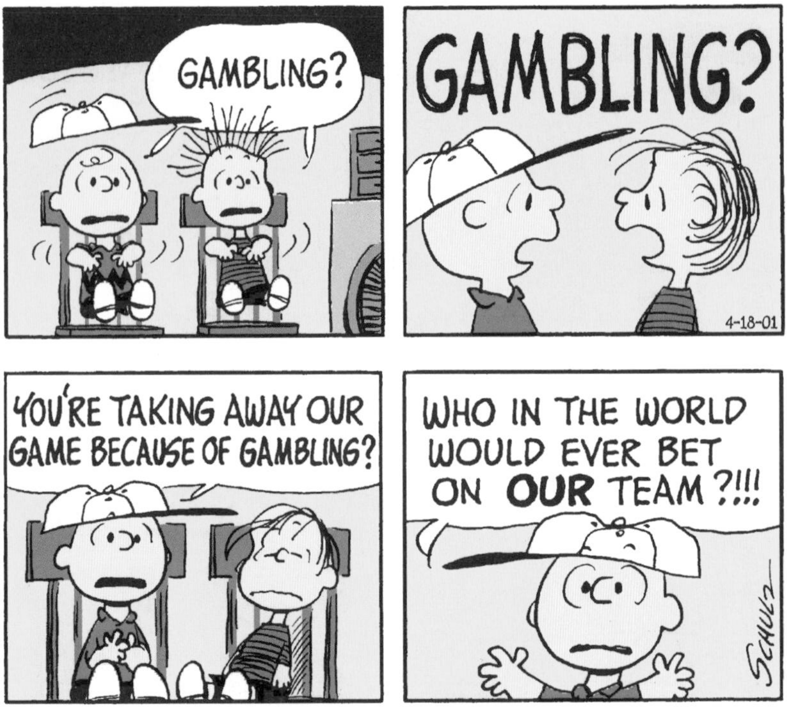
GAMBLING?
GAMBLING?
4-18-01
YOU'RE TAKING AWAY OUR GAME BECAUSE OF GAMBLING?
WHO IN THE WORLD WOULD EVER BET ON **OUR** TEAM?!!!
SCHULZ

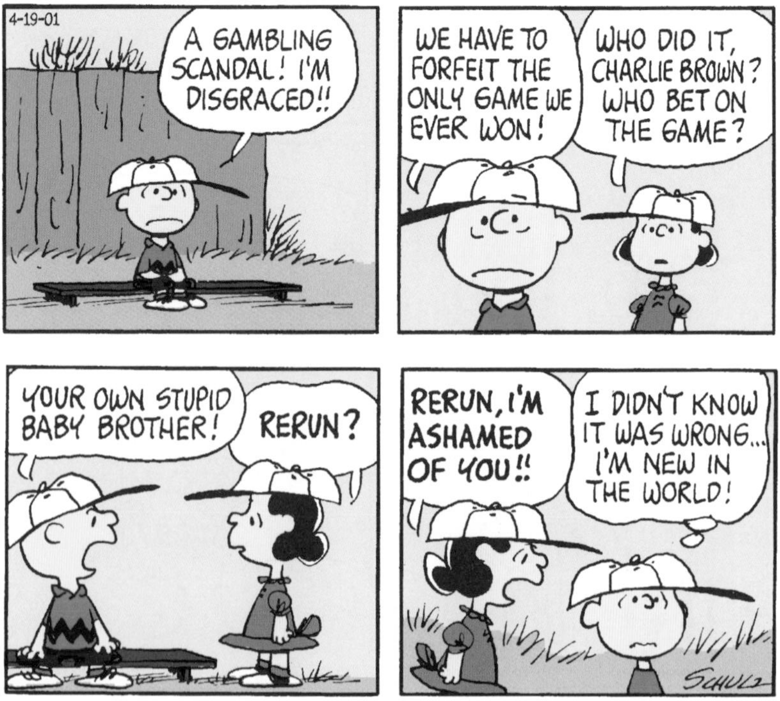
4-19-01
A GAMBLING SCANDAL! I'M DISGRACED!!
WE HAVE TO FORFEIT THE ONLY GAME WE EVER WON!
WHO DID IT, CHARLIE BROWN? WHO BET ON THE GAME?
YOUR OWN STUPID BABY BROTHER!
RERUN?
RERUN, I'M ASHAMED OF YOU!!
I DIDN'T KNOW IT WAS WRONG... I'M NEW IN THE WORLD!
SCHULZ

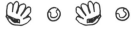

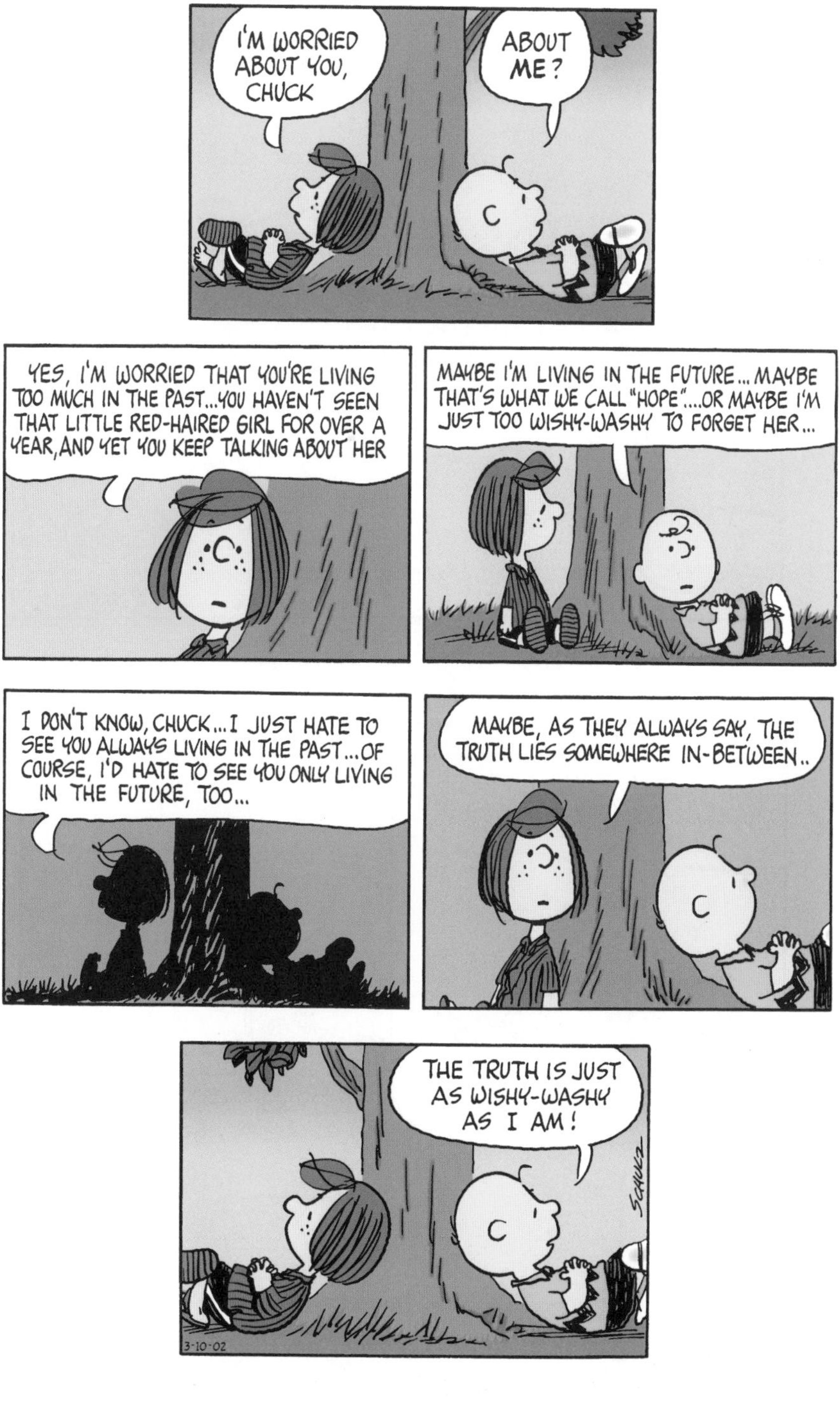
I'M WORRIED ABOUT YOU, CHUCK
ABOUT ME?
YES, I'M WORRIED THAT YOU'RE LIVING TOO MUCH IN THE PAST...YOU HAVEN'T SEEN THAT LITTLE RED-HAIRED GIRL FOR OVER A YEAR, AND YET YOU KEEP TALKING ABOUT HER
MAYBE I'M LIVING IN THE FUTURE... MAYBE THAT'S WHAT WE CALL "HOPE"....OR MAYBE I'M JUST TOO WISHY-WASHY TO FORGET HER...
I DON'T KNOW, CHUCK...I JUST HATE TO SEE YOU ALWAYS LIVING IN THE PAST...OF COURSE, I'D HATE TO SEE YOU ONLY LIVING IN THE FUTURE, TOO...
MAYBE, AS THEY ALWAYS SAY, THE TRUTH LIES SOMEWHERE IN-BETWEEN..
THE TRUTH IS JUST AS WISHY-WASHY AS I AM!
SCHULZ
3-10-02

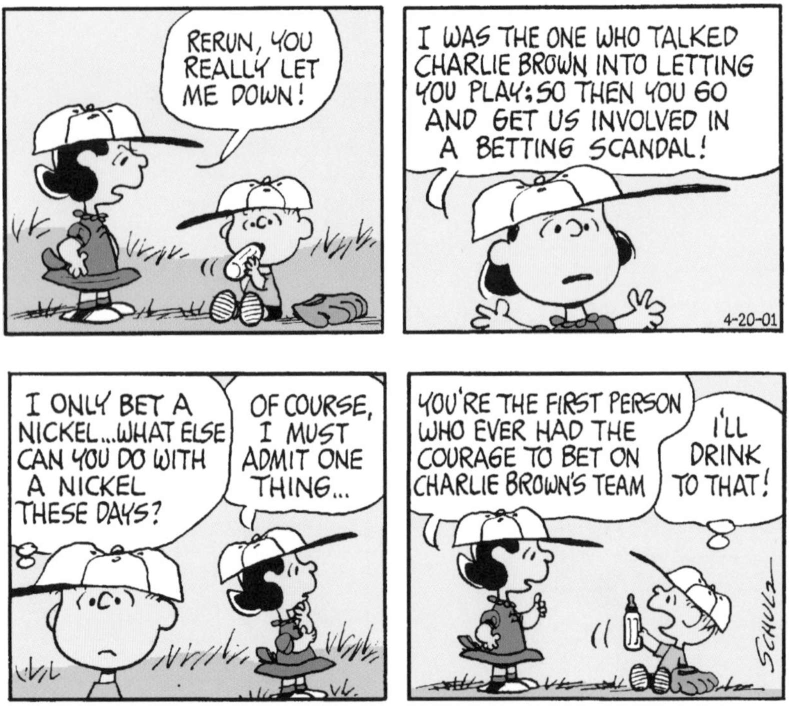
RERUN, YOU REALLY LET ME DOWN!
I WAS THE ONE WHO TALKED CHARLIE BROWN INTO LETTING YOU PLAY; SO THEN YOU GO AND GET US INVOLVED IN A BETTING SCANDAL!
4-20-01
I ONLY BET A NICKEL...WHAT ELSE CAN YOU DO WITH A NICKEL THESE DAYS?
OF COURSE, I MUST ADMIT ONE THING...
YOU'RE THE FIRST PERSON WHO EVER HAD THE COURAGE TO BET ON CHARLIE BROWN'S TEAM
I'LL DRINK TO THAT!
SCHULZ

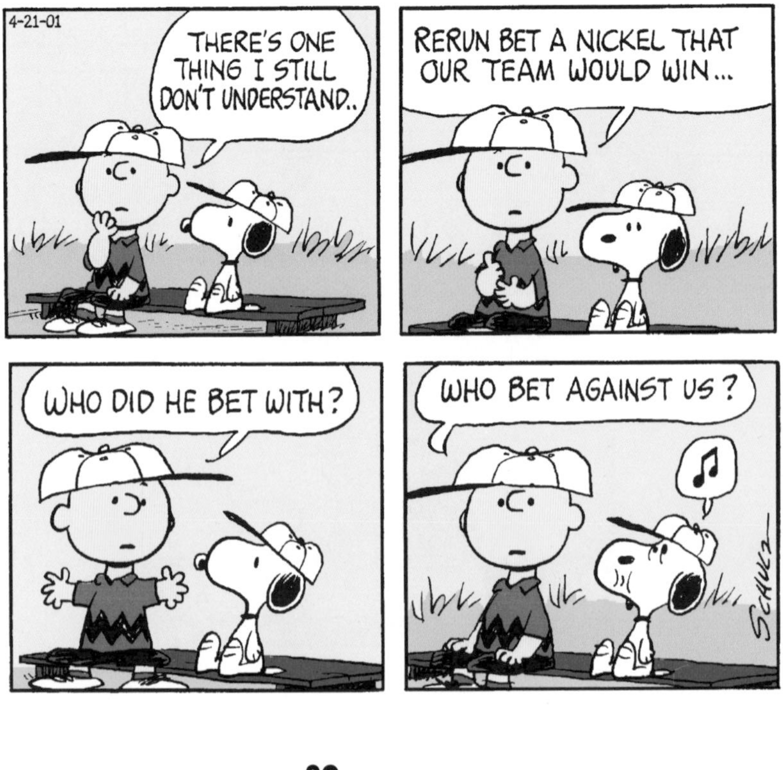
4-21-01
THERE'S ONE THING I STILL DON'T UNDERSTAND..
RERUN BET A NICKEL THAT OUR TEAM WOULD WIN...
WHO DID HE BET WITH?
WHO BET AGAINST US?
SCHULZ

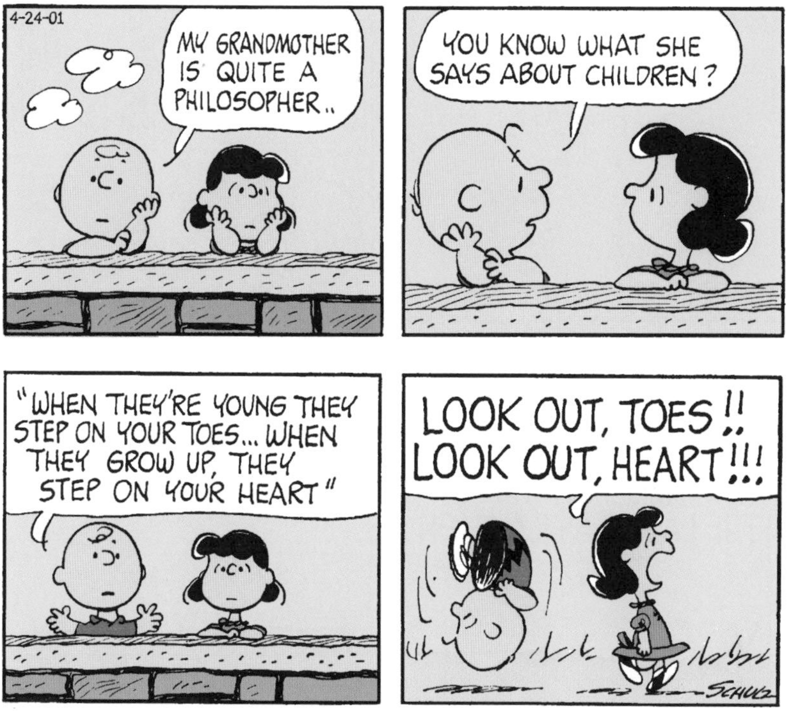
4-24-01
MY GRANDMOTHER IS QUITE A PHILOSOPHER..
YOU KNOW WHAT SHE SAYS ABOUT CHILDREN?
"WHEN THEY'RE YOUNG THEY STEP ON YOUR TOES... WHEN THEY GROW UP, THEY STEP ON YOUR HEART"
LOOK OUT, TOES!! LOOK OUT, HEART!!!

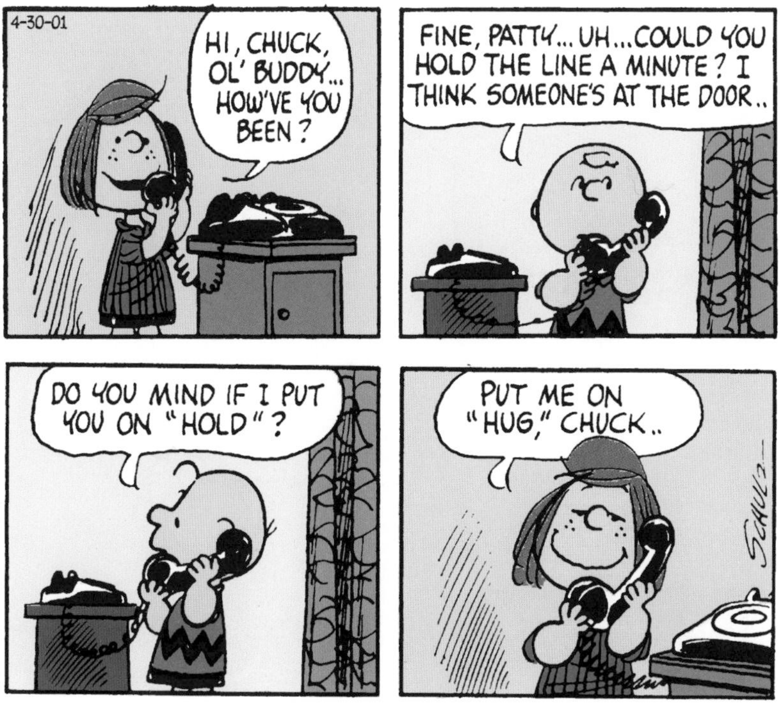
4-30-01
HI, CHUCK, OL' BUDDY... HOW'VE YOU BEEN?
FINE, PATTY... UH...COULD YOU HOLD THE LINE A MINUTE? I THINK SOMEONE'S AT THE DOOR..
DO YOU MIND IF I PUT YOU ON "HOLD"?
PUT ME ON "HUG," CHUCK..

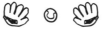

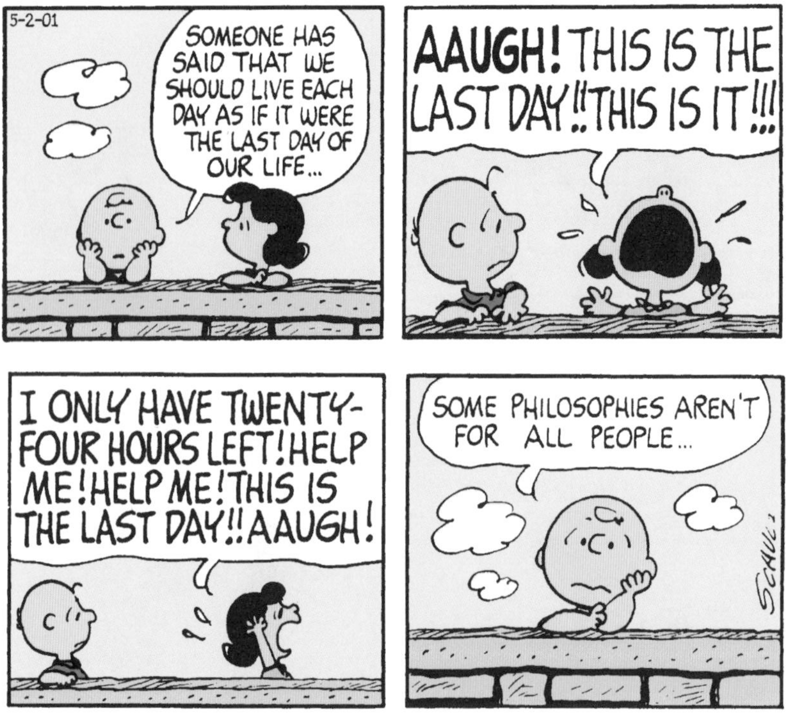
5-2-01
SOMEONE HAS SAID THAT WE SHOULD LIVE EACH DAY AS IF IT WERE THE LAST DAY OF OUR LIFE...
AAUGH! THIS IS THE LAST DAY!! THIS IS IT!!!
I ONLY HAVE TWENTY-FOUR HOURS LEFT! HELP ME! HELP ME! THIS IS THE LAST DAY!! AAUGH!
SOME PHILOSOPHIES AREN'T FOR ALL PEOPLE...

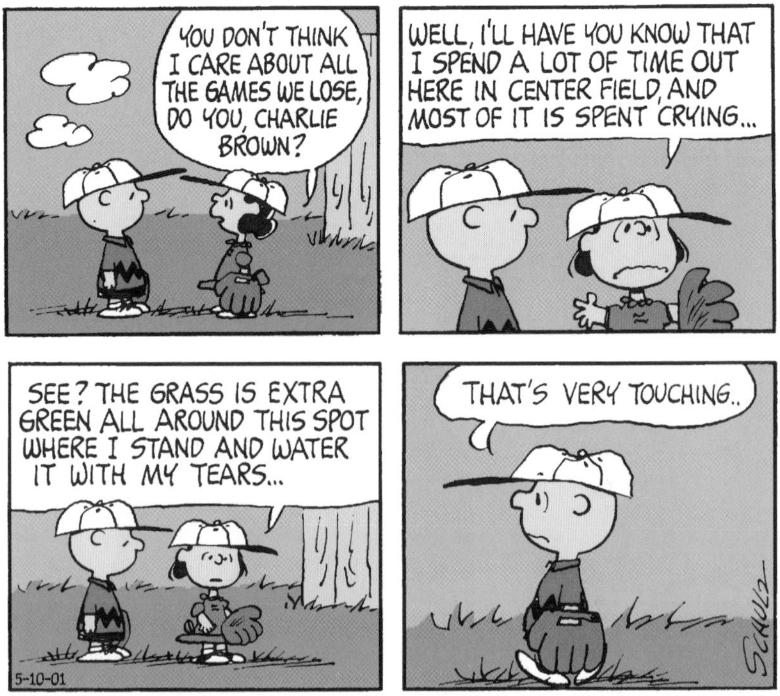
YOU DON'T THINK I CARE ABOUT ALL THE GAMES WE LOSE, DO YOU, CHARLIE BROWN?
WELL, I'LL HAVE YOU KNOW THAT I SPEND A LOT OF TIME OUT HERE IN CENTER FIELD, AND MOST OF IT IS SPENT CRYING...
SEE? THE GRASS IS EXTRA GREEN ALL AROUND THIS SPOT WHERE I STAND AND WATER IT WITH MY TEARS...
5-10-01
THAT'S VERY TOUCHING..

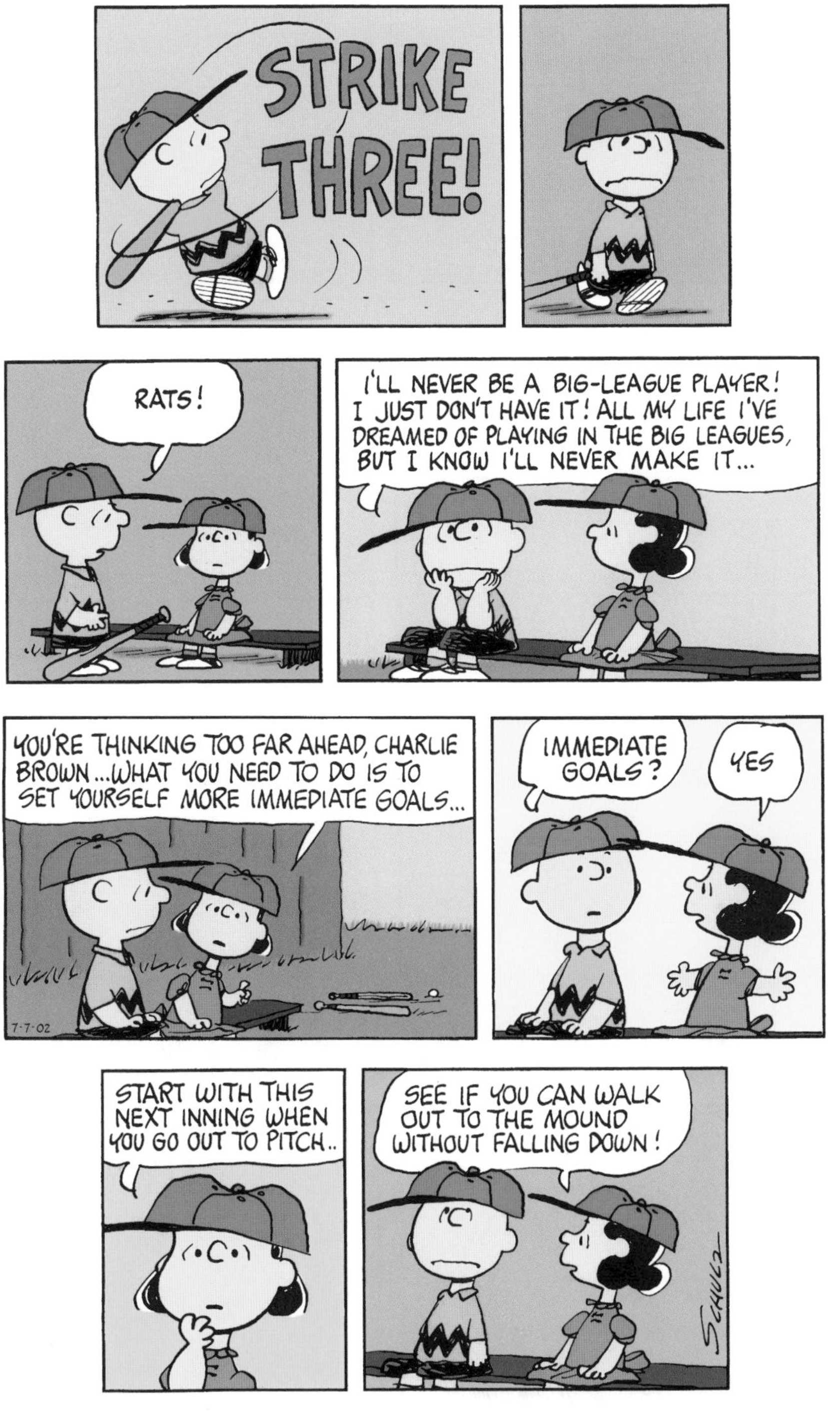
STRIKE THREE!
RATS!
I'LL NEVER BE A BIG-LEAGUE PLAYER! I JUST DON'T HAVE IT! ALL MY LIFE I'VE DREAMED OF PLAYING IN THE BIG LEAGUES, BUT I KNOW I'LL NEVER MAKE IT...
YOU'RE THINKING TOO FAR AHEAD, CHARLIE BROWN...WHAT YOU NEED TO DO IS TO SET YOURSELF MORE IMMEDIATE GOALS...
7-7-02
IMMEDIATE GOALS?
YES
START WITH THIS NEXT INNING WHEN YOU GO OUT TO PITCH..
SEE IF YOU CAN WALK OUT TO THE MOUND WITHOUT FALLING DOWN!
SCHULZ

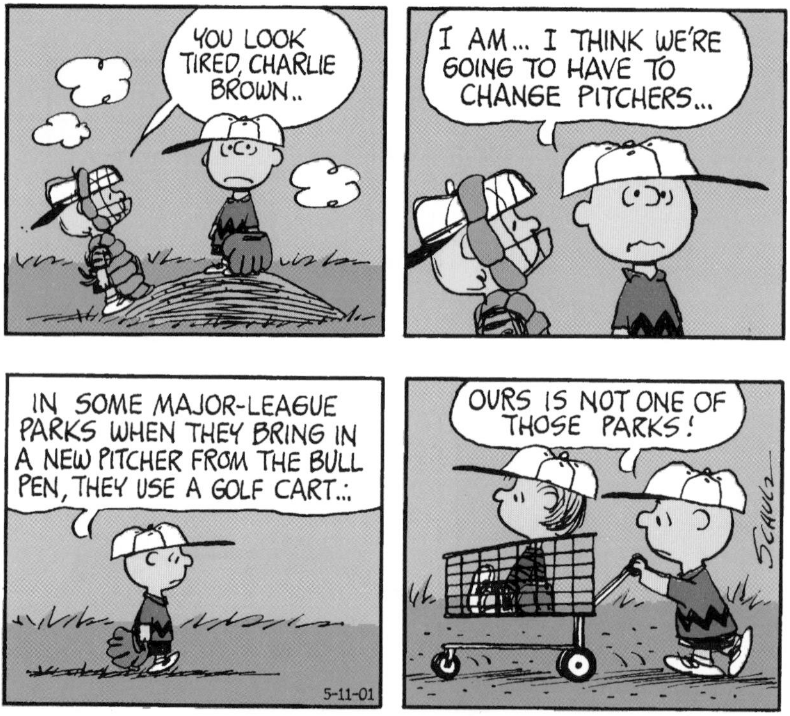
YOU LOOK TIRED, CHARLIE BROWN..
I AM... I THINK WE'RE GOING TO HAVE TO CHANGE PITCHERS...
IN SOME MAJOR-LEAGUE PARKS WHEN THEY BRING IN A NEW PITCHER FROM THE BULL PEN, THEY USE A GOLF CART..:
5-11-01
OURS IS NOT ONE OF THOSE PARKS!
SCHULZ

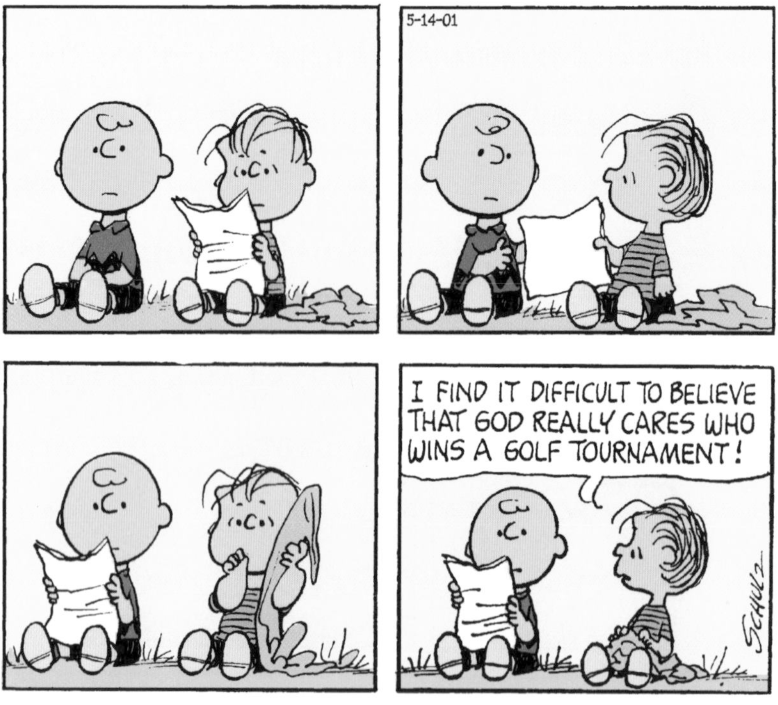
5-14-01
I FIND IT DIFFICULT TO BELIEVE THAT GOD REALLY CARES WHO WINS A GOLF TOURNAMENT!
SCHULZ

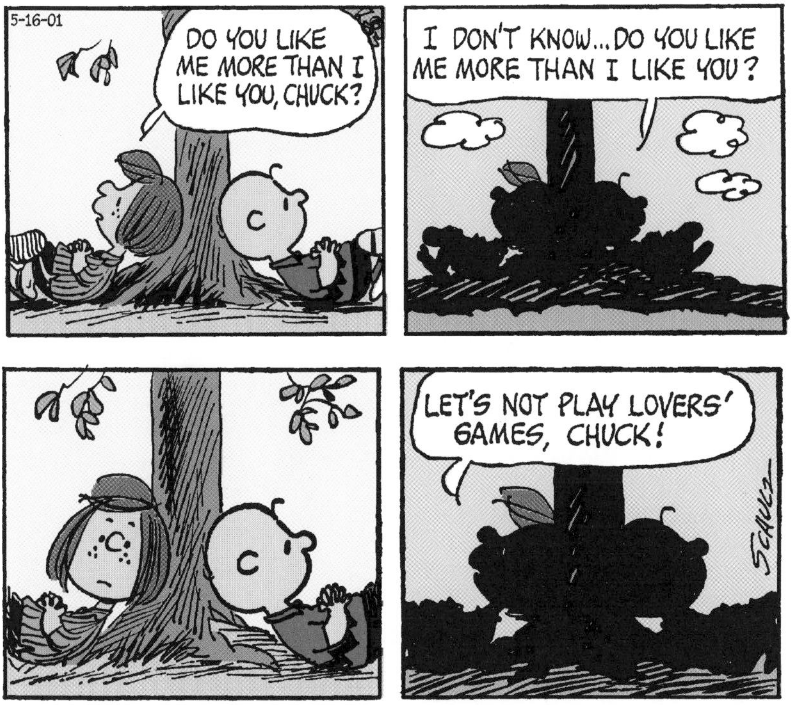
5-16-01
DO YOU LIKE ME MORE THAN I LIKE YOU, CHUCK?
I DON'T KNOW... DO YOU LIKE ME MORE THAN I LIKE YOU?
LET'S NOT PLAY LOVERS' GAMES, CHUCK!
SCHULZ

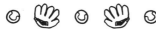

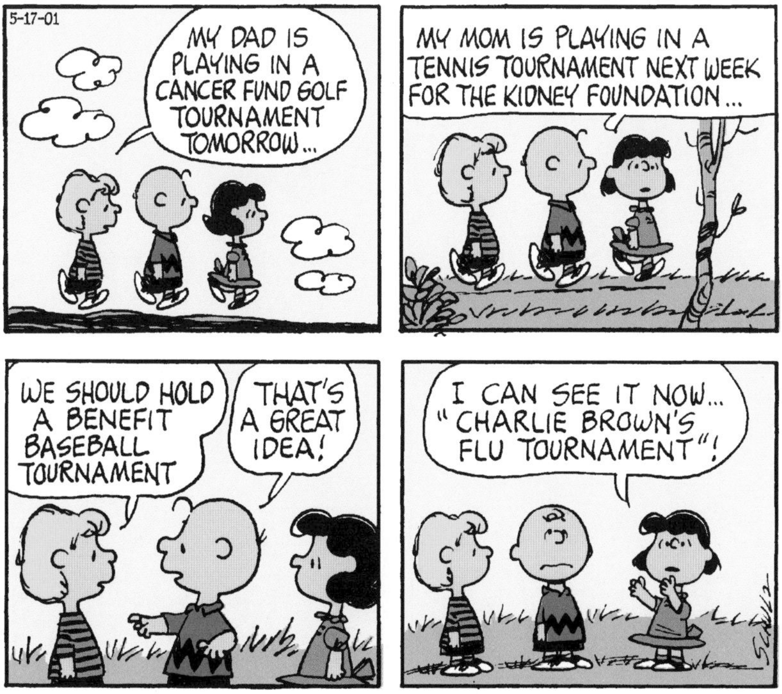
5-17-01
MY DAD IS PLAYING IN A CANCER FUND GOLF TOURNAMENT TOMORROW...
MY MOM IS PLAYING IN A TENNIS TOURNAMENT NEXT WEEK FOR THE KIDNEY FOUNDATION...
WE SHOULD HOLD A BENEFIT BASEBALL TOURNAMENT
THAT'S A GREAT IDEA!
I CAN SEE IT NOW... "CHARLIE BROWN'S FLU TOURNAMENT"!
SCHULZ

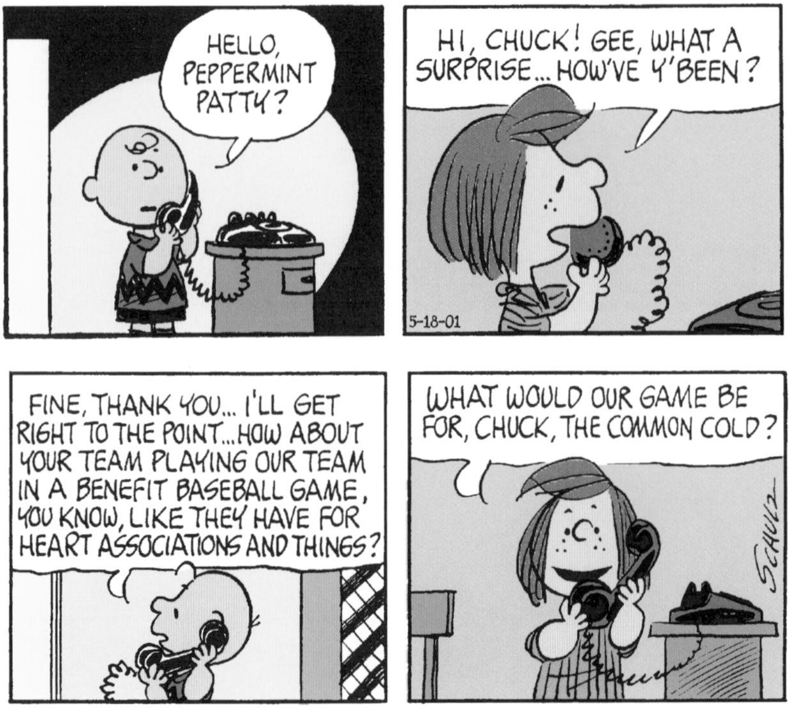
HELLO, PEPPERMINT PATTY?
HI, CHUCK! GEE, WHAT A SURPRISE... HOW'VE Y'BEEN?
5-18-01
FINE, THANK YOU... I'LL GET RIGHT TO THE POINT...HOW ABOUT YOUR TEAM PLAYING OUR TEAM IN A BENEFIT BASEBALL GAME, YOU KNOW, LIKE THEY HAVE FOR HEART ASSOCIATIONS AND THINGS?
WHAT WOULD OUR GAME BE FOR, CHUCK, THE COMMON COLD?
SCHULZ

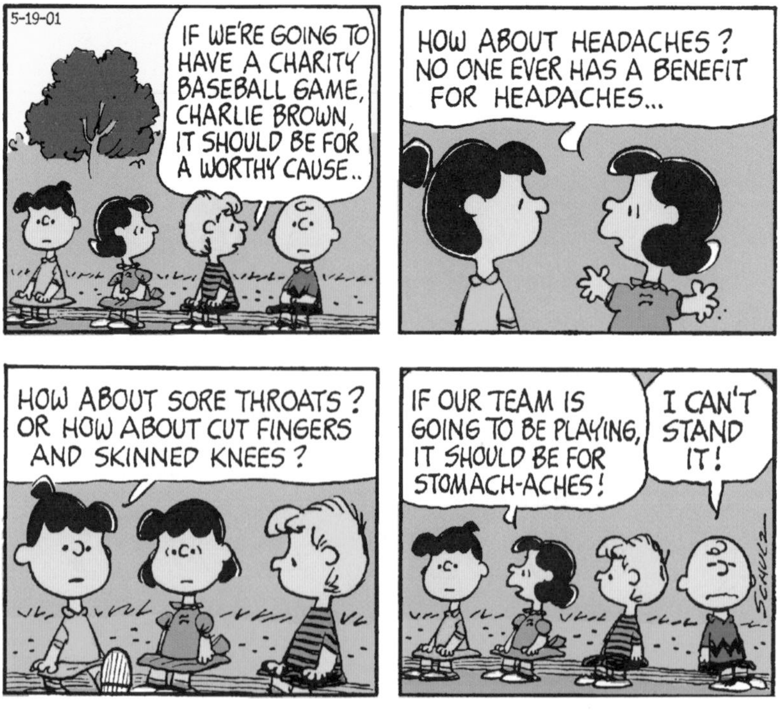
5-19-01
IF WE'RE GOING TO HAVE A CHARITY BASEBALL GAME, CHARLIE BROWN, IT SHOULD BE FOR A WORTHY CAUSE..
HOW ABOUT HEADACHES? NO ONE EVER HAS A BENEFIT FOR HEADACHES...
HOW ABOUT SORE THROATS? OR HOW ABOUT CUT FINGERS AND SKINNED KNEES?
IF OUR TEAM IS GOING TO BE PLAYING, IT SHOULD BE FOR STOMACH-ACHES!
I CAN'T STAND IT!
SCHULZ

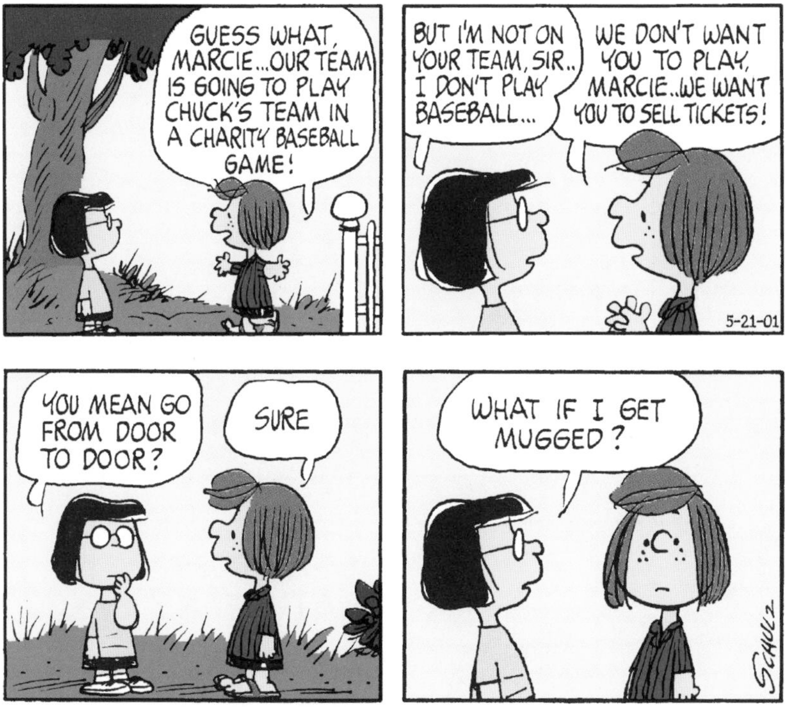
GUESS WHAT, MARCIE...OUR TEAM IS GOING TO PLAY CHUCK'S TEAM IN A CHARITY BASEBALL GAME!
BUT I'M NOT ON YOUR TEAM, SIR.. I DON'T PLAY BASEBALL...
WE DON'T WANT YOU TO PLAY, MARCIE..WE WANT YOU TO SELL TICKETS!
5-21-01
YOU MEAN GO FROM DOOR TO DOOR?
SURE
WHAT IF I GET MUGGED?
SCHULZ

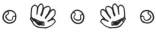

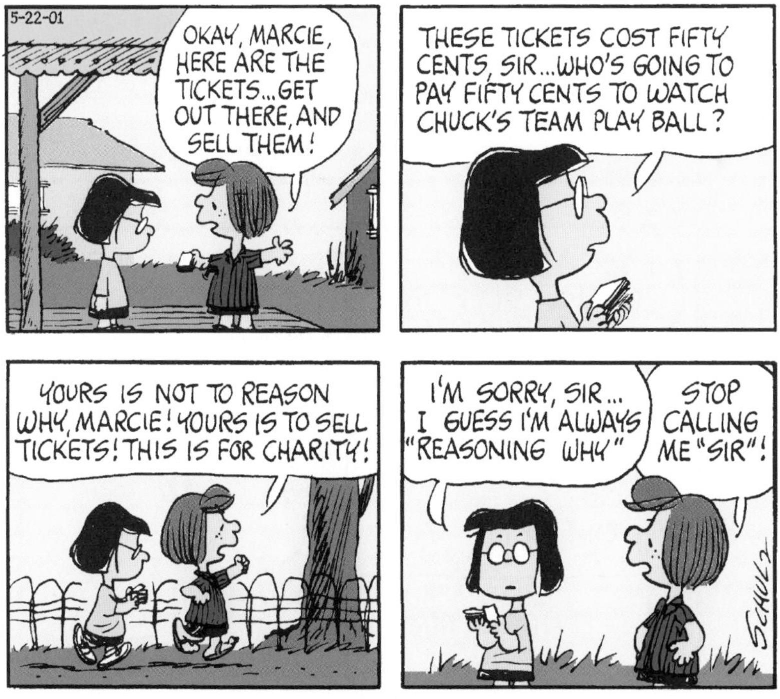
5-22-01
OKAY, MARCIE, HERE ARE THE TICKETS...GET OUT THERE, AND SELL THEM!
THESE TICKETS COST FIFTY CENTS, SIR...WHO'S GOING TO PAY FIFTY CENTS TO WATCH CHUCK'S TEAM PLAY BALL?
YOURS IS NOT TO REASON WHY, MARCIE! YOURS IS TO SELL TICKETS! THIS IS FOR CHARITY!
I'M SORRY, SIR... I GUESS I'M ALWAYS "REASONING WHY"
STOP CALLING ME "SIR"!
SCHULZ

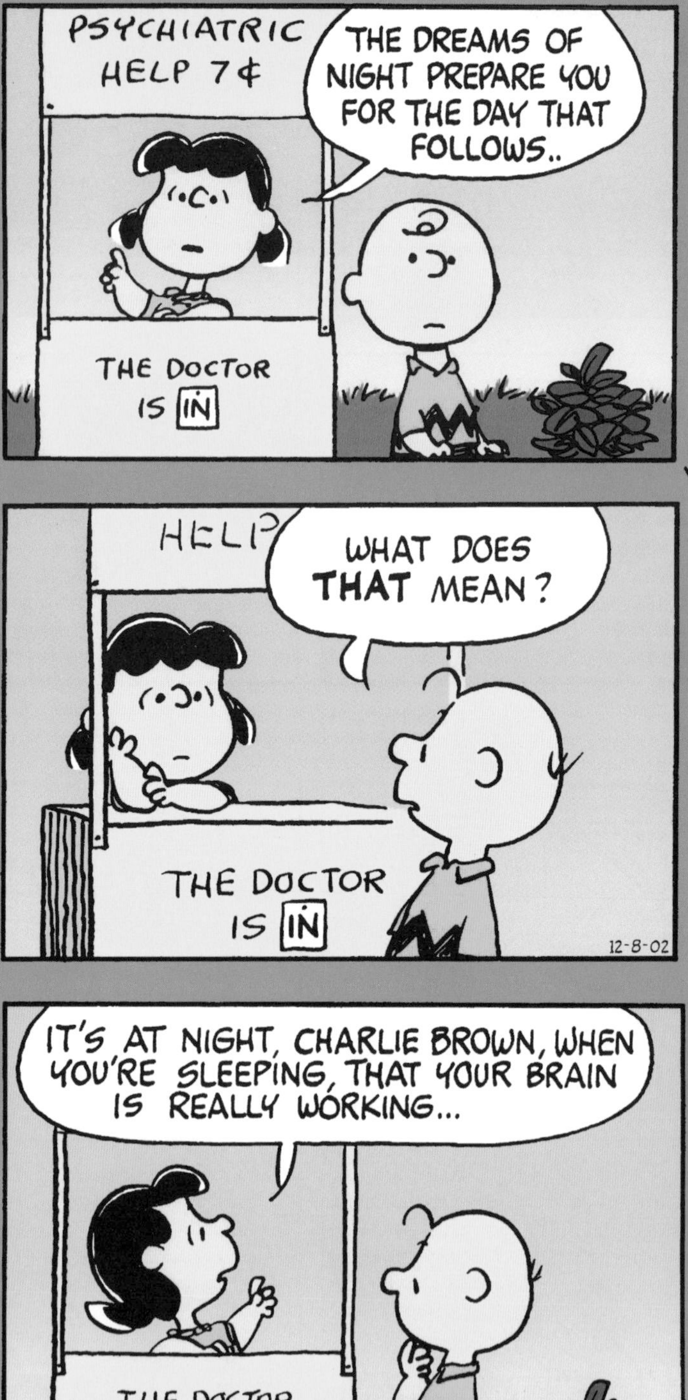
PSYCHIATRIC HELP 7¢
THE DREAMS OF NIGHT PREPARE YOU FOR THE DAY THAT FOLLOWS..
THE DOCTOR IS IN
HELP
WHAT DOES **THAT** MEAN?
THE DOCTOR IS IN
12-8-02
IT'S AT NIGHT, CHARLIE BROWN, WHEN YOU'RE SLEEPING, THAT YOUR BRAIN IS REALLY WORKING...
THE DOCTOR IS IN

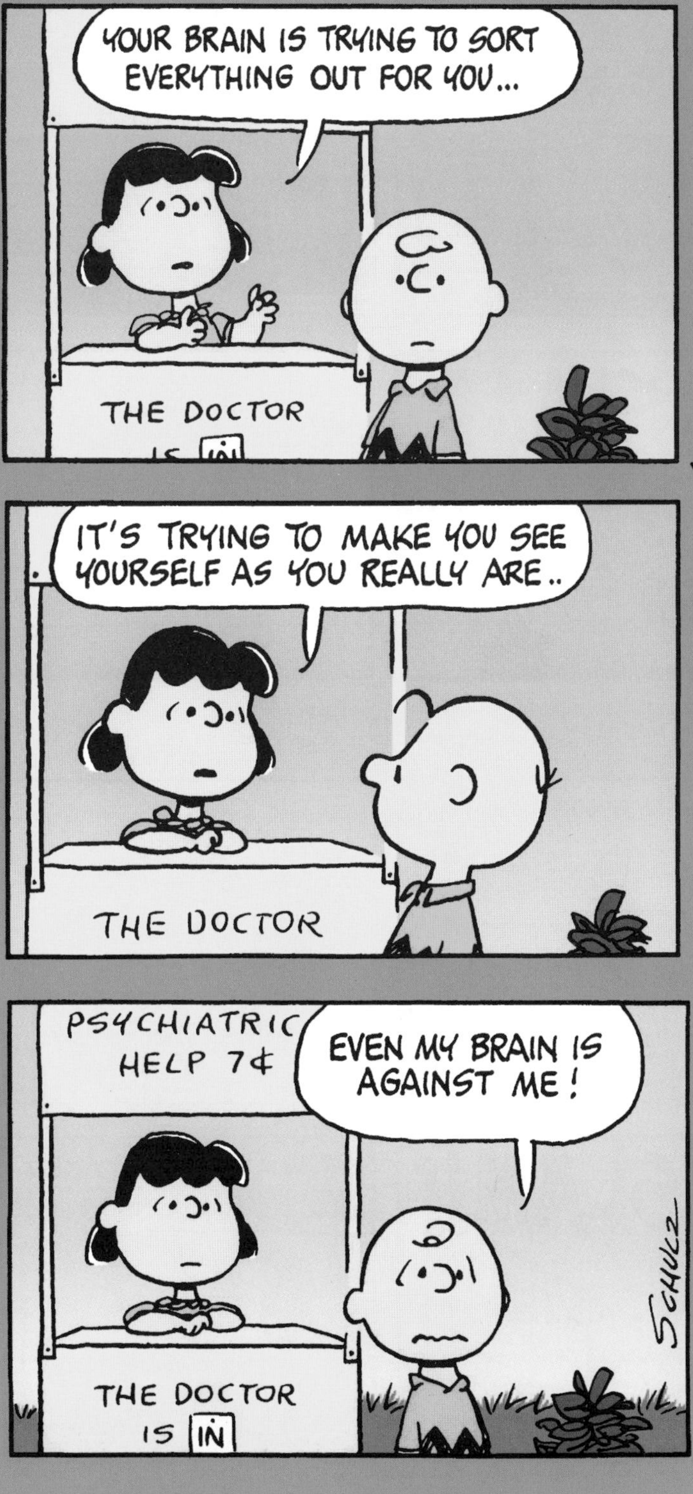
YOUR BRAIN IS TRYING TO SORT EVERYTHING OUT FOR YOU...
THE DOCTOR
IT'S TRYING TO MAKE YOU SEE YOURSELF AS YOU REALLY ARE..
THE DOCTOR
PSYCHIATRIC HELP 7¢
EVEN MY BRAIN IS AGAINST ME!
THE DOCTOR IS IN
SCHULZ

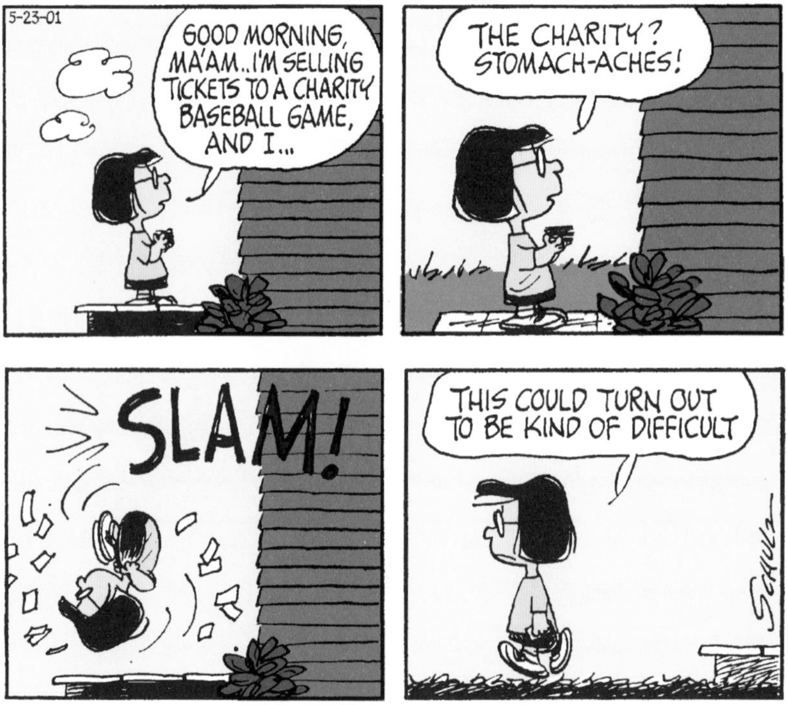
5-23-01
GOOD MORNING, MA'AM..I'M SELLING TICKETS TO A CHARITY BASEBALL GAME, AND I...
THE CHARITY? STOMACH-ACHES!
SLAM!
THIS COULD TURN OUT TO BE KIND OF DIFFICULT
SCHULZ

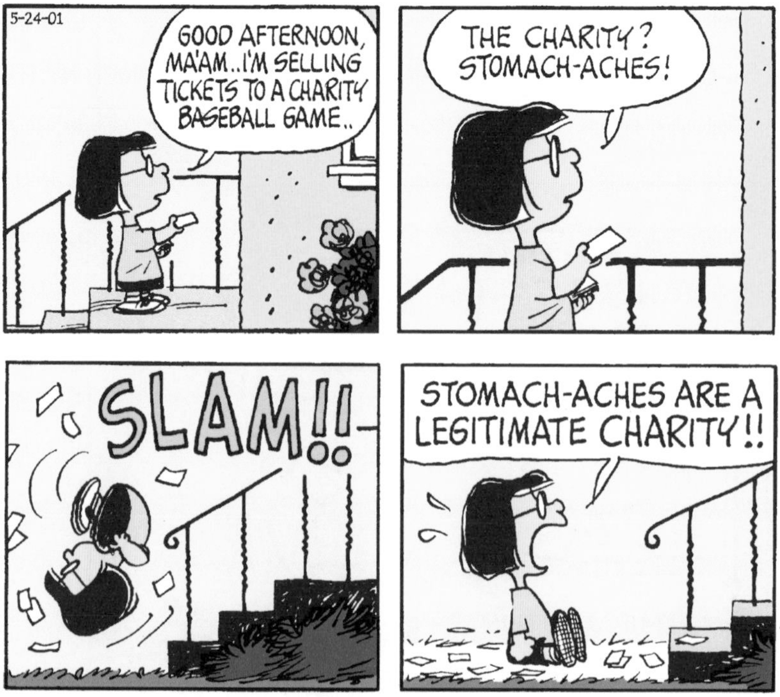
5-24-01
GOOD AFTERNOON, MA'AM..I'M SELLING TICKETS TO A CHARITY BASEBALL GAME..
THE CHARITY? STOMACH-ACHES!
SLAM!!
STOMACH-ACHES ARE A LEGITIMATE CHARITY!!

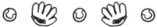

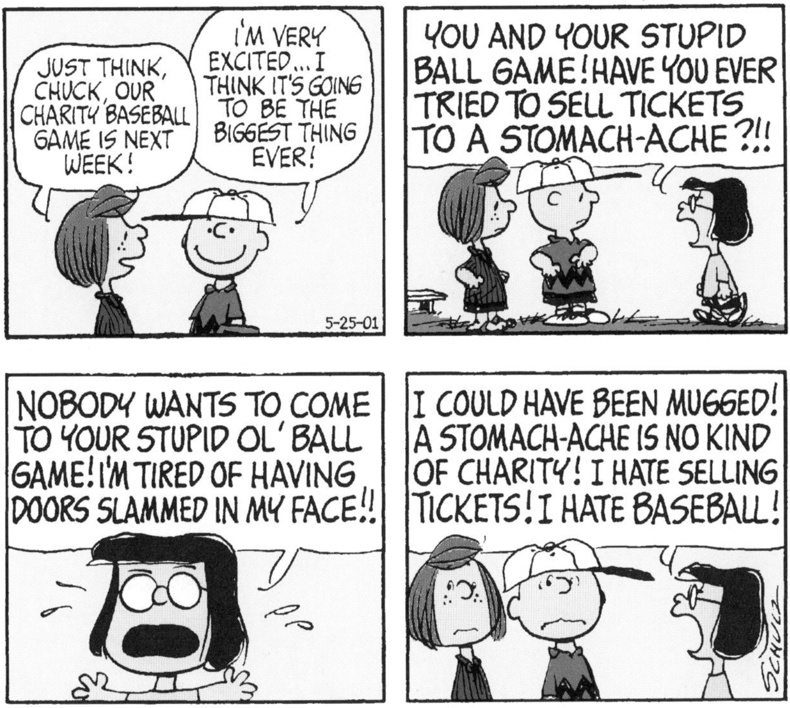
JUST THINK, CHUCK, OUR CHARITY BASEBALL GAME IS NEXT WEEK!
I'M VERY EXCITED... I THINK IT'S GOING TO BE THE BIGGEST THING EVER!
5-25-01
YOU AND YOUR STUPID BALL GAME! HAVE YOU EVER TRIED TO SELL TICKETS TO A STOMACH-ACHE ?!!
NOBODY WANTS TO COME TO YOUR STUPID OL' BALL GAME! I'M TIRED OF HAVING DOORS SLAMMED IN MY FACE!!
I COULD HAVE BEEN MUGGED! A STOMACH-ACHE IS NO KIND OF CHARITY! I HATE SELLING TICKETS! I HATE BASEBALL!
SCHULZ

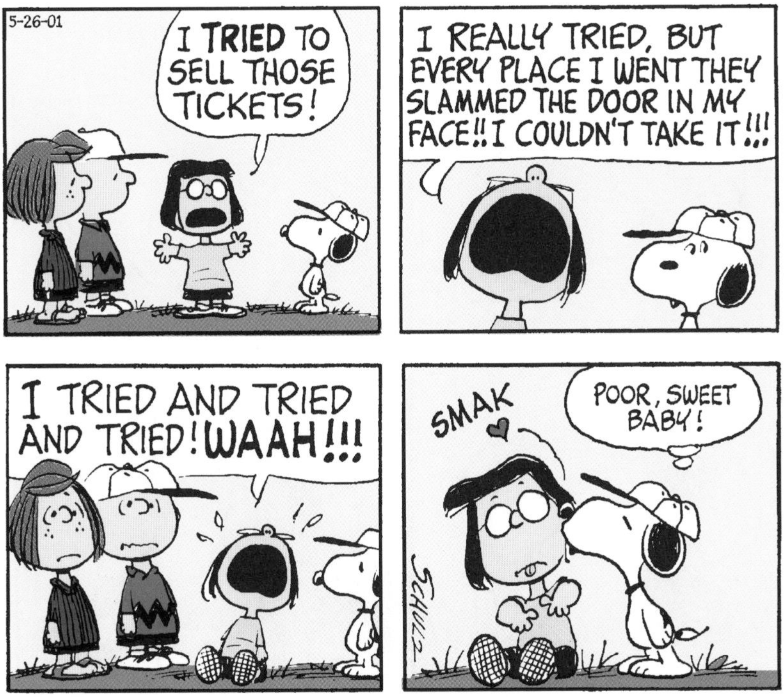
5-26-01
I TRIED TO SELL THOSE TICKETS!
I REALLY TRIED, BUT EVERY PLACE I WENT THEY SLAMMED THE DOOR IN MY FACE!! I COULDN'T TAKE IT!!!
I TRIED AND TRIED AND TRIED! WAAH!!!
SCHULZ
SMAK
POOR, SWEET BABY!

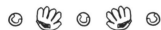

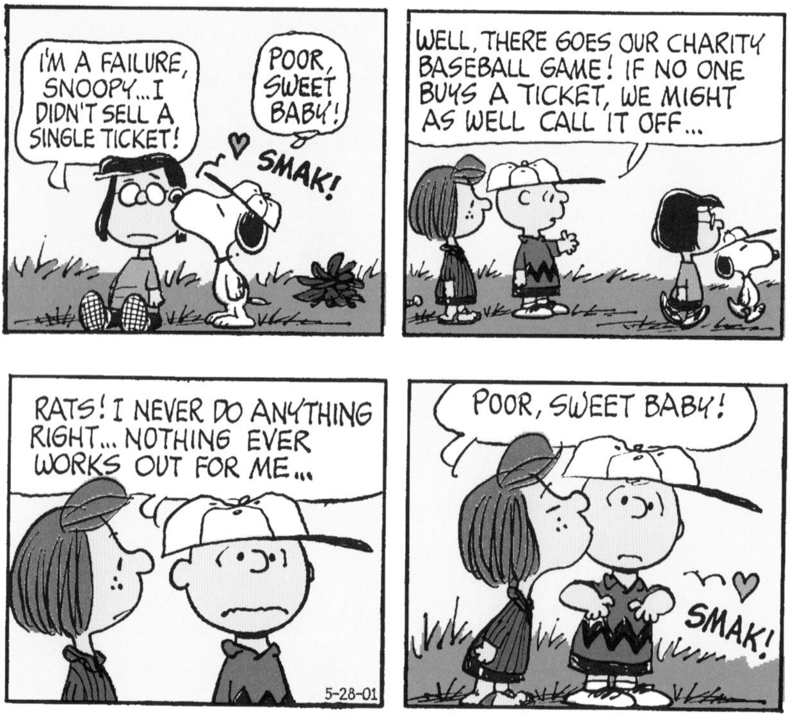
I'M A FAILURE, SNOOPY...I DIDN'T SELL A SINGLE TICKET!
POOR, SWEET BABY!
SMAK!
WELL, THERE GOES OUR CHARITY BASEBALL GAME! IF NO ONE BUYS A TICKET, WE MIGHT AS WELL CALL IT OFF...
RATS! I NEVER DO ANYTHING RIGHT... NOTHING EVER WORKS OUT FOR ME...
5-28-01
POOR, SWEET BABY!
SMAK!

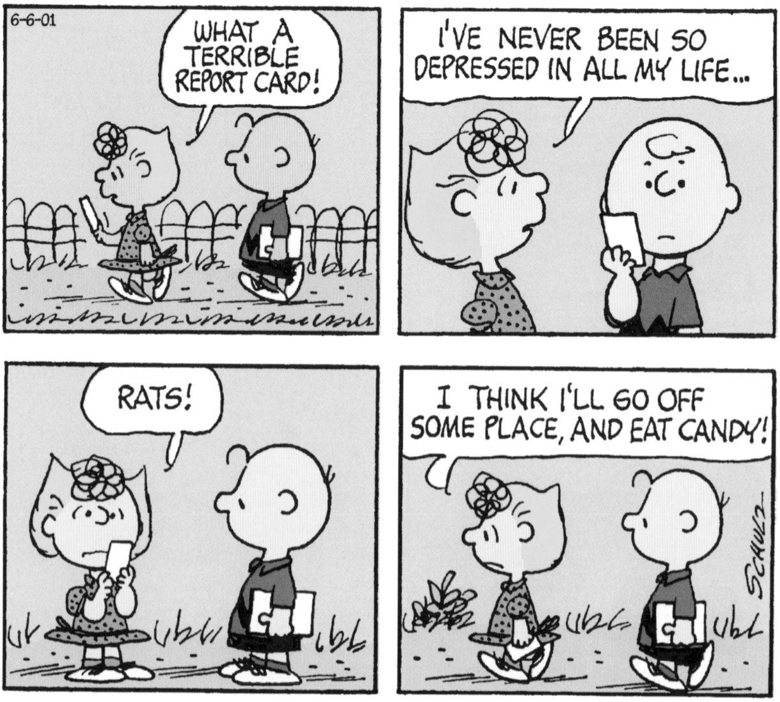
6-6-01
WHAT A TERRIBLE REPORT CARD!
I'VE NEVER BEEN SO DEPRESSED IN ALL MY LIFE...
RATS!
I THINK I'LL GO OFF SOME PLACE, AND EAT CANDY!
SCHULZ

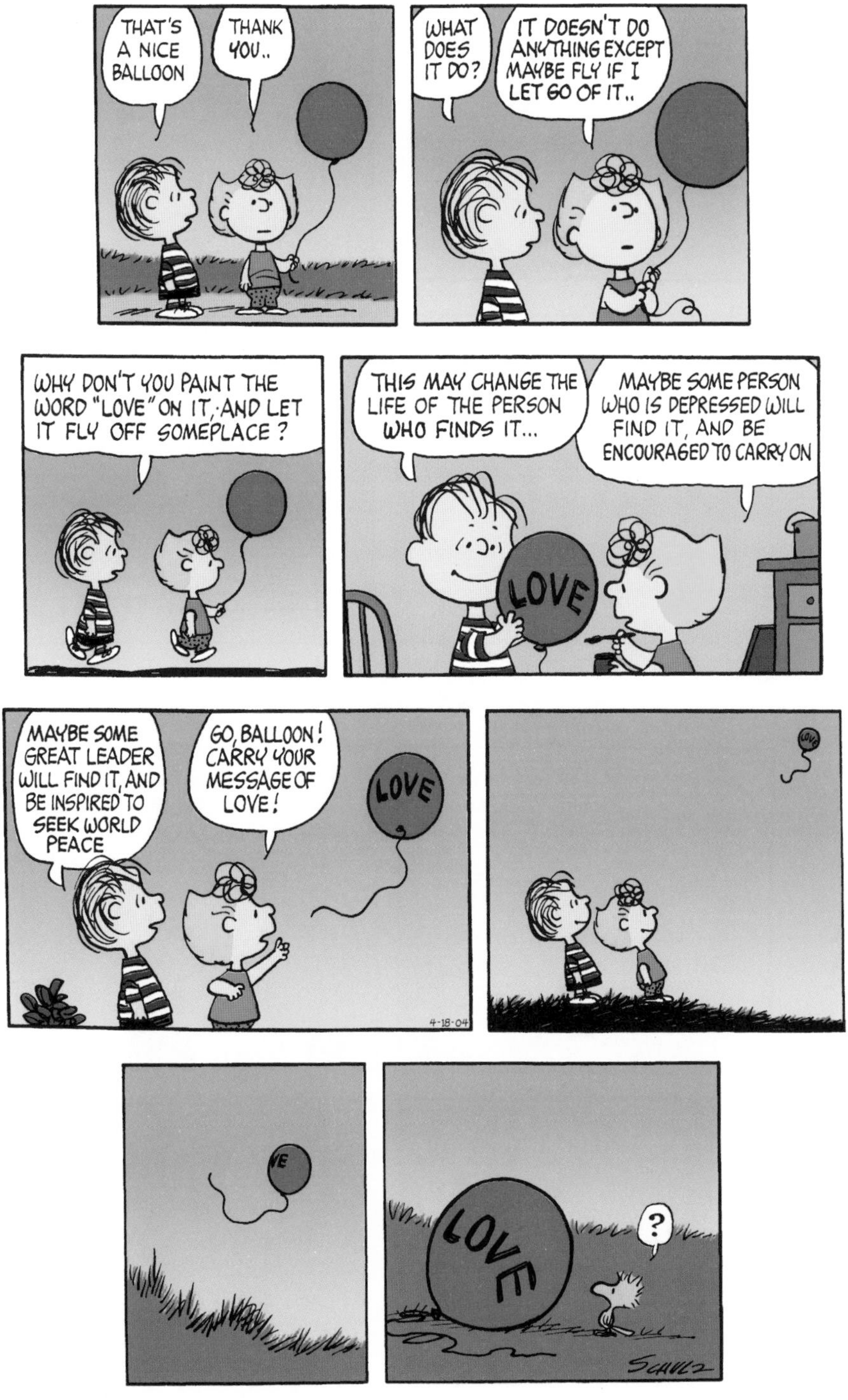
THAT'S A NICE BALLOON
THANK YOU..
WHAT DOES IT DO?
IT DOESN'T DO ANYTHING EXCEPT MAYBE FLY IF I LET GO OF IT..
WHY DON'T YOU PAINT THE WORD "LOVE" ON IT, AND LET IT FLY OFF SOMEPLACE?
THIS MAY CHANGE THE LIFE OF THE PERSON WHO FINDS IT...
MAYBE SOME PERSON WHO IS DEPRESSED WILL FIND IT, AND BE ENCOURAGED TO CARRY ON
LOVE
MAYBE SOME GREAT LEADER WILL FIND IT, AND BE INSPIRED TO SEEK WORLD PEACE
GO, BALLOON! CARRY YOUR MESSAGE OF LOVE!
LOVE
4-18-04
LOVE
VE
LOVE
?
SCHULZ

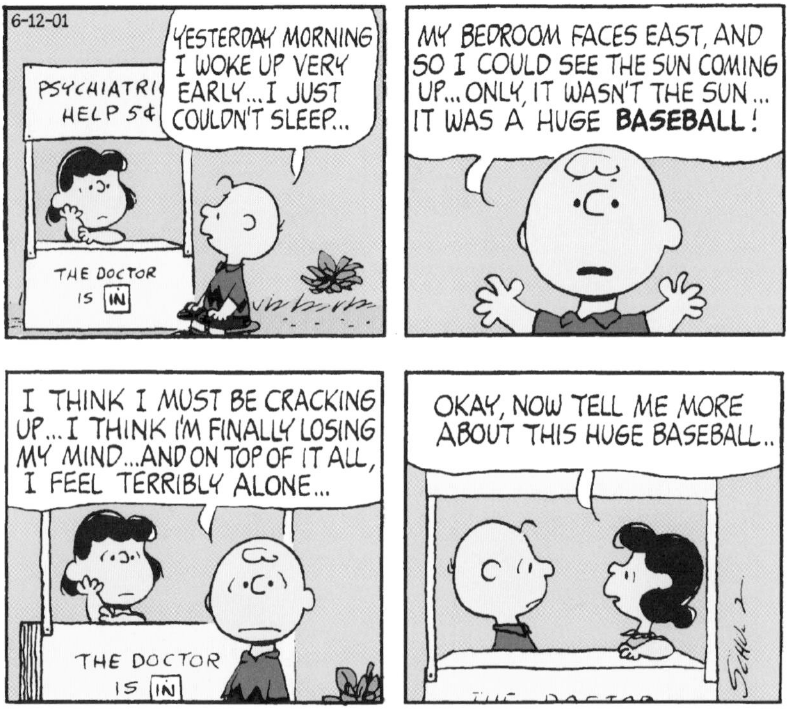
6-12-01
PSYCHIATRI
HELP 5¢
THE DOCTOR IS IN
YESTERDAY MORNING I WOKE UP VERY EARLY...I JUST COULDN'T SLEEP...
MY BEDROOM FACES EAST, AND SO I COULD SEE THE SUN COMING UP...ONLY, IT WASN'T THE SUN... IT WAS A HUGE **BASEBALL**!
I THINK I MUST BE CRACKING UP...I THINK I'M FINALLY LOSING MY MIND...AND ON TOP OF IT ALL, I FEEL TERRIBLY ALONE...
THE DOCTOR IS IN
OKAY, NOW TELL ME MORE ABOUT THIS HUGE BASEBALL..

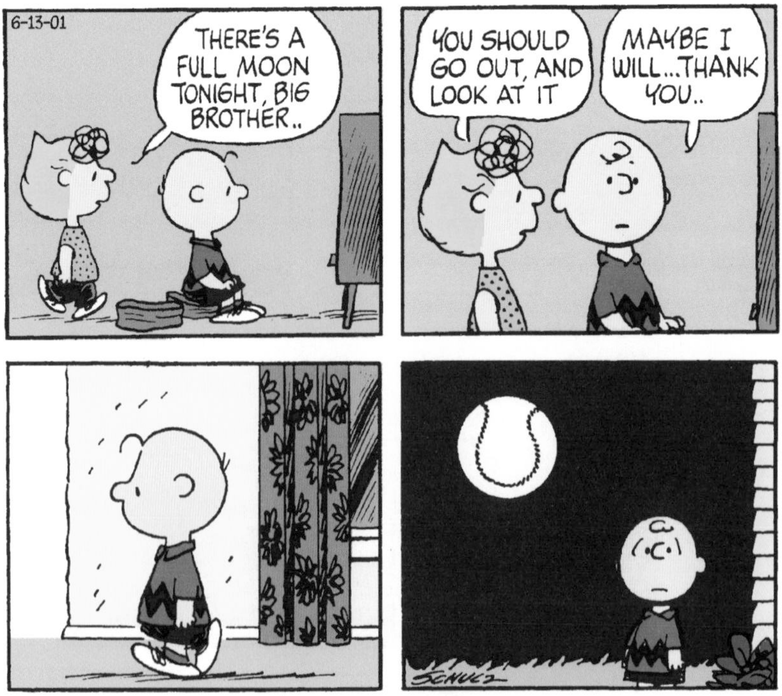
6-13-01
THERE'S A FULL MOON TONIGHT, BIG BROTHER..
YOU SHOULD GO OUT, AND LOOK AT IT
MAYBE I WILL...THANK YOU..

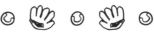

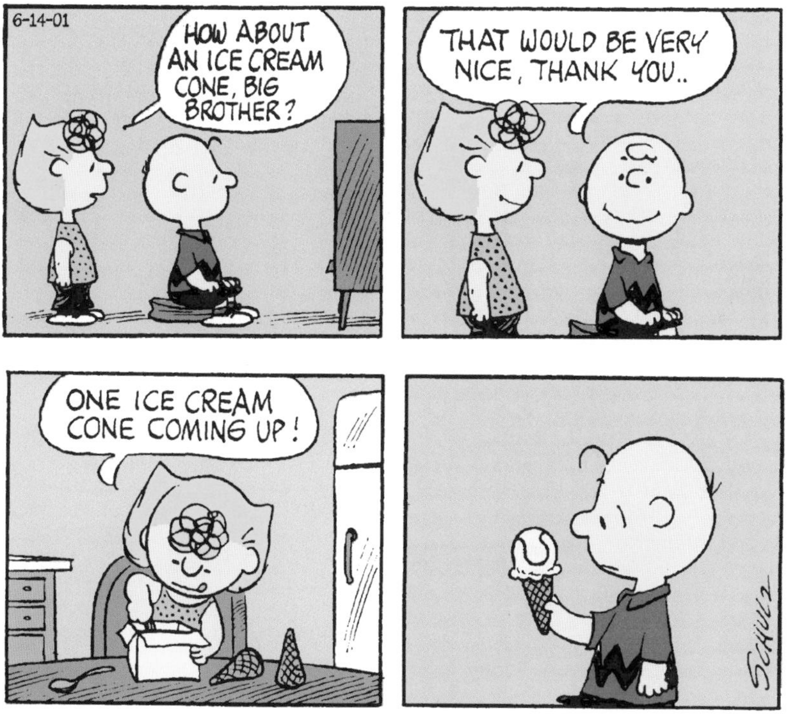
6-14-01
HOW ABOUT AN ICE CREAM CONE, BIG BROTHER?
THAT WOULD BE VERY NICE, THANK YOU..
ONE ICE CREAM CONE COMING UP!
SCHULZ

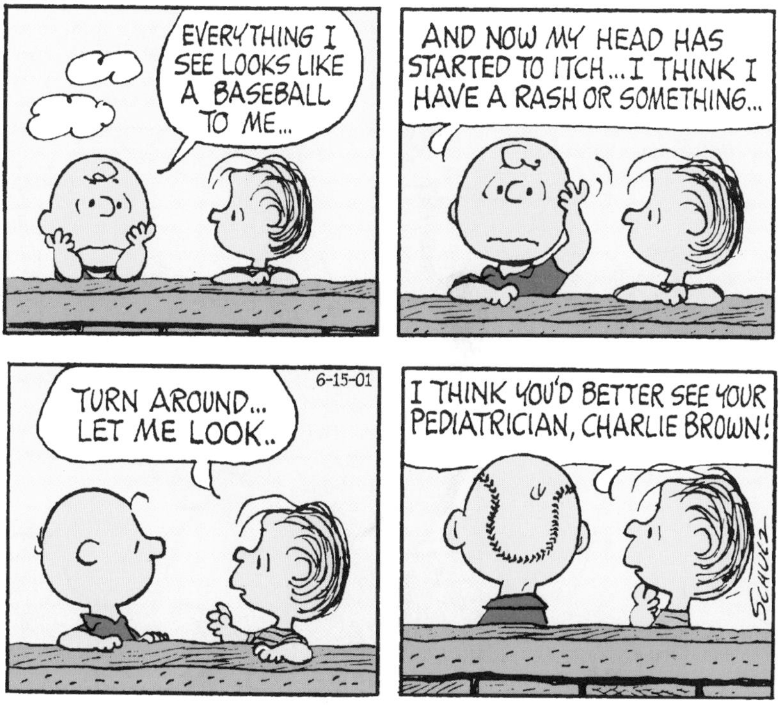
EVERYTHING I SEE LOOKS LIKE A BASEBALL TO ME...
AND NOW MY HEAD HAS STARTED TO ITCH... I THINK I HAVE A RASH OR SOMETHING...
6-15-01
TURN AROUND... LET ME LOOK..
I THINK YOU'D BETTER SEE YOUR PEDIATRICIAN, CHARLIE BROWN!
SCHULZ

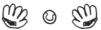

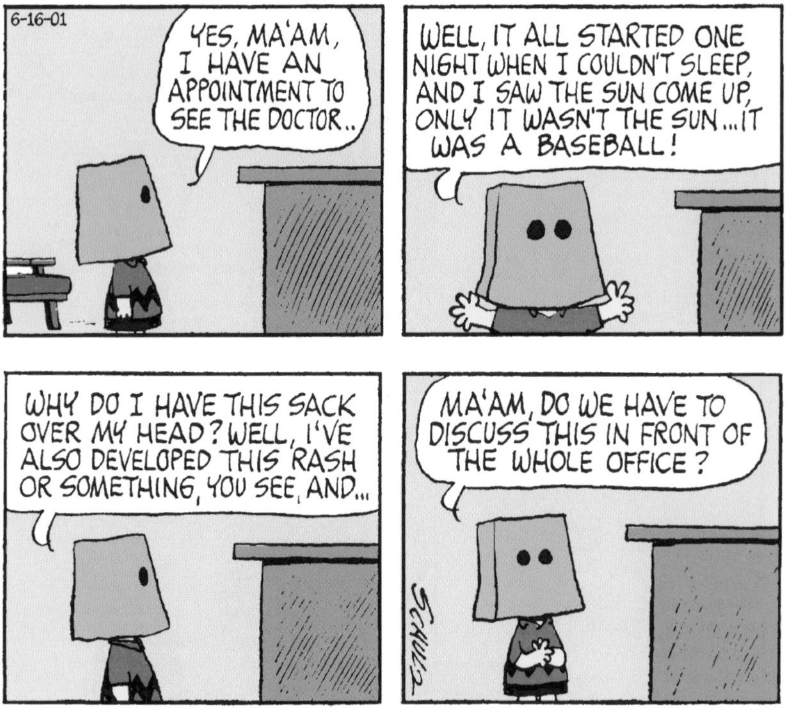
6-16-01
YES, MA'AM, I HAVE AN APPOINTMENT TO SEE THE DOCTOR..
WELL, IT ALL STARTED ONE NIGHT WHEN I COULDN'T SLEEP, AND I SAW THE SUN COME UP, ONLY IT WASN'T THE SUN...IT WAS A BASEBALL!
WHY DO I HAVE THIS SACK OVER MY HEAD? WELL, I'VE ALSO DEVELOPED THIS RASH OR SOMETHING, YOU SEE, AND...
MA'AM, DO WE HAVE TO DISCUSS THIS IN FRONT OF THE WHOLE OFFICE?
SCHULZ

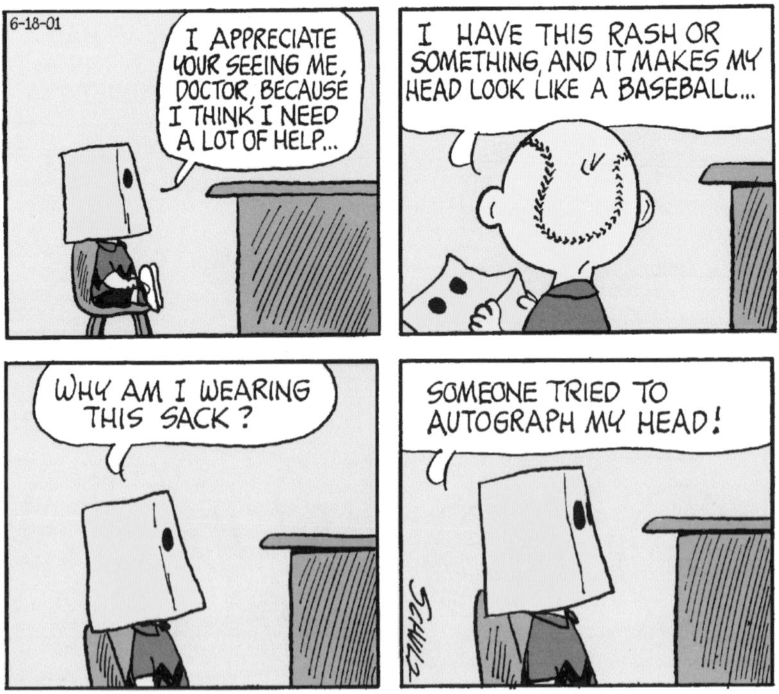
6-18-01
I APPRECIATE YOUR SEEING ME, DOCTOR, BECAUSE I THINK I NEED A LOT OF HELP...
I HAVE THIS RASH OR SOMETHING, AND IT MAKES MY HEAD LOOK LIKE A BASEBALL...
WHY AM I WEARING THIS SACK?
SOMEONE TRIED TO AUTOGRAPH MY HEAD!
SCHULZ

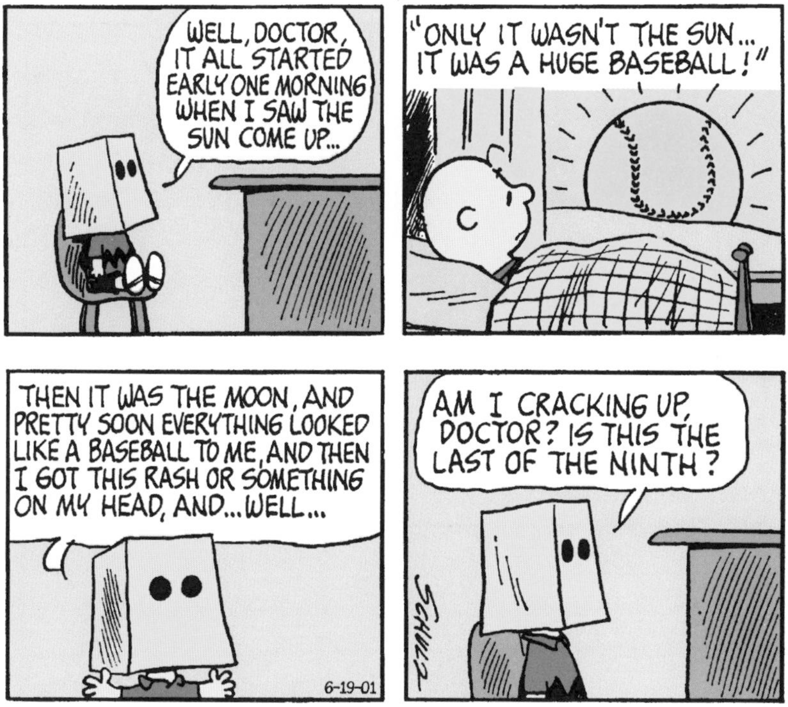
WELL, DOCTOR, IT ALL STARTED EARLY ONE MORNING WHEN I SAW THE SUN COME UP...
"ONLY IT WASN'T THE SUN... IT WAS A HUGE BASEBALL!"
THEN IT WAS THE MOON, AND PRETTY SOON EVERYTHING LOOKED LIKE A BASEBALL TO ME, AND THEN I GOT THIS RASH OR SOMETHING ON MY HEAD, AND... WELL...
6-19-01
AM I CRACKING UP, DOCTOR? IS THIS THE LAST OF THE NINTH?
SCHULZ

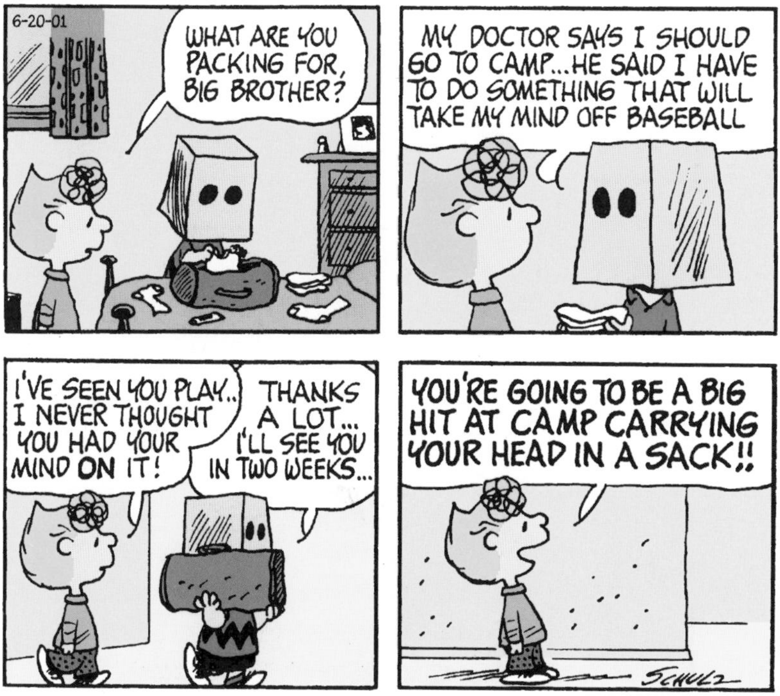
6-20-01
WHAT ARE YOU PACKING FOR, BIG BROTHER?
MY DOCTOR SAYS I SHOULD GO TO CAMP... HE SAID I HAVE TO DO SOMETHING THAT WILL TAKE MY MIND OFF BASEBALL
I'VE SEEN YOU PLAY.. I NEVER THOUGHT YOU HAD YOUR MIND ON IT!
THANKS A LOT... I'LL SEE YOU IN TWO WEEKS...
YOU'RE GOING TO BE A BIG HIT AT CAMP CARRYING YOUR HEAD IN A SACK!!
SCHULZ

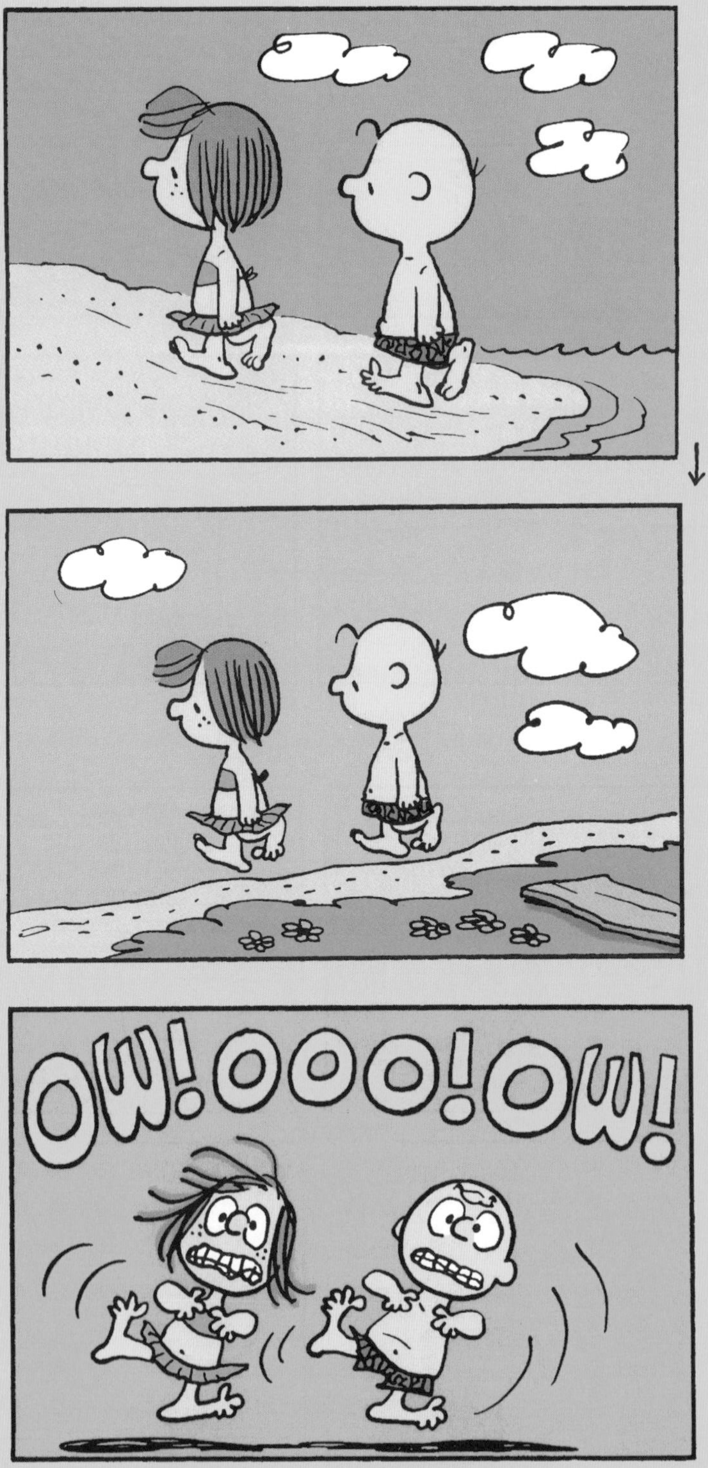
OW! OOO! OW!

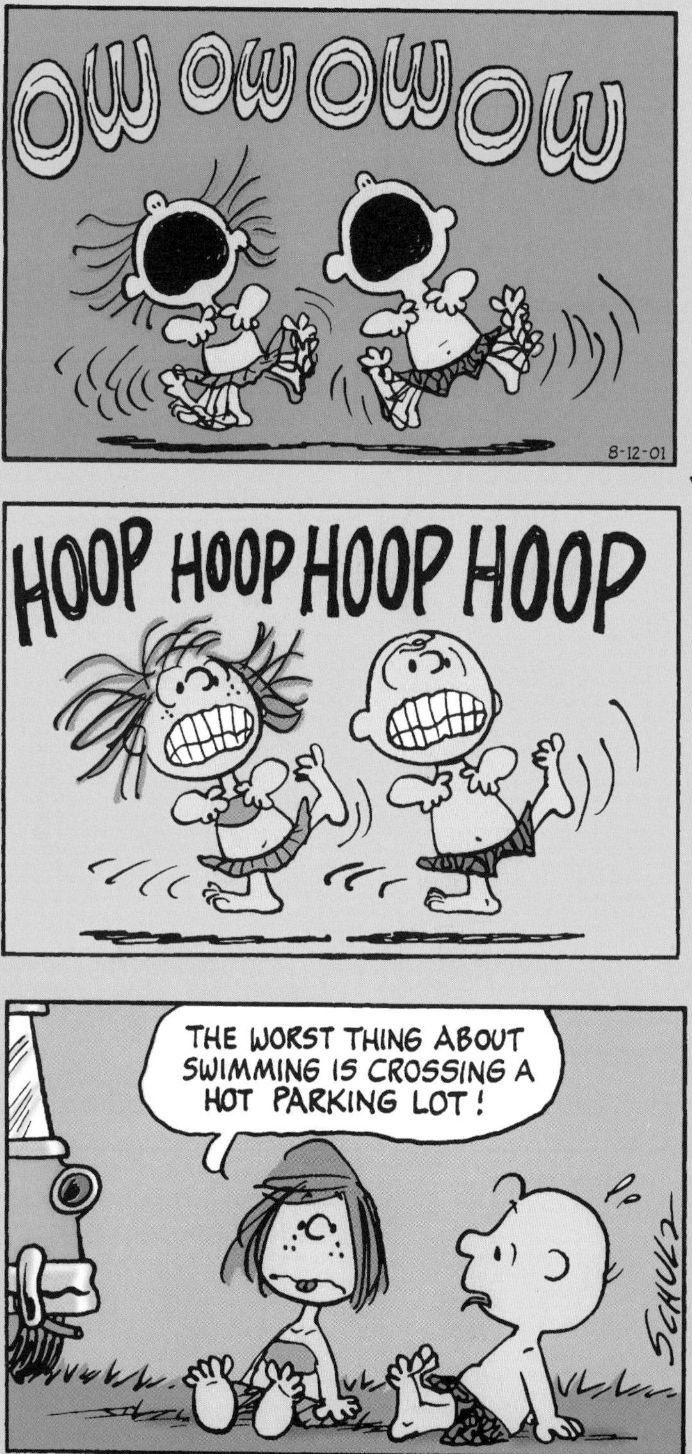
OW OWOWOWOW
8-12-01
HOOP HOOP HOOP HOOP
THE WORST THING ABOUT SWIMMING IS CROSSING A HOT PARKING LOT!
SCHULZ

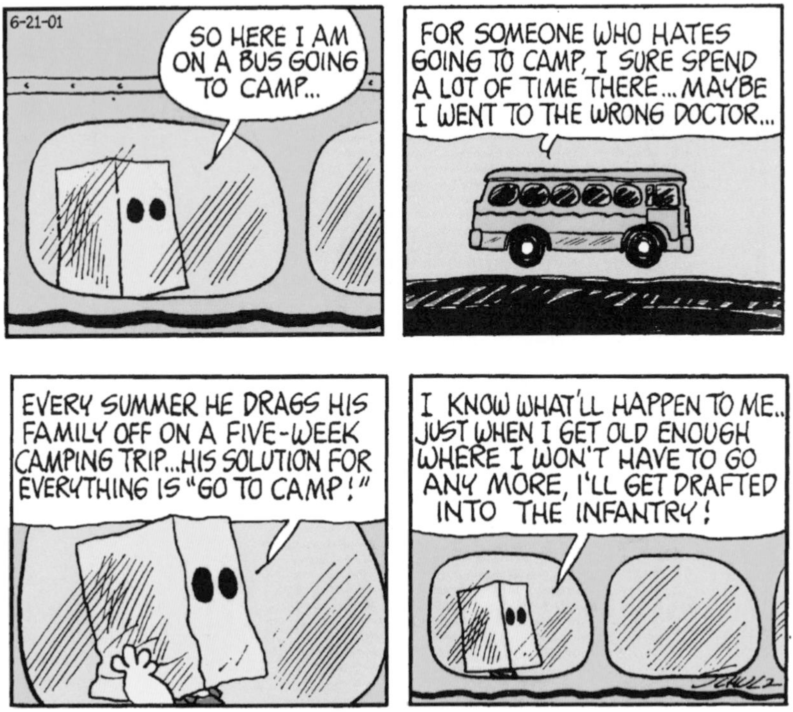
6-21-01
SO HERE I AM ON A BUS GOING TO CAMP...
FOR SOMEONE WHO HATES GOING TO CAMP, I SURE SPEND A LOT OF TIME THERE... MAYBE I WENT TO THE WRONG DOCTOR...
EVERY SUMMER HE DRAGS HIS FAMILY OFF ON A FIVE-WEEK CAMPING TRIP... HIS SOLUTION FOR EVERYTHING IS "GO TO CAMP!"
I KNOW WHAT'LL HAPPEN TO ME.. JUST WHEN I GET OLD ENOUGH WHERE I WON'T HAVE TO GO ANY MORE, I'LL GET DRAFTED INTO THE INFANTRY!
SCHULZ

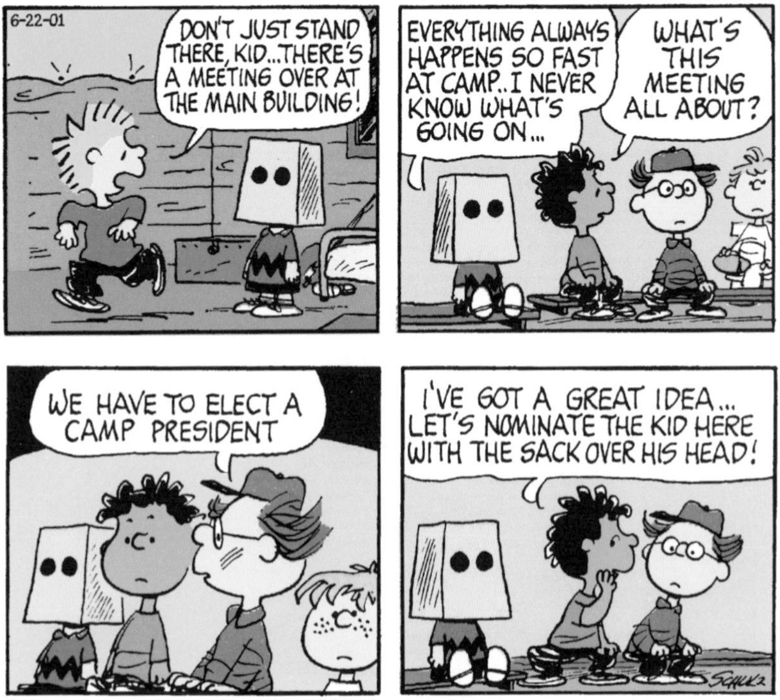
6-22-01
DON'T JUST STAND THERE, KID... THERE'S A MEETING OVER AT THE MAIN BUILDING!
EVERYTHING ALWAYS HAPPENS SO FAST AT CAMP.. I NEVER KNOW WHAT'S GOING ON...
WHAT'S THIS MEETING ALL ABOUT?
WE HAVE TO ELECT A CAMP PRESIDENT
I'VE GOT A GREAT IDEA... LET'S NOMINATE THE KID HERE WITH THE SACK OVER HIS HEAD!
SCHULZ

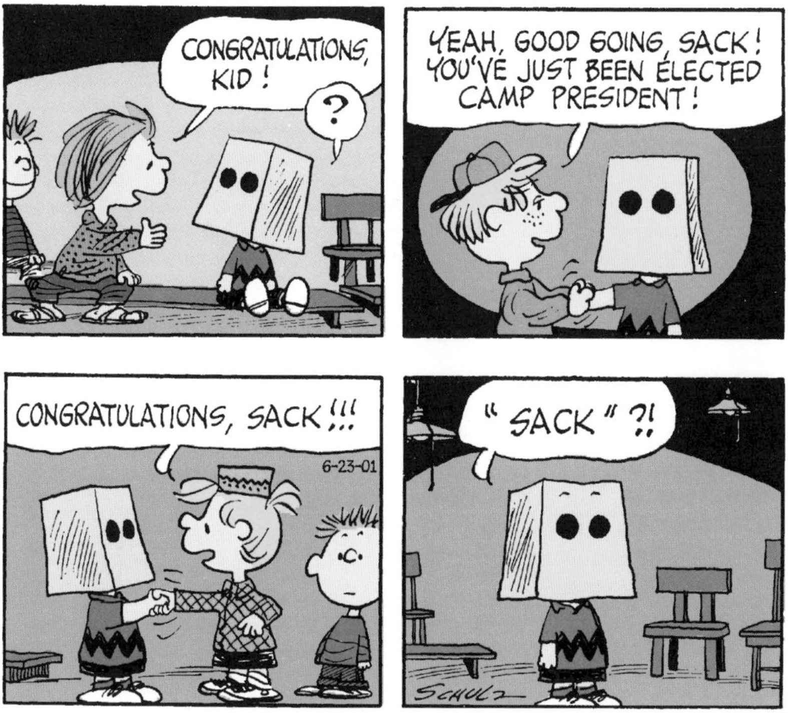
CONGRATULATIONS, KID !
?
YEAH, GOOD GOING, SACK! YOU'VE JUST BEEN ELECTED CAMP PRESIDENT!
CONGRATULATIONS, SACK!!!
6-23-01
" SACK " ?!
SCHULZ

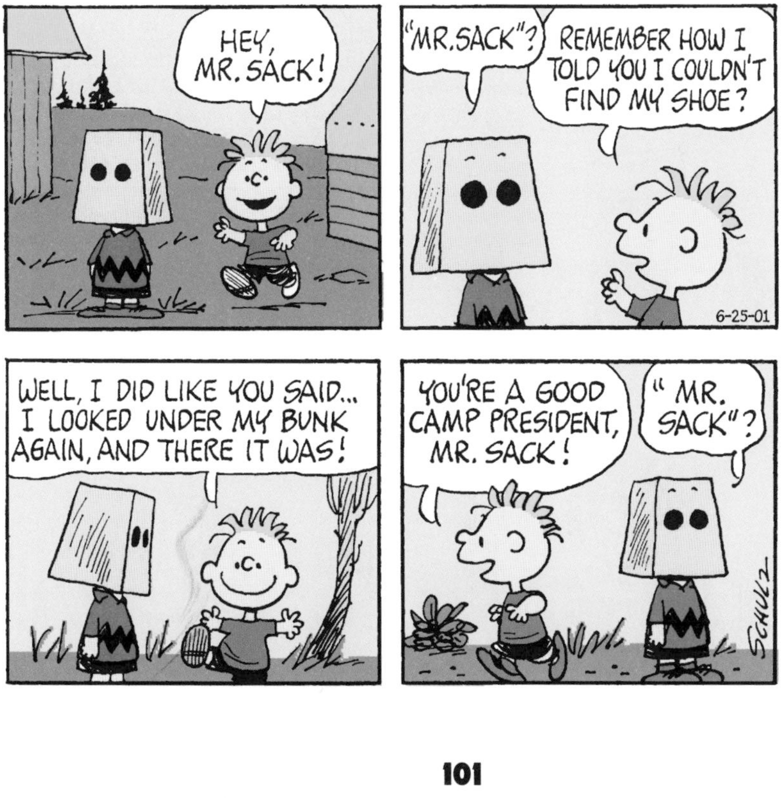
HEY, MR. SACK!
"MR. SACK"?
REMEMBER HOW I TOLD YOU I COULDN'T FIND MY SHOE?
6-25-01
WELL, I DID LIKE YOU SAID... I LOOKED UNDER MY BUNK AGAIN, AND THERE IT WAS!
YOU'RE A GOOD CAMP PRESIDENT, MR. SACK!
" MR. SACK"?
SCHULZ

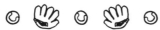

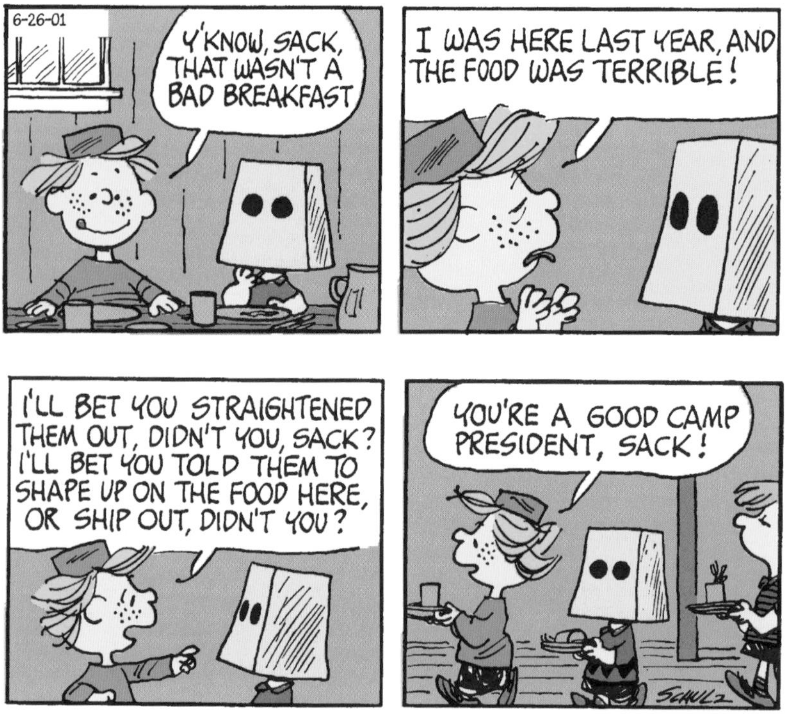
6-26-01
Y'KNOW, SACK, THAT WASN'T A BAD BREAKFAST
I WAS HERE LAST YEAR, AND THE FOOD WAS TERRIBLE!
I'LL BET YOU STRAIGHTENED THEM OUT, DIDN'T YOU, SACK? I'LL BET YOU TOLD THEM TO SHAPE UP ON THE FOOD HERE, OR SHIP OUT, DIDN'T YOU?
YOU'RE A GOOD CAMP PRESIDENT, SACK!
SCHULZ

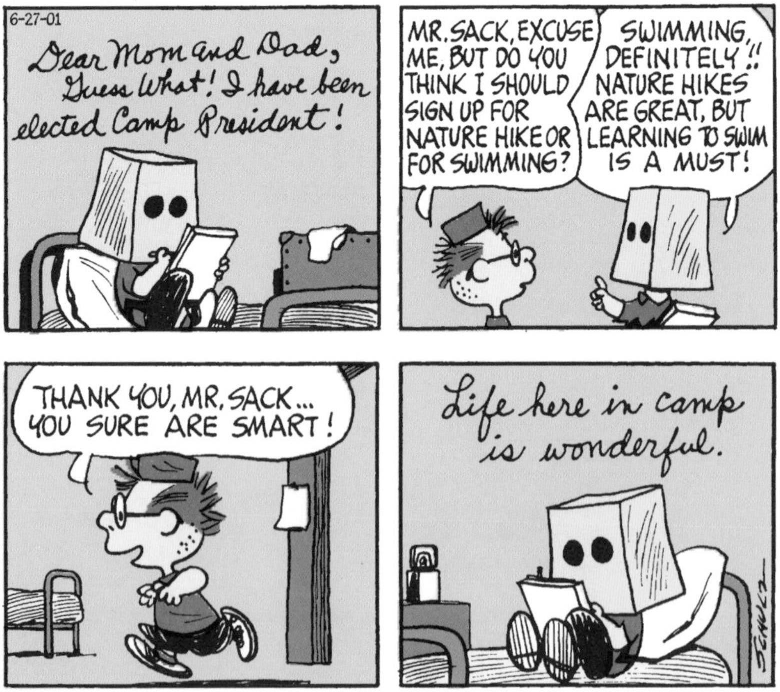
6-27-01
Dear Mom and Dad,
Guess What! I have been elected Camp President!
MR. SACK, EXCUSE ME, BUT DO YOU THINK I SHOULD SIGN UP FOR NATURE HIKE OR FOR SWIMMING?
SWIMMING, DEFINITELY!! NATURE HIKES ARE GREAT, BUT LEARNING TO SWIM IS A MUST!
THANK YOU, MR. SACK... YOU SURE ARE SMART!
Life here in camp is wonderful.
SCHULZ

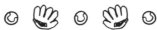

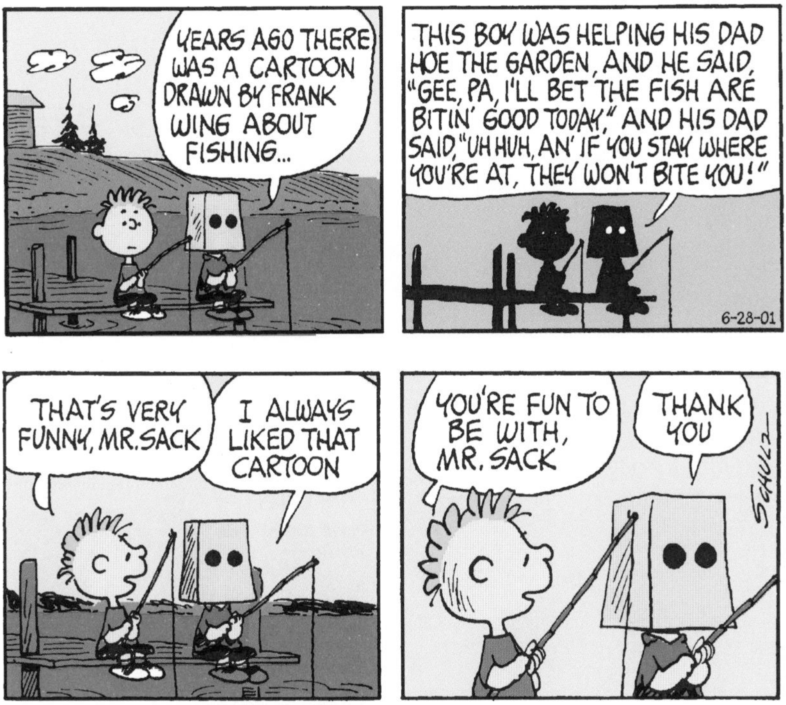
YEARS AGO THERE WAS A CARTOON DRAWN BY FRANK WING ABOUT FISHING...
THIS BOY WAS HELPING HIS DAD HOE THE GARDEN, AND HE SAID, "GEE, PA, I'LL BET THE FISH ARE BITIN' GOOD TODAY," AND HIS DAD SAID, "UH HUH, AN' IF YOU STAY WHERE YOU'RE AT, THEY WON'T BITE YOU!"
6-28-01
THAT'S VERY FUNNY, MR. SACK
I ALWAYS LIKED THAT CARTOON
YOU'RE FUN TO BE WITH, MR. SACK
THANK YOU
SCHULZ

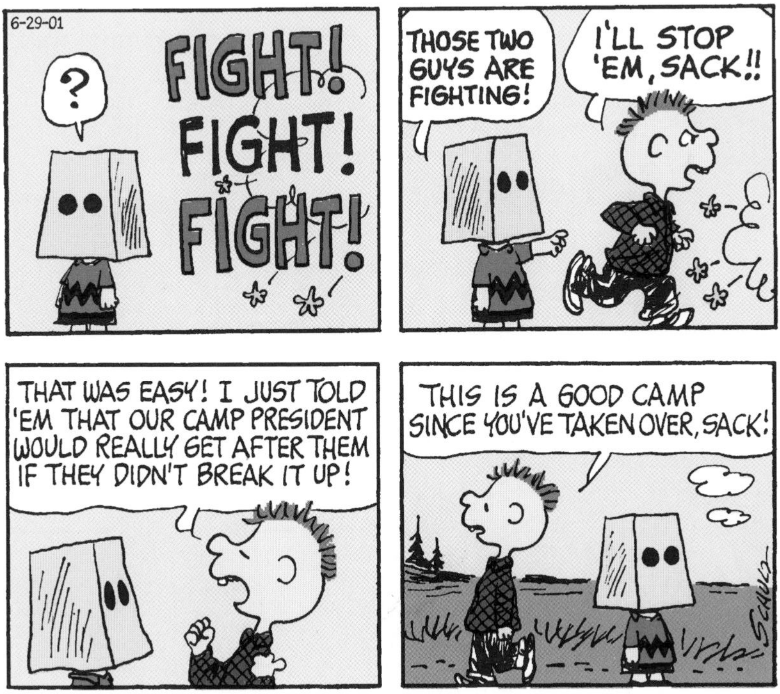
6-29-01
?
FIGHT! FIGHT! FIGHT!
THOSE TWO GUYS ARE FIGHTING!
I'LL STOP 'EM, SACK!!
THAT WAS EASY! I JUST TOLD 'EM THAT OUR CAMP PRESIDENT WOULD REALLY GET AFTER THEM IF THEY DIDN'T BREAK IT UP!
THIS IS A GOOD CAMP SINCE YOU'VE TAKEN OVER, SACK!
SCHULZ

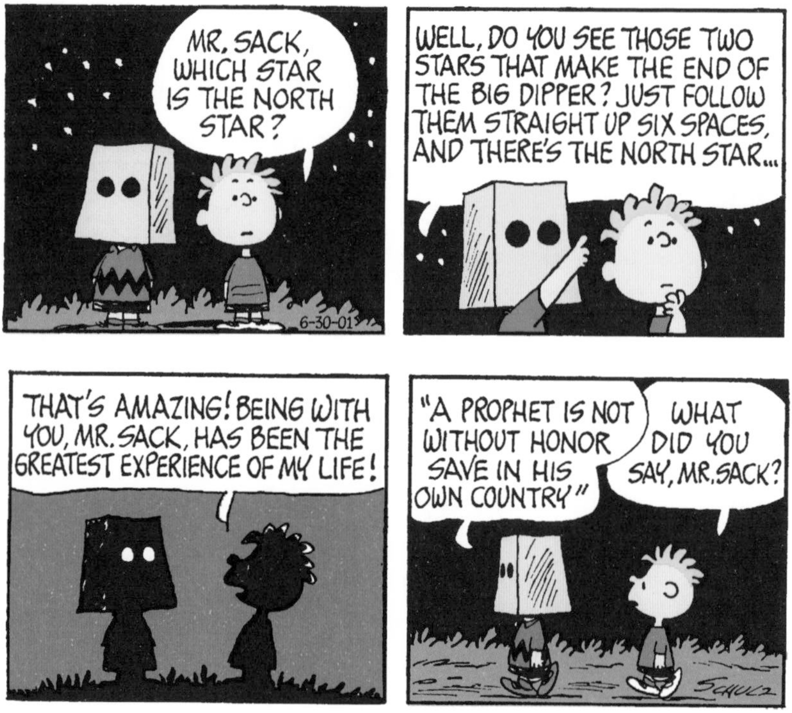
MR. SACK, WHICH STAR IS THE NORTH STAR?
6-30-01
WELL, DO YOU SEE THOSE TWO STARS THAT MAKE THE END OF THE BIG DIPPER? JUST FOLLOW THEM STRAIGHT UP SIX SPACES, AND THERE'S THE NORTH STAR...
THAT'S AMAZING! BEING WITH YOU, MR. SACK, HAS BEEN THE GREATEST EXPERIENCE OF MY LIFE!
"A PROPHET IS NOT WITHOUT HONOR SAVE IN HIS OWN COUNTRY"
WHAT DID YOU SAY, MR. SACK?
SCHULZ

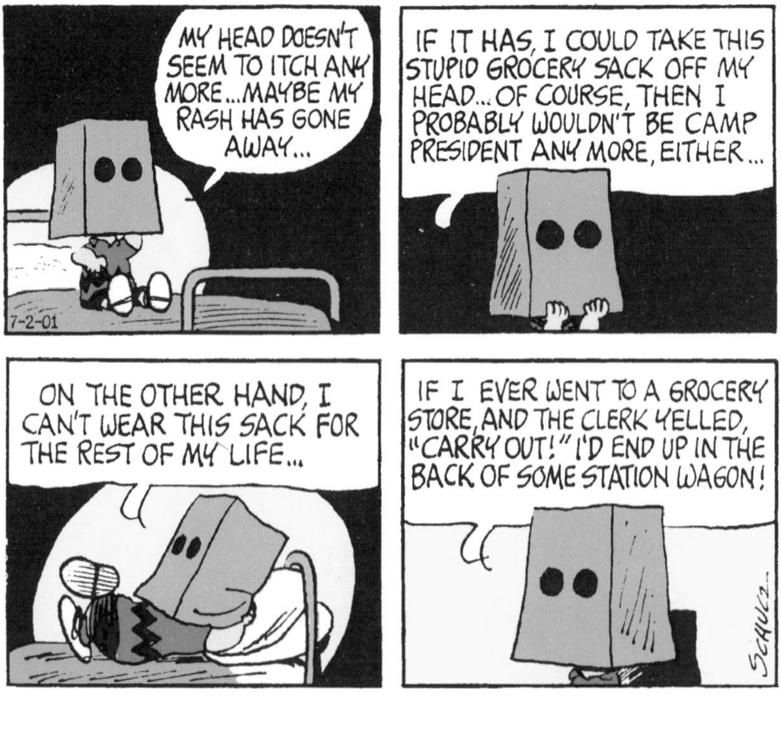
MY HEAD DOESN'T SEEM TO ITCH ANY MORE...MAYBE MY RASH HAS GONE AWAY...
7-2-01
IF IT HAS, I COULD TAKE THIS STUPID GROCERY SACK OFF MY HEAD... OF COURSE, THEN I PROBABLY WOULDN'T BE CAMP PRESIDENT ANY MORE, EITHER...
ON THE OTHER HAND, I CAN'T WEAR THIS SACK FOR THE REST OF MY LIFE...
IF I EVER WENT TO A GROCERY STORE, AND THE CLERK YELLED, "CARRY OUT!" I'D END UP IN THE BACK OF SOME STATION WAGON!
SCHULZ

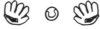

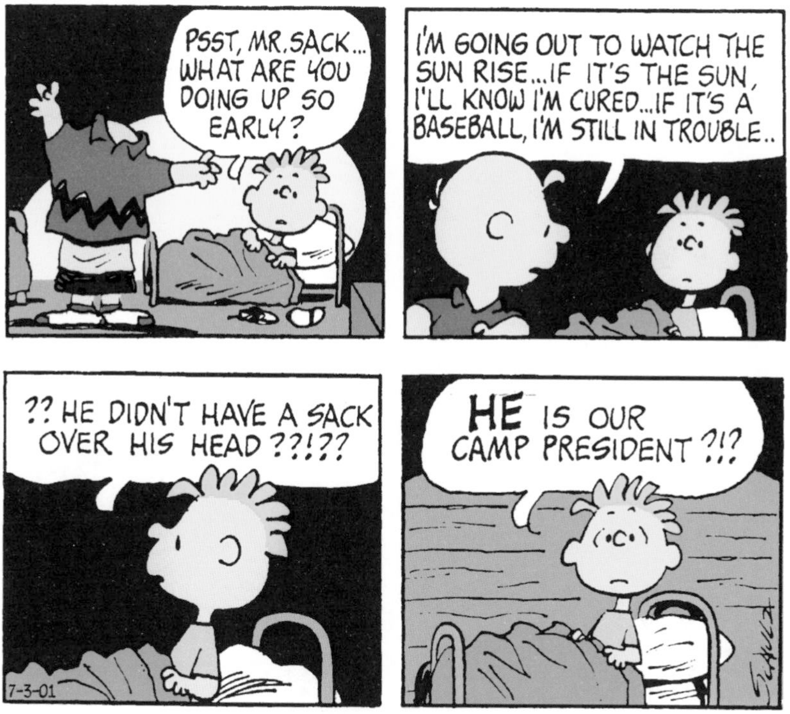
PSST, MR. SACK... WHAT ARE YOU DOING UP SO EARLY?
I'M GOING OUT TO WATCH THE SUN RISE...IF IT'S THE SUN, I'LL KNOW I'M CURED...IF IT'S A BASEBALL, I'M STILL IN TROUBLE..
?? HE DIDN'T HAVE A SACK OVER HIS HEAD ??!??
7-3-01
HE IS OUR CAMP PRESIDENT ?!?
SCHULZ

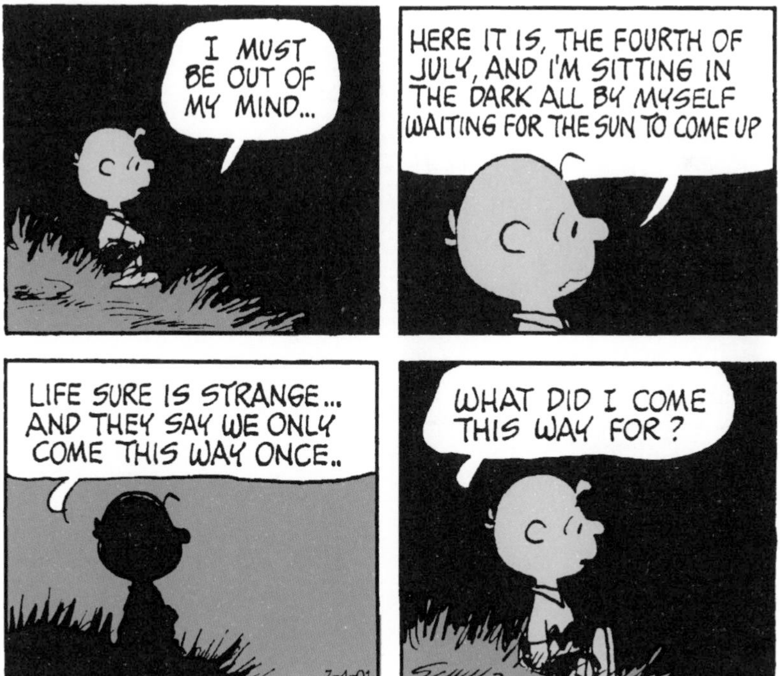
I MUST BE OUT OF MY MIND...
HERE IT IS, THE FOURTH OF JULY, AND I'M SITTING IN THE DARK ALL BY MYSELF WAITING FOR THE SUN TO COME UP
LIFE SURE IS STRANGE... AND THEY SAY WE ONLY COME THIS WAY ONCE..
7-4-01
WHAT DID I COME THIS WAY FOR?
SCHULZ

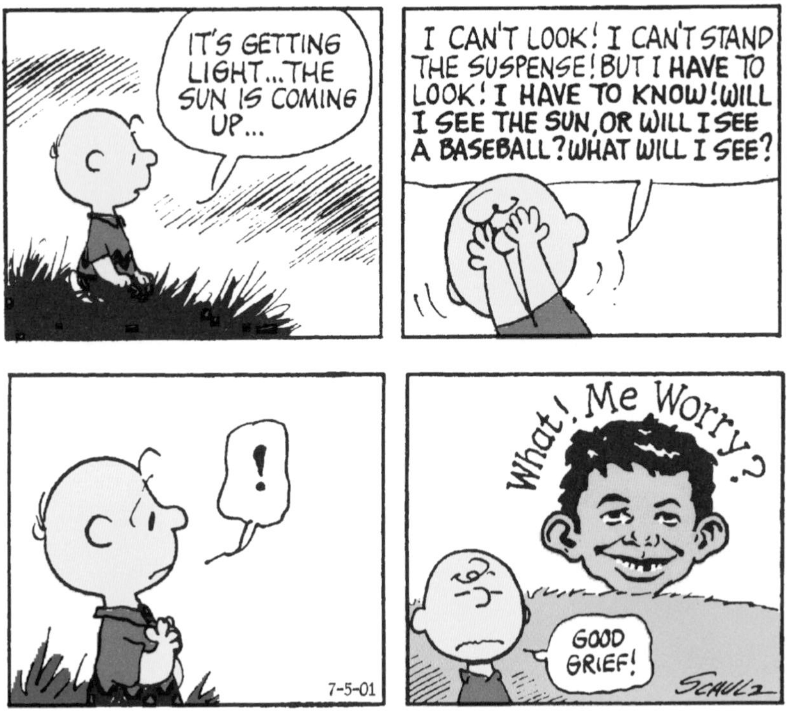
IT'S GETTING LIGHT...THE SUN IS COMING UP...
I CAN'T LOOK! I CAN'T STAND THE SUSPENSE! BUT I HAVE TO LOOK! I HAVE TO KNOW! WILL I SEE THE SUN, OR WILL I SEE A BASEBALL? WHAT WILL I SEE?
!
7-5-01
What! Me Worry?
GOOD GRIEF!
SCHULZ

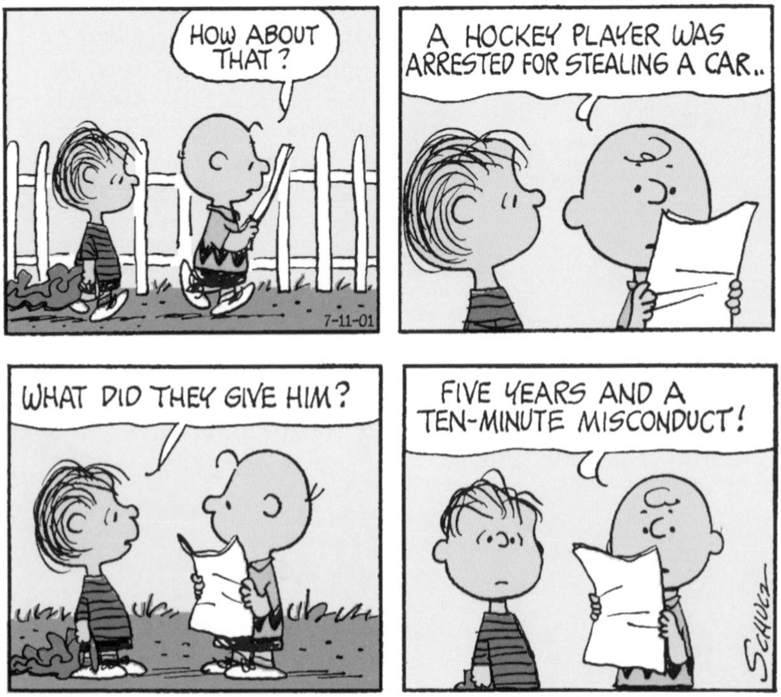
HOW ABOUT THAT?
7-11-01
A HOCKEY PLAYER WAS ARRESTED FOR STEALING A CAR..
WHAT DID THEY GIVE HIM?
FIVE YEARS AND A TEN-MINUTE MISCONDUCT!
SCHULZ

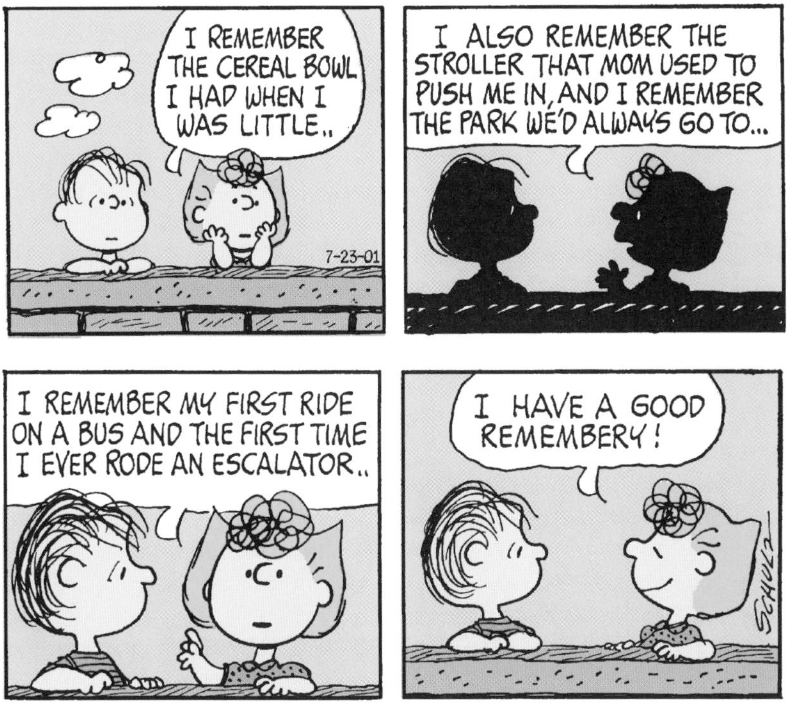
I REMEMBER THE CEREAL BOWL I HAD WHEN I WAS LITTLE..
7-23-01
I ALSO REMEMBER THE STROLLER THAT MOM USED TO PUSH ME IN, AND I REMEMBER THE PARK WE'D ALWAYS GO TO...
I REMEMBER MY FIRST RIDE ON A BUS AND THE FIRST TIME I EVER RODE AN ESCALATOR..
I HAVE A GOOD REMEMBERY!
SCHULZ

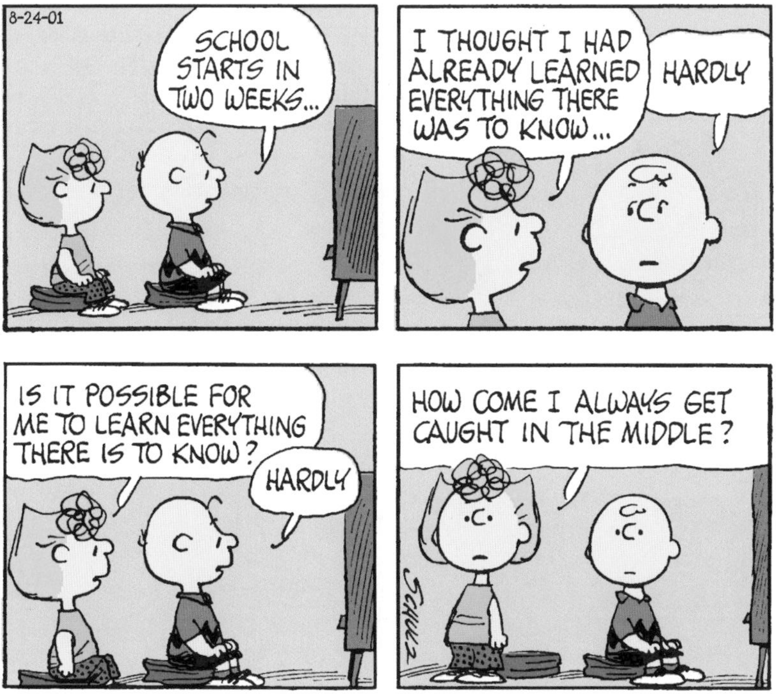
8-24-01
SCHOOL STARTS IN TWO WEEKS...
I THOUGHT I HAD ALREADY LEARNED EVERYTHING THERE WAS TO KNOW...
HARDLY
IS IT POSSIBLE FOR ME TO LEARN EVERYTHING THERE IS TO KNOW?
HARDLY
HOW COME I ALWAYS GET CAUGHT IN THE MIDDLE?
SCHULZ

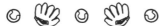

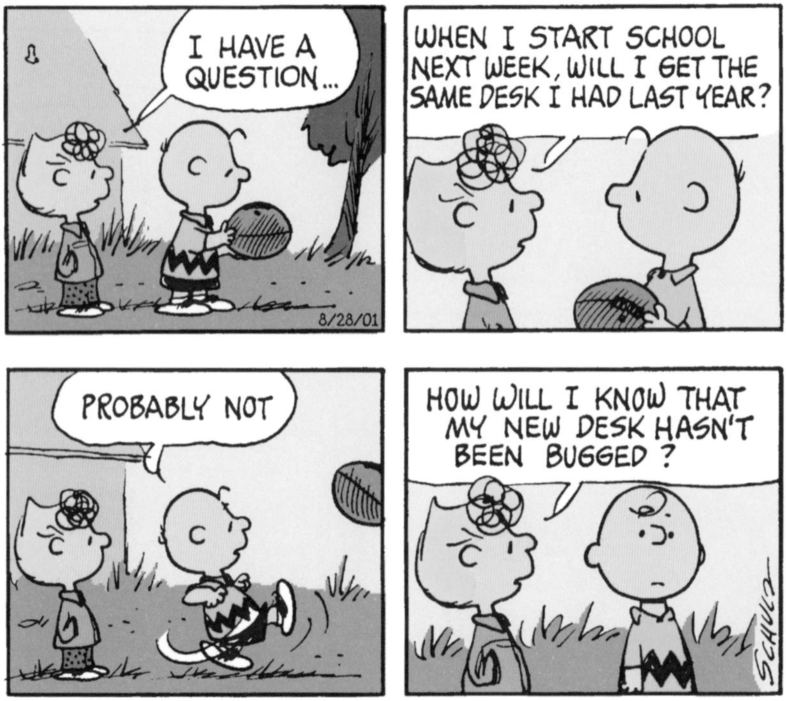

I HAVE A QUESTION...
8/28/01
WHEN I START SCHOOL NEXT WEEK, WILL I GET THE SAME DESK I HAD LAST YEAR?
PROBABLY NOT
HOW WILL I KNOW THAT MY NEW DESK HASN'T BEEN BUGGED?
SCHULZ

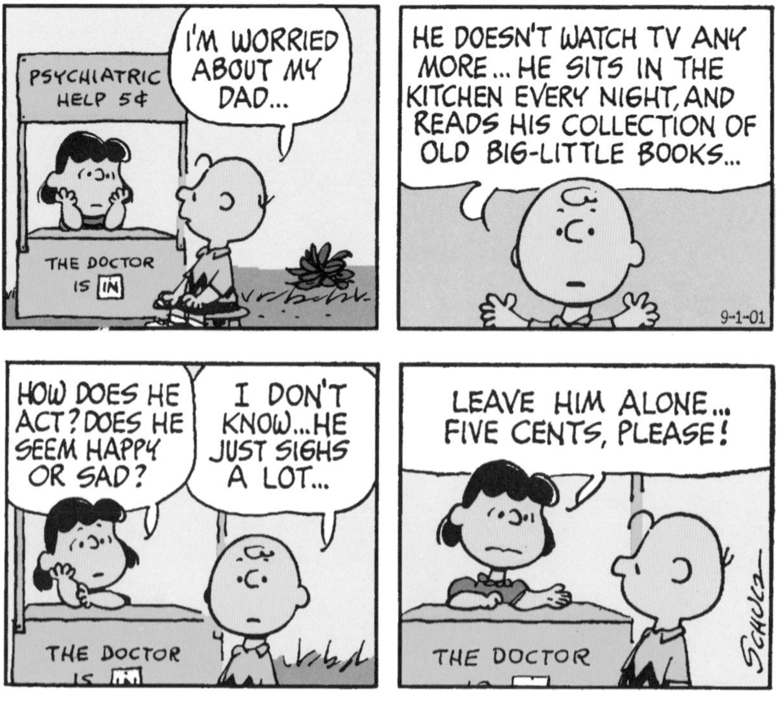

PSYCHIATRIC HELP 5¢
THE DOCTOR IS IN
I'M WORRIED ABOUT MY DAD...
HE DOESN'T WATCH TV ANY MORE... HE SITS IN THE KITCHEN EVERY NIGHT, AND READS HIS COLLECTION OF OLD BIG-LITTLE BOOKS...
9-1-01
HOW DOES HE ACT? DOES HE SEEM HAPPY OR SAD?
I DON'T KNOW...HE JUST SIGHS A LOT...
THE DOCTOR
LEAVE HIM ALONE... FIVE CENTS, PLEASE!
THE DOCTOR
SCHULZ

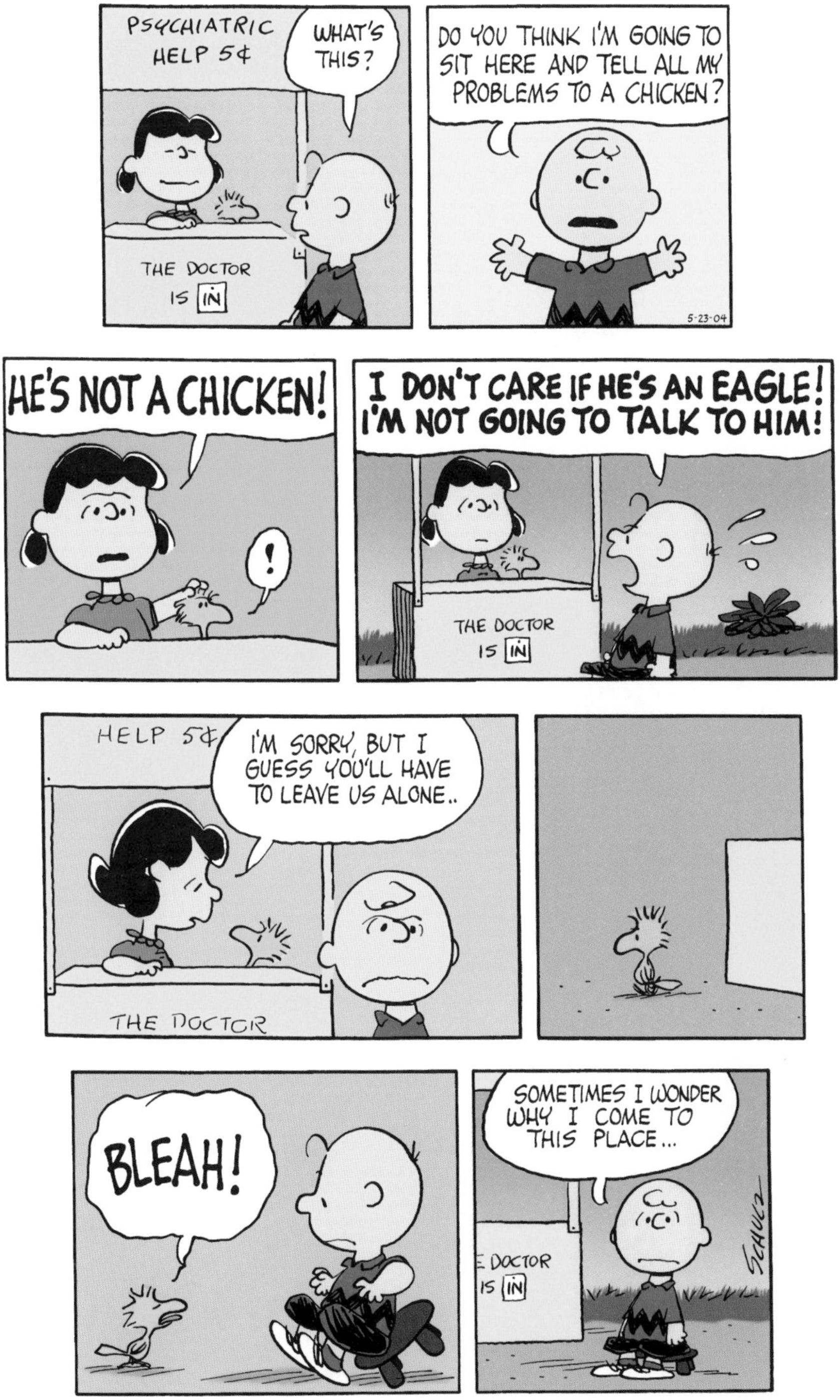
PSYCHIATRIC HELP 5¢
WHAT'S THIS?
THE DOCTOR IS IN
DO YOU THINK I'M GOING TO SIT HERE AND TELL ALL MY PROBLEMS TO A CHICKEN?
5-23-04
HE'S NOT A CHICKEN!
!
I DON'T CARE IF HE'S AN EAGLE! I'M NOT GOING TO TALK TO HIM!
THE DOCTOR IS IN
HELP 5¢
I'M SORRY, BUT I GUESS YOU'LL HAVE TO LEAVE US ALONE..
THE DOCTOR
BLEAH!
SOMETIMES I WONDER WHY I COME TO THIS PLACE...
E DOCTOR IS IN
SCHULZ

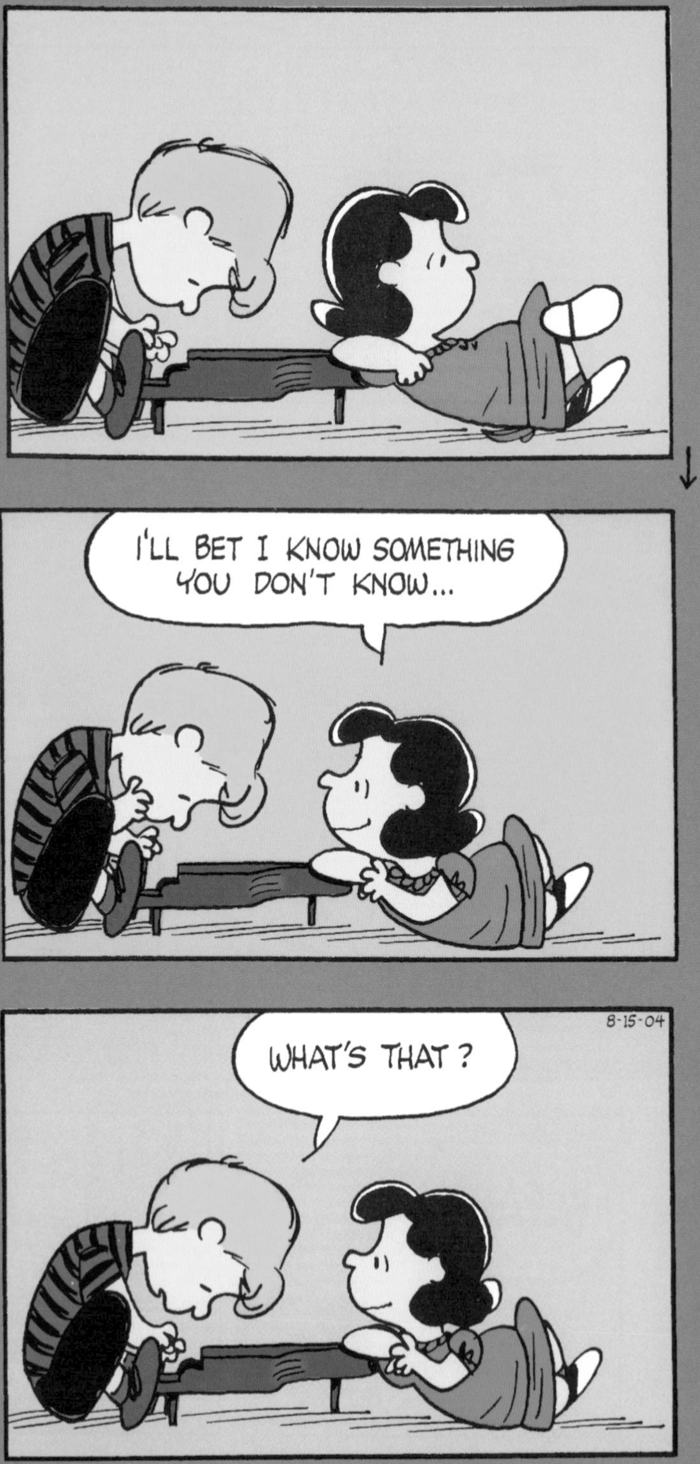
I'LL BET I KNOW SOMETHING YOU DON'T KNOW...
8-15-04
WHAT'S THAT ?

cresc.
BEETHOVEN NOW COMES IN SPRAY CANS!
SCHULZ

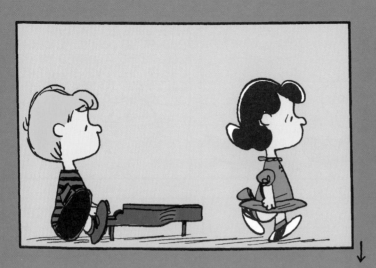

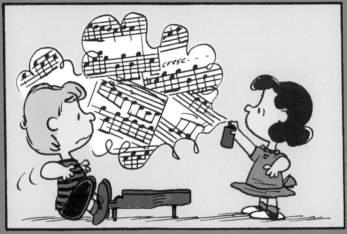

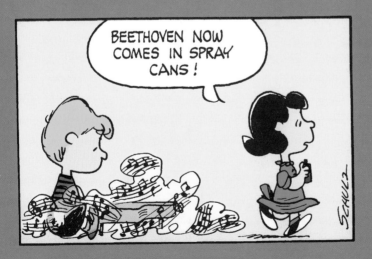

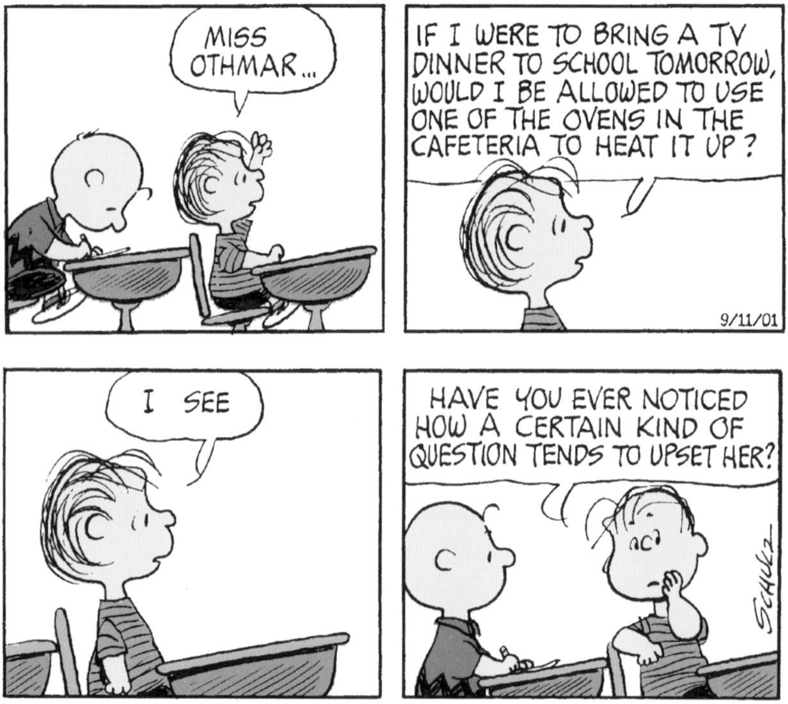
MISS OTHMAR...
IF I WERE TO BRING A TV DINNER TO SCHOOL TOMORROW, WOULD I BE ALLOWED TO USE ONE OF THE OVENS IN THE CAFETERIA TO HEAT IT UP?
9/11/01
I SEE
HAVE YOU EVER NOTICED HOW A CERTAIN KIND OF QUESTION TENDS TO UPSET HER?
SCHULZ

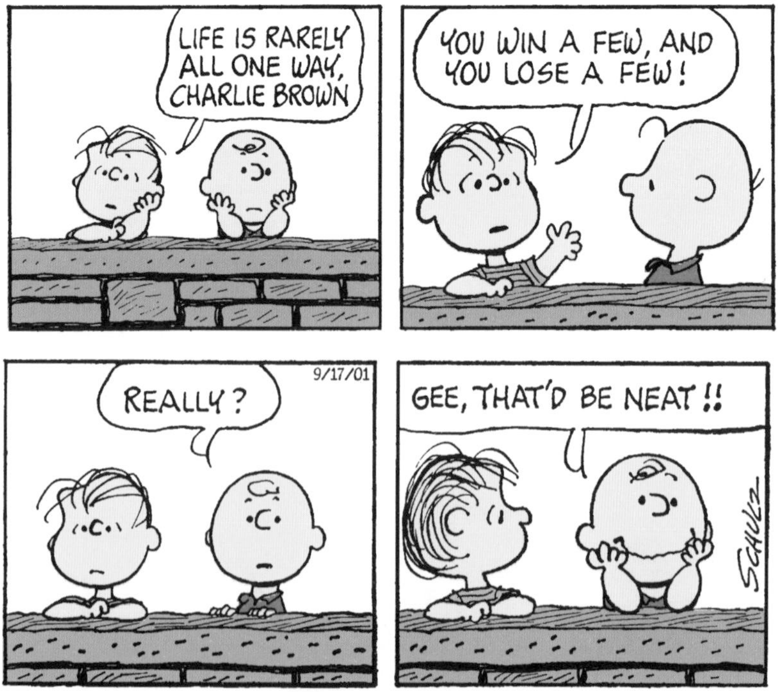
LIFE IS RARELY ALL ONE WAY, CHARLIE BROWN
YOU WIN A FEW, AND YOU LOSE A FEW!
9/17/01
REALLY?
GEE, THAT'D BE NEAT!!
SCHULZ

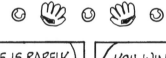

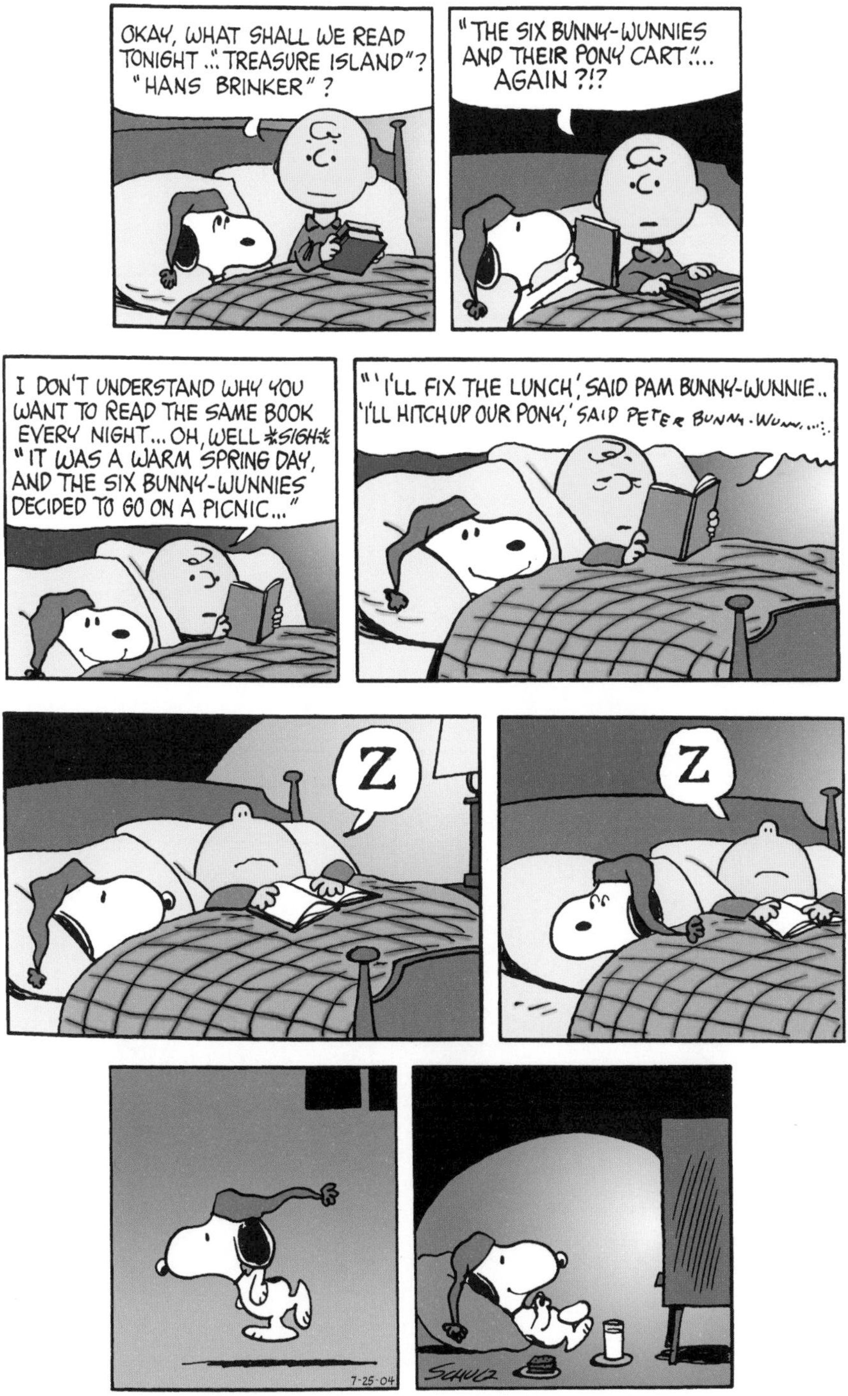
OKAY, WHAT SHALL WE READ TONIGHT..."TREASURE ISLAND"? "HANS BRINKER"?
"THE SIX BUNNY-WUNNIES AND THEIR PONY CART"... AGAIN ?!?
I DON'T UNDERSTAND WHY YOU WANT TO READ THE SAME BOOK EVERY NIGHT...OH, WELL *SIGH* "IT WAS A WARM SPRING DAY, AND THE SIX BUNNY-WUNNIES DECIDED TO GO ON A PICNIC..."
"'I'LL FIX THE LUNCH,' SAID PAM BUNNY-WUNNIE.. 'I'LL HITCH UP OUR PONY,' SAID PETER
Z
Z
7-25-04
SCHULZ

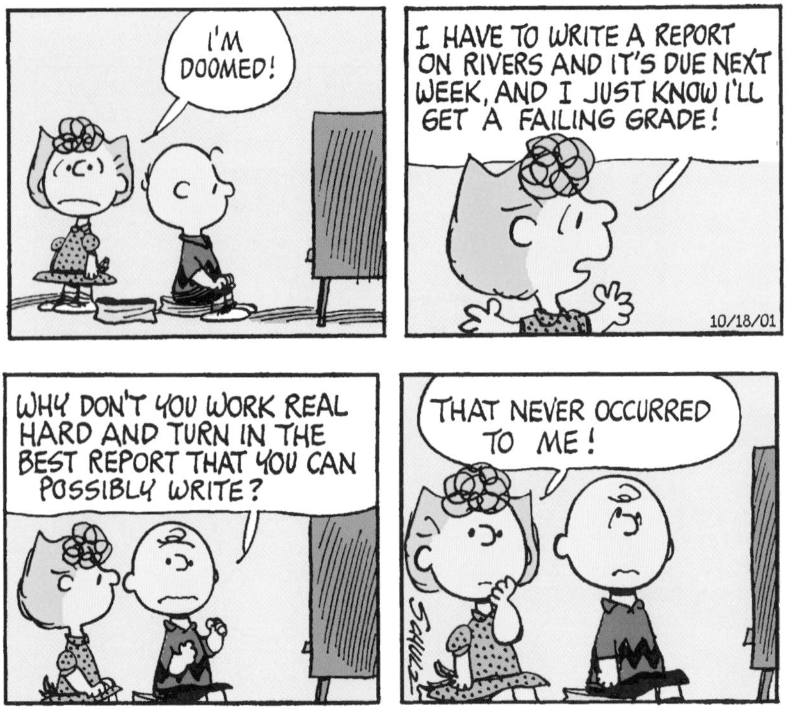
I'M DOOMED!
I HAVE TO WRITE A REPORT ON RIVERS AND IT'S DUE NEXT WEEK, AND I JUST KNOW I'LL GET A FAILING GRADE!
10/18/01
WHY DON'T YOU WORK REAL HARD AND TURN IN THE BEST REPORT THAT YOU CAN POSSIBLY WRITE?
THAT NEVER OCCURRED TO ME!
SCHULZ

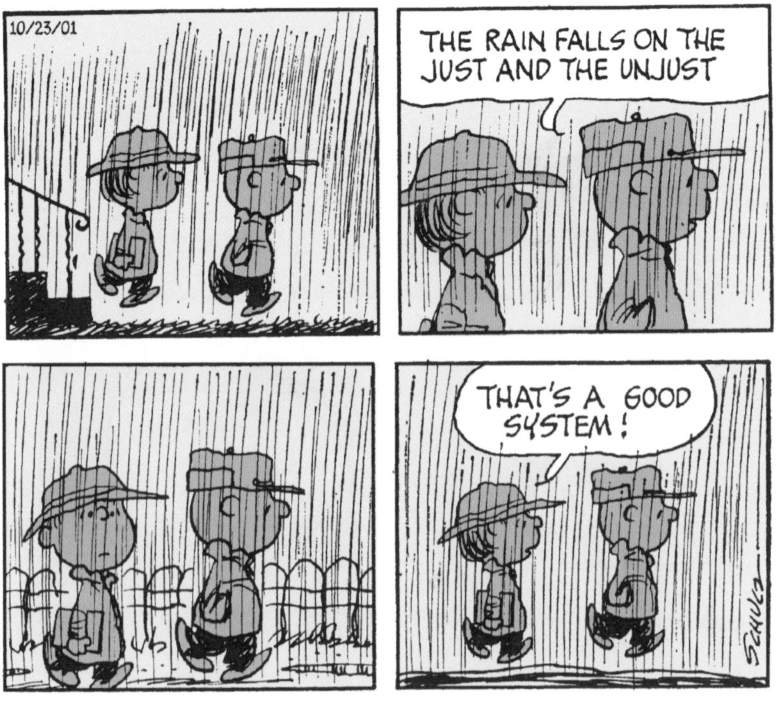
10/23/01
THE RAIN FALLS ON THE JUST AND THE UNJUST
THAT'S A GOOD SYSTEM!
SCHULZ

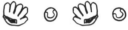

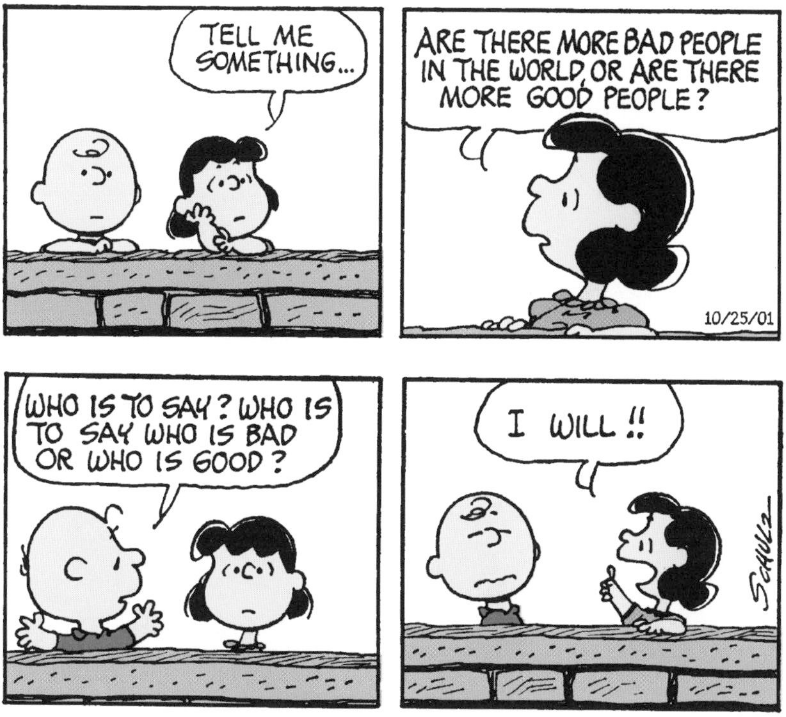
TELL ME SOMETHING...
ARE THERE MORE BAD PEOPLE IN THE WORLD, OR ARE THERE MORE GOOD PEOPLE?
10/25/01
WHO IS TO SAY? WHO IS TO SAY WHO IS BAD OR WHO IS GOOD?
I WILL!!
SCHULZ

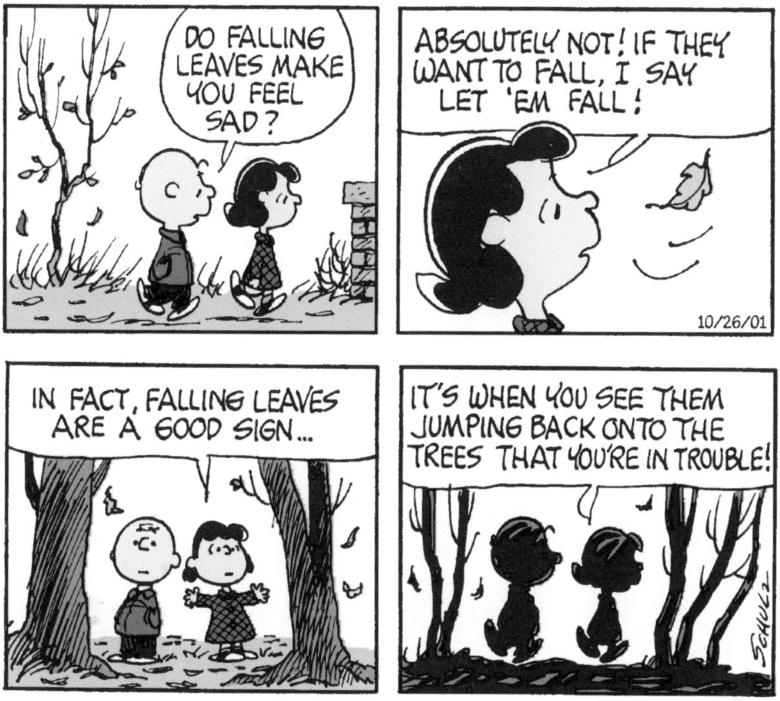
DO FALLING LEAVES MAKE YOU FEEL SAD?
ABSOLUTELY NOT! IF THEY WANT TO FALL, I SAY LET 'EM FALL!
10/26/01
IN FACT, FALLING LEAVES ARE A GOOD SIGN...
IT'S WHEN YOU SEE THEM JUMPING BACK ONTO THE TREES THAT YOU'RE IN TROUBLE!
SCHULZ

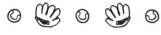

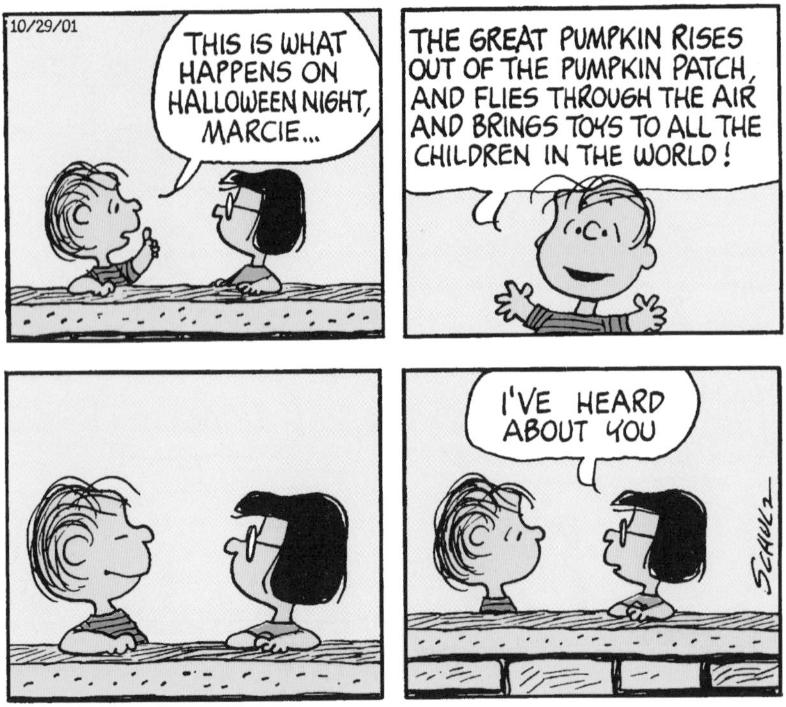
10/29/01
THIS IS WHAT HAPPENS ON HALLOWEEN NIGHT, MARCIE...
THE GREAT PUMPKIN RISES OUT OF THE PUMPKIN PATCH, AND FLIES THROUGH THE AIR AND BRINGS TOYS TO ALL THE CHILDREN IN THE WORLD!
I'VE HEARD ABOUT YOU
SCHULZ

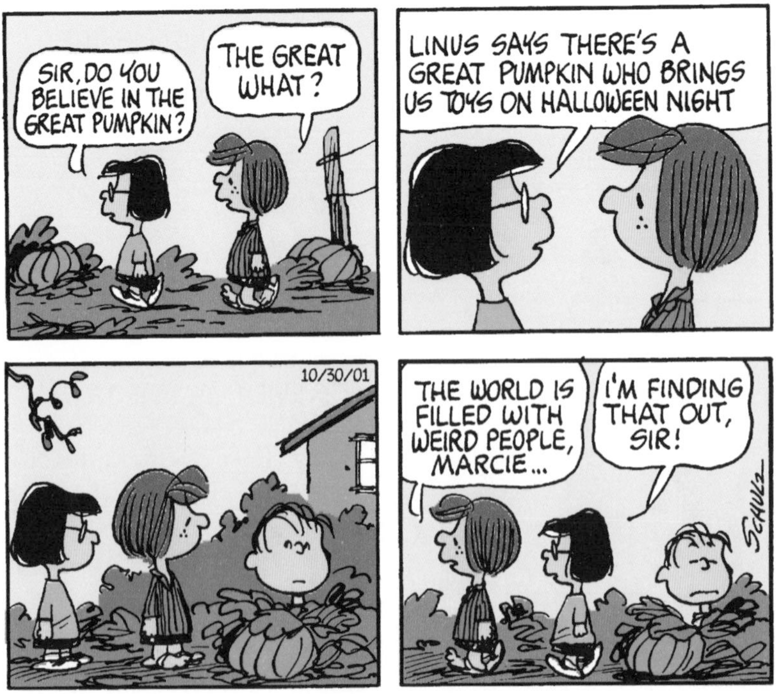
SIR, DO YOU BELIEVE IN THE GREAT PUMPKIN?
THE GREAT WHAT?
LINUS SAYS THERE'S A GREAT PUMPKIN WHO BRINGS US TOYS ON HALLOWEEN NIGHT
10/30/01
THE WORLD IS FILLED WITH WEIRD PEOPLE, MARCIE...
I'M FINDING THAT OUT, SIR!
SCHULZ

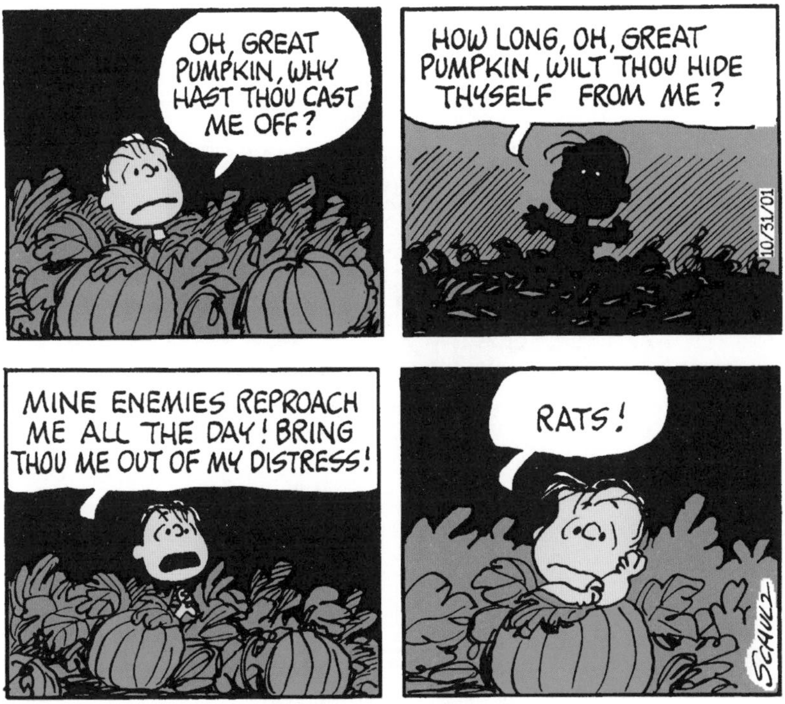
OH, GREAT PUMPKIN, WHY HAST THOU CAST ME OFF?
HOW LONG, OH, GREAT PUMPKIN, WILT THOU HIDE THYSELF FROM ME?
10/31/01
MINE ENEMIES REPROACH ME ALL THE DAY! BRING THOU ME OUT OF MY DISTRESS!
RATS!
SCHULZ

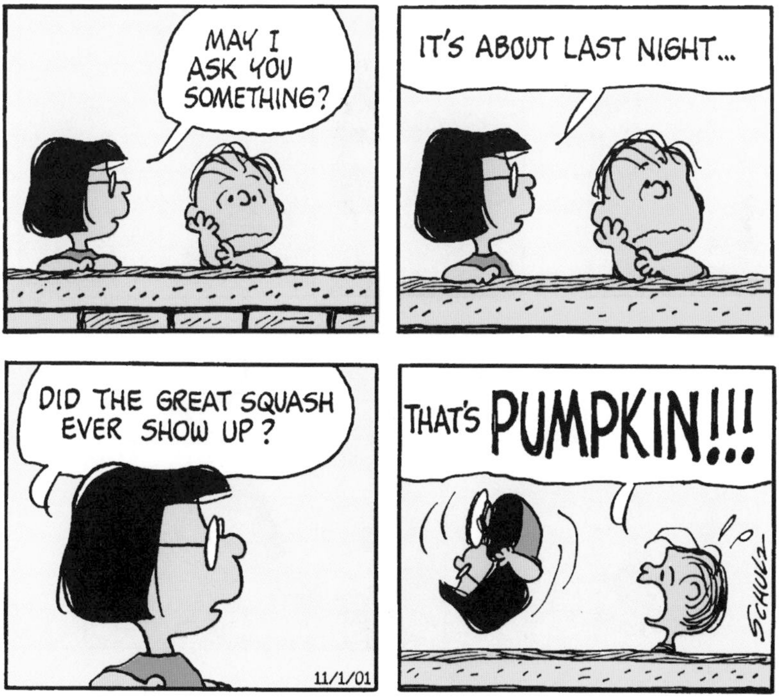
MAY I ASK YOU SOMETHING?
IT'S ABOUT LAST NIGHT...
DID THE GREAT SQUASH EVER SHOW UP?
11/1/01
THAT'S PUMPKIN!!!
SCHULZ

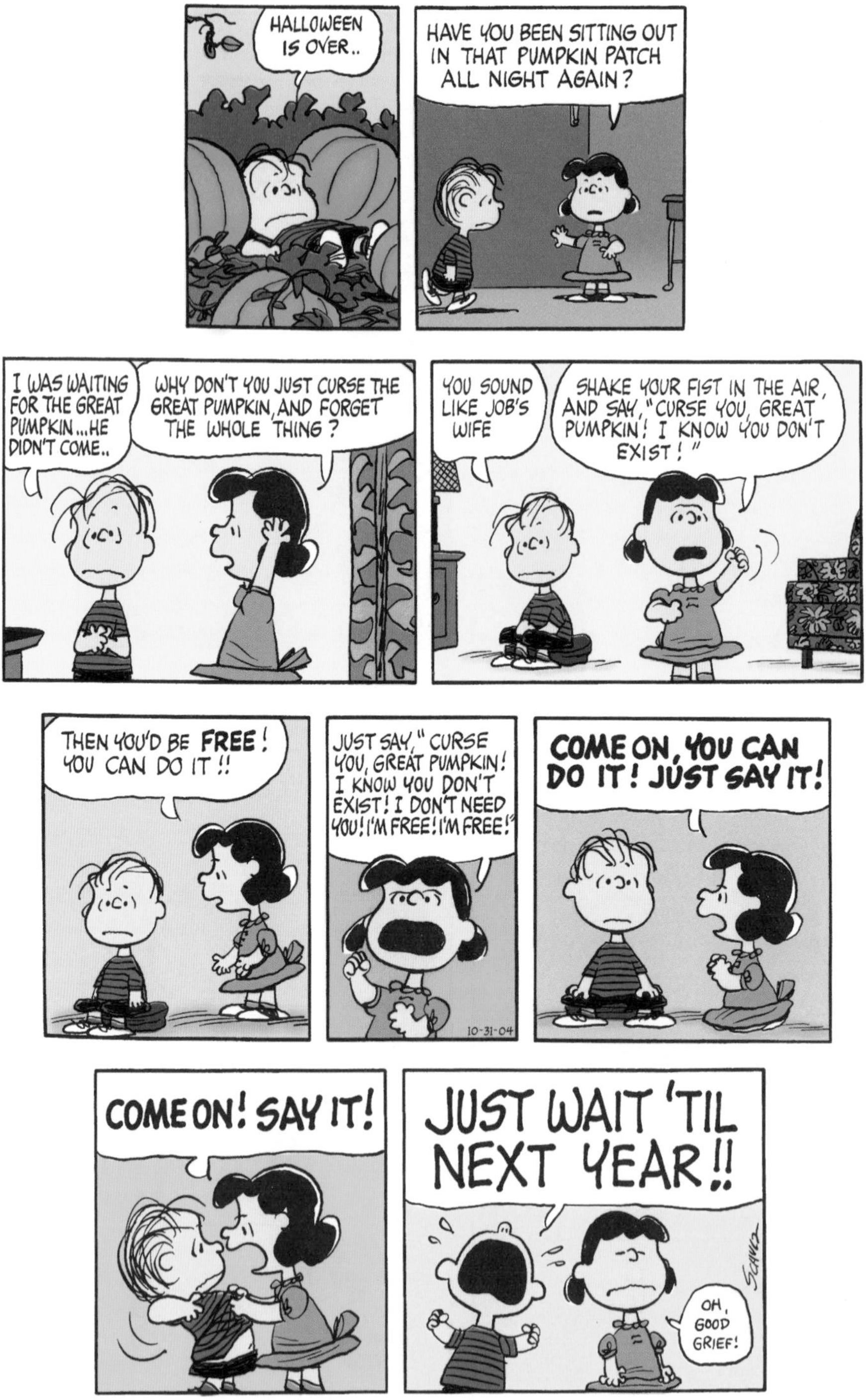
HALLOWEEN IS OVER..
HAVE YOU BEEN SITTING OUT IN THAT PUMPKIN PATCH ALL NIGHT AGAIN?
I WAS WAITING FOR THE GREAT PUMPKIN...HE DIDN'T COME..
WHY DON'T YOU JUST CURSE THE GREAT PUMPKIN, AND FORGET THE WHOLE THING?
YOU SOUND LIKE JOB'S WIFE
SHAKE YOUR FIST IN THE AIR, AND SAY, "CURSE YOU, GREAT PUMPKIN! I KNOW YOU DON'T EXIST!"
THEN YOU'D BE **FREE**! YOU CAN DO IT!!
JUST SAY, "CURSE YOU, GREAT PUMPKIN! I KNOW YOU DON'T EXIST! I DON'T NEED YOU! I'M FREE! I'M FREE!"
10-31-04
COME ON, YOU CAN DO IT! JUST SAY IT!
COME ON! SAY IT!
JUST WAIT 'TIL NEXT YEAR!!
OH, GOOD GRIEF!
SCHULZ

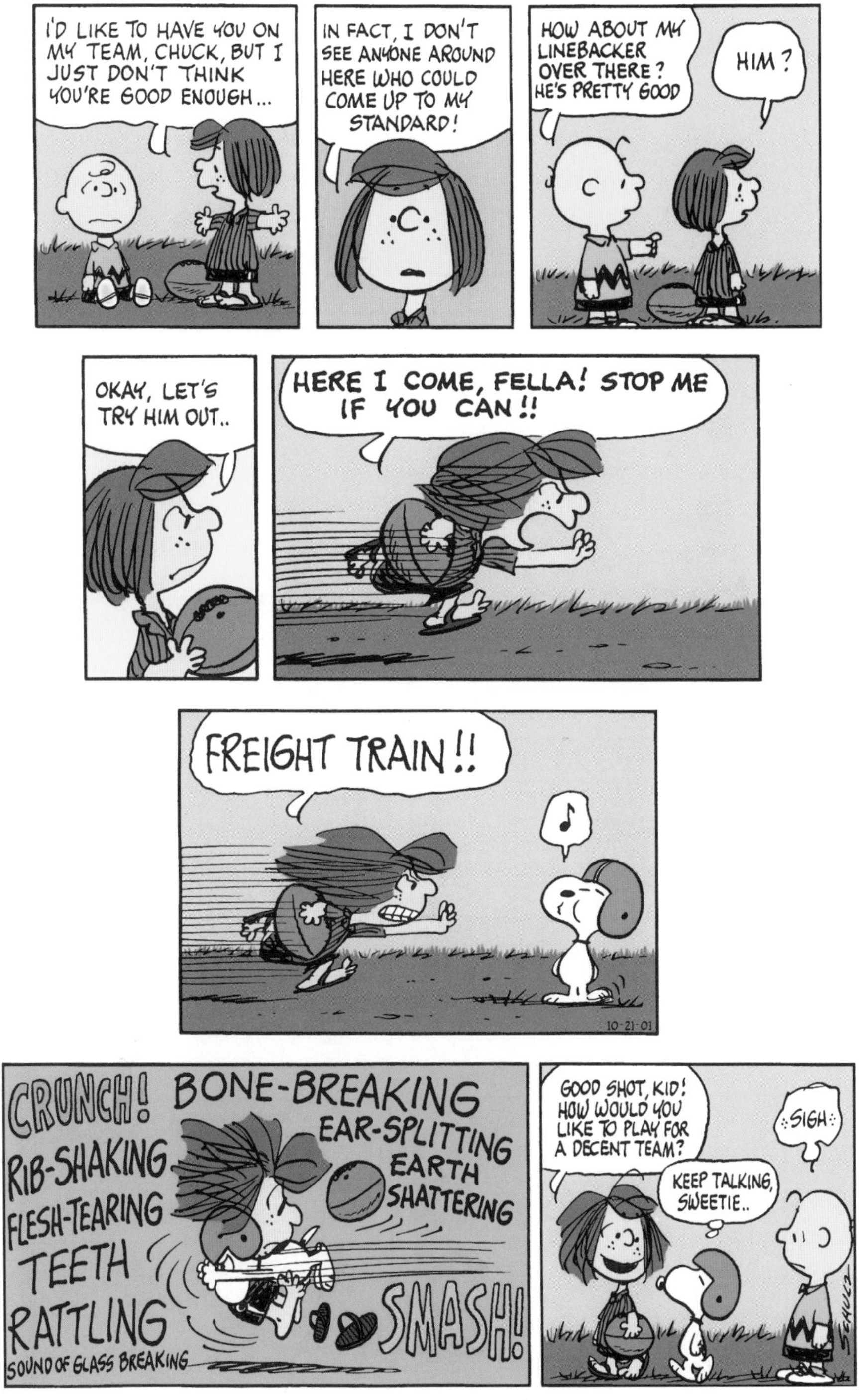
I'D LIKE TO HAVE YOU ON MY TEAM, CHUCK, BUT I JUST DON'T THINK YOU'RE GOOD ENOUGH...
IN FACT, I DON'T SEE ANYONE AROUND HERE WHO COULD COME UP TO MY STANDARD!
HOW ABOUT MY LINEBACKER OVER THERE? HE'S PRETTY GOOD
HIM?
OKAY, LET'S TRY HIM OUT..
HERE I COME, FELLA! STOP ME IF YOU CAN!!
FREIGHT TRAIN!!
♪
10-21-01
CRUNCH! BONE-BREAKING
EAR-SPLITTING
RIB-SHAKING
EARTH SHATTERING
FLESH-TEARING
TEETH RATTLING
SMASH!
SOUND OF GLASS BREAKING
GOOD SHOT, KID! HOW WOULD YOU LIKE TO PLAY FOR A DECENT TEAM?
SIGH
KEEP TALKING, SWEETIE..
SCHULZ

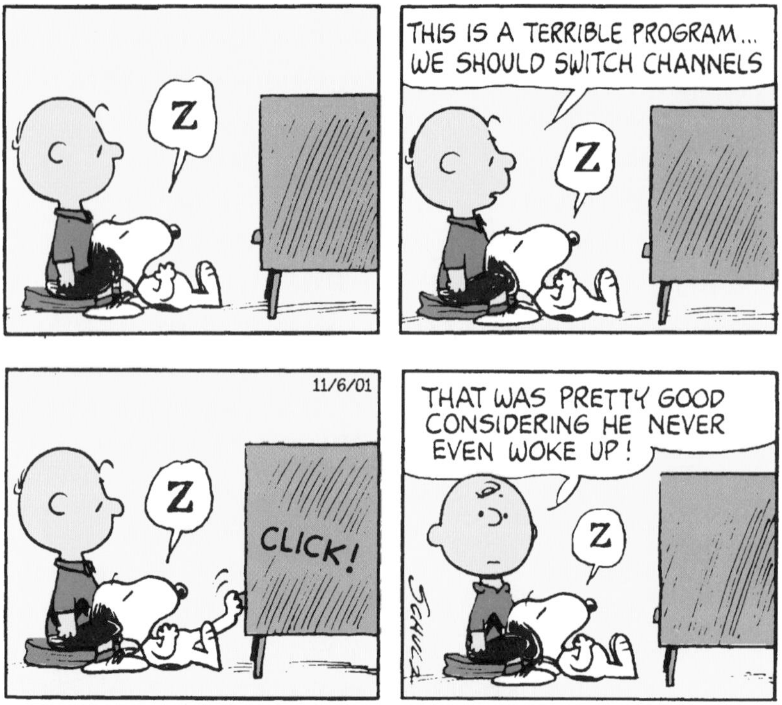
Z
THIS IS A TERRIBLE PROGRAM... WE SHOULD SWITCH CHANNELS
Z
11/6/01
Z
CLICK!
THAT WAS PRETTY GOOD CONSIDERING HE NEVER EVEN WOKE UP!
Z
SCHULZ

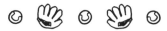

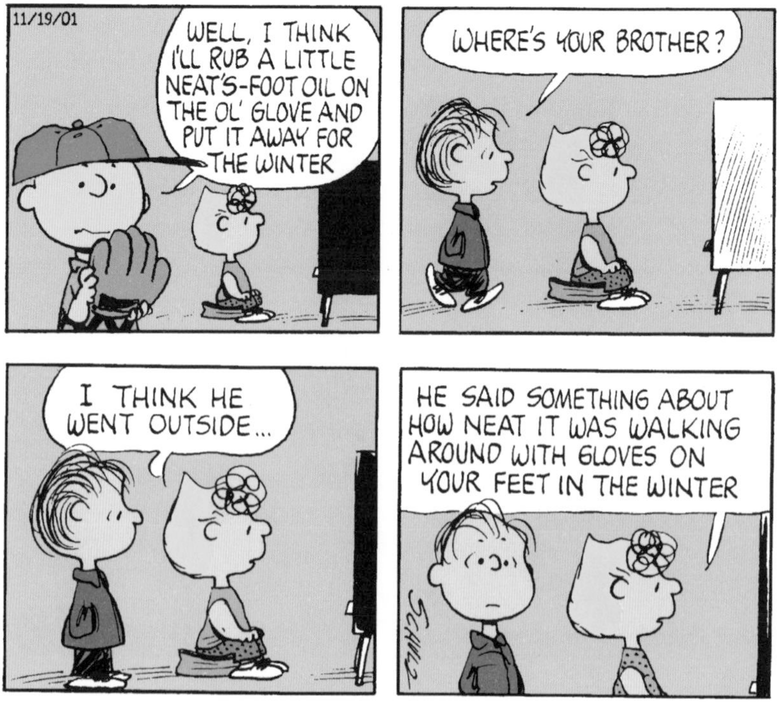
11/19/01
WELL, I THINK I'LL RUB A LITTLE NEAT'S-FOOT OIL ON THE OL' GLOVE AND PUT IT AWAY FOR THE WINTER
WHERE'S YOUR BROTHER?
I THINK HE WENT OUTSIDE...
HE SAID SOMETHING ABOUT HOW NEAT IT WAS WALKING AROUND WITH GLOVES ON YOUR FEET IN THE WINTER
SCHULZ

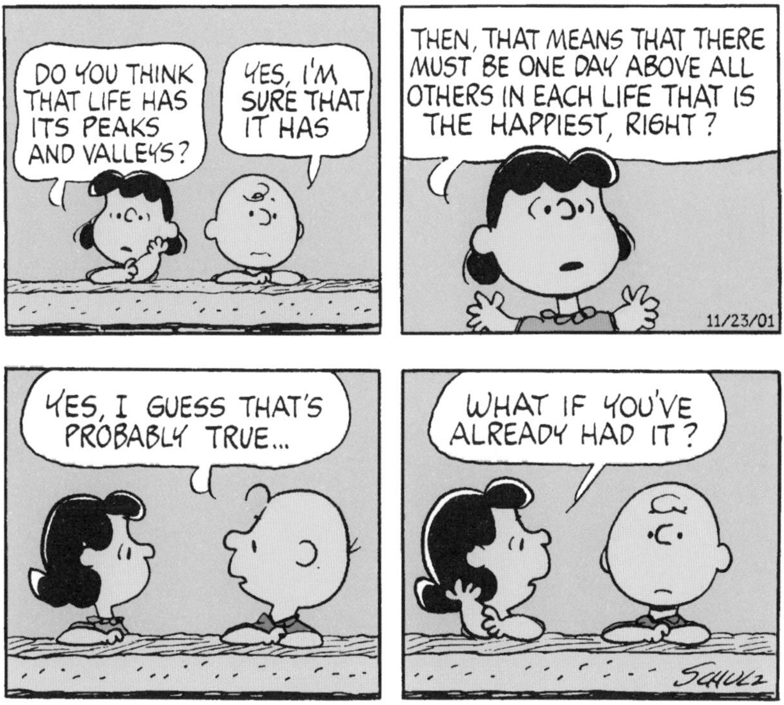
DO YOU THINK THAT LIFE HAS ITS PEAKS AND VALLEYS?
YES, I'M SURE THAT IT HAS
THEN, THAT MEANS THAT THERE MUST BE ONE DAY ABOVE ALL OTHERS IN EACH LIFE THAT IS THE HAPPIEST, RIGHT?
11/23/01
YES, I GUESS THAT'S PROBABLY TRUE...
WHAT IF YOU'VE ALREADY HAD IT?
SCHULZ

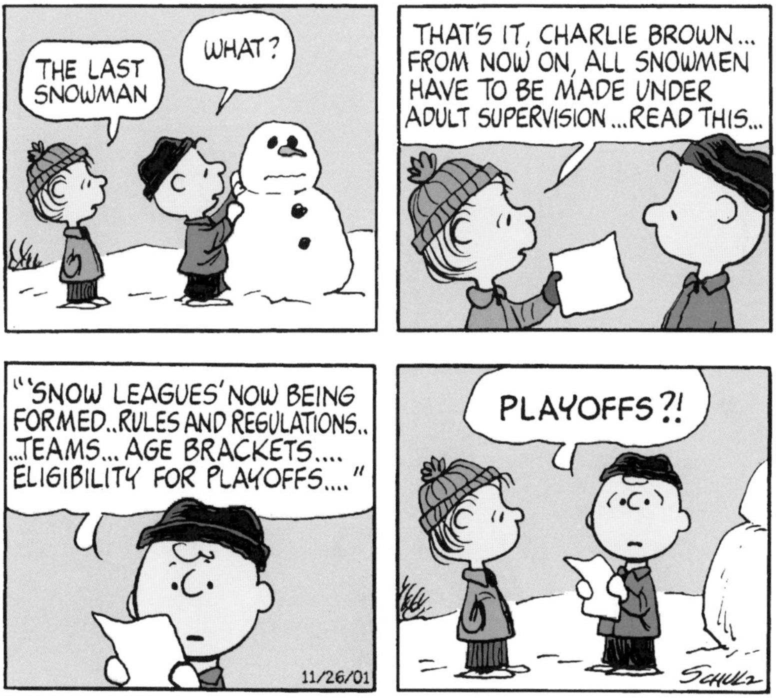
THE LAST SNOWMAN
WHAT?
THAT'S IT, CHARLIE BROWN... FROM NOW ON, ALL SNOWMEN HAVE TO BE MADE UNDER ADULT SUPERVISION...READ THIS...
"'SNOW LEAGUES' NOW BEING FORMED..RULES AND REGULATIONS.. ..TEAMS... AGE BRACKETS.... ELIGIBILITY FOR PLAYOFFS...."
11/26/01
PLAYOFFS?!
SCHULZ

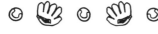

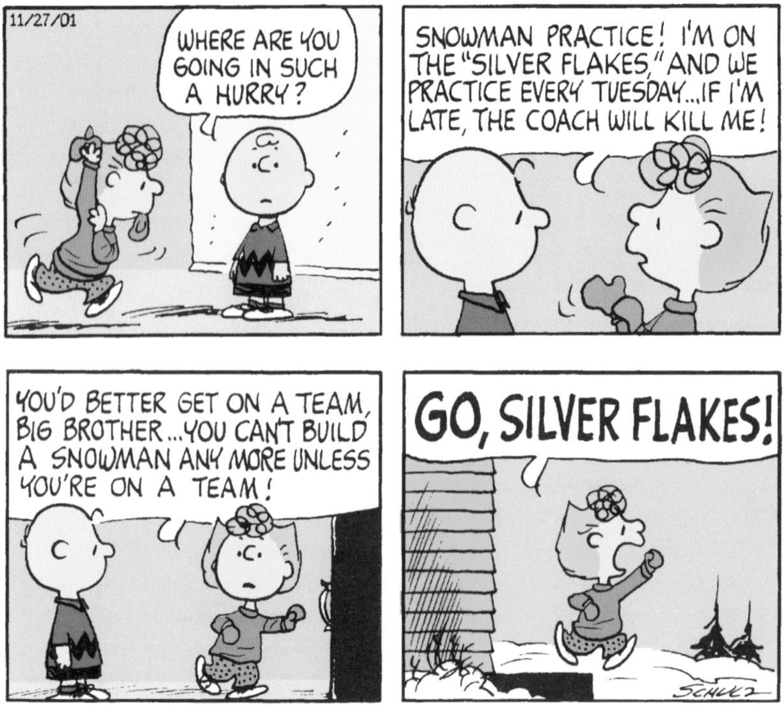
11/27/01
WHERE ARE YOU GOING IN SUCH A HURRY?
SNOWMAN PRACTICE! I'M ON THE "SILVER FLAKES," AND WE PRACTICE EVERY TUESDAY...IF I'M LATE, THE COACH WILL KILL ME!
YOU'D BETTER GET ON A TEAM, BIG BROTHER...YOU CAN'T BUILD A SNOWMAN ANY MORE UNLESS YOU'RE ON A TEAM!
GO, SILVER FLAKES!
SCHULZ

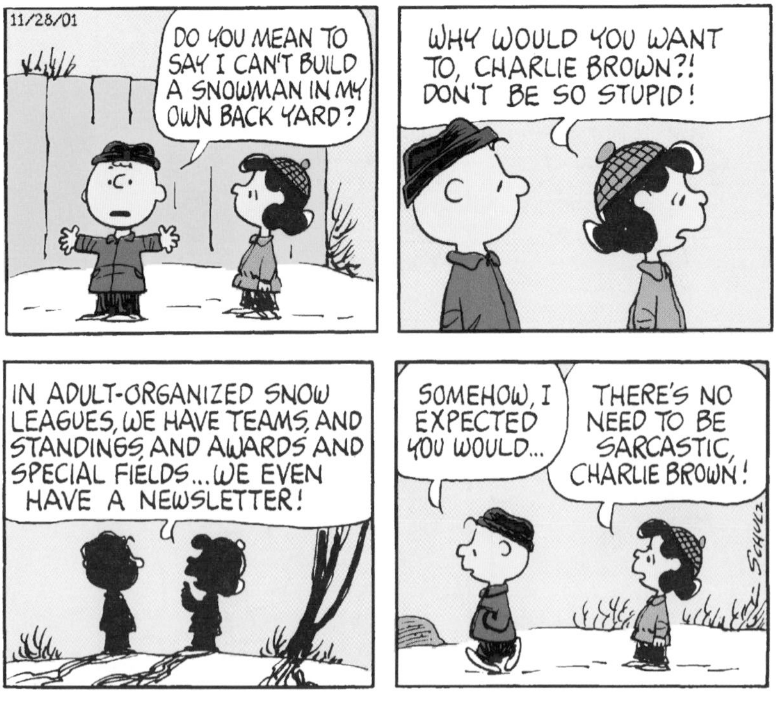
11/28/01
DO YOU MEAN TO SAY I CAN'T BUILD A SNOWMAN IN MY OWN BACK YARD?
WHY WOULD YOU WANT TO, CHARLIE BROWN?! DON'T BE SO STUPID!
IN ADULT-ORGANIZED SNOW LEAGUES, WE HAVE TEAMS, AND STANDINGS, AND AWARDS AND SPECIAL FIELDS...WE EVEN HAVE A NEWSLETTER!
SOMEHOW, I EXPECTED YOU WOULD...
THERE'S NO NEED TO BE SARCASTIC, CHARLIE BROWN!
SCHULZ

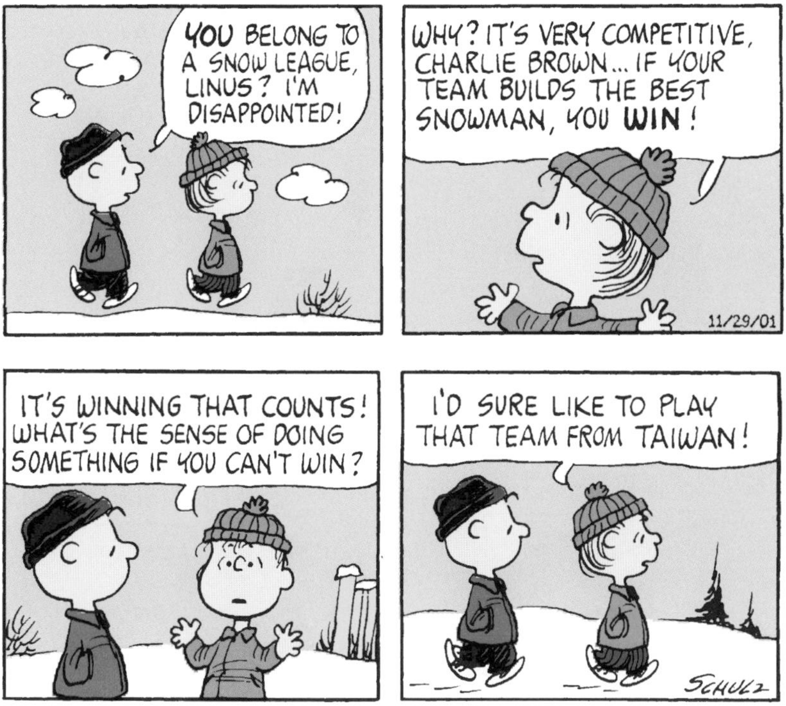
YOU BELONG TO A SNOW LEAGUE, LINUS? I'M DISAPPOINTED!
WHY? IT'S VERY COMPETITIVE, CHARLIE BROWN... IF YOUR TEAM BUILDS THE BEST SNOWMAN, YOU WIN!
11/29/01
IT'S WINNING THAT COUNTS! WHAT'S THE SENSE OF DOING SOMETHING IF YOU CAN'T WIN?
I'D SURE LIKE TO PLAY THAT TEAM FROM TAIWAN!
SCHULZ

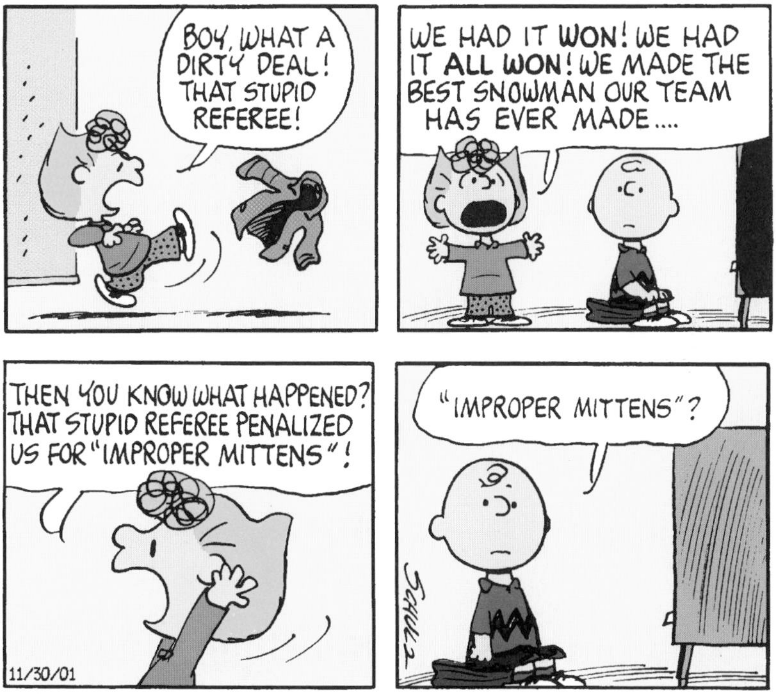
BOY, WHAT A DIRTY DEAL! THAT STUPID REFEREE!
WE HAD IT WON! WE HAD IT ALL WON! WE MADE THE BEST SNOWMAN OUR TEAM HAS EVER MADE....
THEN YOU KNOW WHAT HAPPENED? THAT STUPID REFEREE PENALIZED US FOR "IMPROPER MITTENS"!
11/30/01
"IMPROPER MITTENS"?
SCHULZ

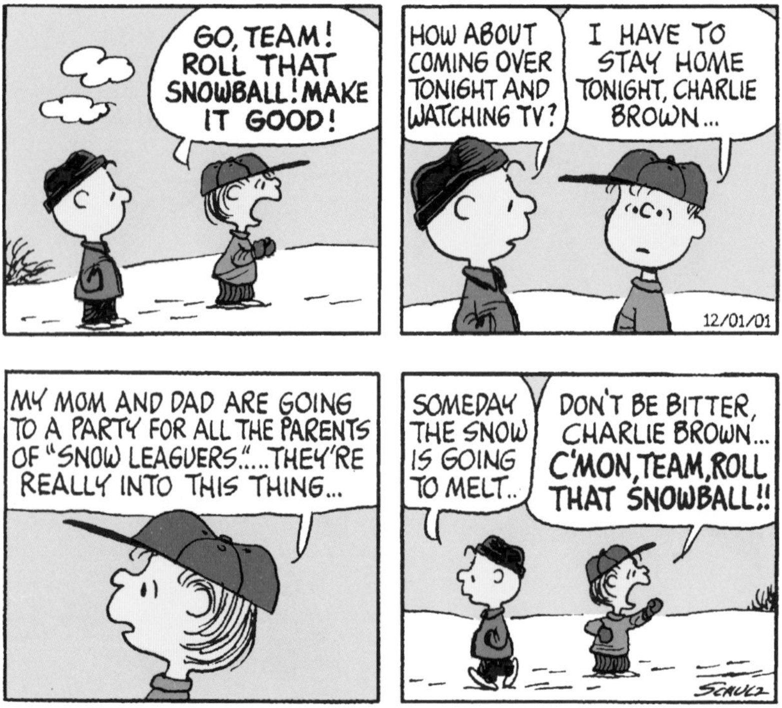
GO, TEAM! ROLL THAT SNOWBALL! MAKE IT GOOD!
HOW ABOUT COMING OVER TONIGHT AND WATCHING TV?
I HAVE TO STAY HOME TONIGHT, CHARLIE BROWN...
12/01/01
MY MOM AND DAD ARE GOING TO A PARTY FOR ALL THE PARENTS OF "SNOW LEAGUERS."....THEY'RE REALLY INTO THIS THING...
SOMEDAY THE SNOW IS GOING TO MELT...
DON'T BE BITTER, CHARLIE BROWN... C'MON, TEAM, ROLL THAT SNOWBALL!!
SCHULZ

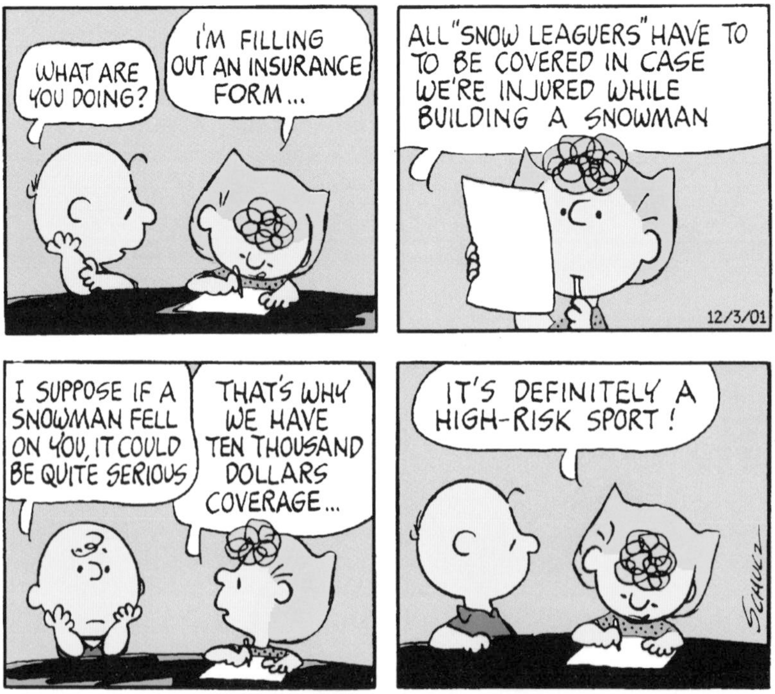
WHAT ARE YOU DOING?
I'M FILLING OUT AN INSURANCE FORM...
ALL "SNOW LEAGUERS" HAVE TO TO BE COVERED IN CASE WE'RE INJURED WHILE BUILDING A SNOWMAN
12/3/01
I SUPPOSE IF A SNOWMAN FELL ON YOU, IT COULD BE QUITE SERIOUS
THAT'S WHY WE HAVE TEN THOUSAND DOLLARS COVERAGE...
IT'S DEFINITELY A HIGH-RISK SPORT!
SCHULZ

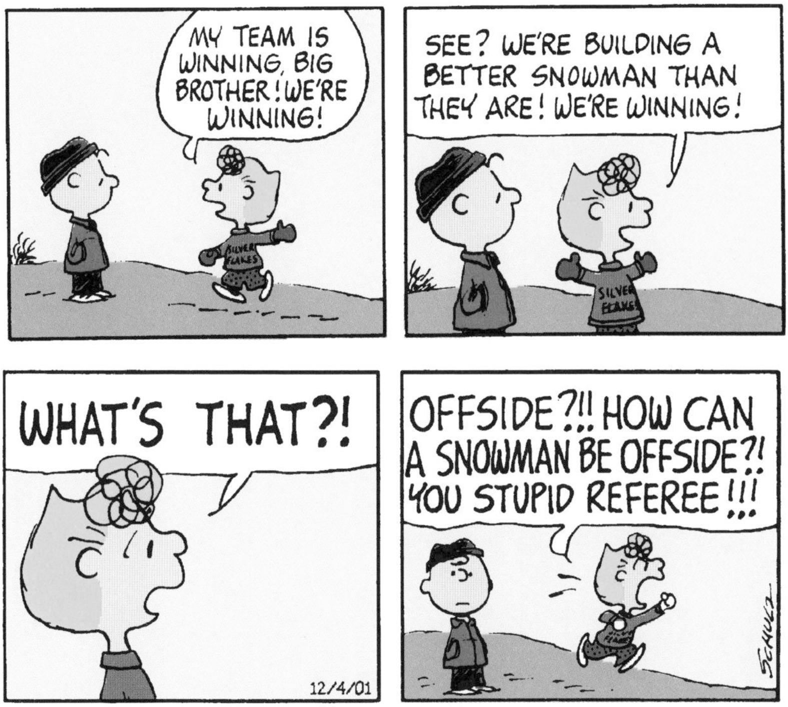
MY TEAM IS WINNING, BIG BROTHER! WE'RE WINNING!
SEE? WE'RE BUILDING A BETTER SNOWMAN THAN THEY ARE! WE'RE WINNING!
WHAT'S THAT?!
12/4/01
OFFSIDE?!! HOW CAN A SNOWMAN BE OFFSIDE?! YOU STUPID REFEREE!!!
SCHULZ

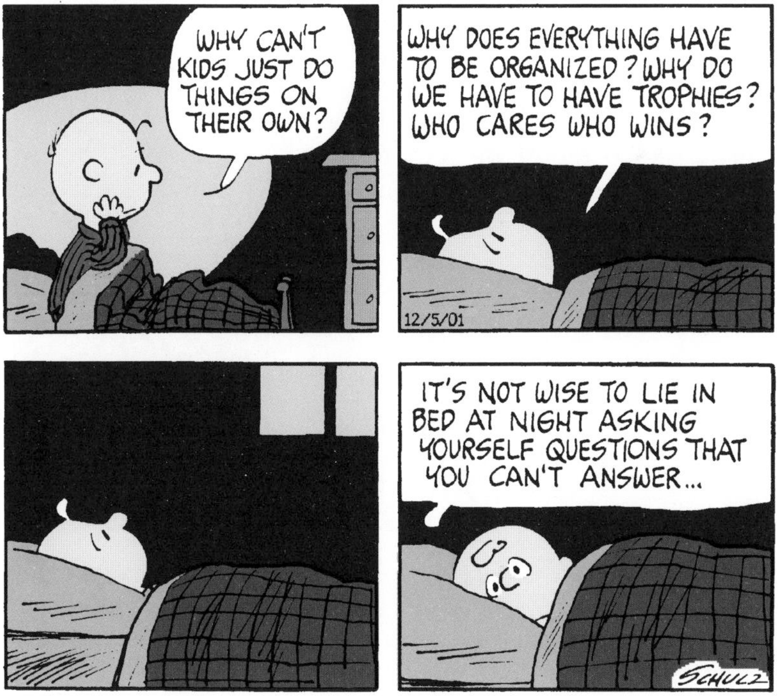
WHY CAN'T KIDS JUST DO THINGS ON THEIR OWN?
WHY DOES EVERYTHING HAVE TO BE ORGANIZED? WHY DO WE HAVE TO HAVE TROPHIES? WHO CARES WHO WINS?
12/5/01
IT'S NOT WISE TO LIE IN BED AT NIGHT ASKING YOURSELF QUESTIONS THAT YOU CAN'T ANSWER...
SCHULZ

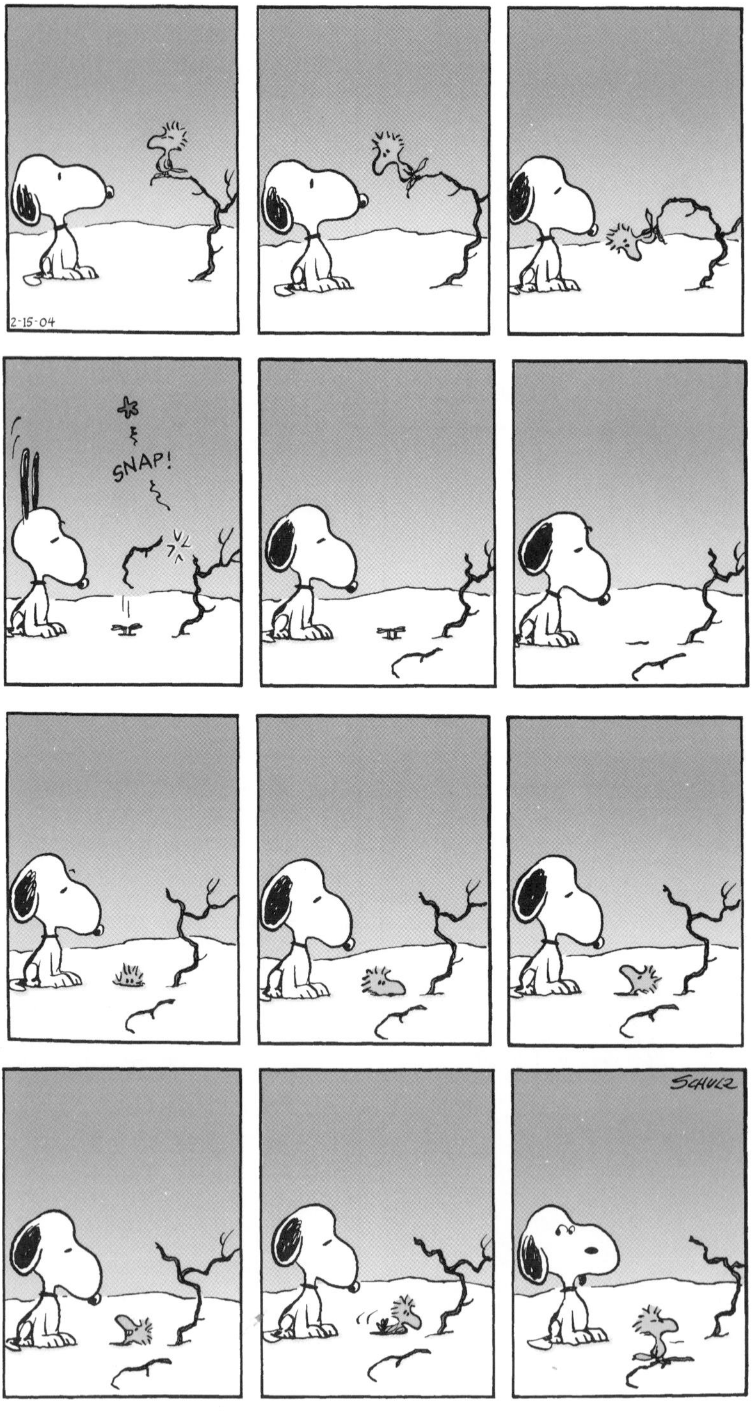
2-15-04
SNAP!
SCHULZ

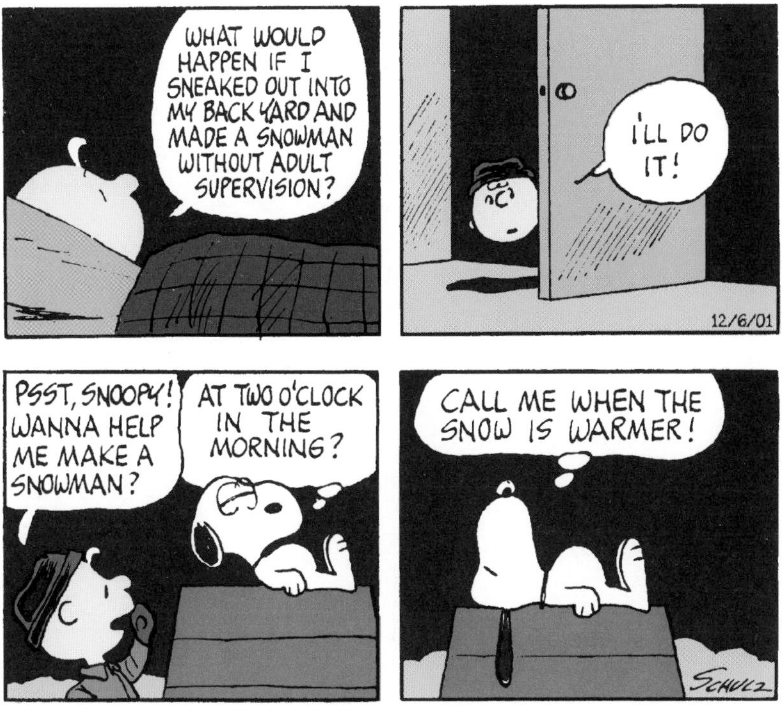
WHAT WOULD HAPPEN IF I SNEAKED OUT INTO MY BACK YARD AND MADE A SNOWMAN WITHOUT ADULT SUPERVISION?
I'LL DO IT!
12/6/01
PSST, SNOOPY! WANNA HELP ME MAKE A SNOWMAN?
AT TWO O'CLOCK IN THE MORNING?
CALL ME WHEN THE SNOW IS WARMER!
SCHULZ

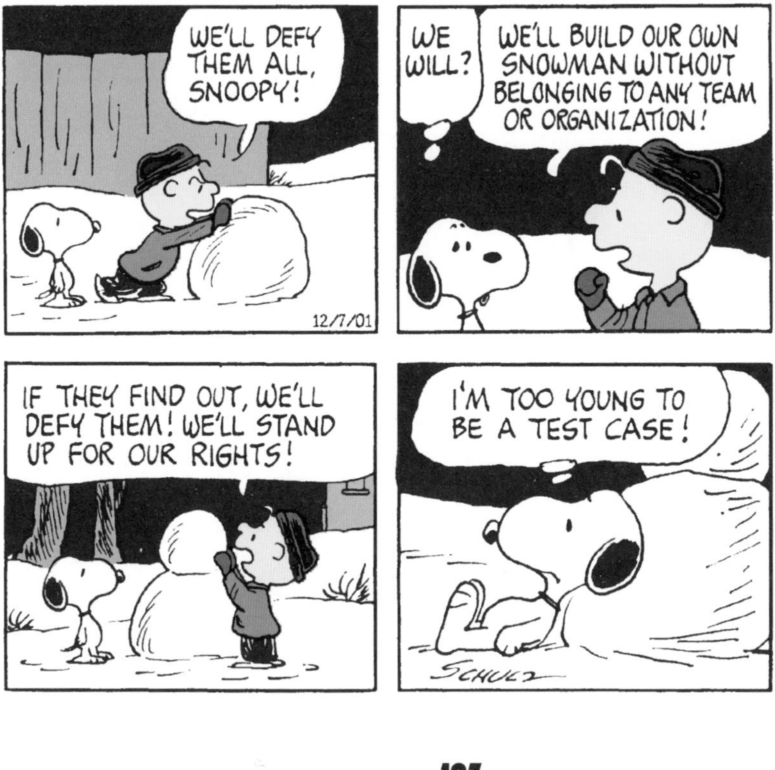
WE'LL DEFY THEM ALL, SNOOPY!
12/7/01
WE WILL?
WE'LL BUILD OUR OWN SNOWMAN WITHOUT BELONGING TO ANY TEAM OR ORGANIZATION!
IF THEY FIND OUT, WE'LL DEFY THEM! WE'LL STAND UP FOR OUR RIGHTS!
I'M TOO YOUNG TO BE A TEST CASE!
SCHULZ

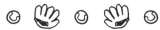

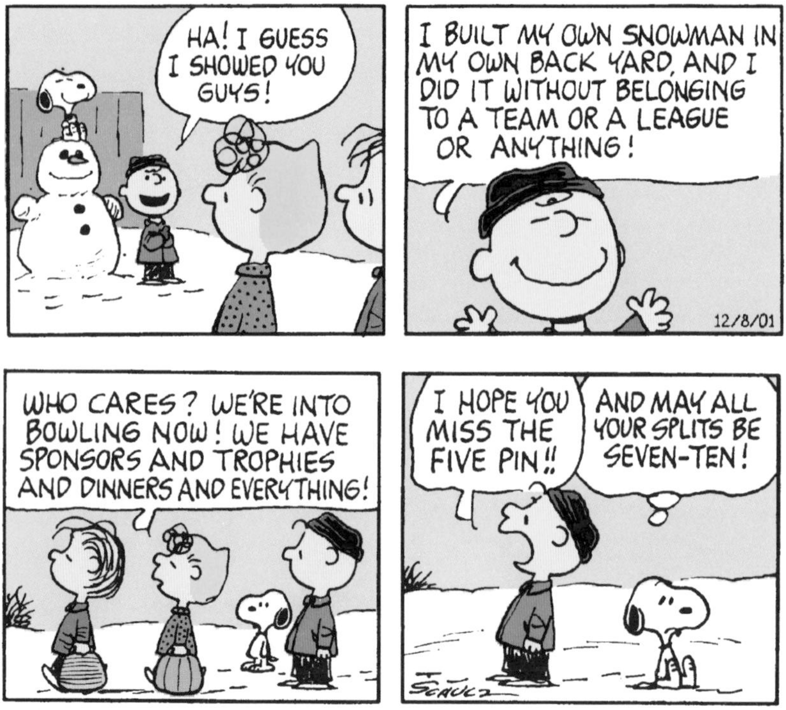
HA! I GUESS I SHOWED YOU GUYS!
I BUILT MY OWN SNOWMAN IN MY OWN BACK YARD, AND I DID IT WITHOUT BELONGING TO A TEAM OR A LEAGUE OR ANYTHING!
12/8/01
WHO CARES? WE'RE INTO BOWLING NOW! WE HAVE SPONSORS AND TROPHIES AND DINNERS AND EVERYTHING!
I HOPE YOU MISS THE FIVE PIN!!
AND MAY ALL YOUR SPLITS BE SEVEN-TEN!
SCHULZ

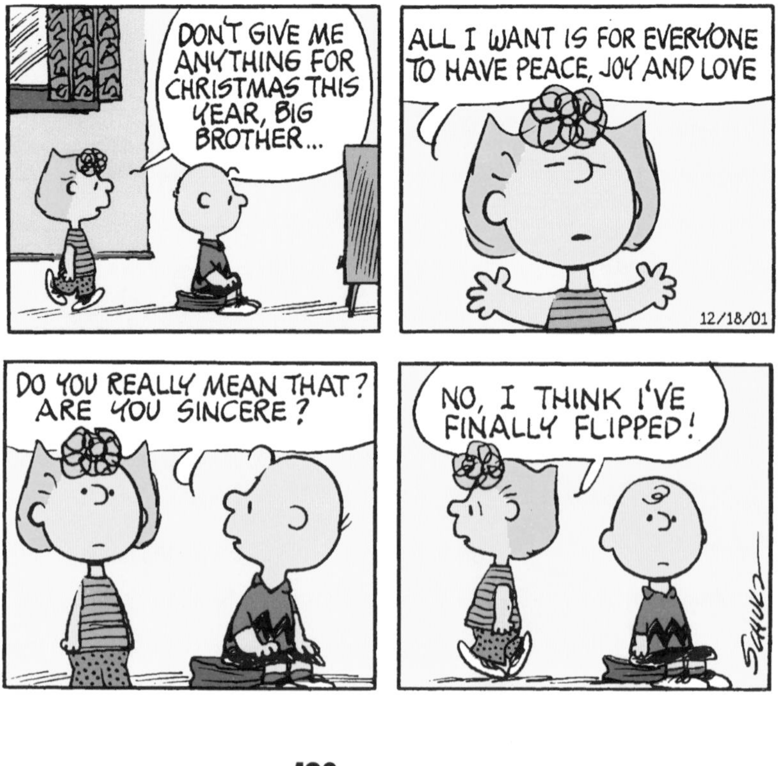
DON'T GIVE ME ANYTHING FOR CHRISTMAS THIS YEAR, BIG BROTHER...
ALL I WANT IS FOR EVERYONE TO HAVE PEACE, JOY AND LOVE
12/18/01
DO YOU REALLY MEAN THAT? ARE YOU SINCERE?
NO, I THINK I'VE FINALLY FLIPPED!
SCHULZ

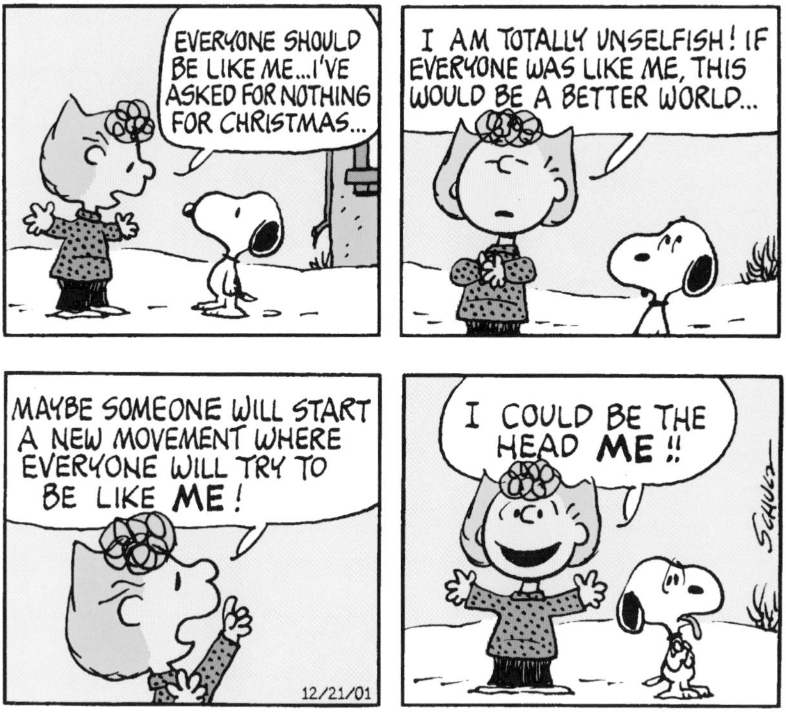
EVERYONE SHOULD BE LIKE ME...I'VE ASKED FOR NOTHING FOR CHRISTMAS...
I AM TOTALLY UNSELFISH! IF EVERYONE WAS LIKE ME, THIS WOULD BE A BETTER WORLD...
MAYBE SOMEONE WILL START A NEW MOVEMENT WHERE EVERYONE WILL TRY TO BE LIKE **ME**!
12/21/01
I COULD BE THE HEAD **ME**!!
SCHULZ

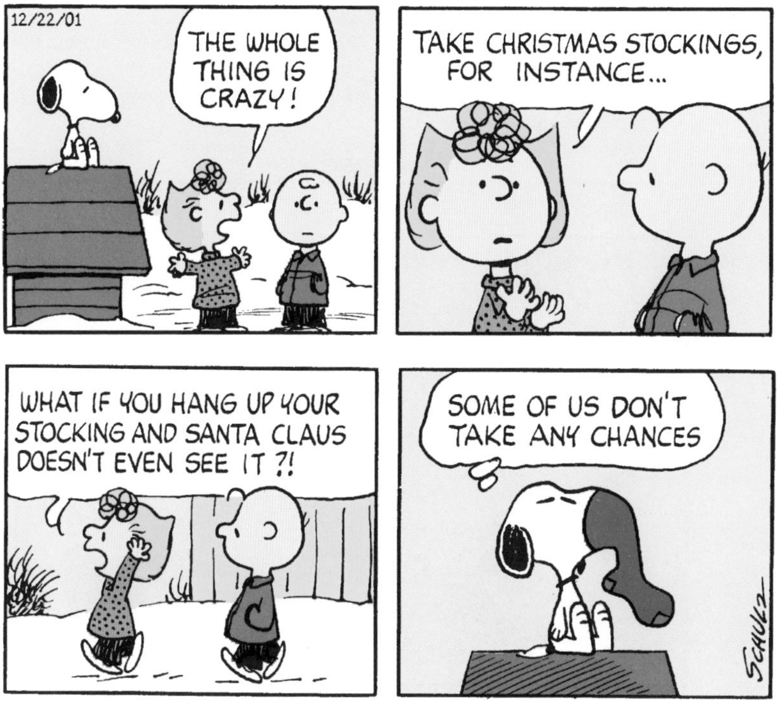
12/22/01
THE WHOLE THING IS CRAZY!
TAKE CHRISTMAS STOCKINGS, FOR INSTANCE...
WHAT IF YOU HANG UP YOUR STOCKING AND SANTA CLAUS DOESN'T EVEN SEE IT ?!
SOME OF US DON'T TAKE ANY CHANCES
SCHULZ

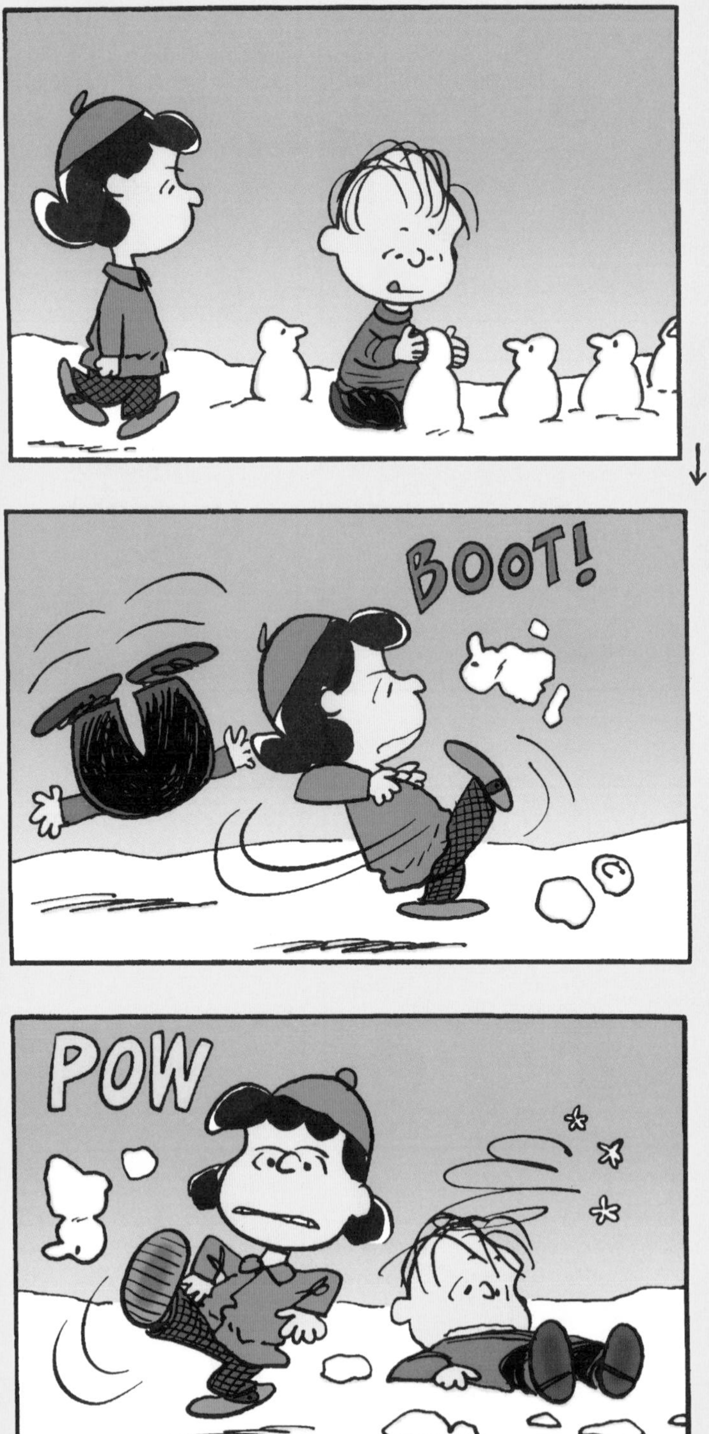
BOOT!
POW

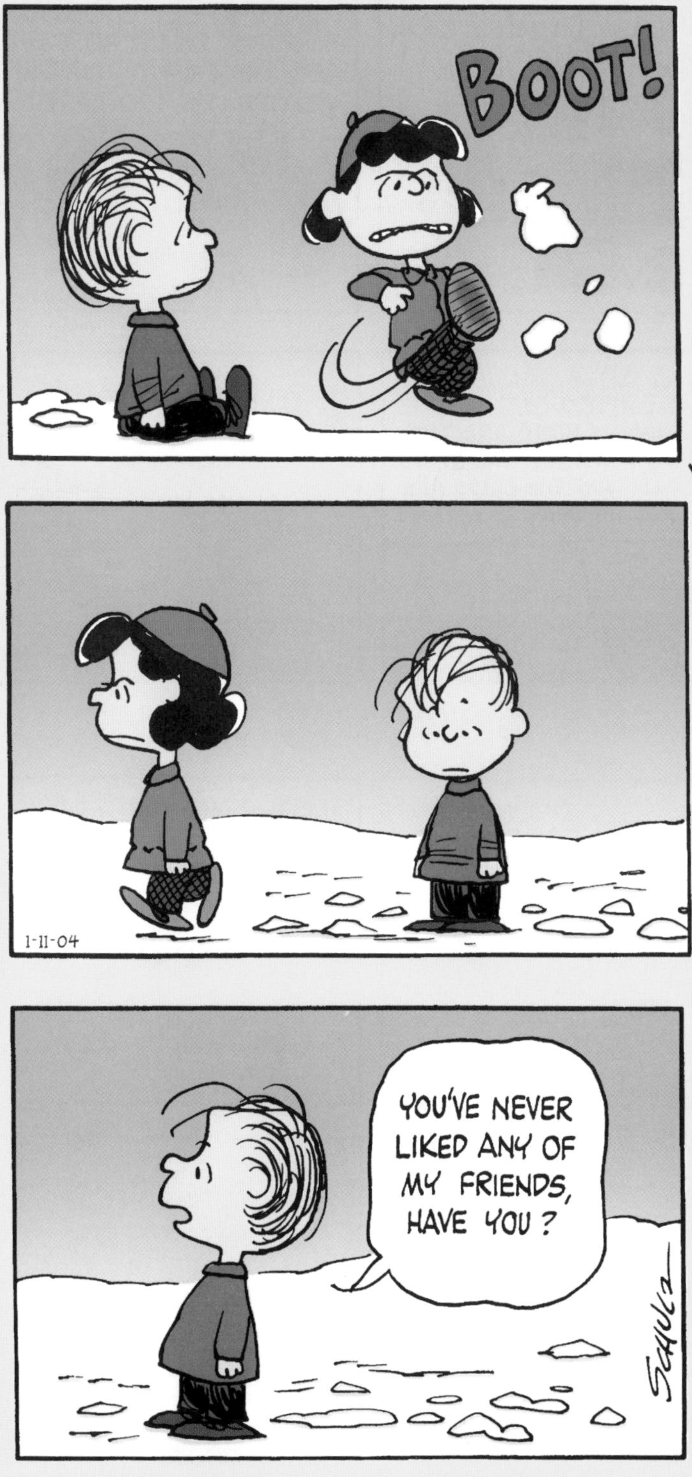
BOOT!
1-11-04
YOU'VE NEVER LIKED ANY OF MY FRIENDS, HAVE YOU ?
SCHULZ

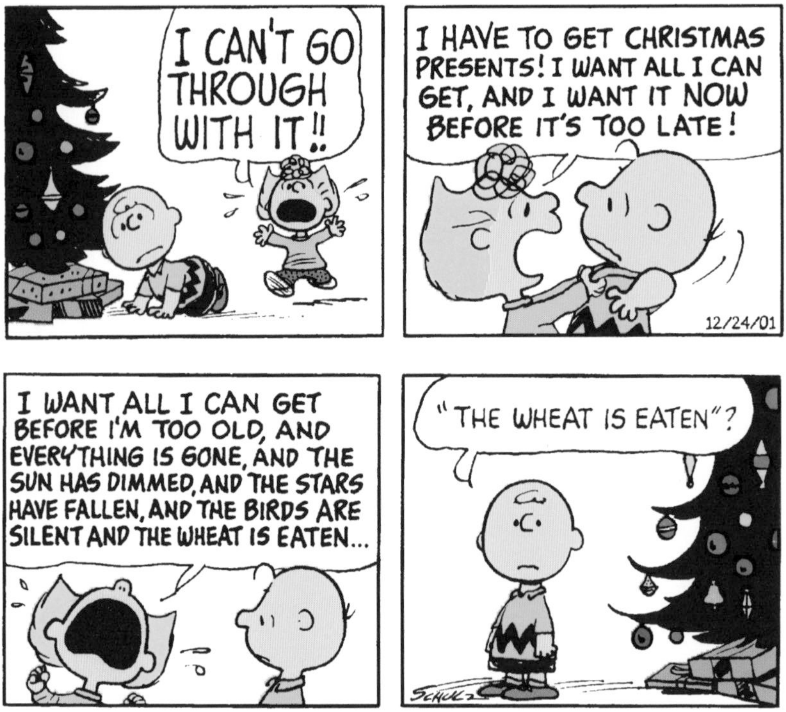
I CAN'T GO THROUGH WITH IT!!
I HAVE TO GET CHRISTMAS PRESENTS! I WANT ALL I CAN GET, AND I WANT IT NOW BEFORE IT'S TOO LATE!
12/24/01
I WANT ALL I CAN GET BEFORE I'M TOO OLD, AND EVERYTHING IS GONE, AND THE SUN HAS DIMMED, AND THE STARS HAVE FALLEN, AND THE BIRDS ARE SILENT AND THE WHEAT IS EATEN...
"THE WHEAT IS EATEN"?
SCHULZ

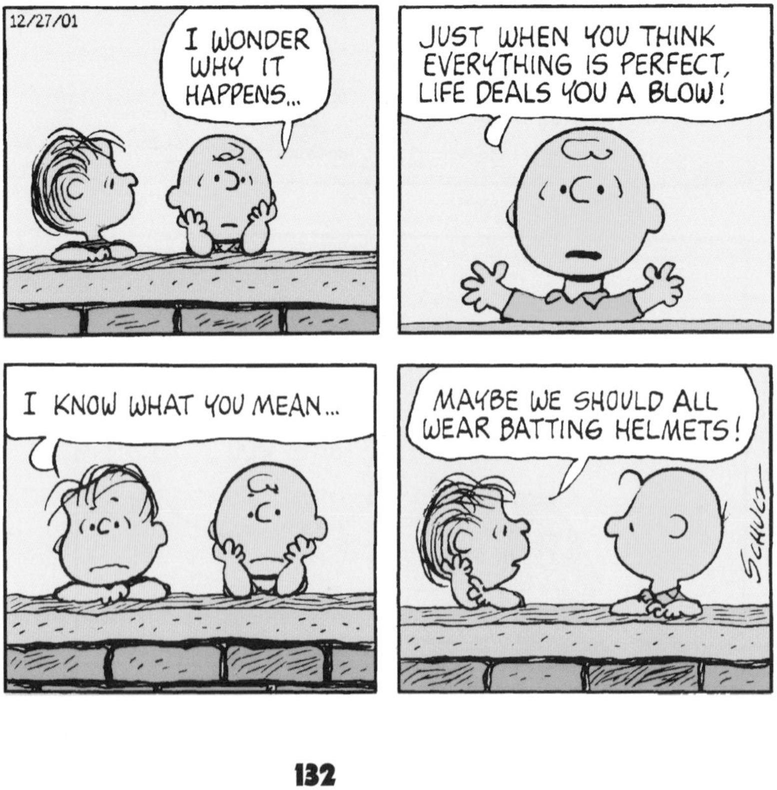
12/27/01
I WONDER WHY IT HAPPENS...
JUST WHEN YOU THINK EVERYTHING IS PERFECT, LIFE DEALS YOU A BLOW!
I KNOW WHAT YOU MEAN...
MAYBE WE SHOULD ALL WEAR BATTING HELMETS!
SCHULZ

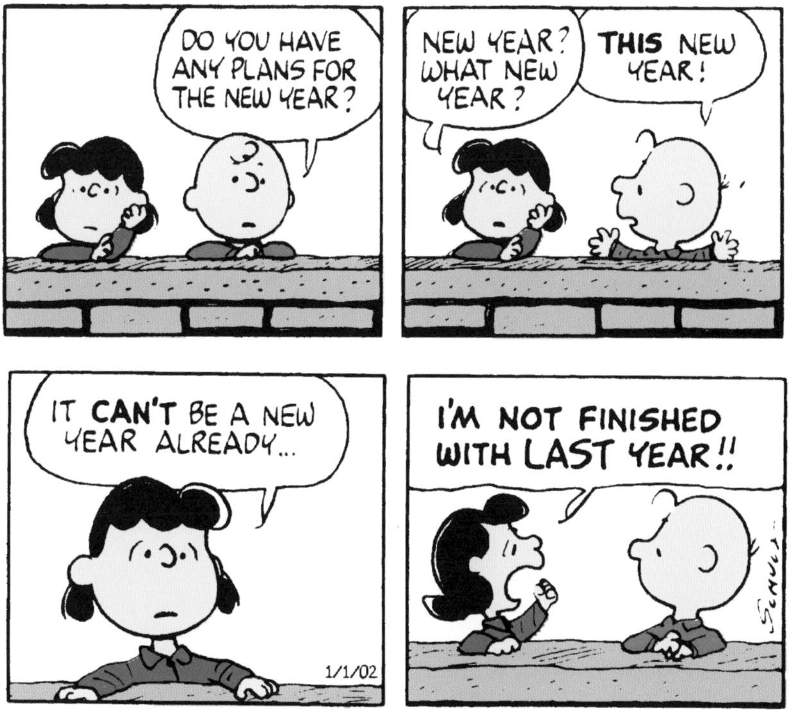
DO YOU HAVE ANY PLANS FOR THE NEW YEAR?
NEW YEAR? WHAT NEW YEAR?
THIS NEW YEAR!
IT CAN'T BE A NEW YEAR ALREADY...
1/1/02
I'M NOT FINISHED WITH LAST YEAR!!
SCHULZ

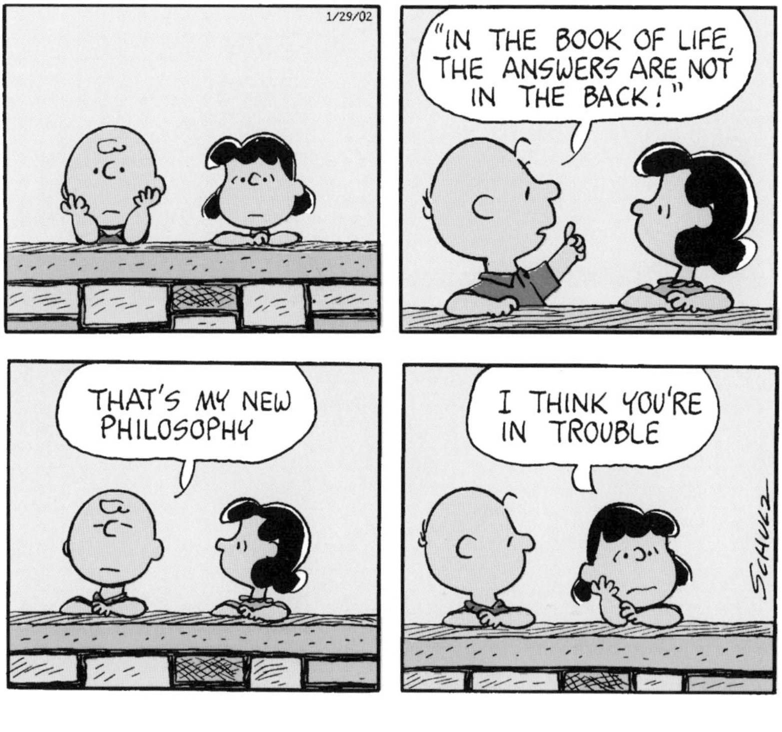
1/29/02
"IN THE BOOK OF LIFE, THE ANSWERS ARE NOT IN THE BACK!"
THAT'S MY NEW PHILOSOPHY
I THINK YOU'RE IN TROUBLE
SCHULZ

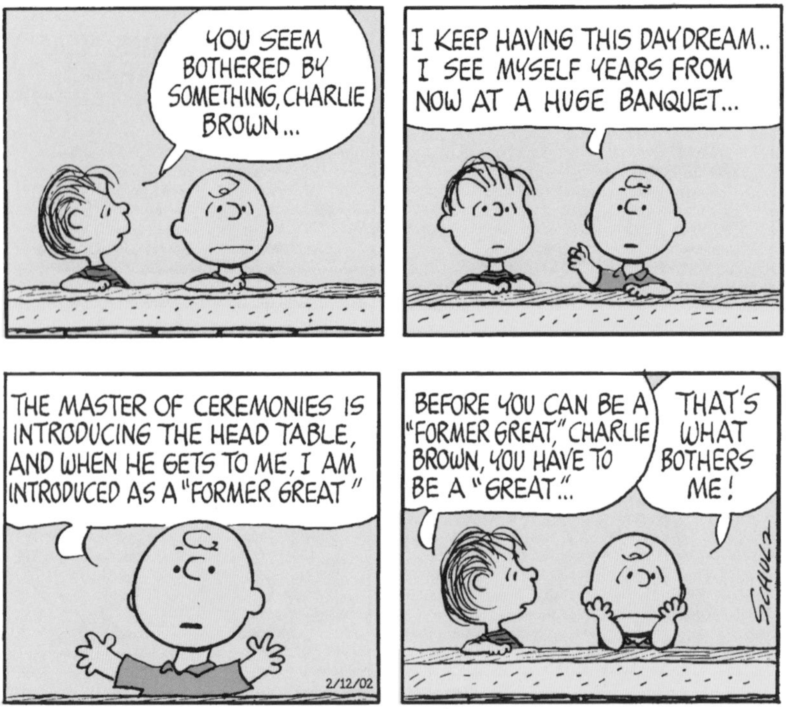
YOU SEEM BOTHERED BY SOMETHING, CHARLIE BROWN...
I KEEP HAVING THIS DAYDREAM.. I SEE MYSELF YEARS FROM NOW AT A HUGE BANQUET...
THE MASTER OF CEREMONIES IS INTRODUCING THE HEAD TABLE, AND WHEN HE GETS TO ME, I AM INTRODUCED AS A "FORMER GREAT"
2/12/02
BEFORE YOU CAN BE A "FORMER GREAT," CHARLIE BROWN, YOU HAVE TO BE A "GREAT."...
THAT'S WHAT BOTHERS ME!
SCHULZ

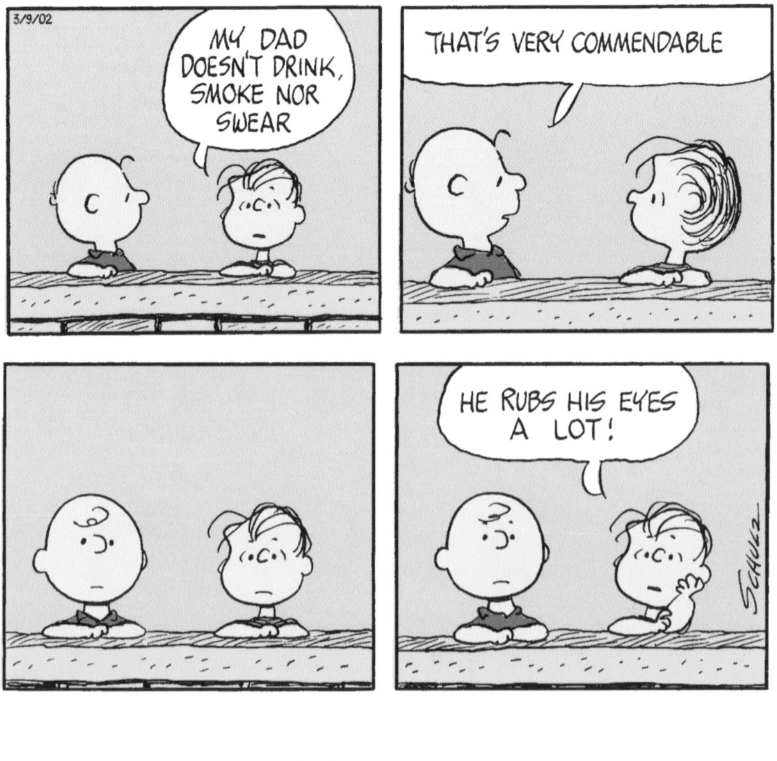
3/9/02
MY DAD DOESN'T DRINK, SMOKE NOR SWEAR
THAT'S VERY COMMENDABLE
HE RUBS HIS EYES A LOT!
SCHULZ

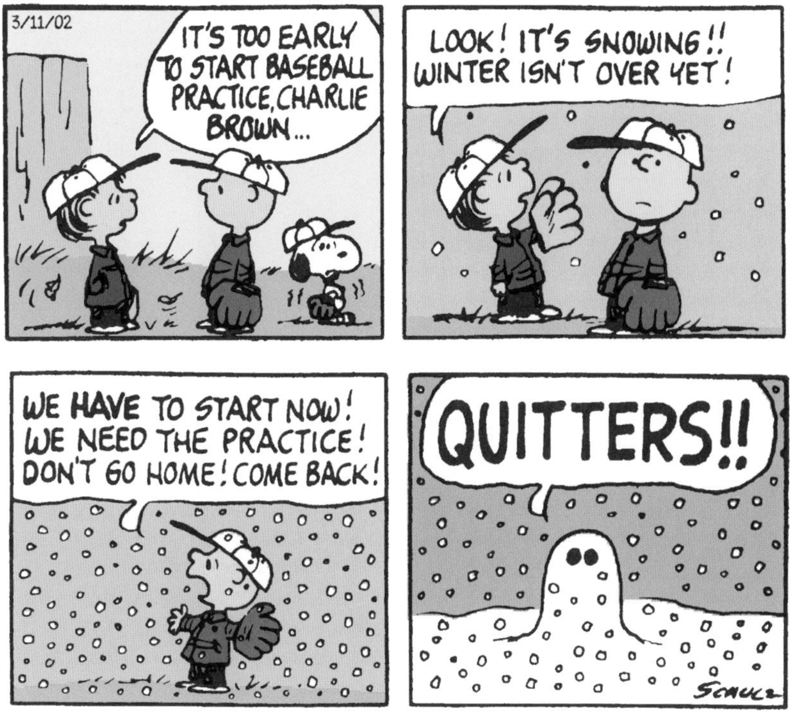
3/11/02
IT'S TOO EARLY TO START BASEBALL PRACTICE, CHARLIE BROWN...
LOOK! IT'S SNOWING!! WINTER ISN'T OVER YET!
WE HAVE TO START NOW! WE NEED THE PRACTICE! DON'T GO HOME! COME BACK!
QUITTERS!!
SCHULZ

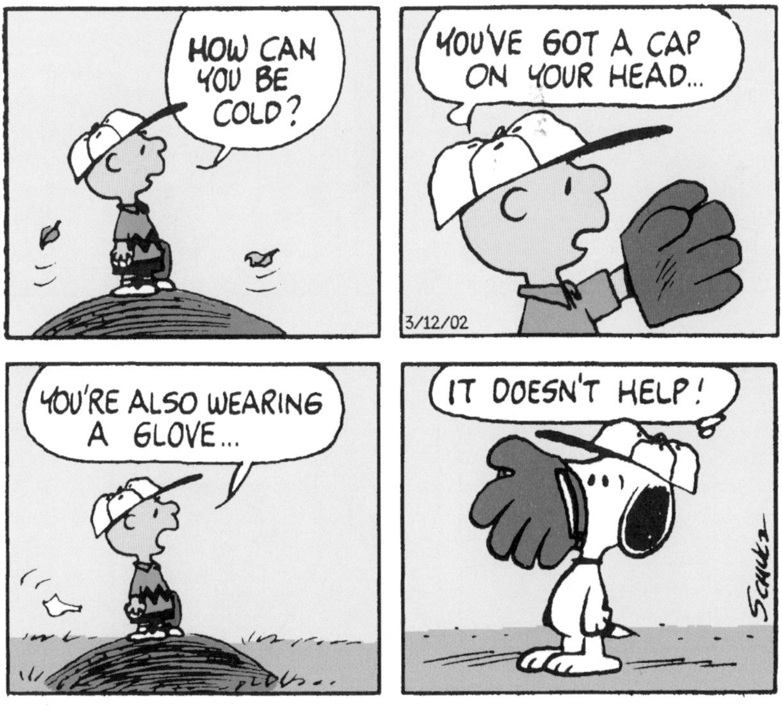
HOW CAN YOU BE COLD?
YOU'VE GOT A CAP ON YOUR HEAD...
3/12/02
YOU'RE ALSO WEARING A GLOVE...
IT DOESN'T HELP!
SCHULZ

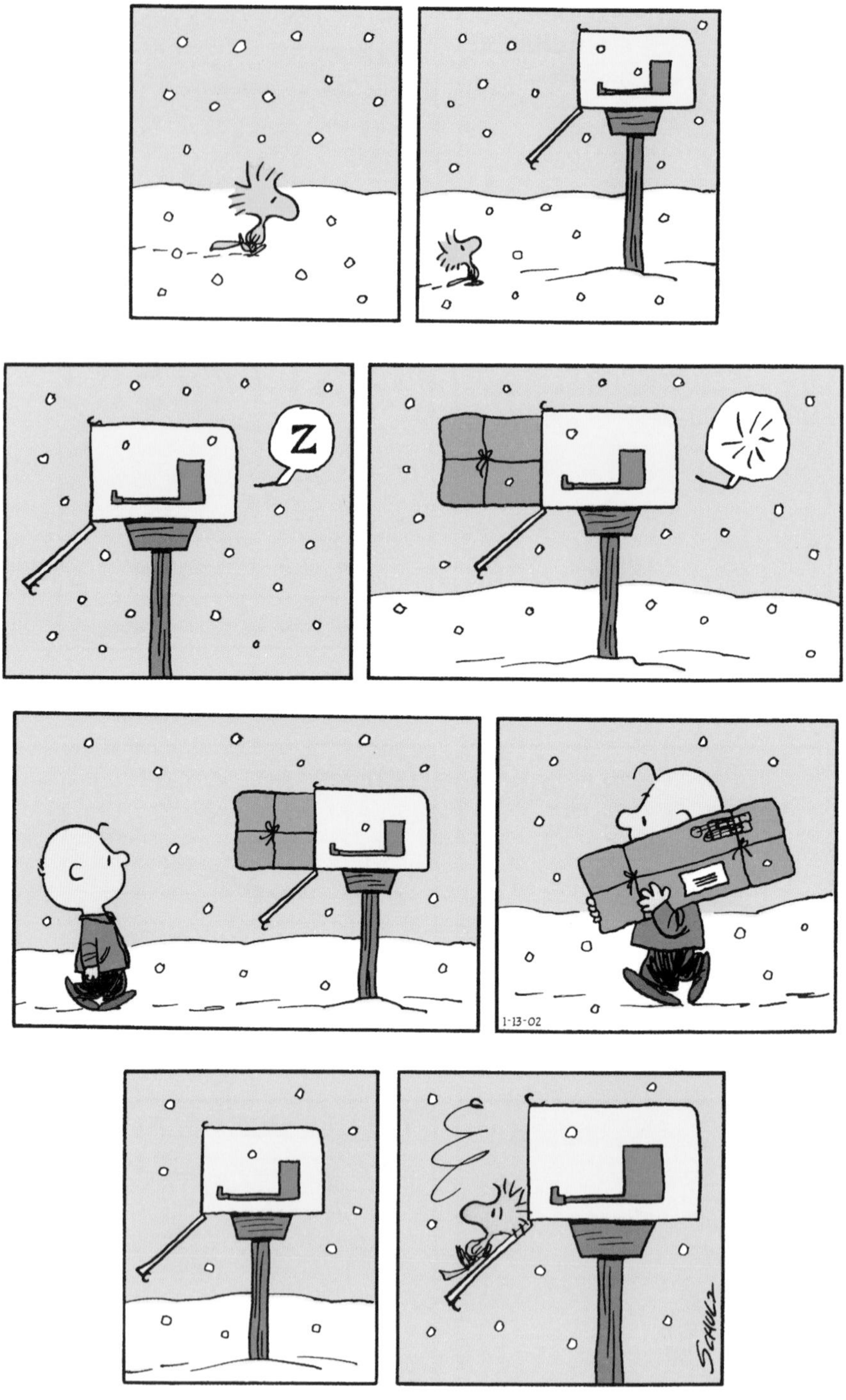
Z
1-13-02
SCHULZ

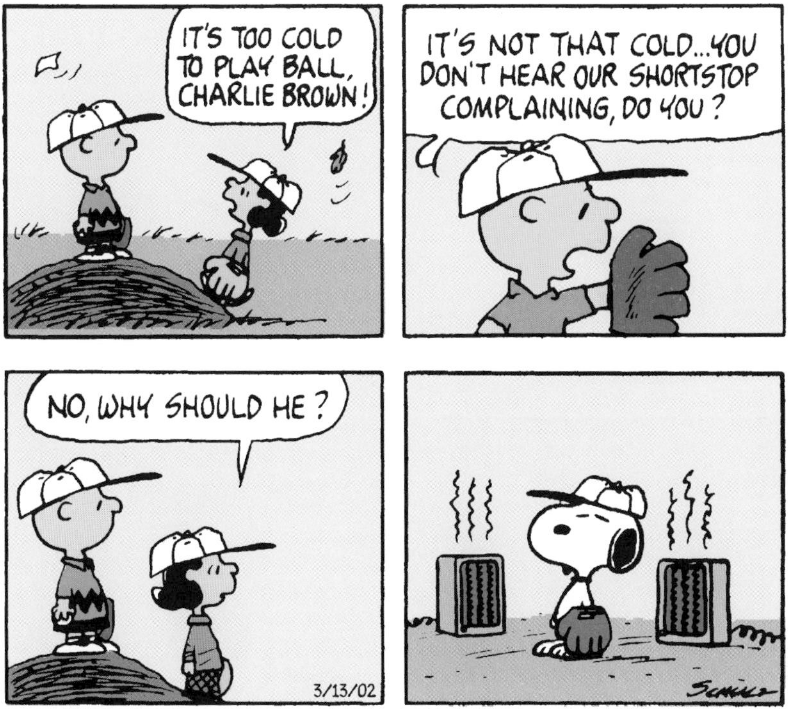
IT'S TOO COLD TO PLAY BALL, CHARLIE BROWN!
IT'S NOT THAT COLD...YOU DON'T HEAR OUR SHORTSTOP COMPLAINING, DO YOU?
NO, WHY SHOULD HE?
3/13/02
SCHULZ

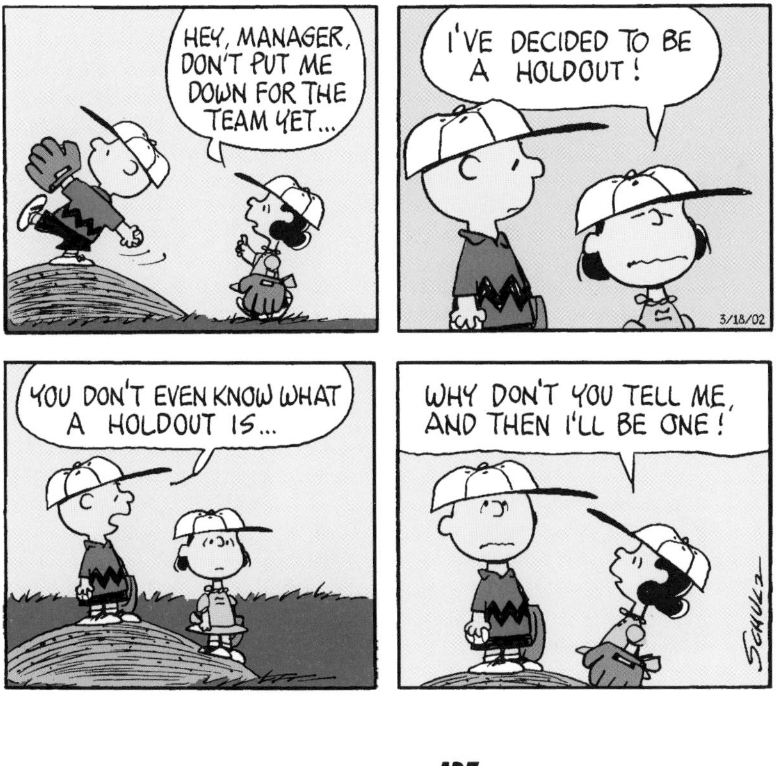
HEY, MANAGER, DON'T PUT ME DOWN FOR THE TEAM YET...
I'VE DECIDED TO BE A HOLDOUT!
3/18/02
YOU DON'T EVEN KNOW WHAT A HOLDOUT IS...
WHY DON'T YOU TELL ME, AND THEN I'LL BE ONE!
SCHULZ

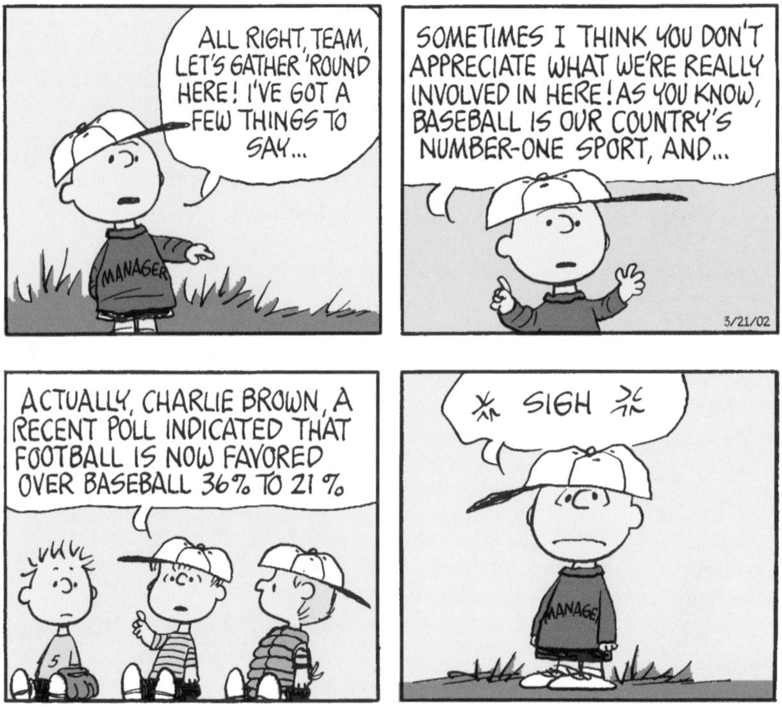
ALL RIGHT, TEAM, LET'S GATHER 'ROUND HERE! I'VE GOT A FEW THINGS TO SAY...
MANAGER
SOMETIMES I THINK YOU DON'T APPRECIATE WHAT WE'RE REALLY INVOLVED IN HERE! AS YOU KNOW, BASEBALL IS OUR COUNTRY'S NUMBER-ONE SPORT, AND...
3/21/02
ACTUALLY, CHARLIE BROWN, A RECENT POLL INDICATED THAT FOOTBALL IS NOW FAVORED OVER BASEBALL 36% TO 21%
SIGH

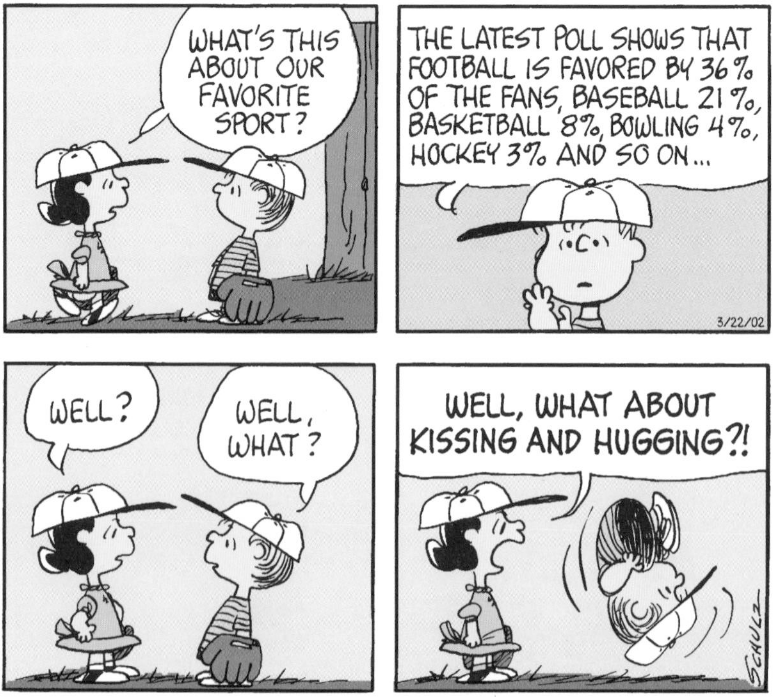
WHAT'S THIS ABOUT OUR FAVORITE SPORT?
THE LATEST POLL SHOWS THAT FOOTBALL IS FAVORED BY 36% OF THE FANS, BASEBALL 21%, BASKETBALL 8%, BOWLING 4%, HOCKEY 3% AND SO ON...
3/22/02
WELL?
WELL, WHAT?
WELL, WHAT ABOUT KISSING AND HUGGING?!
SCHULZ

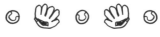

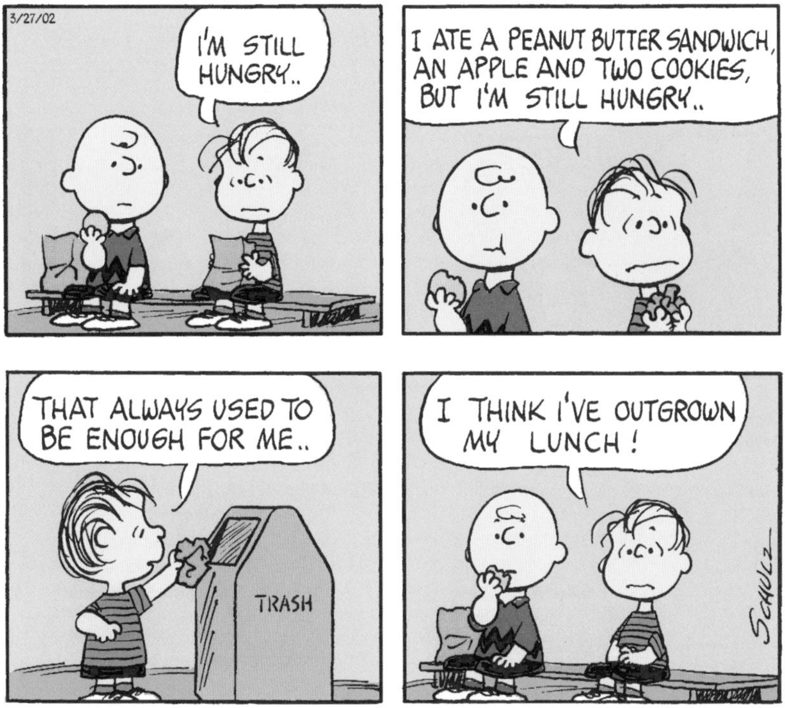
3/27/02
I'M STILL HUNGRY..
I ATE A PEANUT BUTTER SANDWICH, AN APPLE AND TWO COOKIES, BUT I'M STILL HUNGRY..
THAT ALWAYS USED TO BE ENOUGH FOR ME..
TRASH
I THINK I'VE OUTGROWN MY LUNCH!
SCHULZ

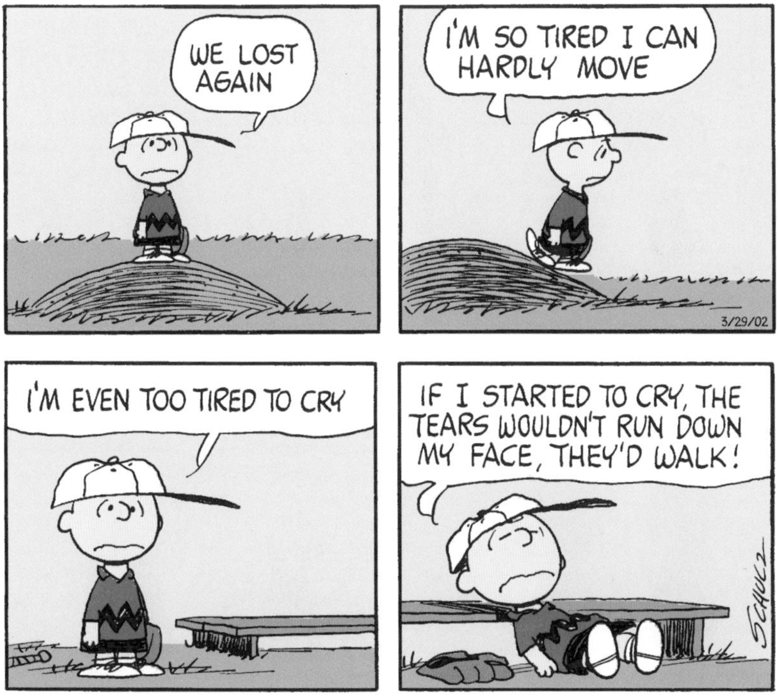
WE LOST AGAIN
I'M SO TIRED I CAN HARDLY MOVE
3/29/02
I'M EVEN TOO TIRED TO CRY
IF I STARTED TO CRY, THE TEARS WOULDN'T RUN DOWN MY FACE, THEY'D WALK!
SCHULZ

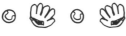

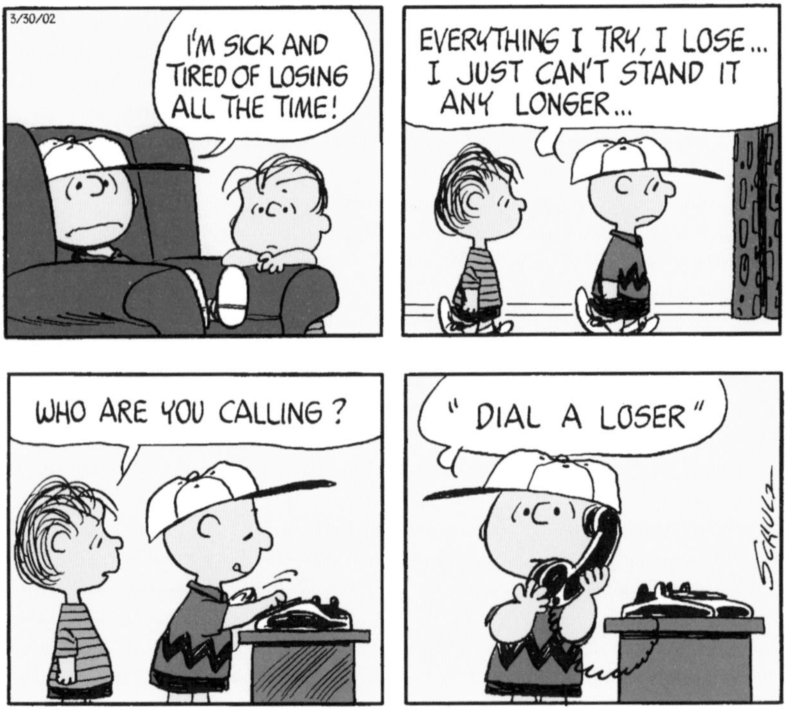
3/30/02
I'M SICK AND TIRED OF LOSING ALL THE TIME!
EVERYTHING I TRY, I LOSE... I JUST CAN'T STAND IT ANY LONGER...
WHO ARE YOU CALLING?
" DIAL A LOSER "
SCHULZ

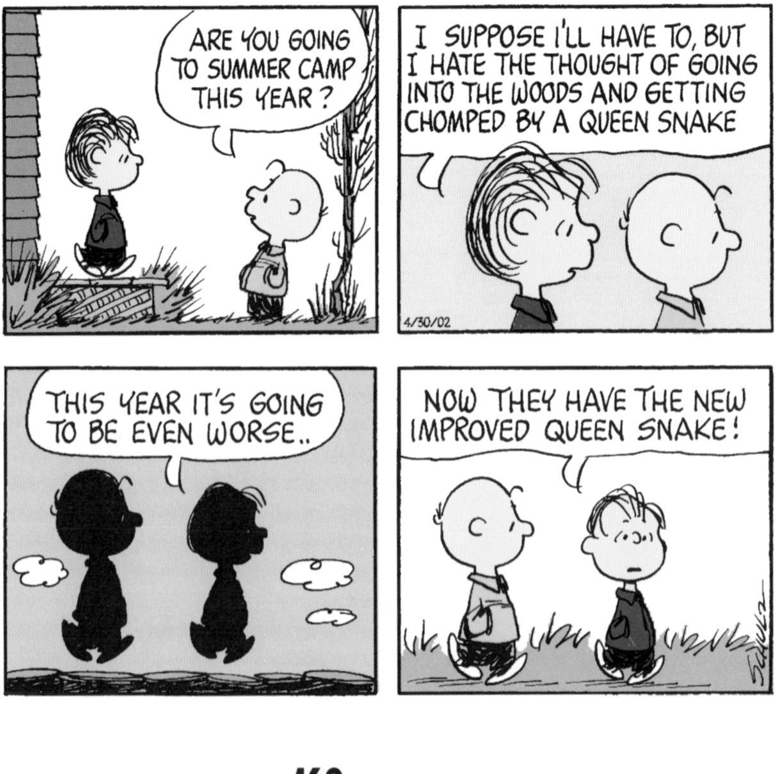
ARE YOU GOING TO SUMMER CAMP THIS YEAR?
I SUPPOSE I'LL HAVE TO, BUT I HATE THE THOUGHT OF GOING INTO THE WOODS AND GETTING CHOMPED BY A QUEEN SNAKE
4/30/02
THIS YEAR IT'S GOING TO BE EVEN WORSE..
NOW THEY HAVE THE NEW IMPROVED QUEEN SNAKE!
SCHULZ

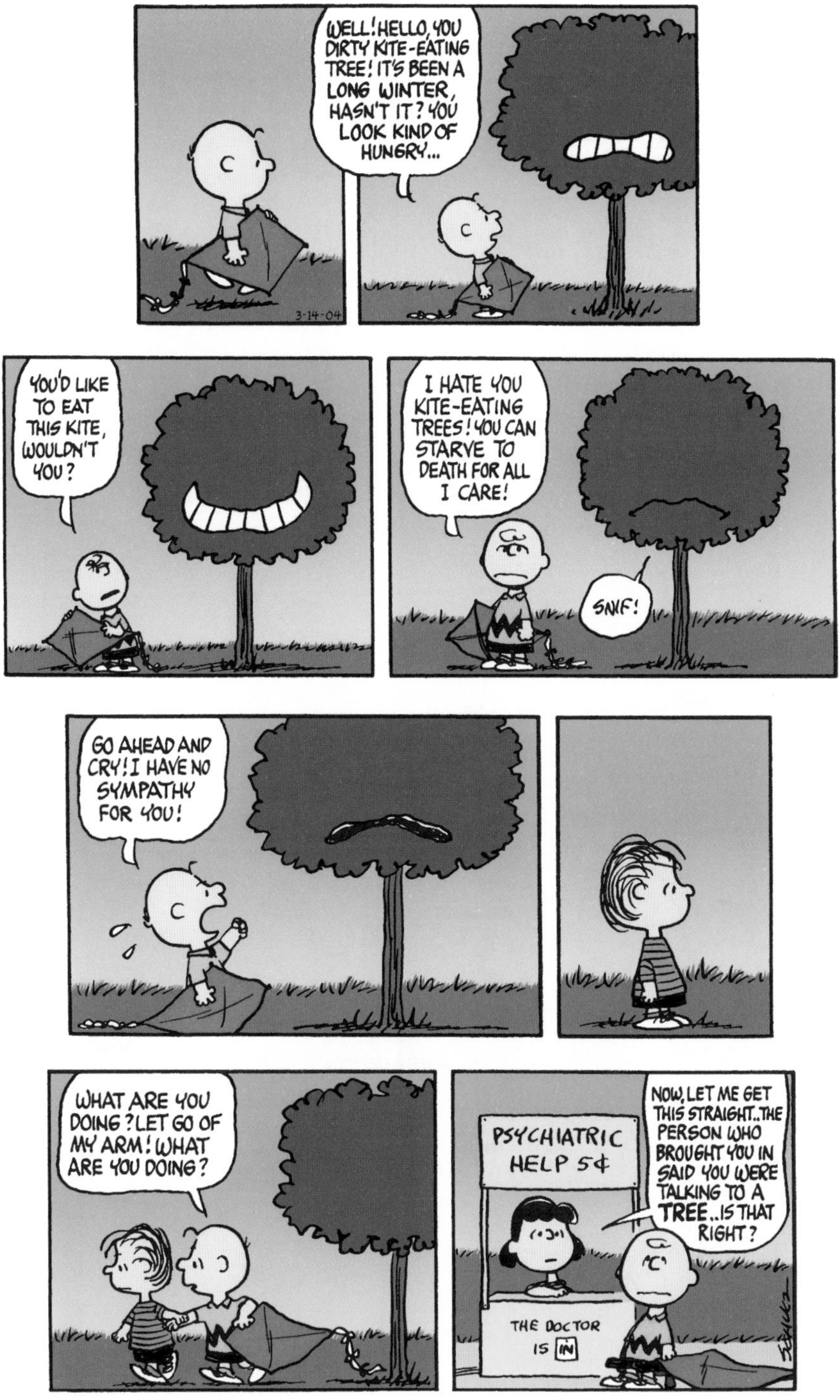
WELL! HELLO, YOU DIRTY KITE-EATING TREE! IT'S BEEN A LONG WINTER, HASN'T IT? YOU LOOK KIND OF HUNGRY...
3-14-04
YOU'D LIKE TO EAT THIS KITE, WOULDN'T YOU?
I HATE YOU KITE-EATING TREES! YOU CAN STARVE TO DEATH FOR ALL I CARE!
SNIF!
GO AHEAD AND CRY! I HAVE NO SYMPATHY FOR YOU!
WHAT ARE YOU DOING? LET GO OF MY ARM! WHAT ARE YOU DOING?
PSYCHIATRIC HELP 5¢
THE DOCTOR IS IN
NOW, LET ME GET THIS STRAIGHT.. THE PERSON WHO BROUGHT YOU IN SAID YOU WERE TALKING TO A TREE.. IS THAT RIGHT?
SCHULZ

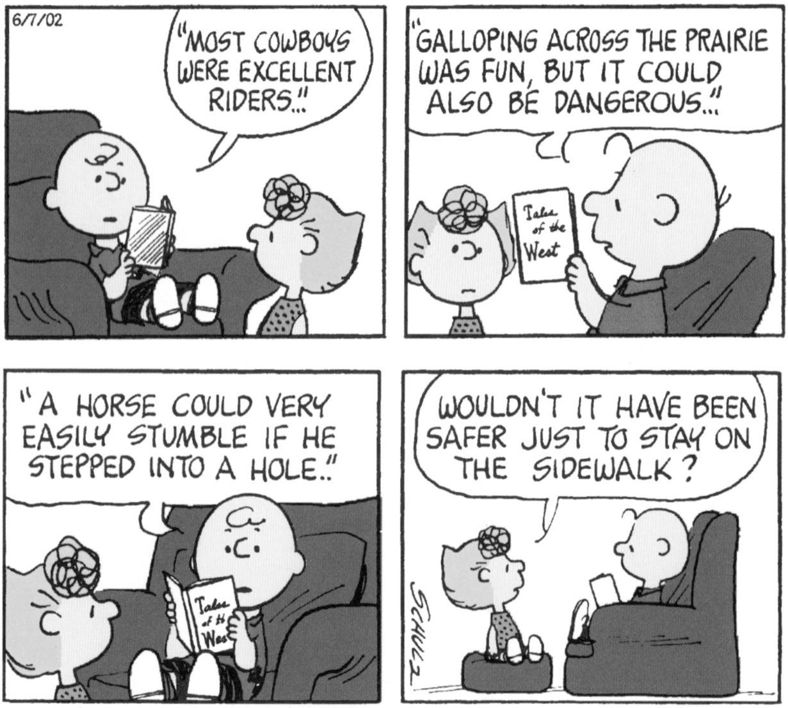
6/7/02
"MOST COWBOYS WERE EXCELLENT RIDERS.."
"GALLOPING ACROSS THE PRAIRIE WAS FUN, BUT IT COULD ALSO BE DANGEROUS.."
Tales of the West
"A HORSE COULD VERY EASILY STUMBLE IF HE STEPPED INTO A HOLE.."
WOULDN'T IT HAVE BEEN SAFER JUST TO STAY ON THE SIDEWALK?
SCHULZ

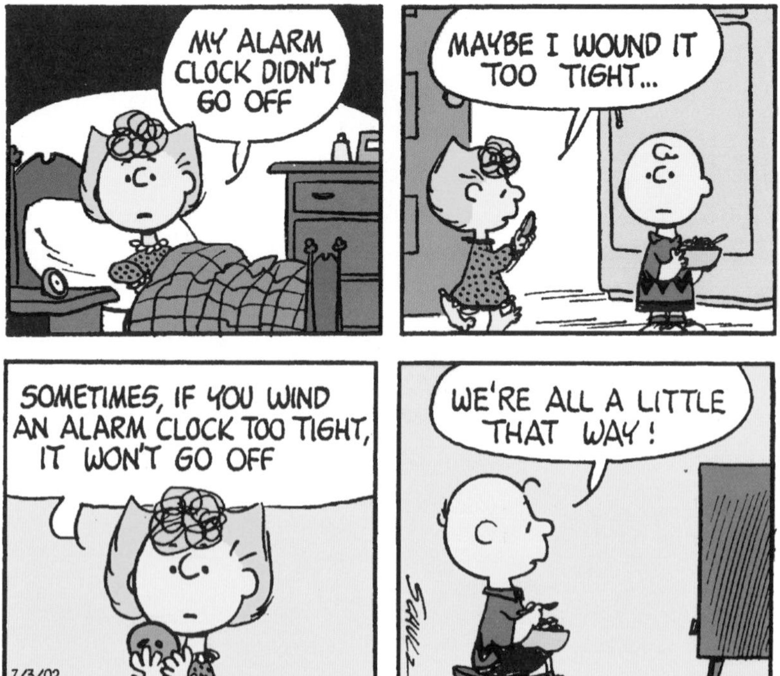
MY ALARM CLOCK DIDN'T GO OFF
MAYBE I WOUND IT TOO TIGHT...
SOMETIMES, IF YOU WIND AN ALARM CLOCK TOO TIGHT, IT WON'T GO OFF
7/3/02
WE'RE ALL A LITTLE THAT WAY!
SCHULZ

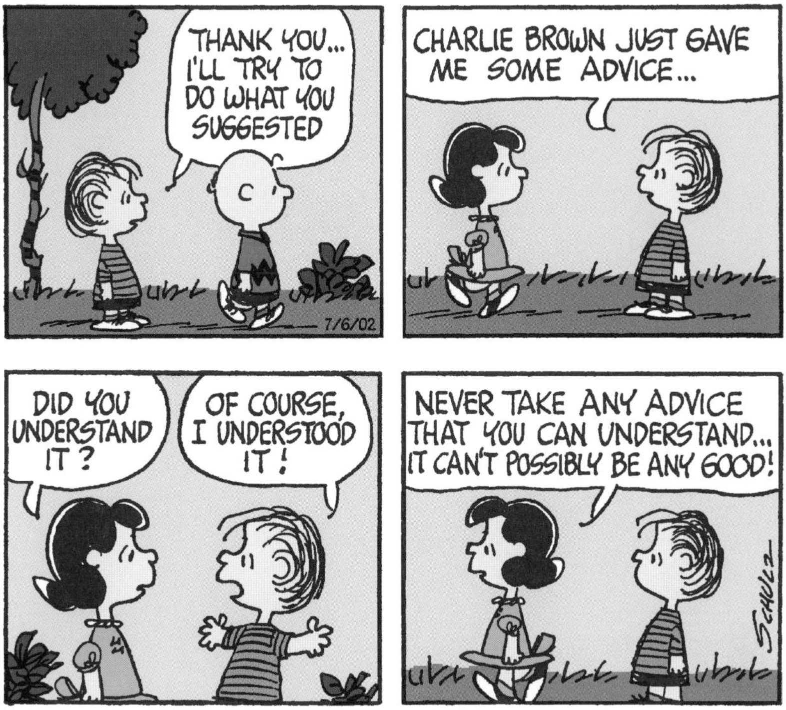
THANK YOU... I'LL TRY TO DO WHAT YOU SUGGESTED
7/6/02
CHARLIE BROWN JUST GAVE ME SOME ADVICE...
DID YOU UNDERSTAND IT?
OF COURSE, I UNDERSTOOD IT!
NEVER TAKE ANY ADVICE THAT YOU CAN UNDERSTAND... IT CAN'T POSSIBLY BE ANY GOOD!
SCHULZ

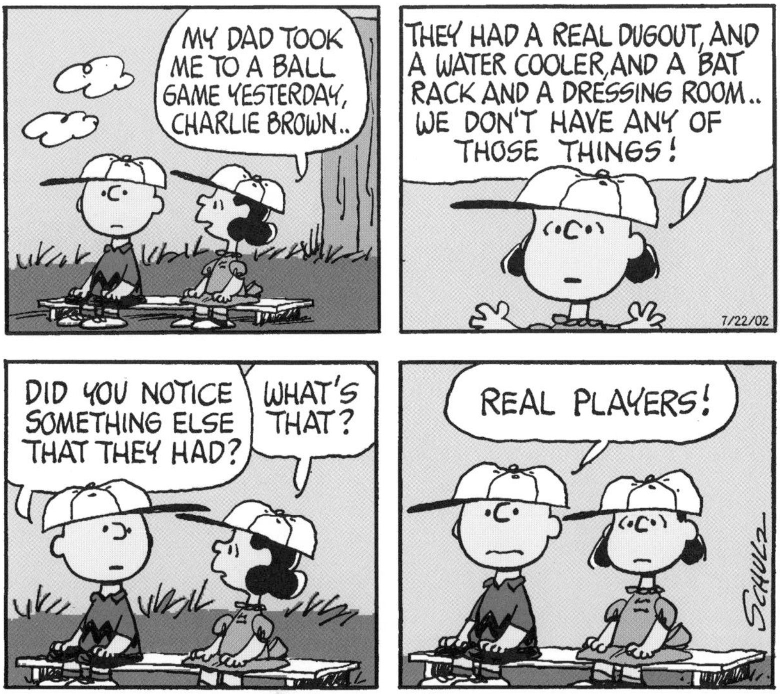
MY DAD TOOK ME TO A BALL GAME YESTERDAY, CHARLIE BROWN..
THEY HAD A REAL DUGOUT, AND A WATER COOLER, AND A BAT RACK AND A DRESSING ROOM.. WE DON'T HAVE ANY OF THOSE THINGS!
7/22/02
DID YOU NOTICE SOMETHING ELSE THAT THEY HAD?
WHAT'S THAT?
REAL PLAYERS!
SCHULZ

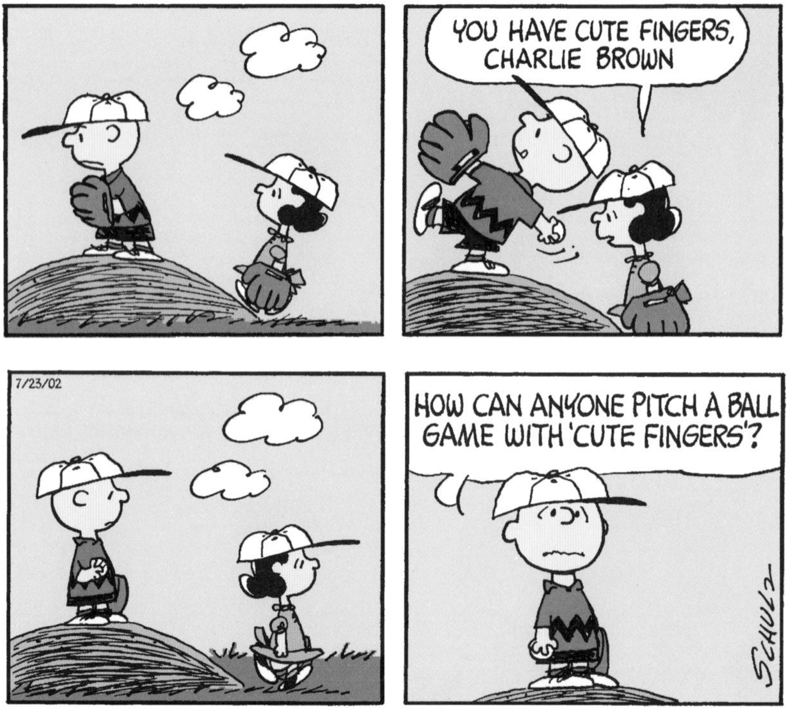
YOU HAVE CUTE FINGERS, CHARLIE BROWN
7/23/02
HOW CAN ANYONE PITCH A BALL GAME WITH 'CUTE FINGERS'?
SCHULZ

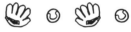

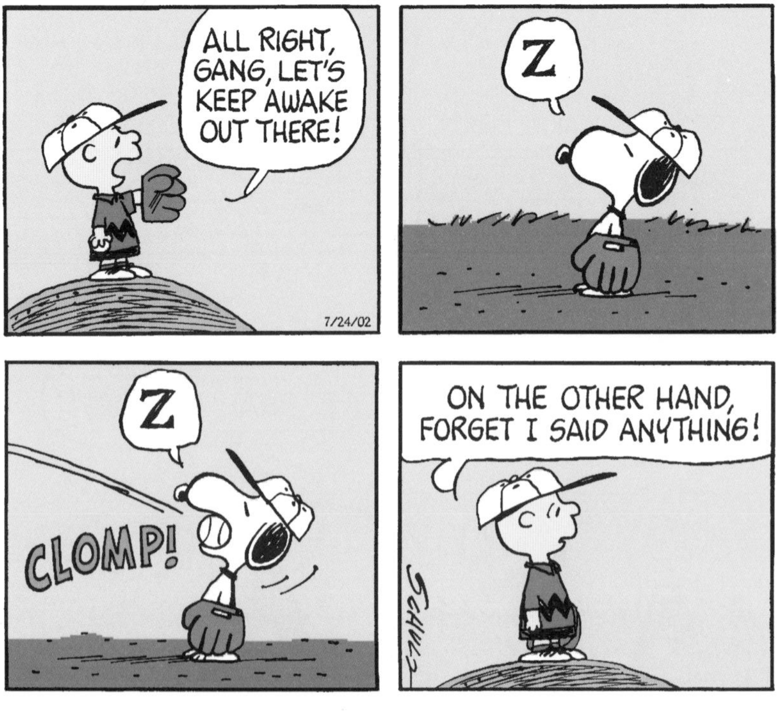
ALL RIGHT, GANG, LET'S KEEP AWAKE OUT THERE!
7/24/02
Z
Z
CLOMP!
ON THE OTHER HAND, FORGET I SAID ANYTHING!
SCHULZ

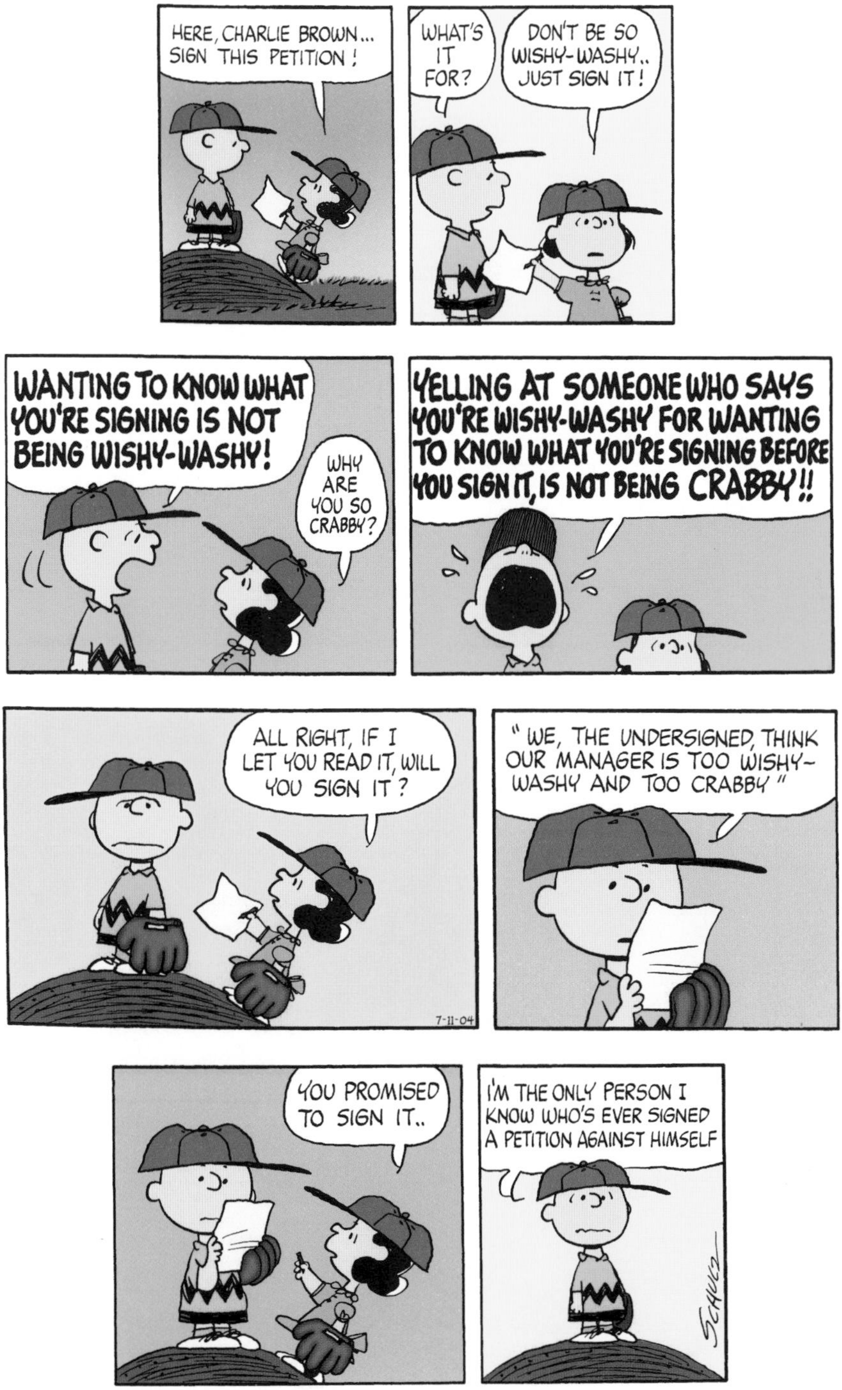
HERE, CHARLIE BROWN...
SIGN THIS PETITION!
WHAT'S IT FOR?
DON'T BE SO WISHY-WASHY.. JUST SIGN IT!
WANTING TO KNOW WHAT YOU'RE SIGNING IS NOT BEING WISHY-WASHY!
WHY ARE YOU SO CRABBY?
YELLING AT SOMEONE WHO SAYS YOU'RE WISHY-WASHY FOR WANTING TO KNOW WHAT YOU'RE SIGNING BEFORE YOU SIGN IT, IS NOT BEING CRABBY!!
ALL RIGHT, IF I LET YOU READ IT, WILL YOU SIGN IT?
7-11-04
"WE, THE UNDERSIGNED, THINK OUR MANAGER IS TOO WISHY-WASHY AND TOO CRABBY"
YOU PROMISED TO SIGN IT..
I'M THE ONLY PERSON I KNOW WHO'S EVER SIGNED A PETITION AGAINST HIMSELF
SCHULZ

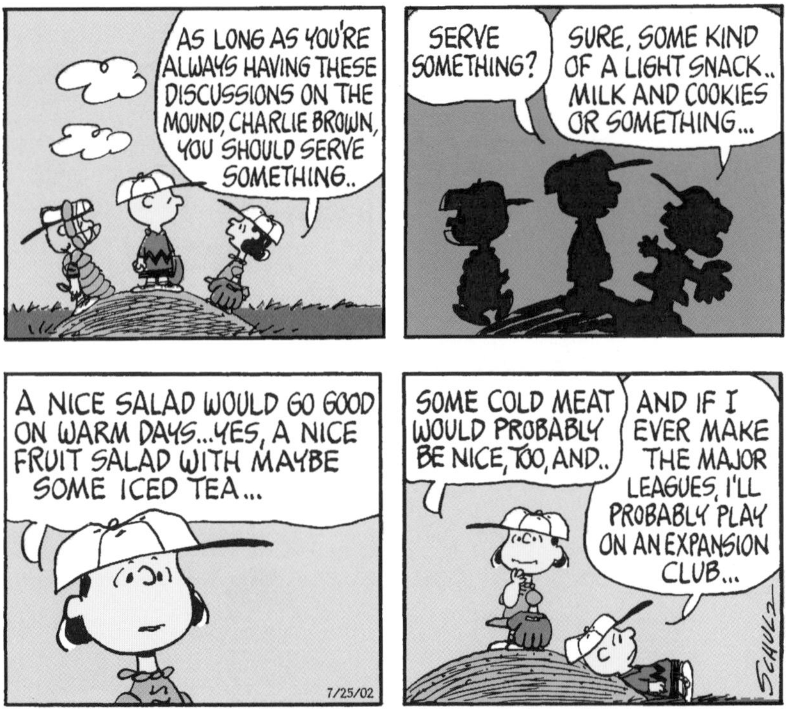
AS LONG AS YOU'RE ALWAYS HAVING THESE DISCUSSIONS ON THE MOUND, CHARLIE BROWN, YOU SHOULD SERVE SOMETHING..
SERVE SOMETHING?
SURE, SOME KIND OF A LIGHT SNACK.. MILK AND COOKIES OR SOMETHING...
A NICE SALAD WOULD GO GOOD ON WARM DAYS...YES, A NICE FRUIT SALAD WITH MAYBE SOME ICED TEA...
7/25/02
SOME COLD MEAT WOULD PROBABLY BE NICE, TOO, AND..
AND IF I EVER MAKE THE MAJOR LEAGUES, I'LL PROBABLY PLAY ON AN EXPANSION CLUB...
SCHULZ

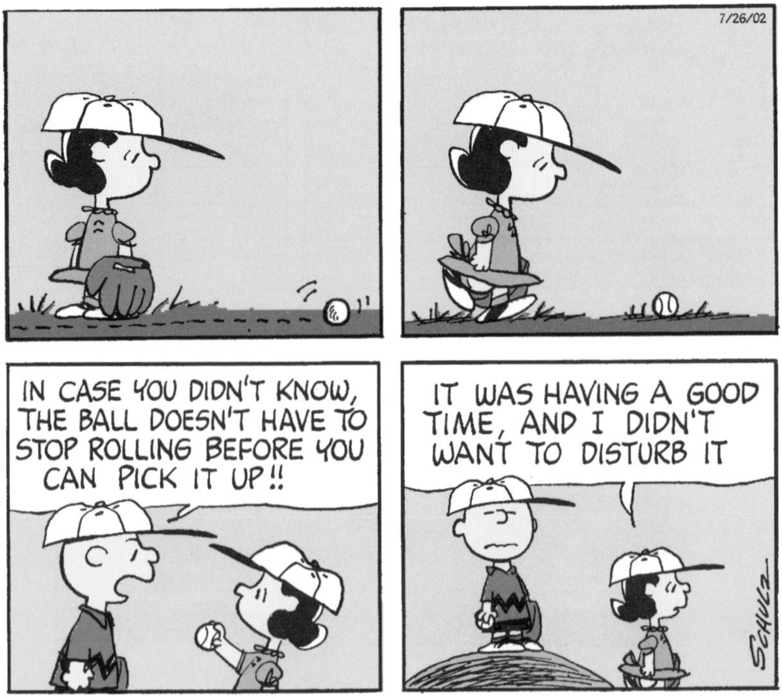
7/26/02
IN CASE YOU DIDN'T KNOW, THE BALL DOESN'T HAVE TO STOP ROLLING BEFORE YOU CAN PICK IT UP!!
IT WAS HAVING A GOOD TIME, AND I DIDN'T WANT TO DISTURB IT
SCHULZ

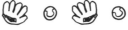

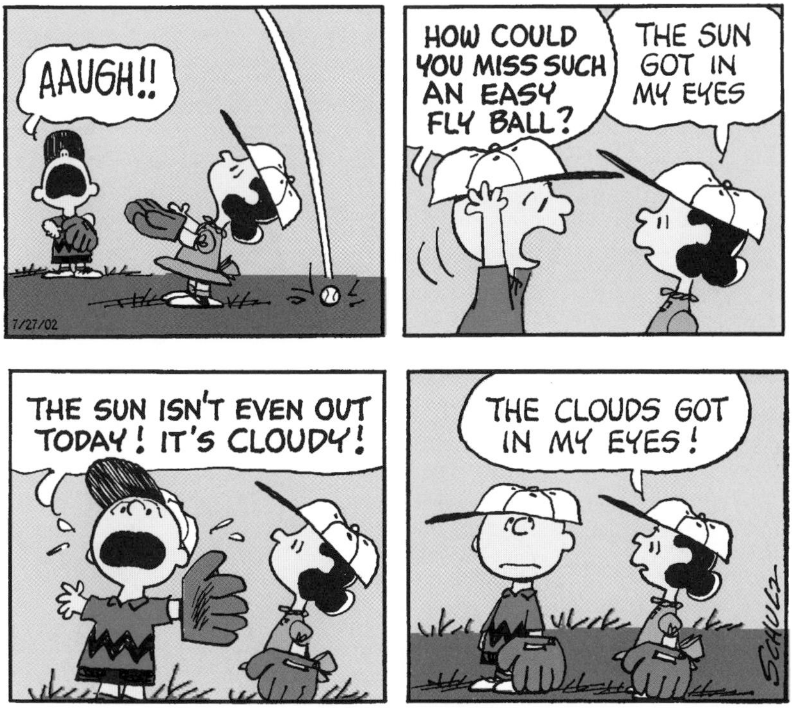
7/27/02
AAUGH!!
HOW COULD YOU MISS SUCH AN EASY FLY BALL?
THE SUN GOT IN MY EYES
THE SUN ISN'T EVEN OUT TODAY! IT'S CLOUDY!
THE CLOUDS GOT IN MY EYES!
SCHULZ

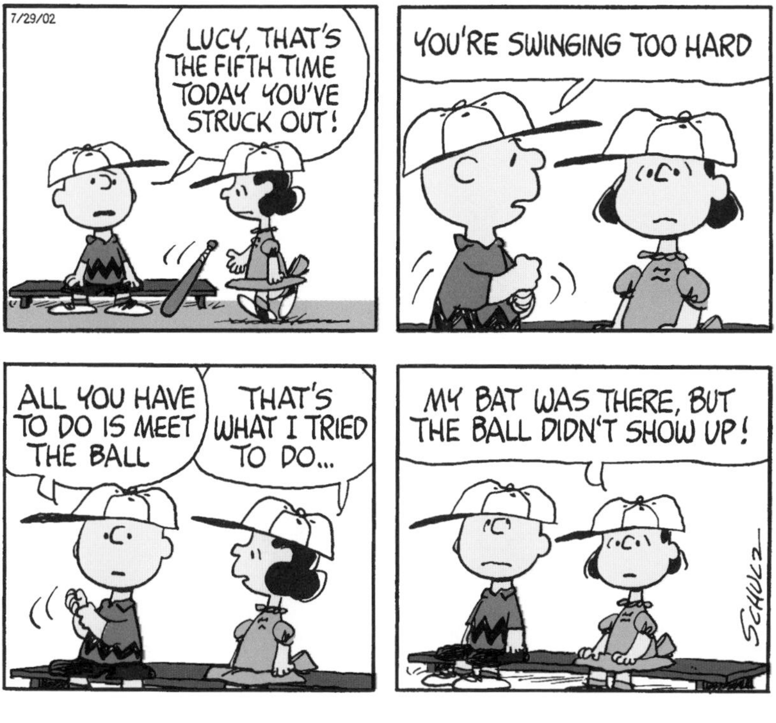
7/29/02
LUCY, THAT'S THE FIFTH TIME TODAY YOU'VE STRUCK OUT!
YOU'RE SWINGING TOO HARD
ALL YOU HAVE TO DO IS MEET THE BALL
THAT'S WHAT I TRIED TO DO...
MY BAT WAS THERE, BUT THE BALL DIDN'T SHOW UP!
SCHULZ

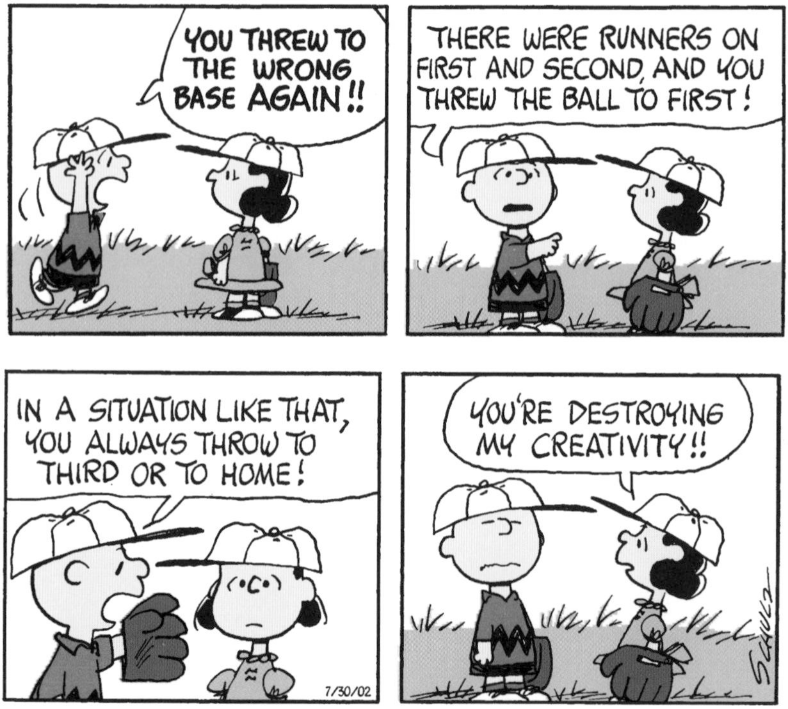
YOU THREW TO THE WRONG BASE AGAIN!!
THERE WERE RUNNERS ON FIRST AND SECOND, AND YOU THREW THE BALL TO FIRST!
IN A SITUATION LIKE THAT, YOU ALWAYS THROW TO THIRD OR TO HOME!
7/30/02
YOU'RE DESTROYING MY CREATIVITY!!
SCHULZ

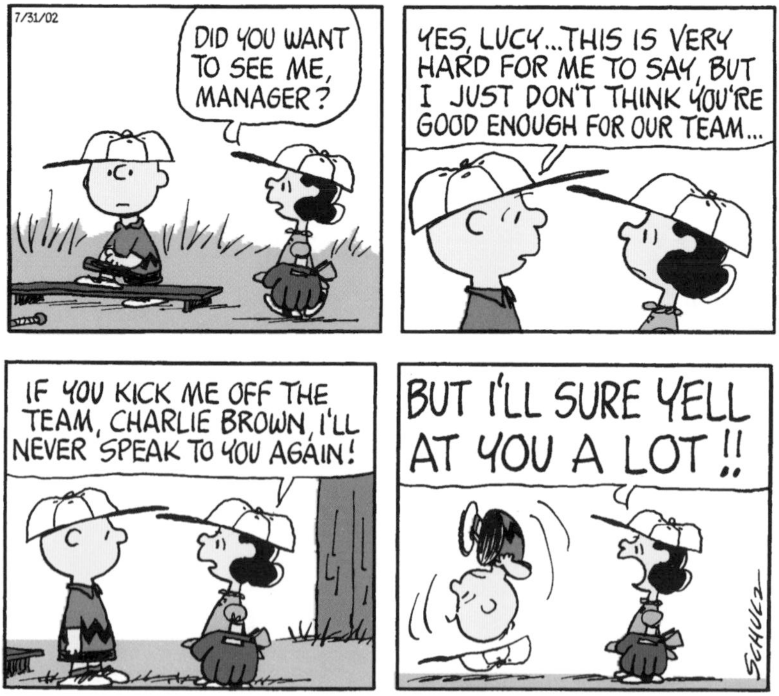
7/31/02
DID YOU WANT TO SEE ME, MANAGER?
YES, LUCY...THIS IS VERY HARD FOR ME TO SAY, BUT I JUST DON'T THINK YOU'RE GOOD ENOUGH FOR OUR TEAM...
IF YOU KICK ME OFF THE TEAM, CHARLIE BROWN, I'LL NEVER SPEAK TO YOU AGAIN!
BUT I'LL SURE YELL AT YOU A LOT!!
SCHULZ

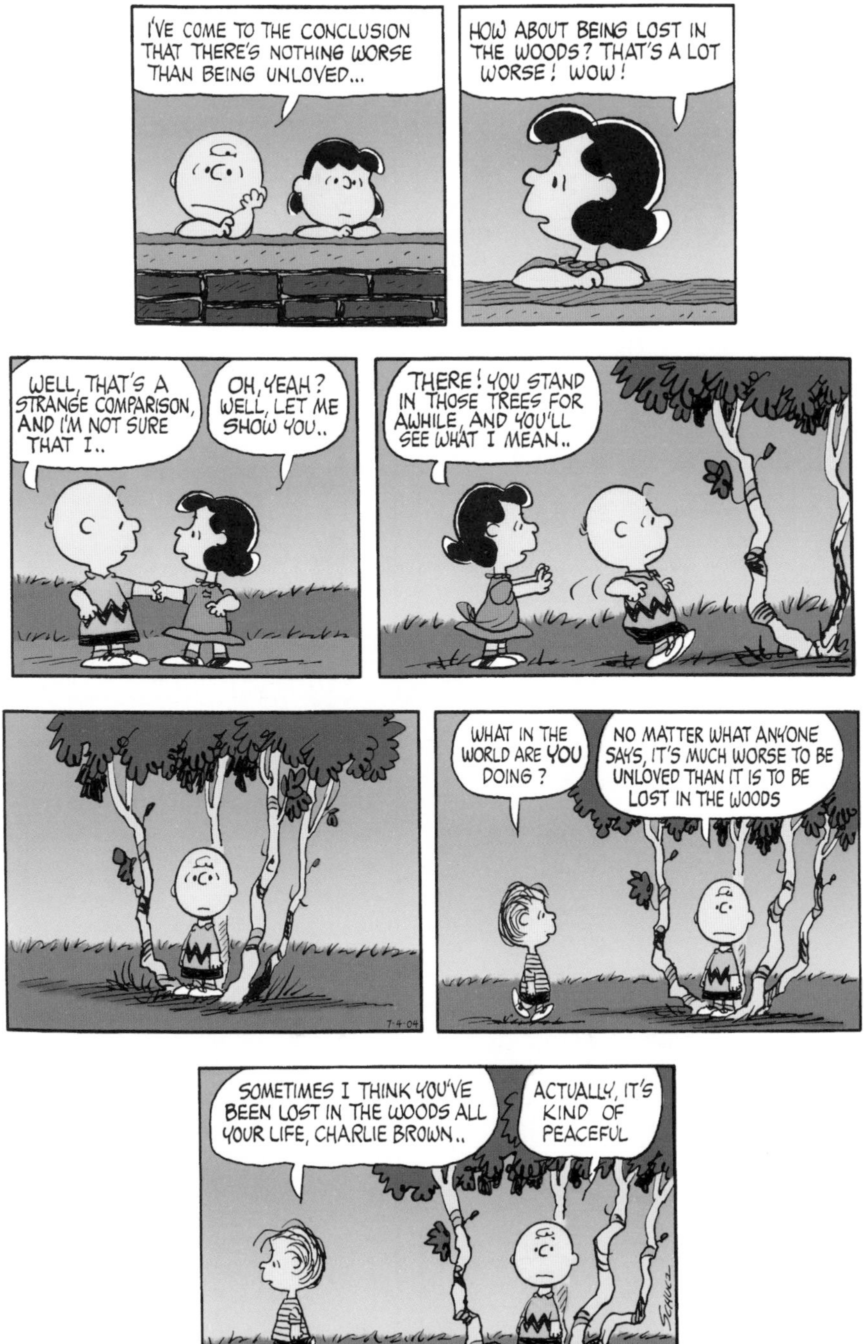
I'VE COME TO THE CONCLUSION THAT THERE'S NOTHING WORSE THAN BEING UNLOVED...
HOW ABOUT BEING LOST IN THE WOODS? THAT'S A LOT WORSE! WOW!
WELL, THAT'S A STRANGE COMPARISON, AND I'M NOT SURE THAT I..
OH, YEAH? WELL, LET ME SHOW YOU..
THERE! YOU STAND IN THOSE TREES FOR AWHILE, AND YOU'LL SEE WHAT I MEAN..
7-4-04
WHAT IN THE WORLD ARE YOU DOING?
NO MATTER WHAT ANYONE SAYS, IT'S MUCH WORSE TO BE UNLOVED THAN IT IS TO BE LOST IN THE WOODS
SOMETIMES I THINK YOU'VE BEEN LOST IN THE WOODS ALL YOUR LIFE, CHARLIE BROWN..
ACTUALLY, IT'S KIND OF PEACEFUL
SCHULZ

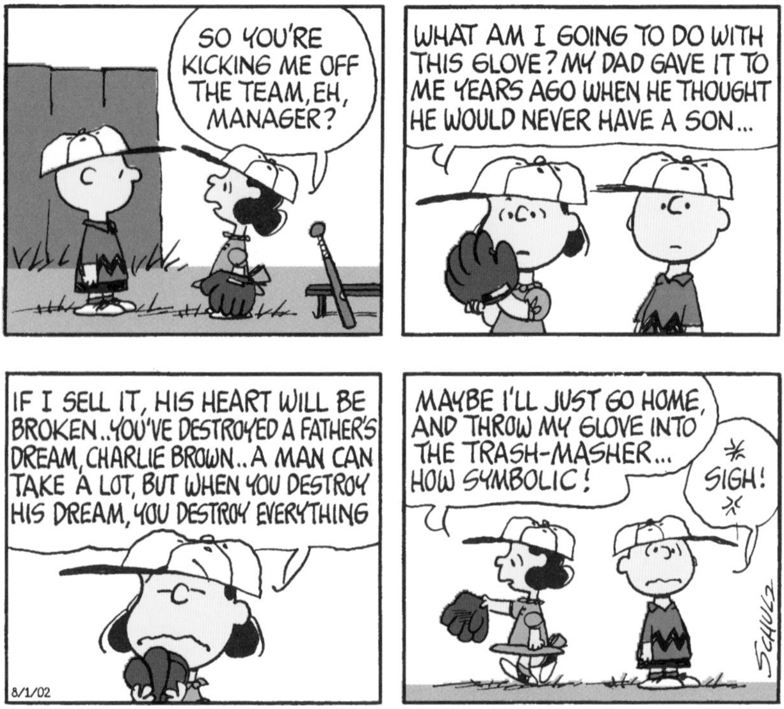
SO YOU'RE KICKING ME OFF THE TEAM, EH, MANAGER?
WHAT AM I GOING TO DO WITH THIS GLOVE? MY DAD GAVE IT TO ME YEARS AGO WHEN HE THOUGHT HE WOULD NEVER HAVE A SON...
IF I SELL IT, HIS HEART WILL BE BROKEN..YOU'VE DESTROYED A FATHER'S DREAM, CHARLIE BROWN..A MAN CAN TAKE A LOT, BUT WHEN YOU DESTROY HIS DREAM, YOU DESTROY EVERYTHING
8/1/02
MAYBE I'LL JUST GO HOME, AND THROW MY GLOVE INTO THE TRASH-MASHER... HOW SYMBOLIC!
SIGH!
SCHULZ

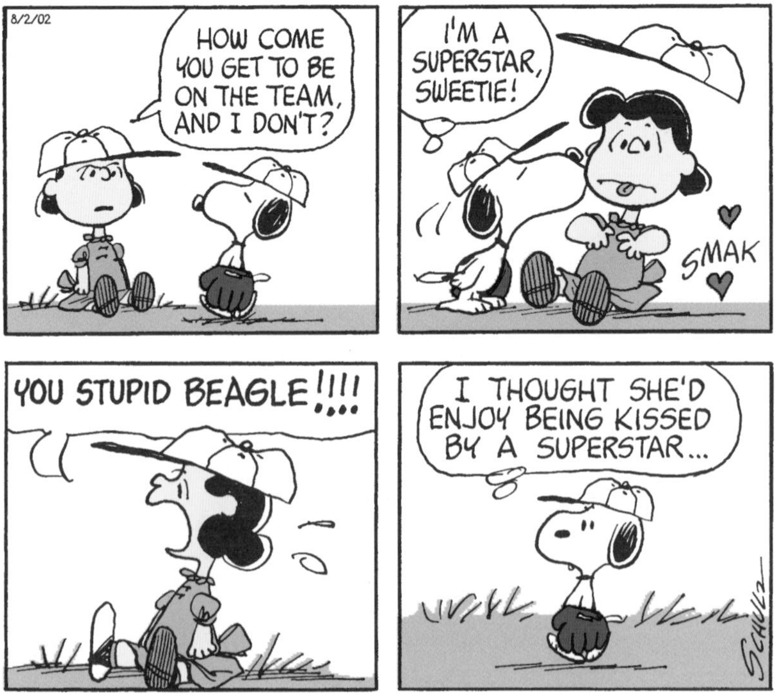
8/2/02
HOW COME YOU GET TO BE ON THE TEAM, AND I DON'T?
I'M A SUPERSTAR, SWEETIE!
SMAK
YOU STUPID BEAGLE!!!!
I THOUGHT SHE'D ENJOY BEING KISSED BY A SUPERSTAR...
SCHULZ

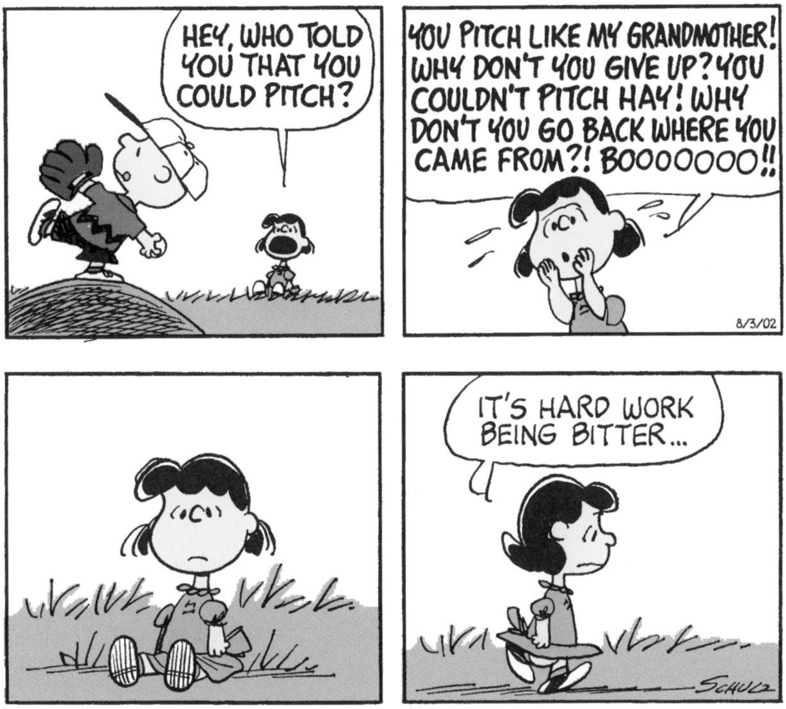
HEY, WHO TOLD YOU THAT YOU COULD PITCH?
YOU PITCH LIKE MY GRANDMOTHER! WHY DON'T YOU GIVE UP? YOU COULDN'T PITCH HAY! WHY DON'T YOU GO BACK WHERE YOU CAME FROM?! BOOOOOOO!!
8/3/02
IT'S HARD WORK BEING BITTER...
SCHULZ

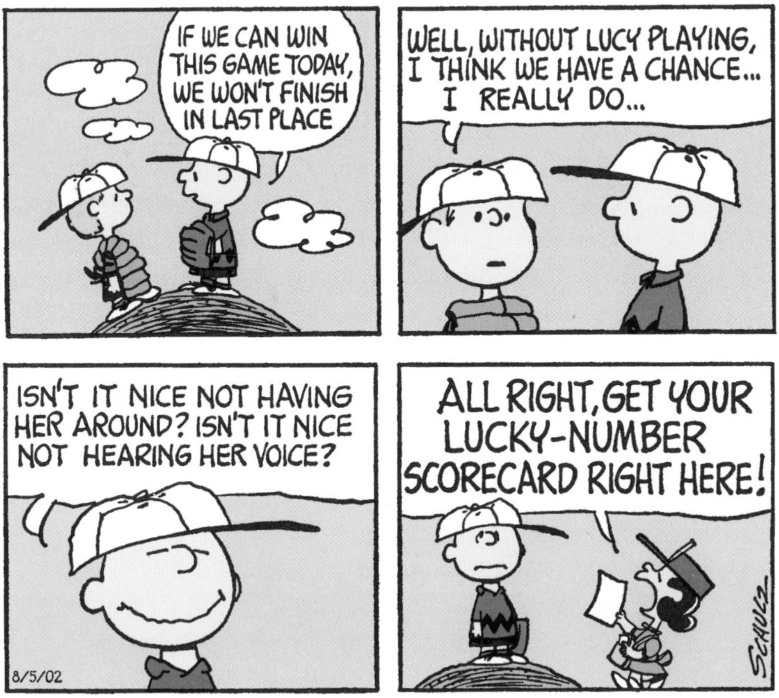
IF WE CAN WIN THIS GAME TODAY, WE WON'T FINISH IN LAST PLACE
WELL, WITHOUT LUCY PLAYING, I THINK WE HAVE A CHANCE... I REALLY DO...
ISN'T IT NICE NOT HAVING HER AROUND? ISN'T IT NICE NOT HEARING HER VOICE?
8/5/02
ALL RIGHT, GET YOUR LUCKY-NUMBER SCORECARD RIGHT HERE!
SCHULZ

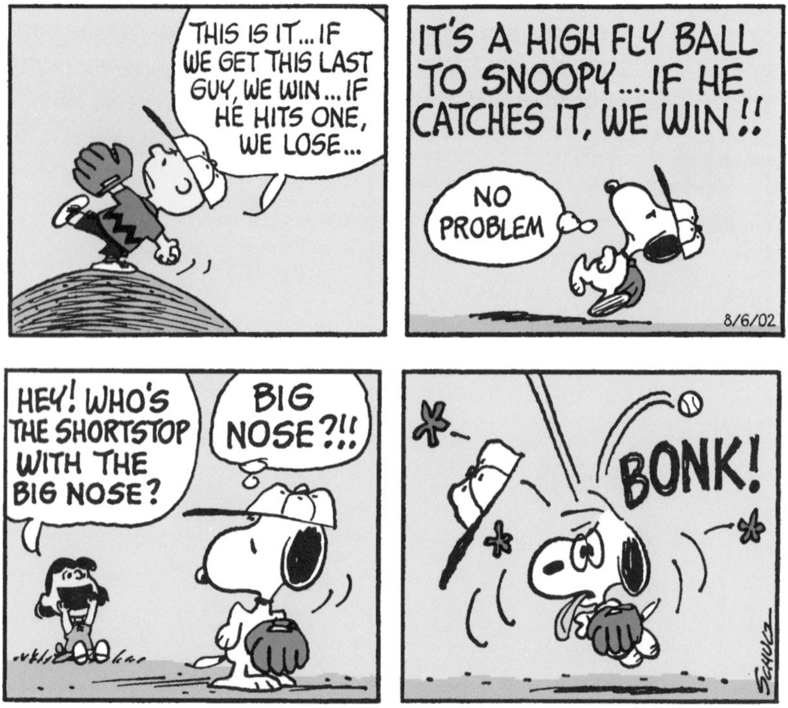
THIS IS IT...IF WE GET THIS LAST GUY, WE WIN...IF HE HITS ONE, WE LOSE...
IT'S A HIGH FLY BALL TO SNOOPY....IF HE CATCHES IT, WE WIN!!
NO PROBLEM
8/6/02
HEY! WHO'S THE SHORTSTOP WITH THE BIG NOSE?
BIG NOSE?!!
BONK!
SCHULZ

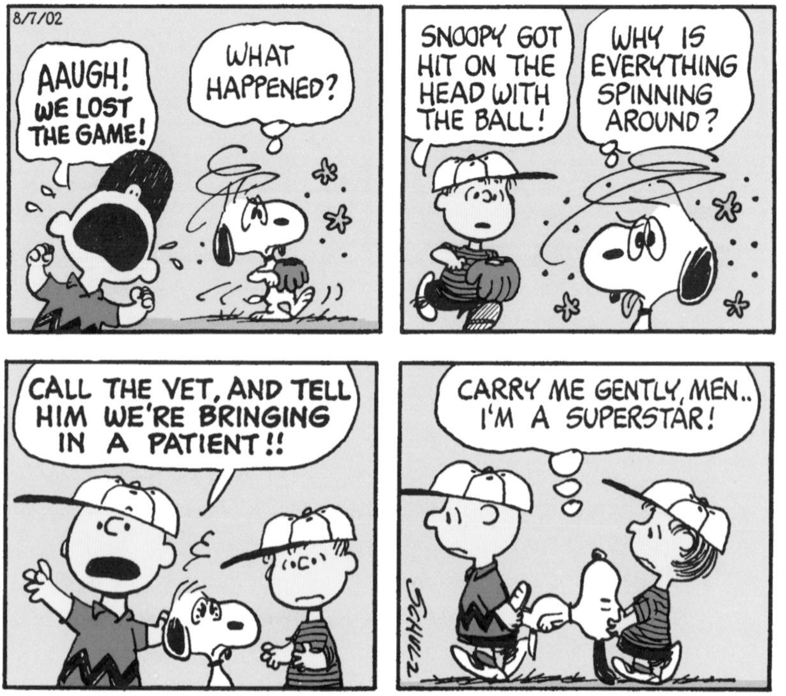
8/7/02
AAUGH! WE LOST THE GAME!
WHAT HAPPENED?
SNOOPY GOT HIT ON THE HEAD WITH THE BALL!
WHY IS EVERYTHING SPINNING AROUND?
CALL THE VET, AND TELL HIM WE'RE BRINGING IN A PATIENT!!
CARRY ME GENTLY, MEN.. I'M A SUPERSTAR!
SCHULZ

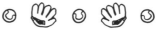

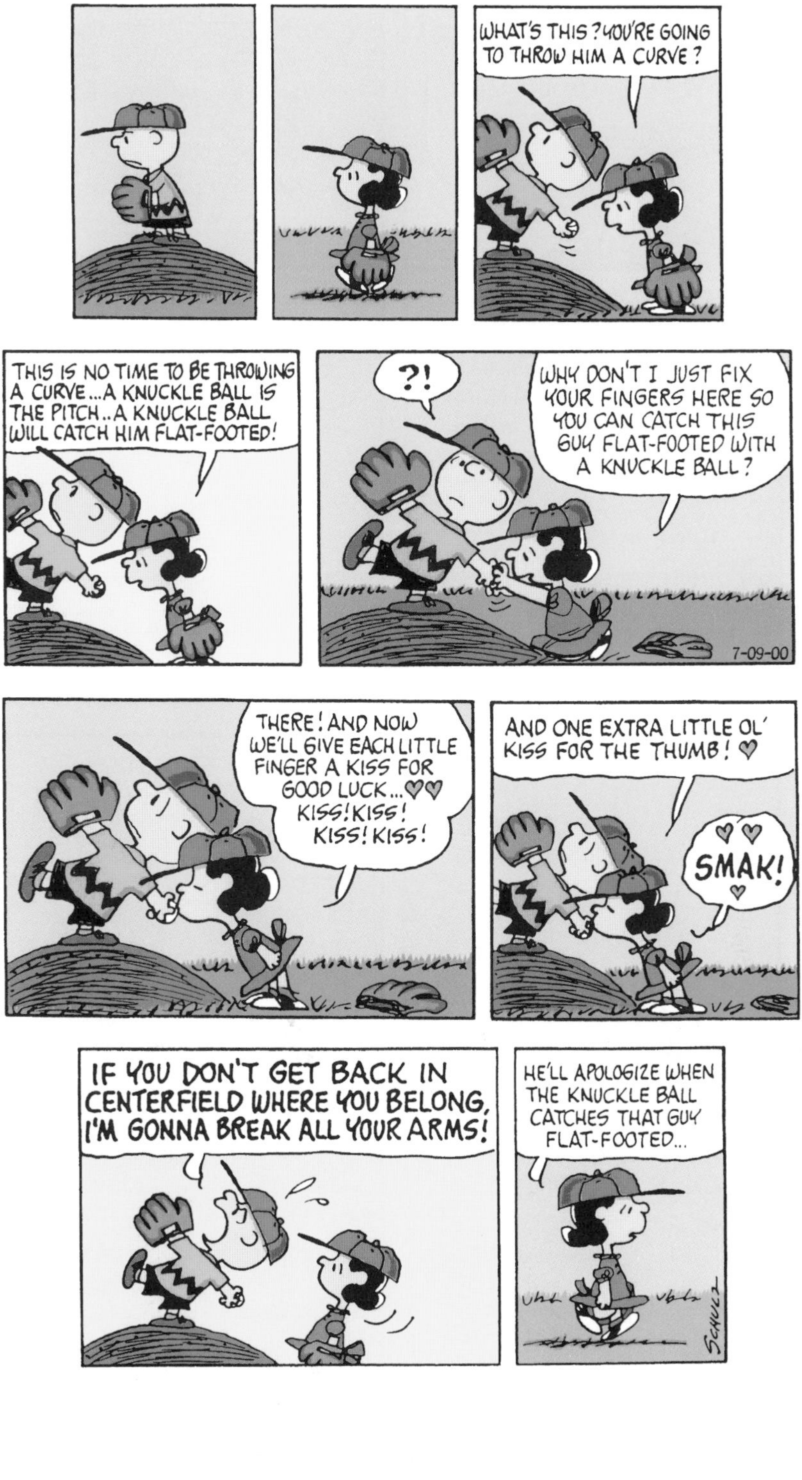
WHAT'S THIS ? YOU'RE GOING TO THROW HIM A CURVE ?
THIS IS NO TIME TO BE THROWING A CURVE...A KNUCKLE BALL IS THE PITCH..A KNUCKLE BALL WILL CATCH HIM FLAT-FOOTED!
?!
WHY DON'T I JUST FIX YOUR FINGERS HERE SO YOU CAN CATCH THIS GUY FLAT-FOOTED WITH A KNUCKLE BALL ?
7-09-00
THERE! AND NOW WE'LL GIVE EACH LITTLE FINGER A KISS FOR GOOD LUCK...♡♡ KISS! KISS! KISS! KISS!
AND ONE EXTRA LITTLE OL' KISS FOR THE THUMB! ♡
SMAK!
IF YOU DON'T GET BACK IN CENTERFIELD WHERE YOU BELONG, I'M GONNA BREAK ALL YOUR ARMS!
HE'LL APOLOGIZE WHEN THE KNUCKLE BALL CATCHES THAT GUY FLAT-FOOTED...
SCHULZ

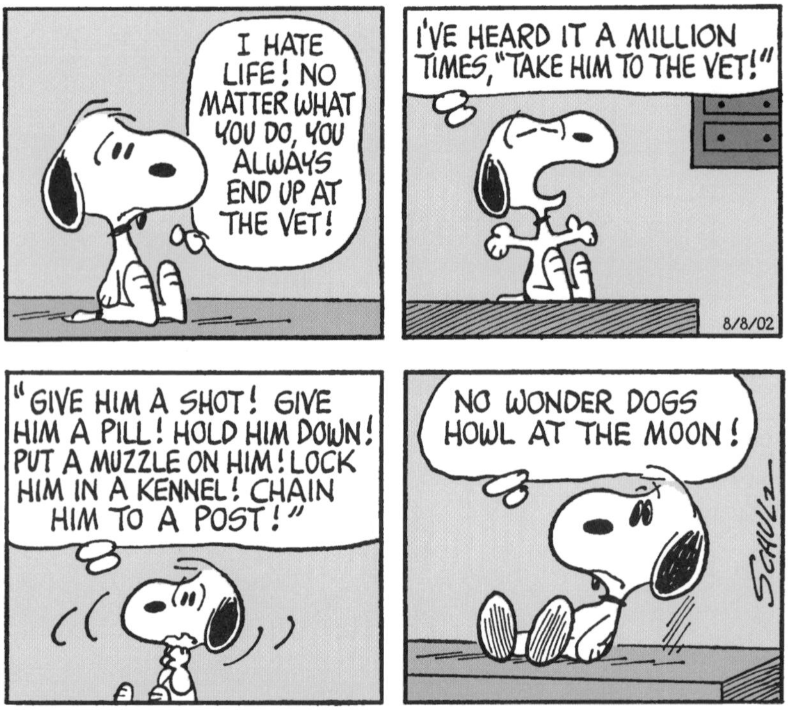
I HATE LIFE! NO MATTER WHAT YOU DO, YOU ALWAYS END UP AT THE VET!
I'VE HEARD IT A MILLION TIMES, "TAKE HIM TO THE VET!"
8/8/02
"GIVE HIM A SHOT! GIVE HIM A PILL! HOLD HIM DOWN! PUT A MUZZLE ON HIM! LOCK HIM IN A KENNEL! CHAIN HIM TO A POST!"
NO WONDER DOGS HOWL AT THE MOON!
SCHULZ

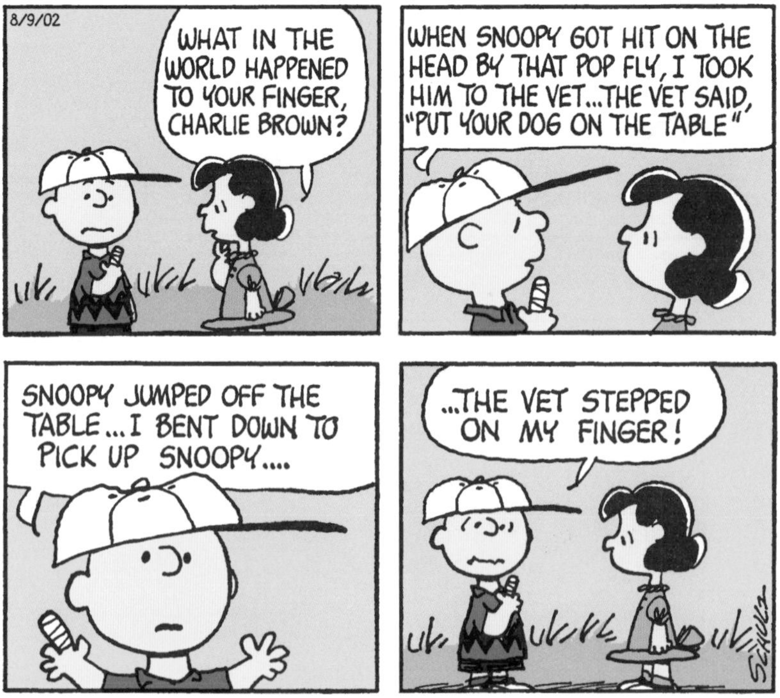
8/9/02
WHAT IN THE WORLD HAPPENED TO YOUR FINGER, CHARLIE BROWN?
WHEN SNOOPY GOT HIT ON THE HEAD BY THAT POP FLY, I TOOK HIM TO THE VET...THE VET SAID, "PUT YOUR DOG ON THE TABLE"
SNOOPY JUMPED OFF THE TABLE...I BENT DOWN TO PICK UP SNOOPY....
...THE VET STEPPED ON MY FINGER!
SCHULZ

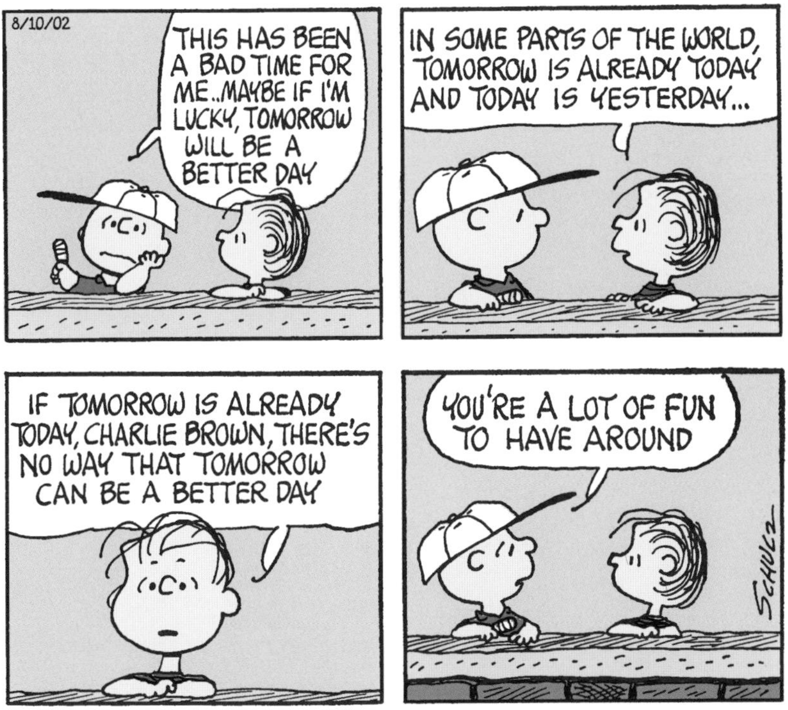
8/10/02
THIS HAS BEEN A BAD TIME FOR ME..MAYBE IF I'M LUCKY, TOMORROW WILL BE A BETTER DAY
IN SOME PARTS OF THE WORLD, TOMORROW IS ALREADY TODAY AND TODAY IS YESTERDAY...
IF TOMORROW IS ALREADY TODAY, CHARLIE BROWN, THERE'S NO WAY THAT TOMORROW CAN BE A BETTER DAY
YOU'RE A LOT OF FUN TO HAVE AROUND
SCHULZ

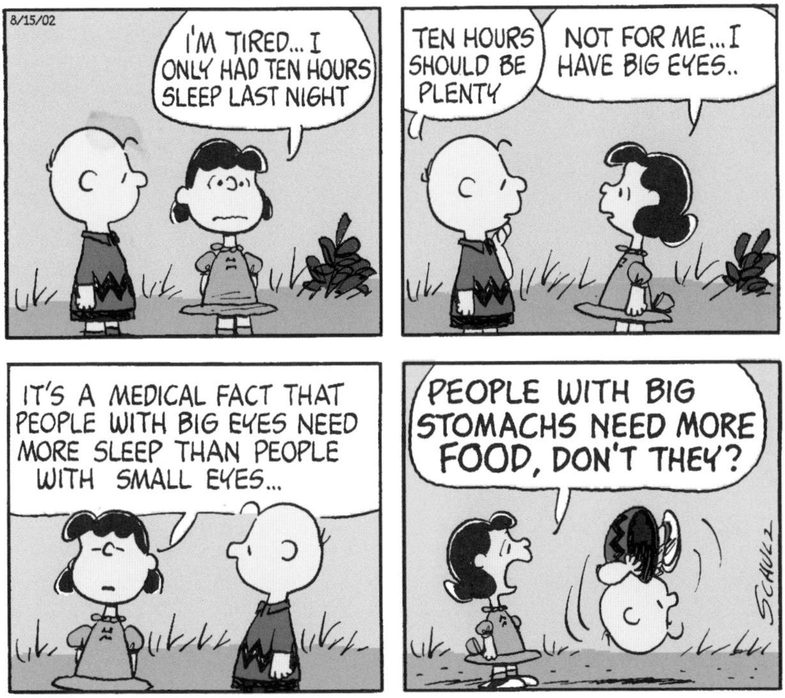
8/15/02
I'M TIRED... I ONLY HAD TEN HOURS SLEEP LAST NIGHT
TEN HOURS SHOULD BE PLENTY
NOT FOR ME... I HAVE BIG EYES..
IT'S A MEDICAL FACT THAT PEOPLE WITH BIG EYES NEED MORE SLEEP THAN PEOPLE WITH SMALL EYES...
PEOPLE WITH BIG STOMACHS NEED MORE FOOD, DON'T THEY?
SCHULZ

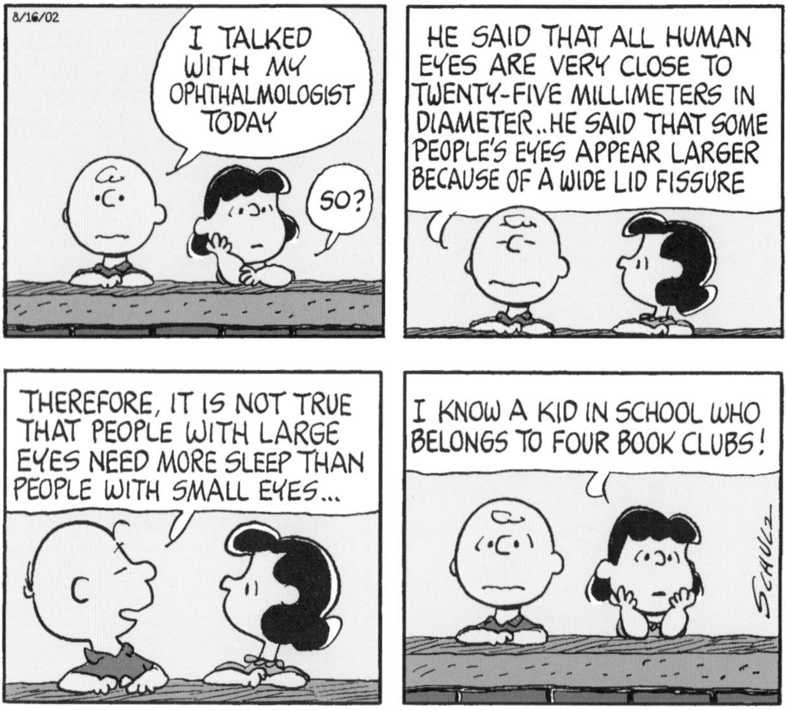
8/16/02
I TALKED WITH MY OPHTHALMOLOGIST TODAY
SO?
HE SAID THAT ALL HUMAN EYES ARE VERY CLOSE TO TWENTY-FIVE MILLIMETERS IN DIAMETER..HE SAID THAT SOME PEOPLE'S EYES APPEAR LARGER BECAUSE OF A WIDE LID FISSURE
THEREFORE, IT IS NOT TRUE THAT PEOPLE WITH LARGE EYES NEED MORE SLEEP THAN PEOPLE WITH SMALL EYES...
I KNOW A KID IN SCHOOL WHO BELONGS TO FOUR BOOK CLUBS!
SCHULZ

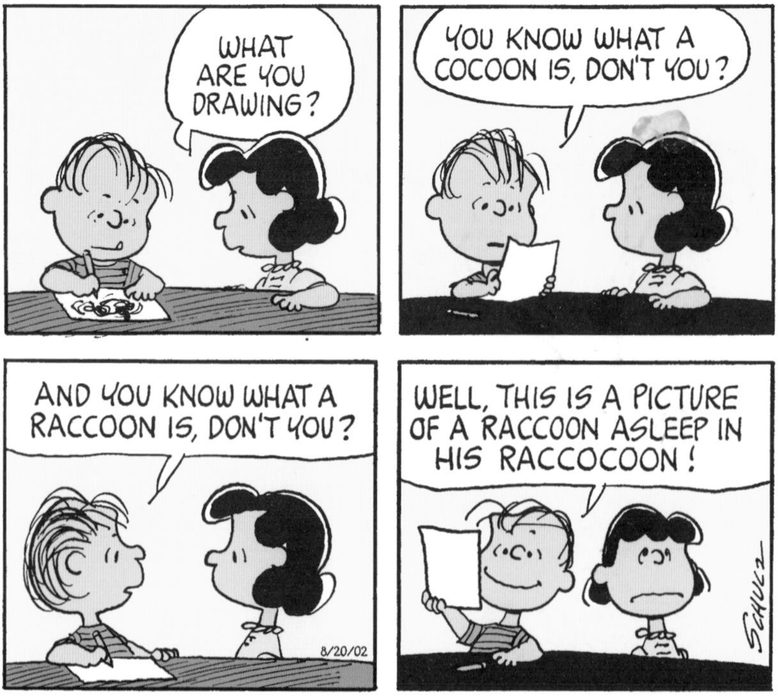
WHAT ARE YOU DRAWING?
YOU KNOW WHAT A COCOON IS, DON'T YOU?
AND YOU KNOW WHAT A RACCOON IS, DON'T YOU?
8/20/02
WELL, THIS IS A PICTURE OF A RACCOON ASLEEP IN HIS RACCOCOON!
SCHULZ

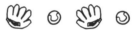

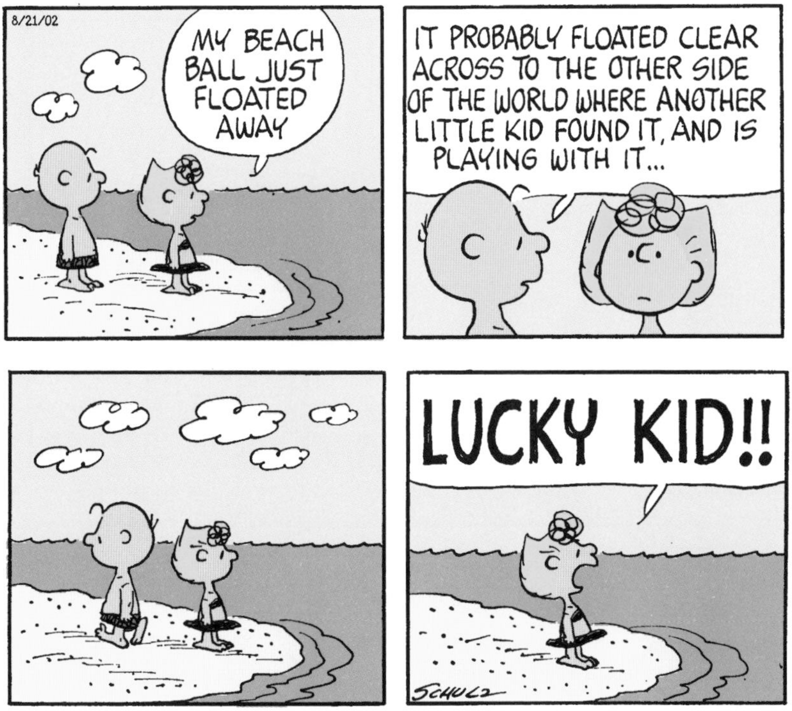
8/21/02
MY BEACH BALL JUST FLOATED AWAY
IT PROBABLY FLOATED CLEAR ACROSS TO THE OTHER SIDE OF THE WORLD WHERE ANOTHER LITTLE KID FOUND IT, AND IS PLAYING WITH IT...
LUCKY KID!!
SCHULZ

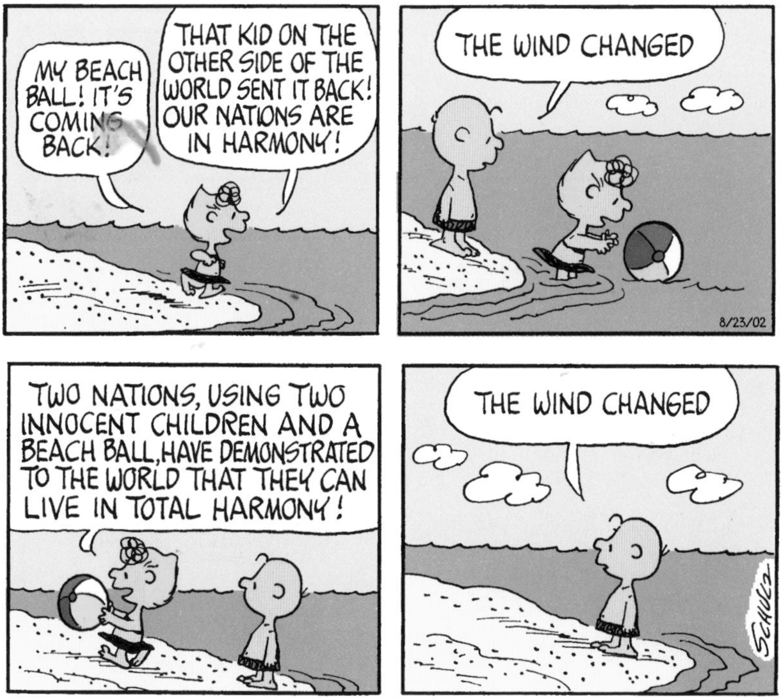
MY BEACH BALL! IT'S COMING BACK!
THAT KID ON THE OTHER SIDE OF THE WORLD SENT IT BACK! OUR NATIONS ARE IN HARMONY!
THE WIND CHANGED
8/23/02
TWO NATIONS, USING TWO INNOCENT CHILDREN AND A BEACH BALL, HAVE DEMONSTRATED TO THE WORLD THAT THEY CAN LIVE IN TOTAL HARMONY!
THE WIND CHANGED
SCHULZ

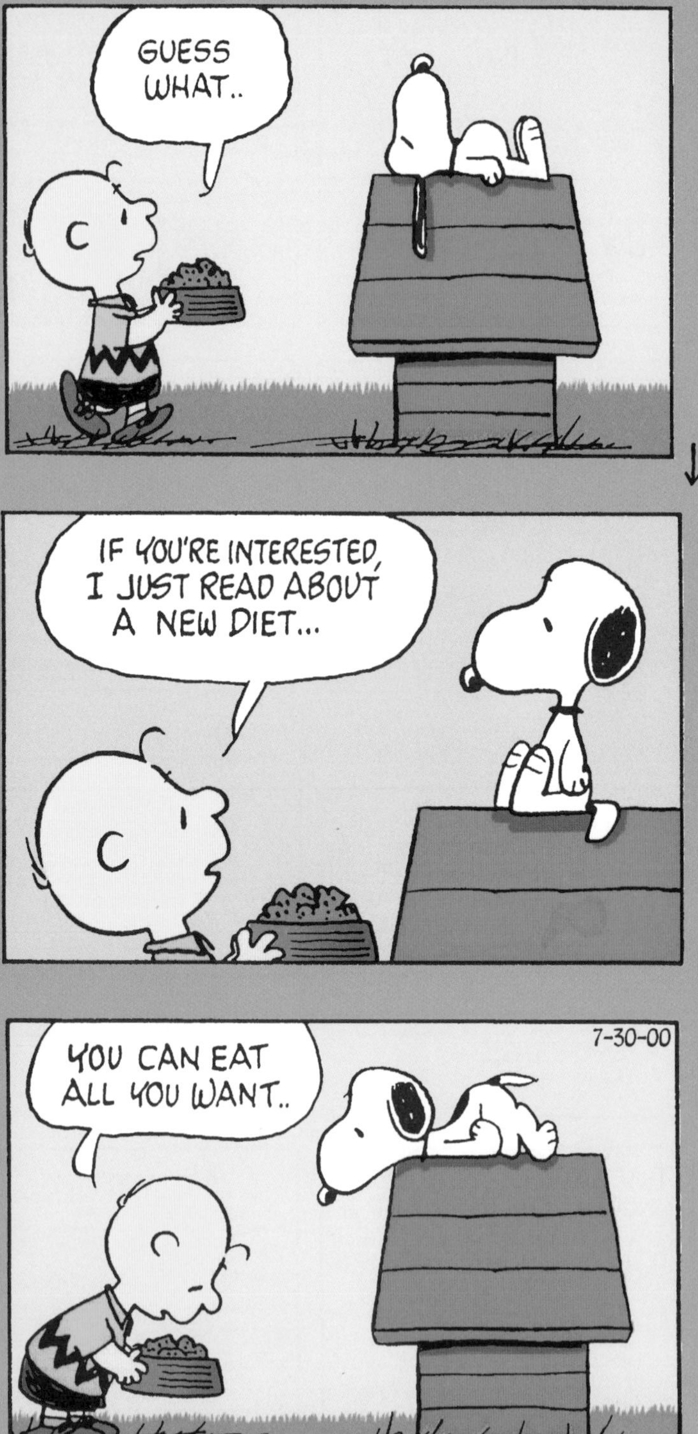
GUESS WHAT..
IF YOU'RE INTERESTED, I JUST READ ABOUT A NEW DIET...
YOU CAN EAT ALL YOU WANT..
7-30-00

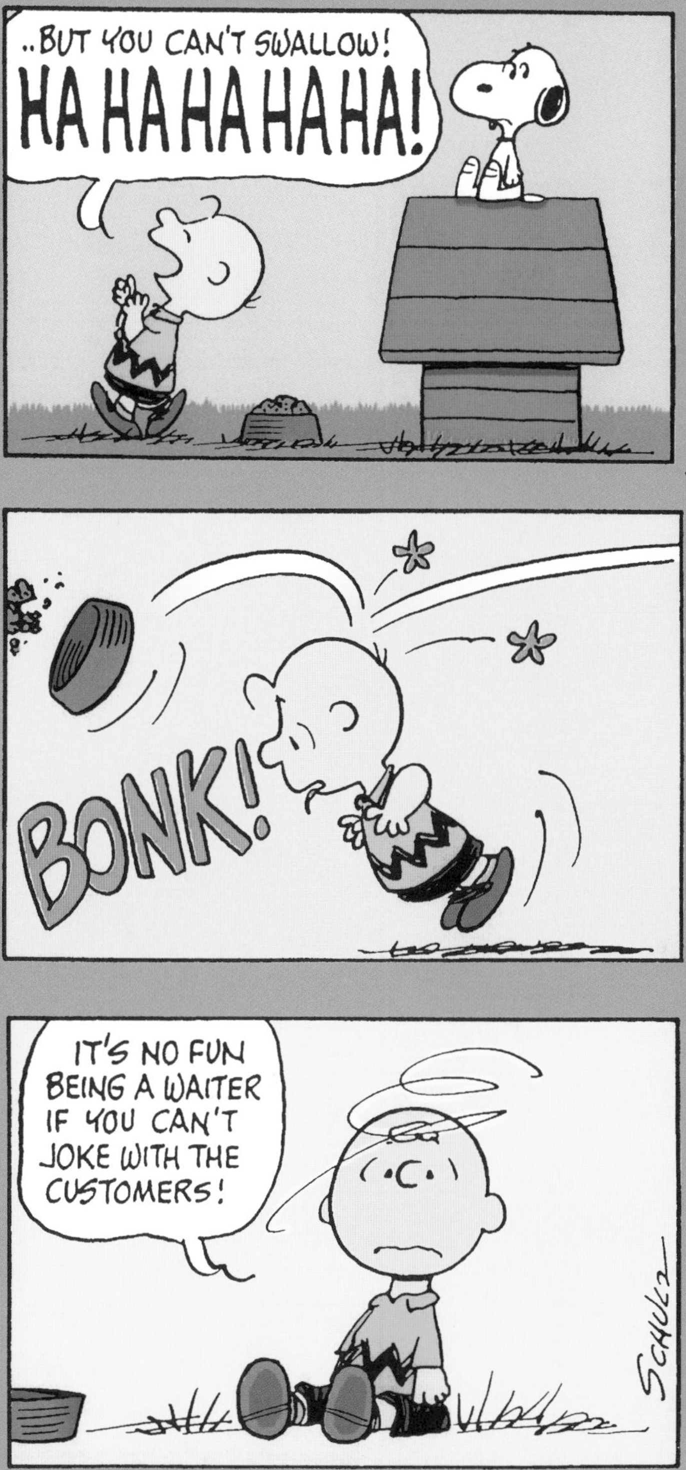
..BUT YOU CAN'T SWALLOW! HA HA HA HA HA HA!
BONK!
IT'S NO FUN BEING A WAITER IF YOU CAN'T JOKE WITH THE CUSTOMERS!
SCHULZ

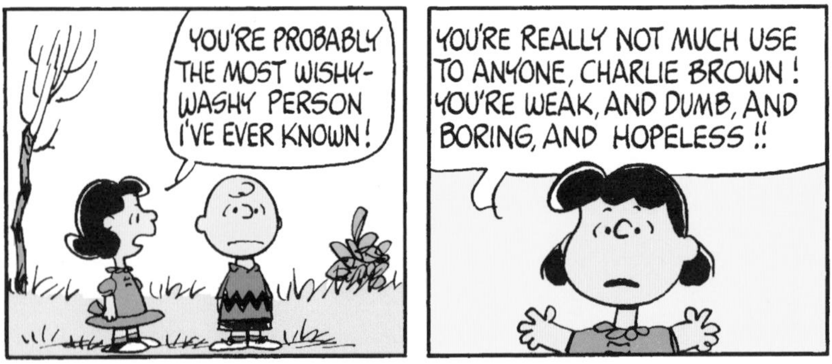
YOU'RE PROBABLY THE MOST WISHY-WASHY PERSON I'VE EVER KNOWN!
YOU'RE REALLY NOT MUCH USE TO ANYONE, CHARLIE BROWN! YOU'RE WEAK, AND DUMB, AND BORING, AND HOPELESS!!

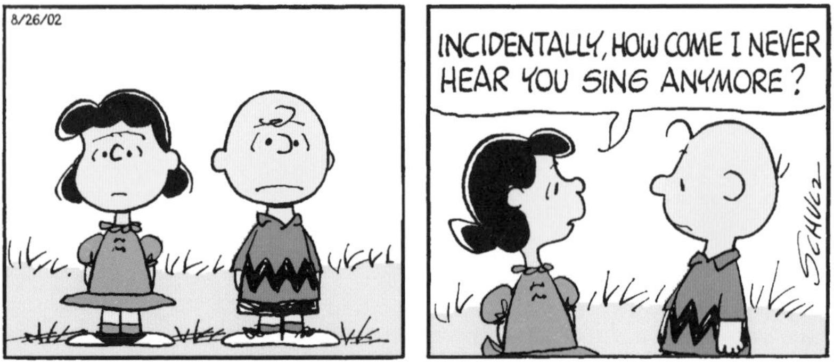
8/26/02
INCIDENTALLY, HOW COME I NEVER HEAR YOU SING ANYMORE?
SCHULZ

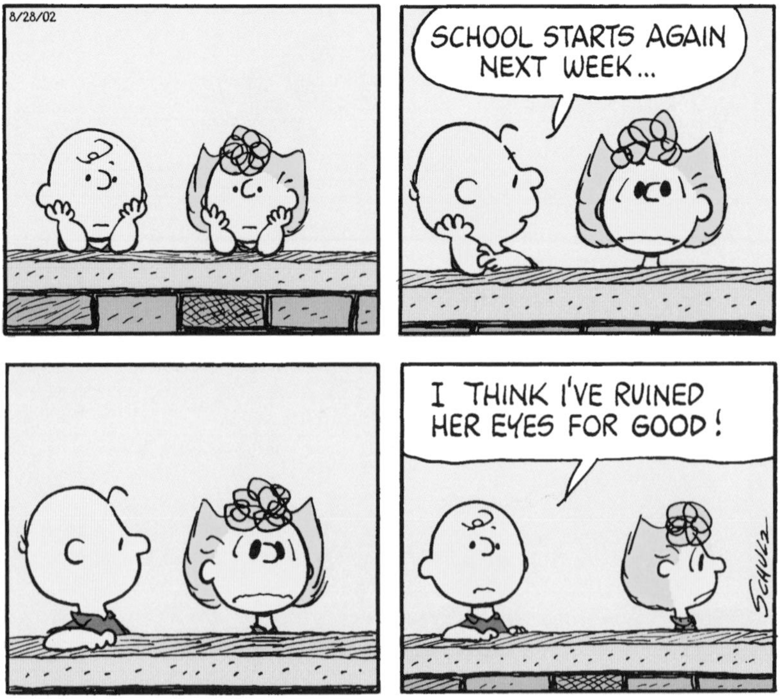
8/28/02
SCHOOL STARTS AGAIN NEXT WEEK...
I THINK I'VE RUINED HER EYES FOR GOOD!
SCHULZ

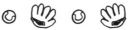

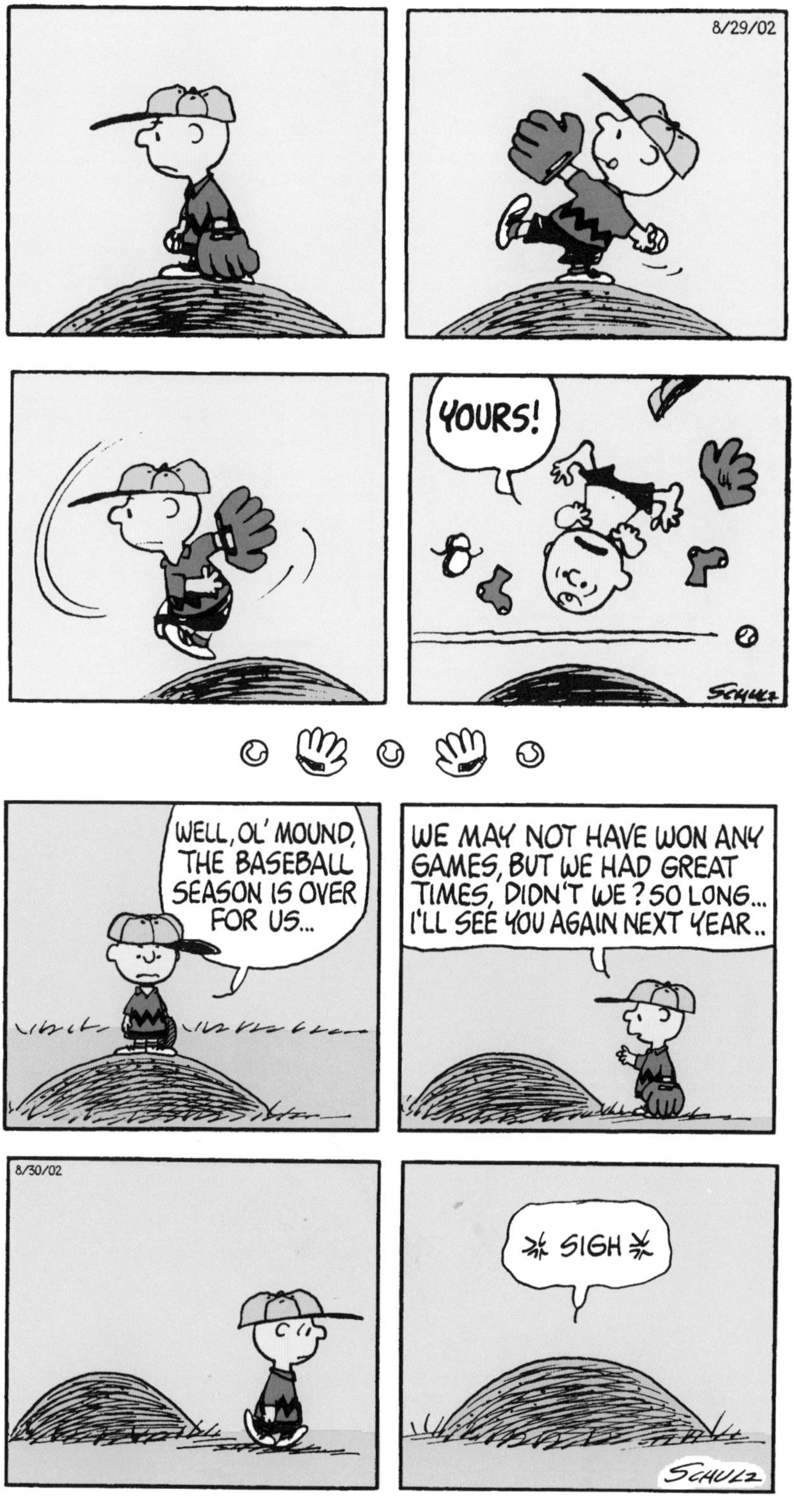
8/29/02
YOURS!
SCHULZ
WELL, OL' MOUND, THE BASEBALL SEASON IS OVER FOR US...
WE MAY NOT HAVE WON ANY GAMES, BUT WE HAD GREAT TIMES, DIDN'T WE? SO LONG... I'LL SEE YOU AGAIN NEXT YEAR..
8/30/02
SIGH
SCHULZ

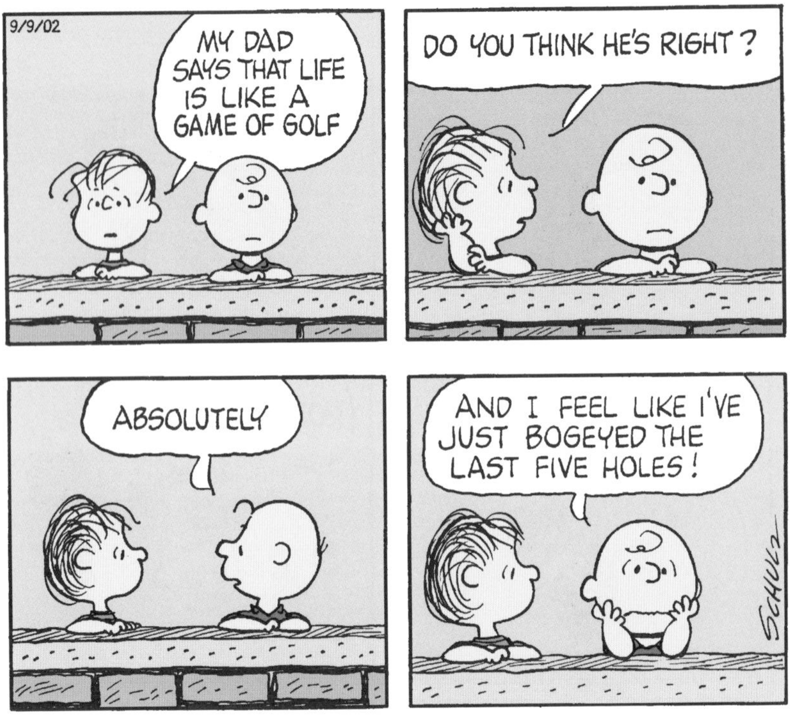
9/9/02
MY DAD SAYS THAT LIFE IS LIKE A GAME OF GOLF
DO YOU THINK HE'S RIGHT?
ABSOLUTELY
AND I FEEL LIKE I'VE JUST BOGEYED THE LAST FIVE HOLES!
SCHULZ

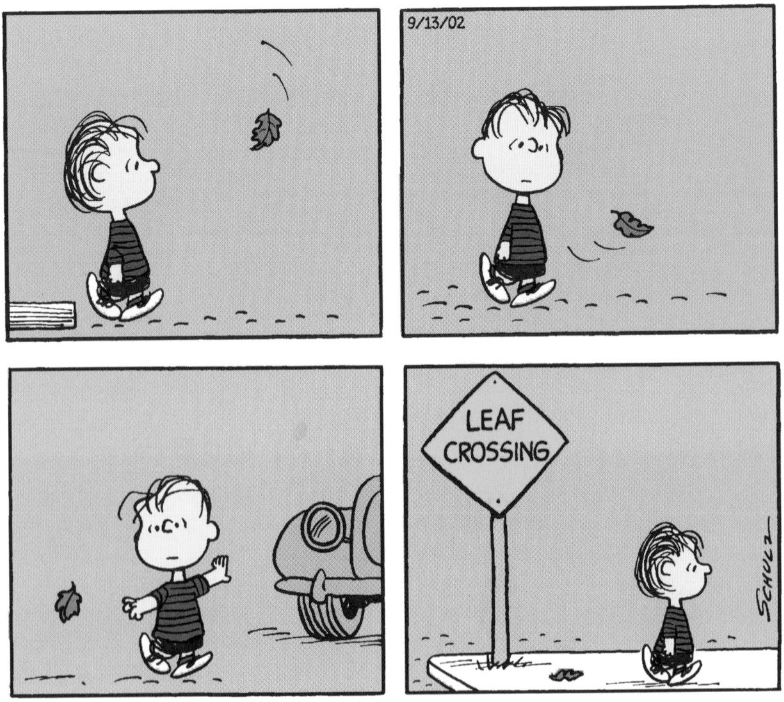
9/13/02
LEAF CROSSING
SCHULZ

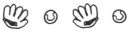

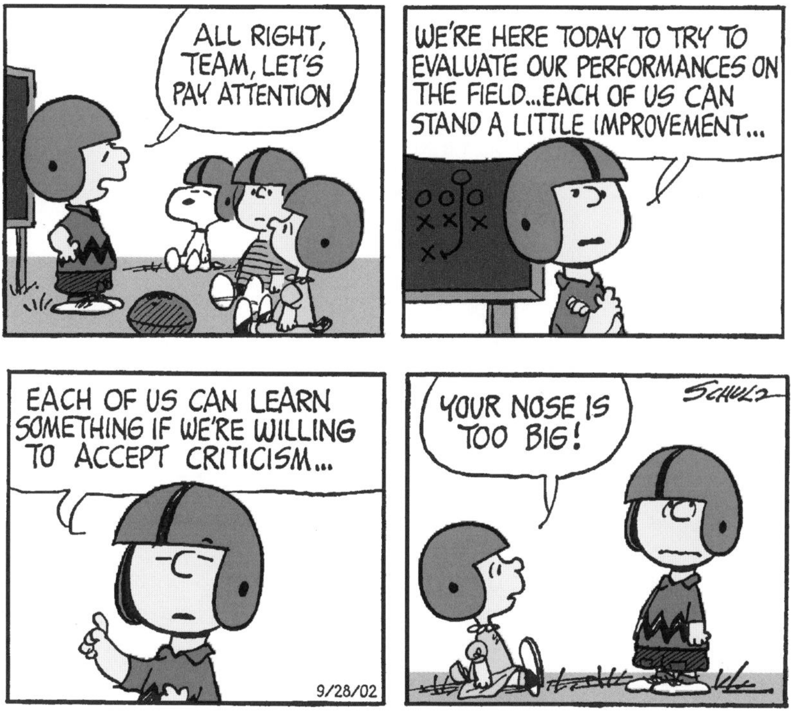
ALL RIGHT, TEAM, LET'S PAY ATTENTION
WE'RE HERE TODAY TO TRY TO EVALUATE OUR PERFORMANCES ON THE FIELD...EACH OF US CAN STAND A LITTLE IMPROVEMENT...
EACH OF US CAN LEARN SOMETHING IF WE'RE WILLING TO ACCEPT CRITICISM...
9/28/02
YOUR NOSE IS TOO BIG!
SCHULZ

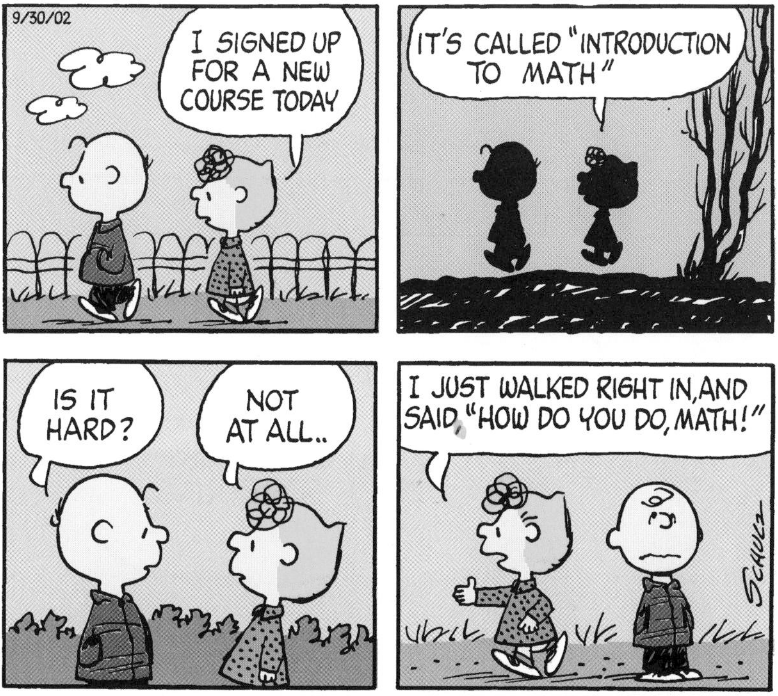
9/30/02
I SIGNED UP FOR A NEW COURSE TODAY
IT'S CALLED "INTRODUCTION TO MATH"
IS IT HARD?
NOT AT ALL..
I JUST WALKED RIGHT IN, AND SAID, "HOW DO YOU DO, MATH!"
SCHULZ

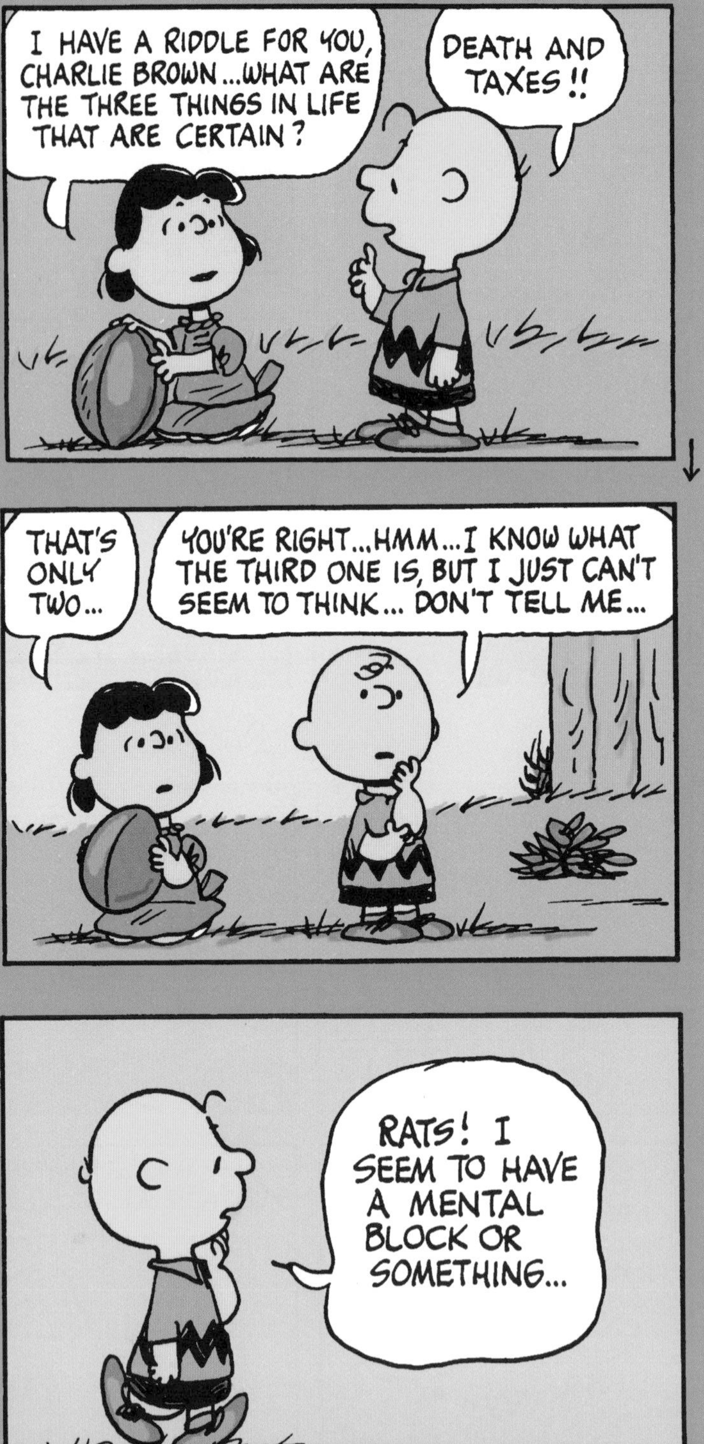
I HAVE A RIDDLE FOR YOU, CHARLIE BROWN...WHAT ARE THE THREE THINGS IN LIFE THAT ARE CERTAIN?
DEATH AND TAXES!!
THAT'S ONLY TWO...
YOU'RE RIGHT...HMM...I KNOW WHAT THE THIRD ONE IS, BUT I JUST CAN'T SEEM TO THINK... DON'T TELL ME...
RATS! I SEEM TO HAVE A MENTAL BLOCK OR SOMETHING...

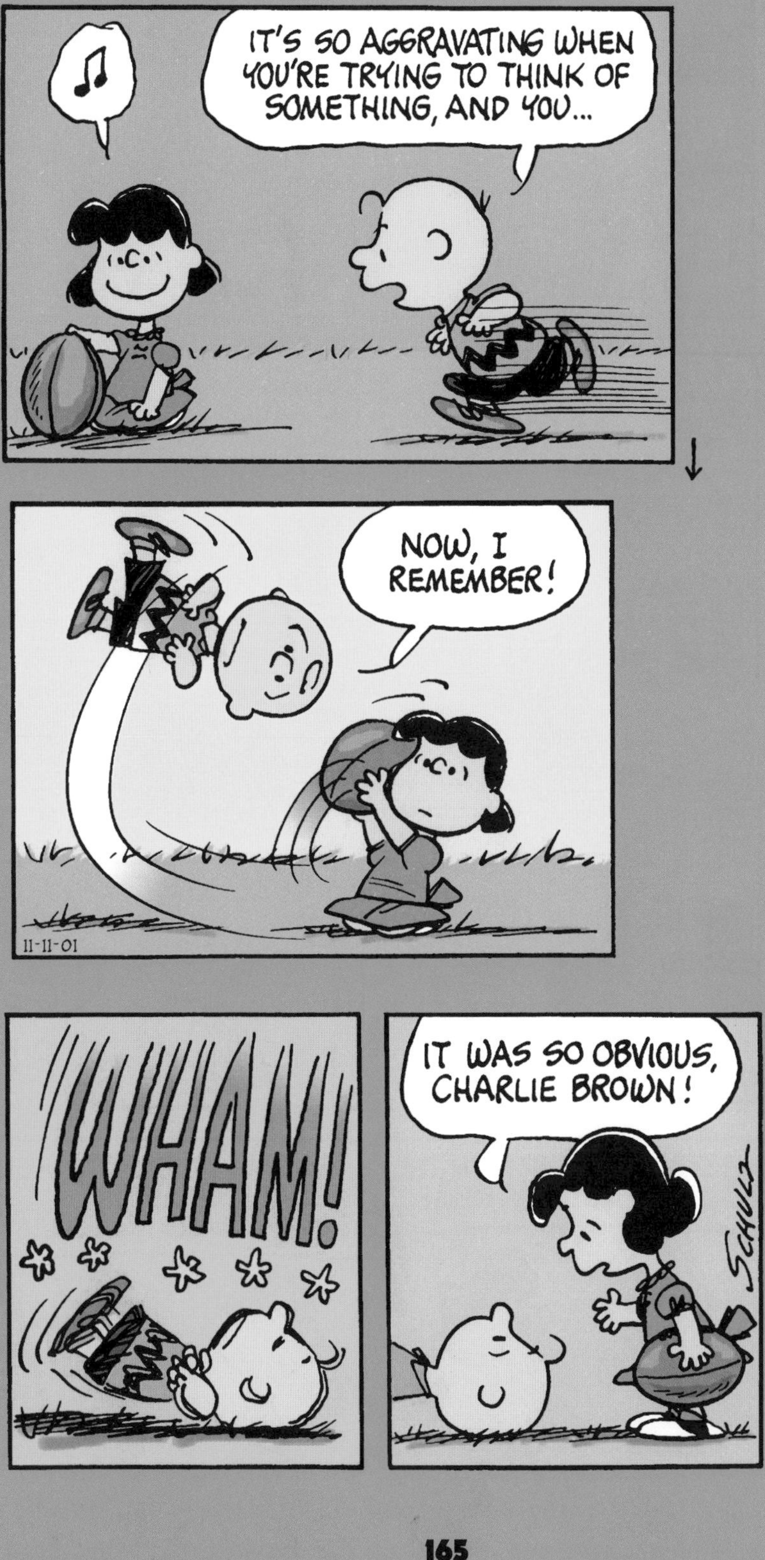
♫
IT'S SO AGGRAVATING WHEN YOU'RE TRYING TO THINK OF SOMETHING, AND YOU...
NOW, I REMEMBER!
11-11-01
WHAM!
IT WAS SO OBVIOUS, CHARLIE BROWN!
SCHULZ

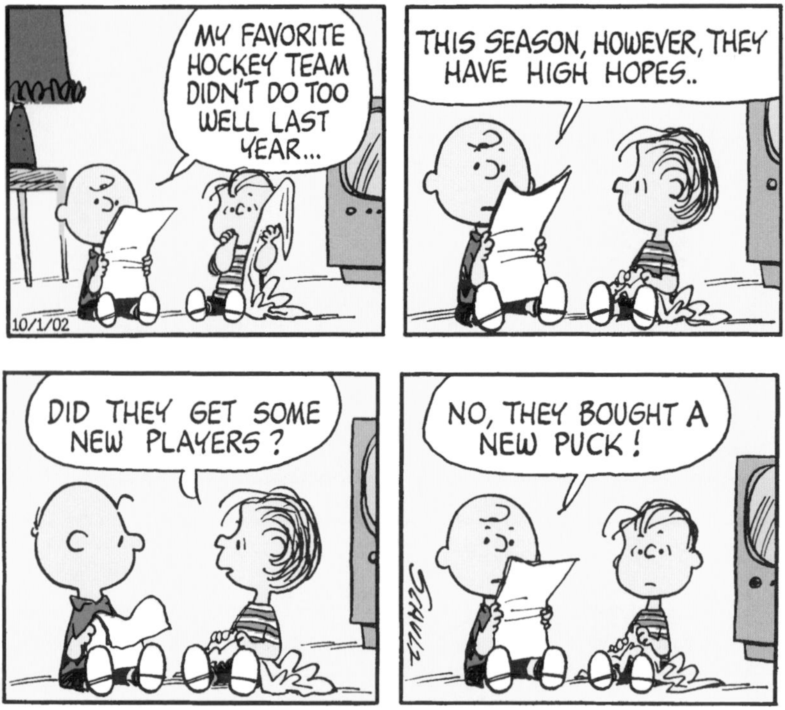
10/1/02
MY FAVORITE HOCKEY TEAM DIDN'T DO TOO WELL LAST YEAR...
THIS SEASON, HOWEVER, THEY HAVE HIGH HOPES..
DID THEY GET SOME NEW PLAYERS?
NO, THEY BOUGHT A NEW PUCK!
SCHULZ

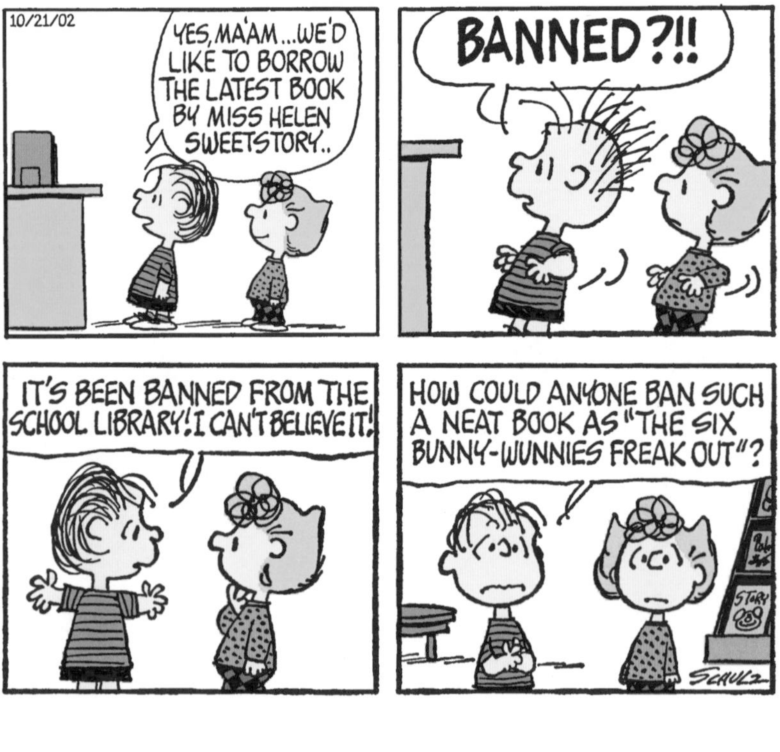
10/21/02
YES, MA'AM...WE'D LIKE TO BORROW THE LATEST BOOK BY MISS HELEN SWEETSTORY..
BANNED?!!
IT'S BEEN BANNED FROM THE SCHOOL LIBRARY! I CAN'T BELIEVE IT!
HOW COULD ANYONE BAN SUCH A NEAT BOOK AS "THE SIX BUNNY-WUNNIES FREAK OUT"?
SCHULZ

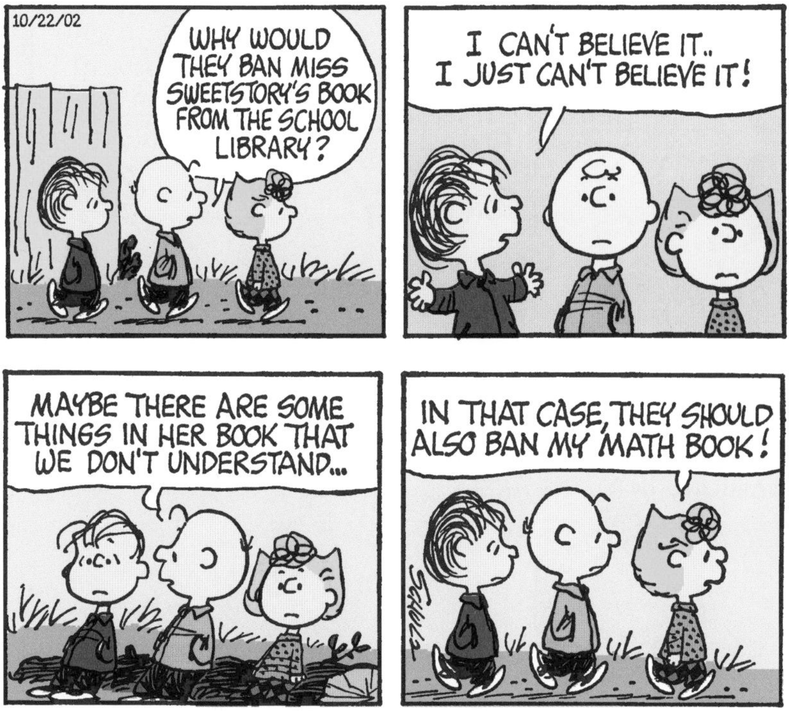
10/22/02
WHY WOULD THEY BAN MISS SWEETSTORY'S BOOK FROM THE SCHOOL LIBRARY?
I CAN'T BELIEVE IT.. I JUST CAN'T BELIEVE IT!
MAYBE THERE ARE SOME THINGS IN HER BOOK THAT WE DON'T UNDERSTAND...
IN THAT CASE, THEY SHOULD ALSO BAN MY MATH BOOK!
SCHULZ

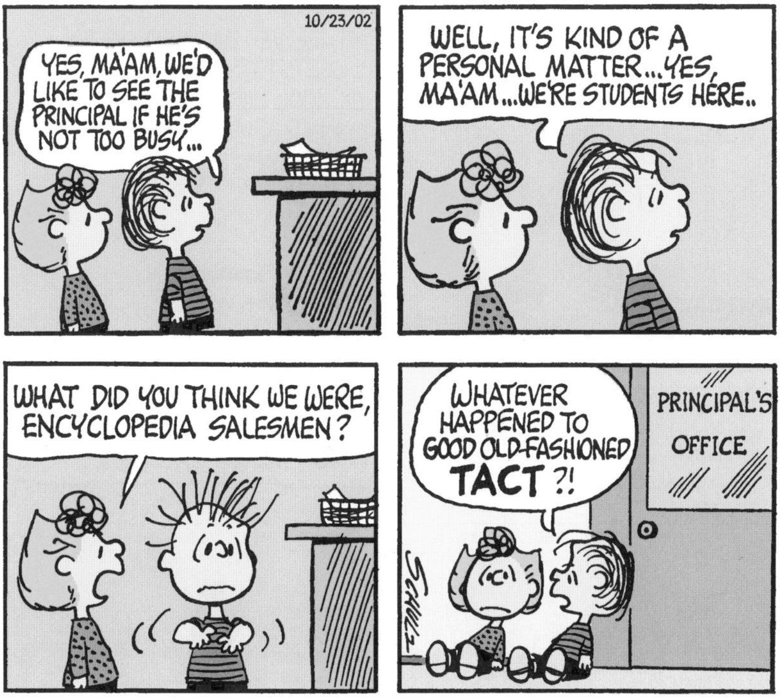
10/23/02
YES, MA'AM, WE'D LIKE TO SEE THE PRINCIPAL IF HE'S NOT TOO BUSY...
WELL, IT'S KIND OF A PERSONAL MATTER...YES, MA'AM...WE'RE STUDENTS HERE..
WHAT DID YOU THINK WE WERE, ENCYCLOPEDIA SALESMEN?
WHATEVER HAPPENED TO GOOD OLD-FASHIONED **TACT**?!
PRINCIPAL'S OFFICE
SCHULZ

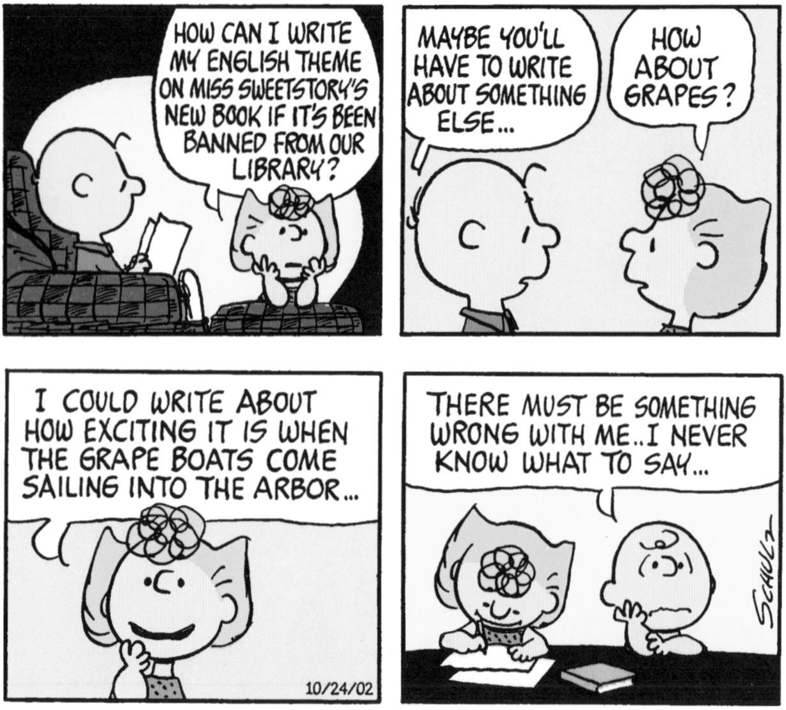
HOW CAN I WRITE MY ENGLISH THEME ON MISS SWEETSTORY'S NEW BOOK IF IT'S BEEN BANNED FROM OUR LIBRARY?
MAYBE YOU'LL HAVE TO WRITE ABOUT SOMETHING ELSE...
HOW ABOUT GRAPES?
I COULD WRITE ABOUT HOW EXCITING IT IS WHEN THE GRAPE BOATS COME SAILING INTO THE ARBOR...
10/24/02
THERE MUST BE SOMETHING WRONG WITH ME..I NEVER KNOW WHAT TO SAY...
SCHULZ

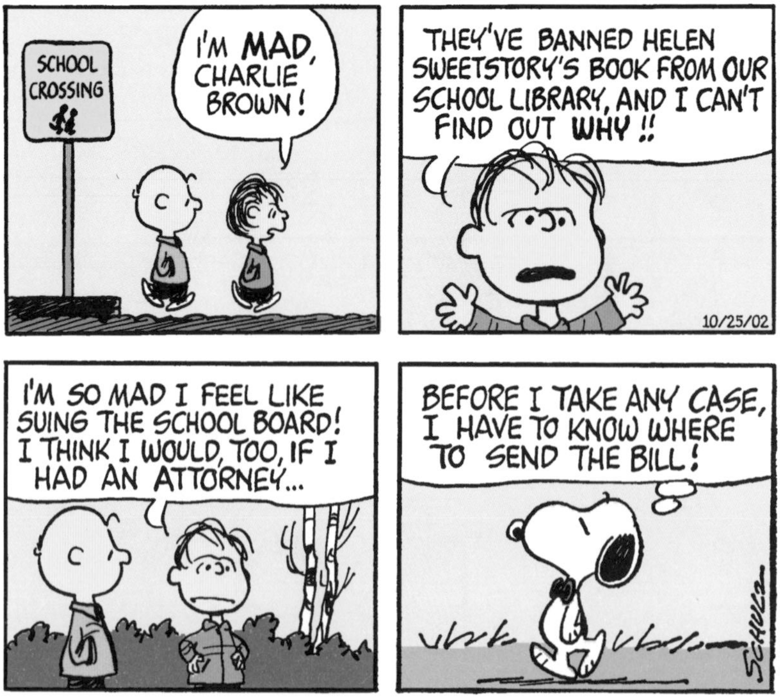
SCHOOL CROSSING
I'M MAD, CHARLIE BROWN!
THEY'VE BANNED HELEN SWEETSTORY'S BOOK FROM OUR SCHOOL LIBRARY, AND I CAN'T FIND OUT WHY!!
10/25/02
I'M SO MAD I FEEL LIKE SUING THE SCHOOL BOARD! I THINK I WOULD, TOO, IF I HAD AN ATTORNEY...
BEFORE I TAKE ANY CASE, I HAVE TO KNOW WHERE TO SEND THE BILL!
SCHULZ

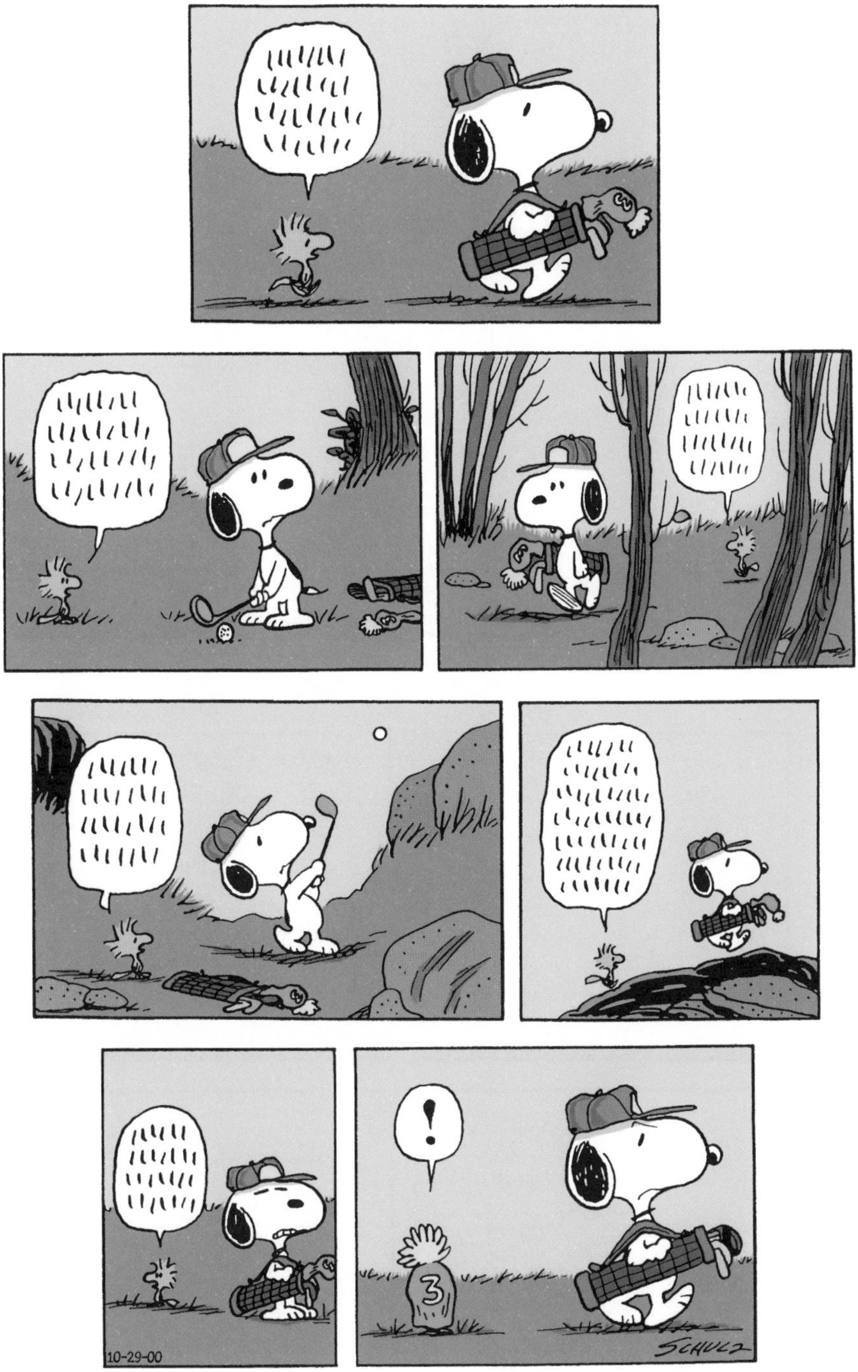
!
3
10-29-00
SCHULZ

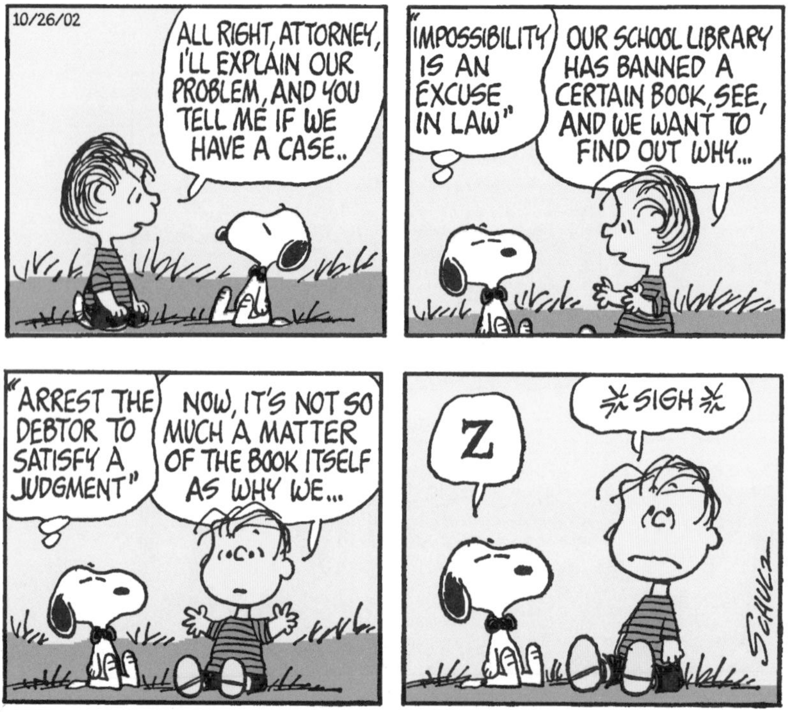
10/26/02
ALL RIGHT, ATTORNEY, I'LL EXPLAIN OUR PROBLEM, AND YOU TELL ME IF WE HAVE A CASE..
"IMPOSSIBILITY IS AN EXCUSE IN LAW"
OUR SCHOOL LIBRARY HAS BANNED A CERTAIN BOOK, SEE, AND WE WANT TO FIND OUT WHY...
"ARREST THE DEBTOR TO SATISFY A JUDGMENT"
NOW, IT'S NOT SO MUCH A MATTER OF THE BOOK ITSELF AS WHY WE...
Z
SIGH
SCHULZ

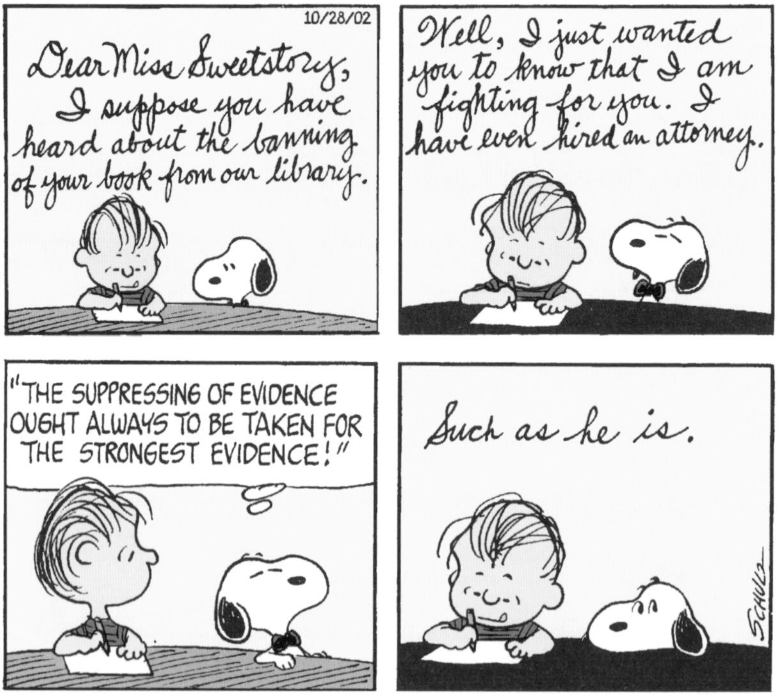
10/28/02
Dear Miss Sweetstory, I suppose you have heard about the banning of your book from our library.
Well, I just wanted you to know that I am fighting for you. I have even hired an attorney.
"THE SUPPRESSING OF EVIDENCE OUGHT ALWAYS TO BE TAKEN FOR THE STRONGEST EVIDENCE!"
Such as he is.
SCHULZ

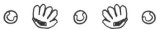

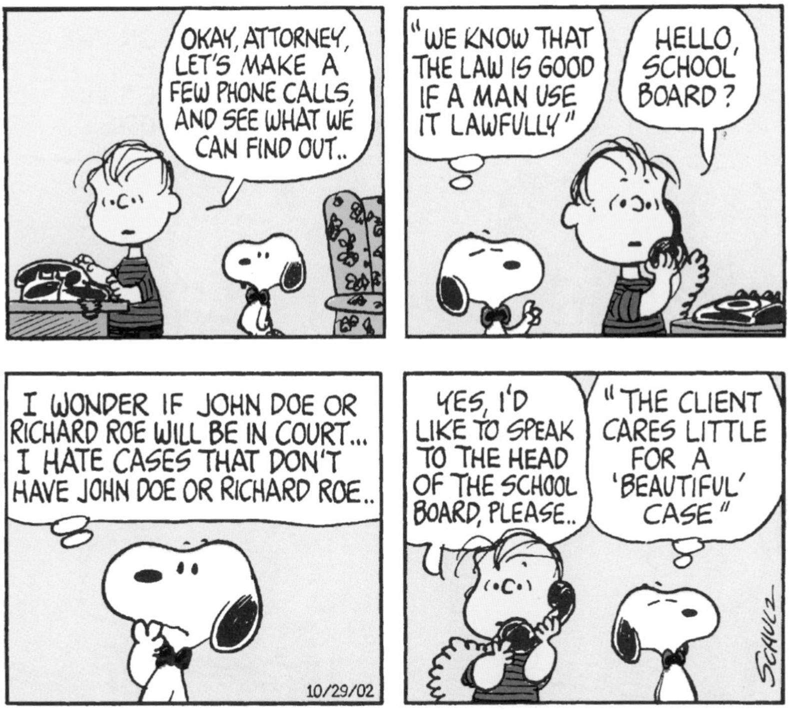
OKAY, ATTORNEY, LET'S MAKE A FEW PHONE CALLS, AND SEE WHAT WE CAN FIND OUT..
"WE KNOW THAT THE LAW IS GOOD IF A MAN USE IT LAWFULLY"
HELLO, SCHOOL BOARD?
I WONDER IF JOHN DOE OR RICHARD ROE WILL BE IN COURT... I HATE CASES THAT DON'T HAVE JOHN DOE OR RICHARD ROE..
10/29/02
YES, I'D LIKE TO SPEAK TO THE HEAD OF THE SCHOOL BOARD, PLEASE..
"THE CLIENT CARES LITTLE FOR A 'BEAUTIFUL' CASE"
SCHULZ

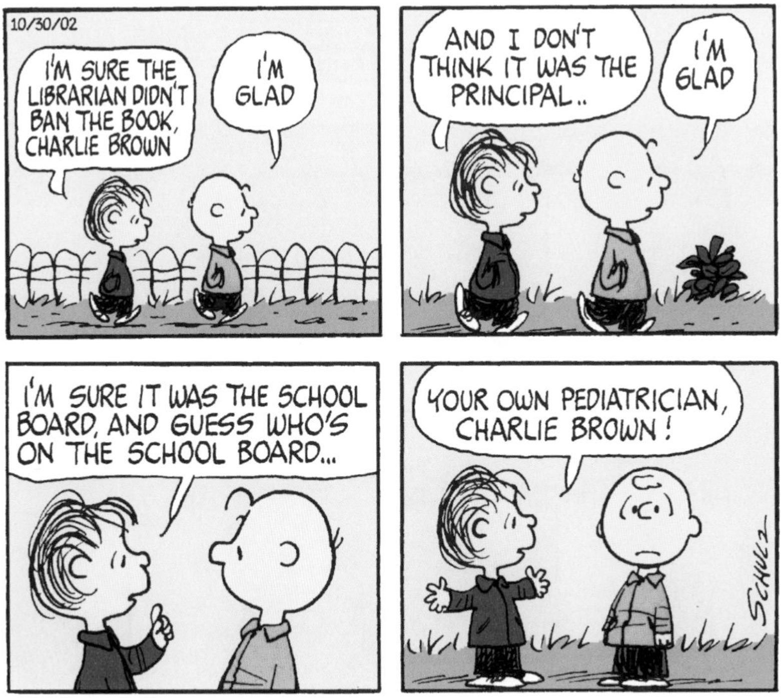
10/30/02
I'M SURE THE LIBRARIAN DIDN'T BAN THE BOOK, CHARLIE BROWN
I'M GLAD
AND I DON'T THINK IT WAS THE PRINCIPAL..
I'M GLAD
I'M SURE IT WAS THE SCHOOL BOARD, AND GUESS WHO'S ON THE SCHOOL BOARD...
YOUR OWN PEDIATRICIAN, CHARLIE BROWN!
SCHULZ

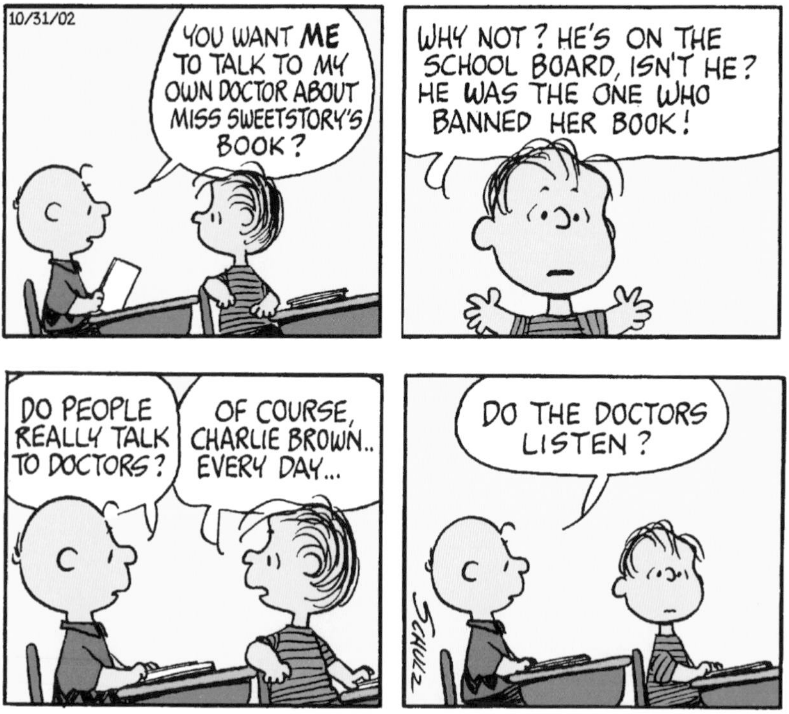
10/31/02
YOU WANT ME TO TALK TO MY OWN DOCTOR ABOUT MISS SWEETSTORY'S BOOK?
WHY NOT? HE'S ON THE SCHOOL BOARD, ISN'T HE? HE WAS THE ONE WHO BANNED HER BOOK!
DO PEOPLE REALLY TALK TO DOCTORS?
OF COURSE, CHARLIE BROWN.. EVERY DAY...
DO THE DOCTORS LISTEN?
SCHULZ

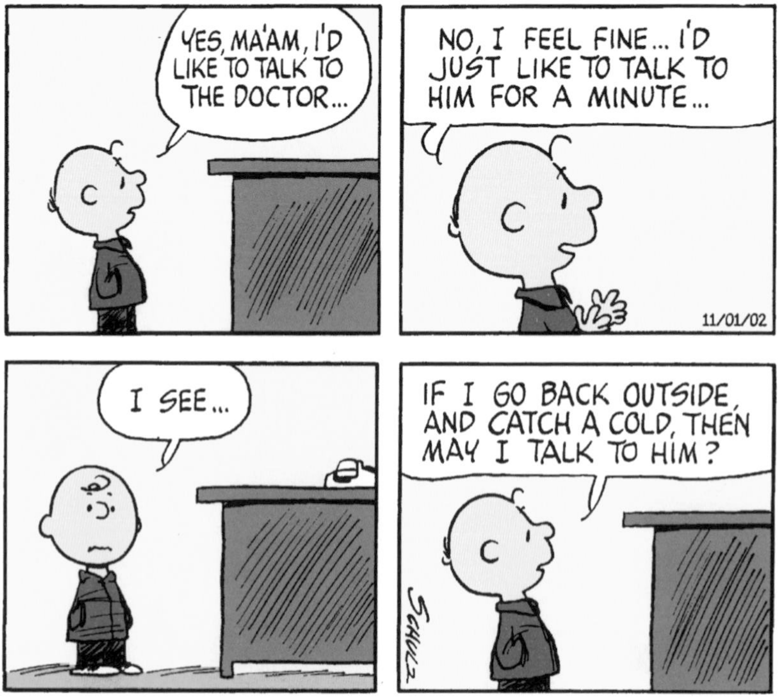
YES, MA'AM, I'D LIKE TO TALK TO THE DOCTOR...
NO, I FEEL FINE... I'D JUST LIKE TO TALK TO HIM FOR A MINUTE...
11/01/02
I SEE...
IF I GO BACK OUTSIDE AND CATCH A COLD, THEN MAY I TALK TO HIM?
SCHULZ

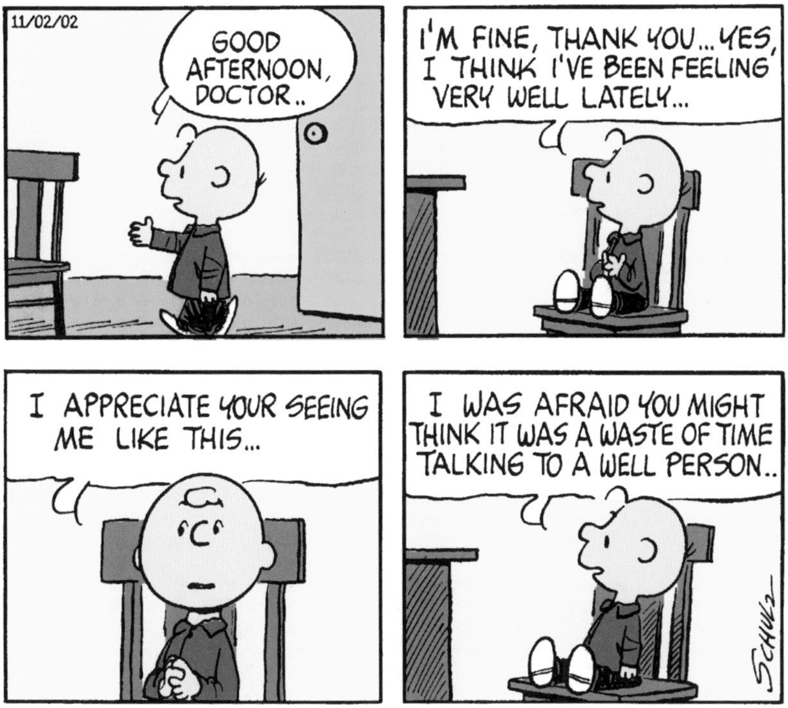
11/02/02
GOOD AFTERNOON, DOCTOR..
I'M FINE, THANK YOU... YES, I THINK I'VE BEEN FEELING VERY WELL LATELY...
I APPRECIATE YOUR SEEING ME LIKE THIS...
I WAS AFRAID YOU MIGHT THINK IT WAS A WASTE OF TIME TALKING TO A WELL PERSON..
SCHULZ

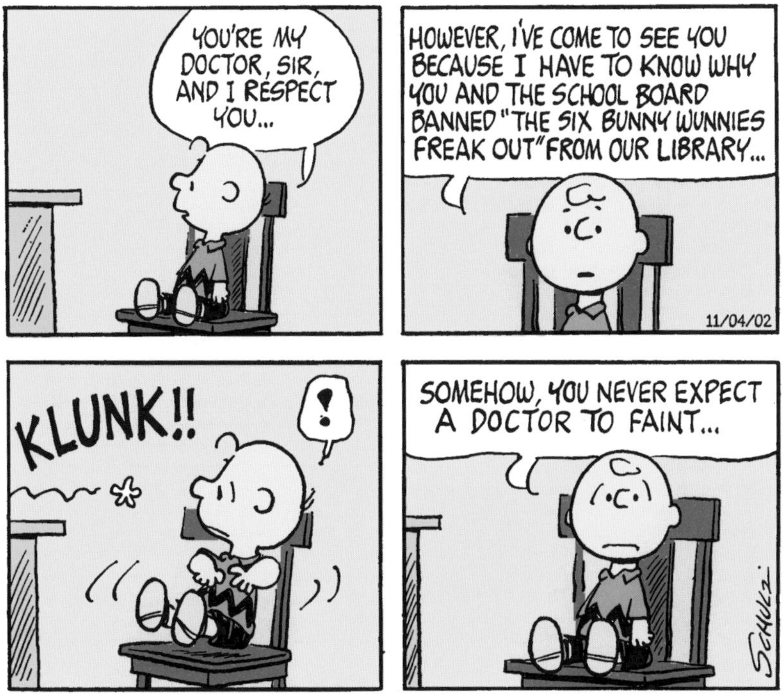
YOU'RE MY DOCTOR, SIR, AND I RESPECT YOU...
HOWEVER, I'VE COME TO SEE YOU BECAUSE I HAVE TO KNOW WHY YOU AND THE SCHOOL BOARD BANNED "THE SIX BUNNY WUNNIES FREAK OUT" FROM OUR LIBRARY...
11/04/02
KLUNK!!
!
SOMEHOW, YOU NEVER EXPECT A DOCTOR TO FAINT...
SCHULZ

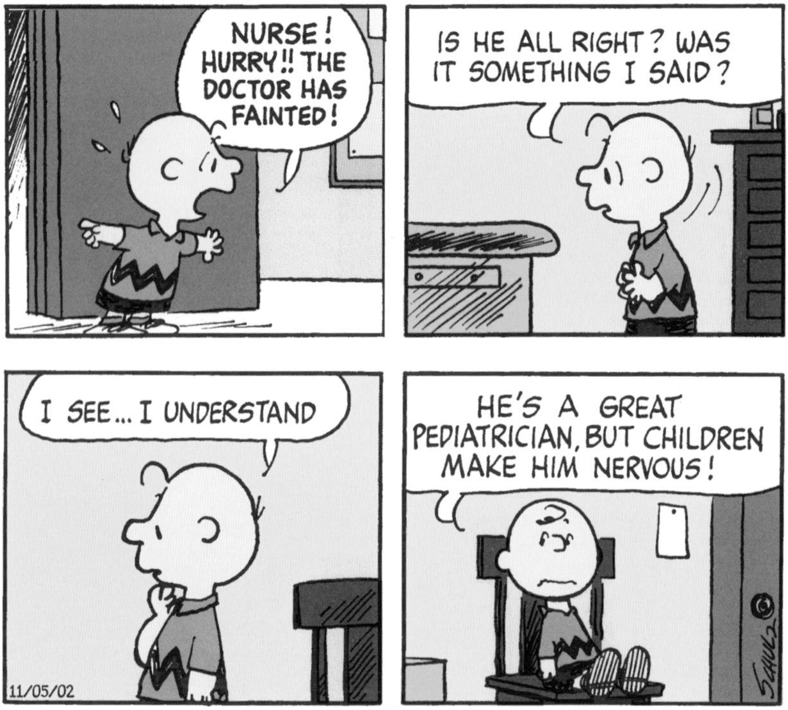
NURSE! HURRY!! THE DOCTOR HAS FAINTED!
IS HE ALL RIGHT? WAS IT SOMETHING I SAID?
I SEE... I UNDERSTAND
11/05/02
HE'S A GREAT PEDIATRICIAN, BUT CHILDREN MAKE HIM NERVOUS!
SCHULZ

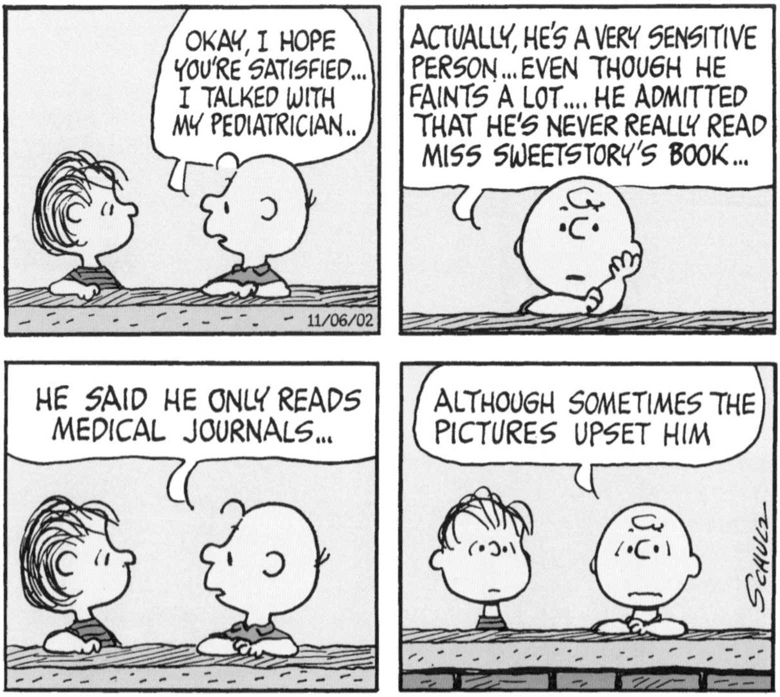
OKAY, I HOPE YOU'RE SATISFIED... I TALKED WITH MY PEDIATRICIAN..
11/06/02
ACTUALLY, HE'S A VERY SENSITIVE PERSON... EVEN THOUGH HE FAINTS A LOT.... HE ADMITTED THAT HE'S NEVER REALLY READ MISS SWEETSTORY'S BOOK...
HE SAID HE ONLY READS MEDICAL JOURNALS...
ALTHOUGH SOMETIMES THE PICTURES UPSET HIM
SCHULZ

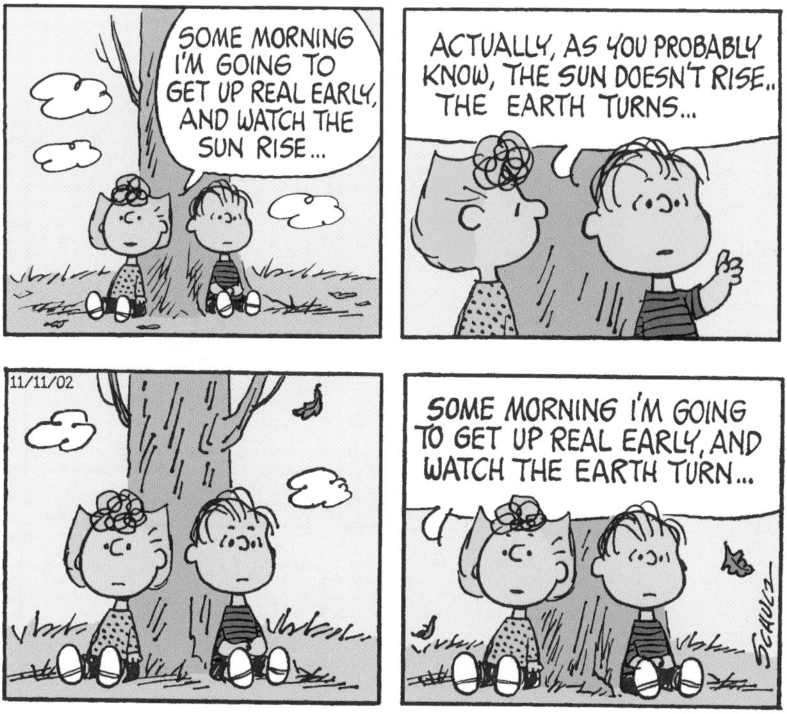
SOME MORNING I'M GOING TO GET UP REAL EARLY, AND WATCH THE SUN RISE...
ACTUALLY, AS YOU PROBABLY KNOW, THE SUN DOESN'T RISE.. THE EARTH TURNS...
11/11/02
SOME MORNING I'M GOING TO GET UP REAL EARLY, AND WATCH THE EARTH TURN...
SCHULZ

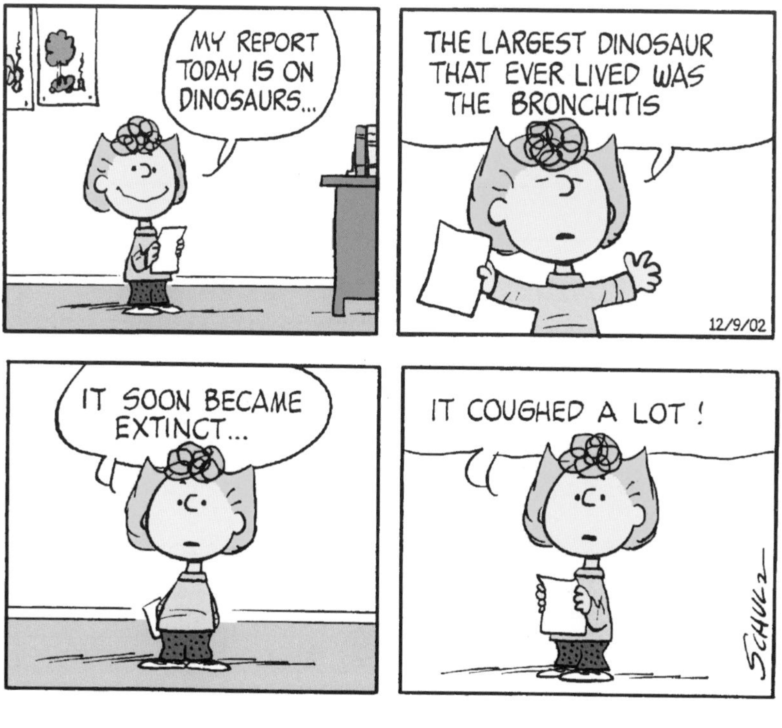
MY REPORT TODAY IS ON DINOSAURS...
THE LARGEST DINOSAUR THAT EVER LIVED WAS THE BRONCHITIS
12/9/02
IT SOON BECAME EXTINCT...
IT COUGHED A LOT!
SCHULZ

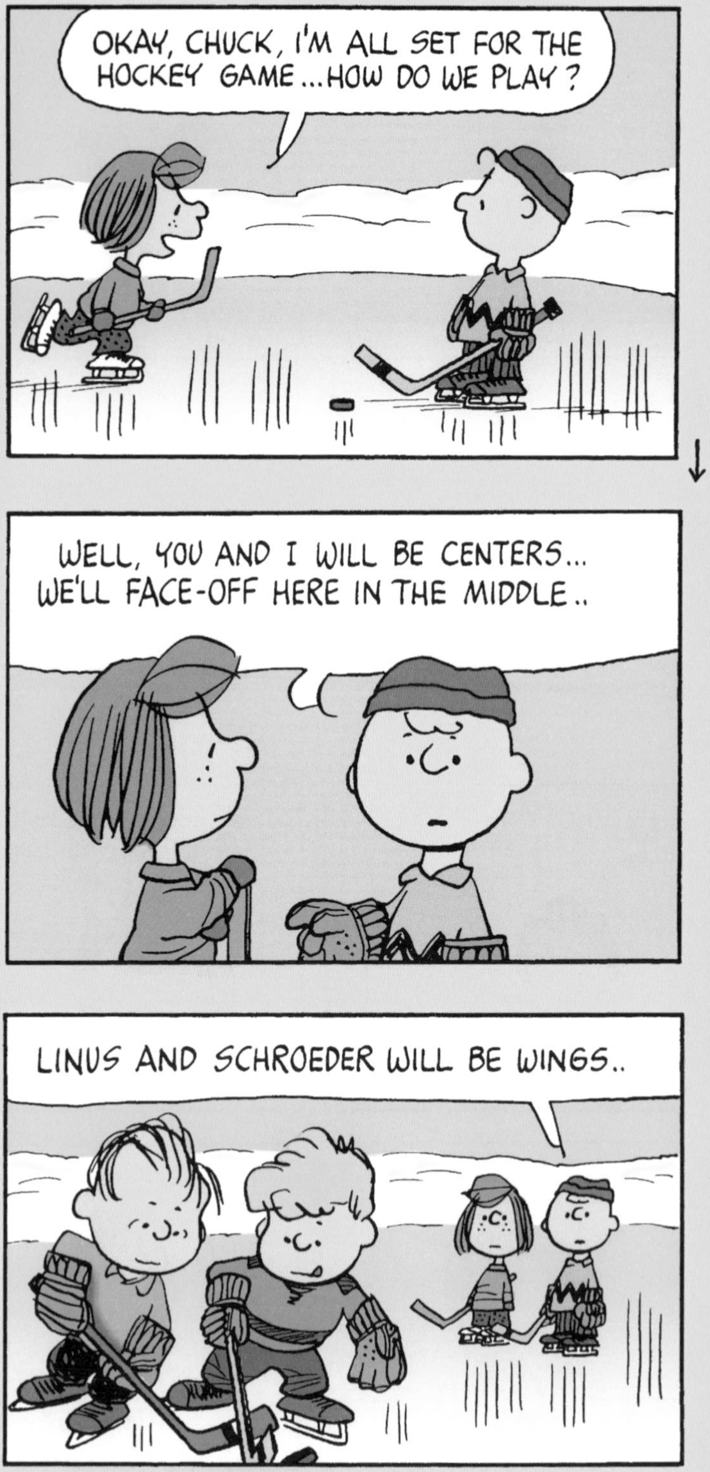
OKAY, CHUCK, I'M ALL SET FOR THE HOCKEY GAME...HOW DO WE PLAY?
WELL, YOU AND I WILL BE CENTERS... WE'LL FACE-OFF HERE IN THE MIDDLE..
LINUS AND SCHROEDER WILL BE WINGS..

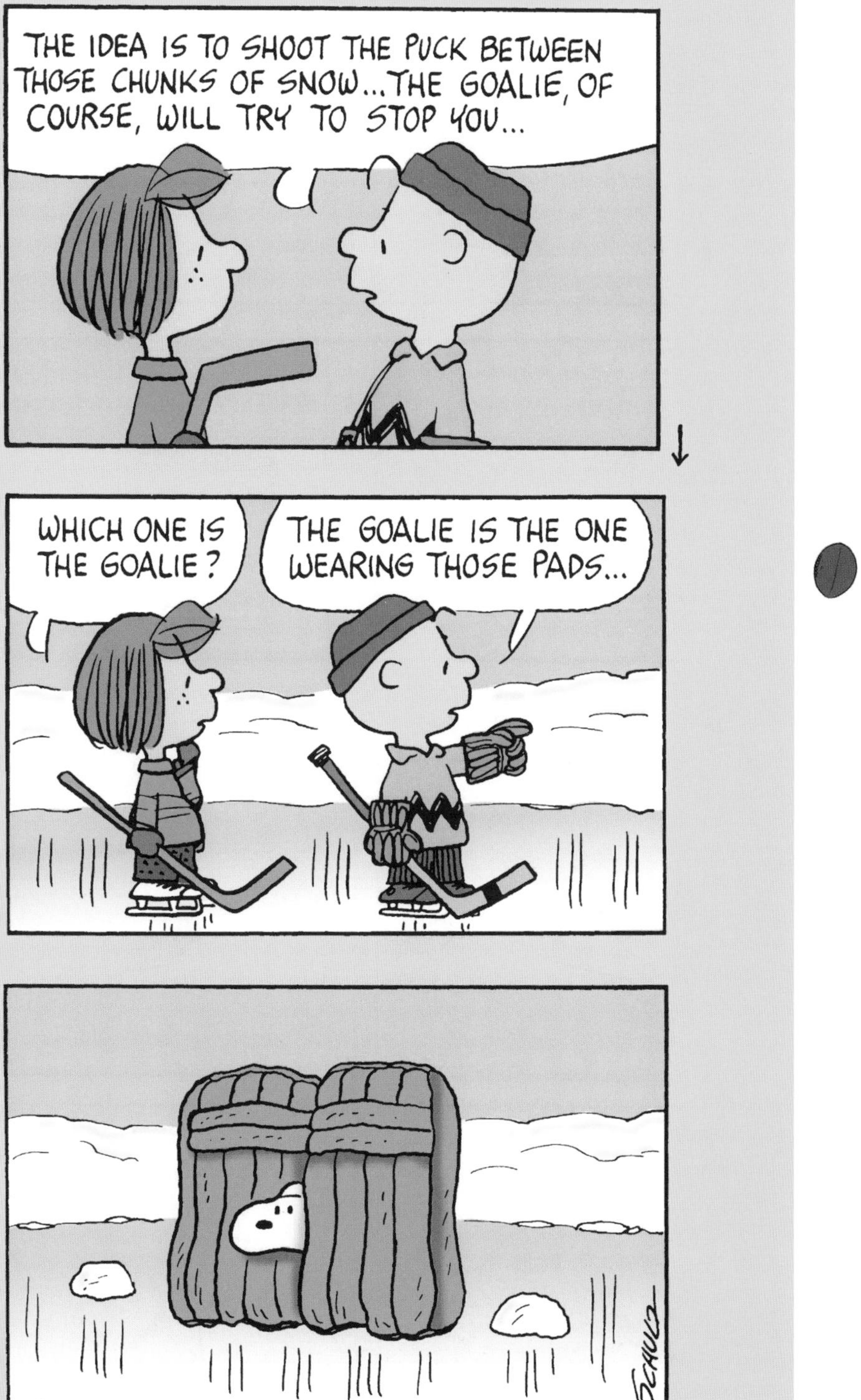
THE IDEA IS TO SHOOT THE PUCK BETWEEN THOSE CHUNKS OF SNOW...THE GOALIE, OF COURSE, WILL TRY TO STOP YOU...
WHICH ONE IS THE GOALIE?
THE GOALIE IS THE ONE WEARING THOSE PADS...
SCHULZ
1-27-02

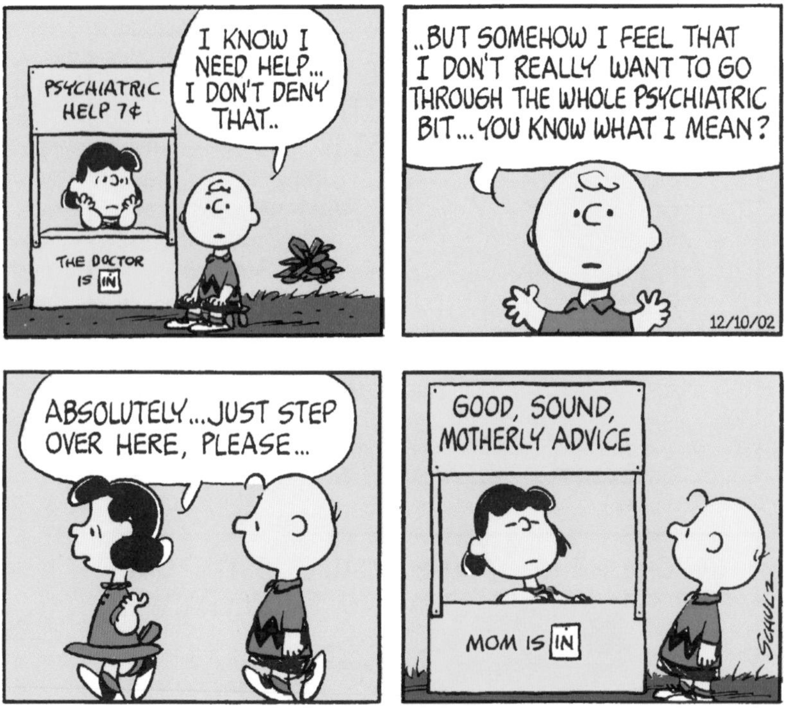
PSYCHIATRIC HELP 7¢
THE DOCTOR IS IN
I KNOW I NEED HELP... I DON'T DENY THAT..
..BUT SOMEHOW I FEEL THAT I DON'T REALLY WANT TO GO THROUGH THE WHOLE PSYCHIATRIC BIT... YOU KNOW WHAT I MEAN?
12/10/02
ABSOLUTELY... JUST STEP OVER HERE, PLEASE...
GOOD, SOUND, MOTHERLY ADVICE
MOM IS IN
SCHULZ

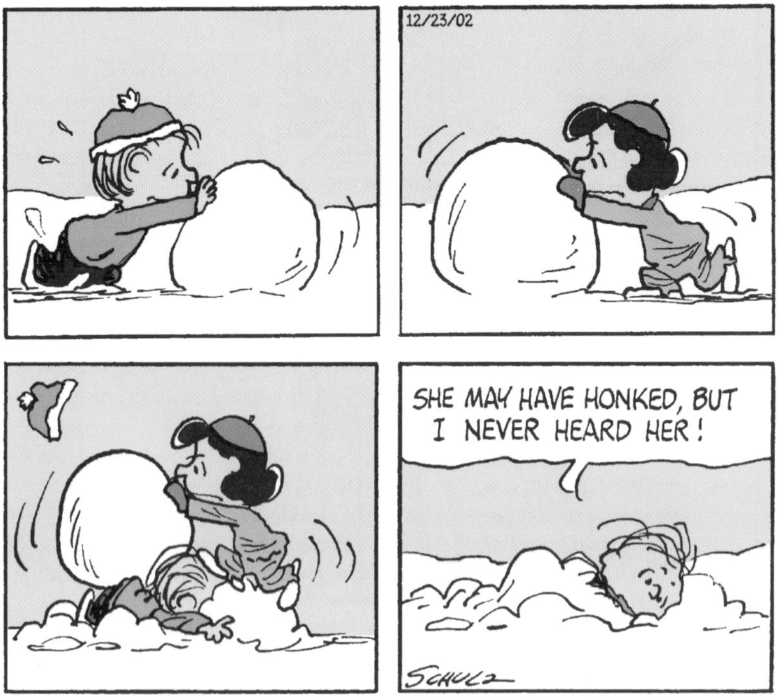
12/23/02
SHE MAY HAVE HONKED, BUT I NEVER HEARD HER!
SCHULZ

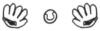

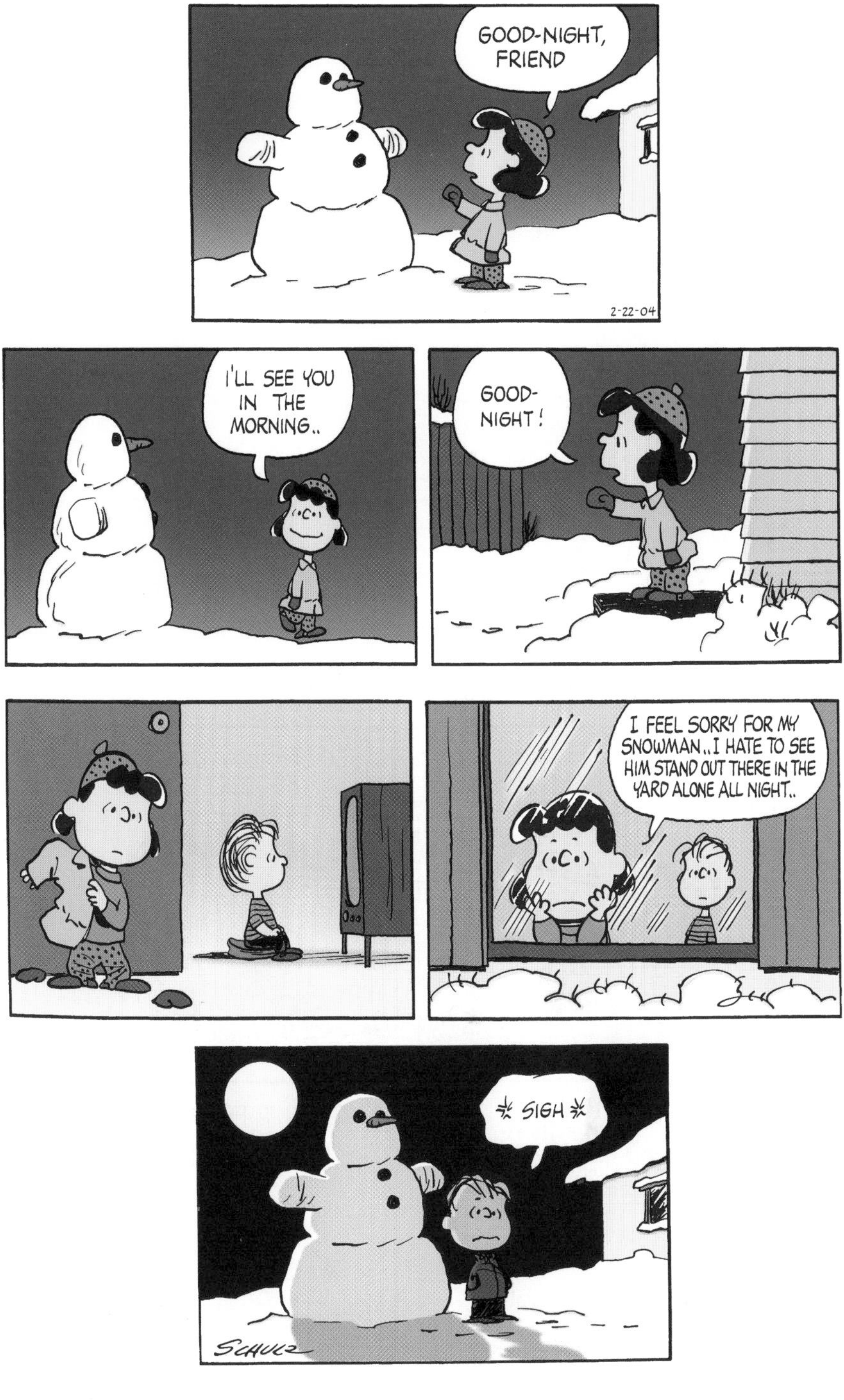
GOOD-NIGHT, FRIEND
2-22-04
I'LL SEE YOU IN THE MORNING..
GOOD-NIGHT!
I FEEL SORRY FOR MY SNOWMAN..I HATE TO SEE HIM STAND OUT THERE IN THE YARD ALONE ALL NIGHT..
SIGH
SCHULZ

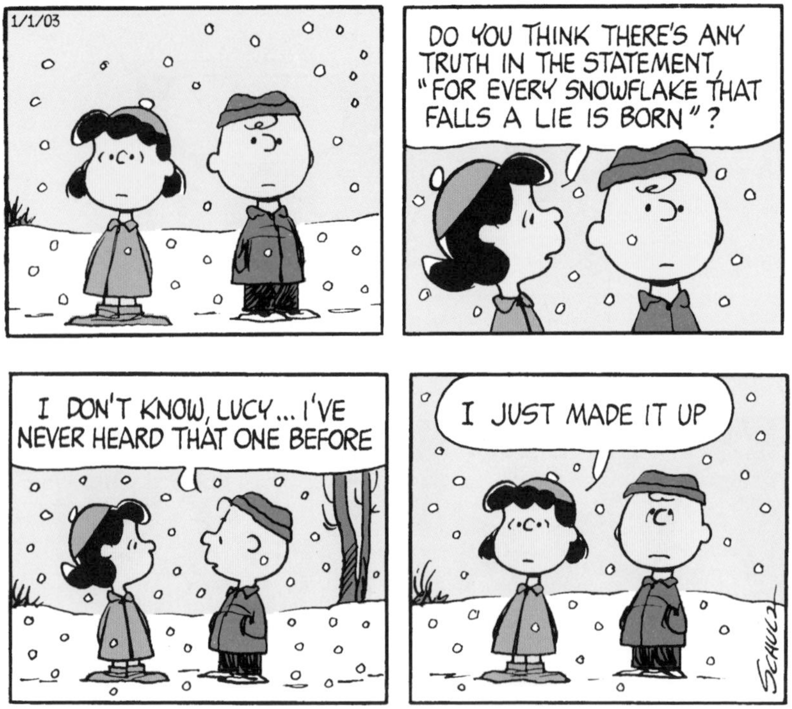
1/1/03
DO YOU THINK THERE'S ANY TRUTH IN THE STATEMENT, "FOR EVERY SNOWFLAKE THAT FALLS A LIE IS BORN"?
I DON'T KNOW, LUCY... I'VE NEVER HEARD THAT ONE BEFORE
I JUST MADE IT UP

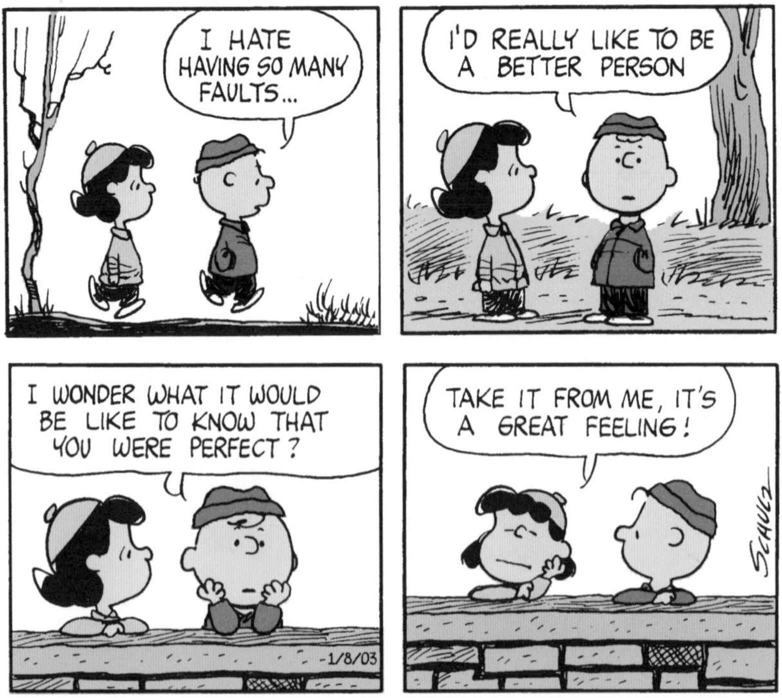
I HATE HAVING SO MANY FAULTS...
I'D REALLY LIKE TO BE A BETTER PERSON
I WONDER WHAT IT WOULD BE LIKE TO KNOW THAT YOU WERE PERFECT?
1/8/03
TAKE IT FROM ME, IT'S A GREAT FEELING!

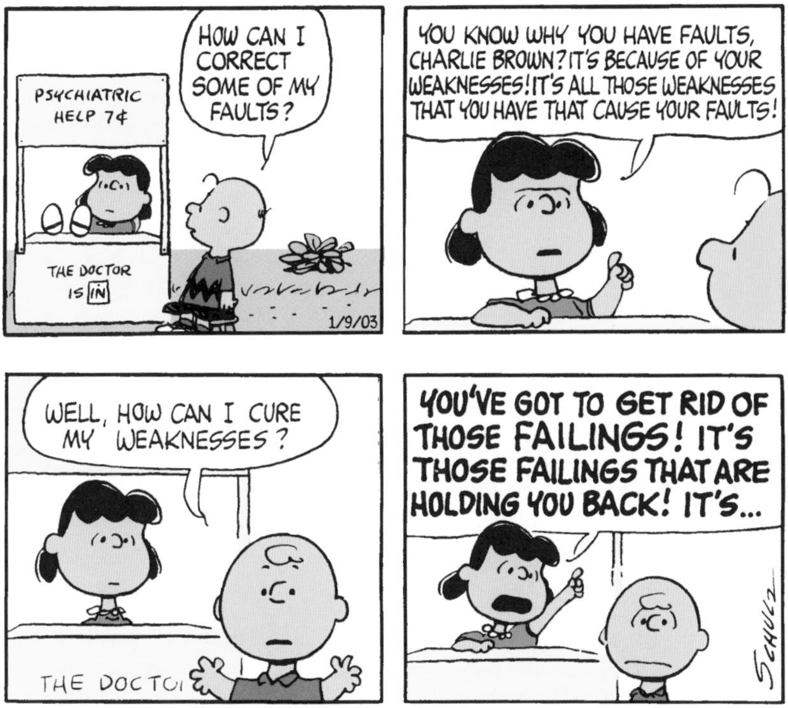
PSYCHIATRIC HELP 7¢
THE DOCTOR IS IN
HOW CAN I CORRECT SOME OF MY FAULTS?
1/9/03
YOU KNOW WHY YOU HAVE FAULTS, CHARLIE BROWN? IT'S BECAUSE OF YOUR WEAKNESSES! IT'S ALL THOSE WEAKNESSES THAT YOU HAVE THAT CAUSE YOUR FAULTS!
WELL, HOW CAN I CURE MY WEAKNESSES?
YOU'VE GOT TO GET RID OF THOSE FAILINGS! IT'S THOSE FAILINGS THAT ARE HOLDING YOU BACK! IT'S...
SCHULZ

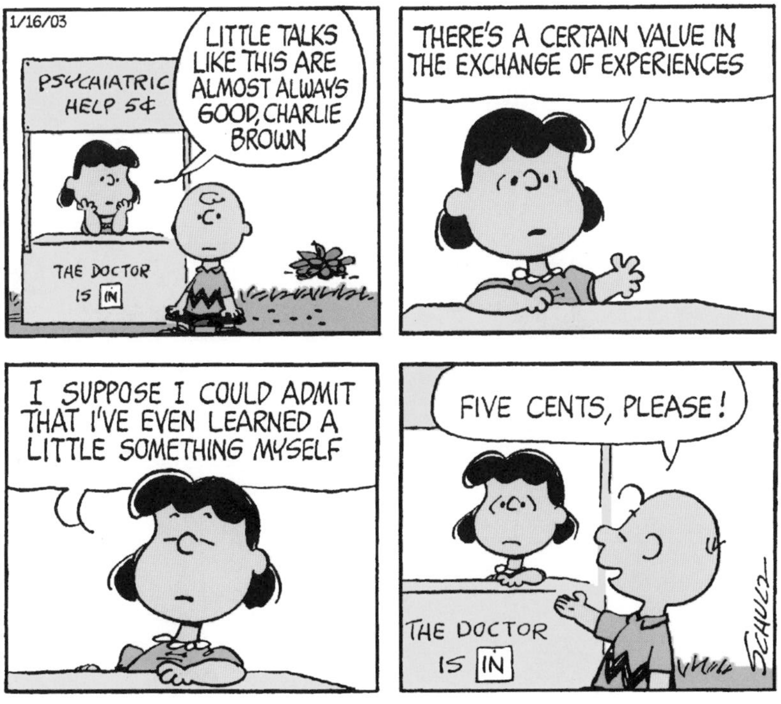
1/16/03
PSYCHIATRIC HELP 5¢
THE DOCTOR IS IN
LITTLE TALKS LIKE THIS ARE ALMOST ALWAYS GOOD, CHARLIE BROWN
THERE'S A CERTAIN VALUE IN THE EXCHANGE OF EXPERIENCES
I SUPPOSE I COULD ADMIT THAT I'VE EVEN LEARNED A LITTLE SOMETHING MYSELF
FIVE CENTS, PLEASE!
THE DOCTOR IS IN
SCHULZ

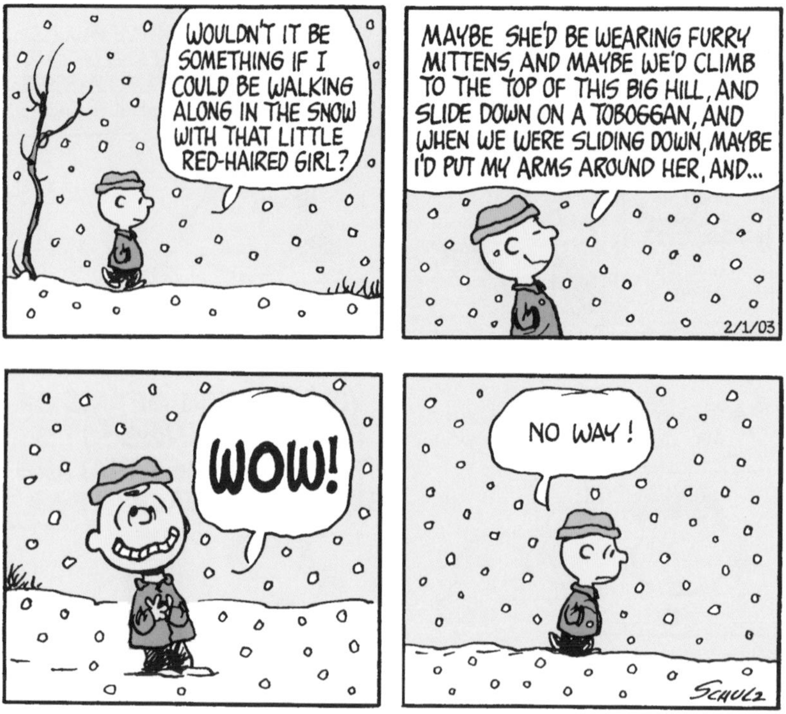
WOULDN'T IT BE SOMETHING IF I COULD BE WALKING ALONG IN THE SNOW WITH THAT LITTLE RED-HAIRED GIRL?
MAYBE SHE'D BE WEARING FURRY MITTENS, AND MAYBE WE'D CLIMB TO THE TOP OF THIS BIG HILL, AND SLIDE DOWN ON A TOBOGGAN, AND WHEN WE WERE SLIDING DOWN, MAYBE I'D PUT MY ARMS AROUND HER, AND...
2/1/03
WOW!
NO WAY!
SCHULZ

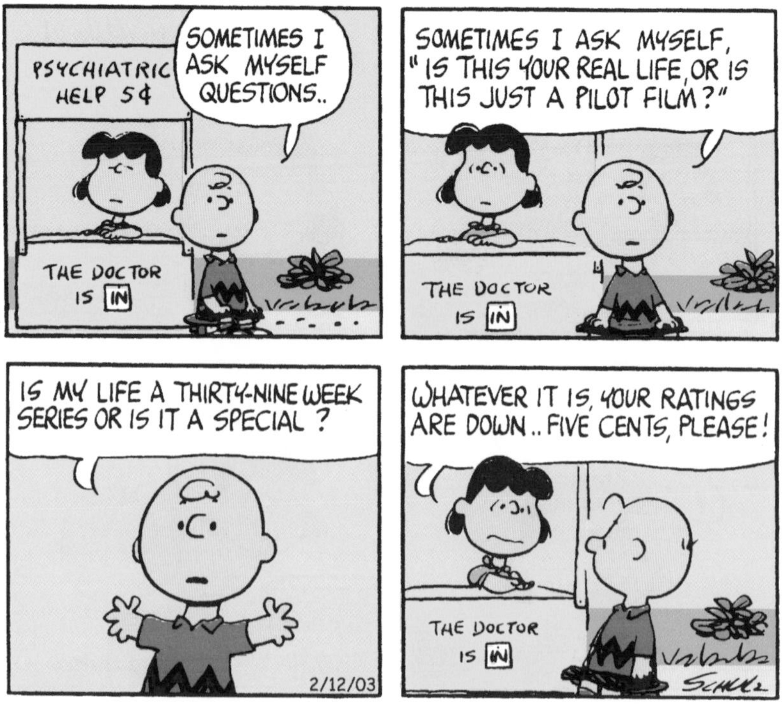
PSYCHIATRIC HELP 5¢
SOMETIMES I ASK MYSELF QUESTIONS..
THE DOCTOR IS IN
SOMETIMES I ASK MYSELF, "IS THIS YOUR REAL LIFE, OR IS THIS JUST A PILOT FILM?"
THE DOCTOR IS IN
IS MY LIFE A THIRTY-NINE WEEK SERIES OR IS IT A SPECIAL?
2/12/03
WHATEVER IT IS, YOUR RATINGS ARE DOWN.. FIVE CENTS, PLEASE!
THE DOCTOR IS IN
SCHULZ

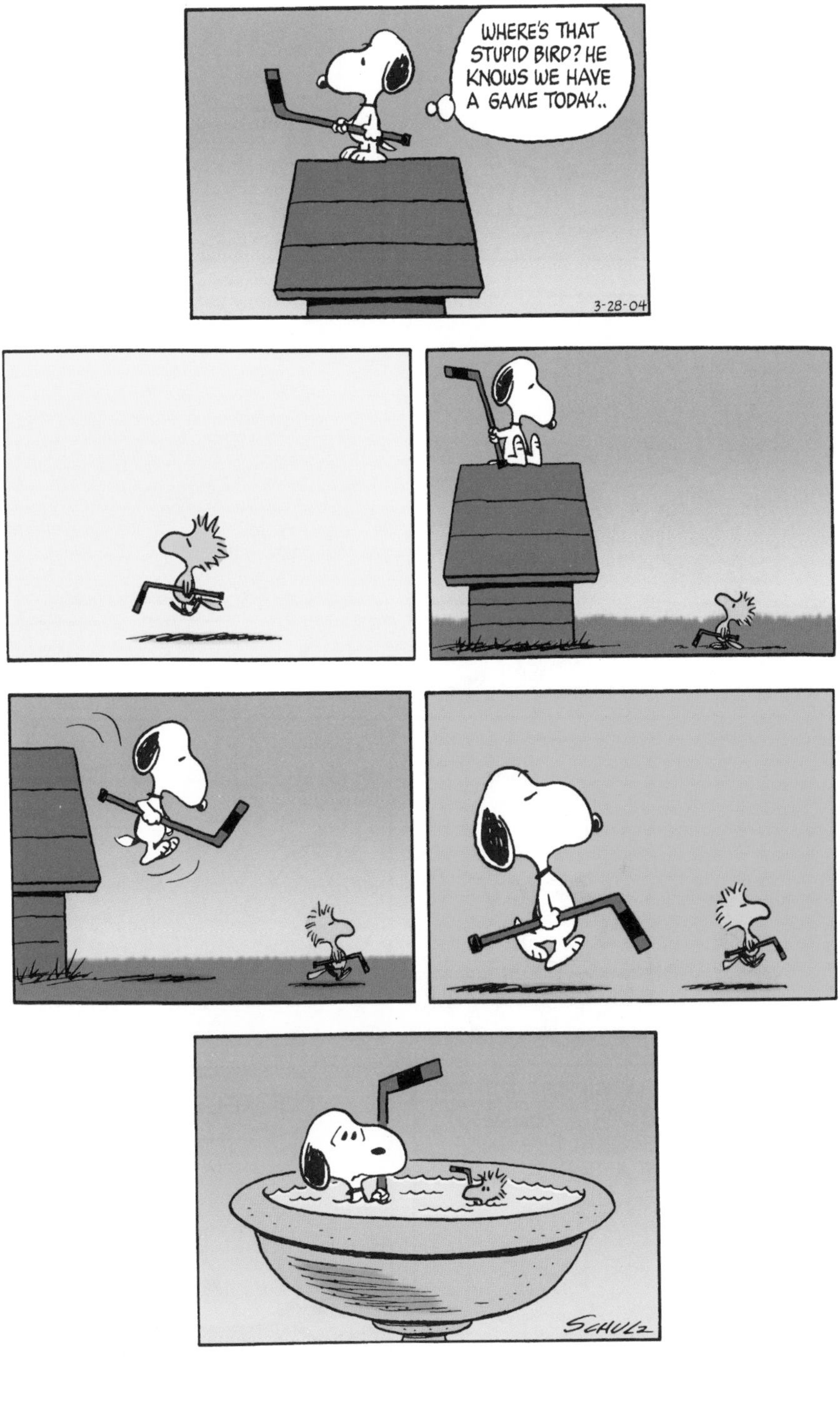
WHERE'S THAT STUPID BIRD? HE KNOWS WE HAVE A GAME TODAY..
3-28-04
SCHULZ

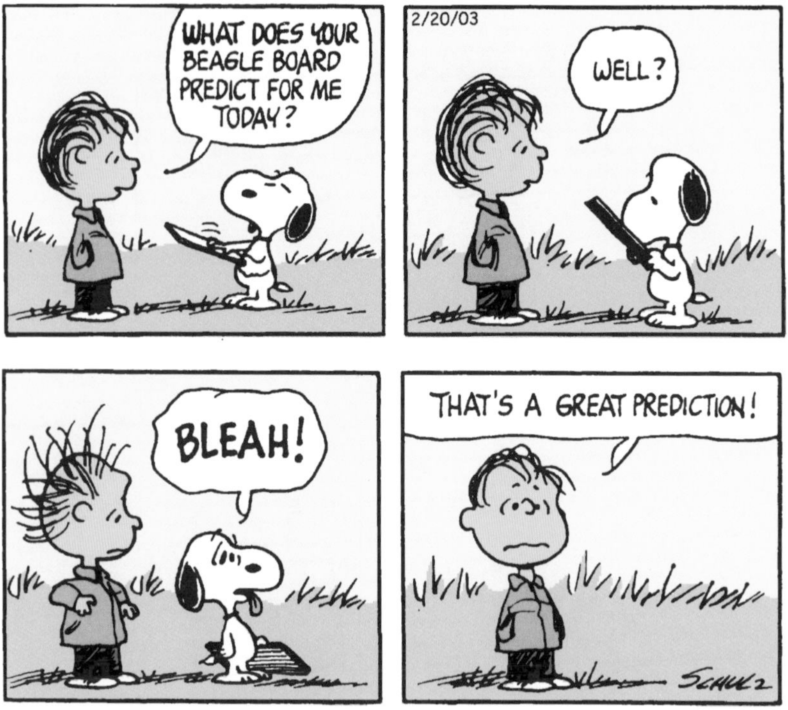
WHAT DOES YOUR BEAGLE BOARD PREDICT FOR ME TODAY?
2/20/03
WELL?
BLEAH!
THAT'S A GREAT PREDICTION!
SCHULZ

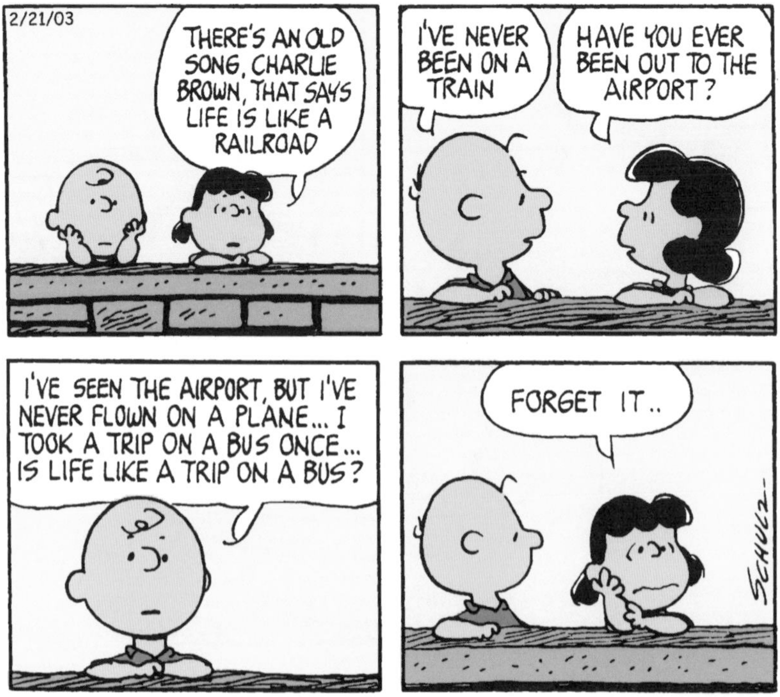
2/21/03
THERE'S AN OLD SONG, CHARLIE BROWN, THAT SAYS LIFE IS LIKE A RAILROAD
I'VE NEVER BEEN ON A TRAIN
HAVE YOU EVER BEEN OUT TO THE AIRPORT?
I'VE SEEN THE AIRPORT, BUT I'VE NEVER FLOWN ON A PLANE... I TOOK A TRIP ON A BUS ONCE... IS LIFE LIKE A TRIP ON A BUS?
FORGET IT..
SCHULZ

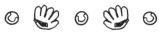

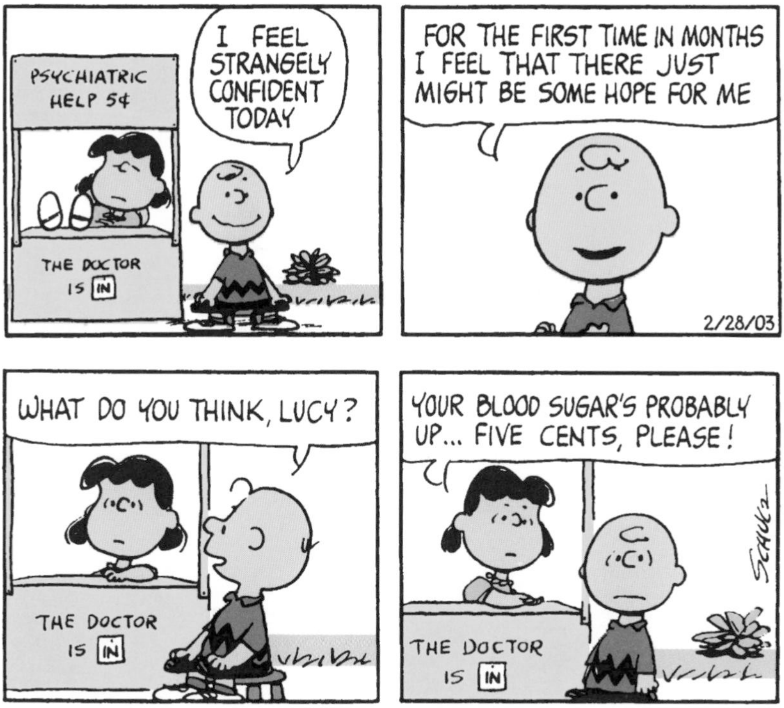
PSYCHIATRIC HELP 5¢
I FEEL STRANGELY CONFIDENT TODAY
THE DOCTOR IS IN
FOR THE FIRST TIME IN MONTHS I FEEL THAT THERE JUST MIGHT BE SOME HOPE FOR ME
2/28/03
WHAT DO YOU THINK, LUCY?
THE DOCTOR IS IN
YOUR BLOOD SUGAR'S PROBABLY UP... FIVE CENTS, PLEASE!
THE DOCTOR IS IN
SCHULZ

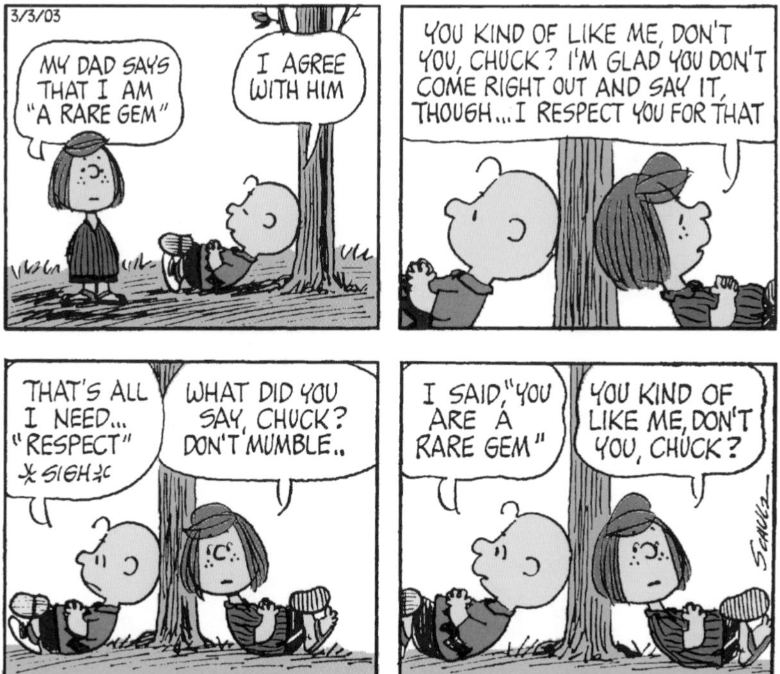
3/3/03
MY DAD SAYS THAT I AM "A RARE GEM"
I AGREE WITH HIM
YOU KIND OF LIKE ME, DON'T YOU, CHUCK? I'M GLAD YOU DON'T COME RIGHT OUT AND SAY IT, THOUGH... I RESPECT YOU FOR THAT
THAT'S ALL I NEED... "RESPECT" *SIGH*
WHAT DID YOU SAY, CHUCK? DON'T MUMBLE..
I SAID, "YOU ARE A RARE GEM"
YOU KIND OF LIKE ME, DON'T YOU, CHUCK?
SCHULZ

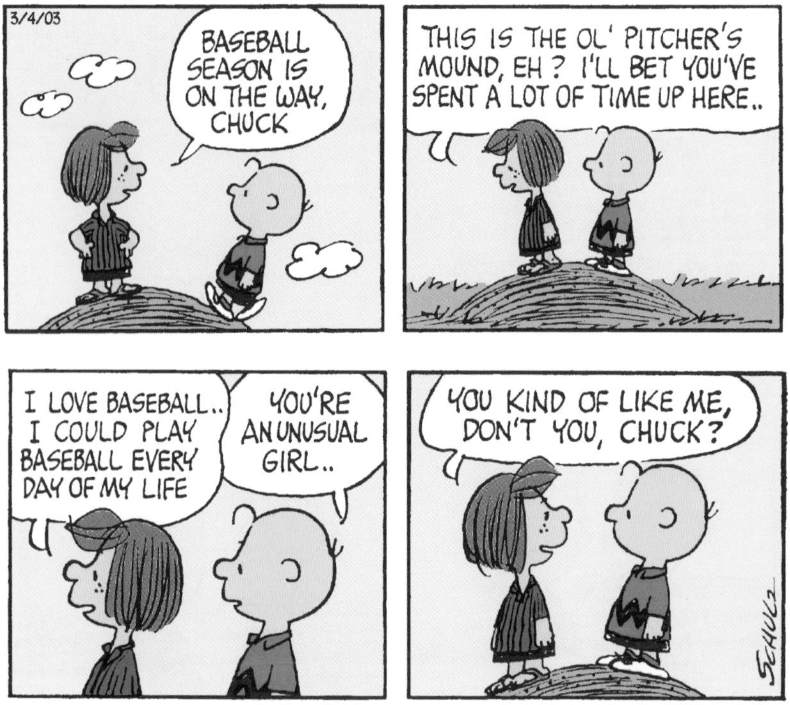
3/4/03
BASEBALL SEASON IS ON THE WAY, CHUCK
THIS IS THE OL' PITCHER'S MOUND, EH ? I'LL BET YOU'VE SPENT A LOT OF TIME UP HERE..
I LOVE BASEBALL.. I COULD PLAY BASEBALL EVERY DAY OF MY LIFE
YOU'RE AN UNUSUAL GIRL..
YOU KIND OF LIKE ME, DON'T YOU, CHUCK?
SCHULZ

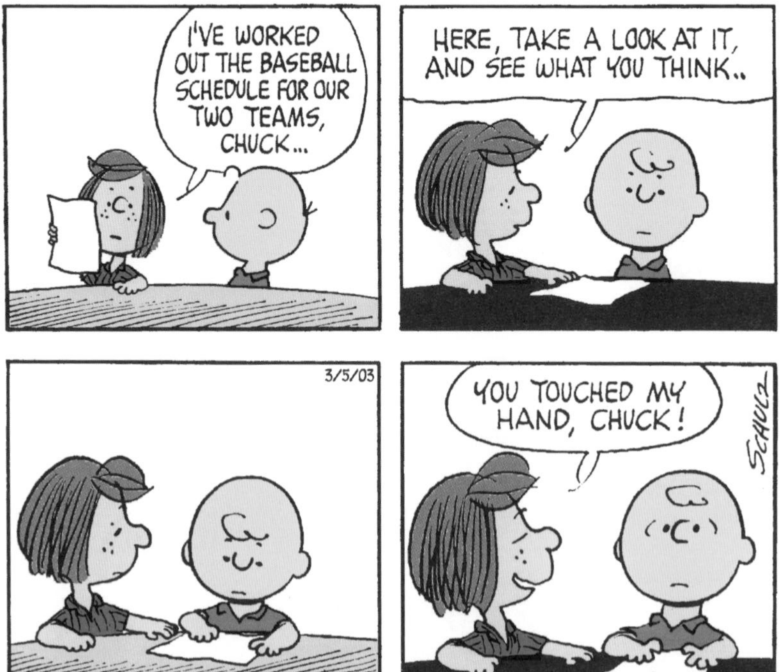
I'VE WORKED OUT THE BASEBALL SCHEDULE FOR OUR TWO TEAMS, CHUCK...
HERE, TAKE A LOOK AT IT, AND SEE WHAT YOU THINK..
3/5/03
YOU TOUCHED MY HAND, CHUCK!
SCHULZ

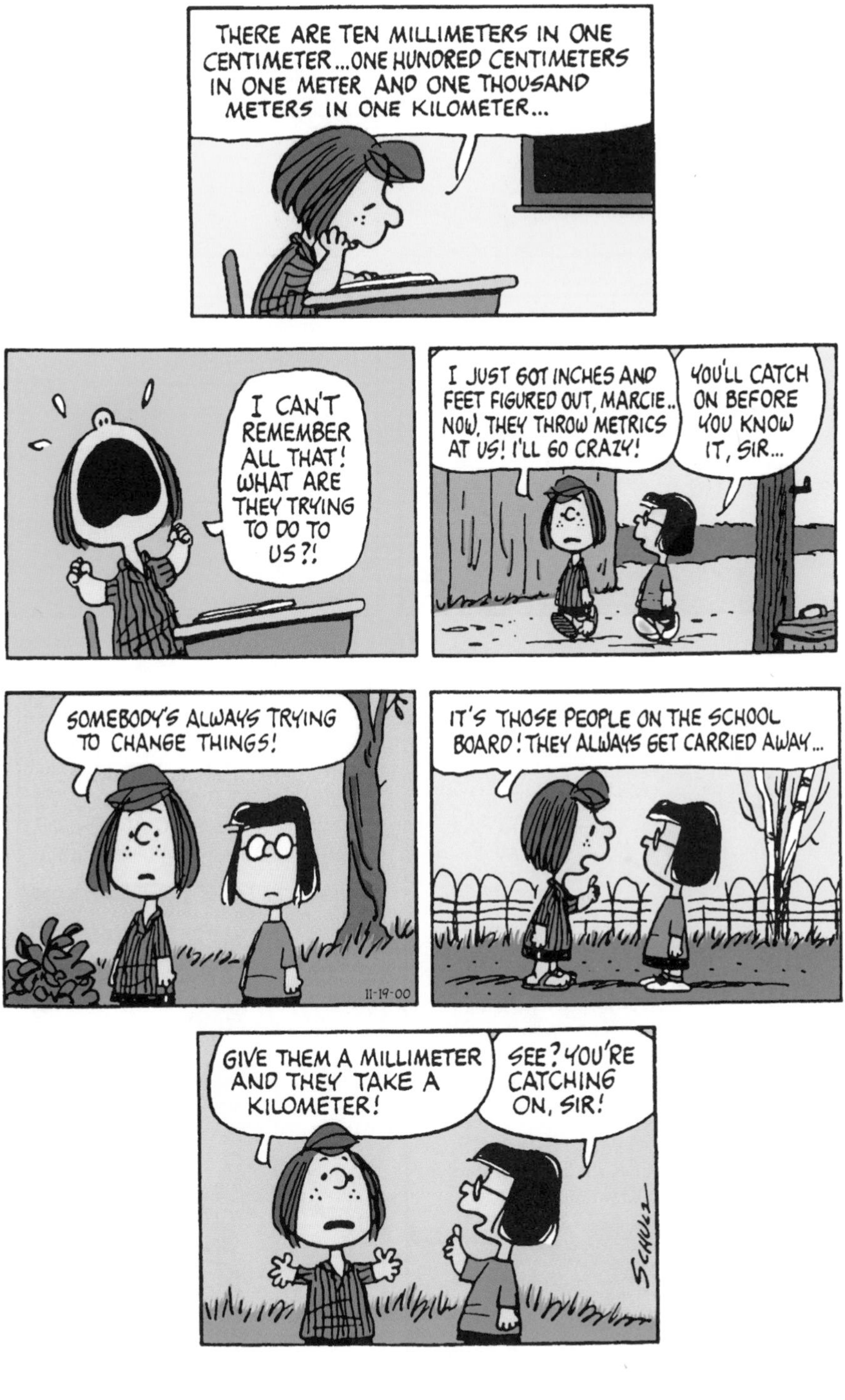
THERE ARE TEN MILLIMETERS IN ONE CENTIMETER...ONE HUNDRED CENTIMETERS IN ONE METER AND ONE THOUSAND METERS IN ONE KILOMETER...
I CAN'T REMEMBER ALL THAT! WHAT ARE THEY TRYING TO DO TO US?!
I JUST GOT INCHES AND FEET FIGURED OUT, MARCIE.. NOW, THEY THROW METRICS AT US! I'LL GO CRAZY!
YOU'LL CATCH ON BEFORE YOU KNOW IT, SIR...
SOMEBODY'S ALWAYS TRYING TO CHANGE THINGS!
11-19-00
IT'S THOSE PEOPLE ON THE SCHOOL BOARD! THEY ALWAYS GET CARRIED AWAY...
GIVE THEM A MILLIMETER AND THEY TAKE A KILOMETER!
SEE? YOU'RE CATCHING ON, SIR!
SCHULZ

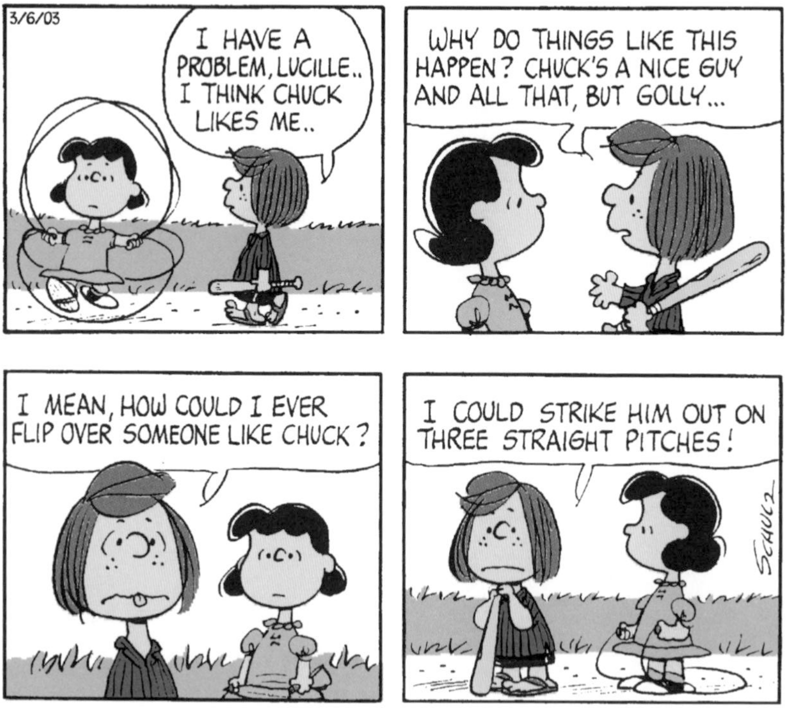
3/6/03
I HAVE A PROBLEM, LUCILLE.. I THINK CHUCK LIKES ME..
WHY DO THINGS LIKE THIS HAPPEN? CHUCK'S A NICE GUY AND ALL THAT, BUT GOLLY...
I MEAN, HOW COULD I EVER FLIP OVER SOMEONE LIKE CHUCK?
I COULD STRIKE HIM OUT ON THREE STRAIGHT PITCHES!

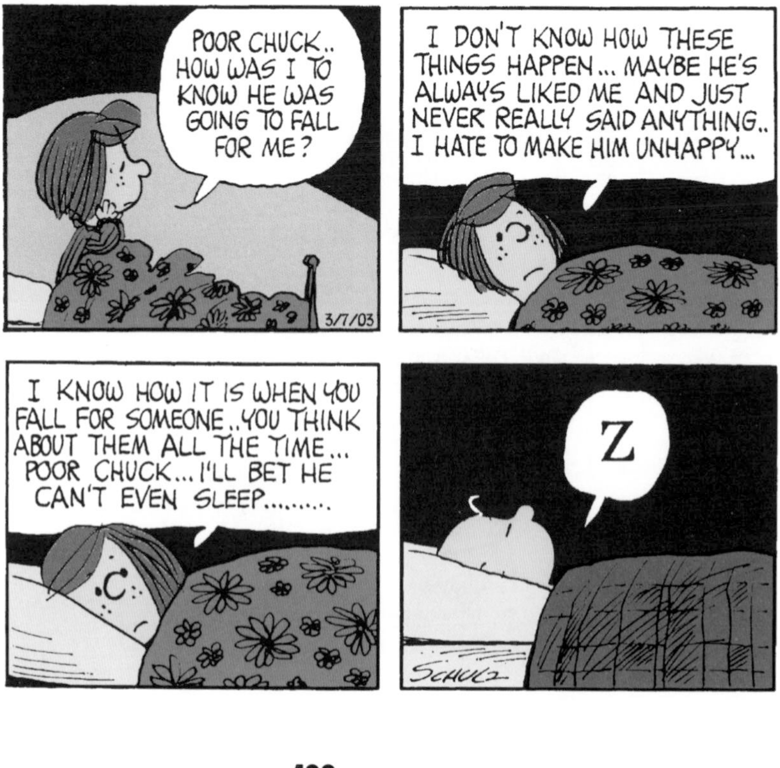
POOR CHUCK.. HOW WAS I TO KNOW HE WAS GOING TO FALL FOR ME?
3/7/03
I DON'T KNOW HOW THESE THINGS HAPPEN... MAYBE HE'S ALWAYS LIKED ME AND JUST NEVER REALLY SAID ANYTHING.. I HATE TO MAKE HIM UNHAPPY...
I KNOW HOW IT IS WHEN YOU FALL FOR SOMEONE..YOU THINK ABOUT THEM ALL THE TIME... POOR CHUCK... I'LL BET HE CAN'T EVEN SLEEP.........
Z

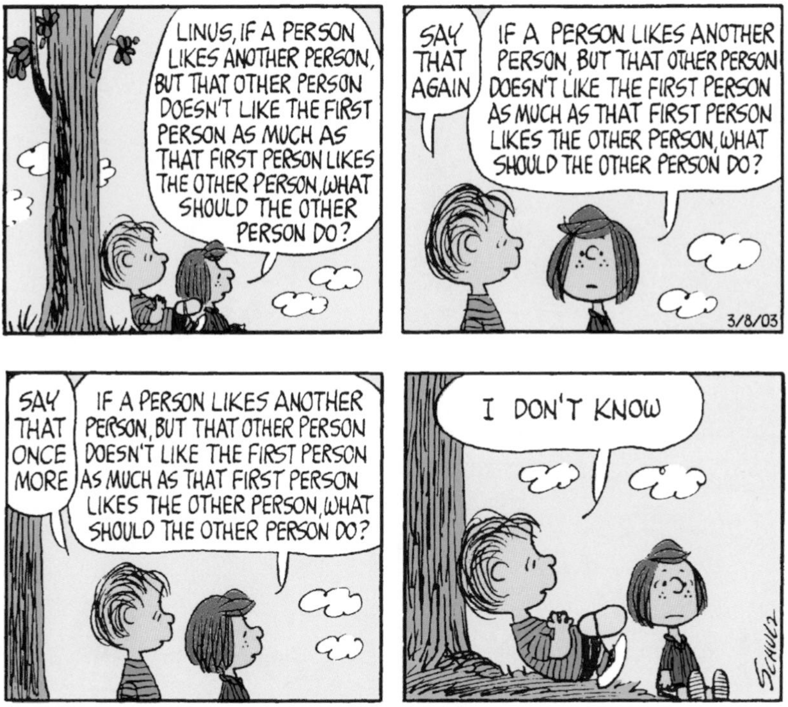
LINUS, IF A PERSON LIKES ANOTHER PERSON, BUT THAT OTHER PERSON DOESN'T LIKE THE FIRST PERSON AS MUCH AS THAT FIRST PERSON LIKES THE OTHER PERSON, WHAT SHOULD THE OTHER PERSON DO?
SAY THAT AGAIN
IF A PERSON LIKES ANOTHER PERSON, BUT THAT OTHER PERSON DOESN'T LIKE THE FIRST PERSON AS MUCH AS THAT FIRST PERSON LIKES THE OTHER PERSON, WHAT SHOULD THE OTHER PERSON DO?
3/8/03
SAY THAT ONCE MORE
IF A PERSON LIKES ANOTHER PERSON, BUT THAT OTHER PERSON DOESN'T LIKE THE FIRST PERSON AS MUCH AS THAT FIRST PERSON LIKES THE OTHER PERSON, WHAT SHOULD THE OTHER PERSON DO?
I DON'T KNOW
SCHULZ

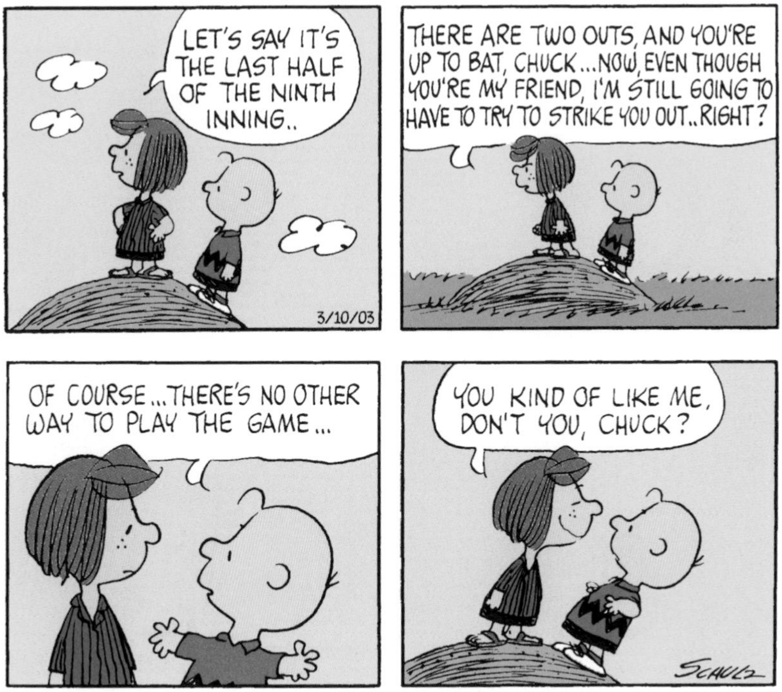
LET'S SAY IT'S THE LAST HALF OF THE NINTH INNING..
3/10/03
THERE ARE TWO OUTS, AND YOU'RE UP TO BAT, CHUCK...NOW, EVEN THOUGH YOU'RE MY FRIEND, I'M STILL GOING TO HAVE TO TRY TO STRIKE YOU OUT..RIGHT?
OF COURSE...THERE'S NO OTHER WAY TO PLAY THE GAME...
YOU KIND OF LIKE ME, DON'T YOU, CHUCK?
SCHULZ

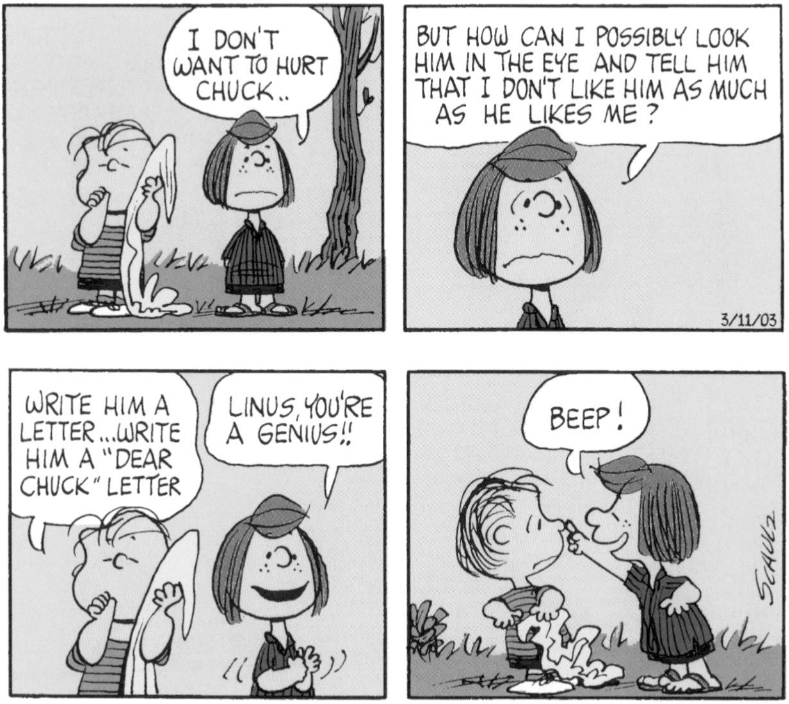
I DON'T WANT TO HURT CHUCK..
BUT HOW CAN I POSSIBLY LOOK HIM IN THE EYE AND TELL HIM THAT I DON'T LIKE HIM AS MUCH AS HE LIKES ME ?
3/11/03
WRITE HIM A LETTER...WRITE HIM A "DEAR CHUCK" LETTER
LINUS, YOU'RE A GENIUS!!
BEEP!
SCHULZ

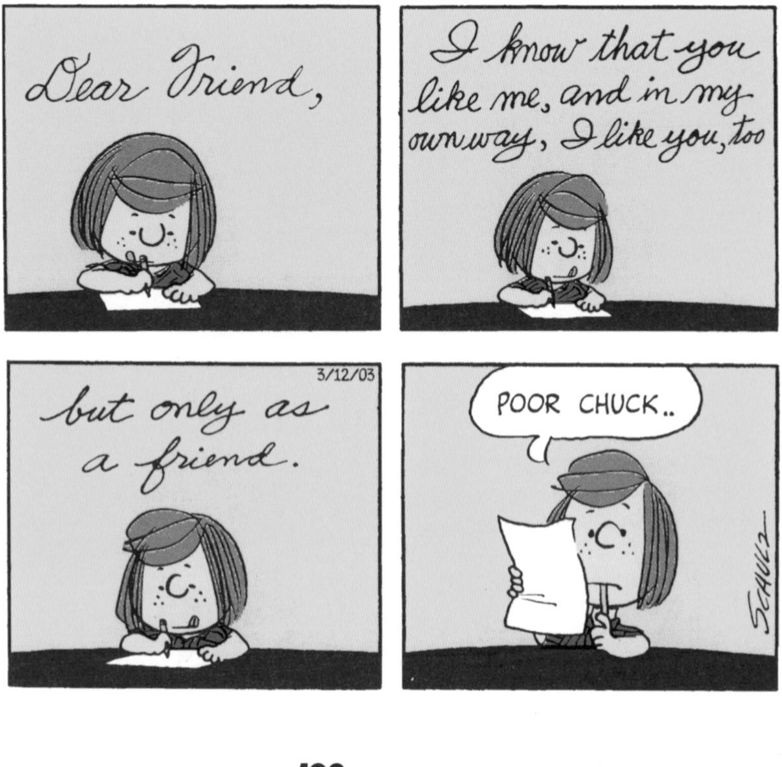
Dear Friend,
I know that you like me, and in my own way, I like you, too
3/12/03
but only as a friend.
POOR CHUCK..
SCHULZ

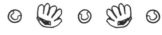

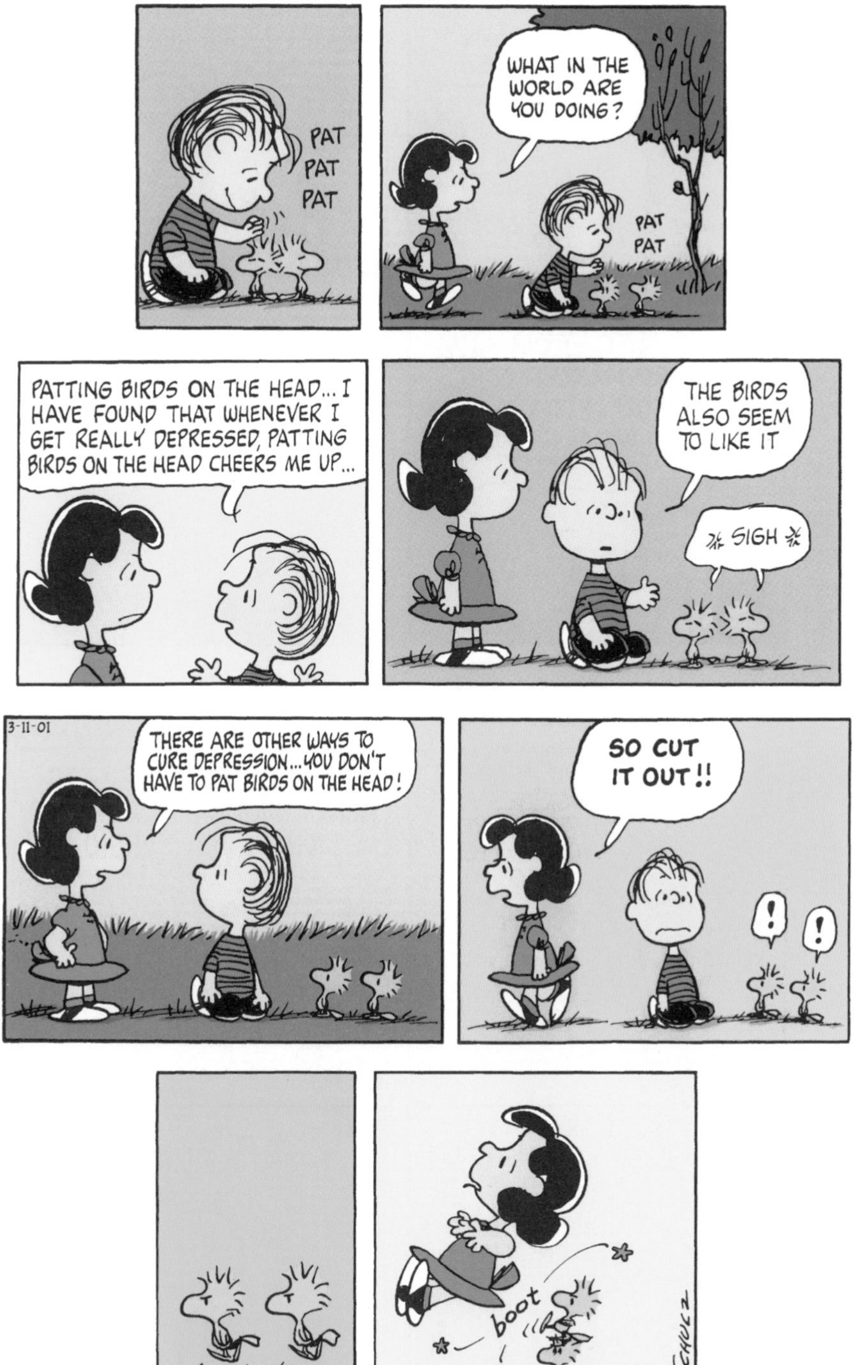
PAT
PAT
PAT
WHAT IN THE WORLD ARE YOU DOING?
PAT
PAT
PATTING BIRDS ON THE HEAD... I HAVE FOUND THAT WHENEVER I GET REALLY DEPRESSED, PATTING BIRDS ON THE HEAD CHEERS ME UP...
THE BIRDS ALSO SEEM TO LIKE IT
SIGH
3-11-01
THERE ARE OTHER WAYS TO CURE DEPRESSION...YOU DON'T HAVE TO PAT BIRDS ON THE HEAD!
SO CUT IT OUT!!
!
!
boot
SCHULZ

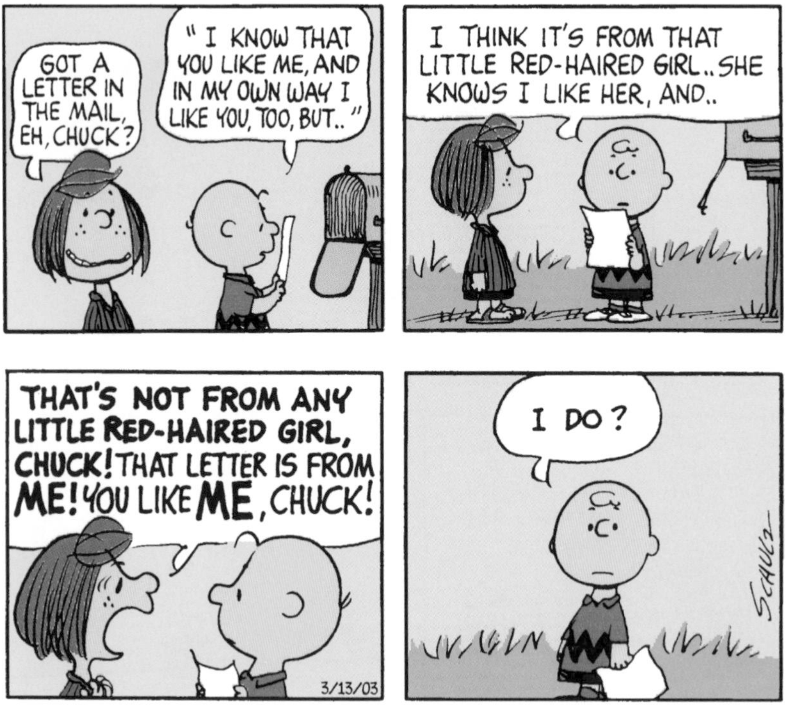
GOT A LETTER IN THE MAIL, EH, CHUCK?
"I KNOW THAT YOU LIKE ME, AND IN MY OWN WAY I LIKE YOU, TOO, BUT.."
I THINK IT'S FROM THAT LITTLE RED-HAIRED GIRL.. SHE KNOWS I LIKE HER, AND..
THAT'S NOT FROM ANY LITTLE RED-HAIRED GIRL, CHUCK! THAT LETTER IS FROM ME! YOU LIKE ME, CHUCK!
3/13/03
I DO?
SCHULZ

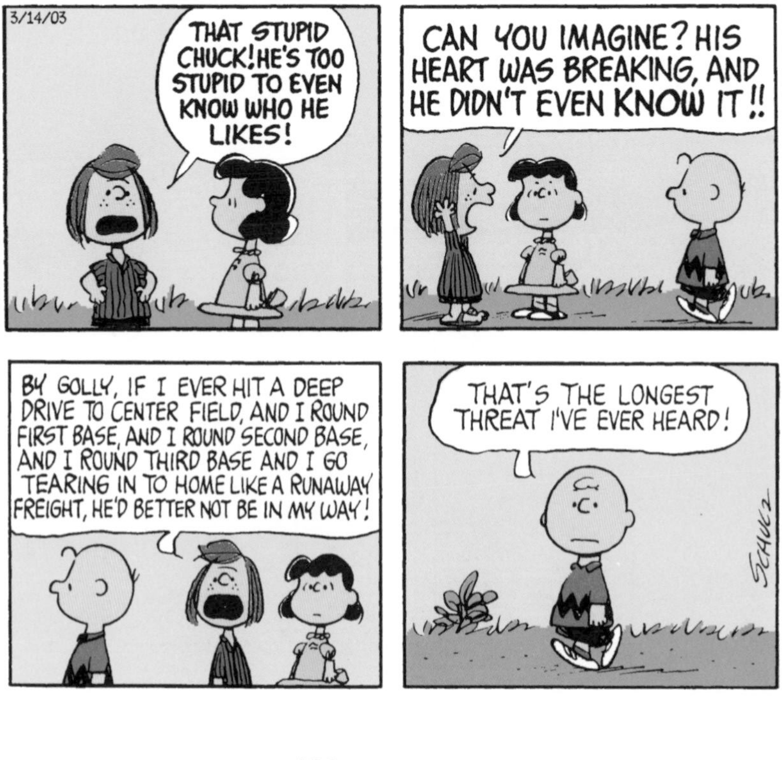
3/14/03
THAT STUPID CHUCK! HE'S TOO STUPID TO EVEN KNOW WHO HE LIKES!
CAN YOU IMAGINE? HIS HEART WAS BREAKING, AND HE DIDN'T EVEN KNOW IT!!
BY GOLLY, IF I EVER HIT A DEEP DRIVE TO CENTER FIELD, AND I ROUND FIRST BASE, AND I ROUND SECOND BASE, AND I ROUND THIRD BASE AND I GO TEARING IN TO HOME LIKE A RUNAWAY FREIGHT, HE'D BETTER NOT BE IN MY WAY!
THAT'S THE LONGEST THREAT I'VE EVER HEARD!
SCHULZ

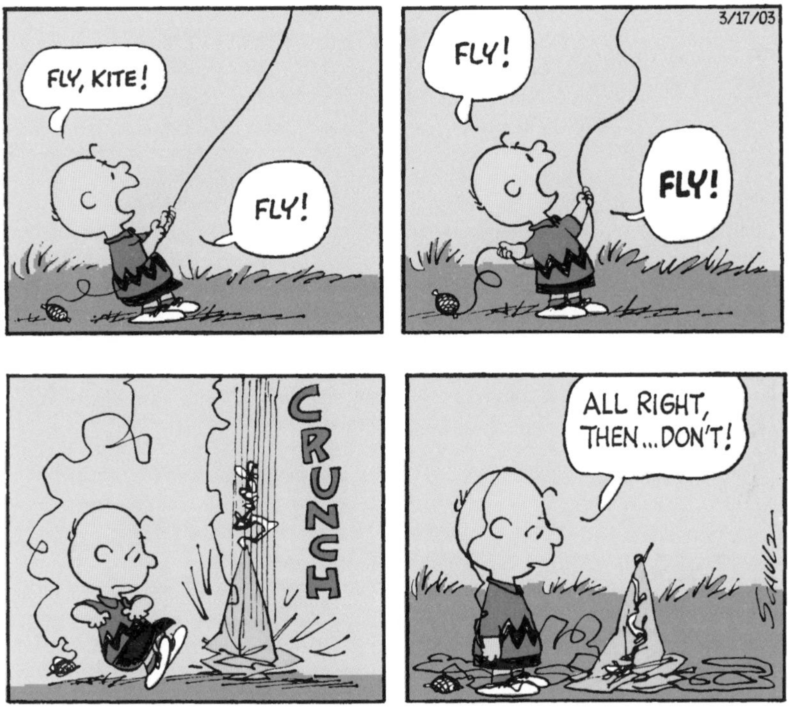
FLY, KITE!
FLY!
3/17/03
FLY!
FLY!
CRUNCH
ALL RIGHT, THEN...DON'T!
SCHULZ

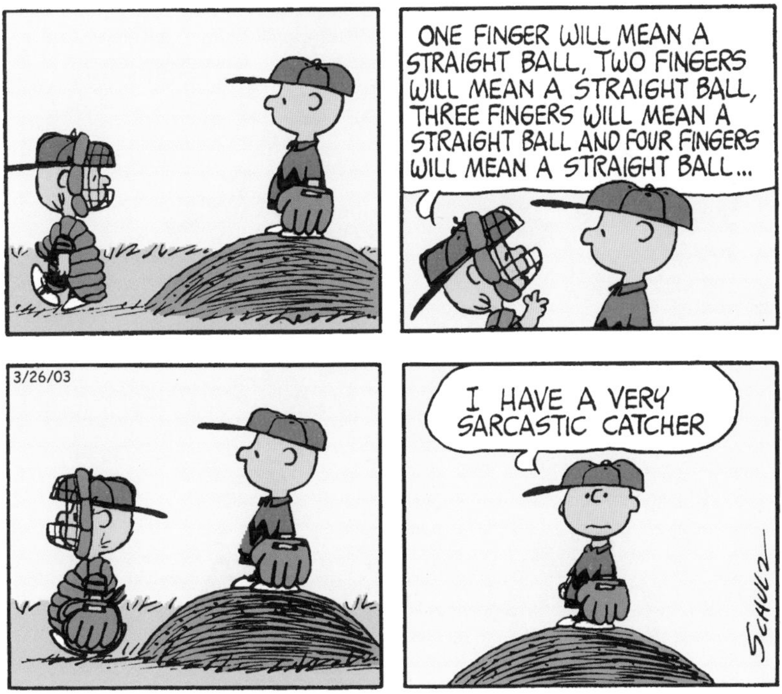
ONE FINGER WILL MEAN A STRAIGHT BALL, TWO FINGERS WILL MEAN A STRAIGHT BALL, THREE FINGERS WILL MEAN A STRAIGHT BALL AND FOUR FINGERS WILL MEAN A STRAIGHT BALL...
3/26/03
I HAVE A VERY SARCASTIC CATCHER
SCHULZ

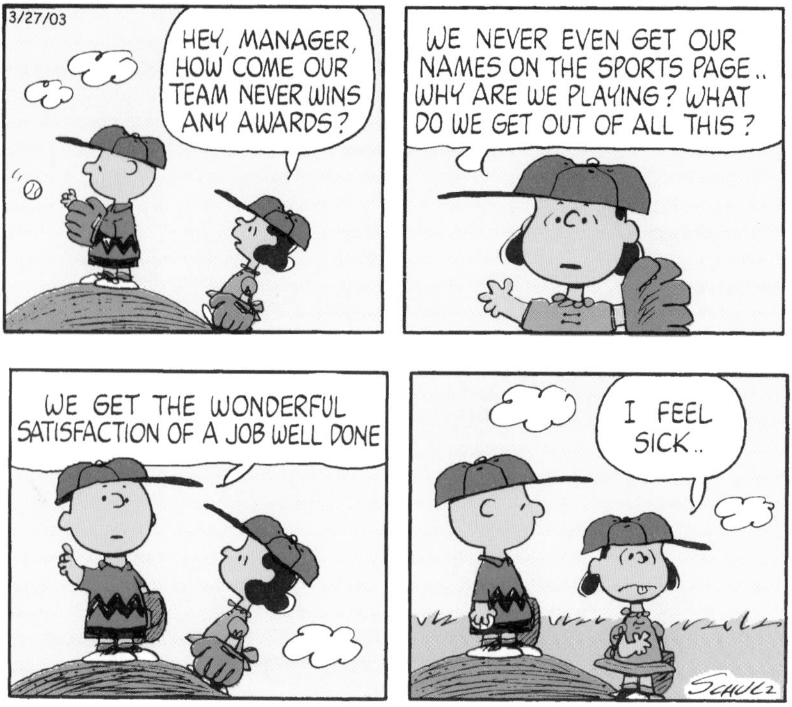
3/27/03
HEY, MANAGER, HOW COME OUR TEAM NEVER WINS ANY AWARDS?
WE NEVER EVEN GET OUR NAMES ON THE SPORTS PAGE.. WHY ARE WE PLAYING? WHAT DO WE GET OUT OF ALL THIS?
WE GET THE WONDERFUL SATISFACTION OF A JOB WELL DONE
I FEEL SICK..

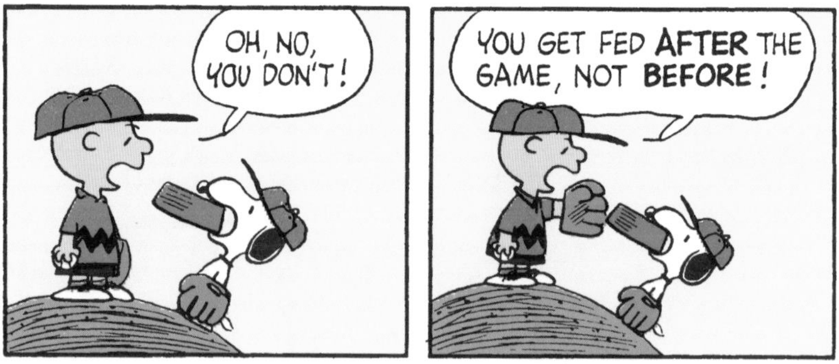
OH, NO, YOU DON'T!
YOU GET FED **AFTER** THE GAME, NOT **BEFORE**!

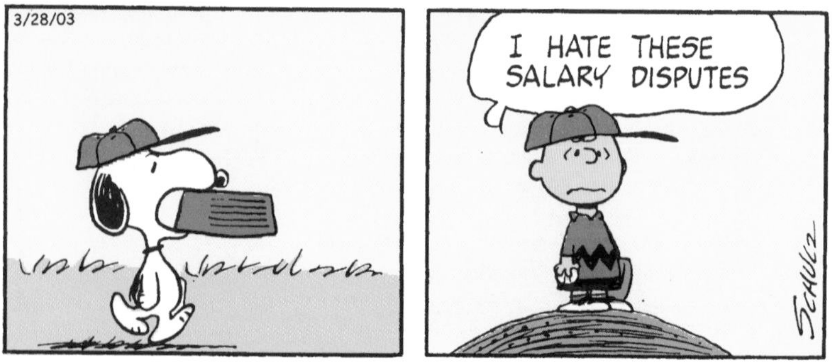
3/28/03
I HATE THESE SALARY DISPUTES

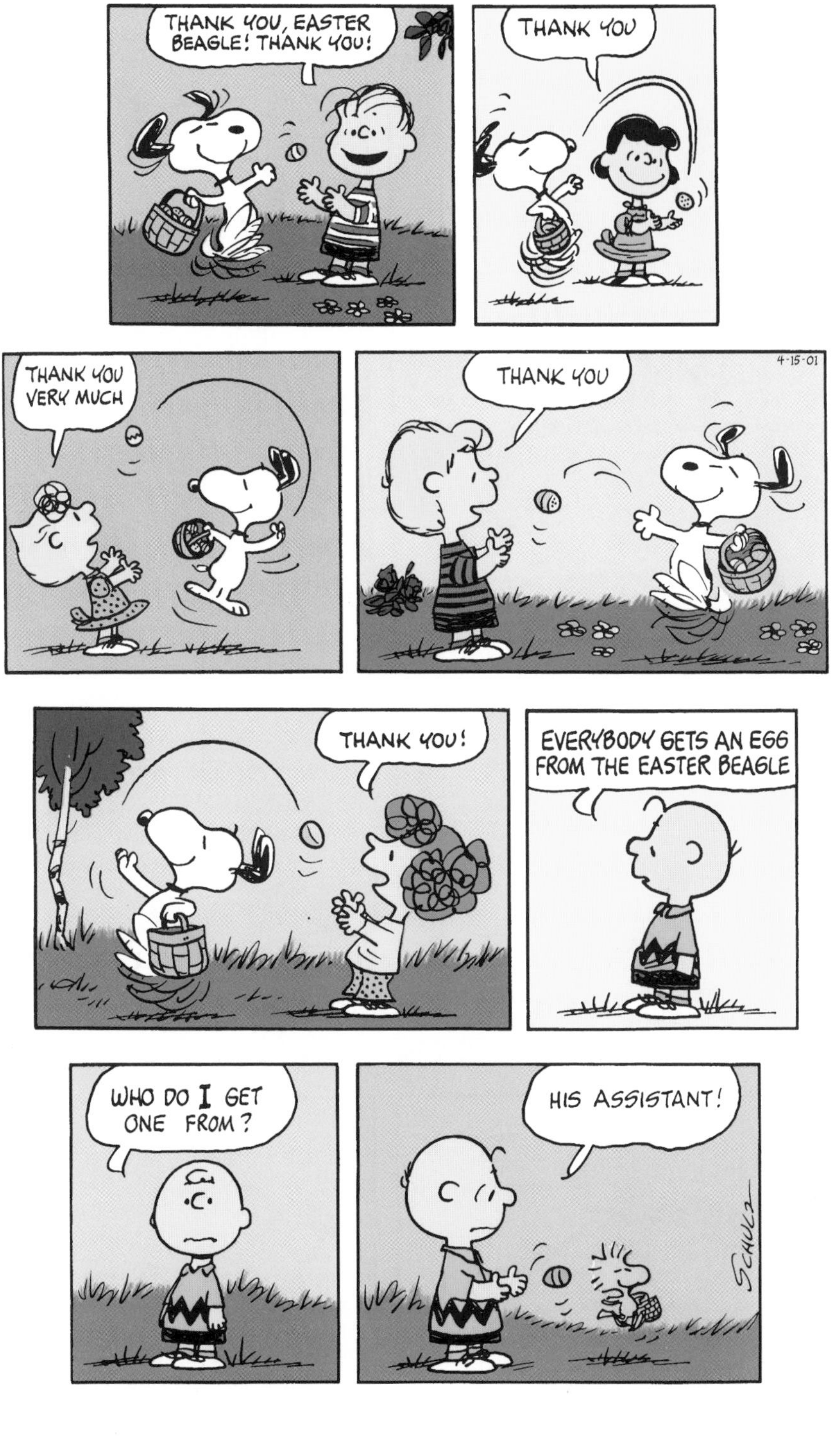
THANK YOU, EASTER BEAGLE! THANK YOU!
THANK YOU
THANK YOU VERY MUCH
4-15-01
THANK YOU
THANK YOU!
EVERYBODY GETS AN EGG FROM THE EASTER BEAGLE
WHO DO I GET ONE FROM?
HIS ASSISTANT!
SCHULZ

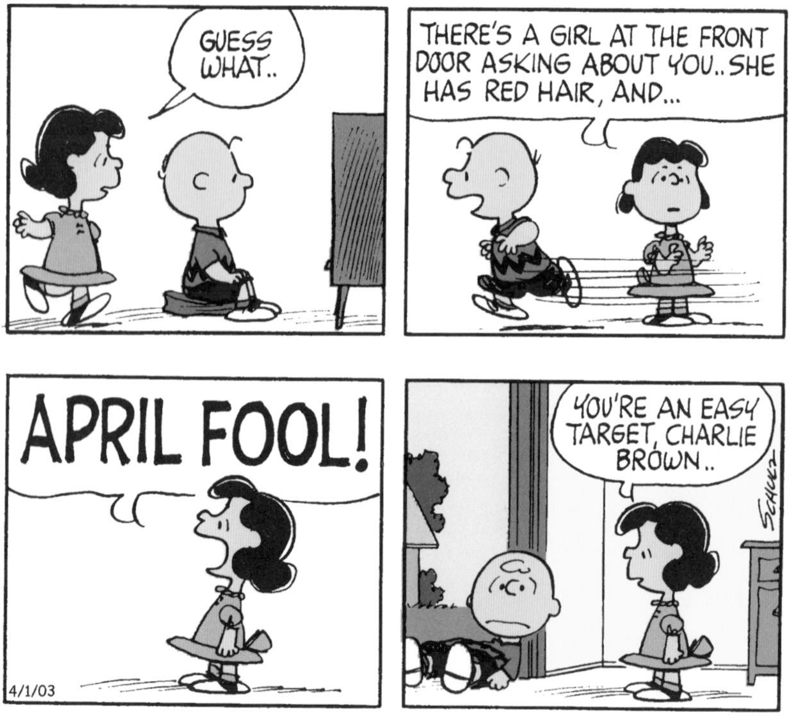
GUESS WHAT..
THERE'S A GIRL AT THE FRONT DOOR ASKING ABOUT YOU..SHE HAS RED HAIR, AND...
APRIL FOOL!
4/1/03
YOU'RE AN EASY TARGET, CHARLIE BROWN..
SCHULZ

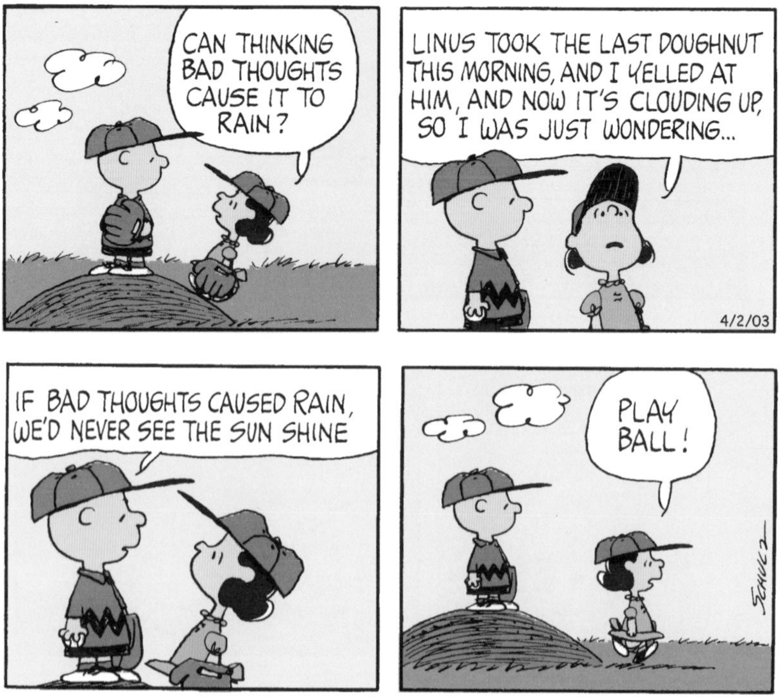
CAN THINKING BAD THOUGHTS CAUSE IT TO RAIN?
LINUS TOOK THE LAST DOUGHNUT THIS MORNING, AND I YELLED AT HIM, AND NOW IT'S CLOUDING UP, SO I WAS JUST WONDERING...
4/2/03
IF BAD THOUGHTS CAUSED RAIN, WE'D NEVER SEE THE SUN SHINE
PLAY BALL!
SCHULZ

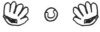

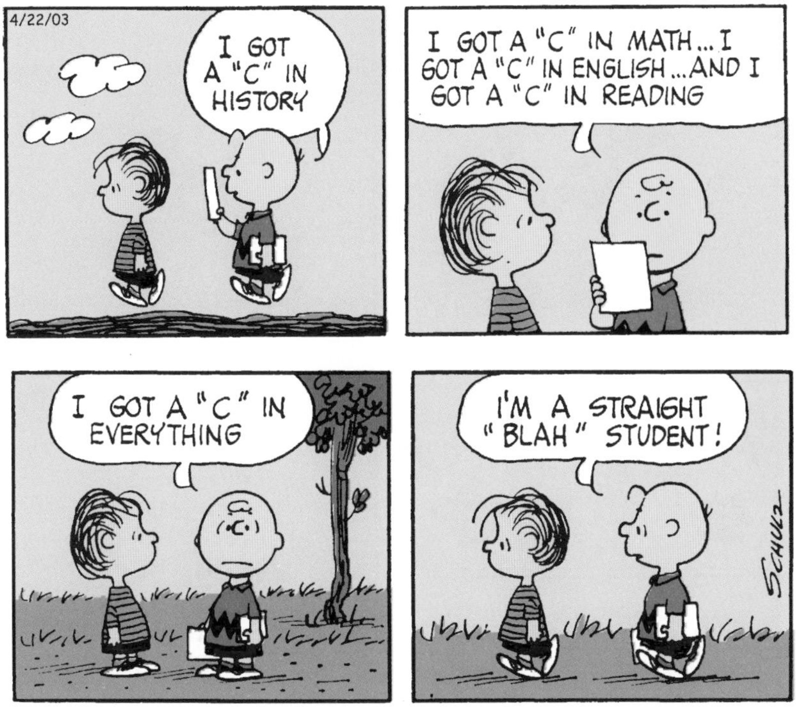
4/22/03
I GOT A "C" IN HISTORY
I GOT A "C" IN MATH... I GOT A "C" IN ENGLISH ...AND I GOT A "C" IN READING
I GOT A "C" IN EVERYTHING
I'M A STRAIGHT "BLAH" STUDENT!
SCHULZ

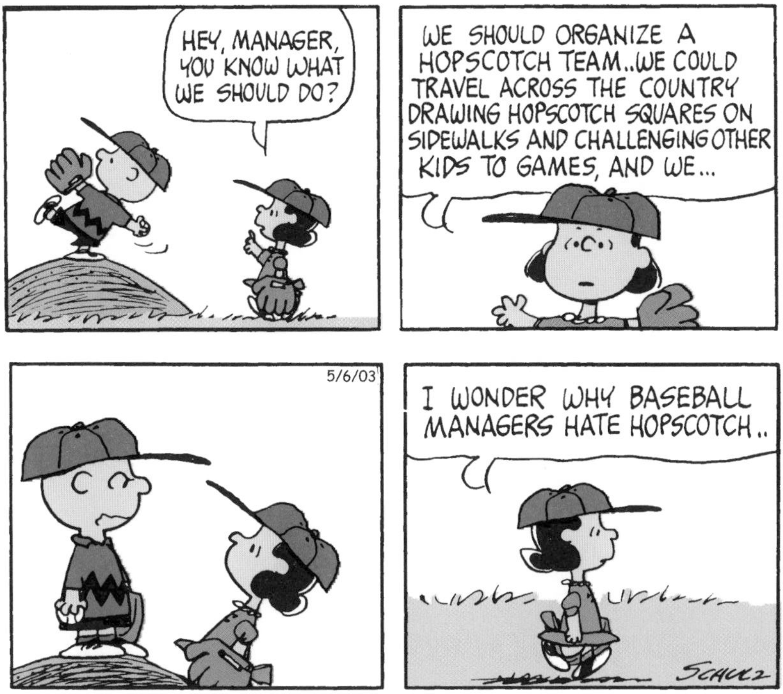
HEY, MANAGER, YOU KNOW WHAT WE SHOULD DO?
WE SHOULD ORGANIZE A HOPSCOTCH TEAM..WE COULD TRAVEL ACROSS THE COUNTRY DRAWING HOPSCOTCH SQUARES ON SIDEWALKS AND CHALLENGING OTHER KIDS TO GAMES, AND WE...
5/6/03
I WONDER WHY BASEBALL MANAGERS HATE HOPSCOTCH..
SCHULZ

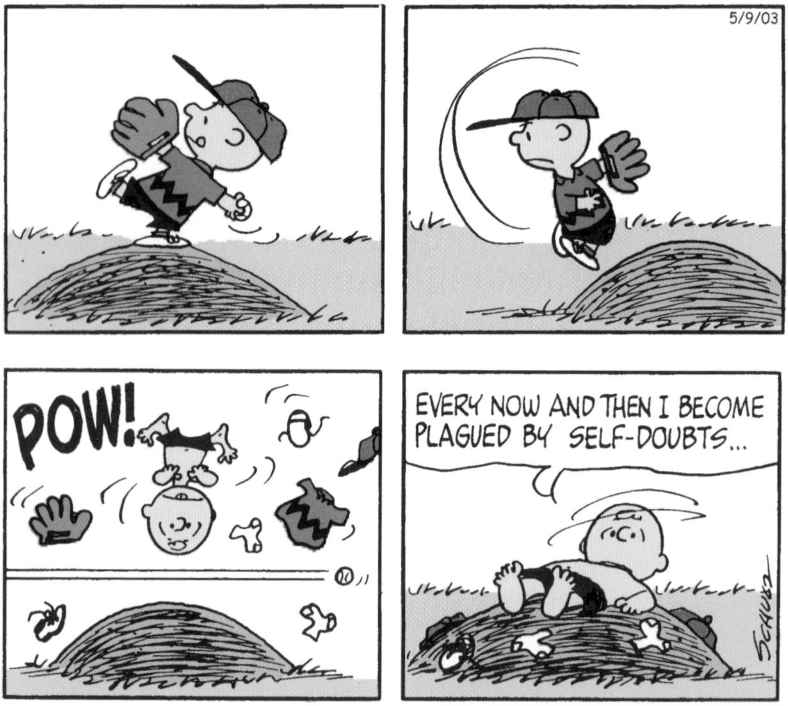
5/9/03
POW!
EVERY NOW AND THEN I BECOME PLAGUED BY SELF-DOUBTS...
SCHULZ

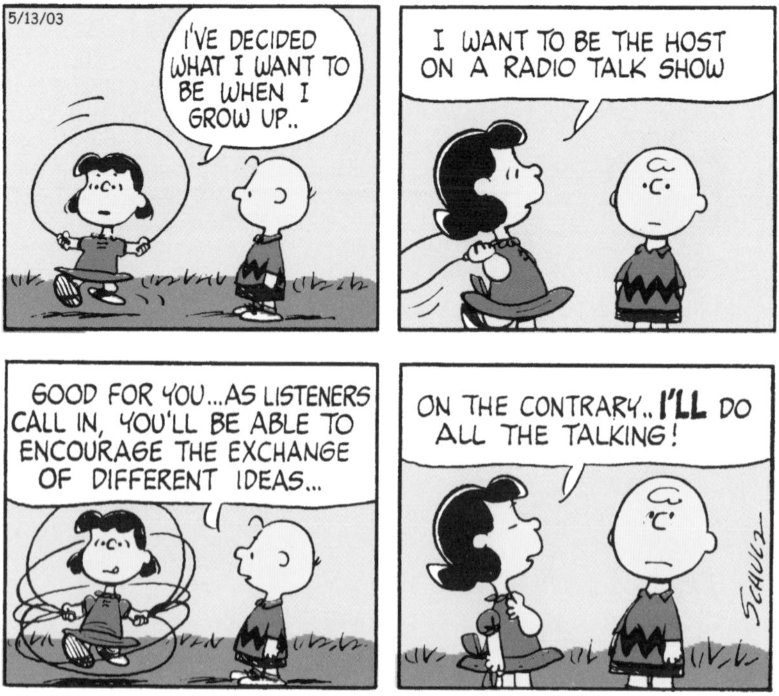
5/13/03
I'VE DECIDED WHAT I WANT TO BE WHEN I GROW UP..
I WANT TO BE THE HOST ON A RADIO TALK SHOW
GOOD FOR YOU...AS LISTENERS CALL IN, YOU'LL BE ABLE TO ENCOURAGE THE EXCHANGE OF DIFFERENT IDEAS...
ON THE CONTRARY.. I'LL DO ALL THE TALKING!
SCHULZ

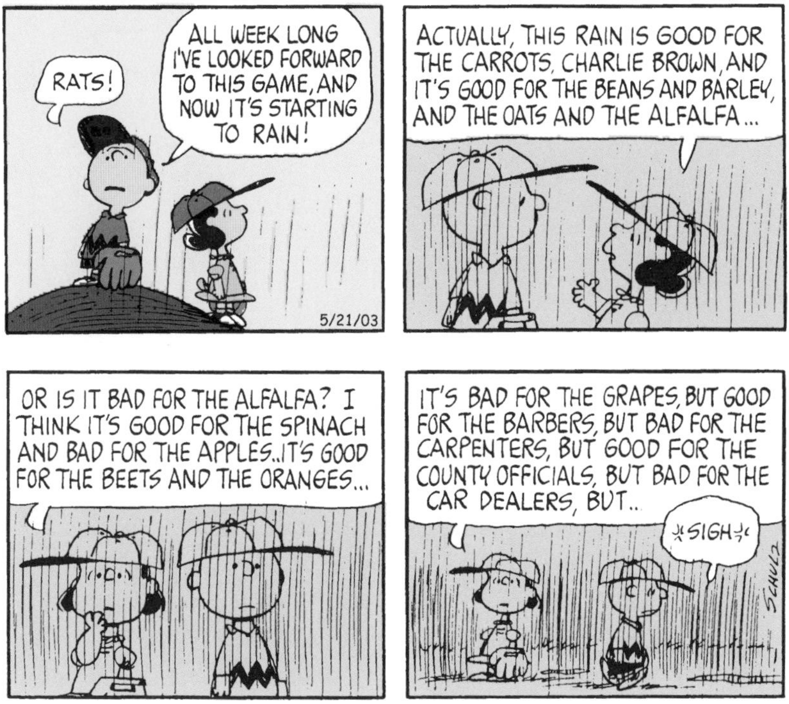
RATS!
ALL WEEK LONG I'VE LOOKED FORWARD TO THIS GAME, AND NOW IT'S STARTING TO RAIN!
5/21/03
ACTUALLY, THIS RAIN IS GOOD FOR THE CARROTS, CHARLIE BROWN, AND IT'S GOOD FOR THE BEANS AND BARLEY, AND THE OATS AND THE ALFALFA...
OR IS IT BAD FOR THE ALFALFA? I THINK IT'S GOOD FOR THE SPINACH AND BAD FOR THE APPLES..IT'S GOOD FOR THE BEETS AND THE ORANGES...
IT'S BAD FOR THE GRAPES, BUT GOOD FOR THE BARBERS, BUT BAD FOR THE CARPENTERS, BUT GOOD FOR THE COUNTY OFFICIALS, BUT BAD FOR THE CAR DEALERS, BUT..
SIGH
SCHULZ

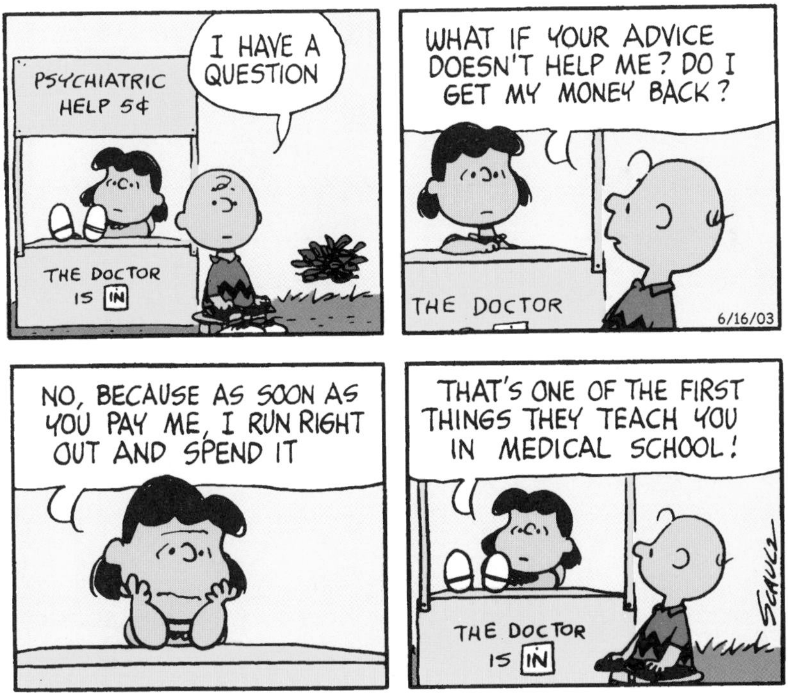
PSYCHIATRIC HELP 5¢
I HAVE A QUESTION
THE DOCTOR IS IN
WHAT IF YOUR ADVICE DOESN'T HELP ME? DO I GET MY MONEY BACK?
THE DOCTOR
6/16/03
NO, BECAUSE AS SOON AS YOU PAY ME, I RUN RIGHT OUT AND SPEND IT
THAT'S ONE OF THE FIRST THINGS THEY TEACH YOU IN MEDICAL SCHOOL!
THE DOCTOR IS IN
SCHULZ

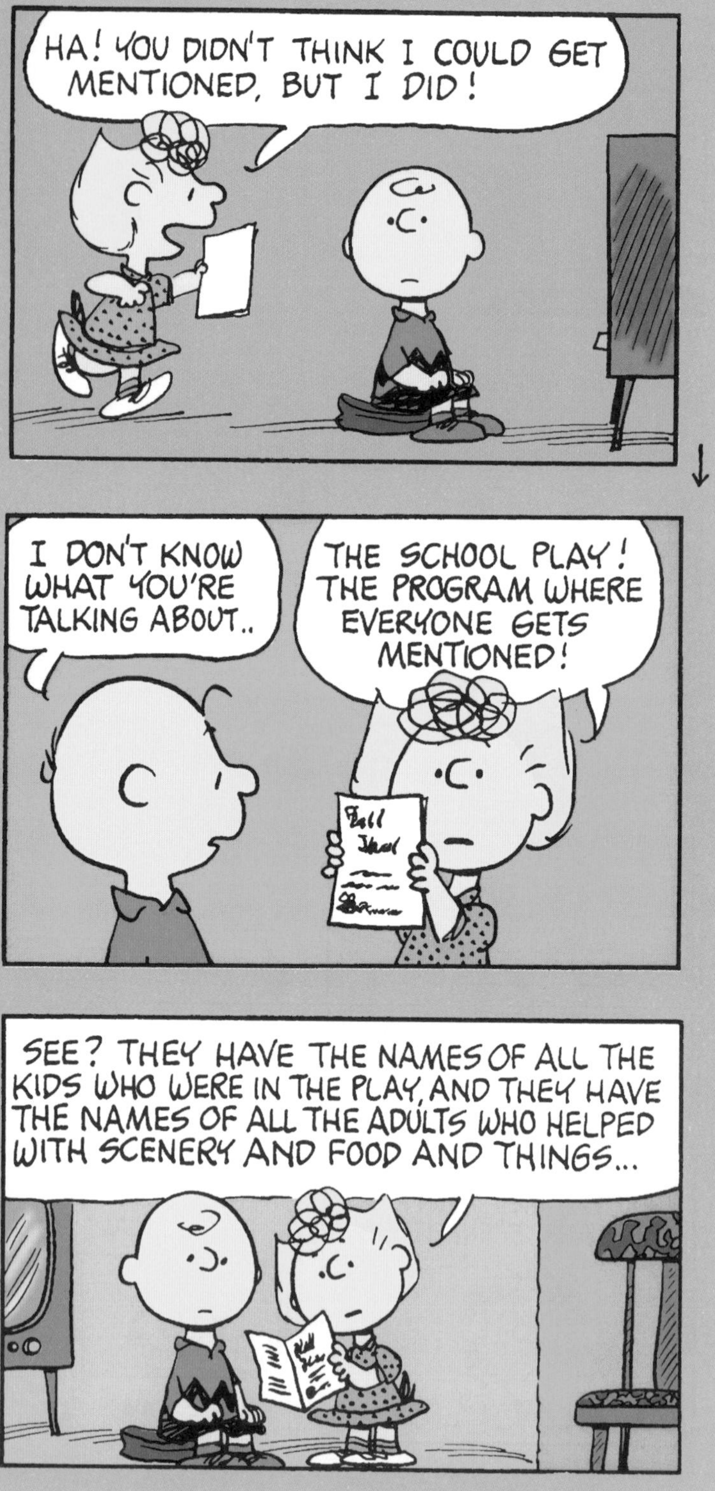
HA! YOU DIDN'T THINK I COULD GET MENTIONED, BUT I DID!
I DON'T KNOW WHAT YOU'RE TALKING ABOUT..
THE SCHOOL PLAY! THE PROGRAM WHERE EVERYONE GETS MENTIONED!
SEE? THEY HAVE THE NAMES OF ALL THE KIDS WHO WERE IN THE PLAY, AND THEY HAVE THE NAMES OF ALL THE ADULTS WHO HELPED WITH SCENERY AND FOOD AND THINGS...

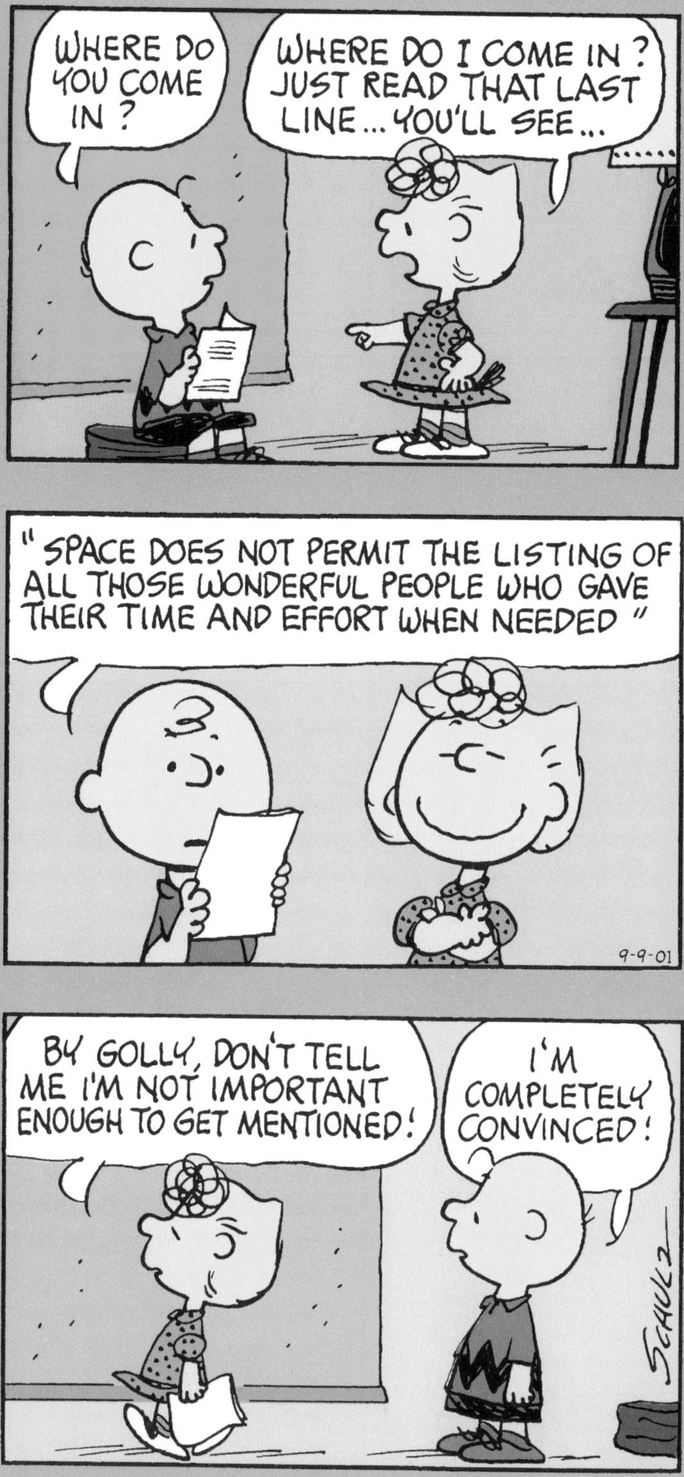
WHERE DO YOU COME IN ?
WHERE DO I COME IN ? JUST READ THAT LAST LINE... YOU'LL SEE...
" SPACE DOES NOT PERMIT THE LISTING OF ALL THOSE WONDERFUL PEOPLE WHO GAVE THEIR TIME AND EFFORT WHEN NEEDED "
9-9-01
BY GOLLY, DON'T TELL ME I'M NOT IMPORTANT ENOUGH TO GET MENTIONED !
I'M COMPLETELY CONVINCED !
SCHULZ

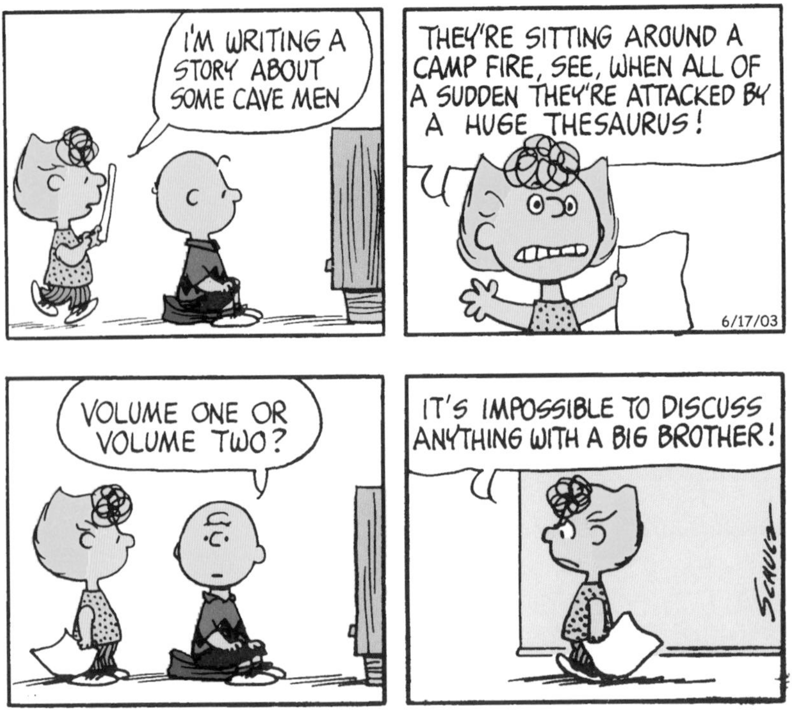
I'M WRITING A STORY ABOUT SOME CAVE MEN
THEY'RE SITTING AROUND A CAMP FIRE, SEE, WHEN ALL OF A SUDDEN THEY'RE ATTACKED BY A HUGE THESAURUS!
6/17/03
VOLUME ONE OR VOLUME TWO?
IT'S IMPOSSIBLE TO DISCUSS ANYTHING WITH A BIG BROTHER!
SCHULZ

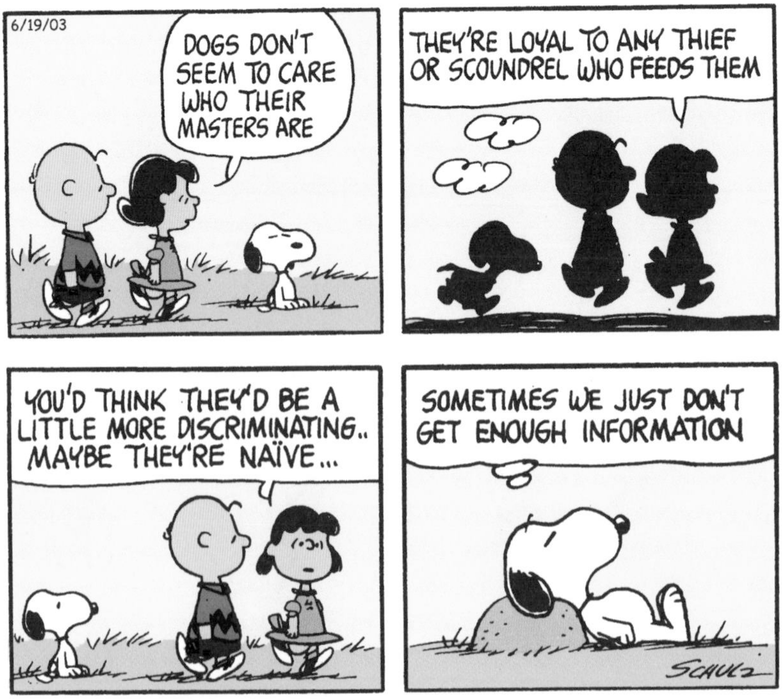
6/19/03
DOGS DON'T SEEM TO CARE WHO THEIR MASTERS ARE
THEY'RE LOYAL TO ANY THIEF OR SCOUNDREL WHO FEEDS THEM
YOU'D THINK THEY'D BE A LITTLE MORE DISCRIMINATING.. MAYBE THEY'RE NAÏVE...
SOMETIMES WE JUST DON'T GET ENOUGH INFORMATION
SCHULZ

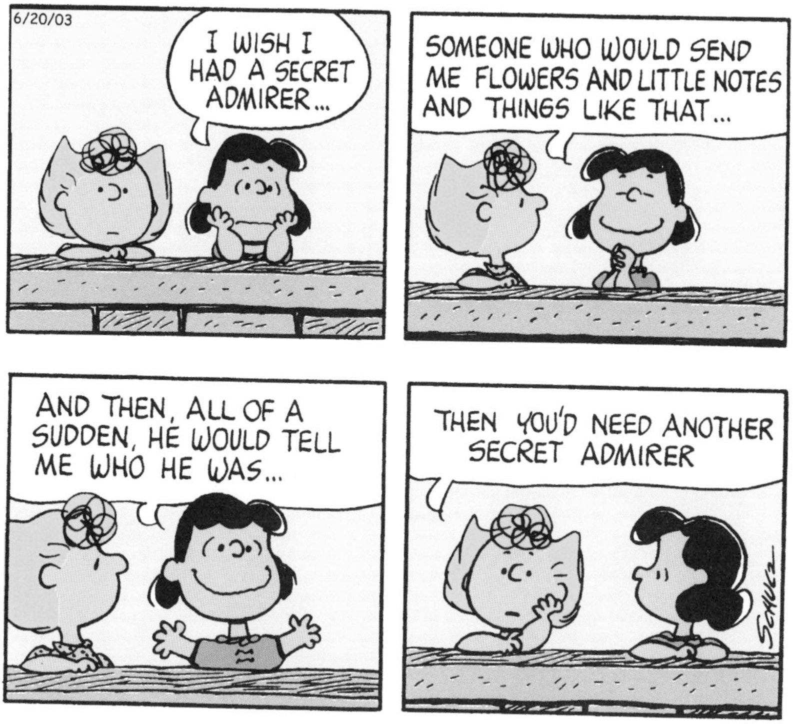
6/20/03
I WISH I HAD A SECRET ADMIRER...
SOMEONE WHO WOULD SEND ME FLOWERS AND LITTLE NOTES AND THINGS LIKE THAT...
AND THEN, ALL OF A SUDDEN, HE WOULD TELL ME WHO HE WAS...
THEN YOU'D NEED ANOTHER SECRET ADMIRER
SCHULZ

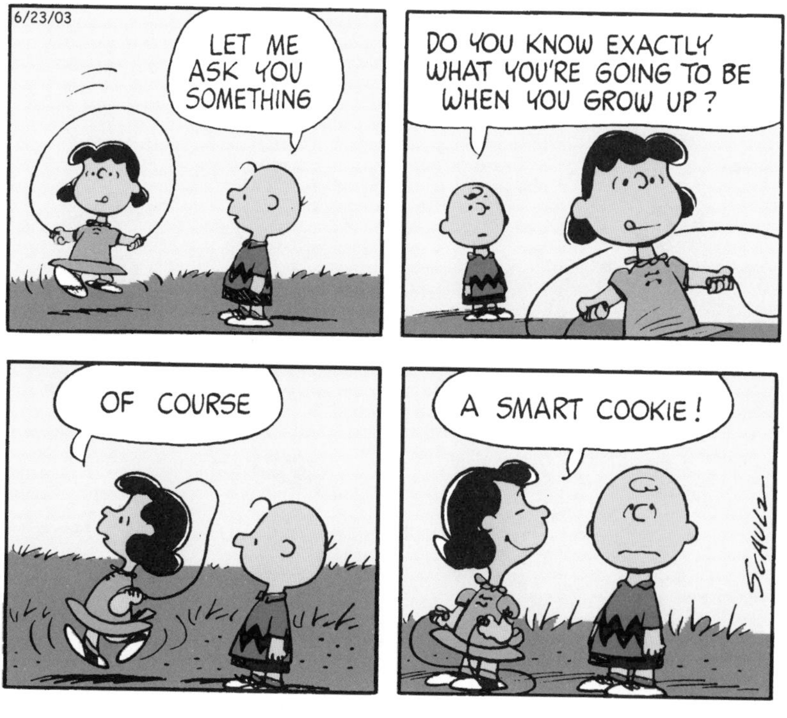
6/23/03
LET ME ASK YOU SOMETHING
DO YOU KNOW EXACTLY WHAT YOU'RE GOING TO BE WHEN YOU GROW UP?
OF COURSE
A SMART COOKIE!
SCHULZ

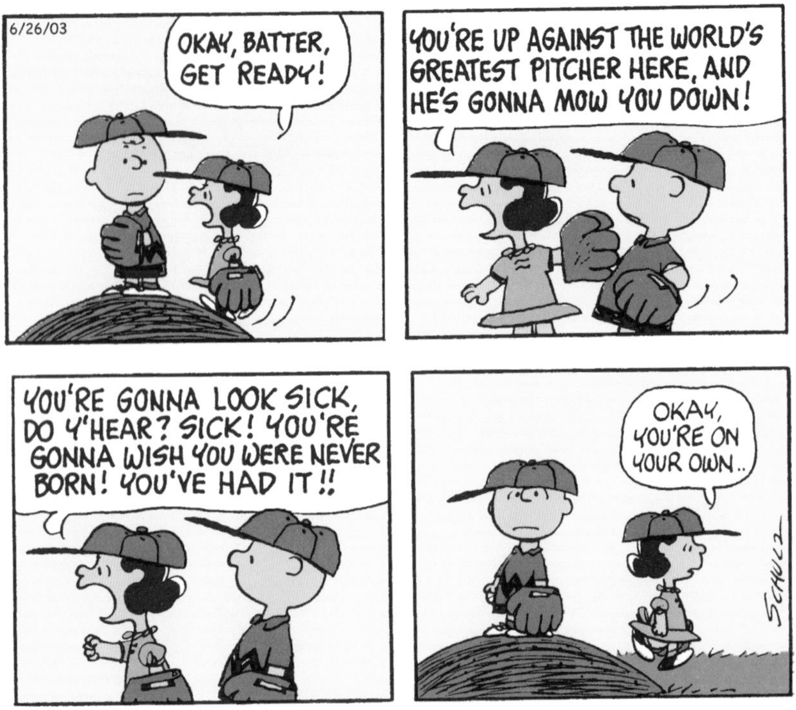
6/26/03
OKAY, BATTER, GET READY!
YOU'RE UP AGAINST THE WORLD'S GREATEST PITCHER HERE, AND HE'S GONNA MOW YOU DOWN!
YOU'RE GONNA LOOK SICK, DO Y'HEAR? SICK! YOU'RE GONNA WISH YOU WERE NEVER BORN! YOU'VE HAD IT!!
OKAY, YOU'RE ON YOUR OWN..
SCHULZ

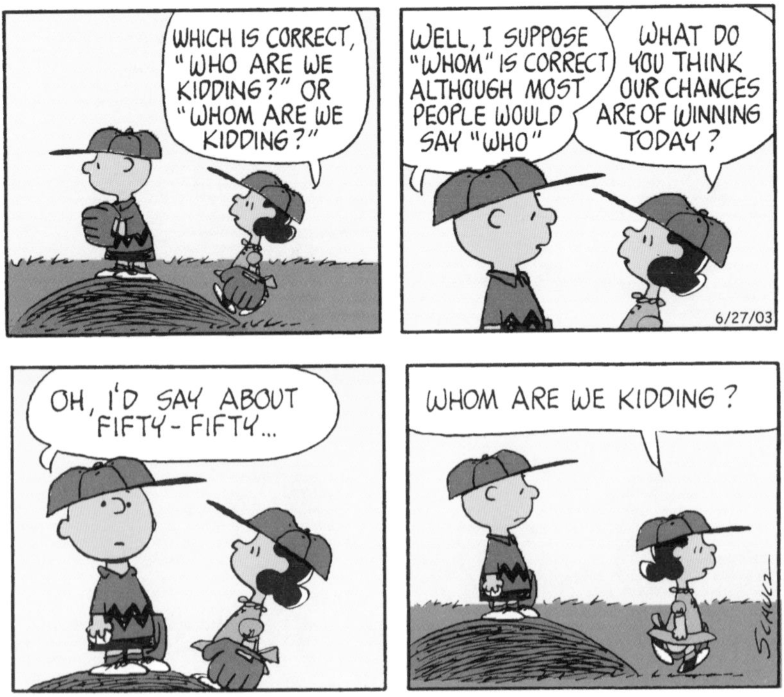
WHICH IS CORRECT, "WHO ARE WE KIDDING?" OR "WHOM ARE WE KIDDING?"
WELL, I SUPPOSE "WHOM" IS CORRECT ALTHOUGH MOST PEOPLE WOULD SAY "WHO"
WHAT DO YOU THINK OUR CHANCES ARE OF WINNING TODAY?
6/27/03
OH, I'D SAY ABOUT FIFTY-FIFTY...
WHOM ARE WE KIDDING?
SCHULZ

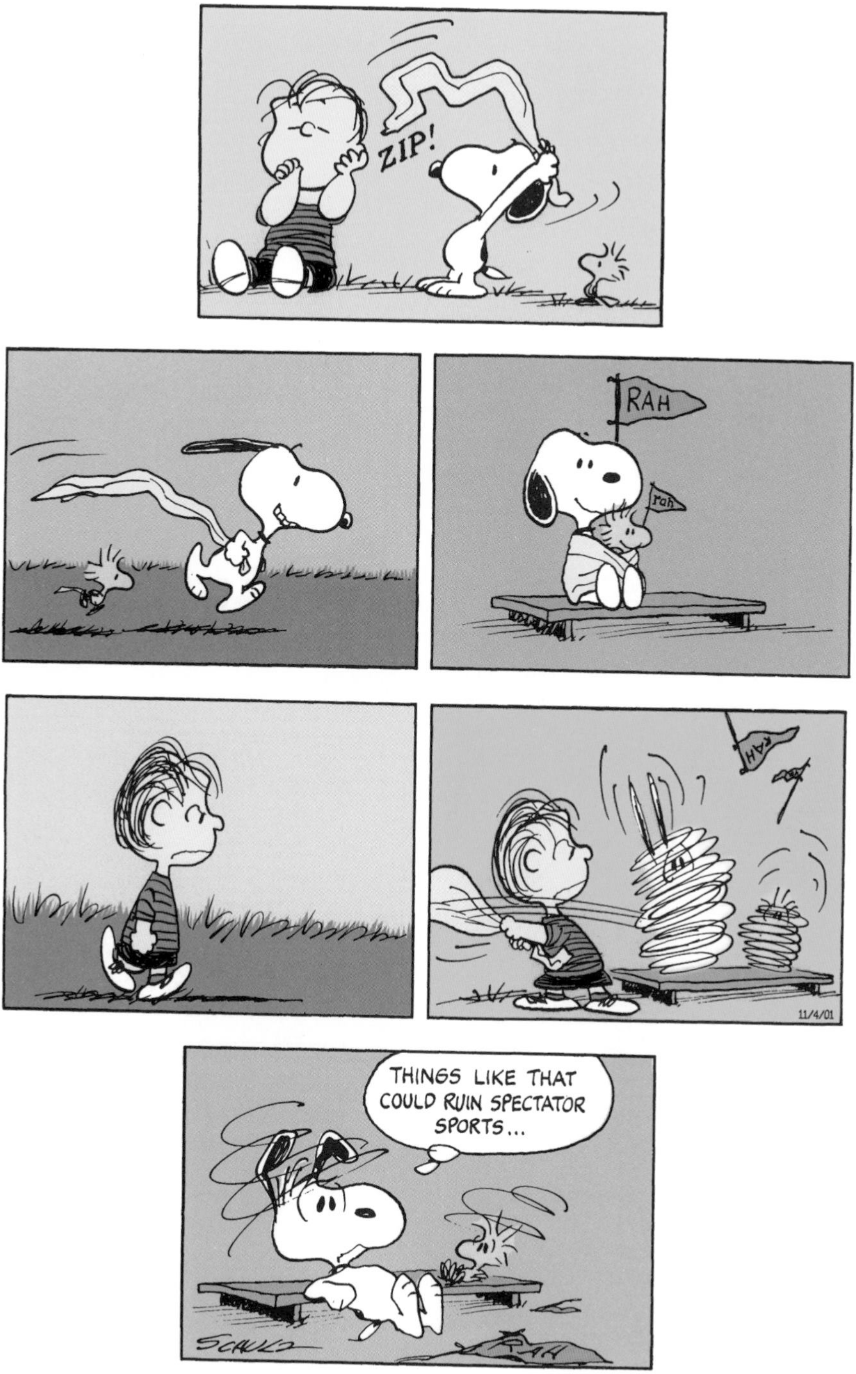
ZIP!
RAH
rah
RAH
11/4/01
THINGS LIKE THAT COULD RUIN SPECTATOR SPORTS...
SCHULZ
RAH

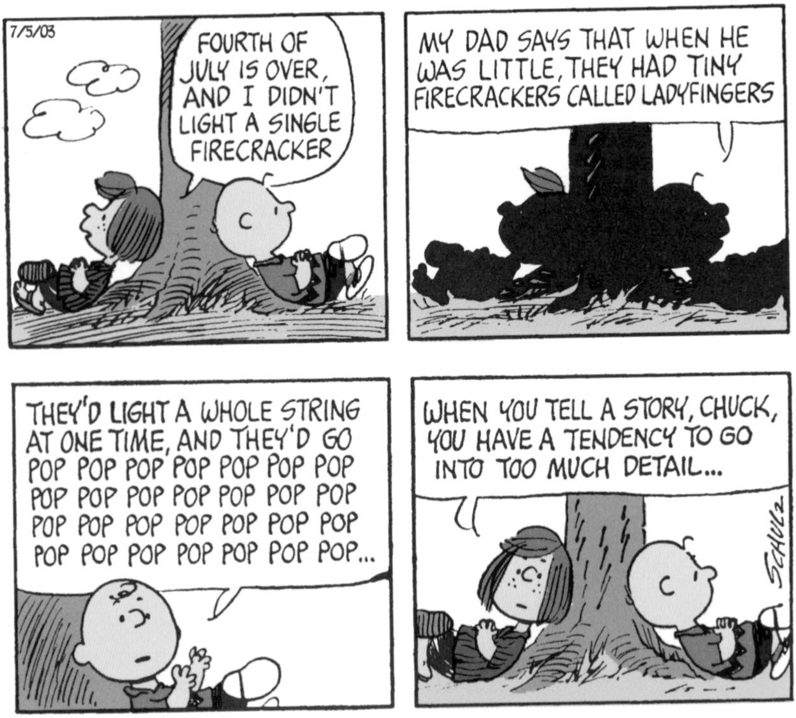
7/5/03
FOURTH OF JULY IS OVER, AND I DIDN'T LIGHT A SINGLE FIRECRACKER
MY DAD SAYS THAT WHEN HE WAS LITTLE, THEY HAD TINY FIRECRACKERS CALLED LADYFINGERS
THEY'D LIGHT A WHOLE STRING AT ONE TIME, AND THEY'D GO POP POP POP POP POP POP POP POP POP POP POP POP POP POP POP POP POP POP POP POP POP POP POP POP POP POP POP POP...
WHEN YOU TELL A STORY, CHUCK, YOU HAVE A TENDENCY TO GO INTO TOO MUCH DETAIL...
SCHULZ

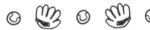

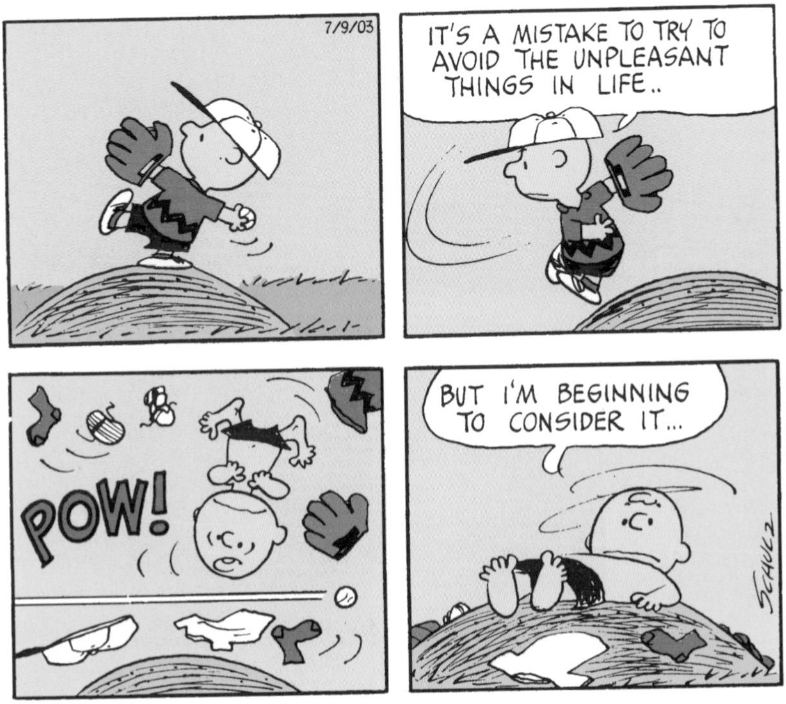
7/9/03
IT'S A MISTAKE TO TRY TO AVOID THE UNPLEASANT THINGS IN LIFE..
POW!
BUT I'M BEGINNING TO CONSIDER IT...
SCHULZ

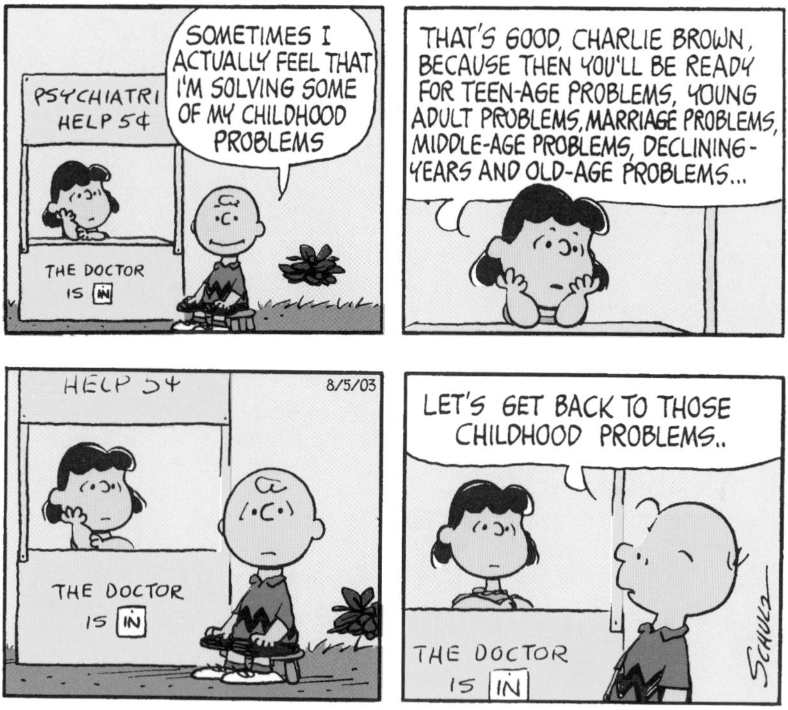
PSYCHIATRI
HELP 5¢
THE DOCTOR IS IN
SOMETIMES I ACTUALLY FEEL THAT I'M SOLVING SOME OF MY CHILDHOOD PROBLEMS
THAT'S GOOD, CHARLIE BROWN, BECAUSE THEN YOU'LL BE READY FOR TEEN-AGE PROBLEMS, YOUNG ADULT PROBLEMS, MARRIAGE PROBLEMS, MIDDLE-AGE PROBLEMS, DECLINING-YEARS AND OLD-AGE PROBLEMS...
HELP 5¢
8/5/03
THE DOCTOR IS IN
LET'S GET BACK TO THOSE CHILDHOOD PROBLEMS..
THE DOCTOR IS IN
SCHULZ

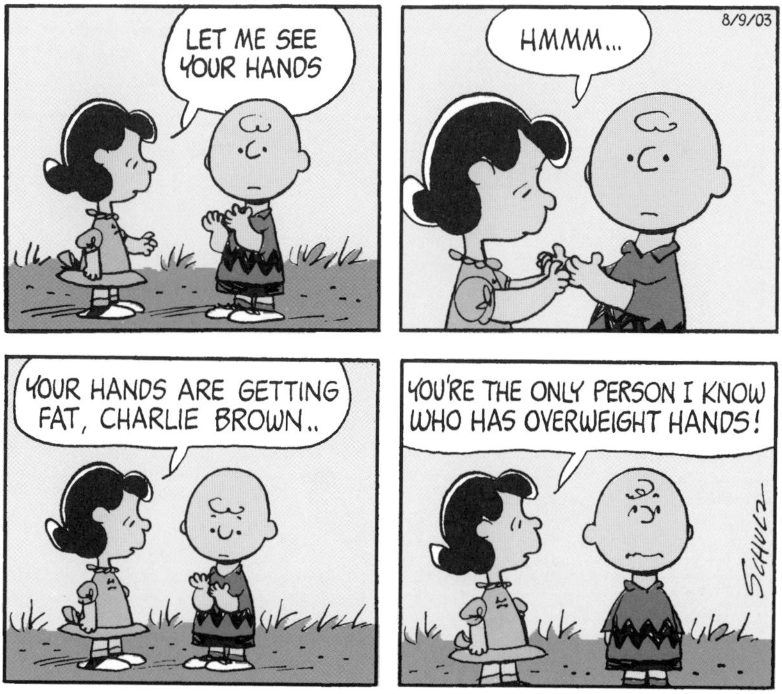
LET ME SEE YOUR HANDS
8/9/03
HMMM...
YOUR HANDS ARE GETTING FAT, CHARLIE BROWN..
YOU'RE THE ONLY PERSON I KNOW WHO HAS OVERWEIGHT HANDS!
SCHULZ

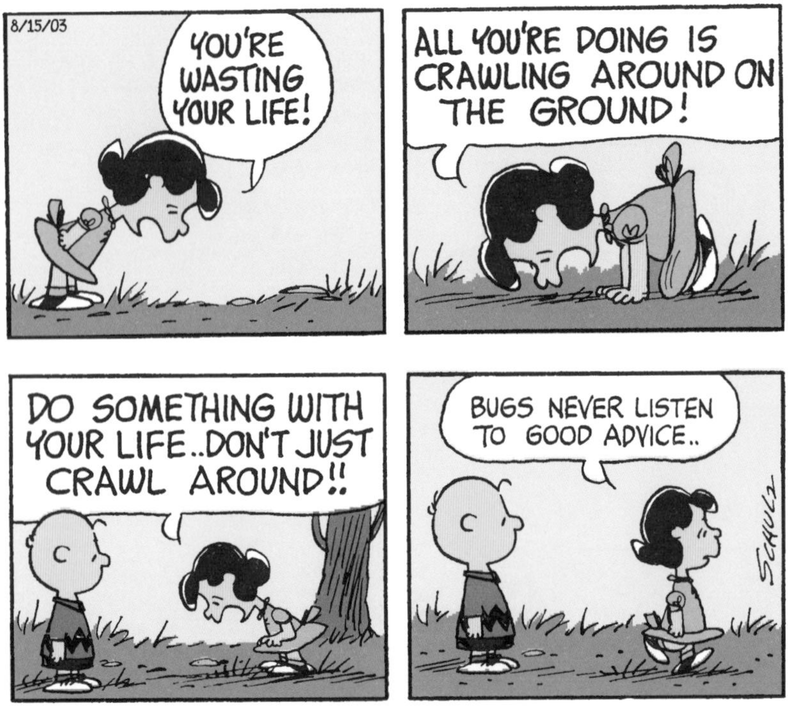
8/15/03
YOU'RE WASTING YOUR LIFE!
ALL YOU'RE DOING IS CRAWLING AROUND ON THE GROUND!
DO SOMETHING WITH YOUR LIFE..DON'T JUST CRAWL AROUND!!
BUGS NEVER LISTEN TO GOOD ADVICE..
SCHULZ

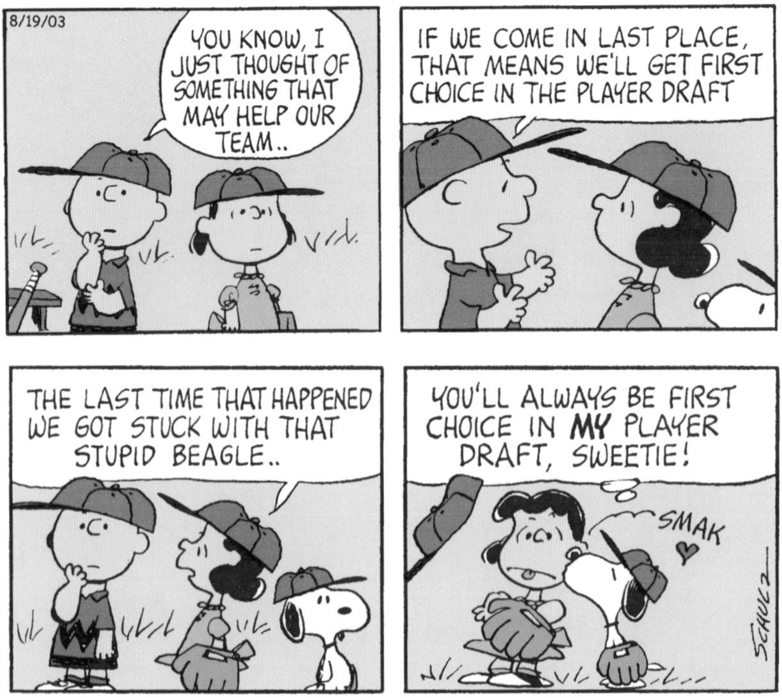
8/19/03
YOU KNOW, I JUST THOUGHT OF SOMETHING THAT MAY HELP OUR TEAM..
IF WE COME IN LAST PLACE, THAT MEANS WE'LL GET FIRST CHOICE IN THE PLAYER DRAFT
THE LAST TIME THAT HAPPENED WE GOT STUCK WITH THAT STUPID BEAGLE..
YOU'LL ALWAYS BE FIRST CHOICE IN **MY** PLAYER DRAFT, SWEETIE!
SMAK
SCHULZ

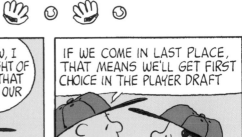

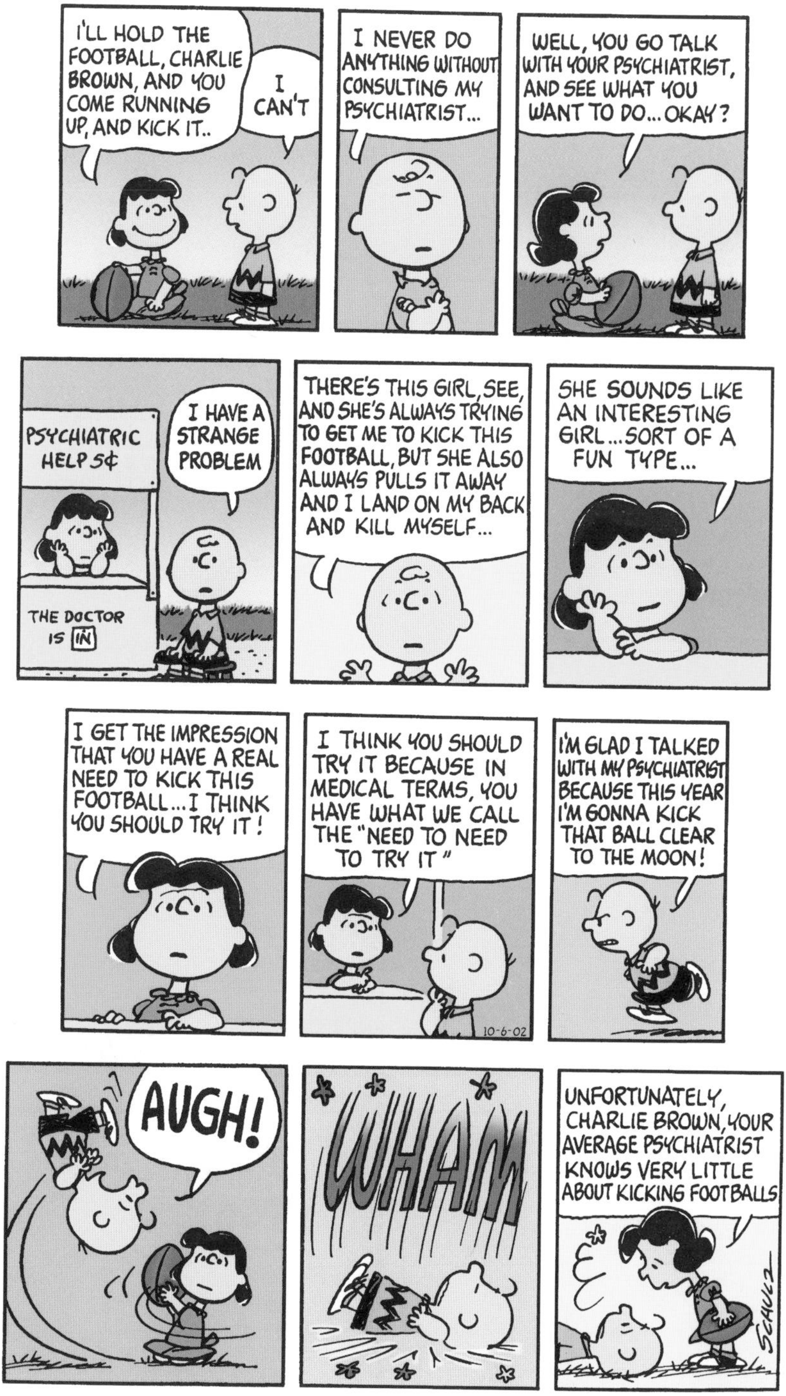
I'LL HOLD THE FOOTBALL, CHARLIE BROWN, AND YOU COME RUNNING UP, AND KICK IT..
I CAN'T
I NEVER DO ANYTHING WITHOUT CONSULTING MY PSYCHIATRIST...
WELL, YOU GO TALK WITH YOUR PSYCHIATRIST, AND SEE WHAT YOU WANT TO DO... OKAY?
PSYCHIATRIC HELP 5¢
THE DOCTOR IS IN
I HAVE A STRANGE PROBLEM
THERE'S THIS GIRL, SEE, AND SHE'S ALWAYS TRYING TO GET ME TO KICK THIS FOOTBALL, BUT SHE ALSO ALWAYS PULLS IT AWAY AND I LAND ON MY BACK AND KILL MYSELF...
SHE SOUNDS LIKE AN INTERESTING GIRL... SORT OF A FUN TYPE...
I GET THE IMPRESSION THAT YOU HAVE A REAL NEED TO KICK THIS FOOTBALL... I THINK YOU SHOULD TRY IT!
I THINK YOU SHOULD TRY IT BECAUSE IN MEDICAL TERMS, YOU HAVE WHAT WE CALL THE "NEED TO NEED TO TRY IT"
10-6-02
I'M GLAD I TALKED WITH MY PSYCHIATRIST BECAUSE THIS YEAR I'M GONNA KICK THAT BALL CLEAR TO THE MOON!
AUGH!
WHAM
UNFORTUNATELY, CHARLIE BROWN, YOUR AVERAGE PSYCHIATRIST KNOWS VERY LITTLE ABOUT KICKING FOOTBALLS
SCHULZ

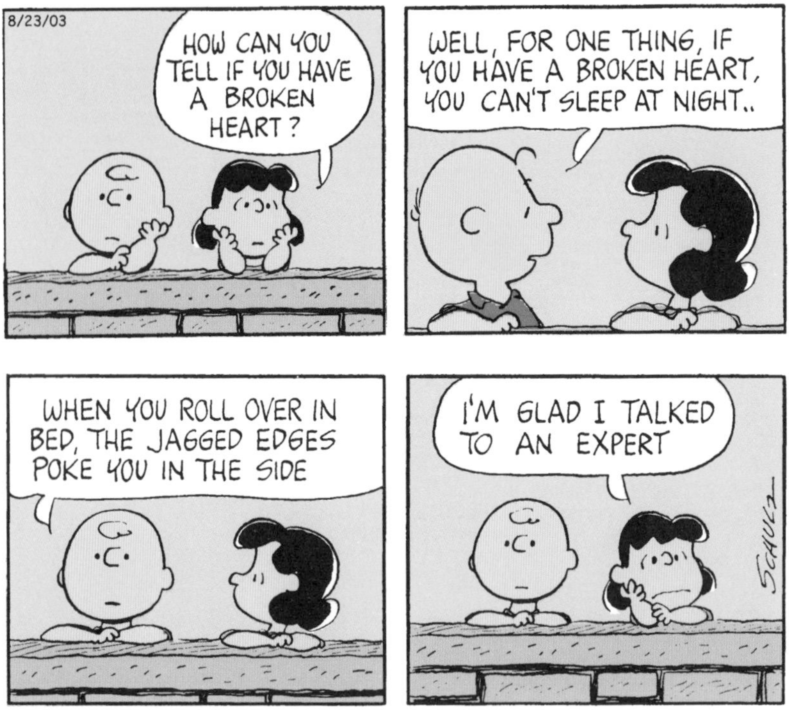
8/23/03
HOW CAN YOU TELL IF YOU HAVE A BROKEN HEART?
WELL, FOR ONE THING, IF YOU HAVE A BROKEN HEART, YOU CAN'T SLEEP AT NIGHT..
WHEN YOU ROLL OVER IN BED, THE JAGGED EDGES POKE YOU IN THE SIDE
I'M GLAD I TALKED TO AN EXPERT
SCHULZ

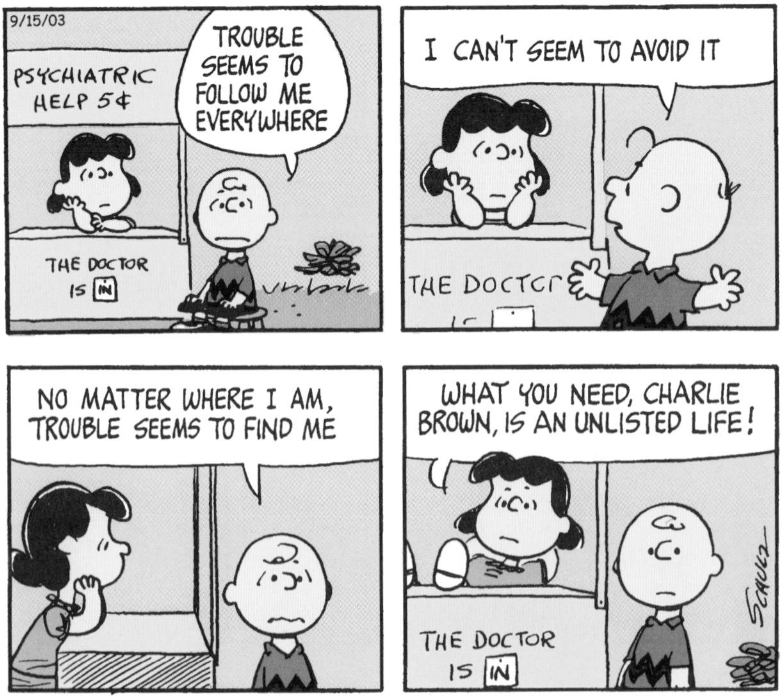
9/15/03
PSYCHIATRIC HELP 5¢
THE DOCTOR IS IN
TROUBLE SEEMS TO FOLLOW ME EVERYWHERE
I CAN'T SEEM TO AVOID IT
NO MATTER WHERE I AM, TROUBLE SEEMS TO FIND ME
WHAT YOU NEED, CHARLIE BROWN, IS AN UNLISTED LIFE!
THE DOCTOR IS IN
SCHULZ

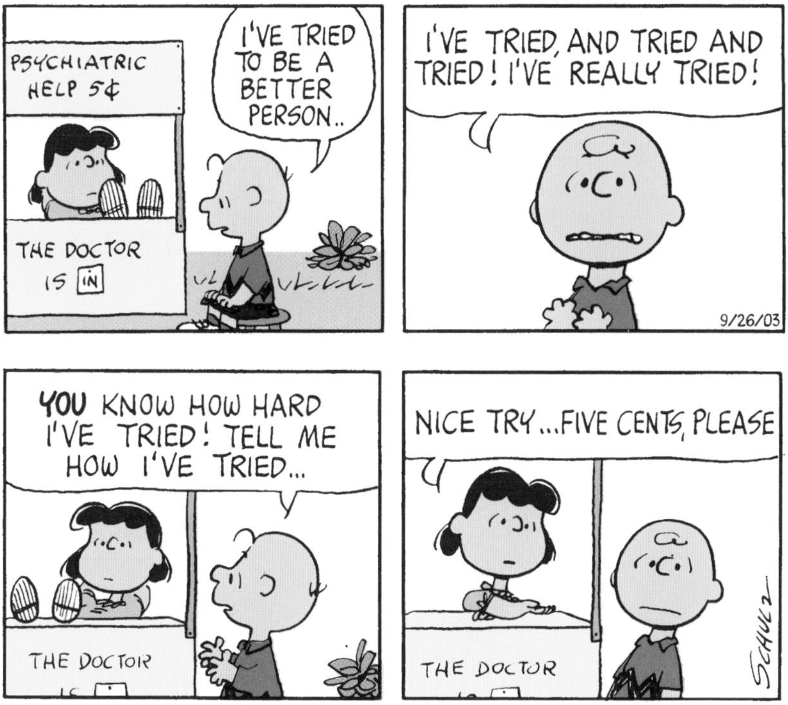
PSYCHIATRIC HELP 5¢
THE DOCTOR IS IN
I'VE TRIED TO BE A BETTER PERSON..
I'VE TRIED, AND TRIED AND TRIED! I'VE REALLY TRIED!
9/26/03
YOU KNOW HOW HARD I'VE TRIED! TELL ME HOW I'VE TRIED...
THE DOCTOR
NICE TRY...FIVE CENTS, PLEASE
THE DOCTOR
SCHULZ

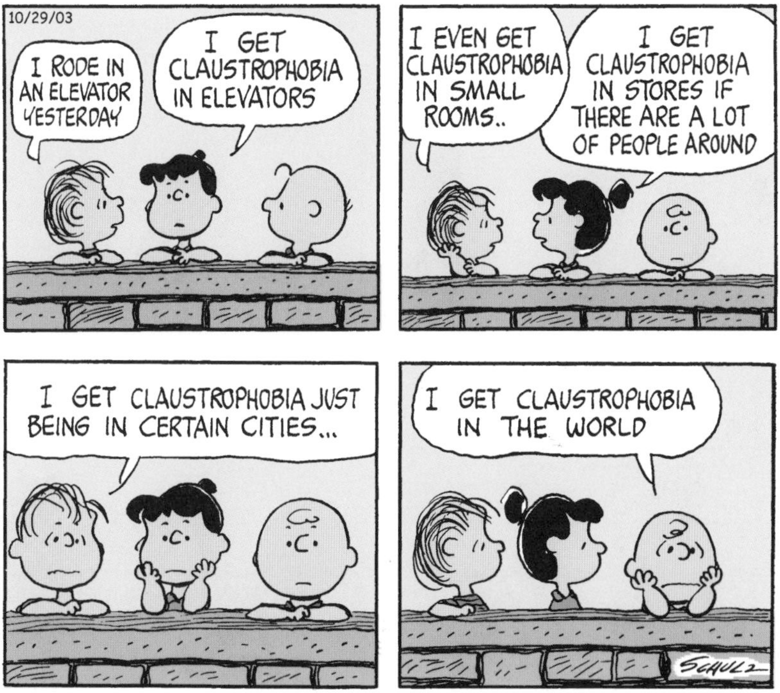
10/29/03
I RODE IN AN ELEVATOR YESTERDAY
I GET CLAUSTROPHOBIA IN ELEVATORS
I EVEN GET CLAUSTROPHOBIA IN SMALL ROOMS..
I GET CLAUSTROPHOBIA IN STORES IF THERE ARE A LOT OF PEOPLE AROUND
I GET CLAUSTROPHOBIA JUST BEING IN CERTAIN CITIES...
I GET CLAUSTROPHOBIA IN THE WORLD
SCHULZ

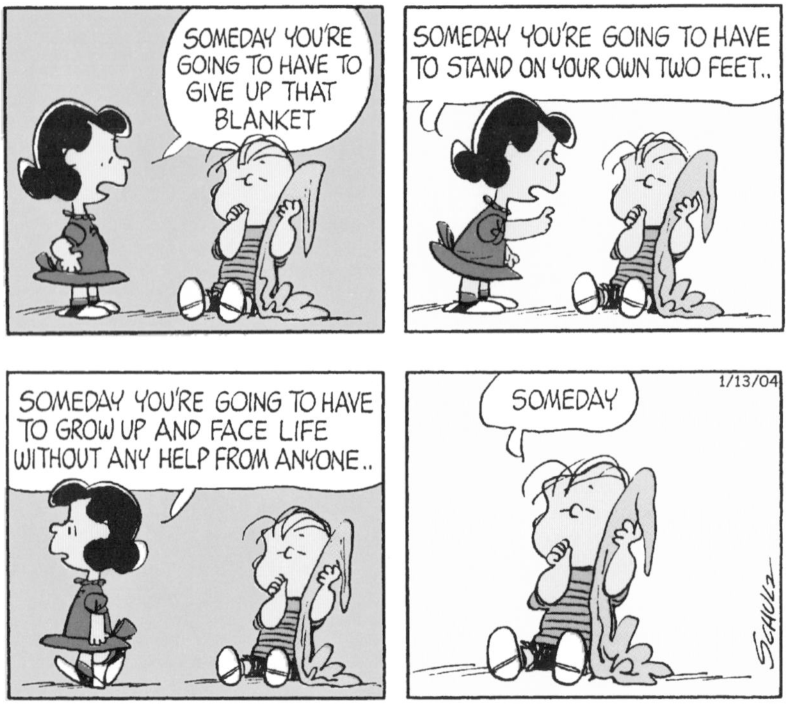
SOMEDAY YOU'RE GOING TO HAVE TO GIVE UP THAT BLANKET
SOMEDAY YOU'RE GOING TO HAVE TO STAND ON YOUR OWN TWO FEET..
SOMEDAY YOU'RE GOING TO HAVE TO GROW UP AND FACE LIFE WITHOUT ANY HELP FROM ANYONE..
1/13/04
SOMEDAY
SCHULZ

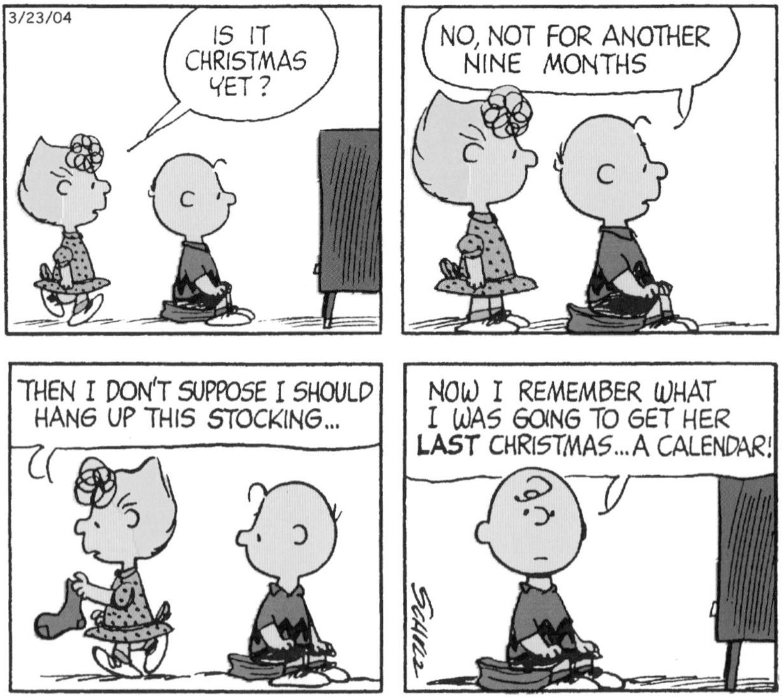
3/23/04
IS IT CHRISTMAS YET?
NO, NOT FOR ANOTHER NINE MONTHS
THEN I DON'T SUPPOSE I SHOULD HANG UP THIS STOCKING...
NOW I REMEMBER WHAT I WAS GOING TO GET HER LAST CHRISTMAS... A CALENDAR!
SCHULZ

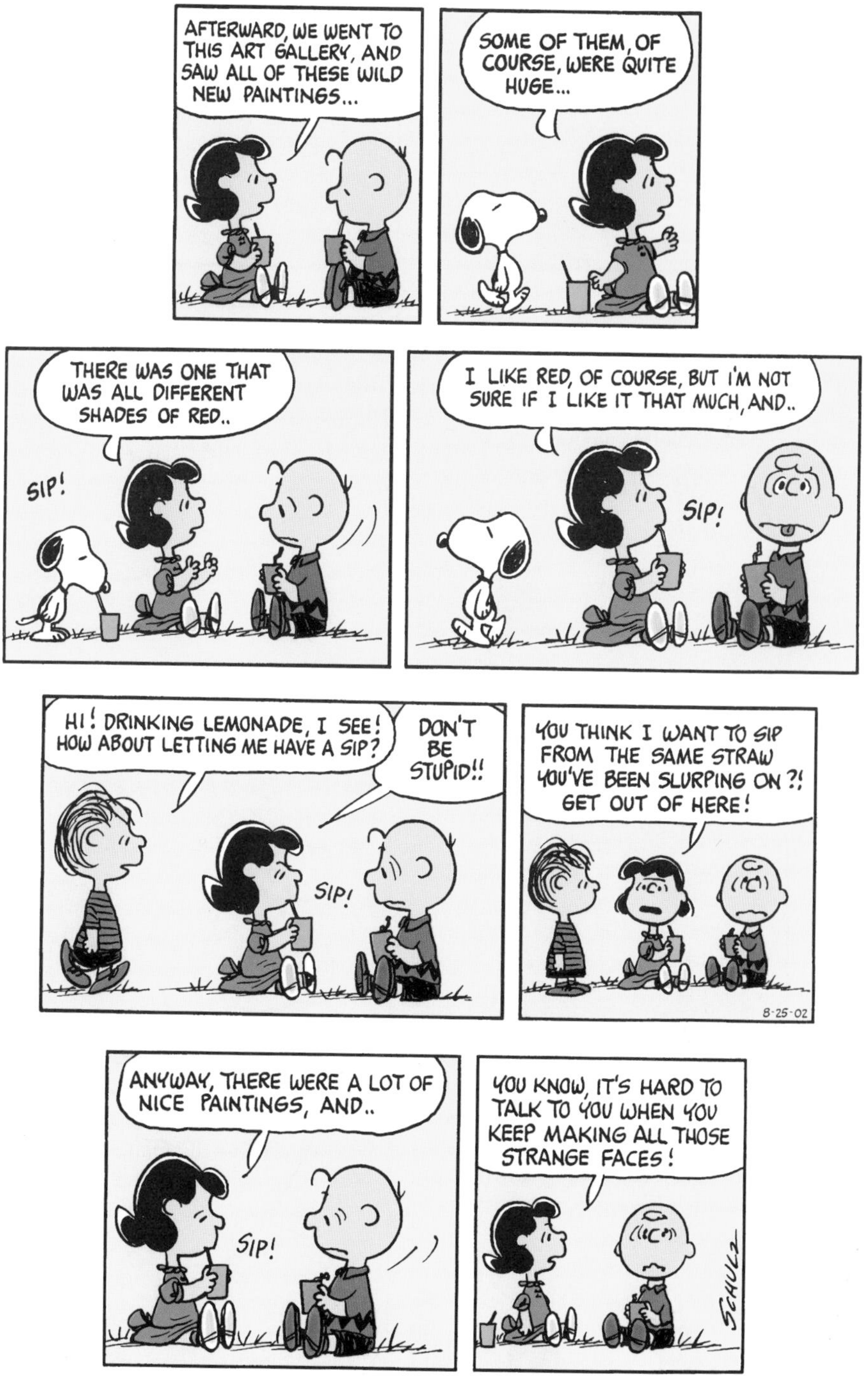
AFTERWARD, WE WENT TO THIS ART GALLERY, AND SAW ALL OF THESE WILD NEW PAINTINGS...
SOME OF THEM, OF COURSE, WERE QUITE HUGE...
THERE WAS ONE THAT WAS ALL DIFFERENT SHADES OF RED..
SIP!
I LIKE RED, OF COURSE, BUT I'M NOT SURE IF I LIKE IT THAT MUCH, AND..
SIP!
HI! DRINKING LEMONADE, I SEE! HOW ABOUT LETTING ME HAVE A SIP?
DON'T BE STUPID!!
SIP!
YOU THINK I WANT TO SIP FROM THE SAME STRAW YOU'VE BEEN SLURPING ON?! GET OUT OF HERE!
8-25-02
ANYWAY, THERE WERE A LOT OF NICE PAINTINGS, AND..
SIP!
YOU KNOW, IT'S HARD TO TALK TO YOU WHEN YOU KEEP MAKING ALL THOSE STRANGE FACES!
SCHULZ

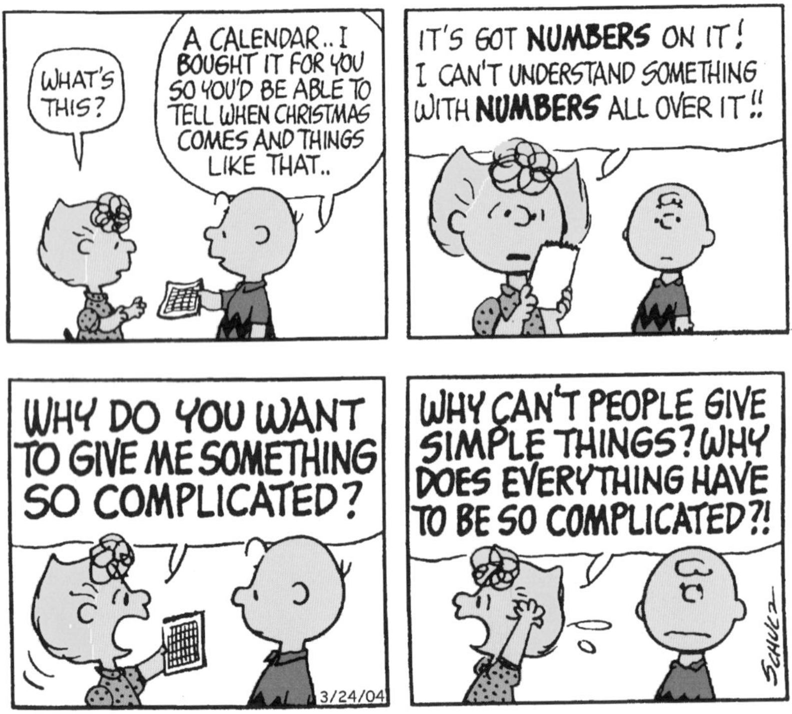
WHAT'S THIS?
A CALENDAR.. I BOUGHT IT FOR YOU SO YOU'D BE ABLE TO TELL WHEN CHRISTMAS COMES AND THINGS LIKE THAT..
IT'S GOT NUMBERS ON IT! I CAN'T UNDERSTAND SOMETHING WITH NUMBERS ALL OVER IT!!
WHY DO YOU WANT TO GIVE ME SOMETHING SO COMPLICATED?
WHY CAN'T PEOPLE GIVE SIMPLE THINGS? WHY DOES EVERYTHING HAVE TO BE SO COMPLICATED?!
3/24/04
SCHULZ

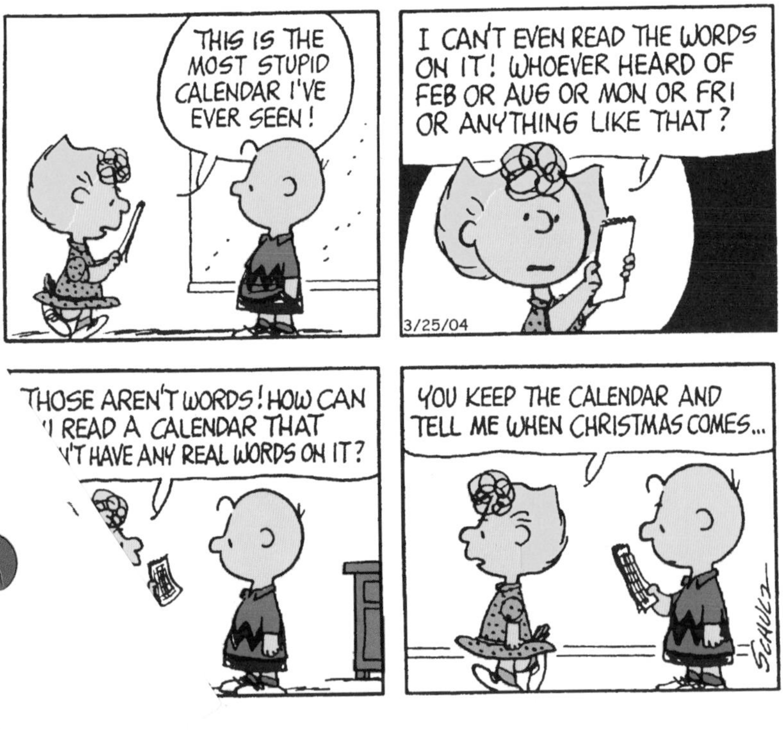
THIS IS THE MOST STUPID CALENDAR I'VE EVER SEEN!
I CAN'T EVEN READ THE WORDS ON IT! WHOEVER HEARD OF FEB OR AUG OR MON OR FRI OR ANYTHING LIKE THAT?
3/25/04
THOSE AREN'T WORDS! HOW CAN
I READ A CALENDAR THAT
N'T HAVE ANY REAL WORDS ON IT?
YOU KEEP THE CALENDAR AND TELL ME WHEN CHRISTMAS COMES...
SCHULZ

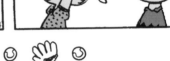

MORE TO EXPLORE!

In addition to all these great *Peanuts* cartoons, here are some cool activities and fun facts for you. Thanks to our friends at the Charles M. Schulz Museum and Research Center in Santa Rosa, California, for letting us share these with you!

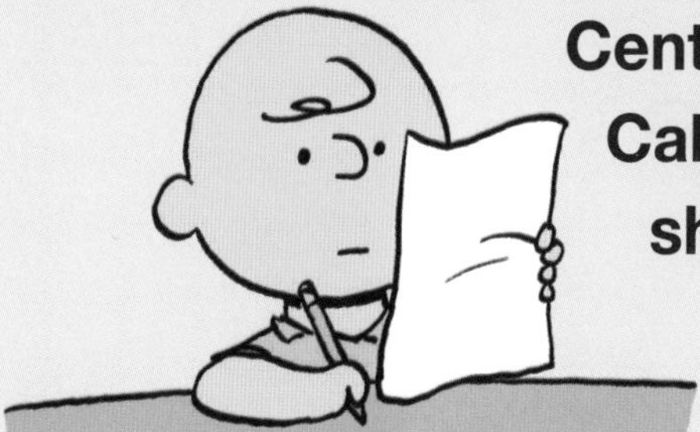

Make a Charlie Brown Mask

MATERIALS: round, white paper plate; scissors; large craft stick; black marker; tape

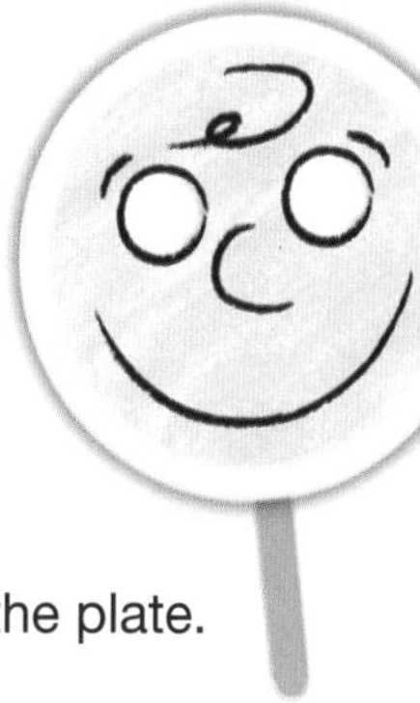

INSTRUCTIONS:

1. Cut out two holes for the eyes.
2. Draw a "C" in the middle of the plate for Charlie Brown's nose.
3. Draw a big, long smile at the bottom of the plate.
4. Draw a curlicue on top for Charlie Brown's hair.
5. Tape craft stick to the bottom of the paper plate for the handle.

Make an Animated Flip Book

An animator must capture a broad range of movements in order for a cartoon to look continuous. Animation is possible because of a phenomenon called "persistence of vision," when a sequence of images moves past the eye fast enough, the brain fills in the missing parts so the subject appears to be moving.

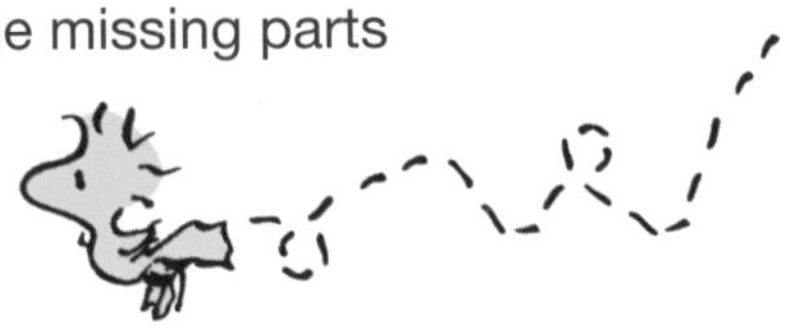

MATERIALS: paper, index cards, or sticky notes; stapler and staples, paper clips, or brads; pencil or marker

INSTRUCTIONS:

1. Cut at least 20 strips of paper to be the exact same size, or use alternative materials, such as index cards or sticky notes.
2. Fasten the pages together with a staple, brad, or paperclip.
3. Pick a subject—anything from a bouncing ball to a flying Woodstock or a shooting star.
4. Draw three key images first: the first on page one, the last on page twenty, and the middle on page ten, then fill in the pages between the key images.

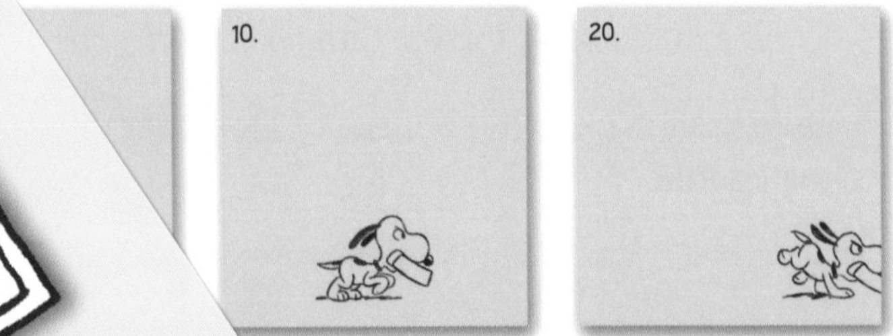
10.
20.

Make Snoopy's Favorite Puppy Chow

Snoopy may be a dog, but we think he'd prefer this fun puppy chow over simple dog food. With an adult's help, make this easy sweet treat for you and your friends to enjoy.

INGREDIENTS: *(for 12 servings)* 3 cups Chex® Cereal (or comparable cereal), ⅓ cup chocolate chips, 2½ tablespoons peanut butter, ½ cup powdered sugar

INSTRUCTIONS:

1. Pour cereal into a bowl.

2. Melt the chocolate over low heat, then add peanut butter.

3. Pour chocolate and peanut butter mixture over cereal and mix.

4. Put powdered sugar in a plastic bag, add cereal mixture, then shake it up! When the cereal is all coated, pour it on a sheet of waxed paper and let it cool. Store in airtight container (if there's any left!).

Go Fly a Kite that You Made Yourself

We hope you're more successful at flying a kite than good ol' Charlie Brown is!

These are directions for a diamond kite, the kind that Charlie Brown tries to fly. Kites are made of these basic parts:

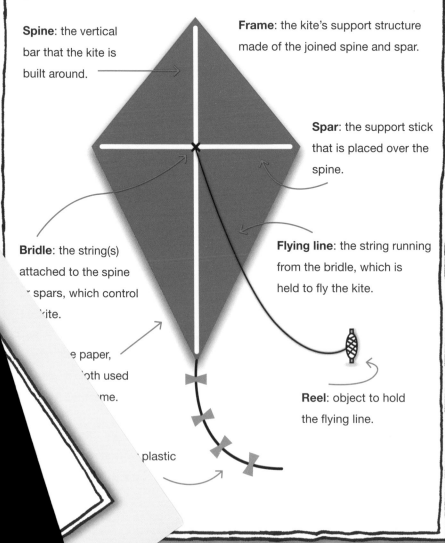

Spine: the vertical bar that the kite is built around.

Frame: the kite's support structure made of the joined spine and spar.

Spar: the support stick that is placed over the spine.

Bridle: the string(s) attached to the spine ⸻ spars, which control ⸻ ite.

Flying line: the string running from the bridle, which is held to fly the kite.

⸻ paper, ⸻ oth used ⸻ me.

⸻ plastic

Reel: object to hold the flying line.

MATERIALS:

- One 24-inch and one 20-inch wooden dowels or bamboo sticks
- String or fishing line
- Sturdy tape
- Cover material (24 inches x 24 inches). You can use newspaper, wrapping paper, or even plastic from a trash bag.
- Scissors
- Ribbons, material, or streamers for tail
- Markers
- Ruler or tape measure

INSTRUCTIONS:

1. Tie the sticks together (tightly) with string at the center of the short stick and six inches down from the top of the long stick.
2. Lay the cover material flat and put the sticks on it. Draw a line between each point of the sticks to make a diamond, then cut the material. Tape the material securely to the sticks at each of the four points of the frame. Reinforce the center of the sticks with four pieces of tape.
3. Punch a hole in the material at the cross-section of the sticks. Attach string through this hole to the cross-section.
4. Decorate your kite and make a fun tail that you can tie to the bottom of the spine.

Be careful when flying your kite. Stay away from tall trees and power lines.

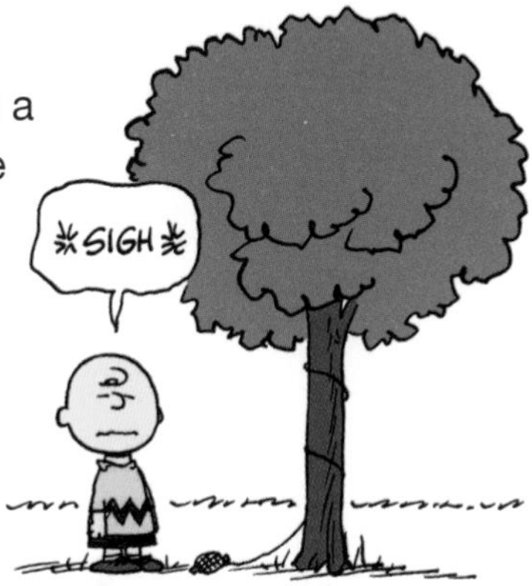
SIGH

Charles M. Schulz and *Peanuts* Fun Facts

- Charles Schulz drew 17,897 comic strips throughout his career.

- Schulz was first published in Ripley's newspaper feature *Believe It or Not* in 1937. He was fifteen years old and the drawing was of the family dog.

- From birth, comics played a large role in Schulz's life. At just two days old, an uncle nicknamed Schulz "Sparky" after the horse Spark Plug from the *Barney Google* comic strip. And that's what he was called for the rest of his life.

- In a bit of foreshadowing, Schulz's kindergarten teacher told him, "Someday, Charles, you're going to be an artist."

- Growing up, Schulz had a black-and-white dog that later became the inspiration for Snoopy—the same dog that Schulz drew for Ripley's *Believe It or Not*. The dog's name was Spike.

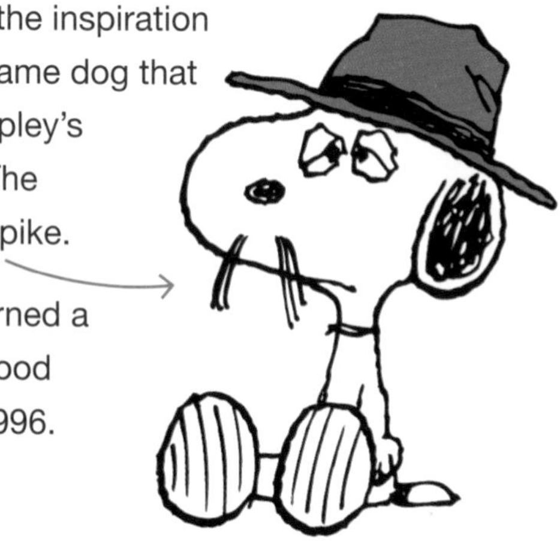

- Charles Schulz earned a star on the Hollywood Walk of Fame in 1996.

Learn How Comics Can Reflect Life

MATERIALS: blank piece of paper, pencil, markers or colored pencils

1. Make four blank cartoon panels, all the same size, on the piece of paper.

2. Look at the example below to see how Charles Schulz used his own life in his strips—even painful experiences like that of loss—and turned them into strips. Think of something that has happened to you at home or school that had a big impact on you.

3. Once you have decided on a story you want to tell, draw it in four panels. Remember, it should have a beginning, a middle, and an end.

An example from Schulz's life:

In 1966, a fire destroyed Schulz's Sebastopol studio. He translated his feelings into a strip about Snoopy's doghouse catching fire:

PEANUTS
SNIF?
I SMELL SMOKE!
SNIF SNIF
9-19
BAM! BAM!
BAM! BAM!
WHAT IN THE WORLD.....
MY BOOKS! MY RECORDS! MY POOL TABLE! MY VAN GOGH!
GOOD GRIEF!
SOB!
SCHULZ

About the Charles M. Schulz Museum

The Schulz Museum and Research Center officially opened August 17, 2002, when a dream became a reality. For many years, thousands of admirers flocked to see Charles M. Schulz's original comic strips at exhibitions outside of Santa Rosa because his work didn't have a proper home. As the fiftieth anniversary of *Peanuts* drew closer, the idea that there ought to be a museum to hold all Schulz's precious work began to grow. Schulz didn't think of himself as a "museum piece" and was, therefore, understandably reluctant about accepting the idea. That left the "vision" work to local cartoon historian Mark Cohen, wife Jeannie Schulz, and longtime friend Edwin Anderson. Schulz's enthusiasm for the museum was kindled in 1997 after seeing the inspired and playful creations by artist and designer Yoshiteru Otani for the Snoopy Town shops in Japan. From that point plans for the museum moved steadily along. A board of directors was established, a mission statement adopted, and the architect and contractor were hired. The location of the museum is particularly fitting—sited across the street from Snoopy's Home Ice, the ice arena and coffee shop that Schulz built in 1969, and one block away from the studio where Schulz worked and created for thirty years. Since its opening in 2002, thousands of visitors from throughout the world have come to the museum to see the enduring work of Charles M. Schulz which will be enjoyed for generations to come.

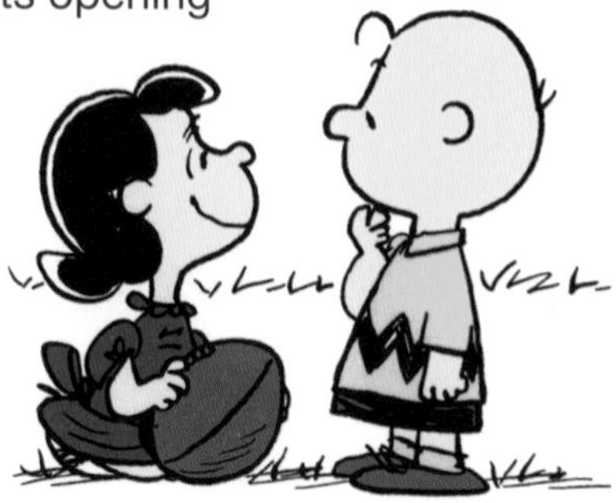

Even More to Explore!

These additional sources will be helpful if you wish to learn more about Charles Schulz, the Charles M. Schulz Museum and Research Center, *Peanuts*, or the art of cartooning.

WEB SITES:

www.schulzmuseum.org
- Official web site of the Charles M. Schulz Museum and Research Center.

www.peanuts.com
- Thirty days' worth of *Peanuts* strips. Character profiles. Timeline about the strip. Character print-outs for coloring. Info on fellow cartoonists' tributes to Charles Schulz after he passed away.

www.fivecentsplease.com
- Recent news articles and press releases on Charles Schulz and *Peanuts*. Links to other *Peanuts*-themed web sites. Info on *Peanuts* products.

www.toonopedia.com
- Info on *Peanuts* and many, many other comics—it's an "encyclopedia of 'toons."

www.gocomics.com
- Access to popular and lesser-known comic strips, as well as editorial cartoons.

www.reuben.org
- Official web site of the National Cartoonists Society. Info on how to become a professional cartoonist. Info on awards given for cartooning.

www.kingfeatures.com and www.amuniversal.com
- Newspaper syndicate web sites. Learn more about the distribution of comics to newspapers.

Check out more *Peanuts* kids' collections from Andrews McMeel Publishing.

SNOOPY
PARTY ANIMAL
A PEANUTS Collection
by Schulz

CHARLIE BROWN
HERE WE GO AGAIN
AAUGH
A PEANUTS Collection
by Schulz

SNOOPY
TO THE RESCUE
A PEANUTS Collection
by Schulz

SNOOPY
WHAT'S WRONG WITH DOG LIPS?
A PEANUTS Collection
by Schulz

I'M NOT YOUR SWEET BABBOO!
A PEANUTS Collection
by Schulz

SNOOPY
BOOGIE DOWN!
A PEANUTS Collection
by Schulz

LUCY
SPEAK OUT!
A PEANUTS Collection
by Schulz

CHARLIE BROWN
ALL TIED UP
A PEANUTS Collection
by Schulz

SNOOPY
FIRST BEAGLE IN SPACE
A PEANUTS Collection
by Schulz

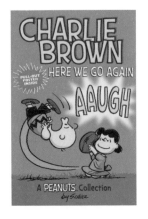

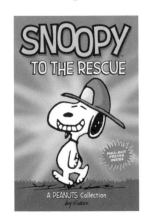

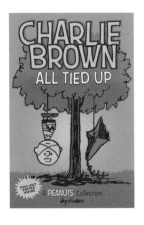